Margaret Mayhew was born in London and her earliest childhood memories were of the London blitz. She began writing in her mid-thirties and had her first novel published in 1976. She is married to American aviation author Philip Kaplan, and lives on the borders of Wales. Her novels, *The Crew*, *The Little Ship* and *Our Yanks*, are also published by Corgi.

Wing Commander David Palmer stared up at the young officer standing before him and did not like what he saw. It wasn't that she was unattractive – she was, in fact, very pretty – but he wanted no part of women being dumped on his RAF station. They were a nuisance

'And just *what* exactly, are you women supposed to be doing here, Company Assistant Newman?' he asked curtly.

Felicity felt the sweat gathering on her forehead.

'Replacing RAF officers and airmen wherever possible to release them for active service, Sir.'

There was an icy silence.

'I appreciate your laudable wish to help your country in wartime . . . but I am *not* in favour of women serving on this station. I did not ask for you. I do not want you. Do I make myself clear?'

'Yes, Sir.'

'Since you are here, we shall have to make the best of it. There may be some areas where you and your recruits can help – cooking, cleaning, that sort of thing. But I'm afraid I am not convinced that women have an active part to play in the Royal Air Force.'

To Felicity Newman his words were a challenge. She was determined to prove that her WAAFS had a heroic role in the battle that was to come. As she began to train the bewildered group of girls – all with their own personal problems – she vowed that one day David Palmer, and the officers like him, would be forced to admit that the 'Bluebirds' were brave, disciplined, and above all essential to the triumphant course of the RAF in the Second World War.

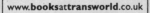

www.booksattransworld.co.uk

Also by Margaret Mayhew

THE CREW
THE LITTLE SHIP
OUR YANKS

and published by Corgi Books

BLUEBIRDS

Margaret Mayhew

CORGI BOOKS

BLUEBIRDS
A CORGI BOOK : 0 552 13910 6

First publication in Great Britain

PRINTING HISTORY
Corgi edition published 1993

10

Set in Linotype Sabon 10/11pt by
Hewer Text Composition Services, Edinburgh.

Corgi Books are published by Transworld Publishers,
61–63 Uxbridge Road, London W5 5SA,
a division of The Random House Group Ltd,
in Australia by Random House Australia (Pty) Ltd,
20 Alfred Street, Milsons Point, Sydney, NSW 2061, Australia,
in New Zealand by Random House New Zealand Ltd,
18 Poland Road, Glenfield, Auckland 10, New Zealand
and in South Africa by Random House (Pty) Ltd,
Endulini, 5a Jubilee Road, Parktown 2193, South Africa.

Printed and bound in Germany by
GGP Media GmbH, Pößneck

For Philip

Acknowledgements

I should like to thank the many ex-WAAF and ex-RAF who kindly gave me their time to tell me about their experiences during the Second World War. I also thank American Eighth Air Force veterans, Bill Ganz and Bill Nelson.

I am particularly indebted to the following: Squadron Leader Tadeusz Andersz, DFC, of the Polish Air Force Association, London, Squadron Leader Jack Currie, DFC, Elizabeth Davies, Peter Elliott, Keeper of Aviation Records at RAF Museum, Hendon, Beryl Green, Edith Kup, Trevor Legg, Eric Marsden, Mike and Cheryl Matthews, Wing Commander Geoffrey Page, DSO, DFC, my editor Diane Pearson, Simon Robbins of the Imperial War Museum, London, Carol Smith, Dame Anne Stephens, Jean Thomson, Anne Turley-George, and to my husband Philip Kaplan, for his support, encouragement and endless help, without which this book could never have been written.

Margaret Mayhew

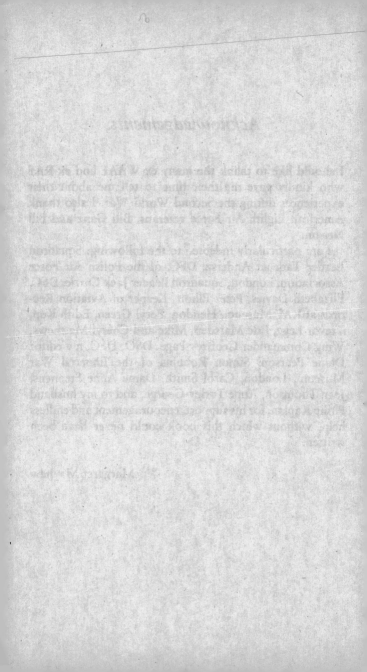

Foreword

The Women's Auxiliary Air Force was formed on 28 June 1939, shortly before the outbreak of the Second World War. At the beginning of the war the WAAF was still very much in its infancy – an unknown and untried quantity. Many in the RAF were doubtful about its value, about the ability of women to undertake work previously done by men, and about the behaviour of women under fire and bombardment.

This is a fictional story about some of those women. It was written in appreciation of the fine service the real women of the WAAF rendered to their country in her time of need.

PART 1

ASSEMBLY

One

The girl sitting beside Anne Cunningham was crying. She had been crying all the way down on the train from London, huddled wretchedly in the corner of the third-class compartment, and she had started up again as soon as the RAF lorry, which had collected them, had swung out of the station yard. Her head was hanging low, almost to her knees, and she kept on dabbing at her eyes with a sodden handkerchief. Her tears matched the rain that was falling steadily outside. Over the lorry's tailgate, Anne watched the wet, black road unwinding. She could see the tall spire of Chichester cathedral poking up into the sky in the distance, beyond the flat brown fields and russet trees. The sea, she reckoned, must be over to the right, a few miles away. Somewhere ahead lay their destination, RAF Colston.

The three-tonner lurched sharply as it rounded a bend, sending its passengers falling about and clutching at handholds. Anne grabbed the slatted bench beneath her and leaned against the canvas tilt to steady herself. A sharp piece of metal dug uncomfortably into her spine and she shifted sideways. The lorry swung into another bend, in the opposite direction, and there was more squealing. Like pigs to market, she thought.

She had never seen such a mixed bag of girls. They were all types and wearing all kinds of clothes. Fur coats, country tweed costumes, smart London suits, school uniform, cheap cotton frocks, expensive silk ones . . . The girl clutching a huge cartwheel hat to her head and smoking a cigarette, looked as though she was going to a garden party. Anne didn't know her name but the peroxide-blonde in the fake leopardskin jacket was called Gloria, and the plump redhead who had been passing round a flask of whisky was Pearl. Sandra, next to Pearl, had a babyish face and was dressed in a grey school coat and felt hat, a plaid travelling rug folded neatly across her knees. The plain, spotty girl with the sour expression was Maureen and the next one along with the eager look and the stutter was Vera. The shy girl sitting by the cartwheel hat was Winnie. Their luggage, piled on the floor of the lorry, was as varied as their clothing – monogrammed suitcases and hatboxes mixed up with cardboard containers, satchels, string bags and brown paper parcels. There was even a birdcage covered with a green baize cloth.

The girl beside Anne was still crying – harder than ever. Her thin shoulders were heaving in shuddering spasms and her head had sunk onto her knees. Anne felt in her pocket for a clean handkerchief and offered it, nudging her with an elbow. What on earth was her name? Edith, Enid, Ena . . . something like that. Her face, when she lifted it, was blotched red and her eyes swollen to slits with all the crying and dabbing. She managed a nod of thanks as she took the handkerchief and Anne saw that there was an engagement ring on her left hand. Perhaps she was crying all those tears for her fiancé, or perhaps she was just plain homesick. The one good thing she could say for all those years at boarding school was that it had cured her of that particular misery.

So, here she was sitting on an uncomfortable bench in the back of a lorry with a load of complete strangers and wondering what she'd let herself in for. Nobody seemed to know a blessed thing about the Women's Auxiliary Air Force, and nobody seemed to know what was going to happen next with the war either. Some people said it would all be over by Christmas and that there was nothing to worry about. The newspapers, though, had horrible stories about Warsaw being reduced to rubble and Poles trying to stop German tanks with horses. There had been

14

gruesome accounts of thousands of people in eastern Europe being slaughtered or taken prisoner or made homeless. She had seen photographs of gaunt, despairing faces, of weeping women, forlorn children, sad old men . . . and pushed them out of her mind. It was all so remote and far away that she couldn't make herself care all that much. It could never happen in England, so there was really nothing to worry about.

The girl was *still* crying. Enid – that was her name, not Ena or Edith. Enid Potter. Would she ever stop? She was like the Mock Turtle and they would soon be drowning in her tears. Anne put an arm round the heaving shoulders. Better try and jolly her up somehow.

The lorry rattled on.

The smoke from her neighbour's cigarette was making Winnie Briggs feel sick – that and the swing and sway of the lorry. Not to mention the nerves in her stomach. So many frightening things had happened on the long journey since she'd left home. Finding her way across London from Liverpool Street Station to Victoria Station had been the worst part. It was the first time she had ever been out of Suffolk and seen a big city, and the Underground had terrified her. She had got hopelessly lost in a maze of passageways and found herself pushed onto a moving staircase and being carried deep down into the earth. She had stood, bewildered, on a platform – not knowing where to go or what to do – and been petrified by trains roaring suddenly out of a tunnel. At last, a strange woman had taken pity on her and turned her back in the right direction. On the train from Victoria she had been too shy to say anything to the other girls, except her name. Several of them, she saw, were from much grander backgrounds than her own, like the girl next to her in the big hat. She wasn't used to mixing with people like that. Nor was she used to ones like the girl with the dyed blond hair and makeup, wearing a spotted, furry jacket.

She smoothed the skirt of her cotton frock and fingered

the little blue ring on her left hand, as though it might give her some kind of strength. Instead, it reminded her painfully of Ken. They had bought the ring in Ipswich, taking the bus there one Saturday afternoon and window-shopping at the jewellers until they had found one that she liked and at a price he could afford. The shop assistant had looked down his nose and Ken had stuttered with nervousness.

The lorry swung round another bend and she was thrown against the girl next to her who nearly dropped her cigarette. She looked cross and said something that Winnie could not hear. She had never felt more miserable in her life, or more uncertain of herself. No-one in her family, except for Gran, had wanted her to join up. Dad had been against it because she was too useful about the farm, and Mum because she was such a help in the house, especially with looking after Ruth and Laura who were still only little. And Ken had been so hurt. He had not understood at all when she had tried to explain to him.

'It's just that I want to do somethin' useful in the war, Ken . . .' was what she'd said.

'You'll go and forget all about me, Winn, I know it.'

How could she forget him when she had known him all her life? When he was almost as much a part of it as her own family? There had never been anyone but Ken. They had been courting since they were sixteen and as soon as the war was over they were going to get married. She had promised him that and she would keep her promise.

The nausea was getting worse and there was a sudden sour taste in her mouth. Winnie put up her hand and swallowed hard. The girl had finished her cigarette and was grinding it out under the toe of her high-heeled shoe, but the lorry was now veering round a succession of bends, swinging one way and then the other. She felt the vomit rise up into her mouth and stumbled towards the rear. There, she was violently and helplessly sick over the tailgate.

*　　*　　*

Wing Commander David Palmer, DFC, AFC, sitting at his desk in RAF Colston Station Headquarters, stared up at the young officer standing before him. He did not like what he saw. Not that the girl was unpleasant to look at – far from it, if he discounted the fact that she was dressed in a hideously unfeminine uniform, but he simply wished that she was not there at all.

He was feeling both angry and irritated. Angry with the fools who had conceived the whole idea of forming a Women's Auxiliary Air Force and irritated by the unwelcome presence of two of them already on his doorstep, and the threat of more to come. He went on staring at the girl, hard and deliberately. She was pink in the face and her eyes were fixed on a spot on the wall somewhere behind his right shoulder. He could tell that she was very nervous and checked his rising temper. It wasn't her fault, after all. She was only obeying orders and she looked intelligent and sensible enough. She couldn't, he guessed, be much more than twenty-one or so – almost young enough to be his daughter, for heaven's sake . . . And what a God-awful, unflattering outfit for any woman. A sort of bastardized version of his own uniform – blue tunic cut just like a man's, shirt, black tie and, instead of trousers, a shapeless skirt. He lowered his gaze to the thick grey stockings and heavy black lace-up shoes. Women, in his opinion, were simply not made for wearing service uniform. They were all the wrong shape and looked ridiculous in it. He directed his stare beyond the girl to the WAAF sergeant standing a pace behind her – cropped-haired, bull-necked, unblinking – and reverted hurriedly to the officer who was a good deal easier on the eye.

He said curtly: 'How many recruits did you say you're expecting, Company Assistant Newman?'

'Twenty, sir.'

'And where do you suppose we are going to put you all?'

She had gone pinker still. 'I don't know, sir.'

'Nor do I,' he said grimly. 'Let's hope Squadron Leader Robinson can sort something out. We had no idea you were arriving yet.'

'I'm sorry, sir. I thought you would have been informed.'

She had a nice voice – well-educated but not affected. It was a point in her favour but he was far from mollified.

'So would I. Evidently they thought it better to take us by surprise. How did you get here?'

'By car, sir. I have my own. Sergeant Beaty came with me.'

He thought sourly: Christ, they'll be cluttering up the place with their bloody cars if we're not careful. Women drivers everywhere. He leaned back in his chair and drummed his fingers on the rim of his desk. A thick-set man of forty-one with a natural air of command, Palmer had served in the Royal Flying Corps towards the end of the First World War and then stayed on afterwards in the newly-formed Royal Air Force. He had spent all his adult life in the Services.

'Just exactly *what* are you women supposed to be doing here, Company Assistant Newman? Perhaps you can explain that to me.'

Felicity Newman could feel the sweat gathering on her forehead and beneath the roll of hair at the nape of her neck. She had been in the Women's Auxiliary Air Force for precisely two months and this was her first posting as a newly-commissioned officer. It was also her first encounter with an RAF Station Commander.

She swallowed. 'As I understand it, sir, our function is to replace RAF officers and airmen wherever possible in order to release them for active service.'

There was silence in the office for a moment. The Wing Commander was picturing his station manned by a pack of females. It would be almost funny, he decided, if the situation were not so deadly serious with Hitler rampaging through Europe like a power-crazed lunatic. This was no time for jokes. The war against Germany had

18

been on for over a month and anything could happen at any time. Every instinct told him that these women were going to be nothing but a damned nuisance, creating far more problems than they were ever likely to solve. They ought to be kept out of it. War wasn't their job. Except for nurses to look after the wounded, it was strictly for men. If they must do something then let it be civilian work — pouring tea, dispensing soup and sandwiches in canteens, knitting socks and scarves for servicemen, all that sort of thing . . .

He took a deep breath. He must be fair. He didn't want to be unkind to the girl but the position had to be made very clear to her from the outset. There was no room for any misunderstanding or tomfoolery.

'I appreciate your very laudable wish to help your country in wartime, Company Assistant, but some things should be explained to you. I am not, personally, in favour of women serving on this station; or on any other station, come to that. I did not ask for you. I do not want you. I do not believe that your place is here, nor that you could possibly replace my men. Do I make myself clear?'

Her reply was almost inaudible. 'Yes, sir.'

He cleared his throat, wondering if he had gone too far. Been too harsh with her. There was always the possibility that she might burst into tears and create an embarrassing scene. He made himself say more gently,

'However, since you *are* here, we shall all have to make the best of it. There may well be some areas where you and your recruits can help us — cooking, cleaning, that sort of thing . . . And clerical work. But I'm afraid I am not convinced that women have a more active part to play in the Royal Air Force, such as you have indicated.'

He saw that her face was now scarlet and there was a glistening trickle of perspiration running down the side of her face. He felt a bit of a rat. But a rat he must be if he were to keep these women under control. Her eyes were still fixed on the wall over his right shoulder. He found that irritating. Damn it, why wouldn't she look at him.

He wasn't going to eat her. He encountered her sergeant's basilisk stare. If they were going to send these females, why in God's name couldn't they send better-looking ones than that? He discarded the gentler tone.

'There is one thing you must understand. This is an operational fighter station in wartime, and you and your recruits will be under my command. I will not tolerate any interference with the efficient running of RAF Colston. Understood?'

'Perfectly, sir.'

He dismissed them with relief and watched dourly as they wheeled about and marched out of the room. Unreasonably, the fact that they both did so smartly annoyed him still further.

In the corridor outside the two WAAFS passed a small group of RAF officers who turned round to stare at them, their faces registering a variety of emotions – astonishment, amusement, disapproval, even downright dismay.

Sergeant Beaty sniffed. 'They don't seem to know what to make of us, do they, ma'am?'

Felicity, badly shaken by the interview with Wing Commander Palmer, did not reply. She had naïvely expected that the RAF would welcome them with open arms. The Wing Officer at her training course had talked enthusiastically during her lectures. *You will be living under the same conditions, sharing the same dangers and carrying out the same duties as the members of the Royal Air Force. You will form an integral and vital part of that great Service.*

There was a burst of laughter from the group of officers. It was a fair guess that it was directed at them.

The lorry swept in through the main gates of RAF Colston, waved on by the guard. It jerked to a halt and the two airmen came round from the front cabin to lower the tailgate. They were grinning broadly.

'Jump to it, girls! Everyone out.'

They clambered down awkwardly, unfamiliar with the knack and hampered by tight skirts, high heels, hats and handbags, exposing thighs and suspenders to the delight of the two airmen. It had stopped raining and they stood on the kerbside with their luggage strewn about them. Other airmen had appeared and grinned from a distance. A window in a nearby building was flung open and more faces gawped and leered. There was a piercing chorus of wolf whistles.

Anne went and sat on her suitcase. She found a cigarette in her shoulder bag and lit up. Pearl, the redhead, squatted on a canvas holdall beside her. Her hat, perched precariously on a mass of curls, had a jaunty yellow feather stuck through its brim.

'Posh place this . . . nice buildings, flower beds, all this grass and trees . . . Doesn't look much like the Air Force, except for *them*.' She jerked her head in the direction of the grinning and gawping airmen. 'What makes all men think they're God's gift to women? I don't fancy any of that lot. Where're all the pilots, that's what I want to know. Fancy a swig?'

She proffered the whisky flask taken from the depths of a large rexine handbag.

'No, thanks.'

'Bit too strong for you, eh? Good for the nerves, though.' Pearl took a swallow and replaced the cap. 'How did you get into this lark, anyhow, a nice young lady like you?'

'I just tagged onto the end of a recruiting queue. Spur of the moment really. Quite honestly I was bored at home.'

Pearl's eyebrows shot up towards her hat brim. 'Blimey! I've never been bored, dear. Never had the time, see. Been working my guts out for six years since I left home. I thought if I joined up it might make a bit of a change.'

Anne said politely: 'Really? What were you working as?'

'Barmaid. Pub called the Red Lion in Fulham. Don't suppose you'd know it. I'd been there two years. Before

21

that I was a waitress in a caff in Tooting. That was hell on earth. Run off your feet all day and treated like dirt. At least in a pub you've got the bar between you and the customers. You wouldn't believe how some of them can behave.' More windows had opened and there was more whistling and yelling. Pearl sighed. 'Doesn't look as though this is going to be much different.'

As Felicity approached the group of recruits, her heart sank. They looked distinctly unpromising. She could see unsuitable frocks and shoes, fur coats, frivolous hats, jewellery, elaborate hair styles . . . all the sort of things of which Wing Commander Palmer would most disapprove. And none of the girls appeared remotely orderly or disciplined. One was sitting slouched on her suitcase, smoking a cigarette, while a blowsy-looking redhead beside her was stowing something away in her handbag that looked suspiciously like a spirits' flask. A small, thin girl was weeping unrestrainedly into her handkerchief and a peroxide blond was twisting to examine a ladder at the back of her stocking, her short skirt hitched even higher. The amount of luggage was alarming, all probably containing even more unsuitable clothing. She hoped her eyes were deceiving her, but surely that was a birdcage among all the rest.

None of her misgivings showed in her face or voice, however, as she addressed the motley little band for the first time.

'You must be tired after your journey. Sergeant Beaty here will show you to your quarters in a moment and you can get settled in . . .' Felicity paused. The blond had turned her attention from her laddered stocking to her painted fingernails which she was studying intently. The rest of them were listening, so far as she could tell, though the thin one was still crying, her sobs and sniffs clearly audible. Felicity raised her voice a little.

'You have been members of the Women's Auxiliary Air Force only for a very short time and it will all seem rather strange to you at first. However, it's not too early to ask you to be sure to conduct yourselves at all times in a quiet and orderly fashion on this Station. You will be closely observed by the RAF – ' Someone at the back of the group sniggered and there was a ripple of tittering. Felicity flushed, realizing the literal truth of her words. The number of airmen in the vicinity had grown considerably as she had been speaking. She went on firmly. 'They are waiting to be convinced that we in the WAAF are capable of playing a serious and responsible part alongside them in this war. Please don't give them any grounds for doubting this.'

She paused again. To her own ears she was sounding horribly pompous . . . like some priggish old school marm. A sudden loud squawking from beneath the birdcage cover caused more giggles. It sounded like a parrot, but whatever kind of bird it was it certainly couldn't be allowed to stay. She must deal with that as soon as possible. The blond girl was now turning round towards the nearest barrack block window where a row of male heads watched the proceedings with interest. One of them shouted something and the blond waved. This was too much. Felicity raised her voice still further.

'What is your name, please?'

The girl's neighbour nudged her. 'She's talking to you. Wants to know your name.'

The blond removed her gaze reluctantly from the window. 'Gloria Gibbs.'

'Well, Gibbs, in future when I'm speaking to you, you will please pay proper attention. And when you answer me, you must call me ma'am.'

Gloria looked sulky. 'Ma'am? I've never called nobody that.'

'All WAAF officers are to be addressed as ma'am. You'll soon get used to it. And you call Sergeant Beaty here, Sergeant. It's quite simple, but please be sure to remember it.'

'Wot about that lot, then?' the blond asked cheekily,

with a jerk of her head in the direction of the airmen. 'Wot're we supposed to call 'em?'

There were more giggles, less subdued, and a whooping whistle from the window. Felicity felt her flush deepening.

'That will do, Gibbs. We'll come to that later.'

She handed them over to Sergeant Beaty who had been glaring ferociously at both the recruits and the men. She found that she was shaking and hoped that it didn't show. In training they had been taught that it was vital for an officer to have control and respect from the start and she was afraid that she had not handled her first encounter with her airwomen very well. She had sensed Beaty's fuming impatience behind her left shoulder and the sergeant had leaped forward to take charge, barking orders like a savage sheepdog released to round up a wayward flock of sheep. The recruits were herded into an untidy crocodile and, as they moved off, there was an enthusiastic chorus of appreciation from all the airmen. Gibbs, Felicity noted, was not the only one, this time, who waved back.

They straggled along behind the sergeant, past more buildings and three huge hangars. Without warning, an aeroplane roared low over their heads. They ducked and Enid fell to her knees, clasping her hands over her ears. Winnie, alone of them, stood stock still, gazing upwards. As the 'plane turned she could see the cockpit and the shape of the pilot's head, and the coloured rings on its side that showed it belonged to the Royal Air Force. She put down her suitcase and shielded her eyes with her hand to watch it fly off into the distance.

'Don't dawdle, you at the back there! Keep up with the rest!'

The sergeant was bellowing at her angrily, the other girls all staring. Winnie blushed. She picked up her suitcase and hurried after them.

At the far side of the station, away from other buildings, lay a small group of wooden huts with corrugated roofs and stovepipe chimneys. The sergeant marched to the nearest hut and they trooped inside and stood staring in dismayed silence. Two rows of iron bedsteads lined the walls, a spartan-looking pile of bedding at each head, and battered metal lockers in between. The windows had no curtains and were criss-crossed with strips of anti-blast brown paper. Unshaded bulbs hung from the ceiling. There was an unlit stove at each end of the hut and water lay in pools on the wood floor where the roof had evidently leaked. It was cold, damp and cheerless, and there was a lingering, unpleasant smell of stale cigarette smoke, sweat and something that might have been old socks.

It was Pearl who broke the hush.

'Holy mackerel!' she said. 'Welcome to the *Ritz*.'

Anne lay awake on her narrow iron bed. Pearl, next to her, had already gone to sleep and was snoring softly. Nothing, she reckoned, would ever keep Pearl awake for long, unlike poor old Enid who was crying yet again over on the opposite side of the hut, making whimpering sounds in between the sobs, like an animal in pain. She put her arms behind her head against the hard bolster and stared into the darkness.

It had all been a bit of a let-down so far, she considered, starting with their sleeping quarters and getting even worse. The ablutions hut nearby was a grim, carbolicky place with cracked basins, rust-streaked baths and slimy duckboards. One of the lavatory chains was missing and so were most of the plugs. The graffiti scrawled large and clear over the walls had brought a blush to some cheeks.

'No use standing on the seat, the crabs in here can jump six feet,' Pearl had chanted, peering into one of the lavatory cubicles. 'Well, I never.'

'Crabs?' Sandra had asked, her baby-face puzzled. 'In *here*?'

'Not the seaside kind, dearie. Nasty little things that a

well-brought up girl like you wouldn't know about.'

'Mummy told me to be sure never to sit on the lavatory seats in case I caught something horrid.'

'Mummy was quite right.'

Anne smiled, remembering. She had never heard of those sort of crabs either but Pearl had explained later. Pearl was going to be rather useful for things like that.

They had been given an evening meal in another hut – a sort of combined tea and supper of bread and butter, sausages, egg and chips, with strong, sweetened tea dispensed from a big urn. The food had all been transported from the airmen's cookhouse and by the time it had reached them it had been only lukewarm, the grease congealing. They had sat at benches at a long trestle table covered with an oilcloth and had each been given an enamel mug, and a knife, fork and spoon and had been told to keep these for their own use and to rinse them in the tub of tepid water by the door as they left. Later, they had been taken over to the NAAFI.

'What's a NAAFI?' Sandra had asked in her high voice. She was always asking questions.

The Navy, Army and Air Force Institute had turned out to be a large brick building beside the parade ground and was, apparently, a place for recreation and refreshment. Their officer, Company Assistant Newman, who had explained this, had said that there was a shop there too, where they would be able to buy all sorts of things like cigarettes, chocolate, soap and so on. It had all seemed quite promising until they had discovered that they were to go in through a side entrance and be shut away in a poky back room. They had sat around on hard chairs, drank more stewed tea and eaten dry buns, served to them through a hatchway in the wall, as though they were lepers. The sound of airmen 'recreating' noisily had reached them from beyond the hatch – loud talk and male laughter, and a piano being strummed energetically. The smell of beer and strong cigarettes had wafted through

26

and Pearl had talked wistfully of the Red Lion in Fulham.

The bedding stacked at the head of each bed in their hut had proved quite as awful as it looked. There were no sheets, the RAF blankets were miserably thin and the bolsters, instead of pillows, appeared to be stuffed with straw. There were no proper mattresses either, only three square pads that were well-named biscuits. Gloria had prodded hers disdainfully with a long, red fingernail.

'Cripes, I'm not sleepin' on them things. They've got stains on.'

Anne turned over restlessly and the biscuits shifted beneath her like ice floes. She tugged them back into place and pummelled at the bolster. Kit hadn't warned her about any of these things, but maybe it was different if you were training as an officer in the Army. She thought about Kit and about the summer's night in June, only a few months ago, when they had sat out on the terrace at home and talked. The dance given for their eighteenth birthday had ended, the last guest gone, and when their parents had gone to bed they had both stayed up to watch the dawn. They had drunk the left-over champagne and she had kicked off her new silver party shoes and lounged in the swing-seat, the skirts of her blue tulle frock billowing softly as she pushed the seat backwards and forwards with one stockinged foot. Kit had been a bit squiffy. He had perched on the edge of the stone balustrade, legs dangling, white tie undone, a glass in one hand and a bottle of champagne in the other. They had talked about lots of things, including the future, which had seemed quite different then.

'Lucky you,' she had told him. 'Going up to Oxford. I've gone and messed things up as usual.'

'You were a chump to get sacked from school. You've got a perfectly good brain, if only you'd use it – to stay out of trouble, for one thing. You could easily have got to Oxford if you'd tried.'

'Don't give me a lecture. I couldn't stick that ghastly

school . . . all those stupid rules and bitchy girls. It was loathsome.'

'You're still a chump. Well, what're you going to do now?'

She had stretched and yawned. It hadn't seemed to matter much then. 'Don't know really. Life's a bit of a bore at the moment. Mummy keeps going on about me going to some finishing school in Switzerland. Honestly, I can't imagine anything more deadly, can you? Flower arranging and French cooking and all that sort of stuff. And girls just like the ones at St Mary's, probably worse. Luckily, Daddy says "No," because of all this scare about there being a war. I'd've refused to go anyway. I've had enough of school. She's still trying to make me do the Season next year, though.'

'So you can bag a husband?'

'That's her idea, anyway. Preferably one with a title.'

'And frightfully rich.'

'And frightfully boring. That's why you're so lucky to be going up to Oxford. You'll meet all sorts of interesting people. Bound to.'

'Matter of fact, I doubt if I'll ever get there.'

'Don't talk rot. You'll get in easily. You'll probably be utterly sickening and get a scholarship.'

He had shaken his head. 'Didn't mean that. The thing is, we're bound to declare war on Germany soon. There won't *be* any Season next year, so you needn't worry about it.'

'I don't believe there's going to be a war. Chamberlain signed that thing to stop it.'

'A piece of paper! What's the use of that? Hitler will just tear it up whenever it suits him. He took over Czechoslovakia and Austria. Now he's got his nasty little eye on Poland. And we've given Poland our guarantee to go to her aid, so that'll be that. War! *Ipso facto.* No getting out of it. Most of the beaks at school say so.'

Anne had been silent for a moment, pushing the swing seat to and fro with her foot. Talk of a war had spoiled all the fun of the evening. She was sick of people going on all about it. Sick of all the talk of trenches and shelters and gasmasks. It was all such a drag. And what had Poland got to do with England, anyway? It was miles and miles away, somewhere in the middle of Europe – she wasn't sure exactly where – and even if it was invaded then surely it was up to the Poles to look after themselves. It was their country. Why should England have to be involved?

She had said impatiently: 'But you could still go up to Oxford, even if there was a stupid war.'

'Not so, old girl.'

'Why ever not?'

'Because I'm going to join up, fathead. Dad's old regiment, if they'll have me. A lot of the chaps at school are going to . . . they're just waiting for the show to start.'

He had spoken as casually as if he were talking about an end-of-term play. She had suddenly felt frightened.

'But Kit, you might get killed!'

He had laughed. 'Not likely. But don't you dare say a word to Ma. She'd flap like anything.'

'She'd try to stop you.'

'Wouldn't be able to. They'll call us up and she won't be able to do a thing about it.' He had waved the bottle at her cheerfully. 'More champers?'

She had watched her twin brother pouring himself another glass of champagne, and she had been very afraid for him. He was the person she cared most about in the world. He was her other half. Her better half. All the things she had somehow never managed to be. He was Captain of Boats and in Pop and almost certain to get a scholarship to Oxford. To think of him being in danger of being killed made her feel sick.

'Kit, do you *honestly* believe there's going to be a war?'

''Fraid so. And to tell the truth, I rather hope there is. Dreadful thing to say, I s'pose . . . Anyway, we can't possibly let old Adolf go on doing just as he likes –

29

marching into other people's countries, shoving them away in camps, all that sort of thing . . . That's what he's doing, you know. S'posing he tries to come and do the same here?'

'Here? In *England*? Don't be daft.'

'It's not so daft. Wouldn't put it past him to have a shot at it. And we couldn't allow that, could we? Just not on.' Kit had taken another gulp of champagne. 'I think it'll all be pretty exciting. A real scrap against an evil little tyrant who's jolly well asking for it.'

She had realized that he meant every word of it. '*Must* you go, Kit? If it does happen. Couldn't you wait a bit?'

He had hiccuped gently. 'Sorry, old bean, but I'd hate to be left out. All my friends are going . . . even old Parker-Smiley and he's still afraid of the dark. Atkinson, Villiers, Stewart, Latimer . . . remember him at the Fourth this year, making sheep's eyes at you? Poor old Latimer. He's got a real crush on you. Keeps asking about you. Must have a screw loose.'

Yes, she remembered Latimer. A tall, thin boy with spots. He'd blushed whenever she spoke to him on that day at Eton, and his spaniel's eyes had followed her everywhere. It had rather amused her at the time. He hadn't been able to come to the dance but the rest of them had been there. She'd danced with them all. Jamie Stewart had kept tripping her up and Noel Atkinson had trodden on her new silver shoes. Peter Villiers was pretty good at the quickstep, really, and little Parker-Smiley, still shorter than her, had surprised her by how well he could waltz. She'd known them all for years – ever since they'd been at prep school with Kit. Now, all of a sudden, apparently, they weren't boys any longer – but men.

She had turned her head to hide the silly tears that had come into her eyes. She had blinked them away. The beech trees at the far end of the garden, beyond the lawn, looked like black cut-outs against the sky. She could hear the first trills of the birds.

'What about me, Kit? What on earth am I going to do?'

'Oh, you'll find something . . . you could always join up as well.'

'Join what?'

'How about the ATS?'

'The what?'

'The Women's Army thing . . . Auxiliary Territorial Service.'

'Ugh! Sounds grim.'

'Shouldn't think they'd have you, anyway. Too bolshie by far.' Kit had inverted the champagne bottle over his glass. 'Damn! Only a drop left. Ah well, all good things must come to an end, as they say. Tell you what, twin, let's drink to us. To us . . . and to the future . . . whatever it may bring.'

They had raised their glasses solemnly to each other in the dawning of that new day, and then Kit had thrown back his head and laughed, as though there wasn't a care in the world. She had tried to laugh too, but she had been so afraid inside herself – so afraid that all the good times they had had together were over. That their childhood was gone and that nothing in the future would ever be the same again.

Pearl had stopped snoring and Enid had stopped crying, at last. But now someone had started coughing down the far end of the hut – a maddening, repetitive sort of cough. It had begun to rain and she could hear it drumming on the asbestos roof and splashing down on the concrete path outside. Anne turned over and pulled the RAF blanket high up over her ears.

Winnie Briggs was awake too. It was so strange to her to be sleeping in the same room as nineteen other girls. At home she slept alone up in the attic, and every sound and movement in the hut disturbed her. She heard Pearl snoring and Anne pummelling her bolster and Enid sobbing. She wasn't far off crying herself. Elmbury seemed as far away as the moon and, in spite of the others around her, she felt dreadfully alone. In the NAAFI earlier she had sat drinking her tea and chewing her bun, hardly saying a word. And undressing before bed had been embarrassing. She hadn't known where to look. Some of them didn't seem to care at all but just peeled off all their clothes in full view of everyone, though the Yorkshire girl next to her had gone off to the ablutions hut to undress and Enid had made a tent of her bedclothes.

She couldn't get to sleep. She kept thinking of home, and of Ken, and worrying about how much she'd hurt him. She'd tried hard to explain things to him that evening when they'd been out walking together, up the little track at the back of the farmhouse, after he'd come to tea on Wednesday, as usual.

'I just don't see why you want to go and join up, Winn,' he'd said, with his sad look on his face.

'I want to do somethin' useful in the war, Ken. Somethin' on my own.'

'Without me?'

'You could join up too, if you wanted. Go into the RAF, p'raps. We might even be in the same place. We could ask.'

He had looked even sadder. 'They wouldn't have me, Winn. Not with my asthma. You have to be fit. I was askin' Mother about it and she said I hadn't got a chance of gettin' in. They'd never even look at me, she says, not with my weak chest. But I've been thinkin' things over . . .'

'What things?'

'Well, why don't we get married now? Let's not wait any longer. Lots of people are gettin' married because of the war. It says so in the papers. We could get married soon as you like.'

'But where would we live?'

He had said awkwardly: 'With Mother . . . just for the time bein'. Just 'til we got settled.'

They had reached the end of the track and stopped at the gate that led into the ten-acre field. She had looked away from him across the corn stubble towards the line of elm trees on the far side and the spire of Elmbury church against the skyline.

'I don't think I could live with your mother, Ken. I don't think she likes me.'

''Course she does. She's just funny about things sometimes. Set in her ways. She's been a bit like that since Dad died.'

'I don't think she'd want you to get married yet. And I don't think it'd work – her and me together.'

'We could try and find a place of our own then – a room or two somewhere in the village. I could still help Mother in the shop.'

'We couldn't afford it, Ken.' She had turned round to face him. 'Let's just wait, like we always said we would. No sense in rushin' things. We're only eighteen, both of us. There's plenty of time. And I want to do somethin' else with my life first, before we settle down.'

He had said bewildered: 'You never used to talk like this, Winn. I've never heard you say anythin' like this before.'

'I haven't thought about it much before, to tell the truth. It's the war's made me think. And talkin' to that lady at the recruitin' place. She made me think a lot. She said things about the Women's Air Force . . . It's goin' to be very important, she said – for England. She said it'd be a chance for women to do somethin' to help win the war.'

'She wanted you to join, that's all. Gave you a lot of sweet talk.'

'No, 'twasn't just that. She meant it. Besides, they've lots of volunteers. There was a great long queue of them. No, 'twasn't just that.'

She had leaned her arms on the top of the five-barred gate. It had been a lovely September. The ten-acre field had looked very beautiful in the evening sunlight, with the harvest stubble like a golden carpet and the skies all pink. A cool little breeze had ruffled her hair. The rooks had been cawing away in the elms and the church clock had chimed in the distance. It had been so peaceful that it had seemed silly to be talking about a war. Hard to believe there was one on. She had gone on looking up into the skies.

'I'll tell you what I'd really like to do, Ken, if you promise not to laugh at me.'

''Course I won't.'

'I'd like to work with the aeroplanes – help look after the engines, an' that. That's why it's got to be the Air Force, see. I love aeroplanes. I watch them fly over here when I'm out in the fields . . . Royal Air Force ones with those rings on. I'd give anythin' to go in one. Just imagine bein' high up there in the sky, soarin' through the air, just like a bird. I want to do that one day, more'n anythin'.'

Ken had stared at her, more bewildered than ever. 'But they'd never let you. They'd never let you near an aeroplane – not to go in, nor even *touch* the engine, Winn. That's men's work.'

'They want women to take over men's work. That's what the lady told me. She said: "We're goin' to train you to do their work, so's they can go to the Front. Three women to do two men's work", that's what she said.'

'Not to look after the aeroplanes, though.'

'Why not?'

He had scuffed at the earth with his foot. 'I told you, that's men's work. You couldn't do it.'

She had said stubbornly: 'I *could*, Ken. I'm sure I could. I'm good with machines. I can mend the Fordson and no-one's ever taught me how. I got it goin' once when Dad couldn't.'

'But that's only a tractor. Aeroplanes are a lot different. Must be. Stands to reason.' Ken had looked miserable. 'It don't seem right to me, Winn, you feelin' like this. None of it seems right.'

He had not understood at all. And now all those thoughts and ideas of hers seemed stupid too. The RAF didn't want them here, except to whistle at and laugh about. Ken had been right. They'd never let her near the aeroplanes. She might as well have stayed in Elmbury. She needn't have married Ken just yet, not 'til they could have a place of their own, but she could have gone on helping at home and on the farm. Dad only had old Jack with his rheumatism now. She thought of her little attic room. If she were there now she'd be able to hear Mum and Dad moving about downstairs. She'd hear the creak of Dad's heavy footsteps on the wooden stairs as he trudged up to bed, Mum's lighter tread, their door latch clicking, their voices in the room below. She'd be able to hear Gran snoring, maybe Ruth or Laura calling out, the mice pattering in the wainscot, Rusty barking in his kennel in the stackyard below . . .

Thinking about it all was Winnie's undoing. Her throat tightened with wretchedness and she turned her face into the bolster and wept.

Felicity Newman was awake in her room in empty warrant officers' married quarters. Sleep was impossible. There was too much to think about. Too much to worry about. The conditions for the recruits were far from satisfactory – damp and leaking sleeping quarters, sordid ablutions, no proper mess of their own, a recreation hut with almost no furnishings at all, let alone comforts, a bleak little backroom in the NAAFI . . . In her notes for guidance it stated clearly that a WAAF officer was responsible for procuring the best living conditions available for the airwomen in her charge. *Officers will, in all cases, consider the health of airwomen and give special attention to cleanliness, sanitation, fresh air, adequate space, recreational facilities* . . . She herself had been as segregated from the RAF officers as the airwomen had been from the airmen, her meals served in the Ladies' Room of the Officers' Mess, while Sergeant Beaty had been isolated in some far corner of the Sergeants' Mess. *You will form an integral and vital part of that great Service* . . .

She had enjoyed her officers' training course – the

interesting lectures, the drill, the companionship – and she had not seriously doubted her ability to do the job; until now. She re-lived her interview with Wing Commander Palmer, seeing again his icy stare and hearing his harsh voice. *Just exactly what are you women supposed to be doing here, Company Assistant Newman? Perhaps you can explain that to me.* She had been as timid and nervous as a school girl and the Wing Officer would have been sadly disappointed in her. *The duty of a WAAF officer is to ensure co-ordination between the Women's Auxiliary Air Force and the Royal Air Force . . . to act as an adviser on WAAF matters to the Station Commander . . . I will not tolerate any interference with the efficient running of RAF Colston . . .* She had been equally green and ineffectual with the airwomen, allowing all that giggling to go on unchecked. *WAAF officers will be responsible for maintaining discipline in their detachments . . .* And what on earth was to be done about their clothes? *Smart appearance is the first step towards smart discipline . . .* But the fact remained that there was no uniform at all available for the recruits. None. And no prospect of any coming soon. She had had her own privately tailored. *The WAAF officer must make herself responsible to the Royal Air Force Commanding Officer for the efficiency, discipline, well-being and training of WAAF personnel under his command . . . I did not ask for you. I do not want you. I do not believe that your place is here, or that you could possibly replace my men . . .*

A heavy vehicle whined past outside, its tyres swishing on the wet road. The sound died away and it was quiet again. It was a long while, though, before Felicity slept.

More than sixty miles away from RAF Colston, Virginia Stratton was also lying awake in her back bedroom in a downstairs flat in Wimbledon, South London. She was still badly upset by the scene with her mother. She had arrived home from work much later than usual that evening and had let herself in very quietly, stopping to hang up her hat and coat in the hall and to peer at herself in the mirror on the stand. It had been raining hard and she had tried to put her hair to rights, re-fixing the combs that held it back on each side of her head. Then she had stood for a moment in the dim hallway, hands clasped, trying to steady herself.

'Is that you, Virginia? You're very late.'

Mother's voice had sounded querulous and she had gone quickly into the kitchen. Cooking always tired Mother. She wasn't used to having to do it at all, as she frequently pointed out, but she would always insist on preparing a three-course meal in the evenings. And the table had to be properly laid and the food formally served, as though they were dining in company, not just the two of them, sitting in a corner of the front room. It was all part of what Mother referred to as keeping up appearances. She had been stirring a saucepan of soup on the stove.

'I was worried, Virginia. Quite upset. Something might have happened to you. They really shouldn't keep you so late. It's most inconsiderate.'

'I'm sorry, Mother.'

'Your hair's very wet. Didn't you use your umbrella?'

'I forgot to take it this morning.'

'You'll forget your head one of these days. I hope you don't forget things at the office.'

'No, I don't . . .'

'Just as well. Good posts are hard to come by these days. You can dry those things now that you're here. It would have been nice if you'd been here earlier to help more.'

She had picked up the tea cloth and begun to dry a mixing bowl from the draining board. Mother had bent to open the oven door and there had been a piece of haddock baking inside, curled up at the edges. She had wondered how she was going to find the appetite to eat it. She had finished the bowl, started on some spoons and dropped one of them with a clatter.

'You're so clumsy, Virginia. It's high time you grew out of it. It gives such a bad impression.'

The oven door had shut on the dried-up haddock and Mother had lifted the lid on a saucepan of boiling cabbage.

'What were you doing so late at the office? It must have been something important.'

She had had to speak up then. Then, or never.

'Actually, I wasn't at the office, Mother – '

Mother had turned to stare, the saucepan lid in one hand. 'Where were you then? Not with some man, I hope. You know my views on that. You're far too young and they're not to be trusted. As I should know.'

'I – I went to the recruiting office. It's very near. Just round the corner, in fact. I've been past it often at lunchtimes and seen the queues . . .'

'What *are* you talking about, Virginia? What recruiting office? What queues? What do you mean?'

'For the Women's Auxiliary Air Force, Mother.'

'For *what*?'

'The Women's Air Force . . . I've applied to join them. It's quite a new thing and they've been asking for volunteers. It's to help the Royal Air Force . . .'

Mother's face had gone frighteningly white. 'Have you gone mad! I hope you're not serious.'

She had held onto the spoons tightly. 'Yes, I am, Mother. I've been thinking about it . . . Every time I saw the queues, I felt I wanted to do something really useful, like those women. Today I talked with one of the officers. She says I could join next month, as soon as I'm eighteen. They'd have me then. But I thought I ought to tell you now – '

'Stop this nonsense, Virginia! Don't be so ridiculous! You have a perfectly good job as an insurance clerk. I shouldn't dream of allowing you to do anything so stupid. A girl of your background joining the Services! I never heard of such a thing. Only the lowest type of girls do that.'

She had said doggedly: 'I don't think that's true, Mother. Lots of women are volunteering now – very respectable ones. I've seen them standing in the queues. I don't want to spend the war working at Falcon Assurance. I want to do something worthwhile. Please try to understand.'

Two red spots had appeared in Mother's white cheeks. 'Oh, I understand. I understand very well. You just want to go off and enjoy yourself, and leave me here all on my own. That's the truth of it, so don't try to pretend otherwise. Worthwhile, indeed! I should have thought it was worthwhile to remember your duty to me, after all I've done for you . . . bringing you up single-handed. You're selfish and ungrateful – and deceitful too, just like your father. Going off to that place without telling me – pretending you were at the office – '

'I didn't pretend that, Mother – '

'You're taking after him, and you're going to abandon me, just like he did. You're going to leave me to face the bombs all by myself. I could be blown to bits for all you care!'

Mother's voice had risen to a hysterical pitch and there had been tears in her eyes. It had been horrible. She had hardly ever seen her cry.

'I do care, Mother. Of course, I do.'

'No, you don't, or you wouldn't even consider leaving me after all I've suffered. You're a heartless, wicked creature and if you go I shall never forgive you!'

Mother had dropped the saucepan lid with a crash and rushed from the kitchen. Her bedroom door had slammed shut so hard that it had shaken the walls of the flat.

She had stood quite still, in shock and distress, clutching the spoons and the damp tea cloth to her chest, feeling her heart thumping hard. The soup had boiled over suddenly, oozing in lava-like streams over the top of the saucepan and down the sides to sizzle on the stove. There had been a smell of burning from the cabbage. She had moved forward blindly to turn both off.

Much later, Mother had come out of her room and they had eaten their dinner in complete silence. Somehow she had forced down the haddock and the burned-tasting cabbage. As usual they had listened to the nine o'clock news on the wireless, as they sat knitting. It had sounded bad. The British Expeditionary Force was in France, German U-boats were attacking British shipping, the Russians were advancing into south-eastern Europe . . . It had seemed clearer than ever to her that she should join up, but she had not dared to raise the subject again.

Lying in bed, she thought about Mother and tried to understand how she felt. The trouble was that Mother had never got over the fact that Father had left her. She had never forgiven or forgotten it, but allowed the wound to fester all these years and to poison her life. And she could never forget that they had once lived in a big house on the edge of Wimbledon Common, with servants. Virginia found she could scarcely remember the house now; nor much of her father. He was only a vague memory of a quiet voice and a prickly moustache and an aroma of cigarette smoke. She thought, though she could not be sure, that he had called her Ginny. She wished she knew more, but Mother hardly ever spoke of him and when she did, like this evening, it was always with a dreadful bitterness. Not only had he been cruelly unfaithful – there had been some other woman, Mother had once said, a brazen, common creature – but he had been a failure as well. The firm he had owned in the City had crashed and he had been made bankrupt. Soon after that had happened he had left them. Abandoned them when Virginia was eight years old. The big house had been sold and the servants given notice. She and Mother had moved into this dreary ground floor flat in a semi-detached house near Wimbledon Park station. She had been taken away from her private school and sent to the High School instead. When she had matriculated, the headmistress had tried to persuade her to stay on to take her Higher Certificate and go to university. She had wanted to badly but Mother had said she could not afford it and so she had left school and started work as a clerk with the Falcon Assurance Company in Holborn, travelling into town every day on the District Line from Wimbledon Park. Perhaps she ought to feel bitter about Father too. She had never found it in her heart to be so, until now.

If Father had not deserted them, Mother would never have felt like this. She would never have become the sad and lonely person she was, and there would not have been this awful burden to carry. Mother had been right when she had called her selfish . . . she *was* only thinking of herself. She had said that she wanted to do something worthwhile in the war but, if she were really honest about it, the chance of getting away from the Falcon Assurance Company meant a lot too. The work was deadly dull. Sometimes she could see herself growing like Miss Parkes who had been with the company for more than thirty years and had grown as drab as the office files she sat among. She could see her own thirty or more years stretching ahead of her . . . the daily journey in on the District Line, changing at Earls Court to take the Piccadilly Line to Holborn, the hours spent in the fusty gloom of the filing department, the solitary lunch at Lyons Corner House, and then more hours with the files. Rush hour back in the crowded Underground and the District Line train rattling out to the suburbs, the walk up the hill from the station to the drab house in Alfred Road, Mother resentful in the kitchen, dinner at the table in the front room, the nine o'clock news on the wireless, the knitting or sewing or reading, and so to bed in this depressing, narrow back room . . .

The rain was splashing down noisily on the concrete yard outside the window, where the dustbins stood. It sounded as though the gutter above was blocked again, which would mean more arguments with the landlord. Virginia lay listening to it and thinking her thoughts, until, at last, she slept.

41

Two

Getting up at six didn't worry Winnie. She was always up by that time at home on the farm and so she didn't moan or groan like most of the other girls in the hut. Nor did she have much difficulty, like some, in stowing her bedding just the way the sergeant had shown them – the three biscuits stacked at the head of the bed, the blankets folded and put on top with one of them wrapped lengthwise round the rest to hold them together, with the join underneath. The bolster topped the pile. Sergeant Beaty had bellowed the instructions the night before, as though they were out on the big parade ground.

'Folds of the blankets to the *foot* of the bed with the edge of the pile *exactly* on the edge of your biscuits ... Are you paying attention, Potter? I'm not telling you again. You'd better get it right if you don't want to find yourself on a charge.'

Of course Enid had started to cry again and Winnie had had to help her make a proper job of her bedding in the morning. At breakfast she sat down beside Winnie and gave her a wan smile. Her eyelids were still red and swollen.

'I don't know how I'm going to cope, really I don't. I wish I'd never volunteered. It's horrible here and I miss Terry ever so much. I cried myself to sleep last night.'

'Terry?'

'My fiancé. I'm engaged.' Enid held out her left hand for Winnie to see her ring. Little chips of red stones formed a flower on her fourth finger. 'They're real garnets, you know. It cost ten pounds, but Terry said it was worth every penny. He's ever so generous.'

Winnie admired the ring. She said shyly: 'I'm engaged too.'

Enid looked surprised. 'Oh! Are you? Can I see your ring?' She inspected the small turquoise stone carefully. 'How much was yours?'

Loyal to Ken, Winnie lied. 'I don't know. I'm not sure.' She put her hand away under the table. The ring had cost less than half the price of Enid's.

She ate some of the lumpy porridge. It was lucky that she felt better and not sick any more or she would never have been able to manage it, or the fried bread and baked beans. The tea out of the urn tasted just as bad as before – sweet and bitter all at the same time. It made her shudder to drink it.

Enid gave her a nudge. 'That girl over there – the one in the blue – she's an honourable. Did you know that?'

'Is she?' Winnie wasn't sure what an honourable was, but the girl looked very smart in her blue costume. She was wearing a pearl necklace and some bright pink lipstick, and her fair hair had beautiful waves.

'Her name is The Honourable Susan Courtney-Bennet and her father is a Lord. Someone told me. She didn't come on the train with us. She has her very own car and she came in that. Fancy! I heard her talking to Sandra last night. She went to Buckingham Palace once and curtsied to the King and Queen. She was telling Sandra all about it.'

Winnie stared at the girl. It seemed extraordinary to be sitting at the same table as someone who had actually met the King and Queen.

Enid was delving into her skirt pocket. 'Would you like to see a picture of my Terry?'

Winnie took the snapshot gingerly between her thumb and forefinger, aware that she was handling something precious. She looked at Enid's Terry who was dressed in some sort of sailor's uniform with a big collar and a round hat. He was standing with his legs planted apart, as if on deck, although the picture had been taken in a garden. His hands were behind his back and he seemed to be squinting into the sun. Privately Winnie thought he wasn't a patch on Ken, but she said politely:

'He looks very nice indeed.'

'Oh, he's lovely! And such a gentleman. I'm ever so lucky.' Enid took the snapshot away and returned it carefully to her pocket. 'I do miss him, though. I only joined up because he's away so much. He's in the Royal Navy, you see. That's his uniform he's wearing. He's an Able Seaman. I thought if I joined up too it'd take my mind off things . . . him being in danger at sea and that. He could be sunk any time by one of those German U-boats and he can't swim . . .'

Her eyes had begun to fill with tears.

Winnie said hurriedly: 'I'm sure he'll be all right. You mustn't worry.'

Enid sniffed and dabbed at her eyes with her handkerchief. 'What does your fiancé do then?'

'He works in a shop. His mother has the village stores at home and he helps her. She's a widow, you see.'

'Oh. Well, I don't suppose he could afford much for the ring. He's not in the Services then?'

'No, he has this asthma. They wouldn't take him.'

'Then you don't have to worry like me.' Enid sounded pleased.

An aircraft went over suddenly, rattling the hut windows. Enid dropped her spoon and covered her ears. 'They make ever such a din those things. It's awful.'

'I don't mind it.'

'Don't you?' Enid looked surprised again. 'It gets on my nerves. I don't know how I'm going to stand it, going on all the time.'

'I expect you'll get used to it.'

'I'm sure I won't. And there's another thing . . . somebody told me we'll all have to get our hair cut short. It's got to be above the collar. I don't know what I'm going to do. Terry'll be ever so upset if I have to. He says it's a woman's crowning glory and he likes it long like this.'

Winnie looked at Enid's straight, mouse-brown hair doubtfully. It straggled wispily on her shoulders. 'P'raps you could pin it up, or somethin'. I expect they'd let you do that.'

'I don't know how. It's all right for you, isn't it? You don't have to worry about yours.'

Winnie felt guilty about her own short, naturally curly hair. And she also felt guilty about not having a fiancé who might be sunk at any moment and who couldn't swim. It seemed odd to her to be a sailor and not be able to swim. As odd as being in the WAAF and not liking the sound of aeroplanes. But she said nothing and started to eat her fried bread and baked beans.

Further up the table, Susan Courtney-Bennet said to Anne: 'I say, where were you at school?'

'A place called St Mary's.'

'*The* St Mary's? The one in Berkshire?'

'That one. But I got chucked out.'

'Heavens, how dreadful! What on earth for?'

'Smoking. I got caught three times.'

Susan blinked. 'Well, you did rather ask for it then, didn't you? It was awfully silly of you.'

'Actually, I was glad to be out of there. I hated the place.'

'But weren't your parents frightfully upset?'

'They were at first. But they got over it.'

'I don't think mine ever would. I was at Parkside. I don't remember anyone ever being expelled from there . . . it's a terrible disgrace, isn't it?' Susan picked up her knife and fork. 'I say, this fried bread is all burned on one side. Honestly! Who on earth does their cooking?'

'RAF cooks, I suppose.'

'I'm Cordon Bleu trained. I expect they'll want me to do dinners in the Officers' Mess – banquets, all that sort of thing . . .'

Anne somehow doubted it. Nothing so far had led her to believe that the RAF had any intention of letting them

45

do anything other than the most boring drudgery. She wondered what dreary job she would be given, and wished she'd joined the ATS, like Kit had suggested. When she had tagged onto the end of the long queue of volunteers in the street, she had thought it was for the Army. It was only when she reached the top and was interviewed by a dragon-like woman in a blue uniform, not khaki, that she had realized that she was volunteering for the Air Force. After all the waiting, she couldn't be bothered to change. The dragon had asked a lot of questions about what she could do. Could she cook? Could she type? Could she drive? She couldn't do any of those things but it had seemed better not to admit it. She had said she could cook – well she had once boiled an egg – and the dragon had written that down. There had been forms to fill in and sign and she had found herself promising to serve for four years, or the duration of the war, to serve in any part of the United Kingdom, or abroad, to obey all orders given by a superior placed in authority over her, and to perform any work required of her by her superior officers. When she thought about it now, she decided that she must have been mad to promise any such thing. Being in the WAAF was probably going to be even worse than being at school. At least at St Mary's they had not had to do the sort of horrible cleaning work which that ghastly sergeant had told them about when she had finished bawling at them about the silly way they had to fold up the bedclothes.

'You will all have daily duties to perform, in rotation. You will take it in turns, in pairs, to clean the washbasins, baths and lavatories in the ablutions, and the floors, windows and stoves in here . . . Each airwoman will be responsible for keeping the floor space round her bed clean and her bed and locker tidy . . .'

The sergeant had reminded Anne unpleasantly of one of the games mistresses at school. She wondered if Army sergeants were as bad, though it wouldn't matter to Kit so much since he was going to be an officer. Lucky Kit. He wouldn't have to clean baths and lavatories or stoves and if his officers' quarters were in anything like the palatial building she'd noticed here, then he'd be in clover. His last letter home had sounded pretty pleased with life.

Atkinson and Villiers are here too, which is a bit of a lark. And Stewart turned up last week, so we're a merry band. They're working us fairly hard but I don't mind that – just so long as we get a chance to have a crack at the Hun. Latimer's going to try and join the RAF. He wants to be a pilot. Bombers, I think. Tell Anne to keep a look out for him.

But RAF Colston was a fighter station, so she was unlikely ever to come across Latimer with the spaniel's eyes. The 'planes that made so much noise overhead, like the one that had just made the windows rattle, were called Hurricanes – so someone had said who sounded as though she knew. They were single-engined fighters and there were, apparently, two squadrons of them stationed here – whatever a squadron might consist of. She hadn't a clue.

Susan Courtney-Bennet was asking something again – whether she knew some girl who had been at St Mary's. She really was a crashing snob and just the sort of type she'd hoped to get away from when she'd left that school. That bit in Kit's letter about him getting a chance to have a crack at the Hun had frightened her all over again. Supposing he were sent to France . . . supposing he ended up at the Front . . . supposing . . .

Squadron Leader 'Robbie' Robinson was in charge of Administration at RAF Colston. Like its Station Commander, he had been in the Royal Flying Corps during the First World War and he had assumed an avuncular role among so many younger men. He had a reputation for solving all problems and it was he who immediately found an office for Felicity in Station Headquarters. Somehow he contrived to re-shuffle things so that she was able to move into a room immediately next door to his own.

'So that you'll be under my antiquated wing, my dear. Somewhat moth-eaten and losing its feathers, but if you

47

need anything you can just pop your head round the door and ask.'

His kind voice, twinkling eyes and the homely pipe, almost permanently clenched between his teeth, gave her reassurance and encouragement, as did the massive copy of King's Regulations which he lent her 'the RAF bible, my dear', which sat at her elbow on her desk. She referred to it constantly and feverishly, riffling through its many pages.

She had assigned her airwomen according to the requirements. It transpired that some could offer much more than the cooking, cleaning and clerical work supposed by the Station Commander. There were half a dozen trained shorthand typists among them, two teleprinter operators, a qualified nurse and a driver who could handle three-ton lorries. Even Gloria Gibbs, who had appeared so unpromising, turned out to be an experienced switchboard operator. She had interviewed each girl painstakingly in turn, and done her best for them with the limited opportunities. It was a great waste, she considered, that some should have to do waitressing and cleaning when they were clearly capable of more. Few, though, seemed to have very high expectations and she had not understood, at first, when Winifred Briggs, the country girl from Suffolk, had asked if she would be able to work with the aeroplanes.

'You mean cleaning them? Something like that?'

The girl had gone very red and shaken her head. It had taken quite a while to persuade her to explain what she really meant.

'I wanted to work on the engines, madam. Help look after them.'

'The *engines*?' She had tried not to look surprised or sceptical. *A WAAF officer must cultivate understanding of, and sympathy with her airwomen* . . . 'Is that something that specially interests you?'

The girl had nodded mutely. She had a fresh country complexion and soft curly brown hair. A pretty girl, shy and unworldly and unspoiled, with a lovely Suffolk way of speaking. She looked strong and capable but it was hard to imagine her working alongside RAF mechanics.

'I see . . . well, Briggs, I'm sure you'd probably make a very good mechanic but unfortunately that trade just isn't open to us WAAFS. Of course, that doesn't mean to say that it never will be. I believe that as time goes by more and more RAF trades will begin to accept us — maybe even that one. We shall have to be patient.'

'Yes, madam.'

'*Ma'am*, Briggs, not madam. Try to remember. In the meantime, I think you would do very well as a General Duties clerk. It's not all that exciting but you'll learn a lot about how the RAF is run.'

A clerk. In General Duties — whatever that was. Filling in forms and such like, most probably. There were forms for everything in the RAF, she'd discovered that already. She'd much sooner have been waitressing or working in the kitchens like some of the others. This then was what she'd left home and Ken for . . . to be a clerk. *I want to do somethin' useful in the war, Ken* . . . She felt like crying again, but what was the use in that? The only thing to do was to be patient, like the officer had told her, and to make the best of things. That, or give up now and go back home to Elmbury. Nobody could stop you leaving if you were a volunteer. One of the girls had gone already. Just packed her suitcase and left. She could take the train to London and then the one to Ipswich and the bus from there home. Mum and Dad would be pleased to have her back to help out, and Ken . . . well, Ken would be happy again and not have his sad face. But if she went back home it would be giving up, wouldn't it? Giving up before she'd even tried. And she didn't want to do that. *I want to do somethin' with my life first, before we settle down*. That was what she'd said to him and she wouldn't give up.

* * *

'You're not seriously trying to tell me that it's a *good* thing having these females here, Robbie?'

Squadron Leader Robinson had known David Palmer far too long to try to tell him any such thing. At least, not directly. He said soothingly:

'I don't think it will be quite as bad as you think. Company Assistant Newman strikes me as a very sensible and efficient young lady.'

'*She* may be, I grant you, but what about the rest of them? I mean what sort of women would join the Services? Remember the reputation most of them got in the last show?'

'Oh, rather unfounded, sir, surely? The girls I came across in the WRAF were jolly good types. Put their hand to anything to help win the war. Did a marvellous job. That's why they got the vote, isn't it, not for chaining themselves to railings?'

Palmer said irritably: 'I know, I know. And it's gone to their heads. They want to get in on everything these days just because they're allowed to vote too. But it still doesn't mean they're going to be any use to us, does it? Any fool can put a cross on a piece of paper and stick it in a box. They'll cause trouble with the men, mark my words, upset everything and be nothing but a confounded nuisance. God almighty, Robbie, we've got a bloody war to fight. It's a serious business and we don't need them causing us difficulties and distractions.'

'Are you so sure they will, sir?'

'Yes, I'm damned sure they will. Where there are women there are always problems, in my experience.'

Robinson thought of the CO's wife. Caroline Palmer could certainly be described as causing plenty of difficulties and distractions among some of the young officers on the station. He was not sure whether Palmer had this also in mind.

He said carefully: 'Once we get everything properly organized, sir, I really think – '

His CO cut across him. 'We can't accommodate them

here satisfactorily, Robbie. We've no proper facilities for females.'

'It'll take a while to sort out, I agree – '

'And they haven't even got any uniform – except those first two. The rest are running round in frocks and high heels and God knows what. Mind you, I don't know which is worse, women *in* uniform, or out of it. All I *do* know is that I don't want them cluttering up my station, whatever they're wearing.' Palmer shuffled some papers crossly on his desk. 'This war's going to be different from the last one. The Front's not going to stay conveniently over there, at a safe distance. An operational station is a target for the enemy and the Hun might take it into his head some day to come and drop a lot of bombs on us. What'll happen with these women then? They'll panic all over the place, having hysterics, and then the men will worry about *them* instead of thinking about what *they* ought to be doing. It's a recipe for disaster.'

The squadron leader cleared his throat. His seniority in years, if not in rank, gave him some authority to speak his mind.

'Personally, I think you're doing them rather an injustice, sir. I don't believe they would *panic*. Women can be extraordinarily calm and brave in a crisis. They're by no means all prone to hysteria – in my opinion, that's a fallacy. Look at the nurses in the WRAF – they carried on with the job no matter what the danger . . .'

'Different breed, Robbie. Totally different. Nurses have a vocation. They're dedicated to caring for the sick and wounded. They're nurses because they're that type of person. But these women . . . this lot we're landed with, they're all kinds and from what I've seen, none of them are likely to be a blind bit of use to us.'

'I think you'll find that's far from the case. They all seem keen to do their best, and surely we're going to need all the help we can get.'

'You'll be telling me next that I ought to be grateful to them for coming here?'

'You may even be that – one day, sir.'

Palmer grunted. 'Trouble with you, Robbie, is that you're prejudiced. You're on their side. It's having two daughters that does it, I suppose.'

The squadron leader thought fondly of his two girls, Heather and Jean. The CO was childless, but whether from choice or misfortune he had never liked to enquire. Meg's looks weren't a patch on Caroline Palmer's. Her hair was turning grey and her waist had thickened, but he wouldn't have traded wives with his commanding officer for all the money in the world. There were times when he felt very sorry for David Palmer. The man had been a superb pilot – still was, for that matter, though these days he mostly flew a desk – and he clearly loved the RAF. But he had married a woman who made no secret of the fact that Service life and Service people bored her stiff – unless the people happened to be young, good-looking and well-connected young officers, in which case her interest far exceeded anything expected of a Station Commander's wife. It was well known. Robinson was not surprised that Palmer apparently expected the worst of women.

The Station Commander had got up from his desk and was looking moodily out of the window behind it, his hands in his pockets.

'That one in charge of them . . . Newley, or whatever her name is – '

'Newman, sir.' Robinson fiddled with his pipe, poking a matchstick round the bowl. 'As I said, she's very sensible and efficient. Rather intelligent, too, I'd say. I gather she was up at Cambridge before she joined.'

'A bloody blue-stocking! That's just what we *don't* need. Well, she may be intelligent, but she's too damned young.'

'She's twenty-two. A lot of our chaps are younger.'

'Nothing to do with it. This one's supposed to be able to control a pack of silly, giggling girls. They should have sent some old battleaxe to cope.'

'I think I'd sooner have Company Assistant Newman any day, sir, if you don't mind.'

Palmer smiled, and the smile transformed his face momentarily, softening the stern features. 'Perhaps you're right about that, Robbie. We don't want any more like that Sergeant Whatsername. God, what a hideous woman! If you can call her one at all. She's got one advantage, though – *she* won't be distracting any of the men from their duties.' He turned away from the window. 'I wish this damn war would get cracking properly. All this hanging around waiting for it to get going. Nothing but practice attacks. The bomber boys have had all the luck so far.'

'Dropping leaflets, sir? Taking a few pot shots at German naval bases? Nothing much to write home about.'

'But at least they're doing *something*. Christ, I wish I were twenty years younger, Robbie.'

'I wish I were too, sir. But I'm afraid there's not much we can do about it.'

'I popped up in a Hurry the other day with Ross's lot. Made me feel about nineteen again. Bloody fine kite. Steady as a rock. Fast as hell. Climbs like a rocket. Turns on a sixpence. I tell you, our young chaps are lucky blighters. I'd give ten years of my life to be in their shoes . . .'

'That sounds as though it would rather defeat the object, sir.'

Palmer gave a short laugh. 'Suppose it would. Do you know, Robbie, sometimes I hate this job of mine. Tied to this desk, missing all the real fun. Being nice to bloody civilians like that woman who wrote to me today complaining about the noise our fighters make. She swears they use her house as a turning point . . . says they're frightening her hunters. And someone else rang to say the low-flying's stopped their chickens laying. God give me patience! They'd be quick enough to complain if we weren't trained and ready for action to defend their blasted horses and chickens when the Huns come. What do they expect us to do? Practise flying on the ground?'

Palmer shook his head in disgust. From outside the window behind him came the sound of high-pitched giggling. He turned round slowly, as though unable to believe his ears, taking his hands from his pockets. He rubbed at the glass between the criss-crossed brown paper strips with the side of one hand. In the roadway outside there was a small group of airmen and two of the WAAF airwomen. He watched in disbelief as one of the girls tweaked off an airman's cap, put it on her own head and ran off shrieking as its owner tried to retrieve it. Louder shrieks reached the two senior officers clearly as the airman caught up with her. Palmer drew a deep breath.

'Now, Robbie, do you see what I mean?'

When Felicity entered the Station Commander's office he was standing with his back to her, staring out of the window by his desk. She stood waiting until he turned, unsmiling, and sat down, gesturing to her to do the same. He clasped both hands together on the desk top in front of him.

'When you arrived here, Company Assistant Newman, I believe I told you my views on having women serving on my station?'

'Yes, sir.'

'And I believe I made them quite plain?'

'Perfectly, sir.'

'They remain unchanged. In fact they have been reinforced a short while ago by the sight of two of your airwomen distracting a group of my men from their duties.'

She coloured. 'In what way exactly, sir?'

'Giggling and horseplay, outside this very window. An appalling display of indiscipline such as I have never witnessed in all my years in the Service. Running about and shrieking as though this was some kind of playground.'

54

'I'm very sorry, sir. I'll do my best to see that it doesn't happen again.'

'You will indeed. You are supposed to be in control of your airwomen, and you are answerable for them and for their behaviour – to me. Under no circumstances is the sort of scene I witnessed ever to be repeated, do you understand? You will speak to your airwomen and make quite certain that it does not.'

'Yes, sir.'

'I do not expect to see airwomen hob-nobbing with airmen, let alone sky-larking with them.'

'Yes, sir . . . I mean, no sir. If I might say one thing, sir . . .'

He raised his eyebrows. 'What one thing?'

'Well, sir, the airwomen will be working alongside the men, in the kitchens, on the switchboard, and so forth . . .'

'I am aware of that.'

'Well, sir, they have to talk to the men, as part of their work. They couldn't very well do it properly without doing so. Then, if they come across them off-duty, about the station, as they're bound to, it would be very difficult not to talk to them then as well . . . not to act in a friendly manner, if you see what I mean.'

'I don't think you see what *I* mean, Company Assistant Newman. I'm not talking about normal exchanges of conversation, in passing or otherwise, but the kind of blatantly flirtatious behaviour that took place before my very eyes. I will not allow that sort of thing at RAF Colston. It is an operational fighter station, engaged in the very serious business of waging war against the enemy. Surely you can grasp that?'

'Yes, sir.'

She was looking distressed but he went on without mercy.

'Which brings me to another point. Clothing. Something has got to be done about it. Your airwomen are parading about the station dressed unsuitably, to say the

55

least. Some of them look as though they are going to a party. It's disastrous for discipline, all round. It can't go on.'

'We have no uniform at all, as yet, sir.'

'I realize that. But that doesn't prevent you from seeing that your airwomen wear more appropriate garments. I surely don't have to spell it out in detail, do I? You must know the sort of thing I mean – sensible shoes with low heels, plain skirts, navy jumpers or cardigans . . . all that sort of thing – not frilly frocks and high-heeled sandals. I don't want to see any more of those on my station, and that's an order.'

'I'll do what I can, sir.'

'You'll do better than that, Company Assistant. You will carry out my orders to the letter. If the airwomen have no proper garments, they must send for them from their homes, or you must get your people to authorize the purchase of appropriate clothing. That's all.'

He reached for his pen and pulled some papers towards him, in dismissal. When she had left the room he looked up at the closed door. How old had Robbie said she was? Twenty-two? That was damned young for the job. Maybe he should have been a bit less hard on her? A bit more sympathetic? It must be pretty tough starting from scratch, with nothing laid down properly, no uniform, no proper accommodation, everything a bit strange . . . No, damn it, he couldn't afford to be anything less than tough. He'd got a job to do as well and that was to make quite certain that the Station was on top line. Nothing else counted. He bent over the papers again.

If they had no uniforms, at least they had numbers. Each had been photographed with a number on a board held beneath their chins – just like convicts, as Maureen Platt complained. She complained as frequently as Sandra Hunt asked questions. The photographs were stuck on their identity cards, called twelve-fifties, and they were told to learn their own numbers by heart.

And they had been issued with paybooks in RAF

blue, and with heavy steel helmets that they carried on their backs like humps, and with cumbersome anti-gas respirators with long elephant snouts that had to be taken everywhere, slung across their chests in canvas holders. As well as these things they had been given identity tags – two flat discs strung on a cord, one red and one green and marked with their name, number and religion, to be worn round their necks at all times.

'In case of you-know-what,' Pearl said darkly.

Sandra looked puzzled. 'What do you mean, you-know-what? I *don't* know.'

'In case they have to identify our bodies.'

'*Bodies?*'

'That's right. These things we walk around in. If Jerry comes and bombs us we might have to be dug out of the smouldering ruins and they'll want to be able to tell who's who.' Pearl tugged at the cord round her neck and fished out her two discs. 'One's rot proof and t'other's fireproof. One of the men told me. This one with the two holes is for nailing on your coffin.'

'*Coffin!*'

'Sorry, dear, but you did ask . . .'

Vera Williams, who stuttered, was examining her paybook closely. 'It says, instructions to airmen. It's not even for us. It should s-s-say instructions to *airwomen*. Listen to this. One, you will be held p-personally responsible for the custody of this book. Two, you will always carry the book on your person both at home and abroad. Three, you must produce the book whenever called upon to do so by a c-c-c – '

Anne leaned over her shoulder. 'Competent authority.'

'S-supposing I lose it?'

'You get put on a charge, I expect.'

Vera turned the pages. 'Oooh! There's a place right at the end for making your will. It says, this is the last will and t-t-testament of . . . and they've gone and left a space for it all.'

Pearl was replacing her identity discs poking them

57

down the neckline of her blouse. 'What did I tell you, Sandra?'

Sandra had gone pale. 'Actually, I don't think Mummy would be very pleased.'

RAF Colston, Anne had discovered, was like a small town. They had trailed round it in the wake of their officer, vainly trying to absorb its geography, but there were so many buildings. There were barrack blocks, cookhouses, workshops, stores, hangars, MT units . . . Station Headquarters, the Operations Room, the Sergeants' Mess, the Decontamination Centre, the Signals and Meteorological Office . . . it was endless and she had forgotten most of them as soon as she'd been told. It wasn't a bad-looking place, she decided, all things considered. It had been built in the late 1920s, mostly from red brick and there was a lot of smart white paint, well-kept flower beds and tree-lined avenues. You'd hardly know it was a fighter station until you saw the great steel hangars, the new wartime camouflage, and heard the 'planes.

The Officers' Mess was an impressive, creeper-clad building with a stone portico at its entrance and a gravel driveway sweeping up to it. Ever so posh, Pearl called it. There were rosebeds and smooth lawns in front, tennis courts at the side and squash courts nearby. A bit like a sports club.

The kitchens, where she was to work, were located, less grandly, round the back – a warren of white-tiled passageways and dark storerooms leading off a big central room. At first sight, this had looked to her like a giant's lair. Everything was oversize. The pans were as big as washtubs, the baking dishes feet square, the knives like medieval battle weapons and the ladles the size of fish bowls. The room was divided down the centre by a row of iron cooking ranges and lit from overhead by a long glass skylight. The atmosphere was hot and steamy with the lingering odours of past meals . . . soups and stews, cabbage and sprouts, fried bacon and onions, fish and a great many chips. Corporal Fowler, the head cook, had been anything but pleased to see them when they had presented themselves at the door. He had turned round from beheading a pile of fish with a huge cleaver.

'Wot the 'ell do you lot think you're doin' standin' there?'

Susan had said haughtily: 'We have been told to report to you for duty.' She might as well have added, my man.

His eyes had narrowed. 'It's *Corporal*, and don't you forget it.'

He had turned his back and they had stood in an uncertain huddle by the doorway while he went on wielding the cleaver. Every chop made Enid jump. When he had finally finished he came over to them, wiping gory hands on a cloth.

He had jabbed a forefinger at Susan and herself. 'You two can do them spuds – in there. That one 'idin',' pointing to Enid, 'can make 'erself useful in 'ere. And you and you,' the finger moving on to Pearl and Sandra, 'can start layin' up tables. Get yourselves some overalls, all of you. You can't work in them fancy clothes.'

She and Susan had found a sackful of potatoes in the scullery and two smelly, rubberized aprons hanging up on a hook. They had begun work, peeling the potatoes and dropping them into huge pans of cold water. She couldn't get the hang of it at all. The peel came off in thick, uneven chunks, leaving misshapen lumps a third of the size. Her arm still ached from the injections the RAF medical officer had given them all, her fingers grew tired and the metal handle of the knife began to rub a sore place in her palm. She had cut her finger badly and the makeshift handkerchief bandage had quickly become a sodden pink mess. Susan had added to her disenchantment with her know-all remarks.

'You're doing it all wrong. Didn't they teach you how to hold the knife properly in cookery classes?'

'I didn't go to any cookery clases.'

'Goodness, didn't you? Why on earth did they put you in here then?'

'Because I lied and said I could cook.'

Susan had looked shocked and disapproving.

Corporal Fowler had been far from satisfied. 'You can take that lot back and get all them bits of peel off; and all them eyes out. Make a proper job of it.'

After the potatoes there had been carrots to be peeled and chopped and cabbages the size of footballs to be washed, trimmed and sliced. And later on came the washing up – a never-ending stream of dirty plates and cutlery and a tottering stack of pots and pans. All had to be washed, scoured, rinsed, dried and, finally, put away in their correct places. Enid, sent to help in the scullery, had cried enough to make everything wet again.

Pearl and Sandra, waitressing in the dining-room, had done better.

'Officers!' Pearl had crowed. '*Pilots!* Whoopee!'

On their one day off a week she and Pearl took the bus into town. They wandered happily round the shops, gazing into windows, and went into Woolworths where Pearl wanted to buy a lipstick. It amused Anne to be entering somewhere ruled strictly out of bounds at St Mary's for its open counters of cheap merchandise, its supposed germ-carrying unwrapped sweets, its dirty wooden floor and its defiantly common shop girls. Pearl spent a long time trying to decide between Pillar Box Red and Flamingo Pink. She daubed two vivid streaks of colour across the back of her hand and considered them at arm's length.

'Which do *you* think, Anne, love? Can't make up my mind.'

'Aren't they both a bit bright?'

'Not for me, dear. Got to go with the red hair, see. I think I might dye it different next time. I'm getting sick of it.'

Anne looked at the massed fringe of russet curls beneath Pearl's hat brim. 'Isn't it really red, then?'

Pearl laughed. 'Gawd, no! Straight out of a bottle. Autumn Glory it's called.'

'It suits you anyway.'

'Ta, very much. Well, I think I'll take the Pillar Box Red. It goes better.'

They progressed to the Regal Cinema to see *The Ghost Goes West* with Robert Donat, and then treated themselves to sausage, egg and chips and a pot of tea for two in the cinema café. Pearl sighed over Robert Donat.

'Now that's what I call a real gent. Class. Lovely manners. He'd make you feel a lady – which I'm not. That voice sends shivers up and down me to hear it. I used to have a picture of him pinned up over my bed – him and Alan Ladd. That's another one gives me the goose pimples. What about you? Who's your favourite?'

'Me? Gosh, I've never really thought . . .' Anne looked at the coloured photographs of Hollywood film stars hanging round the café walls . . .

'That one's rather nice.'

'Robert Taylor? Yeah, he's all right. And I wouldn't say no to Clark Gable. See that picture there of Ginger Rogers? Now *that's* what I'd really like to look like. I keep trying to get my hair to go the same as hers but it's got a mind of its own. Have you got a steady boyfriend?'

'No.'

'Funny, I'd've thought you would have. One of those upper-class johnnies who speak like they've got plums in their mouths. You soon will, I 'spect, with all those officers roaming around. They'll soon spot you.'

'I'm not really that interested.'

'Aren't you? Blimey, that's one reason I joined up. Thought I might get myself a nice pilot.' Pearl lifted the teapot. 'Fancy another cuppa?'

It was pitch dark when they left the Regal café. The town was blacked out and they groped their way along the pavement in the direction of the bus stop. When they passed a telephone kiosk Anne phoned home, fumbling with coins while Pearl, squashed in beside her, held the torch. She dialled for Trunks and gave the number into a receiver that smelled strongly of disinfectant. The operator's voice told her to kindly insert one shilling and sixpence in the box and she dropped her only shilling on the floor. Pearl dived after it. After a moment she heard her mother's voice answering, miles away in Buckinghamshire.

'Darling! What a lovely surprise! How are you?'

She could picture her mother standing beside the telephone in the drawing-room at home, see the room behind her. She saw the whole familiar scene – the big chintz sofa and comfy armchairs, the grand piano by the french windows with all their photographs on the top, the bookcases, the magazines strewn about, the vases everywhere filled with flowers from the garden and greenhouse . . .

'Are you there, Anne? I can't hear you.'

She fought down the sudden huge wave of homesickness that threatened to overcome her. It had taken her completely by surprise and left her close to tears and speechless. She swallowed hard.

'Yes, I'm here. I'm in a phone box in the town. We've just been to the cinema.'

'We?'

'Another WAAF and me.'

'You're making friends then, darling . . . that's nice.'

Pearl's Pillar Box Red mouth was grinning above the torch. Anne knew what her mother would have to say about Pearl. *A barmaid, darling! Surely you could find someone else to be friends with*.

'How are you and Daddy?'

'We're both fine, thank you, darling. Daddy's been asked to do some sort of war work, but I can't tell you anything about it as it's all terribly secret, apparently. He won't even tell me. Some old Army friend of his rang up about it . . . Anne, are *you* all right? Are you enjoying it?'

'It's OK.'

'Are you getting enough to eat?'

'Masses. Lots of stodge and stews. Just like school.'

Someone was rapping impatiently on the phone box door. Pearl swung the torch beam onto a man's face, mouthing widely like a fish against the glass – a beefy soldier in button-to-the-neck khaki.

'Bugger off!' Pearl told him clearly.

Anne covered the mouthpiece quickly and made a warning face at Pearl.

'What on *earth* is going on, Anne? Who was that?'

'Just someone wanting to use the phone . . . they can wait.'

Her mother sounded anxious. 'I hope you're behaving sensibly, darling . . . not getting into any trouble. Do try hard, for once. They won't put up with any nonsense, I'm sure. We got your letter, by the way. Perhaps they'll find something better for you to do soon than peel vegetables and wash up. It does sound rather awful.'

'It is.'

'It's such a pity you didn't take that typing course – '

'Have you had any news from Kit?'

'Yes. We had a long letter from him yesterday. He says he's quite all right. He's hoping to get some leave soon so he'll be able to come home.'

Her mother's voice had lightened at once and taken on an entirely different note. Well, she couldn't really blame her for the fact that Kit was her favourite. Not if she was honest with herself. She must have been a pretty bloody-minded pain in the neck, one way and another, and specially lately. But it always hurt. It always had done ever since she had realized it long ago when she and Kit were still in the nursery. It had dawned on her gradually as she began to notice the special smile her mother reserved for Kit, and the particular tone she always used when talking to him. It was never overt, but it was there. Kit had always said that she was imagining things but she knew that wasn't so.

'Super! I shouldn't think I'll be getting any leave for

ages. Do you think you could send me a decent pillow? The ones here are ghastly bolsters stuffed with straw.'

'*Straw*, darling?'

She started to ask for some more money as well when the pips suddenly went and she was cut off in mid-sentence.

'Pips go?' Pearl asked, juggling coins by torchlight. 'You want to try and get through again?'

'No . . . it doesn't matter.'

The soldier jerked open the door. 'You two goin' to stay in there yakking all night?'

'Oh, belt up!' Pearl snapped at him.

They stepped icily past him, and an accompanying reek of beer and Brylcreem. It had begun to rain and Pearl played the torch over a running wet pavement. She shivered in her thin coat.

'Tell you what, why don't we find a pub. Get a bit of warmth and cheer. Good idea?'

Anne shrugged. 'I don't know . . . I've never been in one.'

'Blimey! Then it's high time you did.'

Pearl located The Saracen's Head down an alley, apparently guided by some natural homing instinct. They fumbled their way beyond the heavy blackout curtain hanging across the door and passed, as though by a magician's trick, from cold, wet darkness into convivial warmth and light. The pub, crookedly ancient, was crowded, mainly with servicemen. The atmosphere was heady with alcohol and thick with cigarette smoke that wreathed the low black beams. Faces turned towards them, wearing lecherous grins.

Pearl was unconcerned. 'Take no notice, love. I can handle 'em easy. Leave it to me. I'm for a port and lemon, then. What's yours?'

Anne remembered that Kit sometimes drank gin and tonic and thought she'd try that. She shook the raindrops from her hair, brushed down her costume and looked curiously about her. She was on more forbidden territory . . . a place designated off-limits by her parents and completely unthinkable by St Mary's – a place even more evil and corrupting than Woolworths; a public house.

Pearl was elbowing her way through the crush round the bar, her feathered hat bobbing jauntily among the khaki, blue and navy, and parrying remarks with sharp retorts of her own that had the men laughing. She returned in triumph, bearing two glasses, and they sat down at an empty table near the fireside.

Pearl raised her port and lemon. 'Bottoms up and down the hatch!' She took a gulp and then nudged Anne with her elbow. 'See those two RAF blokes over there – the short dark one with the fair fella? They're sergeant pilots from Colston. I've seen them around.'

As Anne looked across at the two men with the V-stripes on their arms and wings on their chests, the dark-haired, stocky one smiled directly at her. He strutted over, cocky and confident.

'You two lasses are from Colston, aren't you? The new WAAFS? Mind if we join you, seeing as we're all part of the same happy family?'

Pearl inclined her head graciously. 'So long as you both behave yourselves.'

Two more chairs were dragged up and introductions made. The dark-haired pilot was a Yorkshireman by the name of Dusty Miller and his companion, younger, slighter built and a great deal less sure of himself, was called Jimmy – Jimmy Shaw. Anne soon discovered that he was painfully shy.

'I'm awfully sorry if we barged in on you,' he told her, flushing. 'I hope we're not in the way.'

He reminded her a bit of Latimer, Kit's bashful school friend; he had the same sort of doggy brown eyes. She smiled at him kindly.

'Don't worry, you're not. We could do with some cheering up.'

He was cradling his beer mug awkwardly against his

tunic, just below the wings. She reckoned that he was about nineteen – perhaps twenty. Not much older than herself. His wrists and hands, beyond the blue cuffs, looked too small and boyish to be capable of handling one of those terrifying machines that roared about the skies.

'Do you fly those Hurricane things?'

He said diffidently: 'Yes . . . not very well, I'm afraid.'

He must be pretty good, though, she thought, or he wouldn't be a sergeant pilot. He was different from most other fighter pilots she'd come across so far – swanking about with their top buttons undone. Interesting.

'How did you come to join the RAF?'

He flushed again. 'I just happened to see an advertisement for it one day. There was a picture of some chap looking up at the sky and some 'planes in the background . . . I sort of liked the look of it and I couldn't think of anything else to do when I left school anyway.' He smiled wryly. 'Nothing very noble about it, I'm afraid. It just sort of happened. How about you? Do you like being in the Women's Air Force?'

'Not much. It's pretty dire, to be honest. We're just skivvies and slaves, most of us. It's not a bit like any of us thought it would be.'

He nodded towards Pearl who was engaged in a sparky exchange with Dusty Miller. 'I've noticed her around the station, but I don't think I've ever seen you.'

'I'm in the Officers' Mess kitchens. We don't often see the light of day.'

He set his mug of beer down on the table and unbuttoned his breast pocket to take out a packet of Players, offering them to her. When she took one he struck a match and lit her cigarette and his own very carefully, as though the whole process of smoking was new to him.

'I can't imagine you working in a cookhouse. What do you do exactly?'

'Anything but cook. I'm a spud-basher. I peel potatoes.

66

Sometimes I get to cut up carrots, or slice cabbages or chop onions – that's a killer – or take the outside bits off Brussels sprouts, but mostly I just peel the spuds. If I'm very lucky I'm allowed to put out the breakfast bacon rashers on the trays ready for the oven, if I'm on the early shift. I'm rather good now at making the lean overlap the fat. Oh, and I wash and dry up, of course. That's never-ending.'

He looked shocked and shook his head slowly from side to side. 'It doesn't seem right to me – someone like you doing that sort of work. Not right at all.'

'I don't think the RAF thinks we're capable of much else. We haven't exactly been welcomed with open arms, you know. They've given us all the grotty jobs.'

He said, embarrassed: 'I'm really sorry . . .'

She laughed. 'It's not your fault, so don't worry. They'll change their tune one day probably. Except for Corporal Fowler, of course. He'll never change his.'

'Who's he?'

'Head cook in the Mess. He hates us. Lord knows why. I expect he thinks we're toffee-nosed and look down on him – which we do because he's such a pig. It doesn't stop him asking me out, though. And every time he does and I say not bloody likely, he gives me some other horrible job to do. Perhaps your *ladyship* will *condescend* to clean the ovens . . . And he's always pinching our bottoms.'

The young pilot went brick red. 'That's pretty foul sort of behaviour.'

'He's just living up to his name and there's not much we can do about it.'

They stayed at the pub until nearly closing time and then caught the bus back to Colston with the two sergeant pilots. In the dim-lit interior Anne observed that Dusty Miller's arm had found its way round Pearl's shoulders in their seat ahead. Jimmy, sitting beside her, kept at a respectful distance.

He said suddenly, without much hope: 'By the way, there's a dance in the Sergeants' Mess soon . . . I don't suppose you'd want to come, though.'

'You suppose wrong,' Anne informed him, agreeably under the influence of four gin and tonics. 'I'd love to.'

The squadron CO's party was already in full swing when Felicity arrived at the stone cottage in Colston village where Squadron Leader Ross and his wife lived. She had been surprised to receive the invitation and reluctant to brave the occasion alone, but, in the end, she saw it as part of her duty. She hesitated for a moment at the half open front door, listening to the party sounds within . . . the hum of voices, laughter, glasses clinking. A batman showed her into a large sitting-room which seemed full of strangers. She could see no other women in uniform. Those present were all civilians and some of them turned to stare at her, hostility in their eyes. She had met this before in the Ladies' Room of the Officers' Mess, where she was still condemned to take her meals. Since they had all the advantages of pretty frocks, long hair, jewellery and unlimited make-up, she found this very strange. But then she was quite unaware of how well her uniform suited her.

Squadron Leader Ross appeared before her, genially smiling. 'Glad you could come. Have a drink.' He thrust a full glass into her hand. 'My patent mix. Guaranteed to make you forget all your troubles in one minute flat.'

A sudden roar of laughter behind her made her jump and nearly spill the drink. She turned and saw that it came from a group of pilots standing close by.

'Badger' Ross said: 'Don't mind that lot. They've never learned any proper manners. Too much time in the air and not enough on the ground, that's their trouble. Don't know how to behave like human beings, let alone gentlemen.'

One of the group detached himself. 'I say, sir, I heard that. Bit unfair of you, getting me off on the wrong foot, so to speak.'

The squadron leader touched Felicity's arm. 'I take it you've been lucky enough to avoid meeting this joker before. May I introduce Flying Officer Dutton, a member of my squadron, worse luck. You'd better behave yourself, for once, Speedy. This is Company Assistant Newman, and she's both an officer and a lady.'

The pilot shook Felicity's hand reverently. 'I can see that, sir. Best behaviour and all that, I swear . . . Scout's honour.'

'I doubt if you were ever in the Scouts, Speedy. They wouldn't have you. Too risky for the Girl Guides.'

With that caustic comment, the squadron leader moved away to other guests. Speedy Dutton took out a silver cigarette case and flipped it open to offer to Felicity. She shook her head.

'No, thank you. I don't smoke.'

'What, no vices?'

'Not that particular one.'

He smiled at her. The most striking thing about him was his eyes. They were blue and very bright, and they shone with life and laughter. Otherwise, his looks were not remarkable. He was of medium height, slim and brown-haired with a small, neat moustache. Like many of the fighter pilots, he had a certain look that set him apart from all the grounded penguins on the station . . . an easy confidence, a casual outlook on life, signalled for all to see by the top tunic button left undone. He also had charm. In abundance.

He squinted at her through the smoke from his cigarette. 'Why on earth haven't we met before? Where have you been hiding from me?'

'In Station HQ, actually.'

'Extraordinary!'

'I've seen *you* before, as a matter of fact.'

His eyes widened. 'I must be slipping badly . . . when and where?'

'It was soon after I arrived. You were standing with some others outside HQ when I came out with Sergeant Beaty after seeing Wing Commander Palmer. You all looked at us as though we'd just landed from Mars.'

'Good Lord, I remember now . . . you gave us the shock of our lives. Matter of fact, I only really saw that sergeant. I thought at first it was a chap dressed up for a lark.'

She looked at him severely. 'That was Sergeant Janet Beaty.'

'Almost had me fooled.' He grinned. 'I must say that uniform looks pretty splendid on you, though – much better than it does on us chaps. *Very* attractive. There's something about a woman in uniform . . . on the right one, that is. It didn't do quite the same for that sergeant of yours, I'm bound to say. Look, I can't call you Company Assistant Newman. Too jolly formal. What's your other name?'

'Felicity.'

'I say, that means happiness, doesn't it? Are you happy?'

'Most of the time, I suppose.'

'Not *all* of the time? Bad show that. We'll have to do something about it. I'm happy all the time. Take no thought for the morrow – that's my motto. Live dangerously for today. My real name's Ian, by the way. Far better known, though, as Speedy.'

She asked why and then instantly regretted it. He tried, unsuccessfully, to look modest.

'Because I'm the fastest worker in the squadron – on the ground.'

'Really?' she said coldly.

'Really. Honest injun. No girl can resist me. You might not believe it to look at me, but there it is.' He eyed her appreciatively across the rim of his glass. 'Tell me, what's a lovely girl like you doing in the Women's Air Force thingamijig? Is your father RAF, or something?'

'No, he's a rector. He has a parish in Norfolk.'

'Lord, is he? Never go near the sky pilots myself if I can help it.'

'Sky pilots?'

'Padres. God bods. Devil dodgers. Call 'em what you will. Not really my line at all. No offence intended, you understand.'

'None taken.'

'Good show.' He beamed at her. 'You know, some of the chaps were a bit fussed at first about having popsies round the station.'

'So I gather.'

'Not me, though. I'm all for it. Brightens the old place up no end, and it's jolly nice having them waiting on us in the Mess. Makes the food taste better.'

'We're not here just to brighten the station up, Flying Officer Dutton.'

'*Speedy*, please . . .' His bright eyes danced. 'I rather hoped that was why they sent you. To comfort the brave heroes. Smooth our fevered brows. Boost our morale, and all that sort of thing.'

Declining to rise to the bait, she took a swallow from her glass and coughed as the fiery taste hit the back of her throat. Speedy patted her on the back sympathetically.

'Lethal concoction old Badger brews. Should've warned you. He pours all the bottles in the bath and stirs it with a paddle. I say, look who's just come in. Enter our flint-eyed Station Master. Don't often see him at these junkets.'

Through watering eyes, Felicity caught sight of Wing Commander Palmer at the far side of the room. There was a little eddy of movement around him – as though Royalty had arrived.

'Damn good pilot in his day,' Speedy was saying. 'A real Biggles of the skies, so they say. Bit past it now, of course. Still, he knows how to run the shop all right. Rod of iron stuff.'

'Who's that with him?'

'The blond lovely? Rather a corker, isn't she? That's his wife, Caroline. Our First Lady. Rich too. Her family owned a brewery, or something. Lots of loot. Rich, beautiful and *very* classy. Mind you, I'm not sure I envy the old man that much. She spends most of her time up in the Smoke. Not too keen on us humble RAF types. She's come slumming tonight.

71

Mrs Palmer's long hair was ash blond and her face an oval of pale, smooth skin. She was tall and slim and her plain black dress made every other dress in the room look cheap or dowdy. A little circle of men had surrounded her; a ring of Air Force blue around the black.

'Bees round the honeypot,' Speedy observed.

'I'm rather surprised you're not there too.'

'She's not my type, actually. Bit too much of the cool northern beauty. Besides, I'd be wasting my time for once. She's not interested in any rank below Flight Lieutenant unless you happen to be very closely related to the Duke of Westminster. That little bunch there haven't a hope, if they did but know it.' He smiled at her disarmingly. 'I'd much sooner be where I am. Ever been to the Old Ship?'

'What old ship?'

He squeezed her arm. 'Not a real ship. A pub. First class little place down on the coast not far from here – right bang on the harbour. Very picturesque, as they say in guidebooks. I'll take you there. You'll love it. Jolly good grub and booze and cosy little corners . . .' He gave a sudden groan. 'Oh God, there's old Whitters making faces at me. Wants to meet you. I suppose I'll have to take you over and share you around a bit. Don't let any of 'em fool you, though. Terrible line shooters.'

Felicity allowed herself to be dragged across to the noisy group behind and to be introduced to Whitters, Dumbo, Sinbad and Moses. Flying Officer Whittaker was tall and gangling and his wide grin showed two badly chipped front teeth. He looked like an overgrown schoolboy, with an energetic eagerness to match. His hands wove patterns in the air as he resumed the story he had been recounting.

'So, there I was, screaming downhill, going full bore, when all of a sudden there's one hell of a bang and the old kite starts bouncing around like a bucking bronco. I sit there, hand frozen on the stick, hardly a dicky bird left on the clock, eyes tight shut, preparing to meet my Maker, when, blow me, she pulls out of it, meek as a lamb . . . and I open the old peepers just as I miss this church tower – '

'Norman or Early English Perpendicular?'

'Don't know much about that sort of thing, Sinbad. I'm not an egghead like you. It was sort of square and looked as though it had been there a fairish time . . . where was I?'

'Missing the church tower.'

'Thank you, Speedy. And by a whisker, I can tell you. Knocked off the weather vane clean as a whistle. And there's all these people running about in the graveyard and hiding behind tombstones . . . Sunday morning, you see, so I suppose it was matins. And there's the parson shaking his fist up at me and flapping his cassock like an old hen – '

'Surplice, Whitters, old chum.'

'I must say I did rather get the impression that I was a bit, Moses.'

'No, you've got the wrong word, you clot. You mean his *surplice*, not his cassock. A cassock's that long black job they wear underneath, so he couldn't have been flapping that. Must have been his surplice – the white pinny thing with big sleeves.'

'That was it. Amazing what you know, Moses. Flapped them both like anything. Looked as though he was trying to take off.'

'I expect he was a bit upset about his weathervane, Whitters. Wanted to come up and tell you about it.'

'He may have been, I grant you, Dumbo. Actually, I think they thought I was a Jerry, or something. Anyway, I gave them all a wave to show I was friendly and waggled the old wings before I popped off. Damn close shave, though.'

The short one called Sinbad said airily: 'Reminds me of the time I had a rather close encounter with Lincoln Cathedral . . .'

Speedy sighed deeply. He said in Felicity's ear: 'Don't say I didn't warn you about them.'

She laughed. Their good humour and high spirits were very infectious and she felt better than she had felt at any time since she arrived at Colston – surrounded by these incorrigible young men with their absurd nicknames.

Speedy was squeezing her arm again and whispering once more in her ear. 'Don't forget our date. The Old Ship. First evening we can manage it.' He raised his voice. 'I saw her first, Whitters, so you can buzz off!'

Amid the laughter and Whitters' protests, Felicity suddenly caught sight of Wing Commander Palmer's cold eye upon her across the room.

'And this is a Marshal of the Royal Air Force.'

The airwomen, sitting in a darkened lecture room, stared at the picture projected onto the screen of an RAF cap heavily decorated with gold braid.

The elderly officer who was giving a talk on the history of the Royal Air Force, was explaining how to recognize rank from uniform and the significance of badges and decorations. He traced the cap's peak with the tip of his cane and tried to be jocular. 'Lots of scrambled egg there, as you see. That's what we in the Service call it . . . unofficially, of course.'

They laughed politely.

'Silly old bugger,' Pearl muttered.

They stifled yawns as he droned on at great length about thirty historic years in the air.

The lecture on venereal disease, given by the Station MO, shocked and disgusted them all – even Pearl. They watched in silence as images of ulcerated flesh were flashed onto the screen before their eyes.

The MO was brisk and matter-of-fact. 'The first thing to remember is that promiscuous intercourse can lead to infection,' he tapped at the screen which displayed a face with its features apparently half-eaten away, 'and eventually, if not treated, to this sort of result. The second

74

is to take note of the symptoms of venereal infection, such as I have described, and to report it immediately if you should ever get any of them, so that you can receive early treatment. The third thing to remember is that if you girls keep yourselves for Mr Right then you've got nothing to worry about. None of this will ever happen to you.'

Winnie averted her eyes from the sickening sight on the screen. She had never heard of such diseases and the idea of girls going with lots of different men, like the doctor had said, was completely strange to her. The nearest thing she could think of was when Dot Bedwell at The Pig and Whistle had gone walking out with both the blacksmith and the cobbler and it had come to blows between the two of them. There had been a lot of talk in the village and some had said that Dot lived up to her name. Three months later she had married the blacksmith and it had all been forgotten. Winnie could not imagine going with anyone other than Ken – not even walking out, let alone anything else. It had always been Ken. And Ken had never tried to do anything else other than hold her hand or kiss her goodnight sometimes. Of course, she knew that there would be more than that some day – you couldn't live on a farm and not know how nature worked – but that was all in the future, for when she and Ken got married. It had nothing to do with what the doctor had talked about or these horrible pictures. She stared down into her lap, her cheeks burning in the darkness.

After the lecture, Anne cornered Pearl.

'Do some girls really behave like that – go with any man?'

'Crikey, of course they do. You *are* the innocent, aren't you? Where've you been up 'til now?'

'In a girls' boarding school, actually.'

'No wonder then . . . I take it you *do* know all about the birds and the bees, or didn't they teach you that at that posh place of yours? Don't tell me you still think the stork brings babies or they're left under a gooseberry bush?'

'The subject was never mentioned. It was unmention-able. But they did teach us the reproductive cycle of the rabbit in Biology. It's more or less the same thing, isn't it?'

Pearl roared with laughter. 'I s'pose so, but I bloody hope I never breed like 'em.'

'Pearl, have you ever done it? You know . . . *it*?'

'No, I haven't love, since you ask. Never met any bloke I fancied enough, to be honest. Nothing above the knee is my motto.'

'Waiting for Mr Right?'

Pearl blew a raspberry. 'Waiting for Mr He'll Do. I don't believe there's such a thing as the perfect man for me – just one that's less of a bastard than most of the others.'

Anne thought back to whispered conversations with other girls in the dormitory at St Mary's, after lights out, when they had pooled what meagre information they had. Unfortunately, they'd all been pretty hazy about the whole thing. Any books that might have thrown some light on the fascinating subject were banned at school, though someone had managed to get hold of a copy of *No Orchids for Miss Blandish* during the holidays. Cross-questioned closely, she had been disappointingly vague. One girl had declared solemnly that her mother had told her that when two people got married they were joined bodily as one in a holy union. Someone else's mother had said, less upliftingly, that it was something that women just had to put up with and it was better not to think about it. Nobody could imagine what *it* would really be like, or feel like. The Biology class had provided some interesting facts, including the reassuring one that sperm and urine were never passed at the same time, but Miss Richards, chalking neat diagrams of ovaries and testicles, pipes and passages on the blackboard, had kept her lesson firmly in the animal world. Besides, with her hair netted at the back of her head like a ball of grey wool and her long, sad cardigans, it seemed unlikely that she had ever had any firsthand experience. Even Kit had been unhelpful. *Can't really say, old bean. Different thing for men, isn't it? You'll have to wait and find out for yourself one day.* One day . . . but when, and with whom? He was out there in the world somewhere, walking around, and that was a funny thought, but how was she going to find him?

They were given another lecture on Gas Attacks and later an RAF corporal with leathery skin and a long-suffering expression took them for Gas Drill.

'Pay close attention now, *if* you please. Some of you ladies may think this is all a bit of a lark, but I can tell you it's not. If so much as *one* speck of mustard gets into your lungs you'll never be rid of it. It can blind you and burn the flesh from your bones. So, never mind your hairdos or your make-up, just get those respirators on!'

The heavy rubber masks were foul-smelling and clung suffocatingly to their faces like limpets. The WAAFS filed after the corporal into the Decontamination Centre where thick, acrid fumes rose from a container placed on a table in the centre of a room. They lumbered round and round the table, following their leader in a weird war dance. Outside again, they dragged off their respirators and stood sucking in deep lungfuls of fresh air. Vera was coughing and clutching at her throat, while Enid sank to her knees, moaning.

The corporal shook his head sadly. 'Crikey, what a fuss you females make. What're you all goin' to do when it's the real thing?'

Sergeant Baker, who took them for their first drill, was even more sceptical than the gas corporal. They gathered before him in a timid cluster at the edge of the parade ground. He was a big, beetroot-faced man with a voice like a foghorn and he looked them over with cold eyes, taking in the varying heights, shapes and contours, and the motley array of civilian clothing. Finally, his acid gaze came to rest in disbelief on Gloria's high-heeled, peep-toe shoes.

'You can't wear them things. Go and change 'em.'

Gloria lifted her chin. 'I 'aven't got no others so they'll just 'ave to do.'

He went redder still, an angry purple flush spreading upwards from his thick neck. 'I'm not 'avin' them on my parade ground. It's an insult to the Service and to 'is Majesty.'

Gloria shrugged. She bent down and took off the offending shoes and suspended them from the backs on one forefinger, swinging them gently to and fro. Sergeant Baker glared ferociously as she stood there in stockinged feet on the wet asphalt.

'Catch her death, she will,' someone muttered.

There was a long moment while the sergeant and Gloria confronted each other; at last he gave a snort of disgust.

'Put 'em back on. But next time you come in proper footwear, see, or you don't come at all.' He stared round the group. 'God help us with you women. How're we goin' to fight the war with you lot on our backs? 'itler's secret weapon, that's what you are. 'E won't need to lift a bloomin' finger.' He whacked his stick across the palm of his hand, making some of them jump. 'Well, the first thing I've got to say to you lot is that you're not 'ere to enjoy yourselves. Get that? The second thing is that you don't do *nothin*' 'til I give the order. Is that understood?'

They nodded obediently, huddled together like driven sheep and shivering in the cold wind. Several windows in the barrack block along one side of the square had opened and airmen were leaning over the sills. Whistling and laughter could be heard. The sergeant turned in that direction with a savage yell.

'Pack it up, you lot, or I'll make you tag on the end of these women and see 'ow you like that.' He swung back and pointed at Vera who cringed. 'You there! Come and stand over 'ere. You're the marker. I want you all in a line each side of 'er. Tallest to the right, shortest to the left. Get yourselves in 'eight order. *Fall in!*'

There was a hopeless muddle as they tried to arrange themselves. Exasperated, the sergeant seized those out of order by their shoulders and moved them bodily about like pawns on a chess board until they had formed a row before him, the tallest at one end, down to the shortest.

'Stand still and stop talkin'! When I say *right dress* – and *not* before – you put your right arm out and space yourselves so that your knuckles touch your neighbour's shoulder. That clear, or do I 'ave to say it all over again?'

At his command they all stuck out their right arms obediently, except for Sandra who put out her left and poked Vera in the eye.

After that, they formed themselves into threes, with a good deal of shuffling about and abuse from Sergeant Baker.

'Wot a shambles! Never seen anythin' like it in all me life. Now then, I'm goin' to try and show you 'ow to stand to attention, *if* that's somethin' any of you are capable of, which I doubt. *Stop fiddlin' with your 'air, you at the back there!* Watch closely. You stand on the balls of your feet, 'eels together, feet at forty-five degrees, stomach in, knees back, 'ead up, shoulders back, arms at the side, elbows in, fingers curled with the thumb on the top of the first finger, in line with the seam down your thigh – if you *'ad* a seam, that is . . . *Attenshun!*'

They struggled vainly to remember it all and to imitate the sergeant's ramrod figure before them.

''Orrible! *'orrible!* A bunch of 'ottentots could do it better. Well, let's see if you can stand at ease – that ought to suit the lot of you. Place your left foot to your left, a foot away. At the same time put your arms behind you and bring the shoulders back, placin' the right 'and in the palm of the left with the thumbs crossin' . . .' He twisted sideways. 'See? Simple. Now, let's 'ave you doin' it, just like me. *At ease!*'

They tried their best to copy him. Sandra moved her right foot instead of her left and collided with Vera. Somehow their limbs became entangled and they both collapsed onto the ground. Sergeant Baker turned puce.

'Wot do you two think you're playin' at? This isn't a bloomin' three-legged race! Don't you know your left from your right?'

Sandra had grazed her knees and there were tears in her eyes. 'I'm awfully sorry, Sergeant. I do get them mixed up sometimes.'

'Saints preserve us! And they expect me to drill people like you!'

He took a piece of chalk from his pocket, bent down and wrote a large white letter L on Sandra's left shoe and an R on the other.

'*Now* p'raps you'll remember. *If* you can read.'

He taught them how to turn left, turn right, and about on the spot. They practised the movements many times under his jaundiced eye before, finally, he allowed them to begin marching.

'And I want you *marchin'*, not trippin' along like you was all out shoppin'. Heads *up*, arms swingin', shoulders back . . . Are you all ready? Listen for my commands and don't do nothin' 'til you 'ear them. By the left . . . *quick march!*'

Sandra started off on the wrong foot in spite of the chalked letters on her shoes, and kept hopping and skipping along as she tried to get in step. Blood trickled from the grazes on her knees. Enid's arms and legs moved in stiff and jerky unison instead of as opposites, and Gloria minced along on her high heels, swinging her bottom more than her arms. Winnie, concentrating hard, forgot the cold and felt instead a sudden warm glow of pride as the small band of WAAFS moved together across the vast parade ground. *Left, right. Left, right*. She repeated the words to herself under her breath. Anne, marching at the front, was finding it easy. She had enjoyed the drill, and that had surprised her. She flung her arms out in time with her marching feet and strained her ears for the sound of the sergeant's voice and his next command. The far side of the square was approaching rapidly and still she heard nothing. They were within yards of the edge of the asphalt when, at last, she heard his foghorn voice.

'*About turn!*'

She turned smartly about to face the other way and the other girls in the front rank turned with her. Those behind them, however, had failed to hear the sergeant properly and the ranks collided in confusion and disarray. Enid was knocked to the ground like a ninepin and lay weeping in a puddle. Sandra's grazes were now bleeding in earnest and one of Gloria's high heels had snapped and she was hobbling about, swearing loudly.

Sergeant Baker, a distant and furious figure, could be heard yelling hoarsely while the raucous and delighted laughter from the airmen at the barrack room windows floated to them on the wind like the cawing of crows.

The offices of the Falcon Assurance Company overlooked Holborn. From her desk near the window, Virginia Stratton could watch the endless flow of people walking by on the pavement below. There was a new public shelter now, just across the street. She had seen them piling up a thick wall of sandbags against the building and erecting the 'S' sign, but so far there had been no air raids, only false alarms, and the pessimists who had said that London would be bombed to bits within weeks of the war being declared, had been made to look foolish. In spite of the sandbags and shelters, the blackout and the barrage balloons, a great many people seemed to be living their ordinary, normal lives, going to and fro from their offices and carrying on business as usual. Her mother kept saying that the war would be over by Christmas, but Virginia was not so sure. She had noticed many more uniforms in the street below the window lately – far more khaki, navy and lighter blue among the civilian clothing. And, if the war was going to end so soon, why were the

81

parks being dug up, the statues all taken away, more and more shelters being built, like the one opposite, and all the children evacuated to the country?

She stared out of the window. The subject of her wanting to join the Women's Air Force had not been mentioned again. Mother probably thought she'd given up the whole idea but it had become even more firmly fixed in her mind. She found herself watching for women in uniform among the crowd, and envying them. They walked with their heads held high and with purpose in their step, and she longed to be one of them and not imprisoned in a dreary office. She never saw many in Air Force uniform but there were always a lot in Army khaki. She watched one crossing the street. She looked young and very self-assured. Her tunic buttons and shoes were shiny and her hair was dressed in a beautifully neat roll under her cap. Virginia fingered her own hair and wondered if she could ever make hers go like that. She peered after the girl until she was lost to view.

In two weeks time she would be eighteen and officially old enough to join up. Several people in the department had gone already. Mr Wilson and Mr Platt had joined the Army and Mr Whicker, who spent his weekends sailing, had gone into the Navy. And Mavis, the junior typist, had announced only that morning that she was going to join the ATS.

'I'm going to do my bit, like they asked,' she had told the office smugly. To Virginia she had said later in lower tones, and with a huge wink, 'And it'll be a lot more fun than working here. Chance of a lifetime, that's what it is. Aren't you going to join up, or something?'

'I don't know. I'm not sure yet.'

Mavis had shrugged and picked at the sleeve of her pink angora sweater. 'Loopy if you don't. There'll soon be no-one left here but old men and Miss P.'

Miss Parkes, so disparaged by Mavis, spent her lunch hours knitting long scarves for servicemen. She clicked away briskly in her corner by the filing cabinet and the scarves grew rapidly, snaking onto her bony knees. After Mavis had delivered her news she looked up as Virginia went to one of the cabinets and smiled.

'I expect you'll be leaving us before long, dear. Joining up with all the rest of the young things.'

Virginia coloured. 'I'd like to – as soon as I'm eighteen – but . . .'

'But what, dear?'

'There's my mother, you see.'

'Is she ill then, dear?'

'No . . .'

'Then why can't you? If you want to. I'm sure you'd be very useful to one of the women's services. You've got a good sensible head on your shoulders. And you're intelligent and hard-working.'

Virginia said reluctantly: 'Mother doesn't want me to leave her, that's the trouble. We live alone, you see. Just her and me . . . she rather depends on me.'

Miss Parkes looked over the top of her spectacles. Her hands went on moving busily, the needles click-clicking.

'Is your mother an invalid?'

'No.'

'So, there's no reason why she can't look after herself?'

'No . . . the thing is she spends most of her time by herself in the flat. She hardly ever goes out and it's very lonely for her. She looks forward to my coming home. She got very upset when I told her I was thinking of joining up.'

'I see. Have you suggested she tries joining something like the Women's Voluntary Service? She'd meet a lot of people and keep busy. It might do her good. Try that as an idea.'

'I'll try,' Virginia said doubtfully. 'But I don't think she'd like it very much. She doesn't seem to get on with strangers very well. It's awfully difficult to explain . . .'

Miss Parkes started on another row. 'Which service would you like to join?'

'The Women's Auxiliary Air Force, actually, if I could

83

choose. I don't really know why . . . I've hardly ever seen an aeroplane in my life. But I heard an appeal on the wireless for volunteers, and it's new . . . I've seen queues of girls in Kingsway waiting to join every day.'

Miss Parkes, surprisingly, stopped knitting. The mass of khaki wool lay inert on her lap. She looked up at Virginia earnestly. 'If you want my advice, dear, I should go and join the Air Force as soon as you possibly can. It's a chance to do something else with your life . . . see a bit more of the world . . . meet all sorts of different people . . . do some really interesting, useful work. You shouldn't spend your youth keeping your mother company, or working in an office like this with a whole lot of old people like me; not if there's a good alternative. So long as your mother can look after herself and get out and about there's nothing whatever for you to feel guilty about. That's the way I see it. And I speak from experience. I spent years living with *my* mother, for much the same sort of reason, until she died recently, and every day I came to work in this office. Look at what has happened to me. Or *not* happened, I should say. Life has passed me by. If I were your age again, I'd join up like a shot . . . and I shouldn't let anything stop me. Just find the courage, if you can, to do what you want to do. You'll live to regret it, if you don't.'

She picked up her knitting again, the unexpected exhortation finished. Virginia went on with her work. Mavis, if she had heard Miss Parkes, would have been equally astounded; she would probably, being Mavis, have cheered.

The tube was even more crowded than usual that evening, and Virginia had to strap-hang most of the way to Wimbledon. She walked in the pitch darkness up the hill from the station to the flat in Alfred Road. Her torch battery was wearing out and gave only a glimmer of light but she knew the way so well that it scarcely mattered. Her mother was in the sitting-room, sewing, and she began complaining at once about Mrs Barton who lived in the flat upstairs.

84

'She has her wireless on far too loud. It's so inconsiderate . . . I've told her so several times but she still takes no notice. I had to speak to her again about it today. Do you know she had the effrontery to suggest I should help her in some canteen . . . I told her that, as it happens, I do a great deal of work knitting for the forces, and I can do that perfectly well here in my own home. The war will be finished by Christmas, in any case. I've no intention of becoming involved with people like Mrs Barton . . . such a *common* woman. It's quite bad enough having to live cheek by jowl with someone like her . . . were you going to say something, Virginia?'

'No, Mother . . . no.'

'You looked as though you were. Will you turn on that other lamp, please. I can't see properly.'

On the nine o'clock news that evening it was announced that negotiations between Finland and Russia had broken down. The Russians were accusing the Finns of firing on their border patrols. More trouble seemed to be brewing in the cold wastes of Northern Europe. And Christmas was only six weeks away.

Three

Dear Ken, I hope you are well . . . Winnie chewed the end of her pencil, thinking hard. *I hope your mother is well too.* That was a lie. She didn't really care if Mrs Jervis was well or not. Maybe it was wicked to think like that, but she couldn't help it. Ken's mother was the only person in the world whom she almost hated. It wasn't just because she was always so sharp-spoken and critical, no matter how hard Winnie tried to please her, but mostly because of the way she treated Ken. She was always going on and on about how delicate he was, making him out to be a useless invalid. He was a bit liable to catch chills and get bad chests, that was true, but Mrs Jervis made things much worse for him by the way she behaved.

I'm sitting on my bed in our hut writing this letter and it will soon be time to put the lights out. It's very cold in here, even though we have two coke stoves. They don't seem to give out much heat and everyone crowds round them so you can't get near them anyway. I'm enjoying the work in the Orderly Room . . . That was a lie too. She wasn't enjoying it at all. It was very dull and she hated being cooped up indoors and hardly ever seeing an aeroplane at all. *You wouldn't believe the number of forms that have to be filled in. There's hundreds of them with different numbers for all sorts of different things. You can't do anything in the Royal Air Force without filling in a form for it.*

The RAF corporal in the Orderly Room who had taught her the procedure seemed like an old man to her. He had gone through it all slowly and patiently.

'There's a correct form for every occurrence you can

think of,' he had told her, 'and ones for some you can't. And every one of them's got a number that you've got to learn. That way you can put your hand on the right form for the job straight away. For instance, these are 143s,' he had picked up a sheaf of forms. 'They're for Service Railway Warrants. These over here are 2084s – they're Billeting Forms. Then you've got your 551s, Report of Accident, your 1771s, Travelling Claims . . .' He had worked on steadily through the long list. 'You'll have to learn them all and know how to fill them in properly. It's not difficult but it's got to be done according to Regulations, see?'

Ken wouldn't want to hear about all that . . . there was nothing very interesting about a lot of numbers. Winnie racked her brains. She looked across at the two circles of girls sitting close round the stoves. *The officer in charge of us is always trying to make things better for us. She got us some chairs for this hut and a kettle and teapot so we can make tea on the stoves. And some of the civilian people who live near here have given a whole lot of things for our recreation hut – curtains and armchairs and a carpet, and things like that. One of them gave us an old gramophone and some records and somebody sent an old wireless. It didn't work very well at first but one of the RAF men has mended it and now we can listen to the news and everything.*

Winnie lifted her head again, searching for more inspiration. *The girls are all very nice.* That was another lie really. Some were and some were not. Ruby, two beds away, for instance, was horrible. She pushed and shoved her way around the whole time, ate disgustingly with her mouth wide open and never bathed or washed properly so that she smelled worse than any farm animal. But she didn't want to tell Ken about her. Or about how stuck-up and unfriendly Susan could be. Or how Pearl used swear words all the time. Or how Maureen was always grumbling and complaining. Or the way Gloria went out with lots of different airmen . . . There was no sense in telling him any of that. He'd want her to come straight home.

She pulled up the collar of her dressing-gown round her neck and blew on her cold fingers. She could hear Susan, in the nearest group, telling Sandra all about a dance she had once gone to in a big country house. Sandra was listening to every word and kept on asking questions, as usual. Maureen, beside them, was knitting one of her ever-lasting garments, this time in a dreary grey, and she was wearing a very sour expression on her face from over-hearing Susan. Gloria was filing her nails, her back turned to Maureen. Pearl, who had washed her hair, was curling it up with pipe cleaners and, Anne, her mouth full of hairpins, was showing Enid how to do her hair up with an old stocking. She had cut the stocking in half and tied it round Enid's head. Winnie watched as she brushed the hair upwards and then tucked the ends into the stocking, into a long roll, and fixed it cleverly with the pins. She thought Enid looked a lot better without that lank hair hanging down each side of her face, and her Terry would be pleased if she didn't have to have her hair cut. Not that Enid seemed to talk quite so much about Terry these days, or about what he might think of everything . . . not nearly so much as she used to do.

Winnie sucked the end of her pencil for a moment and then bent over her writing pad again. *We get paid every fortnight. We have to march into the room and go up to a table one at a time and say the last three figures of our numbers. Then we have to take the money with our left hand. The first time I said thank you, but we're not supposed to. There are all sorts of funny customs in the Air Force.*

Maureen was saying something crotchety to Susan and Susan was looking down her nose at her as though she'd just crawled out from under a stone. Nobody liked Maureen, she was such a sour-puss. After the first Pay Parade she had been as bitter as anything.

'Do you all realize that we're only paid two-thirds of

what they give to the airmen, even though we work just the same hours. And I'm much better at my job than they are.'

Anne had laughed. 'Well, I'm not, so I can't really complain.'

Maureen had rounded on her. 'It's nothing to you what we're paid, is it? But *I* have to send money home. So does Gloria. Several of us do. Every penny counts with us. We don't get it sent by our mothers like you. You might remember that.'

Anne had flushed, and said nothing more.

The food's all right. We have things like bacon, eggs and chips, baked beans and kidneys on fried bread, meat pies, toad-in-the-hole and lots of steamed puddings with custard. We're all putting on weight. She wouldn't mention the gristly rissoles, the faggots, the semolina pudding or the frogspawn tapioca, or anything of the things that made her feel sick to look at, let alone eat. *We still haven't got any uniform, except some of the girls have been given shoes because they had only high heels or sandals.* Gloria had made a great fuss about the black lace-ups from Dolcis.

'Schoolmarm's boats, that's wot they are! Beetle-crushers like Beaty wears!'

Maureen had said tartly: 'I sometimes wonder, Gloria, why you joined the Services if you object so much to wearing proper uniform.'

'For the blokes, dearie. Same as you.'

'How dare you say that! Some of us have joined to serve our country in her time of need.'

'Oh, balls!'

'I *beg* your pardon!'

'I said balls! Not that you'd know anythin' about them, Maureen. Not with that lemon face of yours. Enough to put any bloke off.'

Pearl had had to go and stand between them, arms outstretched. 'Break it up, girls. Little birds in their nests should agree . . .'

Our officer has said they've promised to give us some uniform by Christmas. She thinks it will be raincoats and berets and some shirts. We'll have to wait for the tunics and skirts and everything else to come later. One of the girls has had her own uniform made privately at a shop in London. It looks very smart. Susan's beautiful new uniform had been sent by post and they had all gathered round to see her put it on. The blue was exactly the same as the RAF wore and the tunic had shiny brass buttons and a belt with a brass buckle and big patch pockets on the front. It fitted Susan perfectly and the cap sat just right on her head. Her mother had also sent three blue Van Heusen shirts, two pairs of Kayser Bondor grey chiffon-lisle stockings and a pair of hand-stitched lace-up shoes. These had been fingered by everyone in the hut.

Sergeant Beaty had exploded when she had seen it all lying on Susan's bed. 'This uniform's made of officer's material, Courtney-Bennet!'

'Is it, Sergeant? Does it matter? I mean, if I'm prepared to pay for a better quality out of my own pocket, I don't see what difference it makes. That other material is terribly rough.'

'It's against Regulations. And those shirts aren't proper issue either. Nor are those stockings – they're much too thin. And those shoes shouldn't have all that fancy punching on them. I'll have to report this.'

But Susan had been allowed to keep it all and to wear it. She seemed not to notice, or care, that it made her unpopular when nobody else had uniform yet.

Our sergeant isn't very nice and everybody hates her. She's always telling us off and getting people into trouble. If you do something against Regulations they can make you stay in the camp for a week or more and scrub floors and clean windows, and things like that. One of the girls here, called Anne, is always getting into trouble and being given punishments. The RAF call it jankers. They have slang words for everything.

The hut door opened and Winnie looked up from her writing to see Corporal White.

We have a corporal now who sleeps in a room at the end of the hut. She's quite a lot older than us and much nicer than the sergeant. We all like her. She's just come in because it's time to turn out the lights, so I'll have to stop now and finish this letter tomorrow . . .

Later, Winnie lay in bed thinking. She watched the dull reddish glow from the two stoves in the darkness, and listened to the sounds as the hut settled down to sleep – the creaking and coughing and whispering. She had got used to it now. And she had learned to anchor her biscuits so they stayed in place by wrapping one of the blankets tightly round them. She had learned all sorts of other things too, like how to make a bathplug out of a penny and a hanky when there wasn't one, and how to fold and stack her bedding in the morning in a jiffy and so neatly that even Sergeant Beaty couldn't find fault with it. Even though the work in the Orderly Room seemed so dull to her and she hated being shut indoors, she still didn't want to go home. Not while there was a chance of getting to work with the 'planes one day. Company Assistant Newman had said there was and she believed her.

She pulled the blankets round her chin and curled up to get warm. Today was Wednesday. If she had been at home today Ken would have come to tea like he always did on early-closing day. He would have sat at the table beside her, not saying very much, and Mum would have poured the tea from the big brown pot while Dad grumbled on, as usual, about something on the farm. Ruth and Laura would have been wriggling about on their chairs and misbehaving and getting all their own way, and Gran would have been guzzling her food noisily and making sucking noises as she drank her tea. Afterwards Ken would have helped her wash up in the scullery. They couldn't have gone for a walk in the dark so they would have sat in the kitchen for a while, where it was warmest. Gran would have been in her chair close by the range, smoking one of her cigarettes with the ash dropping off the end down the front of her long black dress. And she'd have been making her sharp remarks every so often. Ken was afraid of Gran and Gran knew it. But then everyone was a bit afraid of her – even Dad. That was one reason why he'd let her join up in the end – because Gran had said he must. She'd let fly at him in her old-fashioned Suffolk way of speaking. *Yew let the gal go, Josh, an' doan't be tanglesome and ullus thinkin' o' yarself.* Winnie knew, because she understood Gran better than anybody, that she was really hoping that if she went away then she might not marry Ken. *What do yew want t' wed that tibby for? Can't yew find yarself a better fellah?* She was always saying things like that.

But whatever Gran had hoped, she wasn't going to go and forget Ken, or go out with anyone else. It wasn't easy to keep saying no all the time whenever she was asked. And they none of them liked taking no for an answer. Specially not Leading Aircraftman Jones.

He'd come into the Orderly Room one day to collect something and had stood staring at her so hard that she'd felt herself going red. She'd kept busy with some forms and hoped he'd go away but when she looked up again he was still there, and still staring.

'Where've you sprung from?' he'd asked. 'I've never seen you before.'

She'd gone on with her work. 'I've just started in here.'

'Well, don't you go away again,' he'd said. 'Because I'll be back.'

After that he was always appearing in the Orderly Room on some flimsy excuse. He'd hang around talking to her, even though she did her best to ignore him. He was small and dark and spoke with a sing-song Welsh accent that she sometimes found hard to understand. They called him Taffy, of course, but she'd no idea what his real name was. He'd soon discovered hers, though. And before long he'd asked her to go to the pictures with him. She'd refused.

'Why not?'

'I'm engaged.'

'What's that got to do with it? I'm only asking you to come to the flicks.'

He'd gone on and on asking, and she'd gone on and on refusing. His greenish-grey eyes followed her all the time.

'You may as well give in, Winnie. I shan't give up.'

Once he'd been waiting for her outside. He'd fallen into step beside her.

'Where're you off to in such a hurry then, Winnie?'

'Back to the Mess.'

'Is that all? I thought you were going to put a fire out or something.'

He'd caught hold of her arm to slow her down but she'd shaken herself free and had run ahead to catch up with two other WAAFS. Safe with them, she'd glanced back quickly to see him still standing there, staring after her.

Winnie pulled the blankets almost over her head. She must stop worrying about Taffy Jones. Stop thinking about him at all. Tomorrow she'd finish the letter and post it to Ken.

'I'm awfully busy, Speedy.'

'You can't be busy all the time. Even WAAFS have time off for good behaviour. And you've been behaving jolly well. How about tomorrow? Or the next day? Or next week, if you insist on keeping me waiting?'

Speedy Dutton was sitting on the corner of Felicity's desk. He was wearing a red, white and blue check scarf round his neck and twirled his battered cap round and round on his forefinger. It was one of his frequent visits to her office since they had met at the squadron party. He would breeze in with George his brindle bull terrier in tow. He smiled at her now and the bull terrier wagged his tail. They both looked at her encouragingly. Expectantly.

'Tomorrow evening, then?'

'Well . . .' She sighed.

The cap stopped. 'That's settled then. Isn't it, George? She's seen sense at last.'

He collected her in a bright red MG sports car which bore signs of wear and tear. There was a large dent in one wing and the front bumper was tied on with string.

'Bit of a bone-shaker, the old girl, but she'll get us there and back, never fear. Stand by for take off. Contact! Chocks away!'

They roared out of the main gates and through the village. Felicity grabbed the door handle as they swung round a corner. The wind was blowing through a hole in the hood and there was another blast of freezing air somewhere near her right foot. Speedy whistled happily in the dark and spun the wheel again.

'Don't worry. I know this road like the back of my hand.'

'Do you fly as recklessly as you drive?'

'Rather! Terrific show-offs, us fighter chaps, as you've no doubt discovered.'

'I had noticed – yes.'

As he had promised, he took her to the Old Ship. The pub was down on the harbour front of a small sailing village about fifteen miles away. As she clambered out of the car she smelled the salt and seaweed and could make out the tilted shapes of boats in the moonlight, lying on the low tide mud below.

Inside the pub there were blackened beams and a huge log fire. And Speedy's cosy little corners.

He raised his beer mug to her. 'To your excellent health, Company Assistant Newman. And your blue eyes. Has anyone ever told you how beautiful they are?'

'As a matter of fact, they have. And I didn't take any notice of them either.'

He grinned. 'You haven't told me yet what someone like you is doing in the Women's Watsit. Why on earth did you join it?'

94

'Actually, I didn't join the WAAF. I joined the ATS. The WAAF didn't even exist then. I'd just come down and I was at a bit of a loose end so – '

'Come down?'

'From Cambridge.'

He whistled. 'I say, pretty impressive! What were you doing there?'

'Reading English.'

'Thank God it wasn't Greek. I'd feel no end of a dunce. I once met a girl at a party who could speak Ancient Greek fluently. Kept spouting it at me. Jolly off-putting. She was a pretty girl, too. Look, I still don't see why you went and joined the ATS in the first place.'

She sipped some sherry. 'Well, it seemed obvious there was going to be a war sooner or later, and there was nothing else I had in mind to do . . .'

'So you went and donned the khaki? I bet you looked good in that too. Then what happened?'

'After a bit some of us were attached to the RAF and it sort of grew from there. We weren't even full time at first. We just drilled once a week and went to lectures, and I learned to drive a lorry. I got my commission just before war broke out.'

'Good for you.'

'Not really. It was just a fluke. There weren't many of us and I suppose they were pretty keen to find officers. They asked me the oddest things at my Commission Board – like what would I do if I was shipwrecked on a desert island?'

'Rum sort of question for the Air Force – not as though you were joining the Navy. What did you say?'

'I said I'd build a raft and sail away. Something like that. Actually, I wouldn't have a clue how to do any such thing.'

'No point in telling them that.' He beamed at her. 'None of their business.'

'Why did *you* join the RAF?'

95

'I nearly didn't. The old man wanted me to join the Navy. He was very keen on that.'

'Is he in it?'

'The old man? No, he's a sawbones. GP in Southampton. We live there and we've always had boats and done a fair bit of sailing. I think he thought I'd have a head start, knowing port from starboard.'

'So, why didn't you?'

'Decided I'd have a shot at flying for a change. It's something I'd always wanted to do. Besides, there's nothing like it for impressing the girls, you know. They think you're no end of a fine fellow if you've got these.' He tapped the wings on his chest.

'Really?'

'Really. Drink that up and have the other half. Then we'll have a slap-up dinner.'

He ordered a bottle of wine with their meal and kept topping up her glass. She put her hand over it.

'You're not trying to get me tipsy, I hope, Flying Officer Dutton?'

'Certainly not, Company Assistant Newman. Nothing was further from my thoughts. Shocking bad form! Just a drop more?'

'All right. Just a drop.'

He tipped up the bottle with a flourish. 'Let us have wine and women, mirth and laughter, sermons and soda water the day after. No disrespect to your old man, of course.'

'I didn't know poetry was your line, Speedy.'

'I wouldn't say that. The only poem I can recite all the way through is *Tiger, Tiger Burning Bright*. The thing is, Snodgrass, our English wallah at school was very partial to the stuff. Had a quote for every occasion.'

'*Snodgrass*? I don't believe he was really called that.'

'Cross my heart, it's true. Cuthbert Snodgrass was his name. Terrific sense of humour, as a matter of fact. Looked as dry as an old stick, but he'd come

96

out with some killing things. Who said that about wine and women, by the way? Jolly sensible, whoever it was.'

'Byron said it. It's from *Don Juan*.'

'Ah, that explains it. Both those bods knew a thing or two, didn't they?'

They left the pub at closing time and walked along the quayside, guided by the light of the moon and the stars. There were boatsheds and some buildings at the end of the quay.

'Sailing Club,' Speedy told her. 'Not a bad place, actually. I came here a lot last summer and crewed for old Whitters. He's got his own tub, lucky blighter. When this show's over I've decided I'm going to earn a fortune charming housewives into buying encyclopedias and then I'm going to buy a thirty footer and sail round the world.'

'A tall ship and a star to steer her by?'

'I say, Snodders would have approved of you no end. He was frightfully keen on Masefield. Rousing stuff, he used to say. Good thumping verse. Mind you, you'd need more than one star to steer by . . . I've always wondered about that. Plenty of them out tonight, though, twinkling away up there.'

Felicity looked up into the velvet sky. 'The night has a thousand eyes . . .'

'That's *just* what Snodgrass would have said.'

They stood looking out over the darkness of the harbour. The tide was coming in now, creeping silently across the mud and rocking the anchored boats. Moonlight glittered on the deep water channel beyond.

After a moment Felicity said: 'It's so peaceful here. It's hard to believe that there's a war on.'

'It's on all right. The Jerry U-boats are out there stooging around.'

'But nothing's happening here – that's what makes it so hard to believe . . . no more sirens, no bombs – none of the things everybody thought would happen.'

'Badger reckons they're just waiting for winter to finish. Jolly sensible, really. They have rotten weather over there, you know. You wait, come the spring and they'll be ready for the off.'

'Off where?'

'Search me. Wherever Adolf gets it in his head to go next, I suppose.'

Felicity shivered. He put an arm round her shoulders. 'Cold?'

'A bit. And a goose just walked over my grave.'

'You don't want to let it do that. I never do. Say boo! and it'll go away.'

She moved firmly out of the circle of his arm. 'It's time we were getting back.'

'Must we?'

'Yes, we *must*.'

In the blackness inside the car, he turned to her. 'Do you know, I've never been out with anyone like you.'

'Is that one of your lines?'

'Certainly not. I mean it. I've never met a girl like you . . . clever as well as beautiful, an officer – all that sort of thing. You'll come out again, won't you? There's another wizard little place I know of – '

She said seriously: 'I really don't think it's a good idea, Speedy.'

'Why not? It's a splendid idea. And I swear I'll behave like an officer and a gentleman.'

'I'm not sure you'd keep your promise.'

He said with mock injury: 'You're speaking of my honour, Company Assistant Newman.'

'Actually, I'm speaking of *my* honour, Flying Officer Dutton. You have a terrible reputation on the station, you know.'

'I know,' he said modestly.

'So, you can see that it's not a good idea at all.'

'Tell you what, we'll take a chaperone.'

'A chaperone?'

'George! He'll be just the ticket. Problem solved.'

Felicity opened her mouth to say that it was by no means solved, but he had turned back to start the engine and it roared deafeningly into life. As well as other holes in various parts of the MG, there appeared to be a large one in the silencer. With sublime disregard for any sleeping village inhabitants, or for the feebleness of the shielded headlights, Speedy accelerated noisily away from the harbour. Felicity clutched at the door handle as they veered round a bend and decided to save her breath.

The three-piece band in the Sergeants' Mess was playing a tango with a syncopated thudding that made the floor vibrate. The WAAFS hovered near the door, watching the handful of couples dancing. Gloria did some sinuous, sliding steps up and down, and Pearl, doused in *Evening in Paris,* kept on smoothing the skirt of her shiny green frock over her hips. There had been a struggle previously in the hut to zip her into it. Anne, wearing the long-sleeved, grey woollen dress she had had at St Mary's for school concerts, looked round for Jimmy Shaw among the knots of RAF blue. Vera tugged at her sleeve.

'I've never been to a dance before, Anne. What're we s-s'posed to do?' Her face was taut with anxiety. 'I c-can't dance. I've never learned.'

'Don't worry. Probably, none of them can either.'

Vera wrinkled her nose. 'This place stinks of beer.'

There was no sign of Jimmy and before long Anne was swept onto the floor by a dapper little sergeant with glassy, Brylcreemed hair. He was a good two inches shorter than her and light as a feather on his feet. He spun her this way and that, tango-ing expertly round the room and finishing with a grand flourish that had her bent backwards across his arm. His name was Stan and he'd learned to dance by going regularly to the Hammersmith Palais, he told her, when she complimented him.

'You're not so bad yourself, sweetheart. Fancy another turn?'

After Stan she danced with several other sergeants. They

quick-stepped and fox-trotted, rumba-ed and waltzed to the thudding beat of the band. The haze of cigarette smoke thickened, powerfully laced with beer fumes and wafts of cheap scent. Anne was dragged onto the floor to do the Palais Glide, the Hokey Cokey, a Paul Jones and an Excuse Me. In the middle of this dance, Jimmy Shaw tapped her partner on the shoulder to claim her.

'I'm awfully sorry . . . I couldn't get here sooner. There was a bit of a flap on and the CO wanted to see us . . .'

'Something wrong?'

He shook his head. 'No, not really. Nothing to worry about. Oh Lord, I just stepped on your toes . . . sorry, I'm afraid I'm a rotten dancer.'

Pearl winked as she danced past in the arms of Dusty Miller. The green dress was splitting a little at the seams.

Winnie was sitting in a corner with Maureen and wishing she had never come. She didn't know how to dance and hadn't the nerve to try. She had refused lots of invitations until, at last, they'd left her alone. It seemed silly to be there at all and to have let the others persuade her to come. She should have stayed behind with Susan who had said snootily she had no intention of going dancing with a lot of sergeants. She shifted uncomfortably on her chair and glanced at Maureen sitting rigidly beside her, wondering if it would be very rude to go back to the hut and leave her there by herself. Maureen didn't look as though she was enjoying herself either. Only one man had asked her to dance all evening and she'd said 'No' very sharply, as though he'd insulted her. He'd gone away muttering to himself, and after that nobody had asked her at all. She hadn't said much while they'd been sitting there, except to make nasty remarks now and then, mostly about the other WAAFS. She thought Anne was making a spectacle of herself, dancing in that show-off way, and she had never seen anything so vulgar as Pearl in her tight frock with the side seams splitting so that you could see her petticoat. And what on earth did Vera think she was doing, jumping around like a goat? As for Gloria, the less said about *her* the better. Her behaviour was a disgrace to them all. The way she carried on with all those men . . .

Winnie listened to it all but said nothing. She didn't understand why Maureen had come to the dance if she disapproved of it all so strongly. And she couldn't see what was so bad about the others enjoying themselves dancing. The cigarette smoke was making her eyes sting and she rubbed them with the back of her hand. She had noticed, through the haze, and hoped that Maureen had not, that one or two of the men seemed a bit the worse for drink. There was a crash and the sound of breaking glass from the direction of the bar, followed by loud laughter. Maureen pursed her lips. The band was striking up again after an interval with a bouncy sort of tune. The pianist, jigging up and down on his stool, was grinning round the room. Winnie began to tap her foot surreptitiously. Couples rotated past her . . . Anne dancing with a shy-looking young sergeant pilot who kept tripping over her toes, Sandra plodding round with a tall, serious flight sergeant, a back view of Gloria wiggling her bottom, Vera hopping along and giggling up at her partner . . . and then Enid came slowly into view, sagging against hers like a wilting plant. Her eyes were shut, her head lolled and her hair had come unpinned from its roll and hung stringily down her back.

Maureen drew in her breath with a hiss. 'She's *drunk*!'

Winnie, Anne and Pearl took Enid back to the hut, hauling her along between them, her head hanging low. She was sick three times on the way, once over Pearl's shoes. Susan was sitting up in bed reading.

'What on earth's the matter with her?'

'Some joker laced her orange squash,' Pearl said, swinging Enid's thin legs onto her bed. 'Stupid bugger!'

'You mean she's *drunk*?'

'Clever of you to notice, Duchess.'

'Don't call me that, Pearl. How disgusting!'

'Oh, shut up, Susan,' Anne exploded. 'You sound just like Maureen and about as much help. Why don't you give us a hand?'

'It's nothing to do with me. If you will go to a hop like that, Anne, and mix with those sort of people . . .'

'If you're not careful, Susan, I'll hit you over the head with that bloody book.'

They undressed Enid, peeling off the vomit-stained blouse and skirt, the wrinkled stockings, vest and knickers. She flopped around like a rag doll. Winnie, fumbling with buttons and suspenders, averted her eyes uncomfortably from the white and skinny body beneath. They had just succeeded in putting on Enid's flannel nightgown and in sliding her under the bedclothes, when the door was flung open and Sergeant Beaty strode into the hut. She stood, ham-hands on hips, swinging her big head balefully from side to side.

'What's going on in here, then?'

Anne, the nearest, moved quickly forward. 'Nothing, Sergeant. We're all going to bed.'

'Don't give me that. There's something up, and I *know* it. What've you lot been up to at that dance? What's the matter with Potter?'

'She was tired. She's gone to sleep.'

'She looks funny to me. Stand aside, Cunningham. Let me see . . .'

'I told you, Sergeant, she's asleep. She wasn't feeling very well.'

'Not well? Why didn't she report sick then? Why did she go to that dance? Potter, I want a word with you . . . Out of that bed this minute!'

Anne moved again, blocking the sergeant's path. 'Leave her alone. You've no bloody right to disturb her.'

'*What!* I'll have you on a charge for this, Cunningham. Insubordination! Obstructing me in the course of my duty! *Let go of my arm!* You'll regret this . . .'

Enid groaned loudly and opened her eyes. She reared up, leaned over the side of her bed, and was violently sick on the floor.

'You are confined to camp with extra duties for four days,' Felicity said coldly. She looked up at the girl standing with studied indifference before her desk. 'I'm getting awfully tired of seeing you in here, Cunningham. It's happening far too often and your Conduct Sheet is a disgrace. You're capable of much better things. In fact, I'd say you were officer material, you know, if only you'd give yourself a chance.' She ignored Sergeant Beaty's muffled snort. 'There's a war on, in case that has escaped you, and we're all supposed to be giving our best, not our worst. Think about that and don't let me see you in here like this again.'

Anne left Station HQ jauntily. What did she care? It was all pretty pathetic. A bit of a joke, really. Beaty had been just like an angry bull. She'd felt rather like one of those picadors at a bullfight who stick lances into the bull to make it angry and divert its attention . . .

She stepped into the roadway without looking and the sharp blast of a car horn made her jump back hurriedly. A dark green sports car swept past, driven much too fast and splashing her with muddy water as it ploughed through a puddle. She caught a glimpse of a RAF officer's cap, fair hair to the collar, a spotted scarf . . . and then the car was gone and she was left standing at the kerb, brushing her spattered stockings and swearing indignantly.

Later, Pearl button-holed her. 'How did it go, love?'

'Four days CB and jankers. She really blew me up.'

Pearl made a face. 'And Enid got off scot free.'

'Well, I couldn't say anything about her, could I? I don't care, anyway.'

'I've got some good news for you. This'll cheer you up. A new squadron's arrived and they're all *millionaires*! Auxiliary squadron toffs. Those weekend pilots. Think of that!'

'I think one of them just nearly ran me over, the bastard. It looked a pretty expensive car.'

'If it'd been me, I'd've let him. *Thrown* myself under the wheels. Worth it to get to know one of them. They're nicknamed Croesus Squadron because they're all so stinking, bloody rich. Do you know, some of them have brought their own servants. And their own silk sheets. And they wear silk underclothes . . .'

'Honestly, Pearl, how on earth do you know all this?'

'I've got my spies everywhere, duckie. And I'll tell you another thing, too. We'll be getting some uniform any moment. Newman's gone to Wembley Depot today with a driver to collect it all . . . raincoats, berets, shirts, ties and knickers. That's what we're getting.'

'Is that true, Pearl?'

Pearl drew her finger across her throat. 'As I'm standing here. Anything you want to know that's going on round here, just you ask your Auntie Pearl.'

The weather became bitterly cold. The WAAFS square-bashed on the arctic waste of the parade ground, wearing their new raincoats and berets. Underneath were the crisp blue shirts and black ties, worn with a variety of civilian skirts, and further underneath the voluminous black bloomers that had caused incredulous laughter and dismay in the hut. Pearl had put hers on at once and paraded up and down with the waistband drawn up high under her armpits and the elasticated knicker legs down to her knees, her black beret stuck on top of her red curls like a cowpat. Even Maureen had managed a faint smile. Nobody's raincoat, when they had tried them on, had seemed to fit properly. They were either too big or too small. The shirts had turned out to have separate collars that had to be attached by front and back collar studs. They were fiddly to fix and the stiffened collars rubbed their necks. Some had to learn how to tie a tie.

But to have some kind of uniform at last, however unsatisfactory or incomplete, made them feel differently.

They paraded before Sergeant Baker with a new confidence and pride and he looked them over with a new, if grudging, approval. Magically, their drill improved. Enid managed to synchronize her arms and legs properly for the first time and Sandra remembered her left from her right, though she got in a muddle when she had to salute and march at the same time.

'Wot was you wavin' at me like that for, 'unt?'

'I was saluting you, Sergeant.'

'Thought you was wavin' me goodbye, or somethin'. *Right* 'and, not the left, an' don't flap it around at me. Smarten it up! Right now, let's see if you females can all do it perfect for once. By the left . . . wait for it, Potter, *wait* for it . . . by the left . . . *quick march*!'

They stepped out across the parade ground in unison, arms swinging, heads held high, the pale wintry sun catching the gilt RAF badges on the front of their new berets. Unobserved, their Station Commander watched them from a window.

The station cinema was a cold and draughty hangar that had been fitted out with rows of seats. Winnie found herself next to Vera and surrounded by airmen. They had started off by sitting in quite the wrong place.

'That's the shillin's there, girls,' an airman had called across to them, grinning from ear to ear, as they had taken their places in an area of empty seats. 'Only tapes and rings can sit there. You lot 'ave to sit over 'ere in the sixpennies, same as us.'

They had moved, with red faces, and to a barrage of teasing and laughter as they squeezed their way past airmen to two empty seats.

'Come and sit next to me, darlin'. I'll keep you warm.'

'Over 'ere, love. Don't be shy.'

'Try my lap for size, sweetheart.'

To Winnie's relief the lights soon went out and the banter stopped. She watched the screen as the title appeared: *It's a Wonderful World*.

'They must be joking!' someone called out.

There was more laughter, more shouts and sallies, and then as the film began the noise subsided except for some disturbance in the row behind her which sounded like somebody changing places. She concentrated on the film, gazing, absorbed, at the screen until someone tapped her on the shoulder and whispered in her ear.

'There's an empty seat here beside me, Winnie. You'll see better.'

She recognized Taffy Jones' voice instantly and stiffened. 'I'm all right here, thank you.'

'Don't be daft. You've got that big bloke right in front of you. You can't see properly there.'

His hand was resting on her shoulder and she could feel the warmth of his breath on the back of her neck. She wriggled sideways towards Vera who was watching the film with rapt attention and sucking a strong peppermint.

'Vera, can I change places with you?'

Vera took her eyes reluctantly from the screen. 'What for?' she asked through the peppermint.

'Someone's botherin' me, in the row behind.'

'Oh. All right then. So long as he doesn't go and bother *me*.'

They changed places, climbing awkwardly across each other to groans and complaints from some of the airmen. Winnie tried to enjoy the picture after that but all the time she could feel Taffy's presence there behind her. She knew that if she turned round she would find him watching her.

There was a dance in the Officers' Mess and Anne and Pearl were deputed for duty in the ladies' cloakroom, looking after the furs and wraps. They watched rather sourly as wives and girlfriends in long evening dresses titivated in front of the mirrors. Pearl passed remarks out of the corner of her mouth.

'Don't know why *she* bothers. Nothing'd improve that

face. Blimey, how about her in the red! The back of a London bus looks better . . . See that one combing her locks like she was Helen of Troy? Dyed. Straight out of a bottle. I should know.'

But Pearl was momentarily silenced by the entrance of two women whose expensively sophisticated appearance bore the stamp of London, far removed from the RAF wives. The taller, a slender brunette in a gown that clung to her like a second skin, dumped her mink coat casually on the counter in front of Anne before turning away to inspect her reflection in the mirror. She took out a gold compact and retouched her face.

'I do hope this is going to be an amusing evening, Roz. I've never been to one of these Service dos before.'

Her companion held out her sable wrap in Pearl's direction, looking the other way. 'I shouldn't count on it, Cynthia. It'll probably be fairly deadly. They usually are, in my experience. Thank God, most of the Croesus lot will be here, so we won't have to dance with any of the usual ghastly RAF Regular types, with any luck. You know Willy Langham, don't you, darling?'

'Heavens, yes. Everyone knows Willy. Frightfully amusing.'

'And Johnnie Somerville?'

The owner of the mink coat paused in mid-dab. 'Johnnie? Is *he* here?'

'Well, he's with Croesus Squadron.'

'So he is. I'd quite forgotten. One gets in such a muddle with what they're all doing these days . . . Johnnie's *such* fun. Too divine for words. I saw him at Bunty's party last month, you know. He seemed rather keen, I may say . . .' The gold compact snapped shut. 'In that case, I think I *am* going to enjoy myself.'

When the two women had left the cloakroom, Pearl imitated them contemptuously.

'*Such* fun, darling! *So* amusing! Frightfully, *too, too* divine! Ugh! People like that make me sick.'

Anne had put on the mink coat and was looking at

herself in the long mirror, turning this way and that. She sniffed sideways at the soft fur collar which smelled expensively of the *Arpège* scent her mother wore.

'Who were they, anyway?'

'Girlfriends from London invited by those Croesus fellas, I s'pose. Crikey, they put the others in the shade a bit, didn't they? Wonder what this piece of animal cost.'

Pearl flung the sable wrap over one shoulder and admired herself. The two of them paraded up and down the empty cloakroom in front of the mirrors, wearing the furs. Dance music from the station band playing for the guests in the Mess reached them faintly, and tantalizingly. For a moment they swayed round with imaginary partners, arms outstretched.

Pearl stopped in disgust. 'It's not bloody fair! Here we are, stuck in here while all that rotten lot of cows are out there, having a good time. Let's go and have a butchers at least.'

They put the furs away and slipped out of the cloakroom and across the vestibule. The double doors to the dining hall were open and they stationed themselves at one side, peering round the post. The big room had been cleared of tables for the dance and the band was playing on the dais at one end. A corporal with slicked-back hair stepped up to the microphone in front and started to croon.

Anne watched him with interest. 'Who's that? I've seen his face before.'

'Nobby Clarke. He's an armourer. Oily little tyke really, but he doesn't sing so bad, does he?'

'I wouldn't mind having a go at that, Pearl. It looks fun.'

'Why don't you go for an audition then, love? They were asking for people who could sing the other day for the Station Christmas bash. You've got a nice voice – I've heard you carolling away. You'd be just as good as Nobby.'

'I'm not sure I could ever do it like he does, though.'

"Course you bloody could. You just stand up there, hold onto that microphone thing and warble into it, just like he's doing.'

They went on spying on the dancers. This was a rather different affair from the Sergeants' Mess evening, Anne saw. Far more decorous. Nobody was dancing like Stan with his Palais gliding. There was a good deal of pump handling and quartering the floor stiffly. Cynthia of the mink coat, she was pleased to see, was dancing with a portly squadron leader and looking extremely bored. What had happened to Johnnie who was rather keen and such fun?

Pearl had edged her way a little further round the door post and a pilot officer, coming out, caught sight of her. He was a little drunk and blinked at her, confused.

'I say, I know you, don't I?'

'I'm one of the WAAFS, sir.'

He grinned at her triumphantly. 'Knew I'd seen you somewhere before. I say, what about a dance?'

'You'll get me into trouble, sir,' Pearl said demurely.

'What? Oh, stuff and nonsense! It's Christmas, or jolly nearly. No-one'll notice.'

Pearl winked back over her shoulder as she was led away. Anne stayed by the doorway, watching. Nobby Clarke was on the home straight now, clinging soulfully to the microphone.

Two officers had appeared from behind her and were standing in the doorway. She moved back but they seemed oblivious of her presence so close by. The tall one, nearer to her, leaned against the doorpost, hands in his pockets. The back view of fair hair reaching almost to the collar was familiar and Anne was sure that this was the driver of the green sports car that had almost knocked her down. She was not surprised, when he spoke, to hear that it was in a languid drawl.

'I say, poor old Cynthia's got herself stuck with some frightfully stodgy type. Looks as bored as hell. Go and do the decent thing and rescue her, Willy, there's a good chap.'

The other one laughed. '*You* go, old boy. You're welcome to her. Absolute bloody nympho, if you ask me. I'd sooner not have it *thrust* at me.'

'Still, gift horses and all that . . .'

'Speaking of horses, given or otherwise, old Cynthia's definitely getting a bit long in the tooth, you know. Past thirty, I'd say.'

'Good lord, is she? Doesn't look it, I'll give her that. Not that I've ever actually seen her in the light of day. Last time I saw her at some party she looked all right to me, though I was a bit pissed so I can't remember much about it. I say, what on *earth's* that girl doing in here?'

Pearl and her pilot officer had come into view.

'What girl?'

'The fat one with that awful dyed red hair, dancing with Goofy whatsisname. What the hell does he think he's doing?'

'Foxtrotting, I'd say, by the looks of it. Rather well, actually.'

'I don't mean that Willy. What's he doing with that girl? She's a waitress.'

'A what?'

'A waitress. Serves in the Mess. She's one of those Women's Auxiliary thingummybobs. They wear those RAF shirts.'

'You sure, old boy?'

'Positive. She nearly spilled the soup in my lap, that's how I remember her. Never notice them otherwise. It was that tinned tomato stuff they dish up – missed me by a whisker or I might never've been the same man again. Bloody hot, you know. She should be in the kitchens, or somewhere.'

'Shouldn't worry, old chap, there must be an officer in charge. She'll soon chuck her out. I saw a damned attractive one the other day, as a matter of fact. I always think uniform's pretty sexy on a woman . . .'

'I'd steer bloody clear of the lot of them, Willy, if I were you. You don't know where they've been. Give 'em a wide berth and stick to your own kind.'

'Careful what you say . . . I think there might be one of them standing right behind you, looking absolute daggers at us.'

The fair head turned briefly and without interest in Anne's direction. 'Is there? God, they're everywhere.'

The shorter, darker one laughed. 'I say, Johnnie, if looks could kill you, you'd be a dead man.'

'That'll teach her to eavesdrop. Come on, Willy, we'd better go and do our stuff. I suppose I'll have to dance with Cynthia. God, what a bore! Did I tell you about that girl I met at Sonny's, by the way? She was the most incredible lay. Game for anything. I've asked her down next weekend. Booked a room at the Mermaid . . .'

The two men drifted away out of earshot. The band's tempo had speeded up and Nobby had exchanged his soulful expression for a roguish grin.

You are my sunshine, my only sunshine . . .

So *that*, Anne thought glowering, was Johnnie who was such fun and too divine for words, and Willy who was frightfully amusing. She did not find either of them either divine or remotely amusing. On the contrary. Pearl reappeared, flushed with triumph.

'Bloomin' nuisance . . . I was just getting along like a house on fire with that bloke when Newman shows up dancing with some officer and I have to scarper pretty quick before she sees me. She was all togged up in a civvy frock and I didn't recognize her at first. Don't think she spotted me, though. Hey, what're you looking so pissed off about. What's happened?'

'I've just seen the two those London women were talking about . . . Johnnie and Willy, or whoever they are. They were standing right here in front of me for a while.'

'What were they like?'

'Utterly revolting. They were quite sickeningly pleased

with themselves. I could hear every word they were saying and I can tell you they were bloody rude about us WAAFS – at least, the one called Johnnie was. I was just about to tell him exactly what I thought of him when they moved off.'

'Lucky you didn't, duckie. You'd've been in more trouble. Mustn't cheek officers – remember.'

'It would've been worth it . . . what a creep!'

Pearl took hold of Anne's arm firmly. 'Come on, we'd best get back to our post before anything else happens. Forget those two sods. Let's go and try on some more furs.'

Speedy was manoeuvring Felicity rather erratically round the floor.

'Speedy, this is meant to be a foxtrot.'

'Good lord, is it? Thought it was a waltz. Damn silly name for a dance anyway. Foxes trot jolly quickly. If they mooned about like this they'd get clobbered every time. Sorry, got your toe then. Are you enjoying this caper?'

'Dancing with you? Or the evening?'

'Both. But specially dancing with me.'

'I'm enjoying both, as it happens, though I won't go on doing so if you tread on my foot like that again.'

'I'll try my hardest not to, I swear. Not really my line, dancing, as you may have noticed . . . You know, that frock you're wearing suits you like anything.'

'Thank you.'

'First time I've seen you out of uniform and it knocked me sideways, I can tell you. Mind you, the old uniform suits you too. Fact is, *anything* would suit you. What's it made of?'

'The uniform? It's the same as yours, I think.'

'No, I mean the frock. It's jolly pretty stuff . . . soft and it clings in all the right places.'

'It's georgette.'

'Ah, that reminds me. George is on standby to be your chaperone any evening this week. So, which one is it to be?'

'Honestly, Speedy, I don't think it's a good idea – '

'So you said before, Company Assistant Newman, and I told you that old George is the perfect answer to a maiden's worry.'

'Actually, it's Assistant Section Officer now, not Company Assistant. They've changed the name.'

'What's in a name? That which we call a rose by any other name would smell as sweet.'

'Another of Mr Snodgrass's favourites?'

'Definitely. You can't beat the Bard, Snodders used to say – many a time and oft. Nothing like him for the apt phrase. Amazing when you think about it, isn't it? Three hundred years back and yet the old boy still puts his finger on it . . . if you see what I mean.'

'I think I do.'

'*Romeo and Juliet*, if I'm not mistaken. Now that's romantic stuff, if you like. Romeo, Romeo, Wherefore art thou, Romeo? Damn good. I'm not sure *where* the fellow is, though.'

'He was listening below the balcony.'

'Was he? Poor show that. He shouldn't have been eavesdropping. Eavesdroppers never hear any good of themselves.'

'He did, in this case.'

'So he did. I remember now. It was *his* name she was going on about. Always thought that a bit odd, you know. Rum sort of bloke, smelling of roses.'

Felicity laughed. 'Speedy, this is supposed to be a quickstep now. They've changed the tune.'

'Glad you noticed. Shall we walk a little faster, said the whiting to the snail . . . I say, there's a porpoise close behind us, all right. Lucky I didn't tread on *his* tail. Our revered and respected Station Master is at hand . . . don't look now. He's tripping the light fantastic with some old duck. Bet he wishes he was dancing with you. What are you making that face for?'

'He's not revered by me.'

'What's he done now? Eaten a WAAF for breakfast?'

'It wouldn't surprise me. On toast, probably. He hates having us here. He thinks we just get in the way. I'm only here on sufferance this evening.'

'Bad show. I can't think why they won't let you eat in the Mess, same as the rest of us. If I had my way, you'd sit next to me every day and then I'd eat up all my greens, like a good boy. Whoops, sorry old man . . . didn't see you there. That wasn't *him*, I'm thankful to say.'

'We're second class. Third class, actually. He doesn't believe we're capable of more than cooking and cleaning and filling in forms. He told me so the first day I arrived here.'

'Oh, he'll soon learn. He's one of the old guard, that's his trouble. Getting on a bit and stuck in his ways. As a matter of fact, he's not such a bad chap, you know, when he's in a good mood.'

'When does he *ever* have a good mood?'

'Oh, when the moon is full. Actually, I've seen him positively jovial at some of the Mess nights. Life and soul of the party.'

'I can't believe it.'

''Tis all the cares and weight of responsibility that make him seem so unfriendly. Uneasy lies the head that wears the crown, and all that . . . There you are, the Bard once again. I told you, he always hits the nail on the head. I see our First Lady is running true to form this evening. Dancing with all the millionaires in turn.'

Felicity watched as Mrs Palmer passed them in the arms of one of the Croesus Squadron pilots. Her head was thrown back and she was laughing up into his face.

'Are they really all millionaires in that squadron, Speedy?'

'Bit of an exaggeration, I suppose, but most of them are pretty stinking rich, I'd say. Fresh meat for her. Different breed from us RAF Regulars, the Weekend chaps. She'll go through them like a dose of salts.'

'Speedy, you shouldn't say such things.'

"'Tis true, 'tis pity; And pity 'tis 'tis true. The Bard again! There's no end to his wisdom. Oh lord, was that your toe again . . .?'

At the end of the evening he insisted on walking back to her quarters with her.

'No officer should allow a lady to return home unaccompanied. Rule two thousand and fifty-three, King's Regulations.'

'I'm an officer, too, remember. And quite capable of going home alone.'

'This evening you're a lady – you danced with me, so you must be – and it's my solemn duty to protect you.'

Walking across the darkened camp from the Officers' Mess, he took her arm.

'Wouldn't want you to trip over something.'

'Actually, I can see quite well with my torch, Speedy.'

'You can't be too careful, though. Supposing you broke an ankle . . . jolly inconvenient.'

Unknown to Felicity, all kinds of thoughts were chasing themselves inside the young pilot's head. She was not to know that he was falling deeply in love with her and that he hardly knew how to cope with the unaccustomed feeling. He was afraid that he stood little chance with her. He knew that he amused her and could make her laugh by playing the fool, but he could never be the sort of bloke she must have been used to meeting at Cambridge. The clever sort of chap who could spout Goethe or recite the Iliad, not just pop off a few silly quotes. And yet, he reasoned hopefully to himself in the dark walking along beside her, some of those types must be bloody boring . . . And what's more they couldn't fly a fighter at three hundred miles an hour, bash all over the bloody skies and then cut the daisies upside down with nothing on the clock but the maker's name. So far the old wings had never failed him. The thing was, though, he'd have to play his cards jolly carefully. One false move and it would all be over before it had even begun.

Outside her quarters he released her arm decorously

and then, in an inspired gesture, found her hand and raised it to his lips.

'A fair good night, Assistant Section Officer. And pleasing dreams, and slumbers light.'

The gallant and respectful action touched and surprised Felicity. Even more surprising was the fact that he let go of her hand at once and walked away. She called after him.

'Shakespeare again?'

'Scott,' came the answer out of the darkness.

She watched the narrow beam of his torch bobbing away.

'Good night, Speedy.'

She thought she heard him whistling as he went.

Four

'This way, please, Miss Stratton.'

Virginia hurried after the WAAF who strode ahead down a long and gloomy corridor. The Air Ministry building was busy with people moving about purposefully and she had to dodge between them to keep her guide in sight. A man carrying a bundle of files under his arm collided with her and one of the files slid to the floor, scattering its contents. He swore under his breath as he crawled about retrieving the papers and Virginia, stammering her apologies, tried to help him. Her guide was fast disappearing down the end of the corridor, marching on briskly without a backward glance, and in panic Virginia thrust a handful of the papers at the man and scurried after her.

She was shown into a big, high-ceilinged room with a desk under the window. A grey-haired RAF officer with a line of ribbons on his chest was seated behind the desk, writing something, and a WAAF officer, also grey-haired, sat a little to one side of him. It was several moments before the RAF officer looked up and spoke.

'Sit down, please.'

Neither of them smiled at her as she took her place awkwardly on the chair in front of the desk. The man stared at her through horn-rimmed spectacles and his eyes were two cold blue spheres behind the thick glass lenses.

He clasped his hands before him on the desk top, interlacing the fingers. 'You have asked to be considered for Special Duties, Miss Stratton. Can you tell us why?'

She had no idea what to reply. The whole idea had been suggested to her, not the other way round. In the silence the two of them watched her and waited without expression. More than ever she regretted the day when she had found the courage to go back to the recruiting department, which had led her to this moment. The WAAF officer there had been enthusiastic. She had asked some strange questions, apparently to some particular purpose, wanting to know whether Virginia was quick to learn things, whether she would stay calm in a crisis, whether she could keep a secret . . . She must have given her the right answers because at the end of the interview the WAAF officer had smiled at her with approval.

'I'm going to recommend you to train as a Special Duties Clerk. No good asking me what that is – it's too hush-hush. The only thing I *can* tell you is that you'll be doing one of the most vital jobs in the WAAF – if you're accepted. You'll be hearing from us soon about an interview.'

When the letter had arrived she had hidden it away from her mother. *Dear Miss Stratton, You are instructed to report at eleven hundred hours . . .*

'We're waiting, Miss Stratton.'

The RAF officer was still staring at her. In her nervousness she let her handbag slip off her lap onto the floor. She bent to retrieve it, blushing, and clutched it closely against her body.

'I was told I might be suitable for the work.'

'And do *you* consider that you would be suitable, Miss Stratton?'

'I don't know, sir. I don't know what is required.'

'Then let me enlighten you. These qualities would be required of you: intelligence, alertness, integrity, the ability to think quickly, devotion to duty and absolute reliability. Do you think you can offer all these?'

'I think I have some of them, at least . . . I can only say that I would do my best.'

'Unfortunately your best might not be good enough, Miss Stratton.'

The WAAF officer spoke now in an equally stern voice.

'There is another quality needed . . . are you capable of keeping secrets?'

She could answer this quite firmly. 'Yes, I am.'

'Are you sure? Because if you're the sort of girl who's likely to go round blabbing and gossiping then you'll be no good to us at all. *If* we decide to take you on then you must tell no-one at all about your work or what it involves – and that means *no-one*. Not your parents, or your family, not your boyfriend or any other friends – not even other WAAFs. Nobody at all. Do you understand?'

Virginia nodded. Now the RAF officer spoke again. He was looking at her as though he had no confidence in her at all.

'Women are prone to gossip, as we all know. Why should you be any different?'

She cast a look of appeal towards the WAAF officer but there was no help there.

'I don't really know, sir.'

'You don't seem very sure about anything, do you, Miss Stratton?'

She was silent. Tears were pricking her eyes and she blinked quickly. The officer had unclasped his hands and was looking at the papers in front of him, turning them over.

'You *are* completely British by birth and parentage?'

She swallowed to steady her voice. 'Yes, sir.'

'No foreign grandparents, or great-grandparents. No foreign blood anywhere?'

'Not as far as I know.'

He grunted. It was the WAAF officer's turn again. She had leaned forward a little in her chair. Her grey hair was tightly permed and her eyes matched the tone of her voice.

'What would you do if there was a raid on the station?'

Virginia hesitated. It seemed an odd question. Perhaps there was a catch to it.

'I'd go to the public shelter and wait until the All Clear sounded and then I'd catch the next train.'

To her utter astonishment they both burst out laughing.

'I meant on an *RAF* station, not a railway station,' the WAAF officer said, smiling. 'What would you do if you were on duty there and the Germans came over and dropped bombs on it?'

'I'd carry on with my duties.'

'Good for you!'

When she got back to the office, Miss Parkes, in whom she had confided, looked up from her desk.

'How did you get on, my dear?'

'They accepted me.'

Miss Parkes looked quietly satisfied. 'I knew they would. I should tell your mother when you next have the opportunity.'

And when I next have the courage, Virginia thought. Some time later it occurred to her that she still had no idea what Special Duties actually were.

The Station Commander's house was set apart from the main buildings and stood in its own garden, surrounded by a high beech hedge. The front door was opened to Felicity by a batman and she was shown into a large drawing-room where a group of people in evening clothes stood round the fireside. Wing Commander Palmer detached himself from the semi-circle.

'Good evening, Assistant Section Officer.'

'Good evening, sir.'

She shook hands with him – the first time she had not saluted him. Even off-duty, though, she could not bring herself to drop the 'sir'.

'I don't think you've met my wife.'

Mrs Palmer's handshake was limp and cool. She was wearing a long wine-red gown and her blond hair was caught back in a smooth chignon. She looked at Felicity without welcome or interest. More introductions were made: there were two officers new to Colston, with their wives, two couples from London, a Sir Reginald and Lady Howard who lived a few miles away, and a single young man, also from London, by the name of Charles Savage. Felicity could not imagine why she had been asked to this dinner party which she had not had the slightest wish to attend, but which she had interpreted as a command rather than an invitation. Charles Savage drifted languidly to her side.

'Did I hear right? You're in the Women's Air Force?'

'Yes, you did.'

'You don't look a bit as though you are.'

He was smoking a cigarette through an ivory holder and his hands flapped loosely from his wrists.

'What should I look like?'

He waved the holder. 'Not like you, anyway. I pictured something absolutely fearsome . . . cropped hair, hideous, possibly a moustache . . . that sort of thing, you know.'

'We're quite normal, really.'

'I'd've said *you* were actually rather special . . .'

To Felicity's relief, Mrs Cutler, another of those from London, moved to join them. She had a cupid's bow mouth painted scarlet.

'Do tell me what you're talking about, Charles.'

'I'm talking about the Women's Royal Air Force, Amy, since you ask.'

'Women's Auxiliary Air Force,' Felicity corrected.

'Whatever it is. And this is an officer in it.'

Mrs Cutler's eyes widened. 'Are you really? How extraordinary. Do you have to wear uniform?'

'Normally, yes.'

'Poor you! I should simply *hate* that. I think uniform is super on a man, but I don't think women should wear it, do you, Charles?'

'That all depends, Amy darling.'

The red mouth pouted. 'Everybody seems to be joining something – except you, Charles. This beastly war's spoiling everything. Do you know, Gerald wants me and the children to go to Canada but I simply refuse to. I'd be bored to death there. All that awful snow and people wearing tartan hats with ear flaps and cutting down trees . . .'

'They're not *all* lumberjacks, darling.'

'Well, anyway, I'm not going. The war will soon be over in any case, won't it?'

'How should I know? Ask our officer here. Perhaps she knows.'

Mrs Cutler turned round blue eyes towards Felicity. 'Do you?'

'I'm afraid not.'

'Well, nothing much has happened for ages, has it? And I mean who cares about Poland and those other places? I've never met a Pole in my life, have you? I don't see why we have to go on fighting for them . . .'

Later they went into the dining-room and sat at a polished table lit with candles and set with silver and crystal. The dinner was served by white-coated batmen and a waitress in a starched cap and apron. They began with turtle soup and proceeded to sole crêpes, roast pheasant and orange soufflé. Felicity, listening patiently to Charles Savage's long account of a weekend spent hunting in Hampshire, kept reminding herself that there was a war on. The scene at the dinner table gave no clues. Even Wing Commander Palmer, out of uniform, appeared to have undergone some kind of transformation – and for the better. He was actually smiling at something that Lady Howard was saying to him. Not exactly the life and soul of the party that Speedy had talked of, but a definite improvement on the grim and frightening figure she was accustomed to encountering. If he laughs, she thought, I shall know I'm dreaming.

'Do you hunt?' Charles Savage asked in his loud and irritating drawl.

'No, I don't.'

'Pity. I was going to suggest that you came out some time . . .'

She said coldly: 'There *is* a war on, you know, Mr Savage. We don't have a lot of time for that sort of thing in the services at the moment. I'm surprised that you do.'

He was unabashed. 'You're looking frightfully disapproving . . . Actually, I was turned down for military service. Had a mastoid infection as a child and it left me deaf in one ear. I'm happy to say that my good ear is on *your* side and my bad one on Amy's so that I don't have to listen to all her *bêtises*. Between you and me I wish she'd go off to Canada on the next boat and stay there permanently. I can't imagine what Caroline sees in her. They were at school together, or something . . . Of course, the husband is worth a million . . . trade, though. Not really dear Caro's style, even though all her loot came from beer. She has expensive tastes, our hostess. Just as well she doesn't have to make do on a Wing Commander's pay. Odd that she married someone like him, don't you think? Not her type at all, I'd have said.'

'I really don't know, and I don't think we should discuss it.'

'Now you're looking even *more* disapproving. Very well, let's talk about what you're doing in the Air Force instead. Amy's quite wrong about women in uniform, you know . . .'

Mr Cutler was sitting on Felicity's other side. He had scarcely said a word throughout the soup and fish course, but over the pheasant he began to talk morosely about his business which, she gathered, was something to do with tins. The war, he told her in glum tones, was bound to affect it.

'There'll be a shortage of raw materials, you see. Shortage of everything, come to that. They'll have to ration it all in the end. I tell you, this war hasn't got started properly yet. Things are going to get a lot worse before we're through. I wish I could persuade Amy to take the children to Canada, but she won't. I keep telling her that it'd be a damn sight better being bored over there than living here under the Nazis, but she won't listen.'

'Surely it won't come to us being invaded?'

'I'm very much afraid that it will. The Huns have got to if they want to beat us.'

'But the French – '

'Oh, they'll let us down. The Germans will attack them first and they'll give up, you'll see. No stomach when it comes to a real fight. And once the Huns have taken over France they'll be all set to invade us.'

'They'd have to cross the Channel.'

He gestured tiredly. 'They've got a Navy, haven't they? Not to mention an Army and an Air Force – bigger and better than ours.'

She thought of Speedy's casual words. *Come the spring and they'll be ready for the off* . . . Down the far end of the dinner table, Wing Commander Palmer was talking to the officer's wife seated next to him, his head bent towards her. *This is an operational fighter station in wartime and you and your recruits will be under my command.* If gloomy Mr Cutler was right then it might no longer be a question of the WAAFS taking the men's places to release them for active service. They would soon be in the front line themselves and RAF Colston would certainly come under attack from the enemy. How would they stand up to it? They were all young girls, born in peacetime, whose only experience of gunfire, like hers, had been to hear it safely in the distance in the station butts. Supposing some of them panicked? A girl like Potter, for instance, could easily have hysterics, or at least become a serious liability. Who could say how any of them would behave? She watched the Station Commander thoughtfully for a moment. For the first time she could appreciate some of his reservations – at least in that respect. In every other she was convinced that he was completely wrong. The WAAFS could, and would, cope with most trades just as well as the men. In the end he would have to eat his words. *Cooking, cleaning and clerical work* . . . He'd soon have to change his tune. More recruits were due to arrive after Christmas, and there would be more after that. And more, and more . . . As she thought about this, the Wing Commander turned his head in her direction and she looked quickly away.

After dinner, while the ladies sat in the drawing-room waiting for the men to finish their port, Lady Howard complained stridently about her servant problem. Her cook had given notice and gone to work in a munitions factory, their head gardener had joined the Army, the under gardener had just been called up, and one of the housemaids had insisted on going off to be a Land Girl.

'Left us in the lurch to go and work for some farmer! I told Reginald, I don't know how we're going to manage. We shall just have to shut up both wings and let the garden run to seed.'

Felicity listened to her and to the sympathetic murmurings from some of the other women. All over England, she thought, there must be people who perceive the war only as an inconvenience to themselves. Lady Howard deplores the loss of her servants, Mr Cutler moans about a tin shortage while his wife grumbles that her fun is being spoiled and admits frankly that she doesn't care a fig about the fate of the Poles, nor, presumably, that of the Czechs, Finns, persecuted Jews, or for anyone else whose life and liberty is threatened and for whom we are supposed to be fighting. She doesn't understand, as any Pole or Czech could tell her, and even her husband has tried to, that it's not her entertainment that's at stake but her freedom and very existence.

She was glad when the men came into the room and put a stop to the conversation though this was short-lived when Wing Commander Palmer paused by her chair.

'I hope you're enjoying the evening?'

'Yes, thank you, sir.'

'Good . . . good.' He cleared his throat. 'One of the drawbacks of Service life can be having to be away from one's family at Christmas and so on . . . Does your family live far away?'

'Norfolk, sir. At least my father lives there. My mother died some years ago.'

'I'm sorry to hear that. Brothers or sisters?'

'No, sir.'

He cleared his throat again. 'I believe you were at Cambridge?'

'Yes, sir.'

'Beautiful place. Which college?'

'Girton, sir.'

'Bit out of town, isn't it?'

Mrs Palmer called from across the room. 'David! Lady Howard has something to ask you . . .'

'Excuse me.'

He left her side, to her great relief. The stilted, unnatural exchange had flustered her. She was even thankful to resume a conversation with Mr Cutler who was now talking pessimistically about the inadequacy of the Royal Air Force.

'The German Luftwaffe's twice the size, did you know? I've been told that on good authority. *And* their pilots have had combat experience . . . Spain, Poland . . . those chaps already know a thing or two. Ours are still wet behind the ears. Haven't a clue most of them, I'll bet.'

At the end of the evening, she walked back to her quarters under a glittering, starry sky. It was very cold and felt and smelled as though it would soon snow. She had not enjoyed the dinner party in the least and it was good to be out of the house and in the clean air. It had tired and depressed her, and she still could not understand why she had been asked. Perhaps all Station Commanders considered it their duty to show some sort of bogus Christmas spirit. Mercifully she had only had to exchange a few words with Wing Commander Palmer, and even fewer with his wife. She walked quickly, not needing a torch to see her way, her high heels ringing against the paving. As she passed by the Sergeants' Mess she could hear someone playing 'Hark The Herald Angels Sing' on the piano – strumming it out loudly. In a few days it would be Christmas; the first Christmas of the war.

*   *   *

While his WAAF officer was walking back beneath the stars, Wing Commander Palmer stood in front of the dying fire, finishing his brandy. To his annoyance, Charles Savage had lingered after the other guests and now Caroline was saying a prolonged good night to him at the door. He was very familiar with the situation and it had been a long time since he had cared. They had been married for eight years and for six of those she had been unfaithful with a variety of men. Savage had been only one in a long line.

He drank more brandy and stared into the embers. He had tried his hardest to make the marriage work, but he had failed. He blamed himself entirely for having been foolish enough to marry her in the first place. He was ten years her senior and it was he who had pursued her and not the other way round. He had fallen in love with her the moment he had seen her at a dinner party when he had been on leave in London years ago. She had sat opposite him and he had been almost unable to take his eyes off her throughout the whole meal. He supposed now that it must have been infatuation – the blind infatuation of a long-time bachelor, dazzled by a very beautiful woman. It was several years since he had felt any love for her and doubted that she had ever felt any for him. It remained a mystery to him why she had ever accepted his proposal unless perhaps she had been impressed by the uniform and the medals, and had somehow imagined Service life to be glamorous. He realized now what a disappointment he must have proved – how stuffy and dull he must quickly have seemed to her, and how boring and constricting her life as an RAF wife. He should have foreseen that it could never have made her happy.

Palmer drained his glass and helped himself to more brandy from the decanter on the side table. He sat down in an armchair and rubbed his hand over his eyes. He was very tired and the dinner party had been a strain. He had not felt in the least in a social mood and he had found the effort exhausting. Lady Howard had been particularly tiresome, asking endless questions and complaining about noise from the aerodrome in the early mornings. He had done his best to be placatory. Squadron Leader Forrester's wife, new to the station and sitting on his other side, had, by contrast, been so withdrawn and shy that conversation with her had been equally hard work. On reflection, he thought that he should perhaps have taken the time to talk more to Assistant Section Officer Newman, but somehow the opportunity had not presented itself. She had been deep in conversation with that ass Savage or that fellow Cutler and when he had tried to have a word with her after dinner Lady Howard had intervened with yet more infuriating questions. Pity. He had asked the WAAF officer with the idea that it might help put their relationship on a better footing. Not that he had changed his mind about the folly of having women serving on the station, but because he had accepted that they were here to stay, whether he liked it or not. And he'd been pretty hard on ASO Newman, one way and another.

He heard Savage's flashy sports car start up outside with a low growl. Caroline had taken her time saying good night, as he had expected. He was fairly sure that Savage had been her lover at some point but it was no longer of any interest to him with whom she slept so long as she observed certain basic rules of behaviour and put in a reasonable number of official appearances as his wife. The hot and terrible jealousy and anger that he had first experienced had long since been replaced by a cold indifference. He had even managed to face the fact that her infidelity was common knowledge on the station. He had immersed himself in his work and career and kept up the outward pretence of a normal marriage, so far as it was possible. As he saw it, the only alternative was to divorce her and to him that was unthinkable.

The sports car revved noisily and he heard it drive away, the sound fading into the distance. Thank God Savage had gone! There was a bang as the front door shut and the sharp click of his wife's heels as she crossed the parquet floor in the hall. She came into the drawing-room and he could tell at once that she was in a vile mood. She flung herself into the armchair opposite him.

'Get me a drink, will you, David. A large one.'

He got up to pour her a brandy and handed her the glass. She took a swallow and closed her eyes.

'God, what a boring evening! Those ghastly RAF and their dreary little wives . . . do we have to have people like that?'

'You know we do.'

'I don't see why. Surely you see enough of the men during the day and the wives have nothing to say for themselves. Christ, what a stuffed shirt that Squadron Leader Forrester is! And his wife hardly uttered all evening.'

'She was very shy.'

'Shy! She seemed positively moronic. Can I have a light please?'

He lit her cigarette for her and stayed standing by the mantelpiece. She looked up at him, blowing a thin stream of smoke.

'I have to hand it to you, David . . . I didn't know you were such a dark horse.'

He frowned. 'What do you mean exactly?'

'That WAAF of yours – Newland, or whatever her name is – I thought we'd asked her in the line of duty too.'

'We did.'

'Oh, come off it! I saw you looking at her . . . are you screwing her?'

He kept his face expressionless. He had learned long ago not to react to any of her taunts.

'Don't be absurd, Caroline.'

She laughed harshly. 'You're a pompous prick, David, you know that? Always up on your high and mighty Station Commander's horse, ordering everyone about as though you were God Almighty! Don't tell me you wouldn't like to screw her even if you haven't already done so. I could see it in your face. As a matter of fact I think it's terribly funny! Really rather amusing! You've been ranting on about what a bloody nuisance the WAAFS are going to be and all the time you've had your covetous eye on their officer.'

He said quietly, 'That happens to be quite untrue, but you must think as you like.'

She had drunk nearly half the brandy already. 'Personally I thought she was as dull as ditchwater, and that thing she was wearing was years out of date. Charles was quite taken by her, you know. Extraordinary! I wouldn't have thought she was his type at all. Actually, Charles has become a bit of a bore. I don't think I'll bother to ask him again.'

'I'm thankful to hear it.'

'You're not jealous, by any chance?'

'No, I'm not jealous. I just don't happen to like him.'

'You don't like anyone who's amusing. All you like is your stodgy RAF types . . . preferably ones you can boss around. You can't give Charles orders. He doesn't have to kow-tow and say yes, sir, no, sir, three bagsful, sir, so you don't like him. Give me some more brandy, please.'

'Haven't you had enough?'

'Oh, don't be so bloody dreary! I'm not one of your junior officers. Just give it to me.'

He took her glass and poured more from the decanter. She spoke to his back.

'You should have married someone like your WAAF, David. She'd have made you a good little RAF wife. She'd have polished all your bloody medals and done everything you told her. She'd probably have saluted you after you'd poked her. Mind you, you're old enough to be her father, aren't you? You must seem like Methuselah to her. Still, I suppose it's sort of *droit de seigneur*, isn't it? I mean you can't refuse your commanding officer. Mustn't disobey him. All you need do is give the order and she'll jump into bed. I wonder what she really thinks of you. She must think you're the most frightful old bore.'

He put down his glass. 'I'm going to bed now, Caroline.'

'That's right, toddle off to beddy-byes. You're afraid to listen . . .'

'I'm not afraid to listen. There's just no point in continuing this conversation, and I'm extremely tired.'

'You *are* afraid to. You can't take it, can you, David? You can dish it out all right, but you can't take it.'

He left the room and went slowly upstairs. They shared the same bedroom but no longer the same bed and he lay wakeful in his in spite of his tiredness. She still had the power to hurt, to get under his guard sometimes. He could dismiss the ridiculous remarks about Assistant Section Officer Newman, but others rankled. Was he really so pompous? Did he behave as though he were God Almighty? He supposed that it must seem so, sometimes – certainly to Caroline who had no understanding of what it took to run a station properly. Station Commanders were supposed to engender a healthy amount of respect and fear. It was a necessary part of their job. They were not intended to be popular. He could remember a Station Commander back in the early days who had wanted to be liked, one of the chaps, joking with everybody . . . It had been disastrous for discipline and the station had gone steadily downhill until, eventually, he had been replaced. That had happened in peacetime and so no great harm had been done, but in wartime on an operational station top-line discipline was imperative. To permit anything less was to fail in one's solemn duty. That was the way he saw it. The Methuselah jibe had hurt too, if he were honest. Damn it, he was only forty-one. Scarely an old man yet, though it was true that he was nearly twice the age of a good many of those under his command on this station. He thought, as he'd thought increasingly of late, that he'd give a hell of a lot to change places with some of those young pilots . . . to be in his early twenties with a fast machine like the Hurricane to fly. They were going to be on the centre of the stage in this war and he'd got to watch from the bloody wings.

He heard Caroline come up to bed much later. From the way she stumbled he could tell that she had continued to drink downstairs. She fell asleep immediately and started to snore.

Tomorrow, he remembered, was the Station Christmas Dance.

Anne sat on a chair at the side of the stage. Nobby Clarke, the corporal armourer sat beside her. Behind them the station band, conducted by a sergeant wireless operator called Joe, was playing *Apple Blossom Time* and below them, on the hangar floor, a mass of people swayed to the rhythm. Faces turned up towards her as they passed in front of the stage. She saw grins and winks, waves and mouthings – Sandra giggling at her, Pearl giving her the thumbs up. Her own face felt stiff with nervousness. She fingered the knot of her tie and wished she was down there with them all and not up on the stage about to make a complete fool of herself. She wished she had made a mess of her audition, or got laryngitis.

Nobby shifted on his chair beside her, flicked at the sleeve of his best blue and smoothed his shiny hair with the flat of his hand. *Apple Blossom Time* was drawing to a close and her stomach fluttered in fright. Nobby nudged her – unnecessarily.

'Your turn coming up, love.'

Joe, baton raised, arms stretched wide like the Pope giving his Easter blessing, looked over his shoulder at her expectantly. She forced herself to stand up and take the few steps to the microphone. Every face in the crowd below seemed to be turned towards her – hundreds of white blobs stretching all the way to the back of the hangar. Whoops and whistles came up to her and someone at the front shouted up something unintelligible and probably rude. Then the noise died away as the band began to play. She gripped hold of the microphone, waited for her moment and took a deep breath.

> Look for the silver lining
> When e'er a cloud appears in the blue.
> Remember somewhere the sun is shining
> And so the right thing to do is make it shine for you.
> A heart, full of joy and gladness
> Will always banish sadness and strife.
> So always look for the silver lining
> And try to find the sunny side of life.

To her great surprise her voice sounded quite steady and she began to feel more confident. Her legs stopped shaking and she loosened her stranglehold on the mike. Joe was nodding his approval as he wielded his baton with little flicks of his wrist. The dancers were surging past below the stage and it gave her an exhilarating feeling now to look down on them, as though *she* were propelling the moving mass. She swayed a little this way and that, as she remembered seeing dance band singers in films do, and wished that she were wearing a slinky evening gown instead of her navy skirt, shirt and tie. It was hard to play the part properly, dressed like a schoolgirl. When it was time to sing again, she even managed to smile as well.

> A heart, full of joy and gladness
> Will always banish sadness and strife.
> So always look for the silver lining
> And try to find the sunny side of life.

She finished to loud applause and an ear-splitting volley of whistles. Nobby was clapping his hands at her, Joe was beaming. She'd done it, and by the end she'd almost been enjoying herself.

She went into the wings and downstairs to the back-stage dressing-rooms where she'd left her things. 'We'll try you with just one number,' Joe had said. 'See how it goes. Maybe more next time if you do OK.' Now she could relax and join the others. It was icy cold in the dressing-room. She switched on the mirror lights and sat down, pulling her raincoat round her shoulders. Her eyes looked bright and her cheeks flushed. She fished her compact out of her respirator case and began to apply powder. It was then that she noticed the man reflected in the mirror. He was standing in the doorway behind, watching her. It gave her a fright until she realized that he was not some station ghost, but flesh and blood. And, at the same moment, she recognized him.

He was leaning against the doorpost, a lighted cigarette dangling between the fingertips of one hand, the other in his trouser pocket, one foot crossed over the other. What a nauseatingly affected pose, she thought. Did fighter pilots ever stand upright? They were forever leaning against something – aeroplanes, or walls or doors. Seeing that she had seen him, he smiled at her reflection.

'Mind if I come in?'

She snapped the compact shut and turned to face him. 'You already seem to be. Are you looking for someone?'

'You, as a matter of fact.'

'Me?'

'Yes, *you*. Don't look so surprised. I came to congratulate you. You sang awfully well.'

'Did I?'

'Don't you believe me?'

'I don't think so.'

He laughed. 'I'm Johnnie Somerville, by the way.'

'I know you are.'

'How so?'

'I've seen you before.'

'Really? Do you know, I don't remember seeing you . . .'

'Well, the first time you nearly ran me down in your car.'

134

'Did I honestly? I'm frightfully sorry. That was extremely careless of me.'

'It was rather. The other time was at the Officers' Mess dance last week.'

He looked puzzled. 'You were there?'

'I was standing right behind you when you were with a friend of yours.'

He frowned and then his brow cleared. 'I know, you were the one skulking by the door when Willy and I were talking. What on earth were you doing there?'

'I'd been helping in the ladies' cloaks.'

'Good lord, couldn't they find something better for you to do? Why weren't you singing?'

'This is the first time I've done it.'

He smiled at her. Good teeth, she saw, as well as the rest of the good looks. He pushed back a lock of the too-long fair hair from his forehead.

'Well, you were incredibly good. Cigarette?'

He had levered himself off the doorpost and was holding out an open case – gold, of course, she noted. What else? As it happened she had run out.

'Thanks.'

He lit the cigarette for her with a gold lighter. God, there was even a gold signet ring on his left hand, and a gold watch on his wrist that looked as though it had come from Aspreys. And that uniform certainly wasn't ordinary old RAF issue, but the work of some London tailor. As he held out his arm with the lighter she saw that the jacket sleeve was lined with scarlet silk. On the stage overhead Nobby was crooning his number, 'Blueberry Hill.'

'What's your name?'

'Aircraftwoman Cunningham – sir.'

'For heaven's sake, skip the "sir". We're neither of us on duty. And I meant your Christian name.'

'We're always called by our surnames.'

He had found a wall to lean against now. 'Not by me.

135

You look like a Diana, or a Penelope, or a Portia . . . something like that.'

If he wasn't careful she'd throw up. She put away the compact. The evening would be over before she'd had time to have some fun.

'Sorry, I've got to go.'

He moved to the door with surprising speed and blocked her way. 'Not before you tell me your name.'

'Actually, it's plain Anne.'

'Dinner one evening?'

'What?'

'Will you have dinner with me one evening?'

'No, thanks.'

'Why not?'

'Because I don't want to. Excuse me, please.'

He didn't move and he obviously didn't believe her because he was looking highly amused.

'I may not ask you again.'

'Good. That'll save me the trouble of refusing again.'

'You don't know what you'd be missing.'

'I've a pretty good idea.'

'I often drive up to London . . .'

'Bully for you. Now, would you stand aside, please.'

'When you've told me why you won't have dinner with me.'

She was angry now. The joke had gone on long enough. 'Have you forgotten what you said about WAAFS? I heard you very clearly. You should take your own advice and steer clear of me. You don't know where I've been. Stick to your own kind.'

She pushed past him and he let her go. He did not seem in the least embarrassed or contrite. On the contrary, as she went down the corridor she distinctly heard him laugh.

Winnie was rather enjoying herself at the dance. She had been coaxed onto the floor several times and it hadn't been as hard as it looked. She found that she could sort of walk backwards in time to the music and a sideways step got her round the corners. Nobody minded if she made mistakes. And she loved the music which made her want to dance, even if she couldn't do it very well. She thought Anne was very brave to stand up on the stage and sing. Wild horses wouldn't have dragged her up there at all, let alone to sing in front of the whole station. Everybody came to the Christmas Dance – officers and other ranks, all mixed up together, even the Station Commander. Maureen was dancing too, though she didn't look as though she was enjoying it. Enid, on the other hand, looked as though she was enjoying it a bit too much, pressed close to a tall corporal – at least more than Terry would have liked. They heard less and less about Terry now and Enid no longer carried his photograph round with her in her pocket. It had been put away somewhere in her locker. Once Winnie had found Enid's engagement ring left on the side of one of the washbasins in the ablutions hut. The little red flower that had sparkled so brightly on Enid's finger looked dull and the gold had had a greenish tinge to it. When she had returned the ring Enid had not seemed very worried.

'Oh, thanks, I must have forgotten it,' was all she had said.

Winnie had been rather shocked. If she had mislaid Ken's ring she would have been really upset. What would Terry, far away on the high seas, think about Enid going out with other men like she did? She had always told them how possessive he was. Ever so jealous was what she always said about him. Terry didn't even like her to *look* at another man. So far as Winnie could see, Enid was doing a bit more than looking. Still, it was none of her business and at least Enid didn't cry any more.

A sergeant with a little moustache like Hitler's asked her for the Excuse Me dance. They were only halfway round the floor when someone else tapped the sergeant on the shoulder and she changed partners. She was beginning to get the hang of it all quite well and was laughing with a leading aircraftman from the Orderly Room as they tried to do a rumba, when another man broke in and she saw, to her dismay, that it was Taffy Jones.

It was a shock because she hadn't seen him for a while and had hoped that he'd been posted somewhere else.

'Hallo, Winnie.'

He put his arm around her and she recoiled from him. He tightened his hold.

'Have you missed me then, Winnie?'

She turned her head away from his face and the green eyes that looked at her so intently. He frightened her and all her enjoyment had gone. She was stiff as a poker in his arms.

'I've been away on leave. Home to Wales.'

She said, very politely: 'Oh. Did you have a nice time?'

'Not bad. I'd sooner be here, though.'

'Don't you like goin' on leave?'

'Well, you're here, aren't you? Why should I want to be somewhere else?'

She looked round desperately, hoping that someone would tap Taffy on the shoulder and take her away from him, but there was nobody near.

'Don't look so worried, girl.'

He was a good dancer, she could tell that. Better than any of them so far. But she hated the way he held her so close with his face only inches from hers. She kept her head turned and prayed for the music to end, but the band seemed to play on for ever. When, at last, they stopped Taffy held onto her arm. The band were putting down their instruments to take a break and everyone was moving off the floor in a great tide, pushing and shoving towards the refreshments. Taffy elbowed a way through the crush, pulling her after him and found a space for her on one of the benches at the side of the hangar.

'Sit here. I'll get you something to drink.'

He was gone before she could say she didn't want anything. She sat squashed between two airmen and trapped by the press. There was a glimpse of Enid with her corporal somewhere in the thicket of bodies, and then she was lost to view. There was no sign of any of the other WAAFS with whom she could take refuge.

Taffy reappeared, carrying a beer and an orange squash. Winnie realized that she was very thirsty. He stood over her while she drank, like a dog with a bone.

'What've you been up to while I've been away?'

'Nothin'. . .' She kept her eyes down, avoiding his. 'Nothin' special, anyway.'

'What would that fiancé of yours think about you coming dancing?'

'He wouldn't mind, as it's Christmas.'

'I should hope not. A lovely girl like you ought to go out dancing. Do you go dancing with him?'

There was nowhere to go dancing in Elmbury unless you counted the step-dancing on the table top in the Pig and Whistle on Saturday nights, and that was only two of the men capering in their hob-nailed boots until one of them fell off the table. And Ken didn't know how to dance, any more than she did. She shook her head.

'What's his name . . . your fiancé?'

'Ken. Ken Jervis.'

'Does Ken know what a lucky man he is, then?'

Winnie's cheeks reddened. She looked down into her glass.

'I bet he doesn't. Does he pay you compliments?'

'Yes, of course . . .'

'What sort of ones then? What does he say to you?'

She tried to think. What had Ken ever said? He'd once told her that she had pretty hair, she remembered that.

'You can't think of anything, Winnie.'

'Yes, I can.'

'What then?'

'It's private. None of your business.'

'I bet he never tells you what a beautiful girl you are. Englishmen are no good at paying compliments. They

139

don't know how to treat a woman, like we do in Wales. Have you ever been to Wales?'

'No.'

'You should do. It's a beautiful country. I come from Harlech – that's in the North. It's wild up there . . . mountains and valleys and castles. Have you heard of Harlech castle?'

She shook her head.

'That's near where I live. Have you heard of Owen Glendower, then?'

'I don't think so.'

'He was one of our great Welsh heroes. He fought the English. You should come to Wales one day, Winnie. You'd have to learn to speak the language, though. Not everyone speaks English there, you know. My grandmother doesn't speak a word of it. We all speak Welsh at home all the time, see.'

'It sounds like a foreign country.'

'It is. I told you – we're not like the English. We come from a different race altogether. We feel things differently . . . deeper . . . more passionately . . . not like the English at all.'

The airman sitting next to Winnie stood up and in a flash Taffy had taken his place on the bench. She wriggled away from him. He took a pack of cigarettes from his breast pocket and lit one; he held it in an odd way with his hand cupped round the end as though shielding it from the wind.

'What did you want to go and get yourself engaged for, Winnie?'

'I wanted to.'

'Did you? Are you so sure? It was a daft thing to do. I bet you'd never been out of Suffolk before you came here, had you?'

'No, but – '

'I bet you'd never even left that village where you live. Been anywhere else.'

'I've been to Ipswich.'

He laughed. 'Is that all? You've never really met anyone else but this Ken of yours, have you? How could you be so sure he was the right one for you when you hadn't met any others?'

She said indignantly: 'You shouldn't say things like that. It's nothin' to do with you.'

'All right,' he said, still smiling. 'We won't talk about it, then. What I want to know, though, is what made you go and join up if you were engaged? You're all volunteers, aren't you? You didn't have to. Doesn't your Ken care about you being away?'

She hesitated. 'He didn't want me to go.'

'But he didn't stop you, did he? I would have done. I wouldn't have let you out of my sight if you were my fiancée.'

'Ken's not like that. He – he's very understandin'.'

But she went red again as she said that, knowing that Ken had not understood at all. Taffy Jones, watching the blush spread across her cheeks thought, as he had thought since he had first seen her sitting in the Orderly Room, that she was the loveliest girl that he had ever seen, with her blue eyes and her brown, curly hair and her fresh purity. He drew hard on his cigarette.

'You still haven't told me what made you join up, Winnie?'

'I don't know, really. I just wanted to do somethin' in the war . . .'

'And get away from that village of yours?'

'No. It wasn't like that.'

'Wasn't it? I'd've wanted to get away if I'd been you . . . see the world a bit . . . meet people . . . instead of being stuck in one place all my life.'

Her blush deepened because she knew there was truth in what he said. She *had* wanted to get away from Elmbury and see other places before she and Ken settled down. She knew it was selfish of her, but she hadn't wanted to be like some of them who'd never left the village in their whole lives – not even to go to Ipswich. To be like

Betty Parsons who'd been in the same class as her at the school and had already been married two years and had two children. She'd stay there, most probably, until she was an old woman, never doing anything else but live in Elmbury and look after her children and after Charlie who got drunk every Saturday night. But it hadn't only been for that. Most of all it had been the 'planes. They'd been her secret dream. Something she couldn't tell Taffy who'd laugh like anything.

'Didn't you mind leaving Wales if you like it so much?'

'Oh, I've got used to being away. I was in the RAF before the war started. I've been in a few years already. The life suits me and I can do the sort of work I like.'

'What work do you do, then?'

'I'm a fitter.'

It had never occurred to her to wonder what his trade was.

'You mean you work on the aircraft? The Hurricanes?'

'That's right.'

Although Taffy did not realize it, he could not possibly have said anything that would recommend him more in her eyes.

'I didn't know . . .'

'I like engines. I'm good with them, see, so it's no penance.' He had put his beer mug down on the floor between his feet and he spread out his hands, palms down, the cigarette parked upwards between two fingers. 'I've got a sort of feel for it . . . it comes naturally.'

How could she not have noticed his hands before? They were scarred and grazed and ingrained with oil stains, the nails black-rimmed – a mechanic's hands. She should have guessed long ago what he did.

Taffy sensed a change in her; instead of keeping her eyes down all the time she had lifted her head and was looking up – at him.

'What is it? Have I said something funny?'

'No. It's just that . . . just that . . .'

142

'Just that what? Come on, spit it out.'

'Well, that's what I really wanted to do when I joined up. That's why I chose the WAAF, you see. I wanted to work as a a a mechanic with the 'planes. Only, of course, they won't let us . . . not yet, anyhow. I don't know if they ever will.'

He stared at her. 'Now, there's a novelty and no mistake. I've never heard of a woman who cared two pins about engines. Do you know anything about them?'

'Not the ones in 'planes, but I can mend the tractor on our farm at home when it goes wrong.'

'Has somebody taught you?'

She shook her head. 'No. I sort of know what to do . . . what the matter is. I work it out.'

He nodded, understanding. 'You either have a feel for it, or you don't. It's something you're born with. I don't see why a woman shouldn't have it, just the same as a man, except that usually they don't. I don't see why they shouldn't let you do some of the work – some of the lighter jobs that don't need the strength. You'd be able to do some things easier than us, with your small hands – where it's difficult to reach and fiddly. Mind you, I don't know that some of the boys'd fancy the idea of having women round the machines. I don't think they'd like it much. Now *me*, I wouldn't mind a bit – and I think you'd do a good job.'

'Do you really think so?'

'I do,' he said seriously. 'If you can mend a tractor engine you could work on an aircraft one, if they trained you properly. Same principle. Internal combustion. You could learn easily enough if you've got a feel for it. As I said, some jobs need a man's strength, but you could manage the rest all right.' He looked at her with curiosity. He had known from the first that she was a girl in a million, but this was a surprise. 'How did you get to be so keen on the idea of aircraft, anyhow? It's a funny thing for a woman.'

'I've seen them flyin' over the farm . . . there's an RAF station not far away.'

'Have you ever seen one close up – on the ground?'

'No. I'd like to, but they won't let us near the hangars.'

'Right then, I'll take you. Now's your chance.'

'*Now*?'

'No time better. There'll be no-one around and we'll be there and back before anyone knows it.'

Speedy finally captured Felicity.

'You've danced *twice* with Whitters,' he told her reproachfully, 'and with Dumbo and Moses and all sorts of other chaps. Just about everybody else on this station except me.'

'That's a bit of an exaggeration.'

'No, it isn't. I've been watching you. Rotter after rotter, and never a glance in my direction. You'll be sorry when I'm gone.'

'Gone? Gone where?'

'Mustn't say. But it seems the pen of my aunt may soon be in the garden.'

'What *are* you talking about?'

'You know, *la plume de ma tante*, and all that . . . I'm not much good at the lingo.'

Felicity stopped dead. 'You're being posted to France? Oh, no, Speedy . . .'

He looked pleased. 'I hoped you'd mind. Shall we carry on dancing? We're causing a traffic jam. Actually, it's only a rumour but we're keeping fingers crossed it's true. We're all fed up with stooging around over here. Bit like those greyhounds straining at the leash, as the bod said in *Henry V*.'

'I think they were in the slips, straining upon the start.'

'Were they? Didn't know they had dog racing in those days. Amazing! Speaking of dogs, I was going to ask if you'd look after old George for me, if I have to pop across the ditch.'

'Oh, Speedy, I don't see how I could . . .'

'He's no trouble. Fully house-trained and a model of

good behaviour, unlike his master. He'd sit by your desk all day, quiet as a lamb.'

'Couldn't you send him home to your family?'

'He'd be miserable. He'd miss all the fun. Besides, they already have a dog. An old and very bad-tempered spaniel. He and George wouldn't get on at all. You will, won't you?'

'Well, I – '

'That's settled then. Lucky George.'

'Speedy, this is a waltz now.'

'Is it? I thought something was wrong. One, two, three. One, two, three . . .'

It was pitch dark inside the hangar. Winnie held onto Taffy's hand and let herself be guided by him. Although she could see nothing, she could sense the vastness of the space around her, and she could smell the oil and grease . . . the smell of the machines that were close by, somewhere in the blackness.

Taffy had stopped. He switched on his torch and the beam probed ahead, swinging from side to side until it settled on the nose of an aircraft. Three black propeller blades with yellow tips stood motionless behind a smoothly pointed cone.

'Hurricane,' Taffy whispered.

The torch's beam traced the fighter's outline for her – back across the cowling to the cockpit and its perspex canopy, along each outspread wing in turn, lingering at the gunports, and then back up to the cockpit and aft, over the hump that was like a backbone, and, finally, down to the tail.

'Little beauty, isn't she?'

He went closer and stood by the wing at its root, playing the light upwards. Winnie stepped cautiously after him. She could see inside the top of the empty cockpit where the pilot's head would have been.

'Go on, touch her if you want to,' Taffy said. 'You can't do her any harm.'

She put out her hand and the skin of the camouflaged fuselage felt smooth and tight and hard beneath her fingers.

'Fabric, see,' he told her. 'Metal cowling but fabric fuselage, and fabric tail and wings.' He traversed the beam forward to pick out three metal pipes near the nose. 'Exhaust stubs. Same thing as the stack on your tractor. It's not so very different, see. You'd soon get the hang of it. The engine's under the cowling there, but I can't show you that now – not this time, anyhow. It's a Merlin, twelve cylinder, liquid-cooled.'

The words sounded magical to Winnie. She stroked the Hurricane's cold flank. It was still a mystery to her how something so big and heavy could soar up into the air and fly like a bird. What held it up and stopped it from falling like a stone? She wondered what it would be like to stand this close when the engine was started up – when it burst into life and those three black blades turned round and round so fast you couldn't see them. Sometimes when they were testing the engines she could hear the roar from the Orderly Room. The blades had a kind of twist to them, she saw. That must have something to do with them catching hold of the air and the wings must act like a bird's . . . like the rooks when they were wheeling round over the elm trees up at the ten acre field. But how did it all really *work*? She longed to be able to look at the engine and see if it was anything at all like the Fordson's. A Merlin, Taffy had called it. Wasn't that the name of a wizard in story books? Funny thing to call an engine.

Her WAAF raincoat was poor protection against the bitter cold of the hangar and her teeth were chattering. Taffy put his arm round her.

'You're freezing, girl.'

She pulled away from him at once.

'Don't be scared, Winnie. You're jumpy as a rabbit.'

But she was scared now – alone with him in this dark place.

'Can we go back now?'

'What's all the rush? I'll show you some of the others.'

'No, I want to go back . . .'

She tried to find her way back to the small door they had come in by and tripped over something in the dark. There was a loud clatter of metal on concrete.

'Wait, girl, you'll hurt yourself.' The torch had tracked and found her. He gripped her elbow. 'Don't be daft, Winnie, there's lots of sharp things around. Stay with me.'

He guided her across the hangar, lighting their way. Once outside, she began to feel calmer, her panic ebbing, until, suddenly, there was the sound of heavy footsteps coming along the path towards them.

'Quick! In here.'

Taffy pulled her through a doorway and switched off the torch. They waited, unmoving, while the footsteps went past.

'Snoops!' Taffy whispered in her ear.

Winnie's heart thudded in her chest. If the service police found them out of bounds and together like this, they could get into terrible trouble . . . She began to shiver and shake. How could she have been so *stupid*?

The footsteps died away and there was silence.

'Better wait a mo,' Taffy whispered. 'Make sure they've really gone.'

It was so dark she could see nothing. 'Where are we?'

'Stores hut. Don't worry, there's no reason why they should look in here. It'd be safest to wait a bit, though. They might come back this way.'

She trembled violently, and felt him touch her cheek.

'Why, you're like ice and shaking like you've got the ague. Have this.' He took off his greatcoat and draped it round her shoulders. 'I don't feel the cold, see. I'm used to it – working outdoors so much.'

He was standing very close to her. She could feel the warmth of his body and smell the cigarette smoke on his breath, and she was more afraid of him now than of the service policemen patrolling somewhere outside. He was whispering again in her ear.

'Why don't you like me, Winnie? I'm not such a bad fellow, you know, and you won't even give me a chance.'

She said nothing, rigid with fear . . . trapped.

'You're the little innocent, aren't you? Like the driven snow. What does that precious Ken of yours do then? Hold your hand at the pictures and then give you a good-night peck on the cheek? I bet he never kisses you like this.'

Her lips fell crushed by his and his tongue was forcing itself into her mouth . . . for a moment she was too shocked to move and then fear and disgust gave her the strength to wrench free of him.

'Winnie, wait . . .'

But somehow she found the door and was out of the hut and running, sobbing, down the path – straight into the arms of one of the service policemen.

Except for Pearl, none of the WAAFS had ever spent Christmas away from home before. Some of them were homesick all over again. Their mess hut now had a piano and they sang carols round it – Enid weeping her way through 'O Little Town of Bethlehem'. They had decorated the hut with paper chains and a Christmas tree with painted fir-cones, tinsel and some glittering glass baubles sent by Susan's mother from Harrods. Gloria, to Susan's annoyance, had also strewn cotton wool from sanitary towels along the branches to look like snow.

'*Must* we have that, Gloria?'

'Don't see why not. Looks nice and nobody else'll know it's from fanny rags. Ever so useful they are. Just the job for cleanin' shoes. You ought to try them for paddin' so's you wouldn't look so flat on top.'

Anne, overhearing this, smiled to herself. Gloria seldom missed the chance of a dig at Susan. She thought of the big Christmas tree that would be standing in the hall at home, decorated with all the old ornaments that were brought out of their box each year, and the big star fixed on the very top. The staircase bannisters would be garlanded with holly and a bunch of mistletoe would be hanging over the front door. Just for a moment she let herself picture it all and remember Christmases in the past when she and Kit had been home and they had all been together. And then, because it made her feel miserable, she shut it out of her mind. Closed the door on it firmly. There was no point in wallowing in it. Winnie was looking a bit down in the mouth, she noticed – standing staring out of the window. Perhaps she was thinking about her home in Suffolk. Or maybe she was still upset about that business at the Station Dance. There had been quite a row over her getting caught in a hut with some airman. Everyone had been a bit surprised because it was so unlike Winnie, and nobody thought it was really her fault. Anyway, the airman had taken all the blame, apparently. ASO Newman had come and given them a lecture about not encouraging the men on the station, looking pretty pink in the face herself. As Pearl had said, it was like shutting the stable door after the horses had bolted so far as some of the WAAFS were concerned. There was going to be a concert for the whole station in the evening, as well as a special turkey lunch. All in all, it might not be such a bad Christmas. It might even be quite good fun . . .

Virginia toyed with her roast chicken. She had always dreaded Christmas Day. Mother fussed so much about the preparations for the lunch that it tired her out and put her in a bad mood. It was the same every year. The mood could last for several days and somehow she had to find the courage to tell her about the letter that had come from the Air Ministry, instructing her to report for training on 3 January.

She set down her knife and fork and they clattered noisily against her plate.

'Mother, I – '

Her mother was frowning. 'I do wish you'd try to eat more quietly, Virginia. There's no need to bang your knife and fork down like that.'

'I'm sorry.'

'Table manners are so important. I've always told you that. People are judged by the way they eat. Were you going to say something?'

'No, Mother.'

'If you've finished then we may as well clear away.'

When they had washed up in the small kitchen and put everything away in its place, they sat down to listen to the King's speech on the wireless. His voice sounded quite firm, with little trace of the stutter.

And I said to the man who stood at the gate of the year: Give me a light that I may tread safely into the unknown. And he replied: Go out into the darkness and put your hand into the hand of God. That shall be to you better than light and safer than a known way.

After the National Anthem her mother switched off the wireless and took out her knitting. Virginia found some darning to do. The rest of Christmas Day stretched emptily and bleakly ahead.

'Do the blackout, please, Virginia. I need to switch on the lamp. This bad light is hurting my eyes.'

Virginia rose to pull down the blinds and draw the curtains across the windows. She stood for a moment with one hand still holding the curtain edge.

'What are you doing standing there, Virginia? Come and sit down.'

She let go of the curtain, squared her shoulders and turned round.

'Mother, please listen. I have something important to tell you.'

*　　*　　*

On New Year's Eve there was a talent concert on the station. Volunteers went up onto the big hangar stage to entertain the audience. A flight sergeant did amazing conjuring tricks with playing cards, handkerchiefs and lengths of rope, three of the new WAAFS imitated the Andrews sisters, singing together in close harmony, and another WAAF tap-danced. After her, and when the whistles had died down, an airman from one of the cookhouses juggled with spoons and forks, and balanced china plates on the end of a broom handle. Then a spry little cockney corporal stood up and told a string of jokes that few of the WAAFS understood but had all the men laughing uproariously.

Anne's was the final turn. She sang 'We'll Meet Again' – a Vera Lynn record that was played over and over again on the gramophone in their recreation hut. Afterwards, she led them all in *Auld Lang Syne* and they roared their way through it, arms crossed and linked in long, heaving lines.

The sound carried outside the big hangar where it had started to snow silently and heavily. Soon, the buildings, roads and pathways, hangars, vehicles, aircraft and the great expanse of grass out on the 'drome were all covered in a thick white camouflage. An icy wind began to blow.

It was 1940.

PART 2

PROGRESS

Five

The snow had drifted three foot deep against the north sides of station buildings. Rows of icicles hung like long glass daggers from the eaves, windows were whitely opaque with frost and water pipes everywhere had frozen hard. Leaving one building for another meant braving a razor sharp wind and slipping and sliding over icy ground. There was a 'flu epidemic and the sick quarters were overflowing. RAF and WAAF coughed and sneezed and snuffled. A large party of new WAAFS arrived and one of them developed chicken pox, starting a whole new epidemic. No flying was possible and the station echoed to the ring of picks and shovels instead of to the roar of aircraft engines.

The WAAFS, detailed to help clear the snow, wielded shovels and brooms and were mercilessly snowballed by the men. Ambushes lay in wait for them round every corner as they went about their daily business and they arrived at their destinations with their berets and raincoats plastered with snow and, frequently, a whole lot more of it down the backs of their necks. Anne, in furious retaliation, stockpiled snowballs at secret, strategic points and even carried some round with her to unleash on attackers. It was some consolation to see the pained astonishment on their faces, especially when the snowballs had frozen.

In the evenings the WAAFS huddled round the stoves, taking it in turns to sit nearest the warmest spot in front. At night the hut windows had to be opened in spite of the cold.

'For our health, would you believe it?' Pearl said

bitterly. 'If we don't get 'flu we'll die of pneumonia.'

They piled every available blanket, rug and coat onto their beds. Susan's mother had sent her some angora bedsocks, a soft mohair rug and a pair of navy, fur-lined leather gloves to go with her uniform. Predictably, Sergeant Beaty tried to stop her wearing them.

'Only officers are supposed to wear leather gloves, Courtney-Bennet. All other ranks wear knitted ones, unless they're MT drivers.'

'But there aren't any knitted ones available, Sergeant. And I get terrible chilblains. The Medical Officer told me I must keep my hands warm.'

When they ran out of their ration of coke for the hut stoves Anne and Pearl were caught pinching some from the station compound and confined to barracks for a week. Gloria, more prudently and more successfully, sweet-talked one of the airmen into getting a big bucketful for her. Maureen, sniffing her disapproval, warmed her hands with the rest.

Once a week, on Fridays, they had Domestic Night when they stayed in their hut to clean their own space, to sew and mend, wash their hair, write letters, polish their shoes and do any other necessary chores. It was also the night when the hut was inspected by their officer. Sergeant Beaty would fling open the door with a crash.

'Attention!'

They stood beside their beds as Assistant Section Officer Newman walked up one side of the hut and down the other. Their meagre assembly of uniform was laid out neatly for her inspection.

'There's a button missing off your raincoat, Briggs.'

Winnie stammered. 'It got lost, ma'am.'

'See that you get it replaced. And try to make sure they don't come loose, Briggs. Keep them sewn on tightly so it can't happen again.'

'Yes, ma'am.'

She moved on, pausing at each bed.

'You should have six collars, Cunningham, not five.

What has happened to the other one?'

'Someone took it, ma'am.'

'That's a serious accusation. Do you know who?'

'No, ma'am.'

'So, it may equally well have got lost, like Briggs's button.'

'I suppose so, ma'am.'

'It's not good enough, you know, Cunningham. Mislaying uniform is a grave matter. You are responsible for every item issued to you. Please make every effort to find that missing collar and report to Corporal White when you do.'

'What if I don't, ma'am?'

'I hope you don't mean to be as insubordinate as you sound, Cunningham. If you don't find the collar then the cost of replacing it will be deducted from your pay.'

She stopped next in front of Pearl. 'You haven't swept under your bed properly, Carter. There's still a lot of dust there. See that it's done immediately.'

There were more lectures: First Aid, RAF Customs and Procedures, King's Regulations, Personal Hygiene and, for some curious reason, Anatomy. An RAF MO delivered this talk with the aid of a human skeleton hanging from a hook. He took it to pieces, bone by bone, laying them out casually on a table, and then re-assembled them equally off-handedly as though he were doing a jigsaw.

'Sorry, wrong way up there. This little fellow should go the other way up and then it fits like a glove, see.' He waggled the hand bones at them cheerfully and picked up the skull. 'A skeleton will tell us quite a lot about its owner – height, race, age and so forth, and the skull can give us quite a good picture of what the person looked like. See the shape of the brow over the eye sockets . . . the position of the cheek bones . . . I'd say this chap was somewhere in his mid-forties. If you look at the teeth here – '

There was a crash from the back of the room as Enid slid off her chair in a dead faint.

*　　*　　*

One evening Pearl told their fortunes in the tea leaves. They had brewed up, as usual, boiling the kettle over the open lid of the hut stove. Pearl picked up Anne's mug when she had finished, swished the dregs round, turned it upside down to drain over her own, and then peered into it.

'I see a dark stranger.'

'What?'

'A dark stranger, love. There, in your tea leaves. Plain as the nose on your face.'

Anne laughed. 'Don't be silly, Pearl. You're just making it up.'

Pearl looked injured. 'I'm bloody well not. I always used to read the leaves for people when I worked in the caff. An old gypsy woman taught me. She came in once out of the cold with that lucky white heather they sell, and I gave her a cup of char and a wad for nothing. She was a smelly old thing but I hadn't the heart to turf her out. She read my leaves and then showed me how it's done. As a sort of thank you.' Pearl tilted the mug a bit more and squinted at it. 'He's definitely dark, duckie. And he'll come from across the seas. Fancy that! P'raps he's a Frenchman . . . all Latin passion and lovely manners.'

Sandra had been listening, intrigued. She held out her mug. 'Gosh, Pearl, will you read mine too?'

They all crowded round. Pearl took her time. She swished the dregs in Sandra's mug round three times, drained them over her own and then stared solemnly at the leaves. Sandra hopped from one foot to the other.

'What can you see, Pearl? *Do* tell me.'

'I see money.'

Maureen snorted.

'Golly! How much?'

'Don't know, but you'll be getting some very soon.'

'How super! I've only got sixpence left. Anything else, Pearl?'

'And you'll be getting some good news too. Something that'll make you happy.'

'Gosh . . .'

Others queued up with their mugs. Pearl read each one in turn, intoning gravely.

'I see a journey, Vera.'

'D-do you, Pearl? Where'll I be going?'

'Somewhere in England. And I see a reunion with loved ones soon.'

'That'll be when we get leave. Is there a dark stranger, like Anne's?'

Pearl shook her head. 'Sorry, love . . . wait a mo, though, what's this here? There *is* someone . . . I can see him now. He's not dark, though. More a sort of middling brown . . . That's all I can tell you.'

To Susan she said wickedly, 'I see a pilot.'

'A pilot?'

'A sergeant pilot, Duchess, not an officer. I can see the three stripes. He'll come from the north – '

Susan leaned forward and snatched her mug away.

Pearl took a long time with Winnie's mug. She tipped it this way and that, frowning. 'It's all a bit murky, this one. Bit of a muddle. I think I can see two blokes – one's dark – like your Ken is, isn't he, but there's this other one that I can't quite make out. Looks like he's a long way away . . . overseas, I s'pose . . . don't really know, but he's there all right . . . Hang on, this bit here's clearer. Yes . . . I can see long life and happiness for you, Winnie, love. There's a journey – a long one – and I think that's four kids there, or maybe even five . . .'

Winnie blushed.

Enid was last. 'Hurry up, Pearl. You're taking ever so long with mine. What can you see?'

Pearl said slowly: 'I see someone on the high seas.'

'Oh, that's just Terry. What else?'

'I'm not sure . . . it's not clear at all. I don't think I can see anything else.'

Enid looked disappointed. 'There must be *something*. Everyone else had things.'

But Pearl held out her mug, unsmiling. 'Sorry, love,

that's all. It's like that sometimes. I'll have another go one day.'

Two days later Sandra had a letter from her mother, enclosing a ten shilling note with the news that her pet dog had had six puppies. Pearl looked modest.

'It was in the leaves, just like I said.'

Anne tackled her later on when they were alone. 'Come on, Pearl, tell the truth. You made it all up, didn't you? The whole jolly lot.'

'How did I get Sandra's so right, then?'

'Her mother's always sending her money and she's been talking about that dog of hers having puppies for weeks. And Vera's journey was a pretty safe bet considering we'll be due for leave eventually and she'll be reunited with loved ones because she'll be going home.'

'I told Gloria she'd be having some good news too and she got a letter from her mum today telling her that her dad's gone and walked out. She says it's the best news she's had for years.'

Anne laughed. 'Well, what about Susan's sergeant pilot? Don't tell me you didn't invent *him*.'

'I've got to admit I made that one up. Just to annoy her ladyship. Pity it won't come true. It'd do her a lot of good.'

'Couldn't you have made up something nice for poor old Enid? She looked so disappointed.'

'I couldn't think of anything quick enough – not when I'd seen what I did in her leaves. Never seen it before and it gave me a bit of a turn.'

'Seen what? What're you talking about, Pearl?'

'Death. I saw death in Enid's leaves, that's what. I wish I hadn't, but I did. That old gypsy woman showed me and I tell you, I saw it.'

Anne fell silent for a moment as they walked along, making their way across the station to the new WAAF Mess. Since the fresh intake of WAAFS had arrived, they now had their own cookhouse, with a larger mess, as well as a much bigger recreation hut. In addition to the piano, the gramophone and the wireless, there were more easy chairs and a brand new ping pong table.

'I don't really believe in it, Pearl. Sorry. I mean, I'm sure you do see things . . . shapes in the leaves, or whatever, but I don't believe there's any truth in it.'

'Well, I hope you're right for Enid's sake. Hope it's not Terry. I don't think I'll do it again.'

A lorry passed by, tyres making a crackling sound on the icy road. Two airmen, elbows stuck on the tailgate, whistled and yelled at them. The WAAFS ignored them. They turned into the mess hut and queued up at the counter. Pearl picked up a plate.

'I never finished reading your mug, did I? You watch out for that dark stranger of yours. I saw *him* as clear as anything. He's real all right. Oh, my God, rissoles again!'

There was a mock gas attack. The station siren went suddenly with its frightening banshee wailing, accompanied by warning rattles that sounded like machine-gun fire. They put on their respirators dutifully and carried on working, as ordered, feeling acutely uncomfortable and looking ridiculous. Anne discovered one bonus – it made peeling onions a lot easier. She still spent most of her time in the dark little scullery, with the vegetables and the stacks of washing up, but sometimes Corporal Fowler singled her out for a new task.

"ere you – Lady Muck! Want to learn somethin'? You can come'n make the batter for the toad. Flour, eggs, milk 'n salt. There you are. Mix all that lot up in that thing.'

She looked at the bucket. 'Where do I find a whisk?'

'Whisk? You use yer bleedin' arms.'

She made a face behind his back, rolled up her sleeves and plunged them into the sloppy mess in the bucket.

One of the Hurricanes crash-landed out on the grass and burst into flames. The pilot, trapped in the cockpit, died before anyone could reach him. A pall of black smoke from the wreckage reached high into the air and could be seen and smelled all over the station.

Anne remembered him. He was new to his squadron and had come into the kitchens for a cup of tea early one morning with other pilots from a dawn patrol. They had stood around in their thick fleece-lined jackets, stamping their cold feet in their flying boots and warming their hands round mugs of steaming tea. Like a new boy in school, he had been quieter than the rest – speaking only when spoken to, not pushing himself forward. He had thanked her for the tea very politely, handing her his empty mug with a smile. The thing she remembered most about him, though, was his hair. It had been the colour of ripe corn and was ruffled from wearing his flying helmet, like a small boy's. He had looked about nineteen or twenty – about the same as Jimmy and rather like him. She tried not to think about that corn-coloured hair being burned black like the stubble she had once seen that had caught light in a field. Jimmy had once told her that most pilots dreaded fire above all else. They had been sitting in the bus on their way into town to go to the cinema just before Christmas and he had talked about someone he'd known when he was learning to fly.

'We were doing circuits and bumps one day and he got it wrong. I don't know what happened exactly but he cartwheeled and burst into flames . . . I went to see him in hospital and I didn't recognize him. I went up and down the beds in the ward, looking for him, and one of the nurses had to point him out. He was just a mass of bandages. I sat there and I didn't know what to say . . . The awful thing was that he could speak perfectly well, under all the bandages, and kept asking me what he looked like, and was it very bad? Of course, I said it was fine . . . nothing to worry about. He was there for months. I used to visit him quite often. They wouldn't let him have a mirror to see himself, but one time I went he'd somehow got to one and he was crying and crying . . . he said he just wanted to die. I didn't blame him. I think I'd've felt that way myself. He'd really got no proper features left . . .'

Anne had felt rather sick. 'What happened to him?'

'I don't know. I was posted away in the end and I lost touch. Of course they were doing everything to keep him alive and I suppose they did what they could for his face. His hands were in a terrible mess, too. He kept on having operations but they didn't seem to do much good that I could see. I should think he was invalided out eventually.'

Jimmy had stared out of the bus window for a while in silence. Then he had said suddenly: 'Lucky my parents don't know I'm flying, they'd worry themselves sick.'

'What do you mean – don't know you're flying?'

'I've never told them. They didn't want me to join the RAF in the first place, in case I did any flying. I've never let them know. They think I'm doing some sort of ground job.'

'Won't they find out in the end?'

'I hope not. When I go home on leave I take the wings off my uniform. It sounds pretty stupid, I know, but it's just better that way. I'm an only child, you see. No brothers or sisters, so they count on me a lot.'

She knew so little about him. He so rarely talked of himself.

'Where do you come from, Jimmy? You've never said.'

'Croydon. I've lived there all my life – same house, same street, the local school. Very dull, I'm afraid. To tell you the truth I was rather glad to get away. I feel a bit guilty about that sometimes because I know how much they miss me – specially my mother.'

'I expect you're the apple of her eye.'

He had blushed a little. 'I don't know about that. But it gets a bit much when she fusses . . .'

Anne pictured the Shaw home in Croydon. It would be one of a row of similar houses in a quiet suburban street – pin neat inside and out and very clean. There would be net curtains at the windows, antimacassars on the armchairs, polished linoleum and very prominently

163

displayed, framed photographs of Jimmy – the only child. Mrs Shaw would be thin and nervous, Mr Shaw a silent, withdrawn figure, perhaps with a pipe.

On the day when his squadron had left for France, Jimmy had come to say goodbye. He had managed to get a message to her in the scullery and she had sneaked out to the back of the Officers' Mess to meet him.

'I wanted to see you, Anne, to say goodbye . . . and to ask if you'd do something for me.'

'Of course I will. What is it?'

He had taken an envelope out of his pocket and held it out to her, looking embarrassed. 'It's for my mother. I've written her a letter – just in case anything happens to me. They'd find out then, of course, about me flying and I wanted to try and explain things to her . . . so she'd understand.'

She had said firmly: 'Nothing's going to happen to you, Jimmy.'

'No, I know, but just the same . . . If it does, would you take this to her and give it to her yourself? The address is on there. I wouldn't want it to come through the post for her.'

She had been wearing her work apron and her hands were still wet from the sink. She had wiped them dry and taken the envelope from him, feeling a slight bump beneath her fingers.

'I promise I'll do that . . . but I won't need to. You'll be back safely.'

'Yes, of course.' He had put his hands in his pockets and shuffled his feet a little, kicking at a dead leaf. 'I put my wings in there, for her. The ones off my best blue. Well, she'd know all about my flying by then and I wanted her to have them. It might help.'

That had explained the bump. She had put the envelope carefully away in her skirt pocket. 'I'll have to get back now, Jimmy. If the foul Fowler finds out I'm missing on duty it'll be yet another charge and they'll clap me in irons next time.'

'I'm sorry, I wouldn't want to get you into trouble.' He had looked at her earnestly. 'I wanted to thank you, too, for coming out with me those times and being so . . . so, *decent*. I think you're a wonderful girl . . . one of the best I've ever met.'

'Golly! No-one's ever said that to me before. Aren't you talking about someone else?'

She had laughed, making a joke of it, but he had remained very serious.

'No, I'm talking about you, Anne. And I meant every word of it. Take care of yourself, won't you? And thanks . . . for everything.'

He had taken his hands from his pockets and held her by the shoulders for a brief moment, kissing her quickly on one cheek. Then he had walked away.

She had called after him, 'Goodbye, Jimmy. Good luck!'

But he had not looked back.

Now, travelling into town on the bus by herself on a day off, Anne thought about Jimmy. She sat looking out of the window at the frozen white patches that lay over the fields and at the dirty ridge of snow thrown up along the side of the road. A wintry, watery sun had struggled through the clouds but in the distance the sky looked heavy with more snow. That morning she had received a letter from Jimmy, somewhere in France, and he had said that the weather was bad there too. It was cold, he had said, much colder even than in England, but the squadron had taken over some kind of château and it was very comfortable there with plenty of wood to burn in the fireplaces and good food and wine. There hadn't been much flying and he'd made no mention of any encounter with the enemy. The letter sounded cheerful and she had been relieved. He had seemed so solemn, so resigned to the worst when he had left, that she had been worried for him. She had put his envelope away in her locker — at the back where it was out of her sight and therefore out of her mind. She liked Jimmy. He was very sweet and she had enjoyed their outings to the cinema and the pub. There had never been any hanky-panky, as Pearl called it, and when he had kissed her goodbye like that it had been the first and only time that he had touched her. Other men, she had discovered, were sometimes so pleased with themselves that they couldn't understand rejection. Some even got angry and some, like Johnnie Somerville, apparently refused to believe it. He had sent several notes to her, inviting her out to dinner, but she had ignored them all – to Pearl's incredulous despair.

'What's the matter with you, turning down a bloke like that? Looks like a bloody film star and stinking rich! You want your head examined.'

'I don't like him.'

'You don't have to. Just think of the smashing grub you'd get.'

'You go then.'

'I'd go like a shot if he asked me. Next time you see him, just put a good word in for me – OK? Tell him your old friend Pearl's not such a bloody fool.'

The bus deposited her near the main shopping street and she went to buy some grey lisle stockings at Marks and Spencer and some face powder and soap at Boots. Then she went into a corner sweetshop and bought a bar of chocolate and a quarter of a pound of toffees. At the tobacconist's next door she bought some cigarettes. After that she wandered aimlessly around the town, looking in shop windows and enjoying being free and being on her own for a change. Some goods, she noticed, seemed to be in short supply. The display windows were not so full and there were patient little queues to be seen. Outside the butcher's a woman was complaining loudly that the butcher kept back the best meat under the counter for certain customers. Further on, two women were grumbling to each other about the sugar rationing. She had not realized before that there were shortages in civilian life, or even thought about it. Mess food might be pretty grim sometimes, but there was plenty of it.

She found a telephone kiosk in a sidestreet and asked the Trunks operator for her home number. When she heard her mother's voice answering she pressed button A.

'It's me, Anne.'

The line was rather bad and when any traffic went past she had difficulty hearing what her mother was saying. They had two evacuees from London, apparently – a brother and sister who were settling down quite well. There'd been a burst pipe that had damaged one of the ceilings and the boiler had broken down but they'd managed to get it mended quickly.

She didn't care much about any of that. 'Kit?' she asked. 'Have you heard from him? Is he all right?'

'He phoned us two days ago. He – '

A lorry grinding slowly by in the narrow street drowned the rest.

'What did you say? I couldn't hear that.'

'He's been sent to France. I was going to write today to tell you. The regiment were about to leave. I think it all happened very suddenly.'

She watched the back of the lorry disappearing up the street, seeing it and yet not seeing it, as the words sunk in. Her mother was still talking brightly.

'. . . asked me to give you his love. He says he'll write as soon as he gets a chance.'

'Where is he?'

'I don't know, darling. He couldn't tell me where they were going. Just somewhere in France, like they always say. We haven't heard any more news.'

She could hear the break in her mother's voice then – the strain audible beneath the cheerfulness.

'He'll be all right, Mummy.'

'Of course he will.'

'You mustn't worry about him.'

167

It was amazing how confident and calm she sounded to her own ears.

'I'll try not to.'

They talked of other things – the weather, the blackout, the rationing, Barley, who hated the snow and had refused to leave his warm basket by the Aga, the snowdrops coming up in the garden . . . anything but of Kit being in France. Anne fed more coins into the slot and kept on talking.

After they had said goodbye as though nothing were wrong at all, Anne stepped out of the kiosk onto the pavement. It had started to snow a little – stinging flurries of tiny flakes that made her blink. She stood, unmoving, for a moment.

Kit in France. *Kit in France.*

It was too cold to stand there for long and so she began to walk, not caring much where she was going. All she could think about was Kit. So long as he had been in England, he had seemed safe. But now he was over there, and close to the enemy and to their guns and their aircraft and their bombs, and to their tanks. She had seen newspaper photographs of those tanks – brutal steel goliaths, crushing everything in their path.

She came to a café and went inside out of the cold. There were red-and-white tablecloths, some tired-looking potted palms and elderly women having their tea. She sat down at a table in the corner and ordered tea and toast from a sullen waitress. One or two of the other customers interrupted their gossiping over the cups to glance at her curiously. She ignored them, still deep in her thoughts of Kit. If he were killed she did not know how she could bear it. It was the most terrible thing she could think of that could happen – so terrible that she could not properly imagine it. The world did not exist for her without Kit. He had always been there. They had started life together from two specks. They had formed together inside their mother, been born together, Kit just first, been babies in the same pram together, then in the same playpen, and then toddlers together. Kit had learned to walk first but she had followed quickly by holding onto him. As they grew up they had played together in the nursery at Beechgrove – marching and manoeuvring Kit's lead soldiers across the floor in endless battle formations. She had been station master, guard and porter to his railway trains, petrol pump attendant and garage hand to his toy cars. They had played countless games of Snakes and Ladders and Ludo, of Snap and Beggar My Neighbour and Pelmanism, of draughts and jacks and pick-up-sticks and marbles . . . And, as they had become teenagers and Kit had begun to spend hours making his model aircraft, she had spent hours watching him, her elbows propped on the big nursery table, chin on her hands, passing him pins and knife and glue.

The waitress brought the tea and toast and set it disdainfully before her as though she resented having to do so. Perhaps it was something to do with the WAAF beret and raincoat and the stupid cow looked down on girls in the forces? Anne took no notice. She poured the tea and spread jam on the toast, though she did not feel in the least like eating it.

Even the separation during the school terms had made little difference to them. In the holidays they had still been together, Kit growing a little grander and more lordly in his Eton tails as he progressed so successfully up the school. 'Wotcha, twin!' he'd say casually when they met again at the end of what had seemed to her three interminable months of incarceration at their respective schools. Nothing had really changed. For a short while she had been slightly taller than him – when they had been thirteen – but then he had come home after a long summer term and when they had stood back to back to compare heights he had overtaken her. Now he was more than six inches taller. Taller, wiser and better.

She spun the tea out for as long as she could but the waitress hovered pointedly.

'Will you be wanting anything else, then?'

'No, thank you.'

She paid and left. Outside it was already getting dark and after the warmth of the café it felt bitterly cold. It seemed to have stopped snowing but the wind was just as piercing. There was little point in hanging round the town much longer and so she went to the bus stop and joined the queue there. The woman in front of her fumed impatiently.

'They never keep to the timetable these days. I don't know what everything's coming to. I've been waiting over half an hour. They just don't care.'

They waited and waited but there was no sign of the bus. Anne turned up the collar of her raincoat, stamped her feet and moved around, trying to keep warm. The woman grumbled on.

'Disgraceful, I call it. Just because there's a war on they make that the excuse for everything. The Germans aren't stopping that bus, are they? It's nothing to do with them.'

Anne was too cold to bother to answer her. Cars went by and she envied their occupants. Her feet were feeling numb and she stamped around some more on the pavement and tucked her chin as far as it would go down into her raincoat collar. A green two-seater car, long and low, drew to a halt at the kerb. The passenger door was pushed open and a voice came from the interior.

'Hop in. I'll give you a lift.'

She had recognized both the car and the voice drawling at her. If it had been a warm, sunny day, or even a moderately cold one, she would certainly have refused, but by now she was too miserably frozen to care, and there was still no sign of the bus. She got in.

Johnnie Somerville reached across and pulled the door shut. Inside the car it was blissfully warm and smelled expensively of leather. The seat was wonderfully soft and the thick wool carpeting heaven to her numb feet. They slid smoothly away from the bus stop and its woebegone queue and Anne looked back to see the woman staring after them, her mouth open in affront, her bulging string shopping bag clutched before her.

'I thought for a moment you were going to be ass enough to refuse.'

He was wearing an RAF greatcoat, the collar turned up and his cap pulled down. The car seemed full of his bulk.

'I was cold.'

'Or you would have gone on waiting for the bus?'

'Probably.'

'That would have been a bit stupid. Just because you heard me saying something rude about the WAAF. Are you going to hold that against me for ever? I can't even remember exactly what it was, and you shouldn't have been listening anyway.'

'I couldn't help it. You didn't bother to lower your voice.'

'Well, I apologize. I'm sorry for whatever I said. Now will you have dinner with me?'

'I don't want to – thanks very much. And I can't see why on earth it should worry you in the least. Ask someone else.'

'I'm not used to refusals.'

At least he was honest about it – she had to give him that. Warm air was blowing down blessedly onto her legs and she wriggled her cold toes inside her shoes. She rubbed her hands together to thaw them.

'This is a Lagonda, isn't it?'

'How did you know?'

'My brother's mad on cars. He has models and magazines all over the place.'

'Is he in the RAF too?'

'No, the army. He's just been sent to France.' She kept her voice determinedly matter-of-fact.

Johnnie turned his head towards her, not deceived. 'He'll be OK.'

'That's what I told my mother on the phone. I don't think she believed it. I wish I believed it myself.'

'There's no point in worrying about something that may never happen.'

She thought of the dead young pilot, trapped in his cockpit. 'You sound very cool and calm. Don't you ever worry about what may happen to you?'

'No. I don't even think about it.'

But she wondered if he ever thought about fire and feared it with the rest of them, like Jimmy had said. Feared what it might do to those golden good looks . . .

They had left the town behind and were out in the country. It was dark now and the snow patches on the fields showed up ghostly white. Little lights glowed on the dashboard in front of her. He was driving faster than she cared for, but the Lagonda seemed to devour the miles effortlessly.

He spoke out of the darkness. 'I hear you work in the kitchens. What a waste!'

'Somebody has to peel the spuds for you lot. Or would you sooner it was left on?'

'I'm serious . . . couldn't you get out of there? Do something else?'

'Well, I could apply to re-muster and go off and sew huge patches onto barrage balloons – that's something they want us to do for them now. I suppose they've worked out that it's women's work. Unfortunately, I can't even sew on a button. Actually, I can't even cook.'

He laughed. 'It makes even less sense then – your being in the kitchens.'

'Well, I've learned to make custard. You've probably eaten it. Mine's the one with all the lumps in.'

'As a matter of fact, I rather like lumpy custard. It reminds me of my nursery days.'

'I bet you didn't have to eat it all up, though.'

'Certainly I did. I had a very strict nanny. A clean plate is a healthy plate, she used to say. I never quite understood why.'

Her fingers were aching painfully as they thawed.

She rubbed them hard again. They overtook an RAF lorry, grinding along. The Lagonda purred on smoothly.

Anne twisted round in her seat. 'You've just missed the turning.'

'Have I?'

'The turning to Colston . . . it was back there.'

'Was it?' He made no attempt to slow down.

'Aren't you going to turn round?'

'No.'

'Are you going another way?'

'No. We're going to have dinner.'

'We most certainly are *not*. Would you please turn round and take me back.'

'When we've had dinner.'

'If you don't stop and go back, I'll open this door and jump out.'

'I wouldn't recommend it at this speed. Besides the door's locked and it's a very tricky one to undo.'

'You can't do this.'

'I'm doing it, as you see.'

'I suppose this is your idea of a joke? It amuses you to do this sort of thing.'

'Not particularly. It just happens to be the only way to get you to have dinner with me.'

She gritted her teeth. 'And where are we supposed to be going for this dinner that I don't want and won't eat?'

'London.'

'*London!* Are you mad? It's *miles* away!'

'Not in this piece of machinery. I often pop up there for a quick bite – I told you. Nothing to it. I thought the Savoy might be rather pleasant. There's a good band there and we could dine and dance and have you back by the stroke of midnight – just like Cinderella.'

'Cinderella actually *wanted* to go to the ball – in case you've forgotten. And I'm not hungry.'

'You will be by the time we eat.'

'And she had a pass until midnight, not twenty-three,

173

fifty-nine precisely. And nobody was going to put her on a charge if she didn't make it.'

'Then her coach will return one minute early – at least.'

'There's another thing you've forgotten. Cinderella had a fairy godmother who waved her wand and turned her rags into a ballgown. I can't go into the Savoy dressed like this.'

'There's a war on, haven't you heard? They've bent the rules. You can go anywhere in uniform now, and that's what you're wearing.'

'You know what Cinderella's coachman really was, don't you?'

'A white mouse?'

'No, that was the horses. The coachman was a rat.'

He laughed. She lapsed into a cold and mutinous silence.

It was the first time she had seen London in the blackout. Anne peered out of the car window at what little of the city she could distinguish in the inky dark . . . whitewashed kerbs, the blinking of Belisha beacons, the shielded crosses of the traffic lights, a blue lamp outside a police station, here and there the pale glimmer of a big S marking the entrance to a public air raid shelter and, everywhere, hand torches flickering like fireflies. She heard, before she saw it, the tram rattling towards them down the Embankment.

Johnnie turned the Lagonda into the narrow side street that curved round to the back entrance of the Savoy. He learned across to unlock the passenger door.

'Well, here we are at the ball.'

For a moment Anne contemplated refusing to get out of the car, just as she had contemplated refusing to get in. The hotel attendant was hovering but she was prepared, if necessary, to be parked away with the car. The snag was that on the journey she had somehow acquired an appetite. In fact, she realized that she felt pretty famished. And she liked the Savoy. Her parents had taken her and

Kit there two or three times after a visit to the theatre. Inside, away from the blacked-out streets, there would be soft lights, warmth, nice music and, most appealing of all, nice food. Not rissoles or sausages or baked beans, or any of those canteen things, but yummy, scrummy, civilized fare – cutlets and steaks and game, and afters like crêpes suzettes, ice-cream and meringues. She got out of the car.

They went up the back staircase and along the corridor that led through to the main restaurant – Anne stalking rather than walking beside the pilot to make her point. She could hear a dance band playing in the distance.

In the scented opulence of the ladies' cloakroom she took off her beret and raincoat and surveyed herself grimly in a long glass. Her blouse, skirt, and navy cardigan looked pathetically out of place and about as soigné as school uniform, except that at St Mary's they had worn a revolting shade of bottle green. She took off the cardigan, which made a slight improvement, and then sat down at one of the dressing-tables and applied face powder liberally from a cutglass bowl. The woman at the next door mirror, diamonds sparkling round her neck, was repainting her mouth carefully with lipstick as bright as Pearl's Pillar Box Red. Despondent, Anne rummaged in her raincoat pocket for her Yardley Rose Pink, worn almost to a stub. She thought of the blue tulle frock and silver sandals that she had worn for her birthday dance, and then stopped thinking about them. She couldn't actually care less what she looked like – in fact, the worse the better, in the circumstances. It would serve Johnnie Somerville right to be seen with her looking an absolute mess. Teach him to be such an arrogant pig. She dragged a comb anyhow through her hair and dumped her things with the cloakroom attendant.

He was waiting for her outside, leaning against a pillar – as usual, she thought – and smoking a cigarette. She had to admit, even though she was still angry, that he looked pretty good, standing there in his uniform. A bloody knock-out, Pearl had called him. Well, it was a

175

pity Pearl wasn't here instead because she would have loved it all – the dreamy dance music, the posh diners, the thick carpets, the glitter and the gold, not to mention the food. She would have loved the way the head waiter came forward, bowing and scraping, to lead them to one of the best tables by the dance floor, and she would have loved the way he held her chair for her and then bowed some more. The wine waiter came and went, bowing too. Another waiter flourished starched napkins and large menus were set before them. Anne consulted hers, running through scrumptious possibilities and then decided to pick the most expensive things she could find. She'd run up the biggest bill possible; maybe that would teach him a lesson.

'I'll have the quail's eggs and then Steak Tartare, please.'

'Are you sure?'

'Am I sure what?'

'About the Steak Tartare?'

'Of course I am. It's one of my favourites.' She had never actually tried either but knew they cost a lot and it sounded pretty sophisticated asking for them.

She hummed to the tune that the band were playing while he ordered and tapped her foot under the table. She could have felt quite carefree and gay at this moment if it hadn't been for the man sitting opposite her and looking sickeningly pleased with himself.

The wine waiter returned. A silver ice bucket was placed beside the table, a cork popped.

'Why the champagne?'

'Does one need an excuse to drink it?'

'And *pink* champagne?'

'I thought you might like it.' He raised his glass to her. 'To us. And to many more dinners.'

'I can't drink to that.'

'Very well. Choose a toast.'

She thought for a moment. 'To the Women's Auxiliary Air Force. God bless us every one.'

'I'll second that.'

'Hum!' She put down her glass. 'Don't they mind your having that red lining to your tunic?'

'They don't seem to. It cheers the uniform up a bit, don't you think? How's the champagne?'

'All right. Actually, I think it's rather affected.'

'The champagne?'

'The red lining. So's that tie – blue not black.'

'Blue's nicer, though, don't you think? Less funereal.'

'Pink champagne's actually pretty affected too.'

'There's no pleasing you, Anne, is there?' He stubbed out his cigarette. 'Care to dance?'

'No thanks.'

'Pity. I thought you'd like Carroll Gibbons at least.'

Anne liked the music very much, as it happened. She had been watching the band leader at his white piano and had been itching to dance. But not with Johnnie.

'That woman at the table over there seems to know you.'

'Does she?' Johnnie turned his head. 'Oh, lord, *her*.'

'An old flame?'

'More like a damp squib. Let's ignore her. Tell me more about you. I know your name, but not your age.'

'That's my business.'

'Nineteen, or twenty, I'd say. Thereabouts. I'm an ancient twenty-three. And I now know you've got a brother – older than you, presumably.'

'Five minutes older, to be exact.'

'A twin? That's intriguing. I don't think I've ever met a girl who was a twin before. I have three much older sisters. I'm the baby of the family.'

'And I bet they spoiled you rotten.'

'Oh, I wouldn't say that. They can be very bossy. Fortunately, they're all married now so they can boss their husbands about instead.'

He talked for a while about himself, a subject that usually fascinated his dinner companions who liked to hear all about the family estates in Gloucestershire, the shooting lodge in Scotland, the chalet in St Moritz, the villa near Nice, his other cars besides the Lagonda, his Moth and his penthouse flat in Belgravia. None of these things, however, appeared to interest Anne, still less impress her. On the contrary, she yawned once or twice and interrupted his account of pre-war ski-ing in Switzerland to ask when the food would be coming. He did not know what it was about her that attracted him so much, and made him persevere. She was pretty enough with her funny short upper lip and those large so-candid hazel eyes that looked at him with near scorn, but he had certainly known more beautiful girls, and most certainly ones who were more amenable. Eager, in fact, was a word he would have used about most of them. Eagerness only registered in Anne's face when the waiter finally arrived and the quail's eggs were set before her.

She tried not to fall on the eggs with unseemly haste. They looked very small and were sunk in some kind of clear jelly, like smooth white pebbles at the bottom of a pond. When she tasted them they were rather disappointing. A bit dull. Also, there wasn't nearly enough of them and she still felt ravenous. She picked at the residue of jelly clinging to the sides of the dish. Johnnie was eating some delicious-looking smoked salmon and she watched him with surreptitious envy. When he looked up unexpectedly, she improvised.

'I was just thinking . . . I'm sure I've seen pictures of you in those society mags like the *Tatler*. I look at them when I'm waiting at the dentist. You know the sort of thing they have on those back pages – Lord Bloggs and Miss Blankety-Blank enjoy a joke together at Lady Doodah's dance . . .'

'It's possible,' acknowledged Johnnie who appeared regularly on such pages.

'My mother wanted me to do the Season but luckily the war started.'

'Very obliging of Adolf Hitler.'

'I know I'd've hated it.'

'I must say I can't quite picture you . . .'

'I can picture *you* as a Debs' Delight very easily.'

'I'm not sure I was ever one of those . . . one went to the odd dance when one felt like it.'

She followed a couple wistfully with her eyes as they went past the table and onto the dance floor, drifting off to the music.

'Would you like to dance now?'

'No, thank you.'

'You're quite sure?'

'*Quite* sure.'

The empty plates were whisked away and the Steak Tartare was served to her. Anne stared at her plate in horror. Something horribly resembling a large round rissole sat there, except that the minced up meat was obviously completely raw. In its centre, in a little hollow, lay a raw egg yolk.

'Is anything the matter?'

She shook her head.

He was laughing. 'Anne, you did realize it's not meant to be cooked – steak tartare?'

'Of course I did. I told you, it's one of my favourite things. It's just rather a lot, and I'm not very hungry.'

'Do you want to change it for something . . . lighter? Some fish perhaps?'

'Certainly not.'

She struggled valiantly through it, disguising the taste of the raw meat with the tartare sauce, the vegetables and bits of bread roll, and sluiced each mouthful down with the champagne. Nothing would have induced her to admit her mistake but she could have wept, remembering all the succulent things she might have chosen if she had not been so intent on merely picking the most expensive. The waiter poured more champagne into her empty glass and she took yet another gulp.

Johnnie, fully aware of her struggles, pretended to notice nothing. He talked on easily and tried a subject that he guessed would be close to her heart.

'Was your twin brother at Eton?'

'You're as bad as Susan.'

'Who on earth is Susan?'

'One of the WAAFS. She's as big a snob as you are.'

'I simply thought I might have come across him.'

'As a matter of fact Kit *was* at Eton, but I doubt if you were there at the same time.'

'I'm trying to remember a Cunningham . . .'

'You must have been leaving as he was starting. He only left at the end of last summer term. He was going to try for Oxford if the war hadn't started. He'd have got in easily.'

'He'll be able to when the war's over.'

She looked down at her plate, messy with the remains of raw steak. 'Yes.'

'It'll probably be over by the end of this year. He'll be able to go then. I wouldn't have missed my time up there, I must say.'

'Did you do any work?'

'Some. Mostly I played.'

'I can believe it. Is that where you learned to fly? With the University Air Squadron?'

'No. I'd learned before that. On the Tiger Moth I was telling you about, only you weren't listening. It was a present for my seventeenth birthday.'

'I said you were spoiled rotten.'

He smiled. 'It's come in quite useful, though. I joined the Auxiliary lot as soon as I came down. It was fairly obvious that there was going to be a war, sooner or later.'

She remembered Kit's unashamed enthusiasm on the night of their dance. 'Did you hope there would be?'

'A war? Good heavens, no. I was having far too good a time enjoying myself.'

'Going to deb dances?'

'Among other things.'

'The perpetual playboy?'

'As a matter of fact, I was about to go into the Foreign Office when Herr Hitler rudely interrupted the proceedings.'

'Pretty typical – the Foreign Office.'

'I'm not quite sure what you mean by that, but I doubt if it's complimentary. What have you done to your fingers?'

She took her hand off the table quickly and hid it on her lap. Three fingers were adorned with sticking plaster. Both hands, as she was well aware, were red and chapped from her labours in the scullery. And her hair seemed to smell permanently of cabbage and onions, even after she had washed it.

'I've cut them. I'm always cutting myself with the kitchen knives.'

'You shouldn't be doing that work.'

'So you've said before and I wish you'd shut up about it. It's so boring.'

'Very well, I'll say no more on the subject. Now, take a *good* look at the menu and tell me what you'd like next.'

He smiled with irony as he said this. This time, though, she made no mistake. She chose Meringue Mont Blanc – a gloriously sticky, sickly-sweet concoction of meringue and cream and chestnut purée, all piled up in a lovely little mountain, and which went a long way to obliterating the lingering taste of raw meat. She had scraped her plate clean and was starting happily on the petits fours that the waiter had brought, when Johnnie rose to his feet. He grasped her wrist.

'You can finish those later. Take them all with you. Cinderella didn't go to the ball without dancing at least once before she had to leave.'

She protested through a mouthful of sugared grape as he manoeuvred her firmly onto the floor.

'I don't want to dance.'

'For heaven's sake, Anne, you know perfectly well that you do. You've been tapping your feet under the table all evening.'

He took her in his arms and after a few steps, when she had swallowed her mouthful, she relaxed. She was not at all surprised to discover that he was a very good dancer, considering the amount of practice he must have had. He was quite as good as little Stan of the Sergeants' Mess, only without Stan's showy Palais *glissandos*. All the champagne she had drunk was making her feel light-hearted as well as light-headed and she began to enjoy herself, loving the floaty feeling of moving smoothly across a dance floor to gorgeous, dreamy music.

She was Ginger Rogers dancing with Fred Astaire, except that Ginger Rogers never wore lisle stockings and lace-up shoes. Now, if she had a proper uniform like the Wren who had gone by with the naval officer — smart navy and glamorous black silk stockings . . . Over Johnnie's broad shoulder she caught sight of the damp squib still mooning from her table, and felt rather sorry for her. London was probably littered with similar squibs who had been mad enough to fall for him.

'You dance very well, Anne.'

'They taught us at school. One of the few useful things I learned there.'

'Heathfield? Roedean? St Mary's?'

'You really are an appalling snob. What if I said the local Council school?'

'I doubt if they have ballroom dancing classes.'

'I suppose *you* went to Madame Vacani's?'

'From an early age.'

They danced on and heads turned to watch them. Things would have been perfect if she had been dancing with someone else — someone like the dark stranger Pearl had seen in her tea cup . . . not that she believed that rubbish for a moment. She was quite sorry when Johnnie stopped by their table.

'Pumpkin time,' he said.

The bitter cold outside sobered her up instantly and brought her sharply down to earth. It was snowing again — big soft flakes that tickled her face — and there was an icy wind blowing from the river. Her teeth chattered as they waited for the car and all she could think of now was the long journey ahead in the dark and snow and the awful possibility of being back late. As they drove out of London she sat bolt upright in the passenger seat until, gradually, tiredness took over. Her eyes drooped and she leaned her head against the car window and fell fast asleep.

When she awoke they were still travelling through the night and it seemed to her that it was snowing harder than ever. The wipers were sweeping back and forth across the screen and what little she could see of the road ahead was all white. She rubbed her stiff neck and checked on the petits fours, now rather squashed, in her raincoat pocket.

'Where are we?'

'Still about ten miles or so to go,' he answered shortly. 'Sorry, but I've had to go slowly. The roads are pretty bad.'

She tried to see her watch. 'What time is it?'

'About twenty to.'

'God, I'm going to be late!'

'Don't worry, I'll get you in all right somehow.'

'It's all very well for you,' she told him furiously, 'but it's *me* that'll be doing jankers. Can't you go any faster?'

'Not if you want to get there at all.'

As he spoke the Lagonda skated unnervingly on a patch of ice. Anne sat in grim silence. She was feeling slightly sick, either from the Steak Tartare, or the champagne, or from sheer panic – probably all three. If she were put on yet another charge she would be in serious trouble. She'd been on four in the last three weeks – for cutting across the hallowed, forbidden parade ground, for not wearing her beret out in the town (the snoopy service police were everywhere), for not folding her bedclothes exactly right and for answering Sergeant Beaty back. On the last time ASO Newman had been absolutely livid with her. *You're wasting everyone's time with your silly behaviour, Cunningham, and that's inexcusable when we're all supposed to be doing our very best to help our country win this war. You should be ashamed of yourself.*

It was well past midnight by the time they turned down

the road to the main gates and by then she was fuming with rage. Johnnie seemed maddeningly unconcerned.

'I'll get you in with me. I'll promise them a couple of bottles of whisky and that'll fix it.'

'Supposing it doesn't? I'll get into worse trouble than I am already for being out with a bloody officer! You can drop me further round the side of the 'drome. There's a place there where I can get in under the wire.'

'Are you sure you can?'

'I've done it before,' she said coldly. 'Several times. In and out, as a matter of fact.' She heard him chuckle in the darkness. 'There's nothing to laugh about. If I get caught I'll be doing jankers for weeks. And it'll all be *your* fault.'

'I'm sorry, Anne,' he said. 'Truly sorry. It was the damned snow . . . I swear it won't happen again.'

'It certainly won't as I shan't be coming out with you *ever* again.'

He drove past the main gates and round the perimeter of the 'drome, following the high fence, and stopped the Lagonda where she told him. It was still snowing heavily and she peered through the side window, just able to make out the disused hut a short way inside the fence that marked the point where she and Pearl had managed to loosen the bottom edge of the wire. They had made use of it on a number of jaunts into town, so far without getting caught. The WAAF huts lay further beyond.

Johnnie got out of the car with her but she turned and hissed at him.

'Just *go*! If anyone sees the car they might come over.'

'They won't see it with the lights off and I'm not leaving until you're safely under that wire.'

She stumbled and fell in the ditch but shook him off angrily when he tried to help her up. It took her a while to find the loose section, digging along with her bare hands in a deep drift of snow until she could feel it, and because it was so deeply embedded she was obliged to accept his help in freeing it. He held it for her while she slithered underneath on her stomach and then replaced it after her and kicked the snow back.

'Good luck, Anne . . .'

She heard him call that softly but ignored it and made quickly for the cover of the disused hut a few yards away. His car started up again and turned round, slipping and sliding, before going back the way they had come. When the sound had died away she waited by the side of the hut wall, listening. The wind was making a faint moaning sound, eerie and bloodchilling, and the sky above her glittered icily. She was so cold now that she thought that she would freeze to death where she was standing if she didn't move soon. But, just as she was about to make a dash across the open ground in the direction of the WAAF huts, she heard the trudge of footsteps in the distance and retreated hurriedly round behind the back. Her teeth were chattering so loudly that she was afraid whoever was patrolling the wire would surely hear them, and if they shone their torch down the side of the hut they would be bound to see her tracks in the snow. She clenched her teeth tightly and waited. The footsteps were passing the hut now and stopped suddenly. A torch beam was wandering about, probing the darkness. Anne held her breath, shut her eyes and prayed. Then the boots tramped on again, crunching away over the snow, and she let her breath out in a low whistling sigh of relief.

She waited a few more minutes until she was quite sure that the coast was clear and then moved as fast as she dared across the snowy waste. With luck her tracks would be covered completely by morning. She tiptoed past Corporal White's little room at the end of the hut. It was pitch black inside, the coke stoves cold and dead, the room quiet. She groped her way down the row of beds on her side, counting them carefully until she reached her own. Someone had made up her bedclothes and there was a lump beneath the blankets.

Pearl stirred. 'That you, love? Christ, I was worried about you. Shoved your bolster down so's they might not notice you weren't back . . . bloody lucky it worked. Where the hell've you been?'

Anne told her in whispers as she undressed. There was a sleepy chortle and then a deep sigh.

'Oh, you jammy sod, you!'

'Any questions so far?'

Nobody spoke. The RAF instructor looked at the group of girls gathered round the mock-up plotting table.

'Come on, now. One of you must have *something* to ask. The men always do. Don't tell me you lot know it all first go.'

The girl standing next to Virginia raised her hand timidly. She had frizzy, permed hair and a worried expression.

'I don't think I quite understand . . . the numbers going across and down . . . I don't quite see . . .'

She stared down at the black and white map before her which showed south eastern England, the Channel, northern France and Belgium. It was divided into equal squares. Fighter Command Group boundaries were shown by dotted lines, the Sector boundaries by unbroken ones, and the fighter stations marked by red discs.

'What don't you see?'

'How the numbers work.' She lifted a puzzled face.

'It's perfectly simple. The numbers will give you the exact plot position on the map, just like I showed you. You will be given a four-figure grid reference through your headphones and you mark your plot accordingly, calculating it from these numbers – remember what I said? For example, if you were given 1-5-0-5 you would go *across* one and a half squares and *up* half a square.' The instructor's stick travelled across the map. 'Is that clear?'

The girl's face was red and she looked as though she might burst into tears. 'Not really.'

He sighed. 'Then I suppose we'd better go through it all again, from the beginning.'

Virginia watched and listened, concentrating hard. She

had understood how to plot using the grid numbers easily enough, but that was only a part of it. The metal arrows for marking the plot position and direction were different colours – red, blue or yellow – and a colour-coded clock on the wall was divided into five-minute triangular segments painted in each of those three colours, in rotation. The instructor had explained the point of it. You had to be sure to use an arrow of whichever colour the clock's hand was passing through. It was so that the age of the plot would be clear to the Operations Room Controller on the dais above. And to go with the arrows there were wooden blocks. You slotted plaques onto the blocks to show the height and strength of the aircraft, and whether they were hostile or friendly.

Going patiently over old ground, the instructor made up another block and pushed it over the map's surface to rest beside an arrow somewhere north of Eastbourne.

'There you are. Thirty plus hostile aircraft at fifteen thousand feet, in that position and moving in that direction. All clear?'

They nodded. He looked sceptical.

'Well, we'd better see if it really is. We'll take it in turns.' He pointed to Virginia. 'You first. Now, imagine you've just been given this information . . .'

She listened to him carefully. Then she glanced at the coloured clock and picked up a red arrow. Following the grid numbers she had been given she placed the arrow on the map exactly over Tunbridge Wells, positioning it with the magnetic-tipped rod. Then she made up her block – H for hostile, 40+ for the number of aircraft, and 20 for the number of thousand feet – and pushed that over to stand beside her arrow.

The instructor was lukewarm. 'Not bad. But you were slow. Much too slow. You're all going to have to be a lot quicker than that. Next one.'

They had already learned from the table map that RAF Fighter Command was divided into Groups and the Groups into Sectors. Now they discovered more about

187

how an Operations Room worked. Fighter Command Headquarters, the instructor told them, was like the nerve centre of a spider's web that reached across the country, and information was passed up and down the strands. Messages and orders were sent to the Ops Rooms of fighter stations where the Controller-in-Charge directed his squadrons. He sat high up on a balcony or dais so that he could have an uninterrupted view of the plotting table.

'He can see the whole situation spread out in front of him, at a glance. And your job is to give him the latest information fast and accurately.'

Ops A sat next to the Controller and took down messages as they filtered through and Ops B sat on his other side, assisting. An Army officer was also present to keep the anti-aircraft batteries informed.

'And this,' the instructor continued, indicating a large blackboard on the wall, 'is known as the tote board. As you can see it's marked up to show the state of the squadrons – Airborne, Standing By, At Readiness or Available. The Controller has to be able to see all that as well as everything else.'

They were told about the men of the Observer Corps who kept watch for enemy aircraft and sent in their information over field telephones, and they learned something of the chain of mysterious stations strung along the coastline which could somehow track aircraft by radio waves.

And all the time the importance of secrecy was impressed upon them. Their instructor was blunt.

'If I had my way you girls wouldn't be doing this job. I never yet knew a woman who could keep a secret, so I hope you're all going to prove me wrong. Just remember that what goes on in our Ops Rooms is something the enemy would give a great deal to know about. One silly, talkative girl could give it away. And people will want to know about it – your friends, your family . . . they'll be curious about what you do. They may get angry and upset when you won't tell them, or they may try to guess, draw you out, tease you about it . . . Whatever they do or say *you* must say absolutely nothing.'

Virginia absorbed every word. During her first few days in the WAAF she had wondered how she was going to survive. She had not bargained for the bewildering strangeness of it all. She had been unprepared for the brusque ordering about, the rudeness and unfriendliness of some of the other recruits, the cold and discomfort and the total, embarrassing lack of privacy, and she had found it hard to remember all the peculiar rules and regulations. At night she had wept silently into her bolster pillow, believing that she had made a terrible mistake. She had wept at her own unhappiness and at the thought of her mother sitting alone in the flat, and she had wept again in the day when reprimanded for her clumsy attempts at drill and PT. They had been issued with a sort of uniform – gaberdine raincoats, ugly black berets, men's shirts with stiff detachable collars and sad black ties. None of it seemed to fit her properly and it all made her feel even more ungainly. If it had not been for one thing that eventually happened, her misery would have been complete.

From the moment she had placed that red arrow on the plotting table over Tunbridge Wells, and the wooden block alongside it, Virginia had felt quite differently. She had known then that she had done right. She had been right to leave home and Mother, and none of the other awful things mattered. She had been given an important job to do. Something worthwhile. And she knew that she could do it well.

At the end of their training course they were asked to give a preference for the area where they would like to be sent. Thinking of her mother, Virginia specified the south-east. Later she was told that she was being posted to RAF Colston on the south coast of England.

Six

The journey going home on leave to Suffolk was dreadful. Winnie sat squashed uncomfortably in the third class compartment with seven RAF airmen who teased her all the way to London. Because of a fresh fall of snow, the train was more than an hour late arriving at Victoria Station and then, as before, she got lost in the Underground and had to ask her way at least half a dozen times. Liverpool Street Station, when she finally reached it, was crowded with travellers and she was swept hither and thither like a piece of flotsam on swirling flood waters. The loudspeakers blared out announcements that she could neither make sense of nor hear properly above the hissing and belching of the steam engines. The train she had been supposed to catch had long since departed and the next one to Ipswich did not leave for more than two hours. She sat in the Ladies' Waiting Room where it seemed to be even colder than it was outside. When she boarded the train at last, there were no empty seats left and she had to stand in the corridor with her suitcase wedged between her feet.

As the train steamed slowly out of London, she watched the drab buildings slide by the window and read the big advertisement hoardings . . . *Guinness Is Good For You* . . . *Virol, The Food For Health* . . . *There'll Always be Mazawattee Tea* . . . In a row of back gardens below, she saw lines of sooty washing and the raw humps of air raid shelters poking through the snow like new graves. Presently, the train gathered speed and the terraced houses gave way to semi-detached ones and wider streets and deeper snow. A cemetery flashed past, then a park with allotments and, as darkness was falling, the flat openness of Essex. There were stops and starts and long waits at stations and signals and, as she was drooping with weariness, Essex became Suffolk and the train drew into Ipswich. She queued patiently for the bus which ground its way through treacherous lanes and deposited her outside the Pig and Whistle in Elmbury. Then she walked the remaining two miles home through deep snow and drifts and stumbled up to the farmhouse door.

Her family were sitting round the kitchen table having tea and the oil lamp lit their surprised faces as they all turned towards her. Her mother stopped in the act of cutting into the cake, the knife in mid-air.

'Winnie! What're you doin' here? We weren't expectin' you.'

She set down her suitcase. Her hands and feet were so cold she could scarcely feel them.

'I wrote I was comin', Mum. Didn't you get my letter? They gave me leave.'

'Well, we never know what's happenin' these days, what with the war and the weather. We didn't think you'd get through, it's been so bad . . . What's that you've got on your head?'

'My beret. It's uniform.'

'Funny lookin' thing. Well, you'd better make haste and sit down then while the tea's still hot.'

Winnie took off her raincoat and beret and hung them up by the back door beside Gran's old pattens. Her shoes and stockings were soaking wet but she was too tired to care. She sat down at her usual place at the table. Gran, guzzling from a plate held up to her chin, grunted something and Ruth and Laura stared at her round-eyed as though she were a stranger. Her father passed his plate down for a slice of cake and addressed her indirectly.

'Lost two ewes last week. Six foot drifts. Ground's like iron. Pond's frozen solid. Can't dig anythin' up. Makes no end of work.'

Nothing much had changed since she'd been away. Dad

was grumbling just the same and everything looked just as it had always done. She looked round the room, at the big dresser with its rows of plates along the shelves and cups hanging on hooks, the oak settle along the wall, the ebony clock on the shelf up above the range and the pink lustreware plates each side of it: *Thou God Seest Me* and *Prepare To Meet Thy God*. The kettle was simmering over the fire and there was Gran's chair with its patchwork cushion, and the picture of Ely Cathedral on the wall . . . It was all just the same.

Her mother poured her tea. 'You're lookin' pale, Winnie. Peaky. Don't they feed you properly in that place?'

'I'm all right, Mum. Just a bit cold, that's all. It was a long journey.'

'Well, you don't look it.' Her mother wiped the jam from Ruth's face. 'You never looked like that when you were here. What's that shirt and tie you're wearin'?'

'It's our uniform, Mum.'

'Don't seem proper to me — wearin' men's clothes like that.'

'They're not really. And I wear dungarees here, Mum.'

'That's different. You don't look right at all in those things . . . and all pale like you are. I never did want you to go to that place.'

Gran had finished her plateful and she smacked her lips together. The bib of her long black dress was liberally spotted with food stains.

'Leave the mawther alone, Rhoda. Stop yar fussin'. Yew've no sense at all. She's tired, comin' all that way. Needs her tay. Leave her be.'

Winnie drank the hot tea and ate hungrily. Now that Gran had spoken, she was left in peace. There were floury scones with thick yellow butter, plum jam and seed cake . . . she had forgotten how good home-made food tasted.

Afterwards she did the washing-up out in the scullery. The pipe that brought the water from the pond to the pump beside the sink was frozen solid and so she had to use water from a pail, mixing it with hot water from the kettle off the fire in the enamel bowl. She worked quickly, the old routine resumed as though there had been no break at all and as soon as she had finished she went to change into her dungarees, jumper and woollen socks. She took her old coat off the peg by the back door, pulled on her boots and went out to the stackyard to give her father a hand. He behaved as though she had never been away, leaving all those chores to her which had always been hers, without a word said between them. She drew water up from the deep well, carried the straw and the hay and the feed, and swept clean with the besom. The animals had not forgotten her. Tulip and Buttercup, Cherry and Daisy in the cow byre looked round at her with their soft eyes. Susie grunted in her sty and edged close to have her back scratched with a stick. The ewes in the shed bleated, and butted her with their heads, Prince and Smiler stamped their great hooves in their stalls and swished their tails, and Rusty leaped and barked excitedly at the end of his chain. Even the hens, roosting for the night up in the granary loft, gave soft cluckings and flutterings at the sound of her voice.

Her father, stumping to and fro in his nail boots, grumbled some more. Old Jack was getting worse than useless these days, what with his rheumatism and his slowness, and he couldn't be trusted with the milking any more. As for Barham's lad, the one he'd taken on when Winnie'd gone off and left them in the lurch, he was just a drawlatch, always looking all ways for Sundays.

'Fordson won't budge, neither. Not spark. Been tryin' to get her goin' all week. Blessed if I know what in tarnation's the matter.'

'I'll try her tomorrow, Dad. See if I can.'

'You won't. Dead as a doornail. Just as well we've got the hosses. New fangled machinery . . . don't know why I ever bothered with that dratted thing. Near two hundred pounds she cost me an' all . . .'

By the time she got to bed she ached with tiredness, and yet for a long time she could not sleep. She lay watching the moonlight shining across the foot of her bed – so bright she could see the quilt pattern clearly. Gran was driving her pigs to market in her room below, noisy as anything. They were all asleep. Except for Ruth and Laura who'd taken a while to get used to her again, they'd all behaved just as though she'd never been away. Nothing *had* changed . . . except for herself. That was what was different. She didn't feel like the same person she'd been before. She was glad to be back – to be home again with the family, and to be working on the farm again, and with the animals – but she felt different somehow. As though she no longer properly belonged here any more. Like she was only visiting.

She turned her face towards the attic window. She could see the moon through the gap in the curtains – a full moon, round and soapy white as a cheese, up there in the sky. An owl screeched close by the house and Rusty barked once or twice in the stackyard below – sharp, warning woofs. A fox, most probably, prowling round outside the granary, after the hens. Tomorrow she'd have a good look to make sure it was all secure.

She tried not to think about what had happened with Taffy but it kept coming into her mind. What a fool she'd been, going off with him like that. Such an innocent, just like he'd called her. ASO Newman had been very kind about it, not angry at all, but she'd talked about being careful not to lead the airmen on, about keeping your distance with them, about the fact that she was engaged . . . and that had made her feel a whole lot worse. Made her feel like Dot Bedwell at the Pig and Whistle, or something.

She'd heard that Taffy had got into a lot of trouble and she'd felt bad about that, too, because it had really been her own silly fault – the way she'd gone on about the 'planes, telling him things, acting so eager . . . She ought to have known better. Had more sense. Everyone had got to hear about them getting caught together, about her running out of that stores hut with her shirt torn where Taffy had grabbed hold of her to try and stop her. In the Orderly Room they'd put on false Welsh accents and made jokes about leeks. People had sniggered behind her back and whispered all sorts of untrue things about her and Taffy until, in the end, they'd got tired of it, or forgotten about it. But she couldn't forget, no matter how hard she tried. The very worst thing of all was that she'd let Ken down. That's how she saw it.

She wished she never had to see Taffy again, that his squadron would be posted away. He still kept coming to the Orderly Room, trying to talk to her, but she kept her back turned, pretending he wasn't there. Then, he had cornered her by the entrance to the NAAFI.

'Winnie, give me the chance to tell you how sorry I am. I never meant you any harm . . .'

He had tried to go on, pleading with her, but she'd walked away quickly and taken refuge with Anne and Pearl. Pearl had put an arm round her shoulders.

'Bothering you again, is he, ducky? Some men never learn. Must be barmy about you.'

Winnie closed her eyes. If she didn't stop thinking about it she'd never get to sleep, and she was dog-tired. She had to be up early in the morning. There was a lot to do.

She was up long before dawn. There had been no more snow overnight but carrying the lamp across the yard, she could see the glittering rime of a hard frost. Buttercup's flank was warm against her cheek as she squirted the stream of milk from the cow's udder rhythmically into the pail. She was a good milker and fast and her father grunted a kind of approval when she finished early and went to help him feed and water the other animals.

After breakfast, when it was light, she worked on the Fordson in its lean-to shed. The bucket of radiator water standing beside the tractor had frozen too hard to be broken with a hammer so she fetched some more from the well. Then she pulled the old sacking off the engine and took a look. Dad sometimes switched the tap the wrong way and tried to start on TVO instead of petrol, so maybe that had been the trouble. She unscrewed the little tap on the carburettor to make sure it was properly drained and turned the tap to petrol. Then she went round to the front and swung the starting handle hard. Dead as a doornail, like Dad had said.

She checked the magneto next, taking off the cap and wiping it out with a piece of cloth, and then she rubbed carefully between the points with a bit of sandpaper. When that was done she unscrewed the front spark plug and dripped some petrol down the hole like Mr Stannard at the next door farm had once shown her. She screwed the plug back and cranked the starting handle again. Still nothing. This time she took out all four plugs and put them in an old tin with a splash of petrol and set a lighted match to them. There was a little woomph as the petrol ignited and then died. Another of Mr Stannard's tricks to make them warm and dry. She screwed them back again and tried the starting handle once more. At the third go the tractor's engine sparked and burst into life.

She was pouring the water into the radiator when her father appeared in the lean-to entrance, his face ruddy beneath his brown trilby, his boots and leggings caked with snow. He shouted above the noisy throb of the engine.

'Got her goin', then? Must've bin somethin' cured hisself.'

As she went about the house later, doing more chores, Gran watched her from her chair, puffing on her cigarette. Her upper lip, bristly as Susie's back, was yellow-brown from all the tobacco she'd smoked and her face grimy with soot from sitting close and so long by the range. Her pattens still hung on the big iron nail by the back door but it was years since she'd walked further outdoors than down the path to the privy. When she was a girl, though, she'd told Winnie once, she always wore her pattens out into the yard and everywhere. All the countrywomen had worn them in those days, clopping along the lanes like they'd been shod.

'What's up wi' yew, then, Winifred Briggs?'

'Nothing, Gran.'

'Fiddlesticks! Yew met some feller?'

'No, Gran.'

'Huh! Pity! Hoped yew'd find someone other'n that tibby o' yours. Still, there's plenty o' time. Keep lookin'.'

'I don't want to find anyone else, Gran.'

The old woman snorted.

Ken came to tea. He shuffled into the house in his awkward way and stood twisting his cap round and round in his hands and giving her his shy smile. Gran was at her worst, making her sharp remarks and sucking at her tea loudly. After the meal he helped her take the dishes through to the sink in the scullery and carried the kettle of hot water for her. She tipped some cold water from the pail into the basin and began rinsing the crockery.

'Weather's been bad,' Ken said, drying a plate slowly.

'It's been bad in the south, too, ever since the New Year. Bad everywhere, so they say. Dad says there's six inches of ice on the pond, at least. He has to keep breakin' it for the animals.'

'Must be a bother.'

'Well, you know how he grumbles . . . I don't know what he'd do without somethin' to moan about. That's a nasty cough you've got there, Ken.'

He looked paler and thinner than she remembered, and he kept on with that coughing every so often.

'I've had a bit of a cold, that's all. Don't seem to go away, though.' He picked up another plate. 'I didn't tell you, Winn, but I tried to join the RAF. I didn't tell Mother, either. I just went to the place in Ipswich one day when it was early-closin', quiet like.'

'What did they say?'

'Same as Mother's always said. They won't have me with my asthma. And somethin's wrong with my feet, too. I tried the Army as well, and the Navy, but it's no good – none of them will. I feel such a useless, good-for-nothin'.'

She touched his arm. 'Oh, Ken, what a shame! But there'll be somethin' you can do. I know there will. Somethin' will turn up for you.'

'I hope you're right.' He put down the plate and picked up a cup and began to dry it carefully. 'You said in your letters Winn, that you're still workin' in that Orderly Room place . . .'

'That's right.'

'So, they're not goin' to let you do any work with the aeroplanes, like you hoped?'

'Well, not yet, anyhow.'

'So, what you're doin' – with the forms and all that – it's not so important?'

She saw the way his thoughts were moving. 'Well, it *is* really, Ken. It has to be done so's the station can run properly. All the right forms have to be filled in for all sorts of things, like I told you.'

'Yes, but anyone could do that. It doesn't have to be you. And it's not what you wanted to go and do, is it? Not what you went and joined the Air Force for?'

'No, but our officer says they'll be lettin' us train for all sorts of trades before long. There's lots more WAAFS now.'

'But I don't think they'll ever let you work with the 'planes, Winnie, really I don't.' He coughed again. 'I've been talkin' to Mother. She says she's quite willin' to have you come and live over the shop, if that's what we want. She won't stand in our way. She says another pair of hands might be useful, now she's gettin' on a bit. We could get married soon as the banns are read. If you're not doin' anythin' all that important in the Air Force – well, not what you wanted, anyway – there's not much sense you stayin' on, is there?'

'But I couldn't just leave like that, Ken. For no reason.'

'Gettin' married'd be a reason. Joe Girling was home on leave and he told me the army girls can leave easy if they get married.'

'I wouldn't want to, though, Ken. Don't you see? I want to do more than just help in a shop.'

'That's all I'm doin',' he said quietly. 'Isn't it?'

She turned to him unhappily, aware how she was hurting him. 'I'm sorry, I didn't mean it like that. Really I didn't. You do much more than just help. Your mother couldn't manage without you, the way you do all the post office counter and everythin'.'

'You could do all that too. Learn to.'

She said stubbornly: 'It wouldn't work, Ken. Even if your mother'd let me, and I'm not sure she would, I wouldn't want to leave the Air Force just for that. Please don't ask me to give it up – not just yet. As soon as the war's over I'll come back and we'll spend the rest of our lives here together.'

'The war could go on for years, Winnie,' he said sadly.

Later, when he left, she put on her coat and walked outside a little way with him. The moon had risen over the farmhouse and the snow sparkled frostily and crunched beneath their feet. It was very cold and very clear. They could hear a dog fox barking a long way off in Dersham Wood and the distant, rumbling drone of an aircraft.

'Bomber,' Ken said. 'They've built a new RAF aerodrome up at Riddlesden. Great big place with concrete runways. There's lots of bombers there.'

'I know. Dad told me. There was one came over low this morning. I don't know what kind it was. We only have fighters at Colston. The bombers couldn't land on the grass there.'

She had watched the big aeroplane lumber over the farm, its two engines roaring louder than any fighter. There had been a gun turret at the nose and one at the tail, and she'd seen the guns poking out. She had thought it looked rather a clumsy thing with its blunt nose and high tail fins at the back, but the RAF roundels painted on it had given her a glow of pride – a warm little rush of excitement inside her as though in some way it belonged to her, or she to it. She had waved as it swept over her head. The chickens had scattered about the stackyard, the Suffolks had plunged up and down in the stables and the ewes had barged about, terrified. Her father, far from waving, had shaken his fist angrily at the bomber and sworn he'd be losing all the lambs.

'They say they're bombin' the German battleships,' Ken said. 'I heard it in the shop.'

They listened to the throbbing of the engines fading away into the night. After a moment Winnie spoke again.

'I couldn't leave the Air Force, Ken. I want to be a part of it all.'

'I know, Winn,' he said heavily. 'I understand.'

He coughed again and she tucked his muffler more closely round his throat.

'We'd better not stand out here any longer, Ken. It's too cold and it'll be bad for your cough. You'd better go.'

'I s'pose I had. Well, good night, Winnie.'

He bent to kiss her cheek quickly, as he always did. Taffy's scornful remark came, unbidden, into her mind. *What does that precious Ken of yours do then? Hold your hand at the pictures and then give you a good night peck on the cheek?*

'Winn, there isn't anyone else, is there? Somebody else you've met?'

'No, Ken, there's no-one else. No-one at all.'

He gave a sigh of relief. 'That's all right, then. I just wondered . . .'

'There's no need to worry.'

'You'll still marry me, then?'

'Of course I will. I promise.'

He trudged away through the snow, his cap pulled down and his head bent against the wind. He was coughing again as he went down the lane.

*　　*　　*

Felicity reached home just before dark. She had driven her Ford from Sussex to Norfolk and the roads had been treacherous all the way. The car had skidded and slid about on the ice and snow and it had been a frightening experience. The only thing to be said for the appalling weather, she thought, as she negotiated yet another icy patch, was that it was apparently even worse on the Continent, in which case the Germans would be equally inconvenienced.

George sat patiently in the passenger seat beside her, seeming to enjoy the ride. Speedy had spoken the truth when he had promised her that the bull terrier would be no trouble to look after. George had assumed the part of her protector and spent his days beside her desk, on guard. If he was suspicious of any visitor he took up his bandy-legged stance in front of the door, blocking the exit, until she called him off. He had never bitten anyone, or even tried to, but his fierce expression was enough. It amused her that he invariably did this whenever Sergeant Beaty entered her office, whereas Robbie Robinson could come and go with impunity.

It seemed a long time since Speedy had handed George over into her reluctant keeping. He had appeared in her office, tugging George by his lead, and had flung one arm wide dramatically.

'Fair stood the wind for France when we our sails advance, nor now to prove our chance longer will tarry . . .' He let his arm drop. 'I think that's right. They were off to bash the Frogs at Agincourt, if I remember correctly.'

'Speedy, you're not going?'

'This very day. God for Harry, and all the rest of it. So, I've brought old George for you. You promised to look after him, remember?'

'Did I?'

'Unquestionably. You wouldn't want him to have to go into kennels, would you . . . be put behind bars? You'd hate that, wouldn't you, George? Look how his tail's drooping at the very thought! You can't let him down. I told you, he'll be no trouble. He'll be good as gold.'

The bull terrier had wagged his tail uncertainly and given a little whine.

Felicity had sighed. 'Oh, all right. I'll take care of him for you.'

'Good show! I knew we could count on you. I told you so, George, old chap, didn't I? Said it would be all right. You stand guard while I'm away. Bite anyone's ankles who's a nuisance to the kind lady.'

He had leaned across her desk and kissed her lightly on the mouth. His moustache had tickled.

'Goodbye, Assistant Section Officer Newman.'

'Goodbye, Flying Officer Dutton. And good luck.'

'Thanks.' He had smiled into her eyes, his own shining bright. Then he had bent to pat George. 'Be good, old fellow. Look after your new mistress and do everything she tells you.'

He had blown her another kiss from the doorway, winked, and then he was gone. Beside her, George had given a desolate whine.

The Rectory was shrouded in white and the laurels lining the driveway bowed down under the weight of the snow. The car slithered to a stop somewhere near the front door and Felicity went inside the house, George padding at her heels. The stone-flagged hall was glacially cold, the house in semi-darkness. The grandfather clock ticked loudly in the silence.

She found her father in his study, seated at his desk by the window and working on his sermon in the failing light. When her mother had been alive this room had always been untidy, but now it was chaotic – the worst she had ever seen it. Books and papers were piled high or strewn about on every available surface – shelves, tables, benches, chairs, the old leather chesterfield with the broken springs. They were even under these things, creeping in a slowly advancing tide across the carpet. And since Mrs Salter, from the village, was not allowed to touch anything in the room, the dust lay over it all, in a thick, grey film.

He was so absorbed in his work that he did not notice her presence until she spoke. At the sound of her voice he looked up from his papers, over the rim of his spectacles, and was instantly on his feet, his face alight with pleasure, his arms outstretched to her in welcome.

'My dear child, what a joy to see you . . . I'd quite forgotten the time . . .' He embraced her and then held her at arm's length. 'Let me look at you. You look well. A little tired, perhaps, but that's probably the journey. How were the roads? This wretched weather . . . the snow . . . your hands feel like ice! I meant to light the fire before you arrived. So silly of me . . . Now, where did I put the matches?'

He fussed around, hunting for them. He was still wearing his galoshes, she noticed. The left one was split at the heel so very likely the shoe was damp.

'I generally put them on the mantelpiece, but they don't seem to be here now . . . good gracious, who's this?'

'This is George, Father. I'm looking after him for a friend. I hope you don't mind his coming here. He's very well behaved.'

'Of course not. He looks a very nice dog. Now I *must* find these matches. They're somewhere in this room . . .'

She found them under some papers on a chair and lit the fire in the grate, laid ready by Mrs Salter. The flames flickered feebly over the coal and she shivered in spite of her greatcoat.

'You shouldn't be sitting here in this cold, Father. It can't be good for you.'

'My dear, I never notice it when I'm working. And it does me no harm at all. I'm quite used to it.'

'Shall we close the shutters? Then we could light the lamps.'

'By all means.'

Felicity unfolded the shutters across the windows and lit the oil lamps. The Rectory had no electricity and the only running water was in the scullery; no improvements had been made to the house in the past hundred years. By the time she had done this the fire was burning brighter and they sat beside it for a while with George warming himself at the grate. She studied her father anxiously. He looked well enough, though rather thin. She knew that he frequently forgot to eat the food that Mrs Salter prepared and left for him. Dried out dishes would come to light, left in the bottom of the Aga, or untouched plates of cold food be discovered on the larder shelves. His jacket, she saw, had a hole in one elbow and was missing a button, and he was wearing odd socks – not that that had ever been unusual. She hoped he was not working too hard. The curate had joined the RAF and her father now had to cope with the parish alone. He had never learned to drive and went everywhere on his old bike, riding miles in all weathers and at all hours to visit his parishioners. Typically, he was unwilling, now, to talk about himself.

'I want to hear all about *you*, my dear – not talk about me. How are you getting on and what have you been doing? That uniform suits you so well. Your dear mother would have been so proud.'

She chatted about RAF Colston and told him about some of her problems. He listened sympathetically.

'That's a great responsibility for you – to be in charge of all those young girls. And you're not so much older yourself. But I've no doubt that you do your job to the very best of your ability. It's never easy, of course, to lead . . . You mentioned your commanding officer in one of your letters, I think – what was his name?'

'Wing Commander Palmer. And I'd sooner not talk about him. He's hated us being there from the beginning. He loathes the very idea of having women on his station. We're nothing but a nuisance to him and he's convinced we'll never be any real use.'

'Well, of course, in the end he'll realize that he was wrong. Time will prove the contrary, I'm sure. I have the greatest respect for women and the achievements they are capable of. Your mother was a case in point.'

They both looked up at the portrait that hung over the mantelpiece. The woman who had been taken from them eight years before stared serenely out over the disorder of the study. She had been as serene in life, Felicity remembered – somehow managing to combine the role of rector's wife with that of consultant paediatrician. She wished that she had inherited more of her mother's calm approach to everything.

'I don't think Wing Commander Palmer has much respect for women.'

'Give him time, my dear. Remember that he bears a huge responsibility – for everyone and everything on the station. It must be a heavy burden, especially in wartime. He needs to be very sure of things.'

She smiled. 'Well, I'll try to see it that way, Father. And not that he's just a bigoted old so-and-so.'

He patted her hand. 'And now I'm going to pour us each a sherry – if I can find the decanter and glasses. Then we'll have something to eat. Mrs Salter has kindly left us a pie in the bottom oven, I believe.'

They ate their supper in the kitchen, which was the warmest place in the house. George, fed first with scraps that Felicity had brought with her from the station kitchens, flopped down against the Aga and began to snore gently.

'Where is his owner?'

'Somewhere in France. He's a fighter pilot. I agreed to look after his dog in a weak moment. Actually, I've rather enjoyed having him with me. He stays by my desk most of the day.'

'He seems very fond of you. What about his master? Is he fond of you, too?'

'Oh, it's just a joke, I think, really . . . he's always playing the fool and making me laugh.'

'A great deal better than making you cry.'

She said seriously, 'I hope nothing happens to him in

France, Father. Or to any of the others over there. They're all so decent.'

'I'm afraid you ought to prepare yourself for the possibility that some of your decent young men are going to die, Felicity. It seems to me that it's only a question of time before the Germans advance into France.'

'But surely they'd never get through the Maginot Line. It's supposed to be impassable.'

'I imagine that they will simply go *round* it, and through Holland and Luxembourg and Belgium. Looking at the map, it seems only logical to me.'

'But those are neutral countries.'

'My dear, we are dealing with Evil. And Evil recognizes neither neutrality nor boundaries, as has already been demonstrated. I don't believe that Hitler will rest until he has crushed the whole of Europe – England included – perhaps the whole world, if possible. And it will be up to your brave and decent young men, and others like them, to try and stop him somehow.'

She was quiet for a moment, thinking of the pilots she knew. 'I don't think they quite see it like that. It's almost like a game with them. They make a joke of it all.'

'That's natural. It's their way. And no-one has tried to invade us yet, unlike the poor Poles and Czechs. The youth of England is not yet on fire.'

Speedy would have appreciated the apt quotation. *Just what old Snodders would have said.*

'Supposing the Germans *did* break through the Maginot Line, or go round it, what then?'

'They could drive us back and eventually succeed in occupying France as well. The French don't seem to be well organized in military matters.'

She remembered the gloomy prognostications of Mr Cutler at the Christmas dinner party.

'But if the Germans wanted to invade England they'd have to cross the Channel first.'

'That would present difficulties, I agree, but it might not be impossible, given the likely supremacy of their forces. Especially their air force. It may all hinge on that.'

The Norfolk wind was soughing plaintively round the house and rattling the kitchen shutters. George, warm and comfortable against the Aga, grunted and twitched a hind leg in his sleep. Felicity rested her chin on her hands.

'Do you believe that God is on our side, Father?'

'My dear, I *know* that He is. He will give us the strength to fight this Evil. At the moment there's precious little most of us in this parish can do except pray, but *you* have been given a very clear way to help in the fight. And so has George's owner.'

Her leave passed quietly but busily. She helped Mrs Salter in the house and tried to restore some sort of order to the study. And she drove her father round to make his visits. She had bought the Ford with part of the money her mother had left her in her will, hoping that her father would also learn to drive so that he could make use of the car. But somehow that had never happened. He seemed perfectly content with his bike, travelling about the parish in a stately fashion with his black cape flapping out behind him like a loose sail.

She took George for long walks across the fields. Even in the winter bleakness Norfolk was beautiful to her eyes. She had always cherished its wildness. She loved the wide, open skies and the ever-changing cloud formations casting strange, shifting patterns of light on the land . . . the way a shaft of sunlight would suddenly break through banks of grey cloud like an illumination straight from heaven. And she loved the mewing cries of the birds, the trill of the larks and the clean, salt smell of the wind blowing in from the North Sea. George, happily, if fruitlessly, chasing rabbits, shared her pleasure.

The parish seemed almost untouched by war, tucked away in its remote corner of the county – except for the absence of most of its young men and women and for the presence of RAF bombers lumbering noisily about the skies. The old aerodrome had been a quiet little place in peacetime but all·that had changed. As they drove past it she looked over the hedgerow and saw new hangars and huts and a vast concrete runway stretching away into the far distance. Her father was able to identify the aircraft.

'Those standing over there by the hangar are Wellingtons, and that's definitely a Blenheim, taxiing out – I can tell by the nose.' And, peering upwards out of the car window, 'that one up there coming in to land is a Whitley.'

She was surprised by this, considering his indifference to most machines of any kind, until she discovered that he often visited the bomber station.

'Fine chaps,' he said. 'Very fine chaps. I've had some good talks with them.'

She understood now, too, how he might have gleaned information on the possible course of the war.

The parish church, standing close by the Rectory, was very old and too large now for a community which had once been more numerous and more prosperous. The congregation had shrunk to fill only a few pews and maintaining the fabric was a constant struggle. Felicity, going over to clean the brass, found the sexton's wife sweeping the nave, bundled up in coat, woollen hat, scarf and mittens.

'I heard you were home, dear. The Rector must be pleased. My Peter's gone off with the BEF, you know. In France or Belgium somewhere. We're very proud of him, but of course we do worry.'

Felicity's last memory of Peter was as a schoolboy with a satchel on his back, scuffing his way along the lane.

Mrs Prewitt chattered on, wielding her broom vigorously and raising clouds of dust from the old tiles. The war would soon be over, in any case, wouldn't it? At the last Mothers' Union meeting they'd all thought that. Hitler had gone as far as he could and now he'd stay put. He'd learned he couldn't mess about with people any more. Now the British Expeditionary Force was out there he'd know it wasn't any good. And once this terrible winter was over they'd all feel a lot better. The papers said it was the worst winter this century and it certainly felt like it. All this snow and everything frozen solid. There were some snowdrops out in her garden, though, and she'd even seen a daffodil shoot or two. Spring wasn't far away and Peter would be home again . . .

Felicity began to polish the brass. Mrs Prewitt finished her sweeping and her talking and departed, leaving her alone. She worked on quickly in the damp cold and when it was all done she sat down for a moment in one of the front pews. The altar cross gleamed in the gloom beyond the rood screen. She wanted to pray but she hardly knew what to pray for. For peace? Yes, but only as an honourable end to the war. For victory over Evil? That was more like it. That was what had to be achieved. Somehow. At any cost. She would pray for that. And for Speedy, and for Whitters and for all of them, that they would come back safely . . . and that Peter Prewitt would soon be home again.

It felt like going home from boarding school at the end of term. There was the same flutter of excitement in her stomach; the same feeling of release, as from a prison; the same heartfelt, thankful happiness. Anne feasted her eyes on the changing scenery as the train carried her towards London. The suburban houses had never looked more appealing, the dingy environs of London never more delightful. As the train crossed the Thames on its final approach to Victoria Station she was already on her feet and pulling her suitcase down from the rack. She took the Underground from Victoria across to Paddington to catch another train out to Buckinghamshire. An elderly woman in the corner seat opposite leaned forward.

'Excuse my asking, dear, but is that a uniform you're wearing? What are you?'

'I'm a WAAF.'

'A what, dear?'

'A WAAF. The Women's Auxiliary Air Force. We're sort of part of the RAF.'

The woman was small and drably dressed but her eyes were bright. 'Oh, are you dear? That's nice. I do like the Royal Air Force. So brave the way they go up in those aeroplanes. It's very smart, your beret, with that lovely badge. I did wonder what you were, though . . . there are so many uniforms around these days. You don't fly the aeroplanes, do you?'

'No, they wouldn't let us do anything like that.'

'I didn't think so. That's just the men, isn't it? Still, it's wonderful what you young girls get up to these days. I wish I'd been able to go off and do things like you in my day. You're so lucky.'

'Do you think so?' Anne said curiously. The thought had never occurred to her.

'Oh yes. You were born at just the right time, weren't you? Very lucky. You didn't mind my asking, dear, did you? I was just wondering . . .'

Her mother met her at the station in the Morris and Barley was sitting on the back seat. He wagged his tail furiously and licked her face.

'I'm sure he knew you were coming, darling. He's been waiting by the front door all day. Remember how he always used to do that when you came home from boarding school? Is that your new uniform?'

'It's all we have at the moment. Not the proper thing. We're supposed to be getting tunics and skirts eventually. Horrible, isn't it?'

'Well, I can't honestly say that that raincoat is the most flattering garment I've ever seen. Or the beret! It looks much too big for you. To think you used to grumble about your school hat.'

'Thanks, Mummy! That makes me feel a whole lot better!' Anne pulled off her beret and ran her fingers through her hair. 'We're meant to wear the disgusting things going on leave. One of their hundreds of dotty rules.'

'Well, you can change into your own clothes the minute

you get home. There's a letter from Kit, by the way. He sounds fine. They're billeted in some frightfully grand place, apparently.'

They drove out of the station yard and took the familiar route that would bring them to Beechgrove. Her stomach began to flutter in anticipation again. She watched the scenery go by – sheltered, wooded slopes so different from the open, flat land round Colston.

'Snow's been pretty bad here too, by the looks of it.'

'Perfectly dreadful. We've had more burst pipes in the house. Have you managed to keep warm?'

'Just about. At least it's warm in the kitchens.'

'I wish you weren't doing that sort of work, darling. Can't you change?'

'Don't you start, Mummy. People keep *on* saying that to me.'

'Well, it seems such a waste. You had an expensive education at St Mary's. Surely they could make better use of you?'

Anne thought of ASO Newman's sharp remarks. 'It's not very likely at the moment. Anyway, didn't someone say that an army marches on its stomach? Same with the RAF, I suppose, though you'd think they'd fall out of the sky after some of the food.'

'I think you've put on a bit of weight.'

'We all have. It's the stodge.'

'And you look a bit tired.'

'They work us pretty hard.'

'Well, you must have a good rest while you're here. Catch up on some sleep. I hope Fred and Betty don't disturb you.'

'Fred and Betty? Who are they?'

'Our tame evacuees. Have you forgotten? Well, not all that tame, unfortunately. In fact, they're both little menaces. You wouldn't believe the way they seem to have been brought up. Actually, they haven't been brought up at all – that's the trouble, poor things. It's not their fault. Do you know they'd never seen an inside lavatory before, or a proper bath with taps, or used a toothbrush. And they were absolutely infested with head lice.'

'So were some of the new WAAFS.'

'Good heavens, were they really? Whatever sort of girls are they recruiting now? I do worry about you sometimes, Anne . . . I didn't really want you to join up, you know. It would have been so much better if you could have done something from home.'

'What sort of thing?'

'I don't know . . . VAD work. Something like that.'

'Bedpans and blanket baths? No, thanks. I'd sooner be peeling potatoes.'

She had forgotten all about the two evacuees from somewhere in the East End of London, packed off with thousands of other kids to escape the bombing that had never happened.

'What room are they in?'

'I put them in the old sewing room. They can't do much damage in there. I'm afraid I've let them play with some of your old things in the nursery, darling. I didn't think you and Kit would mind too much. Poor little wretches, I don't think they've ever had any real toys to play with.'

She did mind, in fact, but she didn't say so. Just now the old things in the nursery seemed rather important. She didn't want other children touching them, even though that might be mean-spirited.

The house was waiting for her – solid and unchanged and like a faithful friend. On all her home-comings she had always felt this deep satisfaction at the sight of it standing there at the end of the drive, mellow, beautiful and unchanging.

She went up to her bedroom. That, too, was just the same and very little changed from her childhood. She had insisted on keeping the Three Little Pigs curtains and the Miss Muffet rug and the nursery rhyme picture on the wall. Her collection of china animals still stood on the chest-of-drawers, together with the photographs of Barley's predecessor, Honey, and of her old pony, Rocket.

The faded rosettes that she and Rocket had won together at local gymkhanas hung from ribbons on the wall. Her old books were on the shelves: *Rebecca of Sunnybrook Farm*, *The Wind in The Willows*, *Little Women*, *What Katy Did at School*, *The Water Babies*, *The Secret Garden* . . . Everything was in its usual place. Except Eliza. Where was Eliza? She should have been sitting, propped against the cushion, in her corner of the window-seat.

Anne went along to the nursery. She could hear noises coming from behind the closed door – heavy thuds and a whacking sound. She opened the door. A boy of about seven sat astride Poppy, the rocking horse. He had short dark hair that stuck up in an untidy crest and his thin legs dangled from baggy grey shorts. He was jerking at the reins and making Poppy rock so violently that she was jolting across the floor on her wooden stand. And all the time he whacked at her with a stick.

'*Stop that this minute!*'

He turned his head towards her, startled at first and then defiant. And he went on faster and harder. Thud, thud, thud. Whack, whack, *Whack*! Anne could see the weals he had made on poor Poppy's hindquarters. She went over and grabbed hold of the rocking horse's ears, bringing it to such an abrupt stop that the boy fell forward onto its neck.

'Wot yer do that fer?' His small, sharp face was aggrieved and indignant.

'Don't you dare treat my rocking horse like that! Just look at the damage you're doing!'

She snatched the stick from his hand, opened the window and threw it out into the garden.

He looked at her sulkily. 'It's not yer 'orse. It belongs ter the lidy.'

'This is my nursery. Mine and my brother's. I live here.'

'No, yer don't,' he scoffed triumphantly. 'I never seen yer before. There's only the lidy and the toff lives 'ere. That's right, ain't it, Betty?'

'That's right, Fred.'

A small girl, thin and pale as the boy, but a little younger, was sitting on the floor by the nursery fireguard. Her legs were stuck straight out in front of her and on her lap she held a helpless Eliza who was having the clothes wrenched from her cloth body. Her plaits had already been undone and her black hair straggled wildly about her painted face.

'And that,' said Anne, fuming, 'is my doll.'

She rescued Eliza from the child's grasp and gathered up the scattered clothes and the red hair ribbons. Betty began to wail loudly, screwing up her face and drumming her heels on the linoleum.

'She took my dolly! That lidy took my dolly, Fred, and I never done nuffink!'

Anne ignored her and looked, appalled, round the nursery. Nothing, so far as she could see, was in its proper place. Every cupboard door hung open and toys and games had been dragged out and left higgledy-piggledy all over the floor. Kit's precious lead soldiers lay about like battlefield casualties, some with limbs or heads missing. Engines and carriages, railway track and clockwork cars were all jumbled up together. The old Snakes and Ladders board was upside down in a corner with its spine split, and counters, jacks, bricks, pick-up-sticks, playing cards and marbles were scattered all over the room. The front of her doll's house stood open, its contents a shambles. Only the books in the bookcase were undisturbed.

As she stood looking at it all in silence, tears came into her eyes. The girl had stopped wailing and was staring at her, her mouth still open wide, her nose running. The boy watched slyly from the horse. Anne turned and left the room, holding Eliza in her arms. As she closed the door behind her she heard the thud, thud of Poppy being ridden hard once more.

She went into Kit's bedroom and stood by the window, trying to stop the tears. Through them, with watery vision, she saw that the snowdrops were out round the beech trees at the far end of the lawn, showing bravely through the snow. The terrace where she and Kit had sat and talked that night of their dance was just below the window. It was hard to imagine that now . . . that warm summer evening before the war had started, before any of it had begun.

She found a handkerchief, blew her nose hard and wiped her cheeks. She did not know why she minded so very much about the things in the nursery. After all, they were only toys and games that she had not touched for years. Kit would probably not have minded at all. *Come on, you chump, don't make such a fuss . . . Let the little beggars have some fun in their lives for once. We'll never play with any of those things again.* She could hear him saying it as clearly as if he were standing beside her, and maybe he would have been right. She should have felt sorry for Fred and Betty – underprivileged, deprived, torn from their mother and sent to a strange place far away – but instead she hated them for what they had done. They had wrecked something magical that she and Kit had shared. Even if everything were sorted out and mended and restored to its rightful place, the nursery could never be the same again.

She sat down on the window-seat and re-dressed Eliza in her torn clothes and re-plaited her hair carefully, making bows with the red ribbons.

Kit's room, at least, seemed unplundered. His balsa wood aeroplanes were still safely suspended on their strings from the ceiling . . . the Lockheed, the Ryan, the Fokker, the Ford Tri-Motor, the Junkers JU52, the Tiger Moth, which she supposed must be like the one Johnnie Somerville had bragged about owning, and others in perpetual flight whose names she had forgotten. She looked round the room, making an inventory. The model cars were still ranged in their places along the shelves, the blue-bladed Eton Eight oar was on the wall, together with all the Wet Bob trophies: the winning pennants, the boat lists, the calendar with his name as Captain of Boats. She got up and went over to look at them again. Stuck against the wall at the back of the chest-of-drawers, where he had left them, were the leavers' photographs given by Kit's friends at the end of last summer term. She looked along the row of smiling faces – Villiers, Atkinson, Stewart, Latimer and Parker-Smiley. Villiers, Kit's best friend, was in the same regiment and must be in France with him. Atkinson and Stewart were in the army too. Maybe they were in France as well. Latimer was probably in the RAF now – in bombers, Kit had said. She had no idea which of the services little Charlie Parker-Smiley had joined. He was grinning away at her. Funny how good he had been at the waltz.

She could hear her mother calling from downstairs. Tea was ready. As she left she locked the door and took the key with her. Whether Kit would mind or not, while he was away she was going to see to it that his room was safe from Fred and Betty.

When she returned to RAF Colston at the end of her leave, she found that Croesus Squadron had been sent to France. The station was full of strange faces belonging to the replacement squadron and with their new type of fighters. As well as the Hurricanes roaring overhead there were now Spitfires too.

Pearl was mournful. 'Upped and flew away, just like that. All those lovely millionaires gone! Here, your Johnnie left you this note. Gave it to me in the Mess when I was serving his mulligatawny. I went all weak at the knees when he spoke to me.'

'He's *not* my Johnnie, Pearl.'

'More's the pity, dear. You must have a screw loose.'

Anne opened the envelope. The writing paper inside was headed Officers' Mess, RAF Colston. Beneath that Johnnie had scrawled one line: *Dinner when I get back? Johnnie.* She tore the paper up and threw the pieces away.

Seven

The snow melted away at last leaving a messy legacy of slush and mud. It was still cold but the days gradually grew longer and brighter and the sun shone with a forgotten warmth. Buds began to show on the branches and new grass to spring up on the station lawns.

The remainder of the WAAF uniform and equipment arrived – with the exception of greatcoats, but with spring so near this seemed less important. Far more disappointing was the fact that so few of the garments seemed to fit properly. The airforce blue tunics and skirts were either large, medium or small and their felt-like material wasn't a patch on Susan's privately-tailored uniform. The clumping black lace-up shoes did not come in half sizes and produced blisters, and other clothing issued – more *blackout* bloomers, knicker linings, thick grey stockings, vests, bright pink brassières and suspender belts and striped pyjamas – were greeted with wails of horror. The kitbags, intended to hold it all, were so heavy when loaded up that they could scarcely lift them off the floor let alone swing them over their shoulders as the men did. Vera succeeded after several tries but fell clean over backwards as she did so and lay on the floor, giggling helplessly. As for the caps with their over-risen piecrust crowns and shiny black visors that jutted out like a bird's beak, hardly anybody liked them.

Winnie, though, felt thrilled when she first put on her uniform. She adjusted the tunic belt by its brass buckle, fingered the four patch pockets and the shiny buttons and patted the puffy crown of her cap. Gloria was standing on a chair, trying to see herself in the mirror hanging on the inside of her locker door. Winnie had no idea what she herself looked like but she didn't care all that much. It was enough to have a proper uniform at last. She twisted her head to see the patch she had sewn onto her left shoulder – the RAF eagle with wings outstretched and the A for Auxiliary beneath.

Corporal White inspected them. 'Caps on straight, buttons and shoes shining, ties well tied, stockings straight . . . that's how it should always be. I said caps on *straight*, Gibbs, not on the back of your head like that. Potter, your hair must be off your collar at the back. Carter, there's no need to pull your belt in as tight as that.'

They paraded for the station commander. Palmer found this irksome in the extreme. He should have been pleased that the WAAFS had uniform at last but he still could not rid himself of the idea that it was unwomanly and the sight of them lined up before him in their new blue offended his eyes. The airwomen's version, he saw morosely, was even uglier than their officer's. God, what a horrible hat . . . and those shoes . . . He inspected them grimly, striding along the rows with his newly-promoted WAAF officer a pace or two behind him. It was Section Officer Newman now. She had been away on some administration course and, from the brief look he had given her, he thought she seemed a lot more confident. Rather different from the nervous girl who had stood in front of him on the day she had arrived.

He went down another row. Their numbers had swelled alarmingly since that time. More and more of them kept arriving and he had long ago resigned himself to the fact that they were here to stay. Another row. Christ, they were all shapes and sizes, sticking out here and there . . . it must be impossible to dress ranks . . . From time to time he paused, merciless in his fault-finding.

'Those buttons aren't up to scratch, airwoman. That tie is badly tied. Those shoes won't do.'

Some of them quailed visibly at his approach and he was not displeased. He wanted them to be frightened of him, or at least, have a very healthy respect. That way, they'd behave themselves. He stopped in front of a peroxide blond who eyed him back boldly.

'Am I supposed to be inspecting you, airwoman, or are you inspecting me?'

She still returned his stare. 'You're inspecting us, sir.'

'Then keep your eyes straight ahead. And put your cap on properly in future. And don't belt that tunic so tightly. You're supposed to be wearing a service uniform, not a fashion garment.' He moved on briskly.

'Those SD clerks seem to think they're a cut above the rest of us,' Maureen said with a sniff. She looked down the Mess table at the small group of WAAFS sitting together at the far end. 'Anyone would think we'd got some sort of infectious disease, the way they keep to themselves. I don't see why they should be in quarters while the rest of us are out in huts. What's so special about them, I'd like to know.'

'They're *Special* Duties, aren't they?' Pearl snapped. 'It's all hush-hush. No use your looking sour about it, Maureen. It's not their fault.'

'Well, why should they get off drill? I don't see what's to stop them doing that – like all of us have to do.'

'Same reason as they've been put in separate quarters – they work in watches round the clock. They can't fit in with us and if they put us all in the same huts we'd be waking each other up all the time. You're just jealous, that's your trouble.'

'They plot things on a big map in the Ops Room,' Sandra said brightly. 'That's what I've heard, anyhow.'

Maureen cast another resentful glance down the table. 'If that's all they do, it's nothing so wonderful. It doesn't make them any better than us and there's no call for them to be so snooty.'

Vera sighed. 'But it s-sounds ever so exciting. I wish I could do something like that. All secret and important.'

Susan said: 'Actually, I'm thinking of asking to be re-mustered to Special Duties myself.'

'You *would*, Duchess.'

'There's no need to be offensive, Pearl. I happen to believe that I'm capable of doing more than just cut up cabbages.'

'What makes you think that?'

Anne only half heard the bickering. She was reading a letter from Kit under the table.

We've been on the move again recently and are billeted in the local cinema at the moment. It's full of bugs and stinks of garlic. Bit of a come-down from the last place where we lived like kings. We seem to exist on a diet of corned beef, tinned salmon and sardines here, though Villiers and I, and some of the other chaps, managed to have a pretty good meal in a café the other night – steak and chips and masses of vin ordinaire, which cheered us up no end. The weather's foul! The snow's all gone but it's wet and bloody cold. And the countryside round here's the dullest I've ever seen. Not a patch on dear old Bucks. No sign of any Jerries yet. Altogether, life's a bit grim and dull at the mo. I hope we'll be on the move again soon – out of this hellish place. Villiers sends his best. Have you come across old Latimer yet? Hope you're behaving yourself. Love, Kit.

She folded the letter up and put it away in her skirt pocket. Susan was leaving the table huffily and Maureen was still glaring at the SD clerks, or plotters, or whatever they were. For once she rather agreed with Maureen. Some of them *did* behave pretty snootily and Susan would get on like a house on fire with them. But not all. That tall, gawky girl, for instance – the one who had asked her the way the other day – seemed quite the opposite. She was sitting there now with the rest of them, eating her meal quietly, and looking rather out of things. As Anne watched, she somehow managed to knock her fork off her plate onto the floor. She bent down to retrieve it, red in the face, and went even redder when she caught Anne's eye. Anne smiled and waved.

Virginia gave an embarrassed little wave in return. She recognized the girl at the other end of the table as the one who had come to her rescue when she had got herself thoroughly lost. She looked friendly – unlike the dark-haired one next to her who had been staring in such an angry way. She was uncomfortably aware that a lot of the other WAAFS thought they were a stand-offish group. The trouble was that they had been separated from the moment they had arrived at RAF Colston. The ten of them had been put into former sergeants' married quarters, away from the rest, and it had made for some bad feeling. Only two shared a bedroom and they had their own sitting-room, kitchen and bathroom. Pamela, who shared a room with her, came from London and her family lived in Kensington. She had been a débutante and talked a lot about the dances she had been to and of places like Ascot and Henley that Virginia had only read about. It was obvious after a few days that Pamela would much sooner have been sharing with one of the others who did know all about such things.

Her first encounter with a real Ops Room had been a bit of a disappointment. She had expected a tense atmosphere, a sense of drama, or, at the very least, some feeling of importance and urgency. Instead, it had all been very casual. The Controller up on the dais had been smoking and chatting with Ops B beside him, and the airmen standing round the plotting table had been doing nothing much at all. Some of them were looking bored. She had actually seen one yawning.

And nobody had been particularly pleased to see them. A few of the men had seemed amused by the novelty, but the majority had reacted coolly.

'Look at it this way,' one of them had told Virginia, not unkindly. 'If they sent *you* here, then that means they're going to pack *us* off somewhere else. Well, a lot of us are local lads, or we've got settled down here. We've got families nearby and we don't want to leave them. No offence, but we'd sooner you hadn't come. And how you girls'll ever stand up to the night watches beats me . . .'

They had been told brusquely to put on headphones and to listen to the men and watch them. Instead of the magnetic-tipped rakes they had used in training, they were of plain wood and the trick of moving china arrows with them, instead of the tin ones, had to be mastered quickly. There were other differences, too. They had made mistakes, so that the men either crowed or criticized. At first there had been very little work for them to do. Even so, it was tiring. They worked in a five-watch rota and the night watch was unbearably tedious, as well as the longest. Twice as long. It was hard to stay awake from midnight until eight the next morning in an uneventful Ops Room where the silence was broken only by the ticking of the big clock on the wall or the occasional phone call to test the lines. The officers up on the dais dozed while the plotters sat huddled in blankets, fortified in their break by sandwiches and half-cold cocoa from an enamel bucket. Sometimes, when the Controller turned a blind and indulgent eye, they played a game with pennies to relieve the boredom, tossing them onto the table map and trying to get them in the centre of a square. On all watches they were allowed to pass slack periods knitting or sewing at their posts.

Virginia had begun a diary, recording each day, though at the moment there wasn't much to write down. Twice a week she wrote to her mother and she found these letters very hard to compose. She couldn't write about her work and she didn't think her mother would be in the least interested in hearing details of service life. She wrote a little about Pamela because the house in Kensington and the grand dances would be sure to please her; and she wrote about the netball games they played against teams of other WAAFS because that sounded all right too; and she wrote about Domestic Nights, station concerts, and about lectures, so long as the subject was suitable.

It was impossible to imagine what her mother would have thought about the lectures they had been given at the beginning on personal hygiene and dreadful, unmentionable diseases.

Mother's letters had been full of complaints. The rationing was ridiculous, the shopkeepers insolent, the blackout more dangerous than any bombs would be, the ARP wardens over-familiar and interfering and, worst of all, the house opposite had been taken over by the ATS who drilled up and down the road, making a disgraceful amount of noise. *And such common-looking girls! I can only hope those in the Women's Air Force are a better class. I wish you had joined the WRNS, if you had to join anything at all, though I shall never understand why you were so determined to go off and leave me, without any consideration for how I might feel. It seems to me that you are becoming more and more like your father. The girl you are sharing a room with sounds to be from a good background, so I suppose that is something to be thankful for, at least. Perhaps you could bring her home to tea one day.*

But that was one thing that she would never do – even if Pamela were ever willing, which she doubted very much. She had never forgotten the lesson of Molly. Molly used to sit next to her in class at the High School and she had once invited her home for tea. Mother had gone to a great deal of trouble for the occasion – setting the table with a lace cloth and matching napkins, with the best china and little silver cake forks beside their plates. She had made cucumber sandwiches and a sponge cake, served on paper doilies on the silver cake stand. Molly had wolfed down the tiny sandwiches in one gulp each. She had not used her cake fork and she had spilled crumbs all over the lace cloth. The tea had been one of the most painful experiences that Virginia could remember. Molly had obviously thought it all both strange and very funny. At school next morning, when Virginia had entered the classroom unnoticed, she had found Molly loudly describing the tea to the other girls – the dainty sandwiches, the doilies, the cake forks – and giving an excruciating imitation of her mother to a sniggering audience. At home, her mother had criticized everything about Molly – her lack of table manners and polite conversation, her slovenly deportment, her common accent . . . Pamela would not be criticized for her table manners or her accent, but she would probably find Mother just as much of a joke.

No, she would never ask anyone home again.

The table in the scullery was covered by a mound of dead rabbits. Eyes glazed, fur dull, their forelegs protruded stiffly at all angles, like guns poking from a turret. There was a sickly smell in the air and the buzz of flies.

Anne looked at the pile in revulsion. A fly was crawling slowly and disgustingly over an open eye, another across a patch of blood-matted fur. Enid had hurried over to the sink where she was now making retching noises. Anne went in search of Corporal Fowler.

'What are we supposed to do with all those rabbits?'

'Skin 'em and gut 'em, that's wot yer s'posed ter do. Wot the 'ell did yer think they was put in there fer? I can't cook 'em with their bloody fur on, can I?'

'We can't possibly skin them, or gut them. We haven't the first idea how to. And Potter has already been sick.'

'Too bad. She'll just 'ave ter get used to it. I want all them rabbits ready to cook in a couple of hours.'

'Well, you won't get them.'

'You refusin' to obey an order?'

'I'm saying that we can't possibly do it.'

'Then *I'm* sayin' I'll 'ave you on a charge, Cunningham. This time you've 'ad it.'

* * *

Section Officer Newman wore a weary expression as Anne was marched, capless, into her office; she looked up at her more in sorrow than in anger this time. Anne kept her eyes fixed on the wall during the proceedings. Inwardly she seethed at the injustice and at the whole silly business of it all – a stupid courtroom drama over some rabbits . . .

Section Officer Newman tapped her Conduct Sheet on her desk. 'You don't seem to have learned any sense at all in the time you have been here, Cunningham. You break rule after rule and now, on this last occasion, you actually disobeyed an order, which you have admitted. That's an extremely serious offence.'

'I still don't think we should have been asked to skin and gut the rabbits, ma'am. It wasn't fair.' Beside her, she heard Sergeant Beaty draw an angry breath. She went on defiantly. 'There was a huge pile of them and it was a horrible job. Corporal Fowler gave it to us on purpose. He knew it would make us sick.'

'He gave it to you because it was your job, Cunningham. Skinning and cleaning game may not be very pleasant, I agree, but it's all part of kitchen work. If we all refused to do something just because we didn't fancy it there would soon be anarchy.'

'We had no idea how to do the job, in any case, ma'am.'

'That's absolutely no excuse, and no defence. Corporal Fowler has told us that he would have shown you and you would have learned something. There's no excuse at all for *any* of your misdemeanours over the past months. One week confined to camp and extra duties. Sergeant Beaty, you will assign punishment fatigues, please. Dismissed.'

Later, to Anne's surprise, she sent for her again, on her own. Her tone was quite different.

'Sit down, Cunningham, I want to talk to you. As I have told you before, I believe you're capable of far more demanding and responsible work than you are presently doing. Perhaps, if you are given it, you may turn over a new leaf. Squadron Leader Signals has asked for three WAAFS to train as radio-telephony operators in the Ops Room. I'm proposing to put you forward as one of them.'

Anne was taken aback. 'Thank you, ma'am.'

'You would be replacing the men, once they'd trained you, and you'd be the first WAAFS to do the job. You would also be reclassified as aircraftwoman first class, so there would be a pay increase too. I have to tell you that there's some doubt about our suitability for the job. They're afraid the pilots may lack confidence in a woman's voice, and they wonder if we'll get the technical terms right. I'm counting on you to show them they're wrong.'

'Yes, ma'am.'

Section Officer Newman smiled her nice smile. She really was pretty decent . . .

'Good. But please understand there will be no room for slackness or fooling around, or for disobedience of any kind. You will be concerned with men's safety, and with their lives, not what they eat for lunch.'

'Yes, ma'am.'

'Very well, that's all.'

'Thank you, ma'am.'

'And Cunningham —'

'Ma'am?'

'I've taken a chance on you . . . stuck my neck out . . . don't let me down.'

The Radio-Telephony cabins were at the back of the Ops Room – small, stuffy cells in which two operators worked side by side. Anne's partner and instructor was a leading aircraftman nicknamed Lofty because he was so short. He fitted the headphones over her ears and showed her how to tune in on the RT set and how to move the lever to transmit. He indicated the upright mouthpiece in front of her that looked rather like an old-fashioned telephone.

'You speak into this, see. Very clearly. You'll soon get

226

the 'ang of it. Just remember to write every word down in the log, and you can't go wrong.'

At first she found it very hard to understand the crackling, staccato voices coming into the headphones from miles away up in the skies. And the exaggerated way she was supposed to speak sounded silly: *Niner* for nine, *fife* for five, *foah* for four.

'It's so there's no misunderstandin', see,' Lofty informed her. 'Nine and five, f'r instance, can sound just the same over the RT. You gotta talk like a toff with an 'ot plum in 'is mouth, so's they get it.'

The first time she said anything over the set there was a moment's stunned silence from the Spitfire wanting a course for base.

'Christ, a popsy! Or are my ears deceiving me? What the bloody hell's going on down there? Over.'

She repeated her message primly. 'Hallo Beetle Blue Two. Steer zero-two-zero. Over.'

The pilot's laughter hooted in her ears. 'I say, bang on! What's your name? And what are you doing for dinner tonight? Over.'

Father had been right. The Germans had done more or less exactly as he had predicted. Felicity got up from her desk to open the window. It was a beautiful May morning and the birds were singing their hearts out. The only warlike sounds came from out on the 'drome, in the distance, where the new concrete runway was being built, long enough to take bombers, if necessary. She watched two flight lieutenants stroll past, chatting together as though they hadn't a care in the world . . . as though none of the terrible events of the past month had happened, as though there was nothing to worry about. They were laughing at some joke as they turned the corner out of sight.

It was hard to believe, on such a lovely morning, that things could be so bad: first Norway and Denmark invaded by the Germans, then Belgium and Holland, and then the Germans breaking through the Ardennes and storming their way in tanks across France, driving the French and British troops back towards the coast. Rotterdam had been bombed flat and heaven only knew what sort of carnage was taking place at this moment on the other side of the Channel. Nobody seemed to know what was happening to the RAF squadrons over there, in the thick of it all.

George nudged her with his nose. He was looking up at her uneasily and gave an anxious whine. She bent to stroke his head.

'Do you realize what's happening, Pearl? The whole of the British Expeditionary Force is trapped on the coast, completely surrounded by the Germans . . . and Kit's with them.'

'Steady on, Anne, love. They say the Navy are going to try and get them off the beaches and bring them home. Kit'll be all right. He's with that posh regiment and they'll know what to do.'

'But there must be *thousands* of them. They'll never manage to get them all back.'

'Keep your pecker up, duckie. Never say die.'

'Oh, Pearl, if anything happens to him – '

'Don't even think about it. It won't. Come on, let's go and cheer ourselves up with a cup of NAAFI nectar.'

Winnie found Enid sitting crying on her bed.

'The Germans are going to invade us, Winnie. They're going to bomb us all to bits now they can fly over from France, and then they're going to invade us.'

'No, they're not, Enid. They're not goin' to do any such thing. Lots of our soldiers have got back, haven't you heard? Hundreds of ships went over to fetch them. We've still got an army to defend us. And the Navy. And the RAF.'

'But I heard some of the men talking and they said we're finished. Had our chips, that's what they said. All our tanks and guns and things have got left behind in

France, and we've lost ever so many 'planes. We've got nothing left to fight with.'

'Yes, we have. They'll soon make more guns and tanks in the factories, and we've still got plenty of 'planes over here.'

'But the Germans have got lots more than us – I heard those men saying so.'

'Well, they shouldn't be sayin' such things, Enid, and you shouldn't listen to them. They don't know what they're talkin' about. Besides, we've got Mr Churchill lookin' after things now and he won't let the Germans invade. He says we're going to fight and we'll never surrender.'

Enid had stopped crying. She sniffed.

'Oh, *him*,' she said. 'What can *he* do about it?'

Churchill's voice on the wireless was grave. *'The news from France is very bad and I grieve for the gallant French people who have fallen into this terrible misfortune . . . We have become the sole champions now in arms to defend the world cause. We shall do our best to be worthy of this high honour.'*

'Cor,' said Gloria, filing her nails. 'That's torn it! Just us left alone against the bloody Jerries. Some honour!'

Vera's eyes were shining. 'We shall stand alone and defend our beloved country t-to the death!'

'Speak for yourself. I'm not bloody getting killed if I can 'elp it.'

'You know what'll happen to us WAAFS if the Germans do invade England, d-don't you, Gloria? One of the erks told me. We'll all be raped by ten s-storm troopers!'

'Only ten? What a shame! Just think of that, Maureen . . . something for you to look forward to. You'll be 'aving the bloody time of your life.'

Winnie was sitting in a corner of the WAAF recreation room, struggling with her knitting. She was halfway through a scarf and somehow it looked all wrong. The edges had gone wavy and a hole had suddenly appeared in the very middle. She had begun with thirty stitches and now for some mysterious reason she had thirty-six. She had stopped knitting to listen to Mr Churchill speaking and then she had listened with half an ear to Vera talking about what the airman had told her and Gloria teasing Maureen, while she re-counted the stitches. There were plenty of horror stories like that circulating and anyone could see that things were serious. The army had sent extra men to help guard the station and there were guns everywhere. Almost every day there was a parachutist scare and one of the soldiers had shot some poor sheep dead in mistake for a German. Lots more trenches had been dug and there were roadblocks on all the roads outside the gates. The last time she had been on the bus into town she had seen the concrete pillboxes, and things dotted all over the fields to stop enemy gliders landing – wrecked motor cars, old farm machinery and carts, kitchen ranges, prams and bedsteads . . . all sorts like that. The woman sitting next to her had said that every single signpost had been taken down, all over England, so the Germans couldn't use them to find their way.

Ken had written to tell her that he had joined something called the Local Defence Volunteers. He'd sounded very excited. Mr Eden had broadcast about it on the wireless, he'd said, and that same day every man left in Elmbury had gone straight to volunteer, even old Ebenezer Stannard who must be near ninety. They'd been given armbands and tin hats and they drilled every week on Friday nights in the village hall. They didn't have rifles yet, only some twelve bores and pitchforks and Colonel Foster's punt gun. Some of them drilled with knives tied on the end of broomstick handles – just 'til they got the real thing.

She wasn't frightened for herself, no matter what stories the airmen told, but she was frightened for Ken, and for Mum and Dad, and Gran and Ruth and Laura. They were all in danger too. Ken could get himself shot, trying to be brave with all those old men. And Dad was as much of a worry as the Germans. On the day when war had been declared and they'd been working out in the barn, just the two of them, he'd sworn that if ever the Germans invaded England he'd take his shotgun and shoot the whole family. *You'd be better off dead, you women, if the Germans ever got you.* She had not known whether or not to take him seriously but before she had left home she had taken all the spare cartridges she could find and buried them.

She made it thirty-five stitches this time, and that looked like it might be another hole there . . . How ever did Maureen manage to knit so fast without even looking at her needles? It was hopeless. The only thing to do was unravel all the rows back to past the big hole and try again.

They'd switched off the wireless now and Gloria had wound up the gramophone and was putting on a record. It was *Ramona* yet again – she nearly always picked that one, which drove Maureen mad.

Anne had just come into the room. She looked different these days somehow . . . more serious, and she didn't lark about nearly as much. She'd been so worried about her twin brother who'd been trapped with all the troops in France. Once she'd heard Anne crying very quietly at night. His name was Kit, short for Christopher, and Anne kept a beautiful, framed photograph of him in her locker. He looked a lot like her, with the same eyes and smile, and very handsome. The whole hut had been worried about him, but then the news had come through at last that he was safe in a hospital near Dover. Wounded, but alive. Everyone had been relieved and happy for her.

Winnie pulled at the wool, unravelling the scarf back to near the beginning, then she picked up the stitches and counted them carefully again. This time there were thirty, so that was all right. She started again doggedly with a row of plain. Gloria had put *Ramona* on another time and was dancing round the room, ignoring Maureen who was complaining from her corner. Anne and Vera had begun a game of ping pong and some of the others were laughing at a cartoon in a magazine . . . You'd never guess, to look at them all, that things were so bad.

Eight

As July followed June it seemed to Virginia that the whole of England was holding its breath, and waiting. Invasion was expected at any time. Rumours spread and multiplied. The bodies of hundreds of dead German soldiers were said to have been found floating in the Channel; Hitler had a new secret weapon that could annihilate the whole population; the King and Queen were fleeing to Canada; German spies were everywhere, and enemy parachutists had already landed in Cornwall.

In the Ops Room the plotters' knitting had long since been put away and the atmosphere was electrically tense. The enemy attacks on Channel shipping and convoys were increasing and hostile plots swarmed across the map, advancing from northern France where the Luftwaffe had now taken over the French aerodromes. As Colston fighters scrambled to attack, the voices of their pilots could be heard in the Ops Room over the R/T loudspeaker.

'Hallo Beehive, this is Nutmeg leader calling . . .'

The controller's response was always calm. 'Hallo, Nutmeg leader. Vector one-five-zero. Twenty plus bandits are approaching you from the east, angels one-eight. Over.'

Staccato exchanges between the pilots crackled over the loudspeaker as they searched for the enemy aircraft, until the jubilant cry of *Tally ho*! The confused sounds of the ensuing battle were relayed into the Ops Room with harrowing clarity – the stutter of guns, the shouts of triumph, the swearing and cursing, the cries of warning . . .

'Look out behind you, Red Two! *On your tail!*'

'Break *right*, Mike! OK, I've got him . . . break *quick*! He's right behind you . . .'

'Well done, Red Four. Climb. I'm up here.'

'He's going down . . . I can see smoke . . .'

'Red Two to Red Leader. I've been hit . . . on fire . . .'

'Red Leader to Red Two. Bail out! *Bail out, you clot!*'

Faces round the plotting table, beneath the bright lights, remained expressionless. Rakes pushed markers coolly across the map.

Red Two parachuted into the Channel and was picked up by lifeboat. But two of the other pilots on that sortie did not return.

Virginia had noticed that the WAAF who had waved across to her in the mess hut was now working in the R/T cabins. Once or twice they bumped into each other and exchanged a few words. She wished she had been sharing a room with someone like her and not like Pamela with her casual condescension. As well as the house in London, Pamela's family owned a huge one in Yorkshire. She had shown Virginia a photograph of a mansion set in parkland that had belonged to them for more than two hundred years. The most disconcerting thing to Virginia was that Pamela did not seem to see anything remarkable in her background. All her friends, apparently, lived in similar houses all over England, and their families had owned them for just as long. She talked of them in her offhand way. By some strange process they all appeared to know each other. Pamela had known most of the pilots in Croesus Squadron because they had been her kind and she had been quite put out when they had been posted away to France so soon after her arrival. She had gone out several times with one of them called Johnnie who had been the most handsome man Virginia had ever seen. He had a very expensive-looking green sports car that Pamela had scarcely seemed to notice, perhaps because she was used to travelling in such cars all her life.

Instead of going into town in her off-watch hours, as

many of the WAAFS did, Virginia sometimes borrowed a bike from one of the airmen and rode round the countryside alone. It cost nothing and she liked the freedom and solitude. On a hot July day she set off southwards in the direction of the coast, following a narrow lane that ran between fields of ripening corn. After a few miles she stopped to take off her cap and tunic. It was against regulations but she was too hot to care and there was nobody about. She had leaned the bike against a field gate and stayed there for a while, leaning over it and listening to the larks and watching small puffs of cloud drift across the sky. A squadron of Spitfires swept in suddenly from the direction of the sea. She had seen them take off earlier and counted them out; now she counted them back to make sure that they had all returned safely. The fighters passed directly over her head, drowning the birdsong, and circled above the aerodrome before going in to land. She heard the distant putter of their engines as they taxied on the ground.

She stayed there for a while longer in peaceful contemplation of the scene and then wheeled the bike out onto the road again. She was about to remount when another bicycle came speeding round the corner very fast and on the wrong side. It was ridden by a young man in army uniform. He wore a forage cap tilted on the side of his head and carried his khaki battledress tunic slung over one shoulder, with his shirtsleeves rolled above the elbow. He swerved violently to avoid her and skidded to a halt.

'Gee, I'm sorry! I didn't figure anybody else was around. Guess I forgot to keep left. I'm real sorry.'

Virginia went red and lowered her head. 'That's all right.'

'It sure is a beautiful day,' he went on. 'And I always thought it rained all the time in England.'

He sounded American, or something like that, which was odd because he was in uniform. Virginia hesitated. She did not want to seem rude to a foreigner.

'It's been a very nice summer so far. Are you from America?'

He smiled at her. 'I'm from Canada. You folks always mix us up. There's a whole bunch of us camped about five miles over there. We came over here a couple of weeks back. My first visit to the Old Country, and this is the first chance I've had to take a look round. The name's Neil. Neil Mackenzie.'

He stood astride the bike, holding out his hand. He was quite tall, with sandy hair and freckles. His name was Scottish and he looked like a Scot. It seemed all wrong to her that he spoke with that twangy accent.

She took his hand and shook it stiffly. 'How do you do.'

He looked away from her across the cornfields towards the aerodrome where another aircraft had just taken off and was climbing into the sky. 'Is that RAF Colston over there?'

He was in uniform – more or less – but you couldn't be too careful these days. All those rumours . . .

'It's OK,' he said easily, noticing her wary expression. 'I'm no spy. You don't need to worry about that.'

She began to put on her cap and tunic, fumbling hurriedly with the belt. 'Excuse me, but I really ought to be going . . .'

'Gee, that's too bad.'

'Well, I hope you enjoy yourself.'

He laughed. 'I guess we're not over here to enjoy ourselves.'

'I meant your bike ride . . .'

'Well, I'd enjoy that a lot more if I had some company. Do you mind if I come along with you? For one thing I don't know where the heck I'm going. There're no signs.'

'I'm sorry . . .'

She was wheeling her bike down the lane now, hopping along with one foot on the pedal, gathering momentum to swing her leg over the cross-bar. It was an awkward

236

manoeuvre in a skirt and embarrassing that he would be watching. She glanced back quickly and he was looking so crestfallen that she slowed and stopped. He was a stranger in a strange land, after all, a long way from home, and he had come all this way to help fight the war. It would be ungracious and unkind just to leave him there.

'Well, I'm going this way – towards the coast – if you want to come . . .'

His face lit up and he kicked the pedal forward. 'Any place'll do. Just lead on.'

He kept pace beside her, zig-zagging from one side of the lane to the other as she pedalled along sedately. She regretted weakening almost at once. His presence was an intrusion and flustered her. She did not want him there, steering his bike nonchalantly with one hand, his tunic hooked over his shoulder from the other, whistling snatches from some song. Her skirt kept riding up high above her knees and she had to keep tugging it down.

He zig-zagged widely again and swooped alongside her. 'You didn't tell me your name.'

'It's Virginia Stratton,' she said reluctantly.

'That's a nice name. It's got a good sound to it. And you're in the Women's Air Force – right? That uniform's like the RAF.'

'Yes.'

'And you come from Colston?'

She nodded.

'What do you do there? What sort of work?'

'I'm afraid we're not allowed to talk about it.'

'Sorry. I shouldn't have asked. I was just curious, that's all. I've never met any girls in the services. You been in the Air Force long?'

'About seven months.'

'Like it?'

'It's very interesting.'

'Wish I could say the same for us. As soon as we get over here everythin' stops and we're sittin' around doin' nothin' much. Some of the guys at the camp were in

237

France . . . I'm real sorry I missed that. But I guess our chance'll come . . .'

The lane wound on through the fields until it reached the main road. Virginia stopped.

'This is the road to Bognor.'

He nodded. 'Yeah, we've been through there a coupla times. I remember. Let's go take a look at the ocean. Maybe we'd cool off a bit.'

'You won't be able to go on the beach. There's barbed wire . . .'

'I know. Never mind. We can peek through it and imagine ourselves paddlin'.'

He grinned at her but she looked away.

They went into Bognor Regis and rode along the sea front. Although it was high summer and the Channel glittered enticingly blue beneath the hot sun there were no holidaymakers to be seen. Barbed wire stretched in fat coils for the length of the deserted beach and the promenade was empty except for a woman walking her dog and an old man leaning on his stick and gazing intently out to sea, one hand shading his eyes, as though he expected to sight Germans on the horizon at any moment. They found a bench to sit on.

He stood over her, blocking the sun. 'There's some kinda little store over there – like somethin' to drink?'

'No, thank you . . . really.'

'Aw, come on, now . . .'

He went away and returned with two bottles, straws stuck in their necks. 'Here you are. Root beers. Ginger beer you call it. 'Fraid they're not cold, though.'

'It's awfully kind of you. You shouldn't have bothered.'

He sat down beside her. 'Why not? I had a real thirst and I figured you must have one too – even though you wouldn't say so.'

He drank straight from the bottle, without the straw, and then leaned back, resting it on his knee and shutting his eyes against the glare. She sucked the warm ginger beer through her straw and looked at him covertly. He had put on his battledress tunic and now she could see the Canada flash on his shoulder and a corporal's tape on his arm. She did not know quite how to place him; he wasn't like any of the RAF corporals she'd come across at Colston. He kept his eyes closed for so long that she wondered if he had fallen asleep and was debating whether it would be very rude to slip away and leave him there, when he suddenly opened them again and sat up.

'What part of England do you come from, Virginia? Where's your home town?'

'I live in south London,' she said guardedly. 'In a suburb called Wimbledon. I don't suppose you've heard of it.'

'Sure I have. They play those tennis championships there, don't they? I've heard about those. Never played it myself, though. Hockey's my game. Ice in winter, field in summer. Great game . . . Played some lacrosse too, and some rugby. Done a bit of boxin' as well.'

'Really?' she said politely. 'Where do you live in Canada?'

'Place called Hamilton. You ever heard of it?'

She shook her head. 'I'm afraid not.'

'It's not too far from Toronto. I guess maybe fifty miles or so. Kinda like a suburb too. I was born and bred there. Born with skates on my feet, like all the kids.'

She looked puzzled.

'Ice skates,' he explained. 'All of us kids used to live on the ice ponds. Spent all our time there. You ever skated?'

'Only a few times. There are some ponds on Wimbledon Common and sometimes they freeze over in winter if it gets cold enough, and you can skate on them then. It doesn't happen all that often though.'

'Gee, your winters can't be anythin' like as cold as ours. Our ponds're frozen hard pretty much all through 'til spring. We get a whole lot've snow too. Then we make rinks in our backyards.'

'Do you really?' She had no idea what he was talking about.

'Sure. See, we build the snow up into a kinda small wall all round the yard.' He moved his hands in a circle. 'Then we run the hose over it and let the water inside freeze. You do that maybe a coupla times or more and you've got yourself a great place to play shinny.'

'Shinny?'

'Yeah. Foolin' around on skates . . . practisin' hockey . . . stick handlin' the puck . . .' He crooked one elbow high and twisted his arms to and fro. 'Like that. See?'

'I think so.' She understood vaguely what he meant.

'We used to build igloos, too, when we were kids. Like the eskimos. We'd cut blocks out of the snow and make houses with 'em.'

She stared at him. 'It must be awfully cold where you live.'

'Sure is. I guess it's partly 'cos of the lake.'

She thought for a moment. 'Would that be Ontario?'

'Right!' He looked pleased. ''Course it gets good and hot in the summer for a month or so. Then we go sailin'. Swimmin' too. And we play field hockey instead.' He sighed. 'I guess I'm goin' to miss it all a bit . . . Still, it's great to see the Old Country at last.'

'I expect you came from Scotland originally. Your family, I mean.'

'Right again.' He smiled at her. 'Where else with a name like mine? My Dad's folks emigrated from Dundee way back in the last century. Mum's were English, though. They came from a place called Swineshead in Lincolnshire. Great name, that. I'd sure like to get to see both places if I get the chance while I'm here. You know them?'

'I'm afraid not. I haven't seen very much of England myself. And I've never been to Scotland.'

The only travelling she had done with Mother had been to visit a great-aunt in Bexhill-on-Sea who lived alone in a gloomy house that smelled of mothballs.

'Well, I guess I haven't seen a whole lot of Canada either. Maybe when I get back . . .'

'Do you have brothers and sisters?'

'Sure thing. There's five of us kids. Four boys and a girl. I'm the oldest. If the war goes on another coupla years Andy'll be joinin' me. He's next in line. Like to see a photo of them?'

He unbuttoned the breast pocket of his tunic and passed a crumpled snapshot to her. Virginia looked at the row of smiling children, tallest down to shortest. There was a man and woman standing behind them, smiling too. They were dressed in casual summer clothes and they looked happy and healthy. The Canadian leaned across and pointed them out.

'That's my folks at the back. And that's Sally, the littlest, then Ian, Hugh, Andy and me. It was taken a while back, last summer, so the kids've grown a bit since.'

He was easily recognizable at the end of the line, wearing a plaid shirt open at the neck, with the sleeves rolled up. Though his hair was longer and he looked younger. She handed the snapshot back.

'It's very nice . . . you must miss them.'

'You bet. But they write all the time – even Sal. You should see her letters . . . well, they're mostly drawin's. She draws pretty good for her age. How about you? Any brothers or sisters?'

'No.'

'Gee, that's too bad. Though maybe you like it better that way.'

She had always longed for a brother or sister – someone to talk to, and to share the burden of Mother – but it was not something she could discuss with a perfect stranger. She said nothing. The woman with the dog had disappeared and the old man had given up his vigil and was moving slowly away. She looked at her watch and stood up.

'I'm awfully sorry, but I have to be getting back now.'

He got to his feet as well. 'You haven't finished your root beer.'

'I don't want any more – really. You have it.' She thrust the bottle into his hand.

'I'll ride along with you – if that's OK.'

'I'd sooner you didn't, if you don't mind.'

He shrugged. 'OK, if that's what you want. Sure you'll be all right?'

'Of course.'

'Say, we're havin' a party at the camp Saturday. Will you come? Maybe some of the other Air Force girls, too? We'd pick you up and take you back.'

'I'm afraid I wouldn't be able to. I'll be on watch.'

'Oh. Well maybe another time?'

She backed away towards her bike. 'I don't think so.'

'Maybe we could go out for another bike ride? See some more places round here?'

'I'm rather busy. I don't often get time off.' She tripped over the edge of the kerb and grabbed hold of the handlebars. 'I really must go now, or I'll be late. Thank you for the ginger beer. Goodbye.'

She left him standing there, a bottle in each hand, looking baffled and disappointed.

The language reaching Anne's ears over the R/T was incomprehensible – a garbled collection of sounds that it was impossible to unravel. Lofty snorted in disgust.

'It's them bloody Poles, pardon my French. The ones just arrived. Half of 'em don't speak a word of English. They gabble away to each other in their lingo and keep leavin' their mikes switched on so no-one else can transmit. Blinkin' foreigners!'

Anne listened to a torrent of Polish coming through the air. It was not like any language she had ever heard and after the clipped RAF English it sounded extraordinary. The pilot suddenly broke into singing – a passionate rendering of some Polish song.

'Bloody madmen!' Lofty said.

Anne laughed, amused. The Polish pilots, she discovered later, all spoke some kind of English, including

242

plenty of swear words that they used liberally in the air. They swore in French, too, and, presumably, in Polish. And they sang. Sometimes it was hard to understand their English over the R/T, or for them to understand her. She spoke comically slowly and clearly for their benefit but the answer would often come back, strongly accented:

'Re-peat, plis. Re-peat, plis . . .'

Death no longer shocked in quite the way it had done when the sprog pilot had crashed in flames earlier in the year. Several pilots had been lost defending the convoys and Pearl's Dusty had been among those killed over Dunkirk in May. Pearl had cried a lot for him.

'He was a bloody good bloke,' she had kept saying, wiping away streaming tears. 'A bloody good bloke.'

Most of the original WAAFS had re-mustered to new trades and Pearl was now a parachute packer. She took a huge pride in her work. 'If they have to jump out of the window, I make sure the flipping thing works.'

Anne was sad, but somehow not surprised, to receive a letter from the adjutant of Jimmy's squadron in Kent.

Dear Miss Cunningham, Sergeant Pilot Shaw left instructions that you were to be notified in the event of his death. I am writing, therefore, with great regret to inform you that he was killed in action two days ago . . .

She cried for poor, nice, shy Jimmy who had seemed to know that he would die. He'd been a pretty good bloke too. She went to her locker and found the envelope that he had given her addressed to his mother, with his wings inside. A promise was a promise and must be kept. When she went on leave she would take it to his home in Croydon.

*   *   *

243

George pricked up his ears. He had been lying quietly beside Felicity's desk while she was working on some papers and he suddenly lurched to his feet and cocked his head towards the door. There was a knock and it was flung wide. Speedy stood there, a piece of sticking plaster across his forehead. George scrabbled excitedly for the doorway.

'Steady, old boy . . . down! *Down!*' He smiled at Felicity over the dog's head. 'Well met by daylight, proud Titania.'

'What! Brave flying officer . . .'

'Flight lieutenant, actually.' He came into the room with George still capering around his legs like a puppy, and stuck out his arm to show the two rings on his sleeve.

'Congratulations.'

'Thanks. Bit of a fluke, really. They were getting short of bods. George, skip hence, for heaven's sake! I played Bottom once, you know – under the direction of old Snodders. Paterson minor was Titania, as I recall, and he was nowhere near as pretty as you.'

He leaned across the desk and kissed her cheek. She smiled up at him.

'It's good to see you safe and sound, Speedy.'

'Have you been worrying about me?'

'Naturally, I've been concerned . . . about all of you. We haven't had much news since you went off to France. Just that phone call when you got back . . .'

'Been a bit busy since then, that's the trouble. It's pretty hellish in our little corner at the moment. No peace for the wicked. Up and down the whole day long, smacking Jerry's wrist for trying to sink our ships . . . Actually, I've bagged three of the blighters now – two in France and one into the drink here.'

'Congratulations again.'

He had perched himself on the corner of her desk, in the old way, and was twirling his cap on his finger and looking falsely modest. She thought he also looked exhausted, though his eyes were as bright as they had always been.

'What have you done to your forehead?'

He touched the plaster. 'Oh that . . . Collided with the cockpit the other day when I had to put the kite down in a hurry. I'll tell you all about it over the drink I'm about to buy you. Can't stop long, more's the pity. I managed to wangle a Maggie to flip over to see you and collect old George. I can see he's been in clover – lucky chap!'

George had returned to her side and was panting up at her as if anxious to show that he had not abandoned her. She stretched out her hand to pat him and Speedy caught sight of the new ring on her sleeve.

'I say, what's this? Promotion too?'

'It's Section Officer now, so mind your manners.'

'I can't keep remembering all these different names. Titania will have to do. Come and have that drink with me and I'll tell you all my adventures.'

'I'm actually allowed in the Mess itself now – no more purdah in the Ladies' Room.'

'Station Master changed his mind?'

'About *that*, at least. Pressure of numbers, I think. There are nearly two hundred WAAFS here now, you know.'

'I noticed a fair sprinkling. Haven't I always told you what a jolly good idea they were, Titania? I passed a rather stunning redhead in the corridor just now, on my way in.'

'That would have been Assistant Section Officer Park. She's engaged.'

'I never let that worry me . . . George, stay on guard. We're going to drown our sorrows.'

They walked over to the Officers' Mess in the warm early evening sunshine.

'How's Whitters?' she asked.

'Cracking form. Got himself some new popsie now. Really smitten. He had to take to his brolly the other day. Bagged this 109 and then the Hun's friends went and clobbered him. Matter of fact they travelled down together and landed in the same field. He said they had time for a quiet smoke and a bit of a chat before the local bobby arrived. Turned out this Jerry knew Whitters' eldest sister rather well. He'd met her on some special course at Oxford before the war, apparently. Extraordinary coincidence that . . . Whitters said he was a pretty decent sort of type, actually. He promised to pass on his best regards to big sis when he next saw her. She's in the WRNS, or something.'

'And Dumbo? And Sinbad, and Moses? Are they all right?'

'Fine and dandy. Getting a trifle weary of going once more unto the breach the whole time. Poor old Moses got a bit singed the other day when his kite caught fire, but he hopped out in time. I suppose things will get worse before they get better. Jerry seems to be giving us all his attention now he's got the Frogs out of the way.'

They went into the Mess. In the ante-room Speedy waved greetings at several of those present and flashed a shamelessly dazzling smile at two WAAF officers sitting quietly in a corner. Over their drinks he entertained Felicity with an account of his time in France. Everything had gone swimmingly to begin with, he told her. Five-star accommodation in some château, *haute cuisine*, wine flowing, the odd spot of flying thrown in . . . Then, when the Huns had suddenly got going and started strafing them they had had to move out pretty smartly. It had been tents and corned beef and not much shut-eye after that.

'The fur really started flying, by George! In the end we had to pop off back over the Kanal before they finished us off altogether. That stuck in the old craw a bit, I can tell you, but there we are. We lived to fight another day . . . the next day, in fact. They sent us back over Dunkirk and we were dashing about all over the shop, trying to swat Jerries before they got to the brown jobs on the beaches. That's when I got my brace . . .' Speedy took a thoughtful swallow of his beer. 'Frightful chaos over there, you know . . . lots of fearful black smoke from oil fires so you couldn't see your hand in front of your face, and everyone milling about. Anyway, some blasted Jerry jumped me as I was chasing after a Junkers and winged me. Stopped the engine dead so there was nothing for it but to pancake in Frogland, which is not what I'd planned at all. I picked the nicest-looking field I could find and set her down – rather well, actually, though I say it myself. I missed the cows and stepped out without a scratch, and there was this French girl waiting with a glass of brandy. Jolly thoughtful of her. It went down a treat.'

Felicity laughed. 'Oh, Speedy . . . honestly! What did you do then?'

'Well, I couldn't very well leave the Hurry for the Jerries to nab, so I said to Yvette – that was her name, it turned out – in my best accent: *avez-vous des allumettes, s'il vous plaît?* And she very kindly nipped off and got me some. Luckily there was a good bit of fuel leaking about the kite, and fluid, and so on, and up she went in a trice – *woomph*! Rather sad, really. Still, it was better than the Jerries getting their dirty paws on her.'

'You had to do it, Speedy.'

'Yes . . . Anyway, what with all the commotion – the Guy Fawkes bonfire and the cows charging about in all directions – I thought I'd better make myself scarce and head for home PDQ. Yvette came up trumps again and lent me an old bike. She pointed in the general direction of *la mer* and off I pedalled. The roads were absolutely chock-a-block with all these French people pushing carts and prams and whatnot . . . had to weave in and out of them like an obstacle course.' Speedy turned his head. 'Watch out! Enter the Demon King.'

'What?'

'Don't look now but your favourite man has just come in with old Robbie. I say, it's *Group Captain* now, by the look of things. Promotion all round. You didn't tell me that.'

'Go on with the story, Speedy.'

'Where was I?'

'Bicycling along towards the sea.'

'So I was. Well, I finally got to Dunkirk. It was pretty hairy there – fires raging, buildings bombed to rubble, vehicles abandoned all over the place. I found some navy type who told me everyone was heading for the beach, so off I went again. When I got there it was like the rush hour with everyone queueing up to get on the ships in great long lines . . . I tagged on the end of one behind a lot of army chaps. They were jolly unfriendly.'

'Why?' Felicity asked indignantly.

'Wanted to know where on earth the RAF had been . . . actually they put it a bit stronger than that. Why hadn't we stopped the Huns dropping bombs on them – that sort of thing. I tried to tell them that we'd been up there, above the smoke, doing our little best – and against sticky odds, I might add . . . Whitters, Dumbo and I took on about fifty of the blighters at one point – but I don't think they believed me. We were just discussing it, as it were, when another lot of Stukas came over and we all dived for cover. Bombs raining down, frightful racket . . . made me jolly glad I'd never joined the army. Absolute sitting ducks.'

'It must have been awful, Speedy.'

'It was rather. Anyway, after the dust had settled I happened to see an empty rowing boat bobbing about not far out, so I made a quick dash for it, along with a couple of other chaps. Luckily there were some oars and we took turns in rowing in the general direction of the White Cliffs. The funny thing was that it turned out we were an Englishman, an Irishman and a Scotsman. We told quite a few jokes along those lines to pass the time.'

'You mean you rowed *all* the way across?'

'About halfway, I suppose. Then one of those old Thames barges chuntered by and picked us up. Chap steering called out "any more for the *Skylark*?" Standing room only and a Jerry escort part of the way but he was a rotten shot and we made it all right to Dover. I hopped

248

on a train to London and there I am fast asleep in the first class when along comes a guard who tries to turf me off at the next station – no ticket, see. No money.'

'I can't believe it – how *could* he do such a thing!'

'Well, fortunately, there was this retired admiral in the same compartment. "You'll do nothing of the kind, my man," he says to the guard. "This gallant boy is trying to return to his unit and you should be giving him every assistance." Plain sailing after that. All tickety-boo. When we got to Charing Cross I took the tube out to Elm Park and finally staggered into the Mess, all footsore and weary. There they were – Whitters and the rest of them, lounging about, feet up – and there's me standing there with water running off me, sand in my shoes and seaweed round my neck. And do you know what old Whitters says to me?'

'Something nice, I hope.'

'He says: "Bad luck, old man. You've just missed dinner."'

Felicity burst out laughing. 'I never know whether to believe you or not.'

Speedy pretended to be offended. 'Would I ever lie to you?'

'Probably. But you haven't told me how you hurt your forehead.'

'Ah, thereby hangs another tale. If you're very good and sit still, Titania, I'll tell you. The other day I was screaming along after this 109 . . .'

From where he was sitting, David Palmer could see the two of them talking together and he watched Dutton's hands weaving extravagant patterns in the air, obviously shooting a tremendous line. Section Officer Newman appeared to be falling for every word of it. He drank his whisky and soda reflectively.

Beside him Robbie Robinson said: 'Dutton seems to be living up to his reputation all right.' He sounded amused.

Palmer shifted sideways in his chair, away from the sight of Section Officer Newman laughing at something Dutton had just said.

'I thought Section Officer Newman had more sense.'

'Oh, I think she's got plenty of that. I've never doubted it for a moment.'

'Hum.' Palmer raised his glass again. 'He must be about as hard to shake off as that damned dog of his.'

The squadron leader puffed comfortably at his pipe. 'I imagine Felicity is rather fond of the two of them, but she seems to have them both pretty well under control, from what I've seen.'

'Mmm.' Palmer groped for a cigarette and lit it. 'I still can't get used to having these women here, you know, Robbie. It still goes against the grain with me. I suppose I'm getting too old a leopard to change my spots.'

'Hardly, sir. It's understandable. It's been an added burden for you, having them here – an unknown factor, as it were. But so far I think one can say that it's working out rather well, don't you agree? They're definitely pulling their weight.'

'They seem to do their work well enough, I grant you. I'm not really grumbling so far as that goes. What does concern me, and always has done from the very beginning, is how they'll measure up if this station comes under enemy attack. *When* it does, I should say. It's a virtual certainty now . . . sooner or later. If they panic and have hysterics we're going to be in serious trouble.'

'I don't believe they will, sir.'

'So you told me before. I only hope you're right.'

Dutton and Section Officer Newman were going. He watched as they left the room together and saw the way she turned to smile at him and the way he touched her arm. He thought of the one occasion when he had invited her to a drink in the Mess. Ordered her, might be a better word. It had been soon after he had conceded defeat and allowed WAAF officers into here. He had escorted her over himself and they had entered the ante-room to startled looks and whispered comments. She had asked for a dry sherry and refused the cigarette he had offered her. The conversation had gone stickily, he remembered. He had asked her what part of Norfolk she came from and they had talked about that briefly. She had mentioned that her father was the rector of the parish. Her mother, he knew, was dead.

He had said: 'I'm afraid I've never been to Norfolk. One day I really must try and visit all the places I've never been to in England. I seem to have spent most of my service life in the south, or in France.'

'Have you been in the RAF long, sir?'

'Twenty years.'

It must have seemed like a lifetime to her. In fact, it *was* her lifetime – almost. He preferred not to dwell on that thought.

She had sat upright in the chair, holding her glass stiffly in front of her. He could not recall her smiling, let alone laughing.

She had asked politely: 'Do you miss the flying at all, sir?'

'Very much. As a matter of fact, I still manage to get up now and again – tag along with the chaps and make a nuisance of myself.'

'I'm sure you're not that, sir.'

More careful politeness. Rigid deference to her commanding officer. He knew he had only himself to blame for the fact that she could not relax in his company. He had tried his best to be jovial, to put her at her ease.

'Flying a modern fighter is a young man's job, unfortunately. In my day, of course, we had bi-planes – Camels, Pups, that sort of thing. Much slower than the machines these young men are flying today.'

Young men like Speedy Dutton.

She had gone on being very polite. 'But still needing a lot of skill, surely, sir?'

'I wouldn't say that. The old crates more or less flew themselves. Have you ever been up at all?'

251

'No, sir.'

He had said heartily: 'We'll have to see what we can do about that.'

He had thought of taking her up himself, but so far there had been neither the time nor the chance.

His thoughts switched to Caroline and the last time he had seen her. She had been packing to leave the station, like all the other civilian wives. He had watched as she tossed clothes into the open suitcase on the bed.

'Is it really necessary for you to go back to London, Caroline? It would be perfectly possible to find somewhere reasonably near the station for you to be.'

She had slammed a drawer shut and moved to the wardrobe. 'Don't be ridiculous, David. I've no intention of mouldering away in some damp little cottage miles from anywhere. At least there was *some* sort of life here. Frankly, I think the RAF have a bloody cheek tipping us out.'

'It's a question of your safety, you know that. All aerodromes in the south are prime targets now for the enemy. It would be irresponsible folly to allow women civilians to remain on them.'

She had dragged a green wool costume out and was wrenching it off its hanger.

'What about your WAAFS? Don't they count as women?'

'They're service women, not civilians. Part of the Air Force. They have work to do here.'

She had looked at him over her shoulder as she bundled the costume, anyhow, into the suitcase.

'You've changed your tune a bit, haven't you, darling? A few months ago you couldn't wait to get rid of the lot of them. Now, you're talking as though they were indispensable. You always said they'd have hysterics if someone dropped a bomb anywhere near them.'

'They probably will. But there's nothing I can do about it now. They've taken over a lot of the men's jobs and, with them, the risks as well.'

She had taken a pair of black suede evening shoes from the wardrobe and thrown them on top of the green costume.

'What about your little WAAF, then? Will she be staying too, to keep you company?'

'Who are you talking about?'

Another pair of expensive shoes had followed the black ones — grey glacé kid this time, with bows on the front. 'Don't look so innocent, darling. The WAAF officer who came to dinner here at Christmas . . . the one you lust after.'

He had said coldly: 'If you're referring to Section Officer Newman, yes, she'll be staying.'

'That'll be fun for you, then, David, won't it? With me safely away in London.'

He had controlled his temper. It was pointless to argue. She loved an argument and was much better at it than he. He might well, he reflected now, have pointed out that *she* would undoubtedly have a great deal of fun without him in London, but he hadn't. He had learned over the years that it was far easier to say nothing.

She had snapped the clasps of the suitcase shut and come to stand close to him. The costly French scent that she always wore had filled his nostrils; he hated the smell of it. At thirty-two her skin was flawless, her ash blond hair like silk, her aquamarine eyes brilliant. She was an exceedingly beautiful woman but he had looked at her without desire, or love, or interest.

He had said matter-of-factly: 'I'll come up as soon as I can get away.'

She had given him a tight, dry smile. 'Don't bother yourself, darling. I'm not one of those dreary, clinging service wives. So far as I'm concerned it will be a pleasant change to be away from here. I won't have to be nice to all those RAF bores the whole time. I'll find much more interesting things to do in London.'

'I'm sure you will.'

She had moved forward suddenly and kissed him, her

mouth open against his. He had stood stiffly, without moving, and she had stepped back after a moment and looked at him.

'You're a bloody attractive man, you know, David, but now you've been promoted, I suppose you'll be stuffier than ever.'

'I expect so.'

She had laughed. 'Your little Section Officer is probably madly in love with you, poor thing. Some women like a strong, stern father-figure. They love being ordered about and subjugated. It gives them a thrill.'

He had picked the heavy suitcase off the bed. 'You'll miss your train, Caroline,' he had said.

Palmer put down his empty glass and sighed. Robbie Robinson looked at him.

'You feeling all right, sir? You look a bit under the weather.'

'Just tired.' He signalled the waiter. 'I could do with the other half.'

Lime Avenue was just as Anne had imagined it – a quiet, respectable suburban street, lined with knobbly lime trees. The houses were identical Victorian semi-detacheds with neat little front gardens and brightly-coloured stained-glass panels in the doors. As she walked along the pavement, net curtains twitched and a woman cleaning her windows stopped work to turn and stare. Maybe it was the uniform?

She took Jimmy's envelope from her breast pocket and re-checked the number – thirty-seven. It was further along the road and had one of the neatest gardens. The red tiled path up to the front door looked as though it had been polished and the flanking rows of marigolds had been precisely spaced. She rang the door bell.

The woman who opened the door was also very much as she had imagined. She was small and thin, with tightly permed hair, and was dressed in a plain blouse and skirt. She looked at Anne with dull eyes.

'Yes?'

'Mrs Shaw?'

The woman nodded. The dull eyes seemed to register the Air Force uniform and there was a flicker of some emotion in their depths.

'What do you want?'

The doorstep was not the place to hand her a letter from her dead son; it was not what Jimmy would have had in mind.

'May I come in for a moment? I have something to give you.'

'I suppose so.'

Her voice was as dull as her eyes – flat and uncaring. She led the way into the front room, which felt cold even on the warm summer's day. There had been highly polished linoleum in the narrow hallway and here were the spotless net curtains that Anne had pictured, the starched antimacassars on the armchair backs and, prominently displayed on the sideboard, several framed photographs of Jimmy – ranging from a solemn-faced little boy to one of him in his RAF uniform – without the wings. He was looking straight at her with that earnest expression that she remembered so well. She felt her throat tighten and turned her head away.

Mrs Shaw was standing with her back to the tiled fireplace, her hands clenched together at waist level. She said tonelessly:

'They have already sent me everything that belonged to James.'

James, not Jimmy. His mother was staring at her with her dull eyes and the flicker of emotion, Anne realized now, had been hostility. There was no invitation to sit down. No welcome. No appreciation of the fact that she had come all this way and taken time out of her precious leave. This was going to be much more ghastly than she had expected.

'My name is Anne Cunningham, Mrs Shaw. I'm from RAF Colston where Jimmy – James – was stationed once. I met him there.'

Mrs Shaw's eyes never left her face. 'May I ask, Miss Cunningham, if you were James's girlfriend. He never mentioned you in any of his letters.'

'We were just friends, Mrs Shaw. We used to go to the cinema together sometimes, or to the pub. That's all.'

'James never drank. His father was very strict about that.'

The memory of Jimmy cradling his beer awkwardly in the Saracen's Head and fumbling with cigarettes and matches passed through her mind. There was a pair of men's carpet slippers lined up beside the fireplace with perfect symmetry – the only evidence of Mr Shaw. The room managed to be cold and yet stuffy at the same time, and the silence of the house was oppressive. It was the most depressing place she had ever been in. No wonder Jimmy had escaped as soon as he possibly could. She tried to think of something suitable to say next; something that might comfort this sad woman.

'He always talked a lot about you both, Mrs Shaw, and about his home. It meant a lot to him.'

'I'd sooner not speak of it, if you don't mind. It's a very painful subject.'

'Of course. I'm sorry.'

'You said you had something to give me, Miss Cunningham.'

Anne groped in her tunic pocket for the letter. She held it out. 'James gave me this before he was posted away to France – when he left Colston. He asked me to give it to you personally if – if anything happened to him. I promised him I would.'

There was a moment's silence. At last Mrs Shaw put out her hand and took the envelope. She looked down at it and then up again. Her face was white and set.

'He was very shy with girls. Very reserved. He wouldn't have given you this unless he thought a lot of you.'

It was like an accusation. In some way she was badly at fault in Mrs Shaw's eyes – perhaps because she had not been in love with her son. Or maybe because he might have been in love with her.

'I don't know about that . . . We were good friends, that's all.'

'You must have known all about him being a pilot.'

It was another accusation – full of bitterness.

Anne said apologetically: 'Well, I couldn't really help knowing.'

'Everybody knew, it seems, except *us*. His own parents.'

'He said he kept it from you because he wanted to spare you the worry. He was thinking of you – '

'He discussed that with you?'

'Just a bit.'

'I see. Well, he might as well not have bothered, mightn't he? It was all the same in the end. Worse, because of the shock. I always knew we'd lose him. I knew it all along. It's worse to know he kept things from us, and talked to other people about it.'

Nothing she had said seemed right and yet she had to say something. Keep trying. Jimmy would have wanted her to say consoling things, to comfort his mother.

'I'm terribly sorry about Jimmy, Mrs Shaw – '

'His name was James.'

'James, I mean. He was one of the nicest and kindest people I've ever known. He would never have wanted to hurt you in any way. He asked me to give you that letter because he didn't want you to get it through the post. He wanted to try and explain things, he said . . . about the flying, and not telling you, I think. His wings are inside that envelope too. He told me he took them off his best blue. He wanted you to have them – '

To Anne's horror, Mrs Shaw gave a loud, wild sob – a dreadful animal-like moan that seemed to come from deep inside her. She flung her hands up to her face and collapsed sideways into one of the armchairs.

'Please go! Just go away now and leave me alone. Don't say another word . . . I can't bear it! *Go!*'

Anne looked at her helplessly. She would have liked to have put an arm round her shoulders, but she dared not. She had done far more harm than good in coming here and had somehow made a mess of the whole thing. She tiptoed out of the room and looked back as she closed the door. Jimmy's mother was sitting with her head bowed. She had torn open the envelope, taken out the silk-embroidered RAF wings, and was pressing them against her lips.

'I made a complete hash of it, Kit. Said all the wrong things . . . It was awful!'

'Don't eat your heart out, old girl. It was a pretty tricky assignment, by the sound of it. You did your best.'

Kit was sitting on the window-seat in the nursery, where she had found him when she arrived home. She had flung open the door to see him there, reading a book, one leg crooked up on the cushion, his back leaning against the embrasure, in exactly the way he always used to sit there as a child. It had given her quite a start to see him like that – as though she had suddenly gone back in time. Then he had turned his head towards her and stood up – tall and man-sized – and the illusion had been broken. They had hugged each other, rather clumsily because his wounded arm was still in a sling.

'Wotcha!' he had said, just like he used to do, too, when he had come home for the holidays. 'I nearly didn't recognize you in that uniform. You look frightfully smart and grown-up.'

He was smiling, but she had looked at him with a sinking heart. He was so pale and drawn. And the light seemed to have gone from his eyes: they were as dead as Mrs Shaw's. And yet Ma had said that he had made a good recovery. The arm had been in a pretty bad mess but it had mended well. They had just sent him home for the final part of his convalescence . . .

She had looked at the book open on the window-seat. *'Winnie the Pooh?'*

He had smiled again. 'I'm reverting to childhood. A jolly good book, don't you remember?'

'Almost every word.' She had turned the pages. *'Isn't it funny how a bear likes honey . . .'*

'Buzz! Buzz! Buzz! I wonder why he does.' Kit had picked up the book and sat down again, stretching his legs out this time and looking what he was – a grown man in a children's nursery. 'Have you got a cigarette on you, by any chance? I've run out.'

She had found a half empty packet of Players in her tunic pocket and some matches. He had lit her cigarette for her and she had wandered round the nursery while he sat smoking and watching her.

'When I was last here this was a shambles – those bloody little evacuees had just about wrecked it. Thank God they've gone!'

'I gather they were something of a trial.'

She had opened the toy cupboard and shut it and moved on to inspect her dolls' house. 'Mummy seems to have done her best, but it'll never be the same again.'

He had shrugged. 'Does it really matter? We'll never play with any of the things any more.'

She had known he would probably say that, and that it was the only sensible way to look at it, but it still upset her to see the damaged toys and the weals across Poppy's dappled hindquarters from Fred's stick. She had hitched up her WAAF skirt and got onto the horse, her legs dangling to the ground each side, reins in one hand, cigarette in the other. The wooden stand had creaked under her weight as she rocked gently to and fro. She had watched Kit narrowly. In the car, on the way home from the station, her mother had said: 'He seems rather tired, darling. The arm's much better but he's still not quite himself. He's been through a lot, I think, but he won't talk much about it. He doesn't seem to want to . . . just clams up. I shouldn't probe, if I were you.'

'How are you then, Kit?'

'Alive and kicking, as you can see.'

'The arm's OK?'

'Getting better every day.'

'That's good.'

He had flicked ash out of the open window. 'How's the WAAF?'

She had made a face. 'Bloody awful, really. But at least I'm not stuck in the kitchens any longer.'

'Ma said you were on the R/T, blabbing away to pilots. Sounds interesting.'

'It's all right. A lot better than peeling spuds. It makes you feel quite important, even if you're not. Actually, it's been fairly grim lately. We've all been warned that the Germans could attack the station at any moment. Masses of mock air raids and gas attacks and hours spent sitting around in shelters, wearing our respirators. All that sort of thing. Bloody boring! Do you know, the WAAFS have been told not to put up any resistance if the Germans invade. We're supposed to just do as we're told by them. The general idea is that although we'll probably all get raped we might not get killed if we don't put up any fight. I think that's pretty feeble, don't you? I'm jolly well going to have a bash at shooting a few of them myself, if it comes to it. I got one of the erks to show me how to aim and fire a rifle.'

'Don't try anything of the kind, twin. The RAF are right. Keep out of it. The Huns are complete swine and they wouldn't hesitate to shoot you if they felt like it. Believe me, I *know*. You might think they've got normal, decent, human feelings, but they haven't. They're vicious, rotten scum and I'm going to kill as many of the bastards as I can when I get back.'

His voice had risen and it shook with emotion. She had slowed Poppy down and looked at him in alarm. What had happened to him? In the old days he would have been laughing and joking, making light of everything . . . His face would have been alive, animated, amused . . . not the pale mask it was now. He had turned away from her towards the window, shoulders hunched. To change the subject she had told him about her visit to Mrs Shaw and he had listened sympathetically enough but without any real interest.

She got off the rocking-horse and wandered about the nursery again, touching things here and there. Kit watched her in silence, smoking his cigarette. She tapped the ash from hers into the 'Present from Swanage' mug on the mantelpiece that they had brought back from a seaside holiday long ago.

'I don't suppose Nanny would approve of us smoking in here, would she?'

'Or anywhere.'

'Do you remember all those funny sayings of hers, Kit? I want, never gets. Leave some for Mr Manners. There'll be tears before bedtime . . .'

'There usually were.'

'Yes . . .' Anne lifted the lid of the old musical box – broken, naturally. It used to play *Annie Laurie* and *Here's a Health Unto His Majesty*, before Fred and Betty had got their sticky little hands on it. 'By the way, did you ever come across someone called Johnnie Somerville at school? A good bit older than you.'

'There was a Johnnie Somerville who left just before I arrived. He won quite a few cups, as I remember. Wet Bob and a terrific all-rounder. Held the long-jump record. I know that because I tried to beat it. I think he got a scholarship to Oxford, or something. Why?'

'Oh, I came across him at Colston. He's a pilot with one of the auxiliary squadrons.'

'Have you fallen for him? That would please Ma. The family's probably stinking rich.'

She pulled another face. 'God, no! He's appalling! Disgustingly conceited. The worst sort of Etonian. Nothing like as nice as your friends. How's old Villiers?'

'Villiers is dead.'

She swung round, shocked. '*Dead!* Oh, Kit, I can't believe it . . .'

261

He said tonelessly: 'It's true, I'm afraid. He was killed in France when we were retreating.'

'I'm terribly sorry.'

She looked at Kit, feeling as helpless as she had felt with Mrs Shaw. Villiers had been his best friend since prep school days. Ten years of friendship.

'So am I.' Kit chucked the butt of his cigarette out of the window and stood up. 'Let's go and find a drink before dinner. I could do with one.'

During dinner he was something like his old self. Their mother had turned the meal into an occasion, with candles and silver on the table, and favourite food. She had put on a long gown and her pearls and diamond brooch. From time to time she would lean forward and touch Kit, as though to make sure that he was really there. Their father, back late from his hush-hush job in London, was in a very good mood. The meal passed with a good deal of laughter and reminiscence. It was a long while since they had all been together.

Anne watched Kit. He was smiling too, and making occasional jokes, but she could tell that it was a great effort for him. It was a little show put on to please the parents.

Afterwards, when their parents had finally gone to bed, they went out onto the terrace. They had turned the drawing-room lights off and left the french windows open so that they could hear the record playing on the gramophone. She had chosen the most cheerful one she could find, and danced up and down the terrace to it. In the old days, Kit would have probably joined her and they would have Charlestoned up and down together, waving arms and kicking legs. Now, he sat silently on the balustrade, smoking his cigarette and drinking brandy. When the record had finished she collapsed, breathless, into the swing seat. They were both sitting exactly where they had sat on the night of their birthday dance a year ago. She lit a cigarette.

'What's the matter, Kit? Something's badly wrong. What's happened to make you like this?'

There was a near-full moon sailing high above the beech trees and shining down onto the terrace, but his face was in shadow and she could not see his expression. After a moment he spoke.

'Is it so obvious?'

'To me it is. But then I'd always know. I don't think the parents do. Ma just thinks you're a bit tired – shattered by everything. Still getting over your arm. But it's more than that, isn't it? Is it to do with Villiers?'

Again, he was silent, drawing on his cigarette.

She said: 'Wouldn't it be better to talk about it? To me, at least? It might help and you know I'll never tell another living soul.'

There was another long silence. When, finally, he spoke it sounded as though it was with a great effort.

'As a matter of fact, it is to do with Villiers. Very astute of you.'

'So, tell me about it, Kit. Tell me what happened.'

'Well, I told you he was killed when we were retreating in France . . .'

'Go on.'

'It was all a pretty bloody frightful shambles over there. A monumental cock-up, I'd say. The Hun tanks just kept steam-rollering forward and we just kept on pulling back, digging in, and then pulling back again – scattered all over the place. Communications went to pot. Half the time nobody knew what the hell was going on, or what to do next. There were no proper orders. A bloody disaster!'

'That's what we heard.'

'Yes. We'd dig ourselves in overnight behind some canal or river, fend the Germans off during the next day and then pull back to the next river. That went on day after day. There was no time to sleep. We got totally exhausted. Those bloody Huns never let up – just kept on pushing us back. In the end they got our lot surrounded in a wood. They kept on shelling us and a lot of the chaps were killed, including our CO. He was a damned fine bloke, too.'

There was a long pause. Anne waited. The scent of the roses on the wall behind her was sweet on the night air – an English country garden smell which had nothing to do with what Kit was talking about.

He went on. 'There wasn't much we could do except keep our heads low while the shells went on raining down . . . Then the Stukas turned up and had a go too. That was hell. They make this ghastly whining noise as they dive down – a sort of terrifying screeching – and then the bombs explode all over the shop. It was bloody frightening, I can tell you.'

'I've heard some of the RAF pilots talk about them – '

'The RAF!' Kit said bitterly. 'We never even *saw* the bloody RAF.'

'They must have been there, Kit. They were sent over. They were there all right.'

'Well, I did see a couple of Spitfires – *once*, at Dunkirk, but they were buggering off fast in the direction of home. The Huns had a pretty free field to paste us when they felt like it. Still, I don't blame your chaps. Jolly sensible of them to keep out of it all, really.'

'They *didn't* keep out of it. They were there.'

'The Invisible Men!'

'That's not fair, Kit. They couldn't stay long because of the fuel . . .'

'Well, don't let's argue about it. It doesn't matter much anyway. We'd more or less had it, with or without them. What the hell's that!'

Kit had swung round sharply towards the end of the terrace.

'It's only Barley.'

The spaniel padded towards them and lay down at Kit's feet.

'Sorry, I get pretty jumpy still.'

'Go on with what you were telling me.'

He drew a long breath. 'We managed to break out of

264

the wood at night, under cover of darkness – those of us that were still left alive, that is. We went in small groups. Villiers was with me and about ten of the men. We went along the bed of a stream and got away somehow. After that we kept heading north towards the coast, hiding in ditches and barns, and so on. We hadn't any rations left and the French wouldn't help. Before they'd been giving us wine and throwing flowers, now they wouldn't give us anything – not even water. You'd go through some village and they'd stand in the doorways and spit on you . . . Couldn't blame them either. I felt ashamed we were leaving them to face the Huns.'

'It was their country, after all.'

'I know, but I felt rotten about it. Anyway, we came to this farm. It was miles from anywhere. A filthy sort of place with tumbledown buildings and a yard full of muck. Flies everywhere. There were some loose animals about – pigs and chickens, and so forth, but nobody looking after them. It was deserted. Whoever lived there must have gone off in a hell of a rush. They'd left the door open and everything had been left just as it was. There was a loaf of bread on the table, I remember – half eaten. And a black cat wandering about. It kept following me and rubbing itself against my legs.

'At first we thought it might be a trap so we were bloody careful, but it turned out to be OK. Some French farmer had just vamoosed. We were in clover, really. Killed a couple of chickens and cooked them over a fire – we gave some to the cat and it purred like anything. It was our first decent meal for ages – its, too, I suppose – and there was even some wine in the cellar, Pretty rough, home-made stuff, but it tasted like nectar to us.' Kit lit another cigarette. 'We knew the Germans couldn't be far off but we decided to stay there a few hours and rest up . . . get some kip. Two of the men had been wounded and were in pretty poor shape, and the rest of us were so damned tired that I don't think we could have gone a step further.'

Kit stopped. There was a long silence.

'What happened then?'

His voice was strained. 'We arranged watches, of course. There was an attic in the roof of the farmhouse. You had to climb up through a trap door in the ceiling to get to it, but it had a couple of small windows – one on each side, so there was a fairly good view of the surrounding country. And there was a bright moon so you could see quite clearly. Villiers and one of the others took the first watch and then Corporal Watson and I took over near dawn, while the rest of them kipped down in the cellar.

'We never even saw the Huns 'til they'd surrounded us. Christ knows how they managed it – they must have come up under cover of the trees. I suppose I might have dropped off, though I'd swear I didn't. The first thing I knew was that they'd burst into the house downstairs and caught the others asleep in the cellar. Watson and I could hear them shouting and stamping about. They came upstairs, of course, but they didn't come up into the attic. Maybe they didn't notice the trap door – it was in a dark corner. There – there was silence for a bit and we waited . . . I didn't know what the hell to do next. Then they marched our chaps out into the yard. It was below one of the attic windows so we had a grandstand view, you might say. We could see it all. The Huns were an SS division.'

Kit had turned his head away. His voice was low and she kept very still.

'They ordered them to stand against the wall and then they shot them – machine-gunned them down and then finished them off with pistols and bayonets.'

Anne put her hand over her mouth. 'My God, Kit . . . how horrible!'

'I'll never get it out of my mind.'

'But it wasn't your fault. You can't blame yourself for what the Germans did.'

'Of course it was my fault! Don't you see? I should have

266

spotted the Huns in the first place. I was on watch. I could have warned them. And I could have opened fire when they were in the yard – killed some of the SS, given our lot a chance . . . But I didn't. And I ordered Watson to hold his fire. I was afraid, you see. Afraid we'd be shot, too, if they discovered that we were there. I was a bloody coward.'

'But Kit, what could you have done? Two of you against them all?'

'I've thought about it a thousand times. Been over and over it in my mind. We could have got some of the Huns from where we were. Taken them by surprise. There would have been confusion and some of our chaps might have been able to get away. At least they wouldn't have been shot in cold blood without us lifting a finger to try and save them. All I thought about was saving my own skin and I'll never forgive myself for that.'

She felt a cold horror. It was far worse than anything she had imagined. For a moment she did not know what to say.

'When you're better and stronger, Kit, you'll see things differently. You'll realize that you couldn't really have done anything to help them. What would be the point of getting yourself killed? And Watson too?'

'What I see,' he said sadly, 'is Villiers and those men lying in that stinking farmyard . . . And what I know is that I should have done something. The Germans moved off soon after and Watson and I went down. Our chaps were all dead. Except for Villiers. He was lying in a corner against the wall. They'd shot him in the chest and someone had stuck a bayonet in him but he was just alive. I don't know how. And conscious. I got down and held him and said his name . . . Do you know, twin, he opened his eyes and smiled at me. I felt like Judas. He smiled and told me not to worry about him. To leave him and get out. I held his hand for a bit and kept the flies off him. I could see he was dying . . . The funny thing was he didn't seem to be feeling any pain. He – he talked quite a lot – mostly about school. He kept rambling on about all sorts of things . . . like that time we won the sculls together. Remember?'

She had cheered herself hoarse on the river bank on that sunny summer afternoon. Kit had been flushed and triumphant, Villiers whooping like a Red Indian.

'At least you were with him when he died, Kit,' she said quietly. 'It must have comforted him.'

He seemed to shudder. 'That's the very worst of it, twin – I wasn't. I could tell he was going fast. There was blood coming out of his mouth and he was sort of choking . . . nothing I could do for him. Then I heard the Huns coming back. I could see them coming down the road. And I ran away. I ran away and left him to die there all alone, lying in all that filth, covered with flies. *All alone.*'

Kit's voice broke and he covered his face with his hands. '*Now* can you imagine how I feel? How I'll never be able to forgive myself? Never have any respect for myself again?'

After a moment he took his hands away and somehow got his voice under control. 'Well, we made it to Dunkirk, Watson and myself. I didn't care whether we did or not, but Watson kept me going. We got on one of the ships at the beach – some old paddle steamer. She was so overloaded that she was half sinking. Then the Jerries dive-bombed us offshore and finished the job. That's when I got hit in the arm. Next thing I knew I was in the water. I never saw Watson again . . . I still don't know what happened to him. Somebody fished me out and I found myself on another ship. We crawled back to Dover with Jerries attacking all the way. I kept on hoping they'd kill me so I wouldn't have to go on living with myself.'

'Don't, Kit. You mustn't feel like that. Things like this must happen all the time in war. You've got to try and forget about it.'

'I'll never do that. Never. Nor would you – you know that. I've just got to learn to live with it, somehow. I can't tell the parents. I don't want them to have to know that their brave and wonderful soldier son is just a miserable, bloody coward.'

'That's not so, Kit. You're seeing it all wrong. Being much too hard on yourself.'

But he was sobbing almost soundlessly into his hands. Anne went to put her arms around him and to hug him close. She felt utterly wretched for him, and frightened. Poor, poor Kit who had always been so strong. So sure. So marvellous. For whom everything had always gone so right, and now, suddenly, had all gone so hideously wrong.

She returned to Colston at the end of her leave in time for yet another mock air raid.

'If they carry on like this,' Pearl complained tiredly, 'we won't have time for the real thing.'

In spite of everything, there was an invitation to a party. Someone had decided that a little distraction was needed. One of the Ops Room penguins gave Anne a lift to the rented house a few miles away from the station. The first room she went into was so crowded she could hardly move, and so smoky she could scarcely breathe. She squeezed through the crush of uniforms to another room where there was more air. There she discovered Squadron Leader Robinson who had established himself in a quiet corner, glass in one hand, pipe in the other.

'I'm getting too old for this sort of thing,' he told her. 'Too much noise and too many people. It's all very well for you young ones.'

Anne smiled politely. Everyone liked Robbie Robinson, but he *was* rather old for parties. She looked about her for others she might know and, as she did so, the circle of people nearby shifted so that she was able to see past them across to the far side of the room. A group of RAF officers standing there caught her attention. They were all wearing wings, but had some other emblem that she could not make out pinned to their tunics as well. Something else set them apart, too. They looked older than most of the other pilots, and a lot smoother. More sophisticated. Almost elegant. Men, not boys.

'Who are those pilots over there?' she asked Robbie Robinson curiously. 'They're not ordinary RAF, are they?'

He followed her gaze. 'They're Poles. Poor devils, they've lost everything – country, home, probably family . . . the lot. Amazing chaps, really. Brave as lions. Well, more like tigers in a way. Or wolves. Damned good pilots. They've been in the thick of it a lot longer than us. Those ones there fought with the French Air Force after they had to get out of Poland. Then, when France fell, they showed up here. Real gluttons for punishment. Mind you, they loathe the Germans. Simply loathe them. I'm jolly glad they're on *our* side, not the other one. Frightfully aggressive in the air. They go tearing off if they get even a whiff of a Hun, and nothing will stop them. You can't blame them, I suppose, after what the Germans did to their country.'

She looked, intrigued, at the four Poles – owners of the voices she had heard gabbling incomprehensibly over the R/T, and the ones who did all that swearing and singing as they flew. She stared at one of them in particular, in the middle of the group. He had dark hair, combed smoothly straight back from his forehead, without any parting, and high cheek-bones. It was a brooding, sensitive sort of face. Fascinating. He was lighting a cigarette and as he looked up his eyes met hers across the room. He smiled.

Robbie Robinson murmured beside her: 'I'll introduce you to them, if you like, but beware! Polskis have a terrible reputation with women.'

He conducted her gallantly towards them, but when it came to the point, he had forgotten their names.

'Couldn't pronounce them anyway, my dear. Quite impossible. Anne, these are four unpronounceable Polish gentlemen. Gentlemen, this is Aircraftwoman Anne Cunningham.'

He left her with them. England had gone to war over

their country and yet these were the first Poles she had ever laid eyes on. They bowed to her from the waist, clicked their heels and smiled at her charmingly. The dark-haired one with the cigarette made the introductions.

'Permit me to present Stefan Szulkowski, Henryk Topolnicki, Tadeusz Iranek . . . and my name is Michal Racyński.'

They shook her hand in turn and bowed again. The names had all sounded gibberish to her – except for the last one. She had listened specially hard to hear it. Now, looking at the four of them, she could see the Poland shoulder flashes and that the emblems that she had noticed from a distance were silver eagles with outstretched, drooping wings, holding some kind of wreath in their beaks. Michal Racyński offered her one of his cigarettes and another of them stepped in quickly to light it. She was enchanted by their beautiful manners. And they were all looking at her with open admiration, which was rather nice. The tallest – fair and very handsome – addressed her in slow, heavily accented English.

'Good morning. How are you? Very well, thank you. Good night.'

He beamed at her, showing a glint of gold tooth. Anne laughed uncertainly.

Michal Racyński said: 'That is all the English that Stefan knows.'

'It's very good. Much better than my Polish. Do tell him.'

He translated and Stefan beamed even wider, displaying more gold. He jabbered something.

'He says that he would be very happy to teach you Polish, if you wish. But I do not advise it.'

He smiled at her again as he spoke, like he had smiled from across the room. Close up, his eyes were a very light blue-grey colour. An un-English sort of colour, with un-English sort of depths.

He said: 'I have not seen you before. You are stationed at Colston?'

'Yes. I bet you've spoken to me, though. I'm an R/T operator in Ops. I've probably talked to you when you're flying.'

'Of course! Often we hear women. You are very good. Very clear. Very patient with us and our bad English.'

'You speak it very well.'

'Thank you. You are kind, but is still very bad. They give us all English lessons since we arrive. We try to speak better, but is difficult for us. We cannot say *th* like you. We never say this sound in Polish.'

The one who was called Henryk something or other, added: 'Everything different for us. Language, peoples, food, weather, machines . . .'

He had a thin face and sad brown eyes. The fourth, whose name she couldn't remember at all, nodded vigorously.

'Is very difficult with machines. Speed in miles per hour. Altitude in feet. Fuel in gallons. All different for us.'

'Oh, dear. How awfully muddling for you.'

'No, is not awful. Is good for us. We happy to be here. England is beautiful country.'

'Beautiful girls,' Stefan said unexpectedly and with another huge smile.

In the next room someone had put on a record and people had started dancing. The one whose name she couldn't remember at all bowed to her again.

'Please, you dance with me?'

'Yes, of course.'

She went with him into the next room where they had turned the lights down low and the music was smoochy. He seemed very nice but he wasn't the one she wanted to dance with. She kept him at a distance and talked brightly in stilted English. The awful thought occurred to her that because he had been the first to ask her to dance, some peculiar Polish custom might decree that the others were disqualified. She need not have worried. As soon as they returned to the other room, Stefan clicked his heels and

272

smiled at her hopefully, making twirling motions with his right hand. After him, and some fairly firm controlling in the darkened room, it was the sad-eyed Henryk's turn. Finally, when she was beginning to despair of his ever asking her, Michal Racyński turned to her.

'Now, at last is my turn. Please.'

As she moved into his arms he drew her close against him. He smelled of some delicious cologne and his cheek felt slightly rough and hard against hers. They danced in complete silence, without any need for words. She wished that the music would never end.

When the party ended he drove her back to the station in a very shabby Wolseley.

'I apologize. This car is most old. I get it from dump. The squadron mechanics make it to go.'

She laughed, not caring a fig about the car – whatever it was, or wherever it came from. She felt unbelievably happy.

'It's a very nice car. But what about the others – your friends?'

'Tadeusz has a car too, but much better. He will take Henryk and Stefan. They will understand.'

He turned his head towards her as he spoke and she thought, though in the darkness she could not be sure, that he was smiling.

The Wolseley coughed and spluttered before consenting to burst into steady life. It was very draughty and the springs seemed either badly worn or broken. Comparison with Johnnie Somerville's Lagonda was a joke. An ironic joke, since for all that car's expensive comfort, she had felt none of the bliss she was feeling now in this ancient, uncomfortable vehicle.

She said: 'I like your friends. Do you know, I'd never met any Poles before. Not one.'

'So, how do you find us?'

'Oh . . . very polite. Very charming. Very polished.'

'Polished? I do not know this word.'

'Smooth. Elegant manners . . . that sort of thing.'

He laughed. 'Thank you. Is not so true, I think, but thank you.'

'And very different from most Englishmen. From the other pilots, anyway. I can't explain it exactly.'

'Perhaps we are different because we have lived different lives. And we are older than your pilots. We fight longer. The Germans take our country . . . kill many Poles, destroy our cities, take our freedom . . . We hate them very much for that. So, everything is different for us, like Henryk said.'

'Squadron Leader Robinson told me that you were all in France before – with the French Air Force.'

'Is true. Then we come to England – with some problems. We come with a boat. We arrive at a place called Falmouth.'

'In Cornwall.'

'*Tak*. A beautiful place where all the people are smiling and not afraid. I forget such places exist. They give us fish paste sandwiches and tea. Very kind. We have been many days without food on boat. A woman in a green hat gives me a cup of tea with milk and I am feeling very sick. In Poland we never put milk in tea. So, I ask her, please, is possible to have without milk? She laugh a lot – such a big laugh – and gives me a different cup with black tea. She says to me, soon you are used to it. A very nice lady. Very kind.'

'What about the paste sandwiches? Did you like those?'

'I never have these too. They are good but I cannot eat much in one time, so I eat a little bit and put the rest in my pocket for later. After that, we go by train to Liverpool. Then to Blackpool. Then, at last, they give us RAF uniform and we swear allegiance to your King. We learn first to fly Defiants. For me is like a chauffeur, with gunner in back. Then, they give us Hurricanes and I am very happy. And then we come to Colston. And then I meet you.'

This time she was sure that he was smiling. She

half-hoped that he would stop somewhere en route and live up to the terrible reputation, but he drove her straight to the main gate.

'You permit I take you out one evening, please?'

'I most certainly do permit. But I'll have to meet you somewhere outside the station. We're not supposed to go out with officers. They think it's bad for discipline.'

'That is pity. But I meet you wherever you say. I do not wish you to have trouble because of me.'

'I don't care.'

'We meet soon?'

'Yes, please. *Very* soon.'

'I've met him, Pearl.'

'Met who, love?'

'The dark stranger. The one you saw in my tea leaves. And he's come from across the seas, just like you said.'

'Blimey!'

'I saw him on the other side of the room and I knew he was the one.'

'Just like that?'

'Just like that. His name's Michal Racyñski.'

'Bloody funny name! Sounds like you got something stuck in your throat, then you sneezed.'

'It's Polish. I think his first name is really Michael, but that's how they pronounce it – Me, not My, and with that sort of *ch* in the middle, a bit like a Scot saying *och*.'

'I wish he *was* a Scot. You want to be careful of Poles, duckie. I've heard some stories about them . . .'

'They've got beautiful manners.'

'I bet they have! Did I ever tell you about the Polish airman I met on the train coming back from leave?'

'What about him?'

'Well, *he* was a bundle of charm. All smiles and hot looks, you know . . . Bloody train was packed, as usual, and he got up and offered me his seat.'

'That was decent of him.'

Pearl chuckled. 'Oh, *very* gallant. He bowed to me like

he was Prince Charming, pointed to the seat and said "plis, park your arse," ever so politely. 'Course he hardly spoke any English so he didn't know any better. Must've been some RAF joker taught him that.'

Anne snorted with laughter. 'Michal speaks rather good English. He's got a lovely accent.'

'Yeah . . . You watch it, though, love. Don't go and lose your heart to a pilot, whatever he is. You know what can happen to them.'

'I can't help it. It's too late.'

'It's not worth it, love.'

'Oh, yes it is.'

Pearl sighed and lay back on her pillow. 'Well, don't say I didn't warn you.'

They had been whispering across the space between their beds after lights out. The hut was stiflingly hot and Anne kicked her blanket off. She felt restless and excited and not in the least like sleeping; more like getting up and dancing around, or doing something quite idiotic. Something completely crazy . . . She sat up suddenly.

'I'm going for a swim, Pearl.'

Pearl's bed creaked. 'Now I *know* you've gone bonkers. What do you mean a *swim*?'

'It's much too hot to sleep. I'm going to take a dip in the static tank. Cool off a bit.'

'Don't be such a loony. You'll get caught and there'll be hell to pay.'

'No, I won't. Not if I'm careful.' She was already out of bed and pulling on her knickers.

'You haven't got a swimsuit.'

'Doesn't matter. I won't wear anything. I'm going skinny-dipping.'

Pearl lay back and put a hand over her eyes. 'Christ!'

She carried her shoes until she was out of the hut. Practice with illicit comings and goings had made perfect and she could open both doors, inner and outer, without a sound. The moon gave her enough light to see her way and she moved silently, keeping in the shadow of buildings. The big static water tank stood above ground and its black depths looked rather sinister and less inviting than she had imagined. She hesitated for a moment and then undressed quickly and climbed up over the side and lowered herself into the water. It felt wonderfully cool and refreshing and sinfully free to swim without a bathing suit. Just the sort of thing she felt like doing. She swam across to the other side and then back again, and then to and fro a few more times. After that she lay on her back for a while, floating aimlessly and looking up at the stars and thinking about Michal Racyñski. She thought about his incredibly sexy eyes and how it had been dancing with him and sitting close beside him driving back in the Wolseley . . . to keep herself afloat while she was thinking about all this she paddled at her sides with her hands.

The sharp-eared Station Warrant Officer, making his way late to his quarters, heard the small splashing sound and paused. Bloody rat, he thought. Gone and fallen in the tank. Serve it right! There was another splash. Bloody *big* rat, he thought this time, altering his course quietly. Close to the tank he trod on something soft and clicked on his torch to see his foot on a pair of black WAAF knickers. Near by there was more female clothing – a blue skirt, a blouse and a pink brassière. He stared at them for a moment and then shone his torch over the tank's side onto the water. Not a rat, a *mermaid*! She floundered as the beam caught her and sank quickly from view, but not before he had had a look. He grinned, waiting for her to re-surface as she would surely have to do, and then composed his features into a suitably ferocious warrant officer's expression.

'You in there! I'm turning my back for one minute while you get out and get dressed, then I want your name and number!'

He grinned to himself again as he turned away. There were some compensations, at least, for having these bloody women about the place.

Nine

The Germans attacked the station for the first time on a warm afternoon in mid August.

In the Ops Room, the plot for fifty plus hostile aircraft had moved remorselessly across the map, watched by all eyes. At last the Controller reached for his steel helmet.

'Tin hats on everyone, please. I'm afraid they're coming for us.'

Virginia felt only the smallest flutter of fright in her stomach. Outwardly she moved her plot calmly. Not one of the faces of the WAAFS round the table betrayed any sign of fear. Pamela, directly opposite, was looking almost bored, as though it was no more than another mock attack.

In her office, Felicity was talking to one of the aircraftwomen. The girl's mother was seriously ill and she was arranging compassionate leave, reassuring the tearful ACW.

'Don't worry, Hale, go and get your things packed and we'll arrange for you to be taken to the station so that you can catch an early evening train to London. Corporal Snow will – '

The tannoy blared suddenly into life, cutting off the rest of her sentence.

This is your Station Commander speaking. All personnel, except those engaged on essential services, are to take cover immediately! I repeat, take cover immediately! At any moment we will be attacked by enemy aircraft.

The station siren was wailing as Felicity urged a startled ACW Hale out of the office ahead of her. Above the sound of the siren she could hear the roar of the fighters taking off. The corridors were already full of people hurrying from HQ, cramming their helmets on their heads as they went. She shouldered her way against the stream to check on other WAAFS in the building before she left it herself. Outside, everyone was running full pelt now towards the shelters.

A WAAF on the pathway in front of her tripped and fell and Felicity grabbed her and yanked her roughly to her feet; the girl's knees were bleeding as she limped on. At the entrance to the shelter she shepherded a group of airwomen down into the dugout, glancing anxiously at the sky. She could see the formation of enemy bombers approaching, like a shoal of black sharks swimming on against the blue. An RAF sergeant seized her arm.

'Hurry them up, ma'am, for God's sake!'

She pushed the last two WAAFS down into the entrance and waited for a straggler who came flying down the path, holding her helmet on with one hand.

'Quick as you can, Edwards . . .'

The airwoman gasped at her. 'Sorry, ma'am, but it's Riddle. She wouldn't budge. She's too scared to move.'

'Where is she?'

'Ablutions, ma'am. She's gone and locked herself in the lavatory.'

'Get inside, Edwards. Don't worry, I'll deal with it.'

The airwoman scuttled past her down into the dugout, like a rabbit bolting into its burrow. Felicity raced towards the WAAF ablutions block. Inside, a tap had been left running full on and the water was gushing noisily into the basin. The bombers' drone was much louder now and the station Bofors guns had begun their deep, angry coughing. She hammered on the locked door.

'Riddle! It's Section Officer Newman here. I've come to take you to the shelter. Don't be afraid. You'll be quite safe there, but we must hurry. Open the door, please. At once!'

A fighter shrieked low overhead, drowning the last of her words. She hammered on the door again. An explosion nearby shattered the glass in one of the windows and she flinched as jagged splinters flew about.

'*Riddle! Unlock this door immediately! That's an order!*'

There was still no movement from inside the cubicle. In desperation she thrust her weight hard against the door several times and, suddenly, it gave way. ACW Riddle – very young and very white-faced was sitting on the lavatory lid, her hands clapped over her ears, her eyes tight shut. Felicity put an arm round the airwoman's shoulders and hauled her out bodily; she seemed unable to move of her own accord. She put her own tin hat on Riddle's head and, supporting the girl against herself, dragged her out of the hut and towards the nearest shelter. The dark shape of a bomber swept overhead and there was a terrifying rat-tat-tat of machine-gun fire and the smack of bullets tearing into masonry. They were still yards from the trench when another bomber screamed down and the blast from the mighty explosion that followed picked both WAAFS clean off their feet and hurled them to the ground. Earth and stones showered over them and waves of searingly hot air buffeted them like a rough sea. Felicity found herself clinging for dear life to the grass with one hand, her nails dug deep into the earth, while the other still hung onto the airwoman lying beside her.

She raised her head to see yet another German bomber making its run in, with two fighters in hot pursuit. Yellow flashes spurted from the fighters' wings as their guns fired, but the Junkers came remorselessly on and a stick of bombs dropped over by the hangars sent great eruptions of earth high into the air and made violent shock-waves through the ground. She clutched at the grass again as the world rocked about her.

She began to crawl in the direction of the trench shelter, tugging the girl along with her. Then other hands caught hold of her and she felt herself being dragged painfully across the ground and downwards into the trench, like a sack of coals. She lay there, stunned and winded. Her eardrums felt as though they would burst with the noise and she covered them with her hands. Above the tumult, she could hear the heartening, furious stutter of a fighter's guns.

Anne had been off-duty in the WAAF recreation room when the alarm had sounded. She had been playing a game of table tennis with one of the MT drivers, and listening to Workers' Playtime on the wireless at the same time. Some comedian had been in the middle of telling a joke when the station commander's voice had cut in over the tannoy. For a few seconds she and her opponent stared at each other in disbelief and then, with one accord, they flung down their bats and snatched up their respirators and helmets. As she ran to the door, Anne heard a roar of audience laughter coming from the wireless in its corner as the comedian delivered his punch-line.

In the dugout shelter they took their places on the benches, as they had done so many times in practice. But this time there was no giggling or fidgeting. She looked along the row of scared faces – Maureen beside Vera, Sandra with her hand over her mouth, her eyes wide, Winnie next to Enid at the far end. Enid was looking as though she was going to turn the waterworks on at any moment. Gloria and Pearl would have gone to another shelter. She sat back, her heart thumping in her chest. The WAAF cook sitting beside her in her white hat and overalls had brought her work with her. She was starting to peel potatoes and making a far better job of it than Anne had ever done – paring long, thin spirals of peel away before she lobbed the potatoes into the bucket of water jammed between her stout feet.

Our Father, which art in heaven,
Hallowed be Thy name . . .

The girl sitting opposite had started to recite the Lord's Prayer loudly, her hands clasped before her. The cook leaned her bulk sideways against Anne.

'Don't know what good she thinks *that's* going to do.'

The heavy drone of enemy bombers was clear now and she could hear the ponderous fire of the station guns and the fierce snarl of a fighter. Ominously, a bomber's note changed to a high whine as it began its dive. Two explosions, one after another, made the shelter rock and the water leap in the cook's bucket. Someone gave a choked scream of fear.

Give us this day our daily bread,
And forgive us our trespasses . . .

The girl was shouting now. Why couldn't she shut up? There was enough bloody racket going on without her adding to it. And who cared about daily bread at the moment? Another explosion, much closer, made the hurricane lamps rock wildly on their hooks. Michal would be up there, somewhere in the midst of all that hell, defending them. His Hurricane would be diving on the bombers, guns blazing . . .

For Thine is the Kingdom,
The Power and the Glory,
For ever and ever, Amen.

Thank God, she'd finished her stupid chanting. Enough to get on anyone's nerves. The noise outside was worse than ever. The eerie whistling sound of yet another bomb falling culminated in an ear-splitting explosion that seemed to burst right inside her head. A blast of hot air gusted through the shelter entrance like a blow and knocked them all sideways so that she found herself lying with her head in the cook's lap. The slamming to her body and the searing heat and stench of high explosive left her gasping for breath. The cook was cursing that her bucket had been knocked over and was flailing about with her arms. There were more terrifying whistles and a series of thudding explosions that shook them in violent succession. In all the appalling row going on up above, she could distinguish the scream of one fighter's engine going flat out. She shut her eyes. *Please God, let Michal be all right.*

That bloody girl had started all over again with her maddening chanting.

Our Father, which art in heaven,
Hallowed be Thy name . . .

Anne felt like throttling her. Her feet were soaking from the overturned bucket and her eyes smarting from the dust and dirt that had blown into the dugout. The cook had dropped her knife and was groping about, trying to find it in the semi-darkness. It was her best knife, apparently. As though it mattered when any second they were all probably going to get blown to kingdom come. God, that ghastly screeching sounded exactly like an express train coming . . . She braced herself.

At the other end of the shelter, Winnie was trying to comfort Enid. The racket going on was too loud for any words so she put her arm round Enid's shaking shoulders. She wondered if she ought to change places with her because she was at the very end of the bench, nearest to all the dirt blasting in, but it was hard to get up and move with the shaking going on. The only thing to do really was to sit tight and pray – like that girl was doing up the other end. Only to herself. Not making a song and dance of it, like she was. It was worse, far worse, this than anything she had imagined during the practices. She felt battered by the noise and every explosion made her flinch however much she tried not to because of Enid. It sounded as though everything was being blown to smithereens outside. She shut her eyes tightly as there was yet another screeching whistle overhead, and then the shelter seemed to blow apart round her and the world went dark.

The plotting table was shaking so much that the markers kept sliding out of place. With every bomb explosion a shower of white dust fell from the concrete ceiling and Virginia had to keep blinking it out of her eyes. She pressed her earphones closer to her head to shut out the noise as she listened to the plots. Nobody in the Ops Room had panicked. Nobody had done so much as wince, so far as she could tell. The faces round the table registered only grim concentration. Pamela was looking as though enemy raids were beneath her notice, disdainfully pushing her rake to and fro. There was another violent bang, like a tremendous clap of thunder, and another deluge of dust. The warrant officer standing near winked at her and she hoped he had not seen her shoulders cringe. She looked away from him and, as she did so, the ceiling suddenly seemed to disintegrate. A blast of hot air hit her like a blow and, at the same time, someone grabbed hold of her in a sort of flying rugger tackle that propelled her clean under the plotting table. She lay there, gasping, her helmet askew, a man's heavy weight across her back. The warrant officer who had put her there said apologetically in her ear: 'Beg pardon, miss, but we'd better stay like this 'til the All Clear.'

The bombers had gone, leaving behind them a scene of devastation. Felicity peered out of the shelter at the smoking rubble, the gaping craters, the mangled metal and broken glass, and at the cloud of dust that hung over it all. There was a rotten egg stench of high explosive and a strong smell of leaking gas. Close to the trench a burst water pipe spouted a jet high into the air where the droplets sparkled prettily in the sunlight, like an ornamental fountain. She turned her head towards the WAAF ablutions hut and saw that nothing of it remained but a mound of bricks and broken concrete with a lavatory perched upside down on the top.

The RAF corporal beside her said: 'You all right, ma'am?'

'Yes, quite all right, thank you.'

'Sorry we were a bit rough with you, ma'am. Had to get you down in here as quick as we could.'

'I'm very grateful.'

She could feel blood running down the side of her face and found a handkerchief to wipe it away. ACW Riddle was crouched inside the shelter, still clasping her hands to her ears. An airman had put an arm round her shoulders and was telling her cheerily that it was all over now. She seemed unhurt.

Felicity emerged unsteadily. Other people were coming out of other shelters, clambering over debris and gazing about them. The raid had lasted barely ten minutes but the damage was enormous. Two of the hangars had been destroyed and almost every building seemed to have been hit. Several were on fire – the station armoury dramatically ablaze. As Felicity picked her way through the ruins two of the returning Spitfires flew overhead.

She found Corporal White supervising some airwomen who were filing out of a shelter.

'Anyone injured, Corporal?'

'No, not here, thank heavens, ma'am. Are you all right? There's blood on your face.'

'I'm fine. It's a cut or something. I'll see to it later. Keep them all together here, Corporal. There may be unexploded bombs and we'll have a roll call as soon as we can.'

She hurried on in search of other airwomen, skirting rubble and craters, climbing over a fallen girder. Hot shrapnel and broken glass carpeted the ground. She passed a chain of airmen dousing a fire with buckets of water passed from hand to hand. A party of stretcher bearers came towards her, at the double; one of the bearers called back over his shoulder.

'The shelter by the WAAF cookhouse has been hit, ma'am. They're trying to dig them out.'

She started to run in that direction, stumbling over obstacles in her path. A huge mound of earth marked the site of the shelter. Both entrances had vanished and airmen were digging frantically with shovels; others were tearing at the soil with their bare hands. She started to do the same. There seemed no hope that any of the WAAFS inside could be alive.

'I think it would be better if you left this to the men, Section Officer.'

She turned to see Group Captain Palmer behind her. 'I'd rather help, sir.'

'They'll get them out as quickly as they can.'

'All the same, sir.'

'You've been injured . . .'

With people dead and dying it seemed absurd to have been asked no less than three times already about a silly scratch. She wiped the blood away again with her handkerchief.

'It's nothing, sir.'

'It doesn't look like nothing. Get it seen to as soon as you can. That's an order, Section Officer.'

'Yes, sir.'

To her relief he turned away to talk to one of the airmen. She had noticed vaguely that he was wearing a Mae West over his uniform, so he must have been up with the squadrons. It would have been a case of all hands to the pumps. She went on scraping at the mound of earth, heaving cupped handfuls of it away. The erk digging hard beside her gave a grin.

'Soon 'ave them out, ma'am.'

*   *   *

The warrant officer helped Virginia to crawl out from under the plotting table.

'Easy does it, now. Mind how you go. It's a bit of a mess.'

That was an understatement. The Ops Room roof had been blown open to the sky. Slabs of concrete had crashed down over the table and floor, bringing lights and wiring too in a broken tangle. Incredibly, faint squawking voice sounds were coming from one of the headsets trailing from its jack. The warrant officer extended a hand.

'Careful not to touch any wires. They could be live.'

Her legs felt wobbly and she clung to the firm hand that guided her through the wreckage. There was a buzzing sound in her head and a strange, dream-like feeling about it all. She could not quite comprehend what had happened. The gallery, she noticed dazedly, was still intact and the Controller was up there, together with Ops B and the rest of them. They were mopping themselves down but seemed unhurt. Everyone and everything, she saw, was covered in a thick coating of the white dust, as though bags of cement powder had been thrown around.

A huge piece of roofing had smashed through the edge of the plotting table on the other side. She stepped past carefully and then saw the bottom part of a pair of legs protruding from underneath. She stared at them. They were stockinged legs with black WAAF shoes and the puddle of bright red blood oozing slowly from beneath them was mingling with the dust on the floor. The legs were covered with dust too, and bent at an odd angle, but even so she had no difficulty in recognizing the fine Kayser Bondor stockings that Pamela always wore, or in spotting the deep scratch on the right toe cap that she had tried so hard to polish out.

The warrant officer tugged at her hand gently. 'Come along now, lass. You'll be much better out in the fresh

287

air. Don't you worry, we'll see to all this. Just leave it to us.'

Anne, lying in pitch darkness, could hear the sounds of the rescuers working above – the chink of spades and shovels, the thudding of earth, the faint sound of voices. She could feel space around her, air to breathe, and her groping hand contacted a section of shelter wall still standing firm. She groped further, sweeping from one side to the other, and came across the upturned potato bucket and then something small and sharp – the cook's knife. She could hear the cook groaning and cursing somewhere close in her Liverpool accent, and sounding very much alive. Now, other sounds came out of the blackness – more groans, more curses, some sobs and even a nervous giggle, which was very probably Sandra. Somebody called out heartily, as though on the hockey pitch.

'I say, is everybody all right?'

'I'm bloody well not,' another voice replied sourly. 'I think both my legs are broken.'

Whoever she was, she sounded very calm about it.

'Whatever happened?' a breathy voice squeaked. Even in this situation, Sandra was asking her questions.

'A bomb dropped on us, you silly fool,' the owner of the broken legs told her tersely. 'What the hell do you think happened? The shelter's collapsed on us.'

'They're certainly taking their time getting us out. However much longer are they going to be?'

Anne smiled. That was Maureen, grumbling as usual. Just as well Gloria wasn't here too or they'd have been fighting like cats.

She called out: 'It won't be long. I can hear them at this end. They're almost through, I think.'

'Oh, Anne!' Sandra gasped. 'It's *you*! Thank goodness! I'm so *awfully* glad!'

* * *

288

Winnie could hear them all calling to each other at the far end of the shelter, but the voices were muffled and distant. Part of the roof must have fallen in, between them and her, she guessed. There was no way of telling properly because, apart from the darkness, she couldn't move. At least, she found she could move her upper body, but the lower half was buried deep in earth. It wasn't painful, or even specially uncomfortable, but she couldn't get up from where she was lying. All she could do was feel about with her hands, which she had been doing for quite a while, trying to find Enid. There was nothing around her but earth and stones. She kept calling her name but there was no answer. After a bit she gave up and lay quietly, suspended in a tranquil limbo. Nothing seemed to matter very much – except that she could not find Enid. If she waited here patiently, they would come and rescue her soon. She closed her eyes.

When she opened them again she saw a small round hole of daylight above her. She watched as it grew bigger and bigger until a face appeared in it, squinting and blinking down at her. She smiled at it.

'Blimey! There's one alive down 'ere. Looks OK . . .'

The face disappeared for a moment and she could hear some kind of discussion going on. Then another face appeared and did more squinting at her. It grinned.

'Soon 'ave you out of there, love. Just 'ang on a bit longer. We're goin' to 'ave to go a bit careful, so's we don't shift anythin'. You just stay there nice and quiet and don't move.'

She smiled again at that. It was funny when she couldn't anyway.

The hole grew steadily larger and presently she could see a big bit of blue sky. It was a surprise to see the sun shining quite normally and white clouds going past. From time to time the men spoke to her, asking her name, where she lived, how many brothers and sisters she had, making all sorts of jokes . . . And they kept on telling her to be sure to lie still. They seemed to be digging from the side now.

'Not long now, Winnie, love. 'ave you out of there in two ticks . . .'

There was more digging, the feeling of a great weight gradually lifting from her body and legs, hands reaching her and holding her, moving her gently, lifting her up and out into the bright daylight and fresh air. She looked up from a stretcher at a circle of smiling faces. Two of them she recognized – Section Officer Newman who tucked the blanket round her and wiped her face, and Taffy Jones who was the only one not smiling. He was gripping her hand and swearing under his breath. He looked angry, not pleased. She could see a murderous fury in his strange eyes.

She said to him: 'Enid? Where's Enid? She was with me. Have they got her out too?'

'Yes,' he said. 'They've got her out.'

She searched his face. 'She's dead, isn't she? I know she is.'

He nodded. 'Sorry, Winnie. Her and another one in there. We did our best . . . It's a miracle it wasn't more . . . the whole blooming lot of you.'

She squeezed her eyes shut and, turning away from him, began, quite silently, to cry.

There was no need to open the door to the WAAF hut: it had been blown clean off its hinges. Felicity stood in the doorway and stared at the devastation inside.

Machine-gun bullets had ripped down both rows of beds, tearing through the piles of bedding and scattering them like washing blown from a line. A neat line of bullet-holes punctured one of the locker doors and others, blasted wide open, had spewed forth their contents. Window glass lay in sharp and glittering fragments at her feet and, raising her head, she saw the sky through a gaping hole in the roof. She stooped slowly to pick up a snapshot half buried in the glass – a picture of a young sailor in able seaman's uniform, hands behind his back, squinting into the sun.

By early evening Palmer had a full report of the death toll and damage. Thirty service personnel had been killed, and two civilians. Among those thirty were three WAAFS – two who had been in the shelter and one in the Ops Block when a five hundred pound bomb had gone through the roof. At least fifty more personnel, airmen and airwomen, had received injuries ranging from serious to trivial. The damage to the station had been extensive. All gas, water and electricity supplies had been cut, as well as telephone lines – though, mercifully, not all of those. Two hangars had been totally destroyed and a third severely damaged by fire. Many buildings had been reduced to rubble and those left standing had lost windows, doors and roof tiles. Six Blenheims, four Spitfires, a Hurricane and a Magister had been destroyed on the ground, together with nearly forty motor vehicles. Four more Spitfires had been lost in the air, three of them with their pilots. The runways were a mass of craters.

He immediately set about organizing the necessary repair work. All able-bodied personnel were to help fill in the bomb craters and that included, most *especially* included, so far as Palmer was concerned, the captured crews from the enemy aircraft brought down who were languishing in the guardroom. He took considerable satisfaction in seeing the Germans being marched briskly past his glassless window for this purpose. Some time later, he witnessed a detachment of WAAFS also marching past in the same direction, carrying heavy shovels for the same purpose. They were perfectly in step, shoulders back, heads held high. A group of airmen took their caps off to them and raised a mighty cheer.

Later, he sent for Section Officer Newman. When she came into the office he saw that there was a dressing now over her left temple. She looked pale, he thought, but calm. He told her to sit down.

He cleared his throat. 'I want you to know, Section Officer, that I sent a signal to Fighter Command HQ today, informing them of the exemplary and outstandingly brave conduct of all the WAAF on this station under heavy enemy bombardment.'

A startled blush appeared beneath her pallor. 'Thank you, sir.'

'And I received this signal back just now. I'd like you to read it.'

He handed the piece of paper over and watched the blush deepen as she read the words.

The C-in-C has heard with pride and satisfaction the manner in which WAAF at RAF Colston conducted themselves under fire today. They have abundantly justified his confidence in them.

She looked up and returned the signal to him. She said quietly: 'Thank you, sir.'

Her eyes, meeting his, were very bright. He thought she was on the point of tears. He looked away.

'I want to add my own congratulations to Air Chief Marshal Dowding's. All WAAF personnel stood to their posts today in a magnificent way. And you yourself, Section Officer, set a very fine example. I understand you put yourself at considerable risk during the raid bringing one of your young airwomen to safety . . . I imagine that's how you got that injury. I'm glad to see you've had it dressed. Nothing too serious. I hope.'

'No, sir. The MO stitched it for me.'

'Good, good.' He went on, determined to do full penance. 'As I know you are well aware, I was not, initially, at all keen on the idea of women serving on this station . . .' She was looking at some point on the wall over his shoulder now, as she so often did. He pressed on doggedly. 'I have to say that I *still* have some reservations – in certain areas, at least. I dare say I'm old-fashioned, but I find it very hard to accept the idea of women being so closely involved in active military affairs. I deplore the death of those three airwomen. It seems utterly wrong to me. Goes quite against the grain.'

'I understand how you feel, sir.'

He wished she would look at him. 'However, I was quite wrong about one thing. I was convinced, I must admit, that the WAAF would panic under bombardment – cause us enormous distractions and difficulties . . . That has proved to be completely unfounded and I'm happy to acknowledge it.'

She transferred her gaze from the wall to meet his. 'Thank you, sir.'

He said steadily: 'I have nothing but praise for you all and for the calm way in which you conducted yourselves. As for that airwoman who stayed at her Ops Room switchboard throughout the entire raid at such great peril . . . what was her name?'

'Gibbs, sir. Aircraftwoman Gloria Gibbs.'

'Yes, well, I understand the ceiling was half down and there was an unexploded bomb within feet of her, and yet she kept vital communication lines open for us. I shall see to it that she is recommended for a medal.'

'I'm so glad, sir. She thoroughly deserves it.'

She was not only looking at him now, she was smiling too. The first time, he could swear, that she had ever done so. He smiled back. 'On a more prosaic, but nonetheless important note, I hear your WAAF cooks have been doing sterling work producing an excellent supper for everyone without any water, gas or electricity supplies.'

'Just sausages and mash, sir.'

'Sounds splendid! I shall look forward to having some myself later.'

He could hear himself sounding falsely jocular and patronizing – bloody pompous, Caroline would have said – but he could not help himself. He changed tack briskly.

'I'm afraid we have to face the fact that there will be more attacks, Section Officer. The enemy are obviously planning to do their best to disable our forward fighter stations. In the circumstances, we're going to have to billet personnel away from the station – disperse ourselves and our aircraft as much as possible.'

'I can see that, sir.'

'I'm moving over to the Mess myself and arranging for you to have the use of my house for as many of your WAAF as you can fit in there for tonight. They'll have to sleep on the floor, I'm afraid, but I'm sure you'll make them as comfortable as you can.'

'That's very good of you, sir.'

'It isn't good of me at all, Section Officer. It's the least I can do, since all your buildings have been damaged. As to the rest of your airwomen, Sir Reginald and Lady Howard have been kind enough to offer some space at Eastleigh House . . .' He smiled drily. 'As a matter of fact, they hadn't much option as the house is being requisitioned anyway. Tomorrow we'll have to start sorting ourselves out properly and dealing with the funeral arrangements and so on . . .'

'Is there anything I can do to help now, sir?'

'Not tonight. You've got enough to cope with, and you look very tired already.' She was very pale again. 'That's all for the moment.'

She stood up. 'I believe I should congratulate you, too, sir.'

'Me?'

'I hear you brought down a Junkers, sir. That's what everyone's saying.'

She smiled at him again as she spoke and he felt himself reddening like a schoolboy. He picked up his pen and pulled some papers busily towards him.

'Just a fluke, Section Officer. Just a fluke.'

*　　*　　*

294

He sat up late into the night, sending telegraphs and writing letters of condolence. After a couple of hours of fitful sleep he was up again, ready to face the new day. He went out onto the Mess terrace, broken glass crunching beneath his feet, and surveyed the ruins of his station. Dawn had broken, the birds were singing, and there was a mist rising off the ground. It was going to be hot. Signals Section had worked through the night to restore all telephone links. Electricity was back on and gas and water would follow shortly, with any luck. The craters had all been filled in and the runways were operational. In the distance he could hear a fighter being run up.

Business as usual, he thought, looking up at the empty, pale sky. Let them come. Let them come and do their damnedest. We'll be ready for them.

Ten

Anne and Pearl lay in a dry ditch and watched the dogfight taking place high overhead. Their bikes lay at the edge of the bank where they had abandoned them when the siren had sounded.

Since the big raid on the station, there had been more attacks and the squadrons had risen each time like angry hornets to drive off the intruders. Some raids had come at night which had meant the WAAFS sleeping in cold, wet shelters, huddled together on benches. Gradually, they had grown used to the attacks and would search afterwards for pieces of shrapnel and souvenirs. Vera had the biggest collection, hoarded carefully in an old shoe box. Nobody regretted the move to Eastleigh House; after the huts it was like a palace and Pearl swore she was going to write to Hitler personally to thank him.

Anne tipped back her steel helmet to get a better view, squinting against the glare of the sun. The thin white skeins, drawn by the fighters, made looping patterns across the blue sky, like unravelled wool, and the aircraft, catching the sunlight as they turned, scintillated like tiny diamonds. It looked so unreal. You couldn't hear anything and you could hardly see anything either, and yet they were all trying to kill each other up there, not just drawing pretty patterns in the sky. Pearl, comfortably settled against the ditch bank, was chewing a long piece of grass like a seasoned spectator.

The scrambling had gone on, day after day, from dawn to dusk. All through August and the beginning of September the Spits and Hurries had taken off, time after time. The WAAFS had counted them out and then counted them back anxiously, and there were nearly always some missing. The pilots who survived all looked exhausted and there were stories of them falling sound asleep at the controls when they landed, even before the props stopped turning. In the new Ops Room, moved to an evacuated school building outside the town, it was horrible to have to listen to the sounds of battle over the R/T – to hear the frantic cries of a doomed pilot, the screams of another trapped in a burning cockpit.

'Stop fussing about your Polski, love,' Pearl said, placidly chewing. 'You don't even know if he's up there. Probably sitting on his bum playing cards, safe and sound on the ground.'

'I can't help worrying.'

'Well, I told you not to go and fall for a pilot, didn't I? Bloody stupid thing to do right now. Stick to the penguins and save yourself some grief, that's what I say.' Pearl spat out the piece of grass and fumbled round in her respirator case. 'Come on, let's have a fag while we wait for this lot to see the Jerries off.'

They lit up and then lay back again.

'Anyway,' Pearl said, after a moment, blowing smoke upwards over her head. 'You've only been out with the bloke once. You don't even know him properly, do you?'

But once had been enough. The first time she had caught sight of Michal Racyñski across the room at that party had really been enough. And when, in the middle of all this grisly struggle in the skies, he had taken her out one evening, she had known for certain that she loved him. The country pub had been crowded with other pilots from the station all trying to forget that they might be dead the next day, and there had been so much noise that at times they could hardly hear each other. She had watched him drinking his pint of bitter and smoking his cigarette and had secretly tried to imagine what his mouth would feel like when he kissed her. And she had looked at the hands holding the beer mug and the cigarette and thought about

297

them touching her. They had dark hairs on the backs and long, tapering fingers with nice-shaped nails . . . Polish hands, not English ones. Like his Polish eyes. Bedroom eyes, Pearl had called them warningly, when she had first seen him.

It had seemed out of place, somehow, to see him drinking English beer. A shot glass of vodka would have suited him better, tossed back in one go and then hurled into the nearest fireplace. When she told him so, shouting above the din, he laughed.

'But I like beer,' he had said. 'Is cheap and lasts long time. And is Russians who throw glasses into fire, not Poles. We keep ours to drink more.'

Driving back in the old Wolseley her stomach had been fluttering all over the place in expectation but when he had said good night he had only kissed her hand. True, nobody had ever kissed her hand so delightfully. In fact, she couldn't remember anyone ever kissing it at all. He had made her feel like a princess, but a frustrated one.

She watched a fresh contrail being drawn directly overhead and saw the glint of sunlight catching a wing. It could easily be Michal. There was no way of telling and nothing to be done. She had stopped saying endless little prayers for him since she had discovered that the girl who had been so busy reciting The Lord's Prayer in the air raid shelter during the big raid had been killed. Sometimes she had nightmares about being buried down there and woke in a dreadful, heart-racing panic, struggling with bedclothes. Since Enid's death Pearl refused to read any more tea leaves. Maybe she was afraid of what she might find, or maybe she felt responsible in a strange way.

Enid's body had been sent home for burial, and so had those of the two other WAAFS; but the three dead pilots and the ground personnel had all been buried in the village churchyard. A contingent of WAAFS had marched with the RAF from the station for the ceremony. The Padre's voice had been very firm and clear, ringing out so that they could hear every word. Group Captain Palmer had looked even grimmer than usual and Section Officer Newman, standing beside him, had been serious and sad. Officers had stepped forward one by one to salute the graves and the melancholy notes of the Last Post had floated across the surrounding fields. It had been very moving and there had been a lot of sniffing in the WAAF ranks.

Something, an insect probably, was tickling the back of her neck. She brushed at it with her hand.

'Funny about Gloria, Pearl . . .'

'Why, love?'

'Well, don't you remember her telling Vera that she wasn't going to get herself killed if she could bloody help it, and then she goes and stays at the switchboard with a bloody great bomb parked beside her, and they're going to give her a medal!'

'You can never tell with people, ducks. They say one thing and mean another. And just 'cos Gloria looks and behaves like a tart it doesn't mean she hasn't got guts. If any Jerry tried to rape her she'd probably kick him hard in the privates. Maureen'd probably lie down for him.'

Anne giggled. 'I should think he'd step over her.'

'Could be. Go for someone without a face like a lemon.'

'The ghastly thing though, Pearl, is that it *could* happen. If our lot *don't* see the Germans off then we're going to be invaded, aren't we?'

'It won't happen so don't get your knickers in a twist. Ours are better than theirs. Simple as that. Look, there's one of the buggers coming down now.'

'Where?'

Pearl pointed. 'Over there.'

Anne could make out a small dark shape spiralling downwards and trailing a long plume of smoke.

'How do you know it's one of theirs?'

'I can tell.'

'You can't possibly at this distance, Pearl. Anyway, there's a parachute opening. Thank God.'

'If it's a Jerry it wouldn't be anything to thank God for.'

Anne watched the little mushroom of white that had blossomed in the blue. The falling fighter disappeared behind a wood and orange flames and black smoke erupted spectacularly from the trees.

'I think it was one of ours. It looked like a Hurricane to me.'

'Whatever it was, the bloke got out, so why worry? And stop thinking it was your fella. Polskis are good pilots. Everybody says so. They've been at it much longer than ours.'

'Henryk was shot down and killed yesterday. He went off after some German even when he'd run out of ammo, apparently.'

'Asking for it, then, wasn't he?'

'Poor Henryk. He always looked so sad. Michal told me that his wife and children were all killed when Warsaw was bombed.'

'Yeah, they've had a stinking deal. Must be tough to be kicked out of your own country. But you watch out for yourself. They're not like our fellas. Not from what I've heard. Very passionate. Hot-blooded. That's why they get into such a stew about the Jerries. And they get up to some bloody funny tricks. One of the MT lot was telling me about an ATS girl who'd had to be rushed off to hospital bleeding to death 'cos some Pole had nearly bitten her nipple off.'

'I don't believe a word of it.'

'Laugh away, then, but watch it. No offence, duckie, but you're still wet behind the ears, aren't you? Don't really know what's what. Those Polskis have been around. Me, I'm going to stick to the English blokes with their feet on the bloody ground, like I said.'

'That sergeant you went out with . . . what was he like?'

Pearl flapped a hand in dismissal. 'Married, that's what he was like. Didn't I tell you? Thought I'd got something good going there at first . . . nice bloke with prospects, then he comes straight out with it, cool as a cucumber. A wife and two kids in Macclesfield. Did I mind, he asked.'

'What did you say?'

'Told him to bugger off. I don't play around with married ones. Nothing moral. I just don't fancy someone else's goods. Next time I'll ask before I go out. It'll save time.'

Anne leaned her head against the bank. 'At school some of the girls used to believe that there was only one man in the world who was the right one for you, and that destiny would bring you together.'

'What a load of crap! There's lots of good fish in the sea. Some of 'em are a bit better'n others, that's all. The rest you just chuck back.'

'Like the sergeant?'

'Like him.'

'You *are* unromantic, Pearl. Didn't that old gypsy woman say you'd meet someone tall, dark and handsome one day when she read your leaves?'

'No, she didn't. She said – *Christ! Get down!*'

The Messerschmitt had appeared from nowhere and was streaking towards them at tree-top height. As they ducked down in the ditch it screamed over their heads, the black crosses showing very clearly under its wings. It was followed hotly by a Spitfire, guns blazing. The two WAAFS lifted their heads to peer over the rim of the ditch, and watched the chase low over a field of cornstooks. They saw the German fighter seem to stagger suddenly. One wing disintegrated and pieces flew about. The Messerschmitt hurtled straight into the ground and exploded in a huge ball of fire.

Pearl was on her feet, up and out of the ditch, waving her helmet in the air and dancing up and down, cheering loudly. The Spitfire banked sharply and circled overhead before rocketing upwards. Pearl blew it a smacking kiss.

Anne stood up slowly, staring at the flames, hearing the crack-crack of exploding ammunition. Thick black smoke was billowing from the fire and there was an acrid stench of burning rubber, cordite, fuel . . . She put her hands up to her cheeks.

'Oh, God, how horrible! How *horrible*!'

Pearl was still jumping up and down, waving to the Spitfire.

'Shouldn't we do something, Pearl?'

'What? He'll be done to a crisp. Serve him bloody well right.'

'Pearl . . .'

Pearl stopped jumping and came over, peering at her. 'You look as though you're going to be sick, lovie.' She put an arm round Anne's shoulders. 'Come on, don't go and get soppy over a Jerry. Just think, it might have been the bloke in the Spit.'

The station firetruck was already careering across the fields towards the wreckage. Anne, pedalling shakily along behind Pearl, looked back over her shoulder. Some of the corn stubble had caught fire and little rivulets of flame were spreading out from the German pilot's funeral pyre. She shuddered.

'Have some more wine, Titania?'

Felicity covered her glass quickly. 'No, thank you, Speedy. I've had enough.'

'Never say that.'

They were sitting in the Old Ship, at the same table as before. In his usual way, Speedy had turned up out of the blue. He had driven over from Kent on a forty-eight hour leave and announced that he was taking her out to dinner. The MG now looked more battered than ever. String adorned the rear bumper as well as the front, and the hole in the floor by Felicity's right foot seemed to have got much larger.

'Brought old Whitters along with me,' he had told her as they roared away from the station. 'Just parked him with his grandmother. She's got a ten-bedroomed hovel not a stone's throw from here. I'm staying there myself tonight. Not a bad old girl, as a matter of fact. We used to go round there for a slap-up feed after sailing, back in the good old days of peace and plenty.'

'Where's George?'

'Left him there too. She spoils him rotten. All the best scraps. I knew you'd do without a chaperone for the sake of George's stomach.'

She clutched at the door handle as they swept round a bend. 'How is Whitters?'

'A bit pooped, to tell the truth. We all are. Not a lot of shut-eye lately. Every time we go up there seem to be more and more Huns swarming about all over the place. Can't keep pace with 'em. And most of the sprogs they keep sending us haven't a clue, so we have to play nursemaid. Jolly tiring. Still, Grandmama will tuck him up in beddy-byes nice and early. He's hoping the old girl'll leave him some cash in her will so he'll be on his very best behaviour.'

The thought of the irrepressible Whitters on any such thing made Felicity smile.

It was still light when they drove down the lane leading to the harbour front. The tide was out, as she remembered it had been last time, and there was that same salty seaweed smell that made her think of childhood summer holidays. And think wistfully of how it would be to come here in peacetime.

Over dinner she studied him covertly. She thought he looked even more exhausted than when she had last seen him. There were dark rings under his eyes and the scar on his forehead showed very red against his pallor. He kept propping his chin on his hand and once or twice she thought he was going to fall asleep, sitting at the table.

'Rum sort of war, this,' he said, waving his fork vaguely. 'There you are chasing some Jerry across the fields, hopping over hedges, both of you screeching along like bats out of hell, and you can see people picnicking as though nothing was happening at all . . . White cloths laid out, pouring the tea, passing round the cucumber sandwiches . . . Life going on as per usual with us thrashing about in the skies overhead. I went over a cricket match the other day and they didn't even look up.'

'It must seem strange.'

'Well, it does. It does indeed. And it's just as odd upstairs, sometimes. Do you know we often get BBC broadcasts on our radios, right in the middle of everything. There we are listening to our revered and gallant leader rallying us to the flag, exhorting us to go in and give our all, and suddenly some woman's telling us to take 4 ounces of fat and half a pound of flour and blend well together.'

Felicity laughed. 'I don't believe it.'

'I swear it's true. Last time it was a recipe for rock cakes. Whitters was kindly drawing my attention to some Hun on my tail and this woman starts saying "Bake the cakes for ten minutes at Gas Mark Seven until well risen and golden brown".'

She still wasn't entirely sure whether to believe him, but he seemed quite serious now, turning his wine glass stem round and round between his fingers thoughtfully. Staring at it.

'The weirdest thing of all is to go into the pub of an evening, as we are wont to do. The locals are all there, sitting over their pints, and in we come pretending we've had our feet on the ground all day and that everything's tickety-boo. Nobody mentions what's been going on. Or who's missing. It's pints all round and talk about the weather. Been a lovely summer, hasn't it, and all that . . . To be honest, half the time we pray for a good old peasouper so that we can get a bit of rest.' He lifted his head and smiled at her wearily. 'I didn't tell you I came down in the drink the other day, did I?'

She caught her breath. 'No . . . actually, you didn't.'

'Well, you know me. Always a spot of drama. Some Jerry made a confounded nuisance of himself — they've got no consideration at all. Scored a bullseye in the engine.

Flames all over the shop, and getting warmer, so I had to hop out and take a little swim in the Channel.' Speedy wagged a forefinger at her. 'Don't ever let anyone tell you that the water's warm in summer because they'd be lying.'

She tried to smile. 'Was it long before you were picked up?'

'Not sure. My watch had stopped and I sort of lost track of time. I paddled about a bit and sang a song or two to keep my spirits up. Not ones you'd know, Titania. At least, you might know the tunes, but not the words . . . I kept wishing I had a dinghy like the bomber boys. For some reason they seem to think us fighter chaps are unsinkable. Then I was trying to think of a good quotation for the occasion and I remembered that bit from *The Ancient Mariner*.'

'*Water, water everywhere?*'

'No. Better than that. *Alone, alone, all, all alone. Alone on a wide, wide sea.* Rather apt, don't you think? Old Snodgrass would have given me ten out of ten.'

'Top of the class?'

'Definitely. Anyway, I said that to myself a few hundred times and just as I was beginning to think that everyone had forgotten all about me, this splendid launch turns up. Very decent chaps on board, too. One of them had had the foresight to bring along a bottle of brandy . . .'

Afterwards, as they had done before, they walked along the quayside towards the boatsheds. It was almost dark with just a faint, dull red glow left in the west, like the dying embers of a fire. She remembered how far away the war had seemed last time. Now the Germans were only on the other side of the water. Speedy put his arm round her shoulders.

'When I was waiting to be picked up – or not, as the case might be – I thought about you a lot, Titania. That kept me going.'

'That's a very nice compliment, Speedy,' she said carefully.

He stopped walking and turned towards her. He put his hands on her shoulders. 'You know I'm awfully in love with you, don't you?'

'Oh, dear.'

'The funny thing is I've been out with lots of girls, but I've never really cared two hoots about them until now. I've never met anyone like you, you see. I told you that before.'

'I'm nothing special at all.'

'I think you are,' he said solemnly. 'Very special. The thing is, I know you're not in love with me. Not yet, anyhow. But do you think there's a chance you might be . . . later on?'

'I honestly don't know, Speedy. I like you very much. I'm very fond of you, but – '

'Not quite the same thing, is it?' He sighed deeply. 'Maybe if I'm very good and patient, you will be one day.'

'You'll meet someone else, Speedy.'

'Not like you, Titania. Never like you.'

When he kissed her she hadn't the heart to stop him. He held her close against him for a moment and then sighed once more.

'I suppose it's time to take you back. Then tomorrow it's back unto the flipping breach again. I must say the old ticker sinks a bit at the thought. Ah well. Press on regardless, as they say.'

They walked slowly back along the quayside and he kept his arm firmly round her shoulders all the way.

'Come and have a cup of tea, Winnie?'

'No, thank you.'

But Taffy blocked her way. People were pushing past them in the NAAFI corridor and someone jostled her so hard she almost fell into his arms. Someone else was grinning at her and making some remark she didn't catch.

'It's only a cup of tea, Winnie,' Taffy said pleadingly. 'We could just sit and talk a bit, that's all.'

She gave way. Taffy wouldn't budge and it was hard to make a fuss with everybody going past and staring at them and sniggering. After all, she was safe enough here in the NAAFI and there was nothing wrong with having a cup of tea with him.

They queued at the canteen counter for tea and buns which Taffy insisted on paying for. As he set them down on the table she noticed that there were corporal's tapes on his arm now. The table was sticky with spilled beer and speckled with cigarette ash. He made a face as he took a sip of the tea.

'This stuff's worse than ever. Tastes like sawdust. I bet they do put bromide in it.'

'Bromide?'

'You know, the stuff that makes you drowsy. They're supposed to put it in the tea to keep our passions down.'

She went red.

'I'm only joking. It's just a silly story. You know the rubbish people talk in this place.' He rubbed a hand over his eyes. 'No need for it anyhow. It's been hard enough keeping awake lately. Not much time for sleep.'

She'd watched the fighters taking off time after time since the big raid, craning her neck to follow them as far as she could from the Orderly Room window. She always counted them and crossed her fingers for them. When they came back she counted them again to see how many were missing and watched the ones that had been shot up wobbling and spluttering past, fuselage sometimes in tatters.

Taffy went on. 'All night it is sometimes, with the CO screaming for aircraft and most of them U/S . . . We're beavering away like a lot of lunatics.'

'I've watched them goin' out every day,' she said.

He smiled with a quiet satisfaction. 'We can turn the Hurries round in eight minutes if there's a flap on. Refuel, rearm, engine check, instruments, radio, the whole lot . . . Not bad.'

She'd seen ground crew swarming over a fighter that had just landed. The pilot hadn't even left the cockpit before it taxied off again.

Taffy was watching her intently. 'You look tired too, Winnie. Have they been working you hard?'

'We've been busy.'

Endless forms. Endless queries. Endless filing. So many more people now on the station.

'You're all right, though?' he persisted. 'No ill effects from being in that shelter, I mean?'

She shook her head. She didn't want to talk about it. She had tried hard to forget what had happened and not to think of Enid. Blast did funny things sometimes, everybody had told her. It could get someone and leave the person right next to them quite unhurt. The Hand of God, Vera had called it dramatically, though why should God have chosen just to put His hand on Enid?

Vera was making faces at her now from across the canteen, mouthing widely: *are you all right*? She nodded and gave her a quick little wave to show so.

'Before the raids started,' Taffy was saying, 'some of the boys hadn't a good word to say for you WAAFS. They think differently now, I can tell you . . . the way you've stuck it all and kept going cool and calm as anything. Mind you, I don't know if they'd go so far as to want any of you in the hangars . . . not yet, anyhow. Maybe one day.' He smiled at her. 'See, I don't forget anything you've ever said to me. Do you still want to be a flight mech?'

'I don't think they'll ever let us,' she said wistfully.

'They might.' Taffy watched her face. He said softly: 'I could teach you a bit about aircraft, if you like – so's you'd stand a better chance, if it ever came to it. What would you like to know?'

'Well . . .'

'Just ask away. I'll do my best.'

Winnie blushed. 'I still don't understand how the

308

'planes fly. I can't see how they get up into the air when they're so heavy.'

'That's simple really.' He put down his tea and held his hands out, turned away from each other and tilted upwards slightly. 'The wings are set at an angle, like this, see, so that when the airscrew's turning and pulling the aircraft along fast enough, the angle drives the air flowing past the wings *underneath* them and forces them upwards.'

She tried to follow him, but it still made no clear sense.

He sketched a curve with one hand over the back of the other. 'As well as that, the wing is cambered on the upper surface, like this. That makes the air pressure less on top and greater underneath, where it's flatter, so that sort of sucks the wing upwards. See?'

'I think so,' she said doubtfully.

He dropped his hands and rummaged in the breast pocket of his battle dress tunic. 'Well, there's a lot more to it than that, of course.' He took out a piece of paper and unfolded it, smoothing it flat. 'Look you, I'll give you a demonstration of air flow lifting something. Watch this.'

He let the paper hang loosely from his fingertips, holding it by two corners a little way from him. As he blew gently along the upper surface the paper rose into the air. 'See? Me blowing like that makes an airflow across the top surface of the paper and that causes a decrease in air pressure there. But the air pressure *below* the paper isn't decreased, so the paper rises up, just like you saw. That's the secret of flight.' He smiled at her, holding out the piece of paper. 'Here, you try.'

He stared at her soft lips, pursed to blow. The paper fluttered and then lifted for her. She handed it back to him, looking both pleased and shy.

'Of course,' he said casually. 'There's other things you ought to know about. You've got to keep the aircraft stable in flight so it doesn't swing about in the air, or pitch up and down. And you've got to be able to turn it left and right, and go up and down, and bank . . . But that's all getting a bit more complicated.'

'Would you mind very much explainin' some more to me?'

He grabbed at the chance she had given him, veiling his triumph. Taking a pencil stub from his pocket, he leaned forward across the table and began to draw a picture of an aeroplane on th. iece of paper.

'Well now . . . Your tailplane here gives fore and aft stability. It has to support the fuselage in just the right position, so it isn't nose-heavy or tail-heavy. Then you've got your fin at the back, sticking up like this, with the rudder attached. The rudder's connected to a bar in the cockpit that the pilot pushes with his feet. If he pushes the left side forward, the machine turns left. If he pushes the right, it goes right. Easy.' He sketched on quickly, deftly. 'And here's your elevator on the tailplane, at the side. That's connected to the pilot's control column in the cockpit. When he pulls it towards him this way, the elevator goes up and catches the wind. That forces the tail *down*, which makes the aircraft's nose go *up*, and so she climbs . . .' Taffy demonstrated with the pencil stub. 'If he pushes it forward, the opposite happens and she dives. See?'

Winnie, chin on her hands, concentrating hard, nodded. She had forgotten all about being afraid of Taffy and was quite oblivious to the buzz and clatter of the canteen around her. Vera passed by the table, dragging her feet and coughing helpfully, but Winnie did not even notice her. She was watching the pencil moving across the paper again.

'These flaps on the trailing edge of the wings are called ailerons,' Taffy told her. 'They're attached to the control column too. Push it sideways – to the left, say – and the port aileron goes up and the starboard one down. The wind catches hold of them and makes the port wing tip go down and the starboard wing tip come up. So, the machine banks, like this.'

Taffy stretched both arms wide and demonstrated for her. Winnie watched attentively. He dragged his eyes away from her and went on drawing.

'You've got your airscrew on the nose, of course, and when that's turning, the blades chop at the air and pull the machine along. Same as paddling a boat in water, really . . .'

She listened and watched, totally fascinated. Taffy had opened a new door for her, and onto a world she had longed to discover. When, finally, he put down the pencil, she was transparently disappointed.

'That's enough for now. You'll get muddled, Winnie. I'll tell you more another time.'

After that, it was an easy matter for him to persuade her to go out with him.

He took her to the cinema in town, travelling in on the bus. It was a Betty Grable picture and Winnie enjoyed it. Compared with wartime England, America seemed a wonderful place. Everything on the screen up above her looked dazzlingly beautiful and so full of colour and light. The people were so good-looking and well-dressed that she could scarcely believe that they were real. Everything about them was perfect. And their homes were like palaces. She had never seen such space, such luxury . . .

Afterwards they went to the cinema café and had sausages and chips, and a pot of tea. Again, Taffy paid for her though she tried hard to stop him.

Over the café table he explained a bit more to her, this time about the aircraft engine. She listened entranced to him speaking of pistons and four-stroke cycles; of carburettors and cylinders; of compression and sparks and ignition; of valves and cams and magnetos. They were all magical-sounding words to her and she began to understand what she had only been able to reason instinctively about the Fordson. Taffy drew more diagrams for her on a piece of paper, among the teacups and plates, and, again, he stopped just when she wanted badly to know more.

It was dark and raining when they walked to the bus

stop and they waited in the shelter of a nearby doorway. He screened her from the slanting rain, one arm raised protectively against the wall. Her closeness tantalized him, but he was careful not to touch her. He wished he could see her better. He had always thought her adorable in her uniform. He loved the way her hair curled up round the edge of her cap and the way her large eyes looked at him from beneath its jutting peak. The belted tunic fitted her so neatly at the waist and the severe, masculine cut only made her seem all the more desirably feminine in his eyes. He was not the only one, he knew, to think so.

'You know what some of the lads call you girls?' he told her. 'Bluebirds. From the bluebird of happiness, see? That's what you can bring us . . . if you want to.'

He knew she was blushing in the darkness.

'The bus is comin',' she said, and ducked under his arm as it came swishing along the street towards them.

The chalk mass of the South Downs lay a few miles to the north of Colston, where it curved inland away from the sea. Anne, standing on the top of them, and thinking back to geography lessons at school, remembered that the mass had once been joined to France thousands of years ago. When the Ice Age had ended the melted waters had flooded the depression between England and Europe, creating the Channel. Just as well, in the circumstances. She was still panting from the steep climb up as she surveyed the countryside spread out far below. Everything was in miniature. Little fields, all shapes and sizes, fitting together like pieces of a jigsaw, trees looking just like the toy ones made of lead that she and Kit had played with in the nursery, lead cows and sheep dotted about, and a toy lorry speeding along a road. The houses were Monopoly houses and a toy train, just like Kit's, puffed along at the far side of the jigsaw. The colours were all dusty late summer green and harvest gold, the horizon a hazy, distant border.

She took off her cap and shook her head, letting the

wind blow through her hair. 'We could walk for miles along the ridge, as far as Beachy Head that way, and Hampshire that way.' She waved her arm vaguely east and then west. 'It's lovely, isn't it? Like being on top of the world.'

Standing beside her, Michal Racyñski smiled. 'Beautiful England. The most beautiful country in the world.'

'Do you think so?' she said, pleased. 'More beautiful than Poland?'

'I think so – yes.'

She had no idea what Poland looked like. Not the faintest clue. Forests, most probably. Dark fir trees, though, not leafy English ones. Gloomy clearings, not sylvan glades. Where had she been when the geography lessons had covered Poland? Asleep at the back of the class, most likely, while Miss Carpenter droned on about climate and crops and natural resources.

She admired the jigsaw again. 'Does it look like this from an aeroplane?'

'Yes, but is not the same feeling. We have feet on ground. And is low.'

'What's it like being high up?' She lifted her head. 'Up there in the clouds?'

He spread his hands. 'Is very difficult to tell you. Like to dance in space. Like in paradise. Like to reach for the stars . . . I have not the words in English. Or even, perhaps, in Polish.'

She had watched his face as he struggled to express himself. 'You love flying, don't you?'

'Very much. Since a small boy I want to fly. As soon as I am big I join the Polish Air Force. When Warsaw is bombed we fight the Germans. Many, many die. Many 'planes are destroyed. Our aerodromes are bombed. The army is fighting German tanks with horses. Everything is very, very bad.'

They began to walk westwards along the ridge of the Downs. There were blisters coming on both her heels from her beetle-crusher shoes, but she scarcely noticed them. He had taken off his cap too and the wind was blowing his hair about. It made him look much younger, she thought, stealing a sideways glance. She could imagine him as a small boy.

'How did you come to England?' she asked. 'What happened?'

'Oh, is long story.'

'Tell me, just the same.' She wanted to know everything about him.

He smiled at her. 'You are very curious. If you want so much, I tell you some.' He put his hands in his pockets as they walked along. 'When all is so bad in Poland, I am sent to Rumania with other pilots to fetch French machines. The Rumanian government promise these, but instead, when we arrive, we are all made prisoner and put in camp.'

'How rotten of them!'

'Rotten? I do not know this word.'

'Beastly. Not nice.'

He laughed. 'No, was not nice at all. The camp is place for horses. Was only straw and cold water. We eat soup and black bread one time a day. So, soon I escape. I walk and I walk. I hide in ditch and woods. I sleep in cellars with rats. All the time I walk and then I hide. Then I come to railway station. I have no money for ticket, so I jump on train when is moving.'

It all sounded incredible to her, like a story out of some adventure book. 'What happened then?'

'I sit in train. All are Rumanian people. A man who is opposite look and look at me all the time, and I think I am finished. I was told many Rumanians are for Germans, you see. He speak to me in Polish because he sees my Polish pilot's bag and he knows this. I think he betray me but when the man is coming for the tickets he gives me his ticket and pretends to lose his own. When we arrive at Bucharest he takes me to a restaurant and gives me food. I did not eat for two days before and so was very good.

314

Best food I ever taste. Then he shake my hand and wish me luck.'

'Jolly decent of him.'

'*Tak!* Jolly decent. I like that English.'

'What did you do then?'

'I go to Polish Consulate in Bucharest and get train ticket to Belgrade. Was no longer possible, you understand, to go back to Poland. So, I try to go south west, to go to France. I never think then of going to England. At the frontier station to Yugoslavia there are German soldiers everywhere. Everybody is taken from train and put in room for interrogation. There are two German officers who ask many questions. I speak to them in German and tell many lies. I say I am student. When we go to Rumania we are all given false passports which say we are students, not military. I think because I speak good German they believe me and let me go on to Belgrade, but many others are arrested. I see them march away.'

And all this had been going on, Anne thought, while she had been moaning about cleaning ranges and peeling potatoes, and finding the whole war rather a yawn. She pictured the train thundering across war-torn Europe, the frontier station, the jackbooted soldiers, the cold-eyed German officers rapping out frightening questions, the shuffling queue, women sobbing, children crying, the unlucky ones being hustled away . . .

He went on. 'From Belgrade I go to Athens by train and then go with Polish ship to Marseilles. That bit is easy. I join with the French Armée de l'Air. I speak good French, much better than English, so language was not difficult like here. They teach me to fly Potez – French fighters, you know – and I go north, near Rennes. We do what is called chimney flights . . . We protect factories and power stations . . . things like that. Was the beginning of 1940, before France fell.'

'Poor France.'

'Poor France,' he agreed. 'But we Poles are not understanding them very well. We ask them: Why you not attack the Germans? Why you wait and wait until is too late?'

'My brother says the French think we let them down. Deserted them.'

He shrugged. 'I think the French do this to themselves. They were not well organized. Many stop to fight. A Pole is never like that. We fight to die, even when is hopeless.'

She hated to hear him talk like that. Henryk had died because he had gone after a German without any bullets left. That was crazy. But everyone said the Poles were like that. They hated the Germans. *Loathed* them. She had never met a British pilot who felt such hatred.

'So, when France fell, you came to England?'

He smiled. 'Was not so easy. Not so quick like that. When we are in France the Germans come nearer and nearer and one day when I come back to land I am told I must switch off engine and leave my machine. Germans are coming very soon and we must all surrender. But I do not do this. Instead, I take off again very quick. They shoot at me, but they miss.'

'The *French* shot at you?'

'I do not obey the order, so they shoot. Is natural.' He shrugged. 'I have not much fuel, so I fly south to next aerodrome.'

'Why didn't you go north, towards England?'

'Because I know Germans are already in north, and I cannot go as far as England. So, I go south and then I leave my machine and I walk.'

'More walking?'

'*Tak*. More walking. I walk many, many miles since this war begins. Then I meet other Polish pilots, also walking, with some Czech officers. We try to find transport but the French do not want to help us. With luck we find big depot and make the gate open with guns. We take lorry, fuel, some food, and we drive to Bordeaux. Is all bombed. All ships there are sunk, except one. We get on this ship and the captain he take us to England. Five days on sea and no food except some peanuts that is cargo before. The captain has mascot. An animal . . . I do not know name. Has milk.'

'A cow?'

'No, is too big. Smaller. Little like this.' He held out his hand, palm down. Then he stroked his chin. 'And has little beard.'

'Oh, a goat.'

'Yes, a goat. But she disappear during voyage. People eat her. Captain is very sad. Very cross.' He laughed at Anne's expression. 'Don't be so shocked. *I* do not eat her. Everyone is very, very hungry. You must understand this. You never know what is like. You are lucky.'

She stopped walking and turned to face him. 'I know. I've been thinking just that, listening to you. I *am* lucky. We're all lucky in England. We've never had to go really hungry. And we haven't been invaded by the Germans. Not so far, anyway.'

'It never happen,' he said. 'We stop Germans, I swear. They are never in your country, like they are in mine.'

She saw the sadness in his face, and bitter anger too, and longed to comfort him.

'One day you'll go back to Poland.'

'Of course. First we fight Germans here, then we go back to free our country. And then I think we need you to help us fight Russians. You see, is never finished with Poland.' He ran his hand through his hair. 'Is always war. But we not talk of this now. For now I am happy to be here in England.'

'I'm happy you're here too.'

He smiled down at her, into her eyes. 'Thank you, Anne. I am very glad you say that. You are so English . . . So . . . so simple.'

'*Simple*? That means stupid.'

He frowned, vexed with himself. 'Is wrong word. I certainly not mean this.'

'Straightforward?'

'Perhaps. I wish I speak better English to talk how I

317

want with you. Ah! Decent. *Tak*. Jolly decent. That is something like I mean, I think.'

She said doubtfully, 'It sounds a bit hearty. Jolly hockeysticks, and all that.'

'Hockeysticks?'

'It's a game. We played it at school.'

I can't explain all that to him, she thought. He'd never understand. She was downcast to think that he saw her in such a light. Like a schoolgirl. A jolly English schoolgirl. All giggling and blushing and innocent. He'd be used to other women, of course. Polish ones, French ones . . . slinky Continental women who were not a bit 'so English'.

They walked on and she tried not to stride out too energetically beside him, to make a more graceful impression. Then she began to think about the hatred he must feel for the Germans who had taken his country away from him, and to wonder if she would ever feel the same if they invaded England . . . whether she would be able to kill a German, to fire a rifle like the airman had shown her, without hesitating.

'I saw a Messerschmitt shot down the other day,' she said. 'It was awfully close. Pearl and I were biking over to the station when we heard the siren go. We jumped into a ditch to take cover.'

He exclaimed. '*Close?* What happened?'

'Well, it came over very low and there was a Spitfire chasing it all across the fields. The Spit got it and the Messerschmitt crashed and burst into flames. It was rather awful, seeing it happen like that. I felt rather sorry for the German pilot. It was such a violent, horrible end.'

She didn't add that she had seen it again many times in her mind's eye and had nightmares of it happening to him.

He shook his head. 'I am never sorry when I shoot them. *Never*. In Poland, in France . . . here, in England, always when I see a German go down, I hope he is dead.

318

I say to myself, that is one less of them to fight . . . and I am very glad.'

Because their backs were turned, they did not see the fighter approaching fast from the direction of the Channel. The Pole caught the sound first and, looking over his shoulder, instantly grabbed the girl and flung himself and her to the ground. He shielded her with his own body as the Messerschmitt streaked over them, unleashing a vicious stream of bullets that stitched a pathway along the turf only feet from where they lay. Then, as suddenly as it had appeared, the enemy raider was gone, pelting back towards the coast and France.

Michal lifted his head. A torrent of Polish came from his lips and there was murder in his eyes. He stared after the fighter.

'I kill him,' he said. 'I kill them all.'

Eleven

'Firefly Blue Leader, this is Beehive calling. Are you receiving? Over.'

'Hallo, Beehive. Loud and clear. Over.'

'Vector one-eight-zero. Angels fifteen. Over.'

'Message received and understood. Out.'

Friendly and hostile plots advanced towards each other across the plotting table. Virginia reached out with her rake to alter hers.

'Hallo, Blue Leader. Beehive calling. Orbit. Bandits approaching you from south west. Over.'

There was a long silence. The Controller wiped his face with his handkerchief in the stuffy heat. The Ops Room loudspeaker crackled suddenly again, this time with a different voice. Urgent.

'Blue Three calling Blue Leader. Aircraft two o'clock.'

'OK Blue Three, I see them. *Christ! Hordes of the buggers!* Hallo, Beehive. Blue Leader calling. Tallyho! Going in now . . . Over.'

'Good luck, Blue Leader. Listening. Out.'

The Controller mopped his face again. Beside him, Ops B lit a cigarette. Virginia passed the back of her hand across her forehead. In a moment the battle would begin, against overwhelming odds.

Sometimes she still went on plotting in her dreams. And there was a recurring nightmare in which her hands felt too stiff and leaden to move the blocks and arrows fast enough, and the rake was much too big and heavy for her to lift. She would wake up in a terrible agitation that subsided only slowly as she registered her surroundings — the high ceiling, the fancy plaster moulding, the flowered wallpaper with the patches where the owners' pictures had hung before the WAAF had taken over the house. The other plotters on B watch, who shared the room, slept peacefully and soundly. Madge, next to her, big and noisy when awake, often snored loudly when she was asleep. When they were on nightwatch and trying to sleep during the day, Madge would wear a sanitary towel as a mask across her eyes, the loops hooked over each ear. At first, Virginia had been shocked; now, as with other things that had shocked her, like bad language and nakedness, she had become used to it.

Sometimes, too, she dreamed of Pamela – dreams in which she was still very much alive, walking and talking in her confident way. It was a shock, then, to waken and realize that she was dead. She would remember, against her will, the grey stockinged legs protruding oddly from the rubble, the black shoes, the seeping pool of blood mixing with the white dust . . . And, if she were not very firm with herself, she would start to imagine the rest of Pamela lying beneath that crushing slab of concrete.

It was tiredness, she decided, that was the cause of the vivid dreams and nightmares. They were all dog-tired. The hours of concentration demanded on the day watches, with an incessant stream of plots coming into their ears, had taken their toll. And the night watch, though far less frenzied than the day, could be even more gruelling in its way. The vigil sometimes seemed endless. They would struggle to keep awake round the plotting table during long spells of inactivity and, during their twenty-minute break in the small hours, would often fall fast asleep, their heads resting on each other's shoulders.

Once, at two o'clock in the morning, she had plotted a friendly aircraft from Coastal Command, lost in thick fog over the Channel, and with engine trouble. It had been directed to Colston and she had watched its progress anxiously, as though she herself, by moving its plot across the map, could bring it safely down. At last they had heard it droning overhead, circling unsteadily, and she had waited in suspense until news came that the Hudson had landed safely. Later on, the pilot had come into the Ops Room and she had not been able to help staring at him as he talked to the Controller. He had looked very young to her, hardly more than a boy. Under the bright lights his face was chalk-white and she could see the marks from his mask and flying helmet. He had glanced down from the gallery and, catching Virginia's stare, had smiled at her and raised his hand in salutation. The memory of this salute, as though in personal thanks, had stayed fixed in her mind, sustaining her through further wearying hours.

It was Madge's idea to go to the Salvation Army canteen in the town. She and Virginia had gone to the pictures one rainy evening and, counting their pennies afterwards, two days short of pay day, had found they hadn't enough money to go to a café. As usual, Madge was ravenously hungry.

'Let's try the Sally Ann place. Dirt cheap. Warm and dry. What more do we want?'

The Salvation Army had taken over a church hall in the town centre and when the two plotters entered it was crowded. Army khaki, air force blue and naval navy sat shoulder to shoulder at the long trestle tables. The big room smelled of damp uniforms, cigarette smoke and steam from the big urns at the counter.

They queued for tea and buns and Madge elbowed a space at the end of one of the tables. Three airmen, sitting opposite, nudged each other. One of them leaned across to Madge.

'Wot's your name then, darlin'?'

In her own way, Madge could be quite as intimidating as Pamela. Her background was far less exalted – her father was a dentist and she had been brought up in a small house in Brighton, not a big house in Kensington and a vast mansion in Yorkshire – but she could be as outspoken as she was large.

She looked at the airman coldly. 'Are you talking to me?'

'That's right, sweetheart.'

'Then, please, don't.'

He stopped smirking and glowered. 'Wot's the matter? Same rank as us, aren't you?'

'That has nothing to do with it. I simply don't want to talk to you.'

One of his companions tittered. The other, small and weasel-faced, said sourly:

'Oh, leave it alone, Sid. Bloomin' toffee-nosed WAAFS. Officers' groundsheets, that's all her kind are. She wouldn't give you the time of day.'

Virginia had gone scarlet and was staring at the table, but Madge looked at the little airman as though he were a weevil who had just crawled out of the hall woodwork.

'Do you usually insult defenceless women on their own? What a coward you must be.'

He shifted uneasily. Sid sniggered.

'Squashed you, too, Ron.'

Madge ignored them and turned her attention to her plate. Ron drained his tea and stood up.

'She'd squash me an' all . . . Built like one of them battleships.' He stood up. 'Come on, lads, let's leave their ladyships. Not worth the bloody trouble.'

'Good riddance,' said Madge calmly, when they had gone. 'Now we can have a bit more room, as well as some peace.'

But before she could move round the other side of the table, the spaces left by the airmen were filled at once by three soldiers. They were all Canadian corporals, and one of them was Neil Mackenzie.

Virginia's blush deepened and she did not know where to look. If he felt any awkwardness at the encounter himself, he showed no sign of it. His face had lit up into an easy smile as he recognized her.

'Well, hallo, there! Great to see you again. How've you been?'

Madge glanced at her in surprise. 'You're a dark horse, Ginny.'

'We met out biking . . .' she said lamely.

'Well, introduce me, then.'

Madge was as gracious with the three Canadians as she had been sharp with the airmen. Virginia could tell that she approved of their pleasant manners, and wished she didn't. Before long she was roaring with laughter at some joke.

Neil leaned forward. 'We heard you had some bad raids lately. I was real worried. I tried to find out if you were OK. They said some WAAFS were killed.'

'Yes, three of them.'

'Friends of yours?'

'One of them was.'

He clicked his tongue. 'That's too bad. I'm real sorry. We'll get back at the Jerries for it, when we get the chance. They'll have a taste of their own medicine.' He searched her face. 'Didn't you get my letter? I wrote a week or two back.'

She went redder still. She had got it and had thrown it away in a panic, barely reading through to the end. The rather scrawly writing had asked her how she was . . . told her how great the bike ride had been . . . said something about another meeting . . . another party at the camp . . . asked her to write back.

He went on casually: 'She called you, Ginny. It's cute. Mind if I call you that?'

A lot of the other WAAFS called her the same. Mother would hate it, if she knew. She would probably think it very common. But then Mother would hate her to be in this place and think it very common too – full of Other Ranks and people like Sid and Ron. And Canadians. Not even English. She drank some more tea and stared at her plate again.

'You been on any more good bike rides lately, Ginny?'

She pushed a crumb round the edge of the plate, keeping her eyes down.

'We haven't had much time really. And we do a lot of biking anyway, just getting from place to place. We're billeted right away from the station now.'

'That makes sense. Good place?'

She thought of Eastleigh House, which belonged to titled people, Sir Reginald and Lady Howard. Mother had liked hearing about that, at least. It was a beautiful place. The big drawing-room looked out onto a sweeping lawn with wonderful herbaceous borders. A white squirrel lived in the copper beech at the far end and they fed it with tit-bits. Sometimes it actually ate out of their hands. The dining-room had oak panelling and french windows leading out onto a flagstone terrace. There was a croquet lawn, goldfish pools, a tennis court, a walled garden and a big stable block.

'It's very nice,' she said, still pushing the crumb round with her forefinger. 'Much better than the awful huts we lived in before.'

He grinned. 'We don't even have huts – we're in tents. I figure it's goin' to be a tough winter.'

'Won't you be used to the cold?'

'Sure. It's a whole lot colder back home. But we take care of it pretty well. It's always warm indoors. I guess we have to, or we wouldn't survive.' He paused and added quietly. 'It's just great, meeting you again like this, Ginny?'

In the bus on the way back, Madge said: 'Seems jolly keen on you, that chap, Neil. Rather nice, I thought. Decent manners. I heard him asking you out. Pity you turned him down.'

'I don't know him, really.'

'Well, it's your funeral, Ginny. I'd've gone like a shot. Good sort of chap.' Madge rubbed her stomach. 'Golly, I'm still famished.'

The white squirrel was sitting on the lawn beneath the copper beech tree, nibbling daintily at something held between its front paws. Winnie, watching it from the downstairs window, thought how pretty it was. Much prettier than the grey ones that looked a bit like rats. She had never seen a white one before. An albino, someone had called it. And, less kindly, a freak of nature. Like a black sheep, perhaps, or a cow with only one horn. It seemed to live quite alone and she wondered if other squirrels shunned it because it was different. Animals could do that, she knew. She had seen it with chickens: with human beings, come to that. She had watched WAAFS being treated that way – girls who just didn't fit in for some reason – foreigners, loners, some rookies . . . She had felt very sorry for them, but there was not much that she could do.

Everyone seemed so sure of it all now. It was quite different from the early days when nobody had known anything much. Drill had become easy. They marched about and wheeled and turned and halted, stamping their feet very smartly. She had even learned to salute properly at last, so that meeting officers around the station was no longer the dreaded muddle it had once been. She managed quite well now – saluting three paces before reaching the officer, and holding it for three paces after. Longest way up, shortest way down. And there were all sorts of tricks the WAAFS had learned – softening their hard, uncomfortable shoes in buckets of water, and putting the black boot polish on with hot knives so that they shone better. Some, like Gloria, cut out their pocket linings to flatten their tunics and turned their waistbands over to shorten their skirts. Nobody wanted to be taken for a rookie, so they'd stick new caps in buckets of water, as well, to make them look old and press new uniforms with a hot iron to take the first fluff off.

Vera had come into the room behind her. She addressed it at large.

'Do you know s-something? The p-poor Poles never get *any* post. No letters from anyone, when everybody else does. Isn't it a shame?'

She was looking quite upset, almost tearful. Winnie felt rather grateful to her for being the same old Vera. Nobody took much notice. Maureen glanced up from her knitting.

'Well, they haven't got anyone to write to them, have they? Their families are all in Poland. The Germans aren't going to let any letters through.'

Sandra, busy writing a letter home, had a shocked expression. 'Gosh, how awful! That's *so* sad. The saddest thing I ever heard. I couldn't *bear* not to have letters. Mummy writes to me every single week. Couldn't we do something about it? We could send them postcards and things . . . just so's they have *something*.'

Maureen's needles clicked sharply. 'You know what Section Officer Newman said, Sandra. She warned us to be on our guard against the Poles. You'd only be encouraging them.'

'I don't care. I think it's too sad for words. And I think we should do something about it.'

'S-so do I,' Vera said. 'I've got a postcard of Brighton pier somewhere. It's quite nice. I could send that to them.'

Another girl put down her book. 'I've got one of Buckingham Palace and the changing of the guard. Do you think they'd like that?'

Vera beamed. 'Bound to. They don't have a King and Queen in P-Poland, do they?'

Others in the room began to remember that they had postcards, too, and greetings cards that might do.

'We could make them ourselves, as well.' Sandra was looking happy again. 'Draw pictures or cut them out and glue them on paper.'

Winnie had no postcard but she thought she could manage that. She was glad that Maureen had been ignored. The Poles at Colston always seemed so nice – always bowing so politely. Everyone said how brave they were, and it must be terrible to have lost your home and not even to have a single letter from your family to comfort you. Mum didn't often write, but that was different. She knew they were there, safe at Elmbury. Some of the Poles didn't even know *what* had happened to their families: whether they were dead or alive.

She watched the white squirrel scamper a little way across the lawn to pick up another tit-bit. It sat again with its tail neatly curled, front paws up to its mouth. When Mum *did* write, it wasn't usually very comforting. There was nearly always something wrong – a ewe had died, Susie had squashed her piglets, a crop had failed, either Ruth or Laura was ill, or the Fordson had broken down. In her last letter, though – the one that felt as though it were burning a hole in her tunic breastpocket right now – it hadn't been news of home that had worried her, but news of Ken.

Ken wasn't in the shop when I went in yesterday. His mother said he was in bed and very poorly with his chest again. She says he's not right at all, and she's very worried about him. She wasn't a bit friendly. She seemed to think it was all your fault, with him being so upset at your being away. I told her very sharply that it was nonsense to blame you, but you know how she is about him. I expect she's saying the same thing to everybody in the village. I must say there's plenty of them don't approve of you going off like you did, Winnie, seeing as you're spoken for. I never did see the sense in it myself.

She had re-read the letter anxiously several times. Ken had said nothing about being ill when he'd last written, but then he never complained about his bad chests and asthma. The only time she'd heard him sound bitter was when it had stopped him being able to join up. She'd hoped him joining the Local Defence Volunteers had made him feel happier about that. Mrs Jervis had always been unfriendly, ever since she and Ken had started courting, so that was nothing new. She'd be glad of an excuse to blame her. But could it really be her fault that Ken was so poorly now? If she had been there he might not have been feeling so low, and feeling low could stop people getting better quickly, even if it didn't make them ill in the first place.

There was another reason to feel guilty, too. It was wrong to have gone out with Taffy – not just once, but several times. The aircraft lessons had continued in cafés and in pubs and out on walks near the station. She had listened eagerly while he had talked of coolant systems, superchargers, reduction gear, magneto timing, precision checks . . . she had wanted so much to learn.

And he had sneaked her into one of the hangars to have a close look at one of the Hurricanes with the engine cowling off. She had been able to see the whole side of the Merlin, to stare at the great shining mass of pipes and coils and components. It had made the Fordson look so simple and she had felt a fool to have ever imagined they could be anything like each other.

'What's wrong with it?' she had asked Taffy.

'Nothing, I hope. It's just been changed.'

'The whole engine?' She had gazed in awe. 'Is that difficult?'

'Not if you know how.'

'Isn't it very heavy?'

He had laughed at that. 'I should say so! You have to do it with special lifting tackle. You can't just pick it up by hand.'

Best of all, she had been able to sit in the cockpit for a few minutes. Taffy had shown her how to climb up on the port wing, using the toe-hold, and he had hopped up after her, sure-footed as a cat.

She had sat down gingerly in the pilot's seat and tried to look out of the windscreen, but all she could see was the tips of two propeller blades sticking up each side and the upper part of the hangar wall.

'That's the gunsight up there right in front of you,' Taffy had told her. 'The pilot sits on his parachute pack so he's much higher up than you. Though you can't see much forward when you're on the ground, anyway. He has to zig-zag when he's on the ground, so's he can see where he's going. But when she's airborne, the tail comes up and she's level.'

She had looked in bewilderment at all the switches and levers and dials and Taffy had leaned over the side of the cockpit, his head close to hers.

'Look you now, here's your ignition switches and your starter button. Your throttle's beside you here on the left, and that's your rudder trim control below it – that little wheel. Here's your airspeed indicator in the middle of the panel, with your altimeter below – that tells you how high you are. Then you've got your rev counter up here, your rate of climb here, your turn and bank indicator . . . and this funny looking thing's the artificial horizon I was telling you about – remember?' He had leaned further across, his arm brushing against her breast. 'That's the radiator temperature gauge, the fuel contents gauge, the fuel pressure, oil temperature, oil pressure . . .' He had gone on, pointing it all out to her. 'But don't you go touching anything, see. We don't want her taking off with you.'

She had sat there for a while, just trying to imagine what it must be like to fly away up into the sky. To be climbing, turning, banking, diving . . . doing all the things that Taffy had taught her about. One day, she had said to herself. One day.

He had helped her down off the wing, catching her in his arms, but she had wriggled free as quickly as she could.

Susan had come into the room now. Winnie didn't think she'd be very interested in sending postcards to the Poles. She hardly spoke to any of them from the old hut, now that she was a plotter. Pearl always said it was no loss. Most of them, come to that, had remustered. Sandra was a radio-telephonist like Anne, Vera an Equipment Assistant. And Gloria had her medal. But *she* was still stuck in the Orderly Room, filling in forms.

The white squirrel had finished whatever it had been eating and had bounded away up into the beech tree.

There was a flash of white among the copper leaves as it streaked along a branch.

Winnie took the letter out of her pocket to read yet again.

The Free French pilot was very drunk. He was barely able to stand, let alone dance, and Anne, tired of propping him upright, manoeuvred him towards an armchair and lowered him carefully into it. He fell asleep at once.

She was bored with the party and wished she had not come to it. Without Michal there seemed little point. Most of the other pilots were drunk too and she had been fending them off with monotonous regularity. She decided to leave and began to make her way through the crowd towards the door. On the final stretch Johnnie Somerville barred her way. He was drunk, too, she saw impatiently. He was swaying on his feet and the lock of hair flopped down over his forehead. He pushed it away, out of his eyes which were distinctly bloodshot.

'Been looking for you.'

'Really?'

He looked at her accusingly and wagged a finger. 'You've been avoiding me. Not fair.'

Since Croesus Squadron had returned to Colston she had received various notes from him, all of which she had promptly thrown away.

He was fumbling for his cigarette case and held it out to her, brandishing it unsteadily under her nose.

'No, thanks. I'm just leaving.'

'Not before you've danced with me.'

'Sorry to disappoint you.'

He caught clumsily at her arm. 'Mustn't be beastly to us brave pilots, Anne. Supposed to bring us comfort.'

'Don't be so pathetic!'

There was a brand new Distinguished Flying Cross

ribbon on his chest. She had heard about it but to comment, let alone congratulate, would only ask for further complication.

He looked down at her fuzzily. 'You've got all the wrong ideas about me, you know.'

'Have I?'

'I'm not the arrogant shit you take me for.'

'Then you give a pretty good imitation.'

'Come and dance.'

'You're completely blotto. Don't you think you should sit down?'

'Certainly not. I want to dance with you.'

She looked past his shoulder. 'There's a very glamorous blond standing over there looking absolutely furious with you.'

'Oh, Christ! Forgotten all about her. Must be Penny. Or Patsy. Can't remember her name.'

'Well, whoever she is, she's looking frightfully upset. You'd better go and do something about her.'

As he turned his head, confused, she slipped past him. It was a while, though, before she managed to escape from the party. Other pilots waylaid her to dance and it was hard to refuse them when the next day they might be dead. She came across Johnnie again on her way out. He was fast asleep, lying on a bench in the hall. His tie was undone and he had taken off his jacket which had slid to the floor beside him. The purple and white ribbon of the DFC showed shining new above the pocket. His hair straggled across his face and one hand pillowed his cheek. He looked out for the count, she thought, as she paused beside him. Absolutely all in. How many sorties today? How many in these past desperate weeks? How many life-or-death struggles to earn that medal? There was no sign of the glamorous blond. Anne hesitated. Then she picked up the jacket and tucked it round him before she left.

* * *

The contralto was dressed as Britannia and enormously fat. In flowing robes, burnished breastplate and plumed helmet, and carrying a trident in her right hand, she strode imperiously towards the stage footlights. A line of white-booted chorus girls in Ruritanian soldiers' hats, frogged tunics and very short skirts, marked time behind her, stepping high, arms swinging. The concert hangar was packed with station personnel – officers at the front, other ranks behind. The airmen were whistling delightedly at the girls.

Britannia implanted her trident firmly at arm's length in front of her, and lowered her chins to project the rich, deep voice so that it carried easily to the hangar's very last row.

> I give you a toast, ladies and gentlemen:
> May this fair land we love so well, in dignity and
>   freedom dwell
> For worlds may change and go awry while there is still
>   one voice to cry . . .

She paused dramatically and then launched forth.

> There'll always be an England, while there's a country
>   lane,
> Wherever there's a cottage small beside a field of
>   grain.
> There'll always be an England, while there's a busy
>   street,
> Wherever there's a turning wheel, a million marching
>   feet.

She raised the trident and thrust it forward, shaking it vigorously at her audience.

> Red, white and blue! What does it mean to you?
> Surely you're proud, shout it aloud! Britons away!

The Empire too, we can depend on you! Freedom
   remains.
These are the chains nothing can break.

Felicity, sitting near the front, and to one side of the
stage, looked across at the rows of young pilots below
the stage. They were the chief targets of Britannia's
rallying spear thrusts. And they were the last people
on earth, she thought, who needed any such urging or
reminder. Their faces, illuminated by the stage lighting,
watched the singer impassively. Tired faces belonging to
young men who had already ensured that there was now
a chance of there always being an England. She tried not
to think about all the faces that were missing.

   Britannia was striding back and forth across the width
of the stage, a spotlight tracking her. The soldier girls
marched forward in a ragged line that would have given
a drill sergeant apoplexy. The trident was being flourished
triumphantly aloft, to and fro.

There'll always be an England
And England shall be free
If England means as much to you
As En – gland means to me!

On the final note, a deafening cacophony of applause,
yells and whistles erupted in the hangar. The contralto,
who had finished centre-stage, was bowing graciously, the
chorus girls grinning and waving. Felicity looked along
rows of pilots again. They were clapping hard – one of
them, a pink-cheeked sprog with a touchingly earnest
politeness. In front of them Group Captain Palmer was
applauding gravely. He had been up many times, too,
with them – up fighting one moment and down running
his station the next. She had to admire him for that.

   Somehow the Battle of Britain had been won. They
had hung on, against the odds. She could feel the tears

that had come into her eyes during the song beginning to run down her cheeks and put up her hands to wipe them quickly away. Then she joined in the applause with the rest.

Twelve

'You can only stay for a few minutes. He's not at all well today.'

Mrs Jervis turned her back on Winnie and began rearranging some tins on the shelves behind the counter.

'I'll go on up, then, shall I?'

'If you must.'

Winnie went through the door that led to the living quarters at the back of the shop. She had sat through many a stiff and awkward hour here in the downstairs room, trying to make Mrs Jervis like her better. She had only been upstairs once before, though. Mrs Jervis had been out one day and Ken had shown her his bedroom. It was very small, with only room for the bed, a chest-of-drawers and one chair. His hobby was bird-watching and on the wall he had pinned a collection of wild bird pictures, cut from magazines and newspapers. His mother had come back unexpectedly and found them sitting, side by side, on the bed, looking through a bird book. There had been a horrible scene and she had called Winnie a loose woman. For once, Ken had stood up to his mother, and that had not helped her to like Winnie any better either.

She climbed the steep little staircase that led up from the corner of the living-room and knocked at his door. Ken was lying in bed, holding a book open on the sheet before him, but he was dozing, not reading. He opened his eyes as she went in and his face lit up. She was dismayed to see how drawn and pale he looked.

'Oh, Winnie! It's good to see you! I *am* glad you're back.'

He held out both his hands and she went and took

hold of them in hers and bent to kiss his cheek. He was wheezing badly, his chest rising and falling as though every breath was an effort.

'It's good to see you, too, Ken. How're you feelin'?'

'Oh, fine. Fine. Much better, thanks.'

She sat down on the chair but he patted the eiderdown.

'Sit here, Winn. Closer to me.'

'Your mother might be cross.'

'Let her be cross. I don't care.'

'She says I'm only to stay a few minutes.'

'You're to stay as long as you want. As long as you can.'

She perched on the edge of the bed and held his hand. The sleeve of his pyjama jacket had fallen back and his forearm looked thin as a broomstick.

'I'll stay as long as you like, Ken. I wish you'd told me before that you've been poorly like this. Why didn't you write and say?'

'I didn't want to bother you, Winnie. You've had plenty of more important things to think about. So's everybody, with everythin' bein' so serious. Another one of my stupid chests didn't seem to matter much.' His fingers tightened on hers. 'I've been so worried for you, though. All those bombin' raids . . . knowin' you were in danger.'

She said comfortingly: 'They've stopped comin' near us now.'

'They say it's ever so bad in London.'

She nodded. 'I think it's worst down in the docks and the East End. I saw some bomb damage from the train, though. Quite a bit.'

She had stared down at the gaps in the rows of houses beside the railway line; at the strange sight of odd walls left standing alone, and what had once been indoors now open to the sky. She had seen the patterned wallpapers, curtains flapping at empty windows, firegrates suspended halfway up in space, even a bed roosting lopsidedly on a ledge. Some of the streets had been carpeted with broken glass and rubble.

'They bombed Buckingham Palace,' Ken said.

'I know.'

Somehow that had seemed more shocking than anything. The King and Queen might have been killed. She looked up at the pictures of the wild birds pinned to the walls.

'You've got some new ones, haven't you, Ken? I don't remember that one there in the middle. What is it?'

He turned his head on the pillow. 'A bearded reedlin'. They live in the reed beds. I saw a whole flock of them this summer. It's more of a moustache than a beard, though, isn't it? That black patch.'

He would bicycle for miles, over towards the sea. She squeezed his hand. 'When you're better you must go out bird-watchin' again.'

He started coughing suddenly and turned his head away. When it had subsided, he said weakly: 'Yes, I'll do that.'

She had noticed something else new in the room. There was a steel helmet hanging up on the hook behind the door which must be the one he'd been given as a Local Defence Volunteer. Near it, propped against the wall in the corner was a long pole with some kind of rusty, curved blade on the end of it.

'What on earth's that, Ken?'

'A pike. You know, soldiers used to have them in olden times. Colonel Foster gave it to me. He had four of them hangin' on the walls up at the Hall. And some swords. They were all a bit rusty, but I'm goin' to clean it up. Soon as I can. I'll use it for drill with the platoon, when I get back on my feet again. We're called the Home Guard now, you know. Mr Churchill called us that in a broadcast on the wireless. Instead of the LDV. Sounds better, doesn't it?'

He seemed proud and she was glad for him. Glad that he need not feel so useless with the war effort. It was the pike, she thought, that would be useless against the Germans.

'Haven't you got any proper weapons yet?'

He smiled wryly. 'Well, we're supposed to be gettin' some rifles soon. They keep sayin' so. We'll just have to hope Hitler won't invade 'til then, won't we?'

'I don't think he'll want to invade just now. It's too near winter. The weather'll be bad soon. He'll have to wait 'til next year.'

She could hear some fighters approaching and went to the window to watch them pass overhead, roaring throatily. Hurricanes. Rolls Royce Merlin vee engines. Twelve cylinder, liquid cooled.

'They come over all the time,' Ken told her. 'Bombers too. Your RAF saw the Jerries off good and proper, didn't they? Made sure Hitler didn't get a chance to try it.'

'Yes,' she said. 'They did.'

'That must make you proud,' he smiled up at her. 'I'm glad you joined, Winn. Honest. At the time, I didn't understand it at all, but now I see it was the right thing to do. It was plain selfish of me to want you to stay here.'

She suddenly felt close to tears. 'Don't say that, Ken. It wasn't. And I miss you badly.'

'I was so afraid you'd meet someone else, you see. I mean, I'm not much of a catch. I know that. But there isn't anyone else, is there?'

'No, of course there isn't. I told you so before.'

'I know,' he persisted. 'But if ever there was, I'd understand. I wouldn't blame you, and I wouldn't stand in your way . . . I want you to know that.'

She could feel the colour staining her cheeks. 'Don't be silly, Ken. There'd never be anyone else but you.'

She saw the gladness and relief in his face. He looked brighter, stronger.

'That makes me very happy, Winn. So happy, you can't imagine.'

They could hear his mother moving about in the living-room directly below.

339

'I'd better go now, Ken. I don't want to tire you, or cause any trouble.'

'Don't worry about Mother. She's just shut up the shop, that's all.'

'Just the same . . . I'd better go. I'll come and see you tomorrow, Ken. And every day of my leave.'

She kissed his cheek and went downstairs. Mrs Jervis had taken off her overall – the one patterned with faded red and blue flowers that Winnie had seen her wear for as long as she could remember. In her black blouse and skirt – she'd worn black ever since Mr Jervis had died – she looked even more severe.

'I hope you haven't tired him.'

'I'm sure I haven't, Mrs Jervis. He was pleased to see me. I think it cheered him up.'

'I can't think why. Not after the way you've treated him.'

Colour flooded into her face. 'What do you mean?'

'Going off and leaving him. Breaking his heart.'

She said stoutly: 'I haven't broken his heart. We're still engaged. Nothing's changed.'

Mrs Jervis took no notice. 'He wanted you to marry him decently – not go gallivanting off. You could have stayed here, helped in the shop . . . But no, you had to go and join up. Go miles away.'

'I wanted to join the Air Force, Mrs Jervis.'

'And I know why! You thought my Ken wasn't good enough for you, didn't you? Thought you'd find something better. You've played fast and loose with his affections, that's what you've done. He's suffered torment, wondering what you might be up to with all those airmen. It's *you* that's made him ill. Brought all this on.'

The living-room table with its brown, fringed cloth lay between them like a barrier. Winnie hung onto a chair back, feeling almost sick. Her legs were shaking.

'That's not fair, Mrs Jervis. And it's not possible. I've given him no cause for worry. If Ken's ill, it isn't because of me.'

340

There was a silence. Mrs Jervis's lips were pressed into a thin line and her eyes were hard as stone. She stared at Winnie.

'You'd better know something. Ken's going to die.'

Winnie thought she had misheard. 'What? What did you say?'

'I said he's going to die. He might live a year or two, if he's lucky. He went to the hospital in Ipswich for some tests. He didn't tell you that, did he? He wouldn't want to worry you, however much *you* worried him. The doctor told me last week. He's always had a weak heart, though I never told him that, and the asthma's damaged it even more. A bad attack or infection could carry him off any time. That's what they say.'

She struggled to take in the words: to understand that they were real.

'I can't believe it, Mrs Jervis. It can't be true.'

'Didn't you see how ill he looked?'

'He's been ill so often before . . . I didn't realize it was so bad . . . I'm so sorry, Mrs Jervis. So very, very sorry.'

'I don't want your sympathy. I only want my Ken to be happy for what time remains to him.'

She swallowed. 'Does he know?'

'No. They haven't told him. And I haven't. Wild horses wouldn't drag it from me. And if you breathe so much as one word to him, I'll make you sorry for the rest of your days.'

'I won't. I swear I won't. I'll do anythin' to help make him happy. Anything.'

Mrs Jervis folded her arms. 'You can marry him, that's what you can do. Like you should have done in the first place. He worships the ground you walk on – you should know that. Marrying you is all he's ever wanted since he was a boy. All he's ever dreamed of. You're the only thing he's ever really cared about. I've had to come to terms with that, and it hasn't been easy. I'm his mother but I don't mean half as much to him as you do. But I love my son and all I care about now is that he dies happy. If you marry him they'd let you leave the Air Force with your husband being so ill. Compassionate grounds, they call it. You could come here and help me look after him. Give him some happiness in the time he's got left. If you love him, like you make out, that's what you'd do.'

She stared miserably down at the table. Leave the WAAF? Give it all up – the friends, the company, the new life that she had discovered? Give up any chance of ever working with the 'planes? Come back to Elmbury and live here in this gloomy place with Mrs Jervis who hated her? Her heart sank at the thought of it.

Overhead, Ken started coughing again – a pitiful, sad sound. Poor, *poor* Ken. It couldn't be true that he was going to die. Mrs Jervis might have said that just to punish her. But he had looked very bad . . . worse than she had ever seen him. And, if he was really going to die, how could she be so selfish as to think only of herself like this? Even to hesitate? She was very ashamed and lifted her head to meet his mother's scornful gaze.

'I'll marry Ken, Mrs Jervis,' she said. 'As soon as he wants.'

It was getting dark when Virginia walked up the hill from Wimbledon Park tube station, but not yet dark enough to hide all the bomb damage. She passed clear evidence of the Luftwaffe's night-time visits – fallen tiles, shattered windows, collapsed walls, a mound of broken glass swept into the gutter. Number twenty-three at the corner must have received a direct hit because hardly any of it was left standing. The gate, unscathed, was closed incongruously on a shambles of bricks and glass, pipes and porcelain. Part of the staircase climbed out of the debris to nowhere, and the ginger cat who had lived there was sitting on what remained of the front doorstep.

She let herself into the flat with her key and found her

342

mother in the sitting-room, knitting. The blackout was already in place, the curtains drawn.

Her mother lifted her cheek to be kissed. 'I expected you much earlier than this, Virginia. In your letter you said that you would be home in the early afternoon.'

'I'm sorry, I couldn't help it. The train was held up. How are you, Mother?'

'As well as can be expected, considering the disturbed nights we've been getting.'

'I saw all the damage as I walked up from the station. The house on the corner is a terrible mess.'

'It was hit two nights ago. The woman who lives there was killed, apparently. And a child.'

'How dreadful!'

Virginia sat down, shaken. It was wicked that the Germans were bombing defenceless civilians now – women and children. Number twenty-three was only a hundred yards or so away.

'Mother, don't you think you ought to move out of London – for the time being at least?'

'And where would I go?'

'A hotel, perhaps?'

'I couldn't possibly afford that.'

'A boarding house, then.'

'Full of awful people.'

'It can't be right for you to stay here. It isn't safe.'

Her mother turned the knitting and began another row. 'I've no intention of letting the Germans drive me out of my own home, Virginia. The Government should stop them roaming about the skies all night. All those guns seem to do is to keep us awake. Can't the Royal Air Force *do* something?'

'I think it's difficult for the fighters to see the bombers in the dark.'

'Well, the German bombers seem to find *their* way around, all right. It's all very well for the Air Force, out in the countryside, but we civilians appear to be the main target these days. There'll be another raid tonight, you'll see.'

'We can sleep in the shelter.'

'I *never* go in there. It's extremely damp and it means sharing it with that woman from upstairs. That uniform doesn't seem to fit you very well, Virginia. And it looks poor quality material. Rather cheap and nasty. You never say anything in your letters about this important work you're supposed to be doing.'

'We're not meant to tell anyone about it.'

'How ridiculous! Your own mother! You're only a clerk, aren't you?'

'A special sort of clerk, really.'

'Well, it seems absurd to make such a secret of it. It can't be anything that important.'

Supper was dry, grey liver and tinned peas. Virginia listened patiently to a catalogue of complaints about food shortages, about shopkeepers who kept things under the counter, about long queues for everything and about the ATS girls billeted opposite who had no consideration for anybody.

The air raid siren began its rising and falling wail soon after they had gone to bed. Virginia went into her mother's room, but she flatly refused to go out to the Anderson shelter in the back garden. She went back to bed and lay listening uneasily to the drone of German bombers. The anti-aircraft batteries had started up and she could hear the thunderous crack of their guns and the muffled, distant explosion of their shells. Presently the heavy crump of bombs began. Sleep was impossible. She got up again, put on her dressing-gown and slippers, and pulled aside the curtains and the black-out blind.

Because the house was on a hill she could see clearly eastwards across towards the centre of London. The black mass of the city was dotted with incendiary bomb fires. Searchlights crossed and re-crossed the night sky, groping for the bombers. Their long white beams petered out in misty, cotton-wool like swabs that swept endlessly to and fro. Below, the battery guns winked and flashed, patterning the sky with small starbursts of red. An exploding bomb sent up tongues of yellow and red and another, landing closer, produced a sudden flare of brilliant light that was probably a burning gas main. It illuminated the tall chimneys of Battersea Power Station as clearly as day. Two more explosions, coming closer still, sent her hurrying again into the next door bedroom.

'Are you asleep, Mother?'

'How could I be, with all this noise going on?'

'Would you like a cup of tea?'

She made the tea and carried it through on a tray. Her mother was sitting up in bed, her lamp switched on. She had put on her bedjacket and was straightening it fussily round her shoulders.

'Just because there's an air raid on, Virginia, it's no reason to forget to put a cloth on the tray. We must keep up standards.'

She held her cup and saucer up before her in bed and sipped delicately at the tea. Virginia sat on a chair, balancing her saucer on her lap. She listened to the crump of exploding bombs, trying to gauge their distance, and to the angry crack-crack of the Ack-Ack guns. Somewhere, among it all, she caught a sound she recognized well – the whining, shallow dive of a bomber starting its bombing run. Her mother went on sipping at her tea as though nothing were happening.

She tried to speak calmly. 'I'm going to have a look at the cupboard under the stairs in the morning, Mother. I'm sure we could turn it into a sort of shelter for you.'

'It's very poky and full of rubbish.'

'I'll clear it out for you. It would be much safer than being here. I noticed that the staircase at number twenty-three was still standing.'

'I have already told you that I intend to stay in my own bed – '

Ears pricked, like a dog, for danger, Virginia heard the warning swishing sound overhead, but before she could say anything, or move, the bomb landed with an explosion that rocked the house on its foundations

345

and must have been only a street away. Pictures and ornaments danced and rattled, the lamplight flickered and plaster fell like snow from the ceiling. She had a momentary glimpse of her mother, teacup frozen halfway to her lips, white dust filming her hair and the sleeves of the pink bedjacket, before there was another terrifying, ear-splitting explosion that seemed to take hold of the house and shake it violently. The light went out. She leaped to her feet and the saucer slid to the floor with a tinkling sound of breaking china.

In the darkness her mother said sharply: 'Really, Virginia, how could you be so careless? That was my best tea set. And you can't get replacements now.'

It was several hours before the steady note of the All Clear sounded, along with the frantic jangling of fire engine bells. Virginia peered out of her bedroom window again. The sky was an unearthly ochre colour and the dull crimson glow in the east was not the dawn coming up but London burning. She closed the blackout blind, unable to bear the sight.

'Speedy, you really shouldn't be sitting on my desk.'

'That's no way to treat a weary hero, Titania.'

'Well, as you have some leave now, you'll have time for a rest. Your parents will be so glad to see you. And so proud of your DFC.'

He squinted down at the ribbon on his tunic. 'Actually, they're giving them out like sweeties now – just to keep us happy.'

'I don't believe that. And I think it's wonderful.'

'Thank you, Titania, for those kind words.' Speedy twirled his cap round on his forefinger. 'After this short intermission the powers that be have dictated yet another move for our gallant little band of brothers.'

'Where are they sending you?'

'Bonnie Scotland. That's why I called in en route to the parents. It'll be hoots awa' in no time at all and nairy a chance then of popping over to see you. The idea is that we put the old boots up for a bit. Rest on our ill-gotten laurels. Not much to do up there in the Frozen North, so I'm told. George is looking forward to chasing a few rabbits, though, aren't you, George?'

The bullterrier, sitting by the office door, panted happily.

'I'm just thankful that you'll be out of it for a while.'

'To tell the truth, so am I.' Speedy's cap came to a stop and he considered it carefully, head on one side, as it dangled from his finger. It appeared to be falling to pieces. 'Old Whitters bought it the other day. Don't suppose you heard.'

'Oh, Speedy, *no* . . .' Not Whitters with his toothy grin and tall stories. Not Whitters, so full of life, so amiable, so eager, so nice . . . But she knew better than to say any of this aloud, or to ask how it had happened.

Speedy was still studying his cap. 'Yes . . . bad show, isn't it? Silly blighter should've hung on a bit longer, then he could've come up to Scotland with the rest of us. I'm popping in to see his Grandmama, as a matter of fact. The old girl's bound to be a bit chokker. Favourite grandson and all that. Good sort, old Whitters.'

'I'm so sorry, Speedy.'

He let the cap drop into his lap. 'Oh, well. Can't be helped. 'Tis fate that flings the dice . . . I wonder who said that.'

Felicity shook her head helplessly. 'I've no idea.'

'Nor've I. Must've been one of Snodders'. Dumbo's out of it, too, by the way. His kite went up in flames and he had to jump out of the window pdq. Trouble is it got stuck at first. I went to see him in hospital yesterday. They're moving him to some special burns place. Shouldn't think he'll be doing the Highland Fling just yet.'

Poor Dumbo, she thought. She had seen a badly burned pilot on the station. Poor Dumbo.

'Moses? Sinbad?'

'Not so dusty. Looking forward to a spot of extra shut-eye. But stay, who cometh hither?'

347

George had pricked up his ears and lumbered stiffly to his feet. There was the sound of heavy footsteps in the corridor outside, a brisk knock on the door, and Sergeant Beaty strode into the office. The bullterrier moved forward, his teeth bared in a snarl. Speedy clicked his fingers.

'It's all right, old chap, you can let her pass. She's friend, not foe.'

The dog moved aside reluctantly, still showing his teeth. Speedy put on his cap and slid off the corner of the desk.

'Come on, George, we must continue valiantly on our way.' He touched the cap in a casual salute towards Felicity. 'Fare thee well, Section Officer Newman! And if forever, still forever, fare thee well. The Bard, I believe.'

'Byron, actually,' she said.

'Him again? What a fellow for words!'

He smiled at her from the door, and pulled a dreadful face at the WAAF sergeant's back as he closed it.

Felicity held out her hand for the papers, ignoring the bristling indignation on the other side of the desk.

'Where are we going to exactly, Michal?'

He took his eyes from the empty road ahead to glance at her. 'Is place called Hambledean, in Hampshire. The New Forest you call it. Is little village, I think.'

'To a hotel?' The words sounded unbelievably daring to her ears.

He turned the wheel of the Wolseley. 'No, not hotel. Something better. A little house. Cottage, you say. Is belonging to the family of a pilot I know. He tells me to use this place any time, because I have nowhere to go. He has given key and drawn map. There is no-one there. We shall be alone.' He glanced at her again. 'You want I go back, Anne? You change your mind?'

'No, of course not.'

'You are sure?'

'Quite sure.'

'You look nervous . . . very worried.'

'No, I'm not. Not at all.'

She sat rigidly in the passenger seat beside him. She *was* nervous, there was no use in denying it to herself. But it was a sort of nervous excitement, rather than fear, unless she counted the fear of making a complete mess of things, of being dismally inadequate. The trouble was she had no idea what to expect, or what was expected of her. Not a clue how to behave, or what to say or do. And he must be used to women who knew all those things very well. He'd obviously been around, as Pearl had remarked sagely. He probably expected her to be sitting here nonchalantly, if not elegantly, giving him occasional little significant smiles or smouldering looks, not chewing her nails and staring out of the window.

'Don't do it, duckie,' Pearl had warned her. 'You're not the sort. You'll regret it.'

'Nothing may happen.'

'Give me patience! He's asked you to go away on leave with him – just the two of you! He's not planning to sit and hold your hand, I can tell you that. Even if he was English he'd be thinking of a bit more than that. As he's a Pole, God knows what he's got in mind . . .'

They stopped at a roadside pub and she sat watching him as he went over to the bar. She saw how the barmaid smiled at him as he ordered their drinks and how a middle-aged civilian drinking there turned to talk to him. He is special, she thought, anyone can see that. His looks and his bearing set him apart. And he is from another world than my world. She watched him speaking to the civilian, his dark head bent politely towards him, and her stomach fluttered again. I can't believe it, she thought. I can't believe that tonight I am going to get into a bed with that man who is standing over there and that he is going to do this thing to me – whatever it is exactly . . . He is going to become my lover. That word sounded unbelievably daring, too. Incredibly sinful and worldly. She chewed at a torn fingernail. This time tomorrow I shall know what *It* is like. And, actually, I'm scared stiff. I'm not sure I want to find out.

He came back to the table, carrying brimming mugs.

'You are sure you like beer, Anne?'

'Oh, yes, thanks. I always drink it now. I've got used to it.' She smiled at him brightly.

He raised his mug to her. '*Na Zdrowie!*'

'Cheers!'

She spilled some as she lifted her half pint with a slightly shaking hand.

'Stefan, you know, he puts gin with his beer. He says is tasting much better.'

'What a funny thing to do.'

'For myself, gin is tasting like medicine. Whisky like paraffin.'

'I quite like gin,' she said. 'Actually.'

'You like a cigarette?'

He held out the silver case she had noticed before – heavy, engraved – something saved from his past. She wondered what sort of background he came from. What his family was like. He had never spoken of them.

She coughed a little as he lit her cigarette. 'What was that man at the bar saying to you?'

He flicked the lighter and bent to his own. 'Oh, he sees Poland on my uniform and he asks me about this. He says nice things. A very nice man. Very sympathetic.'

As he raised his head again, she met his eyes – that mesmeric un-English light blue-grey that she had never seen before. Bedroom eyes, Pearl had called them. She thought unsteadily: I love him so much, that's the trouble. I'm mad about him. Nothing else seems to matter. I don't care what other people say or think. I don't give a damn if what I'm doing is immoral or wrong. And I don't even care much about losing my virginity. Underneath being scared stiff, I'm so happy, and I want him to make love to me more than I've ever wanted anything in my whole life . . .

'What are you thinking, Anne?'

She tapped her cigarette unnecessarily against the ashtray between them. 'Oh, nothing special.'

'I think you are very nervous of me. Please . . . there is no need. Believe me.'

Watching them from his place at the bar, the middle-aged civilian saw the way the pretty WAAF looked up and smiled at the Polish pilot. He sighed enviously.

Fallen leaves lay like russet carpeting beneath the beeches of the New Forest. Anne consulted the hand-drawn map on her knee.

'Next left, I think.'

'You only *think*? I never take you as navigator in my 'plane.'

'Navigators have the equivalent of signposts. They've taken all those away now and I don't know this part of the country.'

'Is very beautiful.'

'Do you have forests in Poland?'

'We have many forests, but not exactly like this. Different trees. Everything is different. Poland is much bigger than England. Not so . . . so cosy. In north is sea, in south is hills and mountains, and we have many lakes. But in middle is all lowlands. Poland is *Polska* in our language. That is from *pole* – is word for field. We have many flat fields, you see. Nature is not stopping other people to invade us, like your sea all around has stopped the Germans.'

'What about the climate?'

'In summer is hot. In winter very cold. Sometimes there is a lot of rain. Now, it will already be getting cold. Next month, perhaps, there will be snow.' He turned the car to the left. 'I think you not know very much about my country.'

'Before I met you I wasn't even sure where it was. I had to look you up in an atlas.'

He clicked his tongue and smiled. 'That is very bad. I knew where *you* were.'

351

'Just as well, or you might never have got here. But we're an island, so we're easier to find. You're all sort of mixed up with all those other countries – Czechoslovakia and Hungary and Bulgaria, and places like that.'

'Bulgaria is nowhere near Poland. Is in south by the Black Sea.'

She sighed. 'If you'd been our geography teacher instead of Miss Carpenter I'd've paid much more attention.'

'What else do you not know? What is our capital city?'

'That's easy. Warsaw. What's it like?'

'Very beautiful – once. Many old buildings with very high roofs, painted in colours . . . yellow, pink, orange. Many balconies full of flowers in summer. Many churches. Old streets with . . . I don't know how you say this . . . small stones in the ground.'

'Cobblestones.'

'*Tak*. Cobblestones. And there are cafés and people who sell flowers on the corner of streets . . . And there is a river, like your London has the Thames.'

'I'd like to see it one day.'

'Yes,' he said. 'One day. But is not beautiful any more. All is in ruins.'

'I'm sorry. That was stupid of me. I was forgetting . . .' She bent her head over the map again. 'According to this, we take the next right by a pub called The Green Man.'

'In England,' he said, 'you do not need signposts. Instead you have pubs to tell the way.'

The cottage lay on the outskirts of the village, at the edge of the forest. A thatched roof curved low over the upstairs windows, like two beetling brows, and there was a wellhead, complete with bucket and chain, in the front garden. They walked up the brick path through a wilderness of long neglect. Late roses bloomed blowsily and crimson red on the walls and a thicket of honeysuckle smothered the door.

Inside it smelled musty and, in the dim light of the

fading day, pieces of furniture stood about as shadowy shapes – a table in the centre of the room, some chairs round it, a sagging sofa, a Welsh dresser against the wall, a tall cupboard in the corner . . . There was a copper jug on the windowsill and a row of pottery cows stalked, head to tail, along the shelf above the inglenook. A brass warming pan hung beside the fireplace.

Anne went through to the scullery at the back. She turned on the tap over the stone sink and a gurgling and spluttering heralded a gush of rusty cold water. The iron cooking range looked as though it should have been in a museum. She opened cupboards and drawers, disturbing cobwebs and frightening spiders and wrestled with stiff bolts on the back door which opened onto what once might have been a vegetable patch but was now another jungle of weeds and flourishing stinging nettles. She stared in disbelief at the brick privy and at the tin bath hanging from a nail outside the door.

Every tread of the staircase creaked. Upstairs she discovered two bedrooms – a little one at the back with a single camp bed and a larger one at the front, with a big brass bed that was propped up by bricks at the foot end and covered by a patchwork quilt. The floorboards sloped down towards the window like a pitching deck in a rough sea, and she had to kneel down to see out of the window and beneath the over-hanging thatch. Michal was bringing in the luggage from the car – her kitbag and his suitcase. When she went downstairs he was setting the case down on the table.

'I bring food for us.' He began to take out the contents. 'Eggs, bacon, potatoes, a tin of ham, bread, butter, tea, chocolate . . . Tomorrow we get other things.'

'How on earth did you manage to get all that?'

'I beg. I exchange. I buy.' He delved into the case again and held up a bottle. 'And, most important thing of all, real Polish vodka. Stefan finds this in London. He finds everything. We find glasses and then we drink. But first

353

we must find wood for a fire and fuel for the lamps, before is dark. I am told there is some in a small place outside. There is no electricity, you see.'

'I had noticed.'

'You do not mind? This is not like hotel, I know. Not very comfortable . . .'

She began to giggle. 'I think it's much nicer than a hotel.'

They found logs and kindling and paraffin in a shed at the back, as well as a camping stove that looked encouraging in view of the iron range. Before long the lamps were lit and a fire was crackling in the inglenook grate. The sitting-room had come into soft focus with the warm colours of chintz, oak and brick, and the gleam of copper and brass. Michal found some glasses in the bottom cupboard of the Welsh dresser. He poured vodka into each one.

'Now, you must drink this Polish fashion – very quick, one swallow.' He handed her a glass and raised his own to her. '*Na Zdrowie!*

'*Na Zdrowie!*' she repeated carefully after him and tossed back her glass. She choked as the neat vodka hit the back of her throat and tears came into her eyes. 'Gosh, it's a bit strong!'

He poured some more into her glass, smiling at her. 'You are not used to it, that is all. This is *wyborowa*, a plain vodka, but we have others flavoured with different things – all kinds of berries. I think, perhaps, you like *wiśniówka* best – that has taste of cherries. When you come to Poland after the war you can try all kinds.'

'Yes,' she said. 'After the war.'

His smile faded as he looked at her. 'Oh, Anne . . .'

He put down his glass slowly and took hers from her hand. Then she was in his arms and he was kissing her passionately in the way she had dreamed about and imagined so many times. She put her arms around his neck, eyes closed. Against her cheek he said presently:

'Is better now? Not so much nervous?'

'Much better.'

They drank more vodka, sitting on the rug in front of the fire and talking while they watched the flames flicker and leap, the logs shift and settle as they burned. Later on they made thick sandwiches from the tinned ham and the loaf of bread and ate them beside the fire too, like a picnic. She thought that nothing had ever tasted so good. Nothing had ever been so wonderful.

'You want music?' Michal asked suddenly. 'I remember there was machine where I find glasses. And some records.'

He fetched the portable gramophone and wound it up while Anne went through a box of dusty records.

'Old as the hills . . . Heavens, look at this lot! *Come into the Garden, Maud, I Hear You Calling Me, Take a Pair of Sparkling Eyes.*'

'I do not know these.'

'You haven't missed much.' She stopped on her way through the pile. 'This one's all right, though. Cole Porter – I love him.'

He put it on for her and as the song began he took her in his arms. They danced very close for a while.

When the record had finished he reached out with one hand to lift the needle, still holding her close.

'It is very nice song. I like very much. To dance with you is very nice also . . . but is not enough.' He searched her face. 'Anne, I do not think you have ever been with a man . . .'

She said anxiously: 'Is it so obvious?'

'Is not difficult to tell this thing. But you are sure you want this with me?'

She nodded.

'Very sure?'

'Very, *very* sure.'

* * *

355

She undressed, shivering, in the scullery and washed and brushed her teeth in cold water at the sink. In the flyblown mirror hanging on the wall, her cheeks looked flushed and her eyes bright, as though she had a fever. She peered at herself and wondered if, after tonight, she would somehow look different; whether there would be some subtle womanly change in her appearance that others would notice. The vodka had made her woozy and she had some trouble getting her feet into her pyjama legs.

When she sidled hesitantly out into the sitting-room, he was standing by the fire, one arm raised to the chimney breast, staring at the dying flames. He looked lost in sad thoughts and her heart ached for him in his exile. She gave a small cough and he turned and saw her standing there, the lamp she had taken with her in one hand.

'*Jezus Maria!* What are you wearing, Anne?'

'Pyjamas, WAAF, for the use of. They're issue.' She flapped her free hand which was somewhere inside the too-long striped flannel sleeve. The trouser legs finished in concertina folds around her ankles. 'They're the same as the RAF ones, actually. And much too big.'

He began to laugh. 'Yes, I can see that . . . but I never see a woman wearing these things before.'

He came towards her, his face full of laughter and tenderness. He took the lamp from her and held out his other hand.

'Come.'

She stumbled after him up the creaking staircase, her hand clasped tightly in his, her other holding her pyjama bottoms clear of her bare feet. Her heart was thudding furiously.

The lamplight cast their shadows on the wall – separate and then fused together as he kissed her. He lifted her in his arms. The mattress was lumpy, the sheets damp, but she noticed none of that. All she felt was his mouth on hers, his hands undoing the WAAF pyjama buttons, loosening the cord, the warmth of his skin on her skin, the hardness of his body against hers, the soft touch of his fingers and of his lips . . . She tried not to feel embarrassed or shocked or ashamed, and then, after a while, she didn't care any more.

When she awoke the sun was coming through the little window beneath the thatch. She could see it touching the brass at the foot of the bed, making it glint brightly. Birds were fluttering and chirruping somewhere beneath the eaves, sounding so close they might have been in the room. She shut her eyes, confused for a moment and then opened them again.

He was still asleep, his head turned towards her on the pillow, one arm across her body. She watched him, remembering. Marvelling.

It's worth everything, Pearl. Everything.

Unable to help herself, she touched his hair, smoothing it back from his brow. He opened his eyes and smiled at her drowsily.

'*Kochana* . . . you are happy?'

'Blissfully.'

'I do not know what this means. Is bad? Is good?'

'Good. Very good.'

'Next time I bring big dictionary so I know how you feel.'

She giggled. 'Into bed?'

'*Nie.*' He raised himself on one arm and leaned over her. 'In bed words are not necessary. So, I think we stay here a long time.'

She swept and dusted the cottage and polished the copper jug on the windowsill, filling it with roses from the garden.

'You make home for me,' he said. 'Is wonderful.'

They coaxed the old kitchen range into life and nurtured its sulky beginnings until it was going well enough to heat some water. He carried the tin bath indoors and set it before the fire for her, filling it with water from the big range kettle and from pots and pans. She undressed quickly, stepped somewhat self-consciously

357

into the bath and sat with her arms folded about her body. He teased her, laughing.

'You are *still* shy of me, Anne? Even after everything? That is not sense.'

He soaped her back and then her breasts and began kissing her. She put wet arms around his neck. Afterwards he wrapped her tightly in the towel, like a child, and began to kiss her again. Before long the towel had loosened and fallen to the floor.

That evening he lay on the sofa with his head resting in her lap, smoking a cigarette. He was wearing a thick cream-coloured sweater, like a fisherman's, and it was the first time she had seen him in anything not RAF uniform. She had put on her home jumper and skirt. Just for a while she could pretend they were an ordinary couple and that there was no war. She stroked his hair.

'I wish we could stay here for ever.'

He turned his head to smile up at her. 'Me, also, I wish this. I am thinking the same. It is better not to, because is not possible.'

'All right. Let's talk about something else. You haven't told me where your home is in Poland – unless you'd sooner not . . .'

'No, I tell you about it, if you like. It is near a place called Czersk – in south east of Warsaw. In middle of Poland. Once it was important town, but it has big river that change the way it goes . . . you understand? I don't know how to say this.'

'The river changed its course. Is that what you mean?'

'*Tak*. That is it. And after Czersk was no more very important. There is beautiful old castle high up above the town . . . one day, perhaps, I can show you . . . My home is five miles from there. Is very old place, too. Very dear to me. My family is there a long, long time – since nearly two hundred years. We have much land.'

'It sounds frightfully grand. You're not a count, or anything like that, are you?'

He smiled. 'No, I am not a count. But there are many

counts in Poland. Stefan, he is one. His family is very old, very proud. His mother is like a queen.'

'I hope your mother isn't.'

'No, no. Not at all. She is always laughing, always smiling. Very natural, you know. And very beautiful, to me.'

He was silent for a moment, smoking the cigarette. Presently he went on: 'I must believe that she is still alive. And my father too. And my sister and brother. I *must* believe this – you understand? Most of the time I do not let myself think of them at all, but when I do I always say to myself that they are still alive and well, in spite of everything. Is the only way.'

She tried to comfort him. 'I'm sure they are. I mean the Germans can't have any real reason to harm them.'

'You do not understand what is like, Anne. How can you? Already they kill civilians here in England, I know, but in Poland is much, much worse. There they can do more than drop bombs. They can shoot and kill whoever they want, for no reason at all. They torture, they put in prison, in camps . . . whatever they like. In each town they choose some people to shoot against a wall so that the others will be afraid and do as they are told. My father, he is not afraid to speak, to say what he believes . . .'

He was silent again. She stroked his hair.

'How old are your brother and sister?'

'Helena, she is fifteen. At school – if school is still there. Antek is twenty. He is in cavalry, you know. I am most afraid for him. The Germans have forced Polish soldiers into the Wehrmacht, so maybe I shall fight against my own brother. Or maybe he is prisoner of Russians in labour camp. Or maybe he is already dead. I try to find out. I ask Red Cross but they know nothing. They will tell me perhaps one day, if they learn.'

'Oh, Michal . . .'

'Please, do not look sad for me. To a Pole, is not so strange. Our country has had many troubles. For so many years others try to invade us and we have learned to defend

359

our freedom and our faith. To love our country is part of our religion, you see. To defend her is sacred duty for us all. In Polish Air Force we have flag that says Love Demands Sacrifice. We accept this. I have lost everything, perhaps, but I still have my life to give.'

'Don't talk like that, *please*.'

'I am sorry, Anne. Is stupid of me. Not kind. How can you ever understand?'

She felt hopelessly inadequate, as though a huge gulf lay between them that she could never cross.

'How old are you, Michal? I've never asked you.'

'Twenty-five. An old, old man.'

'How old were you when you first made love?'

'So many questions! I was sixteen.'

'Heavens . . . is that all?'

'She was much older woman . . . married.' He smiled at the ceiling. 'Was very good teacher.'

'Was she Polish?'

'Oh, yes. A friend of my mother. Though, of course, my mother knew nothing.'

'Would she have been shocked?'

'Shocked? No, not at all. She is not like this.'

'If my parents could see me now, they'd be terribly shocked. They think I've gone to stay with another WAAF.'

'I am sorry we deceive them.'

'I'm not. They'd never understand.'

'Why you are with a Pole?'

'No . . . In England nice girls don't do this.'

'I know. The war changes many things.'

'I hope you'll meet them one day. Actually, they're pretty decent.'

'I should be honoured.'

'I love the way you say things like that. So polite and formal. Do all Poles have lovely manners, like yours?'

'I hope we have good manners. We are taught to be so. In our Air Force Academy we are taught that every woman must be treated with same respect as a general.'

360

She giggled. 'I don't know about that, but all the WAAFS love the Poles. They love the way you bow and treat us so gallantly. Like princesses, not generals. Much better than the RAF.'

'The WAAFS are very kind to us. Some of them send postcards and pictures and things, you know, because we have no letters. Stefan, he cry. Never have I seen this before with him.'

She thought of the queenly mother. 'Does he know what has happened to his family?'

'*Nie.* None of us knows.'

The precious days passed too quickly. Time would not wait for them. They went for walks in the forest, shuffling through the dead leaves like children, and for drives round the countryside and over to Beaulieu and Southampton Water. Sometimes they stopped at pubs. But they spent most of the time at the cottage.

'Do you realize, Michal, that we must have spent far more hours in bed than out of it, while we've been here?'

'Naturally.'

'And yesterday we hardly got up at all.'

'I remember very well.'

'I'll never forget these days . . . or this place.'

'Me, also. I never forget. Never.'

She cried in the car when they drove back to Colston. It was worse than going back to boarding school. Far, far worse. The rain poured down. The windscreen wiper swished relentlessly to and fro. Tears rolled down her cheeks.

'I don't want to go back, Michal. I can't bear it.'

He passed her his handkerchief. 'We must go back, *kochana*. There is a war waiting for us. We have to fight. To win.'

She blew her nose and wiped her cheeks. 'Bloody war! I hate it! Bloody, *bloody* war!'

'But we have met because of it. Is one good thing. You must remember this always.'

She was silent. The war had brought him to her. But the war could also take him away.

'I've come to say goodbye.'

Taffy stared at Winnie. 'Goodbye? What do you mean?'

'They're postin' me. I put in for it.'

'Why? You never said. Why did you have to go and do that?'

'I didn't tell you but Ken's very ill. I found out when I was home on leave. The doctor there says he's got a bad heart and he'll die, so I'm goin' to marry him.'

He drew in a long breath. 'Look you, we can't talk here . . .'

He took hold of her arm and steered her firmly round to the back of the station building, away from curious eyes and ears and out of the raw November wind.

'Winnie, why in God's name are you doing this?'

She stared down at her shoes. 'Ken's goin' to die. I told you.'

'But why go and marry him? You were going to wait 'til after the war was over, weren't you? Marrying him won't change him being ill. It won't help.'

'Yes it will. It'll make him happy. It's what he always wanted. He never wanted me to join up. He wanted us to get married when the war started.'

'And you had the sense to say "No", girl. To wait. See a bit of life first. It's selfish of him to want you to marry him now, just to become a widow.'

She raised her head. 'It's not like that! He doesn't even *know*. I was goin' to ask to leave the WAAF as well as marry him, at first, but he didn't want me to do that. He wouldn't hear of it . . . Don't you *ever* say he's selfish!'

He had never seen her angry before. He saw he had said quite the wrong thing. 'I'm sorry, Winnie. So, they're posting you to be near him?'

She nodded. 'I went to see Section Officer Newman and told her about it. I'm going to Mantleham. It's

362

only five miles from home, so I'll be able to visit him all the time.'

He said quietly: 'Don't go and marry him, Winnie. It's a daft thing to do. Even for his sake. It might make him miserable if he finds he can't cope. Might make him worse quicker. Don't you see? It's better left as it is. That way you can pretend with him that everything's all right. And so can he. He's going to guess, sooner or later, even if he doesn't know now. It's better for him, really it is.'

She flared at him again. 'It's nothin' to do with you. You've no right to say anythin'. You don't know Ken, or care about him. You just don't want me to marry him.'

'And *you* don't want to marry him, either. I know you don't. You never have really, only you didn't know it. You found that out when you left home, didn't you? In your heart of hearts you know that's so.'

She gave a small sob and turned away. 'Don't say that! You don't understand anythin'. All you want . . .'

'All I want is you, Winnie,' he said. He put his hands on her shoulders and turned her to face him. An erk going by them made some grinning remark over his shoulder. Taffy ignored him. 'I admit that. I've wanted you since the first moment I saw you. I'd do anything in the world for you – except stand by and see you go through this, without saying something. You're marrying Ken just because you feel guilty and because you pity him. That's all wrong. Believe me, girl, it's all wrong.'

She said stubbornly: 'It isn't. It's the right thing to do. I couldn't live with myself otherwise.'

He looked at her pale, set face and dropped his hands, recognizing defeat. He said fiercely:

'All right, Winnie. Have it your own way, then. But I'll wait for you. I won't let you go, see. And I'll come after you and find you wherever you are.'

Thirteen

Winnie and Ken were married at St Mary's church, Elmbury, in early December. Ken wore his best and only suit and Winnie's mother had altered her own wedding dress to fit Winnie and made bridesmaids' frocks for Ruth and Laura. The church was full of villagers and Ken made his vows without coughing once, while Winnie spoke hers in a quiet but sure voice. Afterwards there was tea at the village hall, with sandwiches and bridge rolls and a two-tier wedding cake with a cardboard base because of the shortages. Gran stayed at home by the range.

When it was all over they were driven in a shiny hired car to Ipswich where Ken had booked a room in a hotel. A waste of money, his mother had kept saying, when they could perfectly well have come straight home, but he had insisted.

'It's what Winn and I want, and I've made all the arrangements.'

They sat in the big hotel dining-room, uneasy in the unaccustomed surroundings, and were served by a waitress who seemed to sense this. She took their order haughtily.

Winnie whispered across the table in the hush. 'Have you noticed how old everyone else is here, Ken? We're much the youngest.'

An old lady sitting alone at the next table was staring at them through lorgnettes.

Ken said: 'Don't take any notice of her. You'd think there was something wrong with us.'

He touched her left hand tentatively. The new gold band gleamed on her fourth finger beside the little blue ring. 'You look so lovely, Winnie. I can't believe you're really my wife. I'm the luckiest man alive.'

The happiness shone from his eyes and she was never more certain than in that moment that she had done the right thing. They were married and Ken was happy. And now that she had been posted so near she would be able to see him quite often. Never mind that she missed Colston and that RAF Mantleham was a bleak place by comparison, or that she had had to start all over again with a lot of strangers. It was a small price to pay and she paid it willingly for his sake. She would have left the WAAF willingly, too, but he had refused to hear of it.

'I won't let you do that, Winnie. It wouldn't be right. There's a war on and they need you.'

They were to live over the shop with Ken's mother, of course. No other arrangement was possible. They couldn't afford a place of their own and Ken would need to be looked after while she was away. Winnie knew she would just have to make the best of it and try to get on with Mrs Jervis.

'Two Brown Windsors.'

The haughty waitress set down the plates before them, but for all her superior air and the grandeur of the dining-room, the soup was tepid and tinned.

Later, in their bedroom – a chill and gloomy chamber with dark, heavy furniture and wallpaper like cold porridge – they faced each other shyly.

'Will I come back later, Winnie?'

'No, it's quite all right, Ken.'

They undressed on each side of the double bed, their backs turned considerately to the other. Winnie put on her new flannel nightgown, shivering. The springs creaked and twanged as they got in. Ken pulled the cord to switch out the overhead light and put his arms carefully around her as though she were made of very delicate porcelain.

'Winnie, oh Winnie . . . how I love you.'

He kissed her gently and held her close, but he could not manage to make love to her. She did her best to help him but without knowing how. After a while he lay back, overcome with a long bout of coughing.

'I'm so sorry, Winn . . . so sorry. I think I'm just too tired, that's the trouble. And now this wretched cough . . . I'm so sorry.'

She touched his arm, dismayed at the anguish in his voice. 'Don't worry, Ken. I'm tired, too. It's been a long day. I'd go to sleep if I was you. It'd be the best thing.'

Gradually his breathing became slow and regular and she knew he had fallen asleep beside her. She lay wide awake in the darkness of the unfamiliar hotel room. She was not disappointed at Ken's failure; in some ways it had been a relief. She was only sorry for his sake because he had sounded so upset. The truth was – and she had faced it at last – that Taffy had been quite right when he'd said that she had never really wanted to marry Ken. Somehow it had just always been expected. Seemed natural. Ken had always been there, for as long as she could remember, and she'd never known any different until she'd gone away. She was fond of him, of course she was. Very fond, or she wouldn't be here. Couldn't have gone through with it. She cared very much about his feelings and his happiness and she felt such a terrible, deep pity for him being so ill . . . it wasn't fair when he was such a good, kind person. Taffy had been right about that too – she was so sorry for him. But she didn't love Ken – not in the way she now realized that people could love each other. Taffy had given her an inkling of that. Not that she loved Taffy either. She didn't even like him really, though she'd felt better about him lately – not so scared of him. But he'd taught her a lot more than all those things about 'planes. He'd shown her how you *could* feel about somebody . . . how it might be. *I bet he never kisses you like this*. If she'd felt the same way about Taffy that he felt about her and it was him lying here in this bed beside her, she would have remembered this night for the rest of her life.

Winnie blushed with shame in the darkness at even thinking such a thing. Ken was coughing in his sleep and she leaned over to tuck the bedclothes closer about him. Then she lay back and tried to sleep too.

In the morning Ken was feverish and too poorly to go down to breakfast. He lay on the pillows, flushed and miserable.

Winnie felt his forehead anxiously; it was burning hot. 'P'raps I ought to call a doctor.'

'No, don't. Please don't. It's only a chill, or somethin'. I'm always getting those. It's my stupid chest. It picks up everythin'.' He coughed and closed his eyes. 'Poor Winn. This isn't much of a honeymoon.'

She held his hand. 'Don't you worry, Ken. Just you lie there and rest.'

He slept for most of the morning, though the hotel staff didn't seem to like it. She kept guard beside his bed and bravely sent the chambermaid away. By lunch time, when he woke, he said he felt much better, though the flush was still in his cheeks.

'I only booked the one night but we could stay another, if you'd like to Winnie.'

'No,' she said. 'It costs such a lot and I think we'd better go home. It'd be for the best.'

They caught the bus to Elmbury and when they arrived at the shop Ken's mother took one look at him and put him straight to bed. Winnie was left downstairs, waiting. She sat by the table in the living-room, twisting the fringed ends of the brown cloth in her fingers, not knowing what else to do.

Mrs Jervis came down the stairs, her tread heavy on each step. Her face was stiff with disapproval. 'I told you both it was a waste of money going off to that hotel. I knew it would make him ill. But you would have it.'

Winnie stood up. 'Ken wanted it, Mrs Jervis.'

'And *you* should have known better. Talked him out of it. Him in his condition! He's not up to things like that. He's not up to *anything*.'

The implication was clear and Winnie went red.

'I understand that, Mrs Jervis. And I'll do everythin' I can to take care of him.'

'It's nursing he needs now and you don't know much about that, do you? He's got a high temperature and I'll have to get the doctor.' Mrs Jervis moved towards the door and then turned, her hand on the knob to deliver her parting shot. 'I'd given over my room to you both — moved into Ken's — but you'd better sleep on the couch down here, so he can get some proper rest.'

She went out, shutting the door behind her. Winnie sat down again and covered her face with her hands.

'Christmas is coming and Pearl is getting fat.' Pearl patted her widening hips. 'Well, *fatter*. Look at this skirt. I'm bulging out of the bloody thing and I've already taken it out as far as it'll go. I'm going to look a right sight at the ball in this! Where's my Fairy Godmother to do something about it?'

Anne finished tying her tie. 'We'll all be in uniform, so who cares?'

'*I* do. It's all very well for you, love. It suits you. But my prince is never going to come while I have to wear these togs. And how can we waltz divinely in clodhoppers like ours?'

Pearl clumped heavily round the room in her black lace-up shoes.

'You could try going on tiptoe.'

'*Tiptoe through the tulips, through the tulips . . .*' Pearl went up on her toes, arms extended wide, and pranced her way towards the dormitory door. 'Come on, ducky, or all the best blokes'll have been nabbed. It's OK for you. *Your* Prince Charming'll be waiting for you.'

The brassy notes of the station band and the shuffle and drag of hundreds of dancing feet echoed in the cavernous wastes of the hangar, which was decorated overall for Christmas. This year the singer clinging to the microphone was a professional brought down from London — a platinum blond in silver lamé.

'Not a patch on you, love,' Pearl remarked. 'And forty if she's a day. The hair's dyed too.' She cast her eye round. 'Crikey! Wonders never cease. There goes His Majesty, tripping the light fantastic with one of the *cooks*.'

They stared in amazement as Group Captain Palmer went past with the fat cook who had been beside Anne in the shelter beaming in his arms.

Pearl whistled. 'Well, I never. You could knock me down with a feather. That settles it. When it's the Ladies' Excuse Me I'm going straight for *him*. Always thought he was a bit of all right. I like the strong, silent, masterful type.'

Anne was searching the crowd in vain for Michal.

'Looking for someone?' Johnnie Somerville blocked her view.

'As a matter of fact, I am.'

'Well, come and dance with me while you're looking. You'll see better.' He held out his hand to her. 'It's Christmas, Anne. Goodwill to all men.'

'If she won't, then *I* will,' Pearl informed him.

He turned to her with an easy smile. 'May I have the pleasure of the *next* dance with you, then?'

Pearl held out the hem of her WAAF skirt and curtsied as low as its tightness would permit. 'Thank you kindly, sir.'

'You've changed your tune a bit, haven't you?' Anne said as she went with him reluctantly.

He took her in his arms. 'What tune?'

'You know jolly well. A year ago you wouldn't have been seen dead dancing with someone like Pearl. I remember what you said about her.'

'What did I say?'

'You were extremely rude and loathsomely snobbish.'

'That was a long time ago, Anne.'

He steered her through the milling, jostling mass smoothly. She had forgotten what a good dancer he was but, naturally, he knew it. To be fair, Pearl was in for a treat in that respect. For a while Anne gave herself up to the pleasure of it.

He manoeuvred her deftly past a near-stationary couple who were causing a log jam. 'I hear you've been seeing a lot of one of the Polish pilots.'

'Do you?'

'True or false?'

'None of your business.'

'Wolves in wolves clothing, you know.'

'That's rich, coming from you! How's Penny?'

'Penny?'

'The blond who was with you at that party – the one where you were smashed.'

'I'm often smashed at parties. But I remember you refused to dance with me. I was very hurt. Patsy, not Penny. And I've no idea how she is. I haven't seen her since then.'

'I'm not surprised. Who's the latest?'

'Nina.'

'From Argentina?'

'No, from Kensington, as a matter of fact. She's an actress. Walk-on parts at the moment, but I've no doubt she'll go far.'

'Far away from you, if she's got any sense.'

He smiled, unperturbed. 'It's the season of goodwill, Anne, remember.'

Over his shoulder, she caught sight of Michal standing talking to Stefan in a far corner of the hangar. She could hardly wait for the dance to end so that she could get away.

Palmer relinquished the cook with relief. It felt like dancing with a barrage balloon. She was light on her feet, as fat people often are, but there was too much of her for comfort. And she had scarcely stopped talking throughout the whole dance. Other WAAFS might still quake before him, but the cook had shown no signs of awe or nervousness to be dancing with the Station

Commander. He had smiled grimly to himself as he propelled her round and wondered if he had lost his touch and got too soft. Just because the WAAF had done well so far it didn't mean that discipline should slip one jot.

He danced next with one of the plotters – a tall, rather gawky girl who, in contrast to the cook, hardly uttered a word and kept stumbling clumsily. He had picked her at random from a row of wallflowers and she had seemed horrified to be asked and looked at him in near panic. She seemed to find the whole experience a frightening and unpleasant ordeal.

He had intended from the first to dance with Section Officer Newman but there was no shortage of others who had the same idea. He finally managed to approach her as she finished dancing with Robbie Robinson and caught a look of dry amusement in the squadron leader's eyes, which he ignored.

To hold her in his arms was a strange irony when they usually encountered each other in confrontation across his desk. Only very rarely had their meetings not been on formal station matters. He sensed that she was ill at ease at the situation, though she did not betray it outwardly – any more than she betrayed it standing in front of the desk. She had learned a lot since that first day when she had blushed and stammered and been close to tears.

To his annoyance, he realized suddenly that it was a Ladies' Excuse Me dance but reasoned that it was most unlikely that the Station Commander would be interrupted dancing with the senior WAAF officer. He set himself out to be encouragingly relaxed with her, to remove any awkwardness she might feel, but for the life of him he couldn't think of anything to say except the most banal question.

'Are you enjoying the evening, Section Officer?'

'Very much, thank you, sir.'

'Good to get everyone on the station together like this,' he said heartily. 'Makes a proper Christmas spirit. A lot of them must be missing their families at this time.'

'Yes, sir. I think they appreciate it very much.'

Oh God, he thought, we might as well be in my office. I must sound a boring old buffer to her and she must be wishing she was dancing with one of the young chaps . . . with someone her own age. He consoled himself with the fact that at least he could show some of those how to dance properly – a lot of them didn't seem to have a clue – and that he'd also shown them that he was still more than capable of flying with the best of them, as well as shooting down Huns. The Distinguished Service Order that had been added to his medals was gratifying, but he wore his two flying crosses with the most pride.

She felt as light as the cook on her feet, but a great deal nicer to hold. His right arm fitted easily about her slim body. Her hand was resting lightly on his shoulder and the other felt small and cool in his. He was diverted to notice that her hair had come unrolled a little. It gave her a kind of vulnerability that pleased him, oddly, and made him wonder how she would look with it all loose . . . how she would be when she was not being a WAAF, saluting and standing to attention and always on duty and on her guard.

He was about to say something else when, to his intense annoyance, a plump, redheaded airwoman tapped him boldly on the shoulder. He thought she had a colossal cheek, even though it was an Excuse Me and smiled with difficulty. She seemed quite unabashed. Section Officer Newman had detached herself much more readily than he cared to see. Rapidly, in fact. He watched her move away and before she had gone very far, a young flying officer had claimed her for a dance.

'I am so sorry, Anne. The car does not start . . .' Michal took her hand and kissed it. 'Stefan helps me to push it and in the end she goes. But I am very late.'

Stefan gave her his wide, gold-toothed beam and bowed. He gestured round the hangar, at the coloured paperchains and streamers.

'Very interesting. English Christmas.'

She wondered what on earth they both made of it — of the rowdy, irreligious jollity of it all.

'I expect Christmas is very different in Poland.'

Stefan nodded. 'With us is evening before Christmas. Not day. So, we think to give big party then — all Poles here. Michal and me, we talk of this. A real Polish Christmas party. And you are honoured guest.'

Later, dancing with Michal, she asked: 'What was Stefan talking about? Are you really going to give a party, like he said?'

'Certainly. On the evening of Christmas. Is all now decided and arranged. Is to be in village hall. We Poles are invited to many English parties. Now is our turn to give back hospitality.'

'With vodka?'

'Naturally, with vodka. A great lot of vodka. Stefan he is finding this. And wine. And Polish food.'

'What sort of thing do you eat?'

'Always questions, Anne.' He smiled down at her. 'You will see.'

'I got him,' Pearl said, patting cold cream into her face.

Anne buttoned her pyjama jacket, yawning. 'Got who?'

'God Almighty. Group Captain Palmer. Told you I was going to make a beeline for him in the Excuse Me. I danced the foxtrot with him. He's not half bad at it either — almost as good as your Johnnie.'

'He's *not* my Johnnie. What on earth did you talk about?'

'This and that. Not much of a talker, he ain't. Matter of fact I think he was a bit pissed off that I butted in when he was dancing with Newman. I think he rather fancies her.'

'You're making it up, Pearl. He's got a heart of stone.'

'Still waters run deep, even with stones at the bottom.

I saw the way he was looking at her. I can tell these things.'

'But he's *years* older than her. And he's married.'

'Still the little innocent, aren't you?' Pearl sighed. 'Even after everything. Good luck to him, I say, with that cow of a wife. Wonder what she thinks of *him* – Newman, I mean.'

'Couldn't you tell that, too?'

'Don't be sarcastic, ducky. She didn't seem to be looking at him at all, which could be a lucky sign for him.'

'Surely if she liked him, she'd look at him.'

'If she liked him, she might. Or even if she *dis*liked him. But if she was falling for him, she might not look at him at all. See what I mean?'

'No, I don't. What are you hitting yourself under the chin like that for, Pearl?'

'So I don't get a double one.'

Anne climbed into bed. 'Anyway, I think you imagined the whole thing.'

The village hall had been transformed into a foreign land. Branches of winter greenery decorated the walls and ceiling and dozens of candles burned on the window sills, giving a shimmering light. Long trestle tables had been strewn with golden straw and a miniature Christmas tree, decorated with glass balls and candles, stood in the centre of each one.

Michal watched Anne's face as she stood in the doorway and stared. 'You like it?'

'It's wonderful! *Magic!* The WI would never recognize this place.'

'WI? What is that?'

'The Women's Institute. A sort of women's club. Most villages have one. They meet and make jam and things.'

'We do not eat jam tonight.'

'What *do* we eat then?'

He took her arm. 'Come and look.'

At the end of the hall, below the small stage, dishes had been laid out on two more long tables. Many dishes, all different.

'How in heaven's name did you do all this?'

'That is our secret.'

She looked curiously along the loaded tables. Nothing was familiar.

'It's different from English food.'

He laughed. 'No fish and chips? No bangers and mash? Nothing like that?'

'No turkey either. Don't you have that at Christmas?'

'You will not find meat here at all. We do not eat meat on this evening because it is a fast.'

'A *fast*! With all this lot?'

'Everything is vegetables, or fish, and so on.' He took her along the tables, pointing out dishes. 'Herrings . . . smoked eel . . . another fish, but I do not know the name in English. And this is *flaki* – a soup of tripe and paprika and other spices.'

'Tripe? Yuk!'

'You will like this, I promise. Is not like your tripe. Is very good. But here is another soup made with lemon, if you prefer. And we have cheese dumplings, mushroom dumplings and *chlodnik* – that is sour cream and cucumber. And, at the end you can see *kiesel* and *tort* and *babka* . . . all kinds of Polish puddings.'

'Well, I think it looks marvellous. When do we start?'

'We begin when the first star shows in the sky. That is our Polish custom.'

'I hope it's not cloudy.'

She had been one of the first guests to arrive but before long the hall was crowded and the vodka flowed. When they sat down at the long tables to eat, the Christmas tree candles were lit and wine replaced the vodka. She found it hard to believe that she was in England, sitting in an ordinary English village hall, scene of ordinary English events – flower shows, mothers' meetings, jumble sales . . . The golden straw, the forest greenery, the magic-making candlelight had turned it into some European folklore place. She ate the strange food and listened to the jabber of Polish spoken all around her, and felt like an alien in her own land. Polish faces, some gaunt with suffering, Polish voices, Polish names, Poland shoulder flashes everywhere, the Polish eagle glinting on uniforms, someone with smouldering eyes leaning right across the table to kiss her hand, Stefan raising his glass rather drunkenly to her from further down and calling out something incomprehensible to Michal beside her.

'What did he say?'

'He says you are very beautiful. And he is envying me very much.'

Towards the end of the meal one of the Poles, an older man than the rest, went up onto the stage and sat down on a chair to play the accordion. Presently, he began to sing quietly, as though to himself. It was a sad song, full of yearning.

'He is singing of Poland,' Michal said in her ear. 'He wishes he was there and he swears to return one day. He sings for us all.'

Afterwards all the Poles gathered together and sang a carol to their guests.

> *Jezus malusieński, Leży wśród stajenki*
> *Płacze z zimna, nie dała mu Matusia sukienki,*
> *Płacze z zimna nie dała mu Matusia sukienki.*

Anne listened, watching their faces. It didn't matter that nobody else understood a word. It was about Christmas and that was the same in any language.

When they had finished, the accordionist shed his solemn mood and began to play a fast polka. The tables were moved aside and people took to the floor with abandon. They danced until the village hall shook to its foundations. The polkas were nothing like the sedate hops that Anne could remember from childhood dancing classes. These were wild, whirling gypsy dances where the Polish men changed partners constantly. The room blurred dizzily about her as she was handed, spinning, from one man to the next. The music got faster and faster and the ring of onlookers clapped their hands loudly to the beat and stamped their feet. Finally, it was Michal who caught her in his arms and kept her there until the music stopped. She leaned against him, laughing and gasping.

When the evening was over they walked out to the Wolseley, beneath a starry sky.

'It was a lovely party, Michal. Thank you.' She stopped to look up. 'Either I'm plastered, or I'm still dizzy from all that polka-ing. Some of those stars seem to be moving.'

'Stars can move . . . sometimes they fall.'

She went on gazing upwards, awed by the glittering vastness of the heavens. 'It's been the best Christmas ever so far. Seems a funny thing to say when we're in the middle of a rotten war, but it's true. Last year I missed being at home so much. But this year I don't seem to be missing it at all.' She turned to him. 'I'm sorry. That's a stupid thing to talk about, when you must miss your home terribly.'

He put his arm round her shoulders. 'I do not miss it so much since I meet you, Anne. For me, too, this is a good Christmas. Because of you. And because of England. But specially because of you.'

He kissed her as they stood there together beneath the stars. And in the car he kissed her again. And again.

'I have small present for you.' He put a package into her hand and closed her fingers over it with his own. 'Wesołych Świat! Happy Christmas, Anne.'

She was half-dismayed, half-delighted. 'I've got something for you, too, but I wasn't going to give it to you until tomorrow.' She had saved up for weeks from her pay to buy him a silk scarf.

'I give now because in Poland we do this. Open, please.'

He held a torch for her while she undid the paper.

Inside there was a small cardboard box and inside the box a silver brooch in the shape of the Polish eagle with outstretched, drooping wings, exactly like the one he wore on his breast. She held it cupped in her palm and it shone bravely in the torchlight.

'Oh, Michal . . . thank you. It's beautiful. But I won't be able to wear it when I'm in uniform. We're not allowed to.'

'Wear it inside your tunic, where nobody can see.'

He unbuttoned her greatcoat and then her tunic and pinned the brooch to the lining on the left side. 'Next to your heart, you see. Why are you crying?'

She wiped her eyes. 'I don't know . . .'

'You must not. It is Christmas and you should be happy.' He took her hands in his and held them up to his lips. 'I want you to be happy always, Anne. And I ask you something now that I have no right to ask. I am a foreigner with no home, no money, perhaps no country, and maybe a short life . . . but I ask you to marry me, Anne. I am trying to tell you that I love you with all my heart, and I want so much I am your husband and you are my wife. I say this very bad . . . I am sorry. *Kochana*, you are crying again. I should not ask this.'

'Yes, you should. And I'm not crying because I'm upset or anything, but because I'm so happy.'

'You mean . . . you marry me?'

'Oh, *Michal*!' She flung her arms round his neck. '*Tak! Tak! Tak!*'

'Well, congratulations, duckie. Can't say it's a big surprise.' Pearl gave Anne a big hug. She grabbed her left hand to inspect it. 'No ring yet?'

'Just this, for the moment.' Anne opened her tunic and showed the brooch. 'It's not official. Not 'til he's met the parents. He insists on asking Daddy for my hand formally. Bit of a bore.'

'And what's Daddy going to say, do you think?

378

When he hears his daughter's planning on marrying a foreigner?'

'He'll be all right. Once he's met Michal.'

'Won't he think you're a bit young?'

'I'm nineteen.'

'Old Mother Riley!'

'I'll stay on in the WAAF, of course. I suppose they'll make us be at separate stations – that'll be grisly, but I'm not going even to *think* about that now . . . Oh, Pearl, I'm *so* happy! So terribly happy!'

'I can see that, love. You've got bloody great stars in your eyes. No need to wish *you* a Happy Christmas.'

He wore the silk scarf she had given him, tucked inside the neck of his RAF shirt, and she thought as she sat beside him in the Wolseley on the drive to Buckinghamshire in January, how wonderful he looked. So special. Her parents would be bound to think so too and to like him from the very first and make him welcome. On the way he stopped to buy flowers for her mother and when they arrived at the house and she had introduced him proudly, he bowed and kissed her mother's hand before he presented the bouquet. Her father came out of his study, all smiles, and Barley pushed himself forward to be patted, wagging his tail in approval. She only wished that Kit could have got leave from his camp up in Yorkshire to be there too, and that their leave could have been more than a forty-eight. It was so little time.

She took Michal all round the house, revelling in the chance to show him her home and her other life – to share it all with him and to make him somehow a part of it. In the old nursery he admired Poppy, pushing the rocking horse to and fro and looking about him.

'In Poland, in my home, we have room very like this, with many toys and books.' He picked up a lead soldier in a scarlet tunic. 'My brother, Antek, and I, we fight many battles with soldiers like these.' He stared down at it in his palm.

'Kit and I did, too. Well, he did all the commanding, and I just moved things round, actually. Come on, I'll show you his room.'

The model 'planes still flew from the ceiling. Michal exclaimed in surprise and examined them closely.

'He did not want to join the RAF, your brother?'

'No. He wanted to be in the army, like my father.'

'Your father is army?'

'Was. He left it ages ago. He works in the City — of London, that is. Or he did until the war started. Now he's doing some sort of hush-hush work. I don't know what exactly. He never talks about it and we never ask.'

'And all these things on the walls — these things for boats . . .?'

'They're sort of prizes. Kit rowed at Eton — the school he went to. He was rather good at it, actually. That's him in the middle of that group there . . .'

'He looks so much like you. Same eyes, same shape of face. Same smile.'

'Does he? People always say we're awfully alike, though we're not identicals, of course, so we needn't be any more alike than any ordinary brother and sister.'

'But a twin must be special, I think. To know you have been together since the very beginning of life.'

She nodded slowly. 'Yes, it's true.'

He smiled. 'I think I am jealous of him.'

'Actually, I've felt jealous of him myself sometimes. He's definitely my mother's favourite. She adores him.'

'I cannot believe she adores him more than you.'

'I can. I used to mind a lot, but I don't so much any more. In fact, I can understand it now. I must have been an awful drag sometimes — always bolshi about things and arguing. Kit's always been the easy one and done everything so well. Never been any trouble, like me. Are you your mother's favourite? I bet you are.'

He smiled. 'She always says she loves us all the same. I am sure is true. And is the same for you.'

She watched his smile fade and could have kicked herself for bringing up the subject of his family. When would she ever learn to guard her tongue? He had turned away and was looking at the row of school photographs along the back of the chest-of-drawers.

'Who are these?'

'Kit's special schoolfriends. They all give each other photographs of themselves when they leave. It's a tradition.'

'Such fine clothes for school . . .'

'They always dress like that. It's a sort of uniform. Only they don't usually look so clean and tidy.' She pointed at the photograph of Villiers. 'He was killed in France. At the time of Dunkirk.'

'I am so sorry. He was very nice, I can see. And so young.'

'Yes, he was very nice. I liked him the best of them, I think. He was great fun. A great sport. He'd have been about nineteen when he was killed. Kit's age, and mine.'

She took her eyes away from Villiers' smiling face. What had happened at that farmhouse in France was between Kit and herself. She would never tell another living soul. Not even Michal.

At dinner she was anxiously ready to smooth over any awkwardness for him, to help with his English, if necessary, to fill any gaps in the conversation . . . but everything seemed to go well. Her father poured some of his best wine.

'So, you're on Hurricanes, then? How do you find them?'

'Very good aircraft, sir.'

'Ever flown Spitfires?'

'No, sir. Not yet. One day, I hope. Then I see if they are so wonderful like everybody says. But I am very happy with Hurricanes. It is a wonderful fighter. Very steady for aim and shoot, and you can see very well. She climb fast and she turn, like you say, on a sixpence. That is big advantage. And because the fuselage is fabric, she goes on flying with many holes.'

He was making it sound so casual, so unremarkable. There was no clue to the ferocious battling that she knew lay behind his words – to the frantic twisting and turning, the desperate corkscrewing, the screaming dives, the deadly rattle of machine guns, bits of aircraft flying off, fireball explosions . . . Her mother was feigning interest, her head inclined politely as to an unusual guest whom she couldn't quite make out; her father, genuinely curious, was asking more questions. She caught Michal's eye and smiled.

After dinner she went to help her mother clear up and make coffee in the kitchen. Only the daily cleaning woman remained now out of the domestic servants. The cook, the parlour maid and the gardener had all left to join up. Her mother who had hardly ever washed up a cup in her life, much less cooked, seemed to have got quite used to working in the kitchen. She even spent hours helping in some canteen, apparently, making tea and sandwiches and dishing them out.

'What do you think of Michal, Mummy?'

'He's very charming, darling. Impeccable manners. I haven't had my hand kissed for years . . . it was rather nice. Lovely flowers, too. And, of course, one feels so sorry for the wretched Poles.'

'I don't want you to feel sorry for him, Mummy. I want you to like him.'

'Well, I do, darling. Such a brave young man.'

'Because we want to get engaged. He's asked me to marry him and I've said yes. He's speaking to Daddy about it right now, while they're alone.'

She hadn't meant to blurt it out like that, but she couldn't keep the secret any longer. She wanted to see the delight on her mother's face when she heard the news. Instead, she saw shocked dismay.

'Oh, Anne! I didn't realize . . . I thought you had just brought him home because he had nowhere else to go. I

382

thought you were rather sorry for him – like that girl at St Mary's whose parents lived abroad, and you used to ask to stay here in the holidays.'

'Mummy, what *are* you talking about? I'm not sorry for Michal. I *love* him. And he loves me. I told you, we want to get married.'

'But, Anne, you don't know what you're talking about. You're only nineteen. Much too young. You've had no experience of life.'

'I've been away from home for more than a year. I *do* have some experience of life, as a matter of fact.'

'Yes, but in the WAAF – that's not the real world.'

'Well, it seems pretty real to me. People *really* get killed. We've had *real* bombs dropping on us. *Real* things like that happen all the time.'

'Don't be sarcastic, Anne. That's not what I meant.' Her mother was looking appalled. 'I can see why you like him, of course. That type can be very attractive. He's very good-looking, very . . . worldly. Much older than you.'

'He's twenty-five, that's all.'

'He seems more.'

'He's suffered a lot, that's why. He's lost his home and his country, and perhaps his family too. And he's been fighting the Germans for a long time.'

'Yes, well, as I said, darling, I feel very sorry for him – for them all. But he's a foreigner, Anne, and from a country you know nothing about, not even somewhere like France. You can't know much about him either.'

'I know a great deal about him, as it happens. We've been seeing each other for more than six months, whenever we could.' She met her mother's eyes steadily. 'I know him very well.'

They faced each other for a moment in silence before her mother looked away. She said coldly: 'I hope you've remembered, Anne, that we've brought you up to have certain moral standards . . . I expect that of you, at least. It seems to me that in all this you're letting us down yet again. Being wilfully difficult and headstrong. You're far too young and it's quite ridiculous for you to think of marrying an RAF fighter pilot in wartime, even if he were English. Apart from the fact that he could be killed any day and leave you a widow, how is he going to support you properly on service pay?'

'I'd far sooner be his widow than never have been his wife. And I don't care about the money.'

'There's no need to raise your voice like that at me. You're speaking like the child you still are. You've never had to worry about money, never had to count every penny or go without. You don't know what you're talking about. Daddy will never hear of your marrying him. What could this Pole possibly offer you? What sort of background does he come from anyway?'

'It's just as good as mine – probably better. His family have a big estate in Poland.'

'So he *says*. It might be a complete lie for all you know. It almost certainly is – '

'I'm not going to listen to you speaking like that about Michal.' She was shouting now. 'Just because he's not one of those chinless wonders out of Debrett that you've always wanted me to marry . . . he's worth *ten* times any of them!'

She blundered furiously from the kitchen. Upstairs in her bedroom she sat on the windowseat, hugging Eliza in her arms and letting her angry tears fall on the doll's head.

Her father came in search of her later, knocking quietly on the door. He sat down beside her and offered his silk handkerchief.

'Dry your tears, poppet. I've given my permission for you and Michal to get engaged because, knowing you, if I said no you'd simply go and elope. But I'm making one condition of giving my blessing. I want you to wait until your next birthday before you actually get married.'

She stared over the handkerchief. 'But that's six months away at least! Why?'

'Because I want you to be very sure of what you're doing – both of you. I like your Pole, Anne. I know a brave and decent man when I see one, but he's a foreigner and you're foreign to him.'

'You sound just like Mummy. You'll be telling me he hasn't got the right sort of background in a moment.'

'It's nothing to do with right or wrong backgrounds, but of two different ones. Two different countries. Different languages, customs, ideas, religions – he's Roman Catholic, of course. And I'm thinking ahead to the future. When this war is over, he may want you to go and live in Poland. To leave England and your family and everything you've known all your life. Have you really thought about that? Because you should.'

'He might stay on here. Live in England.'

'He hasn't said that. All he has spoken of is returning to Poland one day. And who knows to what conditions? His country will have been devastated by war. His family may all be dead, his home destroyed . . . he may have nothing material whatever to offer you . . . and yet he may still want you to live there with him. You will need to be very, very sure, if you do that. I can see that you are very much in love with him, and he with you, but it must be able to stand the test of time, and everything else as well.'

She screwed the handkerchief into a ball in her fist. 'Michal may not even survive six months, Daddy. Have you thought of that? I don't want to wait. I can't *bear* to wait! I want to be with him as much as I can.' She was sobbing.

He put his hand over hers. 'Calm down, poppet. You must think of Michal too.'

'I *am* thinking of him.'

'No, you're not. Not clearly. The Battle of Britain is over but the RAF still has a vital part to play in this war. And a dangerous one, as you know only too well. If Michal is worrying about you when he's flying, as his wife and his responsibility, then it will make it even more dangerous for him. Don't you see? A fighter pilot should have nothing on his mind but the job in hand. Now, in another six months things may be a lot easier. We're not doing too badly in North Africa . . . Who knows, the Americans may even come into the war to help us. That's another good reason for waiting a while.'

She gulped and sniffed. 'I suppose so . . .'

He patted her hand. 'I'm talking sense, poppet, believe me. Now, come downstairs and we'll open a bottle of champagne to celebrate.'

'I don't think Mummy's going to want to celebrate much. I just had an awful row with her. She's dead against it.'

'She just needs to get used to the idea, that's all. I've spoken to her and she's in the drawing-room right now, talking to Michal.' He kissed the top of her head. 'We do have your happiness at heart, Anne, even though you may not believe it.'

Her mother had pinned on a false smile. Anne watched her being very gracious to Michal. She is smiling at him, she thought, but all the while, inside, she is saying to herself that, with any luck, he may be killed before Anne can marry him. Then she thinks I'll end up marrying the sort of stuffed-shirt drip she's always hoped I will, and she'll be able to plan the sort of wedding she's always wanted. Not a mixed, hole-in-the-corner affair with a Catholic foreigner, but a full-blown one in the village church. Me in clouds of white, bridesmaids, flowers everywhere, 'Praise my Soul the King of Heaven,' a huge marquee on the lawn, all the smart friends . . . She moved to Michal's side and put her arm defiantly through his.

That night she tiptoed barefoot down the passage to the spare bedroom and slid, shivering, beneath the bedclothes into Michal's arms. She snuggled close against his warmth. They talked in whispers.

'Kochana, your feet are like ice.'

'Sorry. I didn't bother with slippers. I just couldn't sleep at all, knowing you were here in this house —

so near to me. I wish we hadn't agreed to wait six months.'

'It is right to do as your father asks. He has good reasons and it is not for very long.'

'It's too long for me. I hate the thought of it.'

He stroked her hair. 'We must be patient. I do not wish you to quarrel with your parents because of me. That would be sad. And now, I can buy you a ring. Tomorrow we go to the next town and look in shops. I have saved money. It is not so much, but we find something you like and one day I buy you one much better.'

'I won't want anything better. I'll want to keep that one and wear it always.'

'So many women would not say that. Are you more warm now?'

'Yes, thanks to you.'

His hand moved down her body. 'More pyjamas, Anne?'

'Old school ones, this time.'

'So many buttons . . .'

She crept back to her own room in the small hours, skirting the floorboards that always creaked. Her bed was cold and lonely without him.

Fourteen

The winter days lengthened gradually into spring. Winnie, doing her turn as Orderly Room Duty Clerk one evening, looked out of the window at the sun still shining, and listened to the birds singing. It made her feel better.

RAF Mantleham was nothing like as nice as RAF Colston. The fighter station was just a collection of huts hurriedly erected in flat and muddy Suffolk fields that took the full force of the prevailing wind. The hut where she slept with other WAAFS was even worse than the first one they had lived in at Colston. It was never warm, condensation streamed down the walls and the concrete floor was always wet. She missed the WAAFS she had known at Colston badly – Vera, Anne, Sandra, Pearl, Gloria . . . even Maureen and Susan. The ones at Mantleham were not very friendly and she felt like an outsider. She had arrived alone and in the hut she was a new girl among airwomen who all knew each other well. And the only one who was married. They looked at her curiously and treated her as though she were somehow different from the rest of them. She would have liked to tell them that she wasn't – that she wasn't really like a properly married woman at all, that she didn't know anything more about what that was like than they did. But she couldn't. That wouldn't have been fair to Ken.

She went on looking out of the Orderly Room window, thinking about poor Ken. She had a bike now because the Waafery was sited so far away from the rest of the station, and she used it to ride over to Elmbury to see Ken whenever she could. Lately she thought he had seemed better. Now that the weather was beginning to warm up, perhaps he might be able to go outdoors a little. They might be able to go for a walk, or even do some bird-watching. Anything would be better for him than just being at home, either upstairs in bed or sitting in that dark dreary room behind the shop. Next time, if it was fine she'd suggest that, though Mrs Jervis would probably try to stop it.

So long as Ken's mother had anything to do with it, there was no chance of any sort of normal married life. She never let Ken forget for one minute that he was an invalid, or Winnie how much she was resented.

'I've given Ken his tea, Mrs Jervis. You don't have to bother.'

'I'd sooner you didn't, if you don't mind. I know just how he likes it. If you make it too strong it's very bad for him.'

'He said it was all right. I was very careful.'

'Just the same, I'd sooner you didn't.'

At night her presence in Ken's old room, just across the narrow passageway from theirs inhibited them hopelessly. Every sound could be heard and she thought that even if Ken had not been so weak and ill, nothing could have happened between them. Lying wakeful in Mrs Jervis's uncomfortable marriage bed, she could not imagine her here with Ken's father, as they must have been. Her cold disapproval seemed to seep through the very walls.

The sound of a fighter taking off made Winnie crane her neck to catch a glimpse of it. She could just see the Spitfire rising into the air and watched its wheels go up as it climbed rapidly into the evening sky. Now she understood exactly how and why it flew. The air flowing under the wings and the reduced pressure over the camber on the top of them would be combining together to lift the aircraft upwards . . . that was how it worked. The pilot would be pulling back on the control column, forcing the tail down to make the machine climb upwards, like it was doing now . . .

'Day-dreaming again, aircraftwoman? This won't do.'

The WAAF corporal was glaring at her from the doorway. 'I've told you before to keep your mind on your work. You're not supposed to stand gazing out of windows when you're on duty.'

Winnie went red. 'Sorry, Corporal.' She hurried back to her desk.

At Colston the trees on the station were coming into leaf and there were daffodils in bloom outside the Officers' Mess. Felicity, returning to her office after lunch, found four airwomen waiting outside her door. They stood at attention and saluted. The first in line, an aircrafthand, followed her inside and shut the door. Felicity sat down at her desk.

'Well, what can I do for you, Jones?'

'I want to re-muster, please, ma'am.'

'To what trade?'

'I'd like to train to be a telephone operator, please, ma'am.'

'Why is that, Jones?'

The girl hesitated. 'I've been scrubbing floors and cleaning things for nearly a year, ma'am, and I'd like the chance to do something else now. I always fancied working on a switchboard but there weren't any vacancies when I joined. I'd like to try, and I think I can do it.'

'I see.' Felicity turned it over in her mind. Jones had a clean slate. She seemed sensible and hard-working and she had a clear speaking voice. Other aircrafthands would be arriving soon who could take her place. She deserved to be given her chance. 'Very well, Jones. Write a formal letter in the proper way, giving your reasons and let me have it. You must start it: Ma'am, I have the honour to request . . . and so on. Then let me have it. It will all depend on vacancies still, of course, and it might mean you being posted to another station. Would you mind that?'

Jones shook her head. 'I'd miss it here, ma'am, but I think it'd be worth it.' She beamed her thanks and saluted smartly before she went out.

ACW Hollis who came in next was far from smiling. Felicity who knew the reason, told her to sit down and the airwoman, who was a cook, started immediately to cry. Her mother and two sisters had been killed when their home in London had been bombed. Only her father and her small brother had survived. She was leaving the WAAF to go and look after them, and doing so with a heavy heart.

'Your discharge has come through, Hollis, and you'll be cleared to leave early tomorrow.'

'I don't want to go, ma'am.'

'I know, Hollis, and we'll miss you. But your father and brother need you.'

The cook nodded. She blew her nose hard and wiped her eyes. 'Thank you, ma'am. I'll do my best for them, of course, but I'm ever so sorry to be leaving the WAAF. I've been happy here. It's a good life – better than I've ever known.'

She was not the first WAAF who had had to leave for a similar sort of reason. Many of them had lost homes and relatives in the bombing of London and other big cities – Southampton, Bristol, Plymouth, Coventry, Portsmouth, Birmingham, Liverpool . . . the Luftwaffe had pounded them all. Some, like Hollis, had been needed by their families to help cope with disaster. And some, like Hollis, had been reluctant to go. Felicity had come to realize that joining the WAAF had provided a heaven-sent escape route for girls trapped in joyless, dreary, dead-end circumstances. They had seized the chance and flourished in their new life. Then, sometimes, they had to go back.

ACW Stratton was the next to enter. She tripped on her way in, fumbled a salute and stood blushing. Felicity smiled at her.

'There's nothing to worry about, Stratton. Quite the contrary. There have been excellent reports on you, which is why you are here. I've been asked to put forward the names of two WAAF SD clerks suitable for special training on top secret work, and I'm proposing that one of them should be you.'

The airwoman looked completely astonished and taken aback; she obviously had a low opinion of herself. Felicity mentally reviewed what she knew about Stratton: Christian name, Virginia, nineteen years old, good education record, worked as an insurance clerk before volunteering, no charges or misdemeanours of any kind while serving and, apparently, completely reliable. The self-confidence would probably come in time.

'I'm afraid I can't tell you very much about the work because I don't know a lot about it myself and it's very hush-hush indeed. All I can say is that it would be related to the kind of work you are doing at present – concerning tracking aircraft and establishing their position. That sort of thing. It's very responsible and demanding work, I'm told, and absolutely vital. I already have one suitable candidate and I think you should be the other. Would you like to be put forward?'

The girl's brow furrowed anxiously. 'If you really think so, ma'am . . .'

'I most certainly do, Stratton,' Felicity said, encouraging her firmly. 'I think you will do extremely well.'

The last airwoman waiting outside had plenty of self-confidence but, unfortunately, lacked self-discipline. As ACW Cunningham marched in and saluted, Felicity wondered if she was about to make a bad mistake. There was still trouble of some sort with her every so often – still complaints of lateness, lost kit, insubordination, dumb insolence, larking about . . . the night when she had been caught swimming naked in the static tank was still talked about all over the station. On the last occasion she had been caught climbing through the window of Eastleigh House at two in the morning and had refused to say where she had been. Presumably with the Polish pilot to whom she was now engaged, which meant that her mind would probably be even less on the WAAF than before. And yet she had always believed that Anne Cunningham

watch it, talking to it softly in Polish, turning to smile at her, taking her in his arms . . .

All these thoughts went through her mind as she bicycled along the lane. A Bedford tooted as it went past and she waved at the airmen in the back. She began to hum, and then to sing.

> *Look for the silver lining*
> *When e'er a cloud appears in the blue.*
> *Remember somewhere the sun is shining*
> *And so the right thing to do is make it shine for*
> *you . . .*

She swept into the driveway of Eastleigh House, sending gravel spurting out from under the wheels, and swerved to avoid the cook's cat who was strolling across. As she skidded to a halt near the front door, a new WAAF whom she hardly knew leaned out of a downstairs window and called to her.

'There's a man in the garden to see you.'

The silly clot had pulled her head in and gone before she could ask who it was. Michal? But he wouldn't come in here. The Waafery was out of bounds to RAF except for special reasons. Kit? He was miles away in Yorkshire. She left the bike and walked round the side of the house to the gardens. Someone in RAF uniform was sitting on the seat in the rose arbour at the end of the pathway. At first she couldn't see him clearly, but as he stood up she recognized the tall figure of Stefan. She thought, puzzled: what on earth's *he* doing here? Then, as he began to walk slowly towards her, without his usual beaming smile, and she saw the look on his face, she knew.

They stood facing each other on the path. He lifted his hands and let them fall again. A gesture of despair.

'I am very sorry, Anne. Very, very sorry . . .'

He was unable to speak more. She saw that he was weeping, the tears sliding down his cheeks. She couldn't cry with him. She couldn't seem to do anything but stand there and stare at Stefan, as though he weren't real and this wasn't happening at all. If she stood perfectly still he would vanish and everything would go on as before.

But now he was taking holding of her hands and leading her towards the garden seat, making her sit down, though she didn't want to in the least. She went on staring at him. At last she found her voice and it sounded so calm it might have been someone else talking. Another person who had taken over and was asking a question for her.

'Is there any hope, Stefan?'

He shook his head. 'None. I am there. I see.'

The other person spoke again. 'Tell me what happened.'

He hesitated, very troubled.

'I want to know, Stefan. Please tell me.'

He gave a deep sigh. 'Very well. If you want. We were on patrol. Many patrols we have done these days, and we see nothing. But today we are vectored to intercept bandits. We find them. We go after them. Michal, he is shooting one and I see another coming from high at back of him. I try to tell him quick on R/T, but is too late, or he not hear. Then he is hit very bad. One wing is gone. His Hurricane go down fast . . .' Stefan twisted his hand downwards. 'I go down too, so I am with him. There is fire and much smoke . . . All the time I am hoping to see parachute. I call him again and again on R/T but there is no answer. Many times I try. I shout . . . I am in terrible fear for him . . . Then I see him go into sea. There is big splash with aircraft. I fly low to see if perhaps he gets out . . . but the Hurricane she sinks very quick and there is nothing. I fly round and round. I look and look but there is just water . . .' He put his hands to his face. 'I am very sorry, Anne. I could not help him. I could do nothing. *Nothing.*'

She looked over his bent head at the white squirrel scampering merrily across the lawn. After its winter hibernation it was full of the joys of spring. She watched it whisk up the trunk of the big copper beech and into the branches where the buds would soon burst into young leaves. The whole garden was full of new life – birds nesting, green shoots sprouting, flowers opening, grass growing. It would all burgeon and blossom and bloom into a summer that Michal would never see.

'Thank you for telling me, Stefan. And thank you for coming to give me the news yourself.'

He lifted his head. 'Michal ask me to do this, if it happens to him. I promise. He was my very good friend. I never forget him.' He spread his hands helplessly and sadly. 'He ask also I give you this.'

She hadn't noticed the suitcase tucked away beside the seat. Stefan placed it before her, at her feet. It looked scratched and well-used. A label hanging from the handle bore Michal's name. She remembered how he had opened it up on the cottage table in the New Forest. *I bring food for us. Eggs, bacon, potatoes, a tin of ham, bread, butter, tea, chocolate . . . and, most important thing of all, real Polish vodka.*

'Here is key,' Stefan was saying. 'I put everything he has in suitcase. There is not much. We Poles have not many things.' He paused awkwardly. 'The car he give to me. He write letter to say this, but it is for you, if you want . . .'

She shook her head firmly. 'No, thank you, Stefan. I want *you* to have it. I'd have no use for it. And I couldn't bear to see it.'

'You are sure?'

'Quite sure.'

'There is letter for you too, in suitcase.' He groped in the breastpocket of his tunic. 'I have also something for you. Is photograph. I make one day last summer. I think you like.'

She took the envelope he offered without opening it. Jimmy's mother had done the same and now she understood why.

Stefan was looking at her anxiously. 'You want I find someone to be with you before I go?'

397

'No, thank you. I'd much sooner be alone.'

He stood up, towering over her, sad but in command of himself again. 'Michal always speak of you Anne. He love you very much.'

He bowed to her gravely and she watched him walk away down the path.

After a while she put the suitcase on the seat beside her and opened it. Inside she found Michal's few possessions – his RAF kit, with his best blue uniform, an English-Polish dictionary, a Bible, his silver cigarette case, a bottle of the cologne he used, and the thick, cream-coloured fisherman's sweater he had worn at the cottage. She lifted it out and held it against her cheek for a moment; it smelled faintly of his cologne. His letter lay at the bottom of the case.

> *My darling,*
> *If ever you read this, I shall be dead. Stefan has promised he will give it to you. I leave these few things for you, to keep what you wish. I do not want you to be sad for me. You must not be so. I am not afraid to die and I always understood this could happen. I told you once that I had only my life left to give. I give it willingly, for my country and for yours.*
> *There is only one regret and that is that if this happens I shall never know a life with you. And our children will never be born. We would have had the happiest life together, I am very sure of this. But I think your father and mother were right. It is better you are not a widow. Better we had never begun. You must now make a different life. A new beginning. Promise me to do this. One day you will marry some nice Englishman who loves you as much as I do, and who will take care of you and make you very happy.*
> *Remember me sometimes, but only with a smile.*
> *Michal.*

She opened the flap of the envelope that Stefan had

given her and drew out the snapshot. Michal was standing in flying clothes beside his Hurricane, one arm resting on the fighter's wing. He was holding his helmet in the other hand and the wind had ruffled his hair. He looked like he had looked on the walk on the Downs – young and carefree. And he was smiling at the camera, and straight at her.

The tears came then, quite suddenly. She buried her face in his sweater and gave herself up to a terrible grief, crying as though her heart would break.

PART 3

ACHIEVEMENT

Fifteen

Virginia's special training course took place at RAF Yatesbury in Wiltshire and lasted for several weeks. The other WAAF put forward by Section Officer Newman had turned out to be Madge and, big and noisy as she was, Virginia was glad of her company. It made being sent away from Colston less of an ordeal. Before being accepted they had been given another eyesight test. Whatever the mysterious secret work might be, it required perfect vision.

RAF Yatesbury was a huge camp with an enormous number of people. Virginia thought it a grim place. The WAAF huts were two miles from the training building and they had to march there and back while the RAF whistled at them along the way.

Their first lecturer was a middle-aged man who looked and sounded like a kindly, absent-minded schoolteacher. He smiled round at them.

'You are going to learn all about something called radio direction finding, or radio location. None of you will know anything about this, so let me explain as simply as possible, and from the very beginning.'

He picked up a piece of chalk and turned to the blackboard behind him. First he drew a human head turned sideways, in profile, and marked in an eye. Then, at a short distance, he drew a house and then, above and between them, a sun surrounded by rays. It was like a small child's picture. He began to make dotted lines, linking the three in zig-zags. 'The human eye sees an object because the light rays from the sun are reflected from that object to the eye, like this . . .' The chalk made dot-dot noises across the board. 'Unfortunately, light waves can't travel through cloud or fog, or solid walls, and at night, when there's no sun at all, we have to use artificial light to send that reflection to our eyes.' He drew another head turned towards a vase of flowers, and then an electric light bulb suspended overhead. There were more dotting sounds as he joined the three. Then he turned round with a dry smile. 'Luckily, I never wanted to become an artist.'

There was a ripple of amusement round the room. He was much less frightening than most of the RAF instructors she had come across, Virginia thought. Even though she couldn't imagine what the childish drawings could have to do with some important, secret work, she was hanging onto every word, like the rest of the class.

He continued in his mild way, making it all seem no more complicated than a cookery class. 'So, you can see that light waves have their drawbacks when we want to see objects. However, another means has been discovered of enabling us to locate them and in all kinds of circumstances. By using a different kind of wave.'

He paused, and it was a dramatic pause. The room was completely still.

'Wireless, or radio waves travel at the same speed as light and, like them, are electro-magnetic. And, like visible light waves, they can be reflected from objects in a kind of echo. And they are not affected by the weather.' He turned to the blackboard again, with an apologetic smile over his shoulder. 'As a matter of fact, Mother Nature developed this technique millions of years ago to help bats fly at night without bumping into things.' The chalk squeaked excruciatingly as he drew a rather good picture of a bat, wings outstretched in flight, and then a lamp post beside it. He dotted another line from the bat's mouth to the post and back again to the ears. 'Bats send out short bursts of squeaks – inaudible to us, unlike my chalk – and catch the echo when it bounces back at them from an obstacle in their path. Not only can the bat tell there's something there but where and how far away it is.'

He put down the chalk and brushed his hands together, beaming at them. 'And you are all going to learn to be like a bat. Only it won't be squeaks but radio waves. And the objects you will be locating with these echoes won't be lamp posts . . . but aircraft.' He paused again as there was a murmur round the room. 'We know, you see, that the speed of radio waves is one hundred and eighty-six thousand miles per second. So, if we send out a wave from a given point and then measure the time it takes to travel to an object and then bounce back again to us, we can easily work out how far away that object is. To give a very simple example, if a radio wave has taken one thousandth of a second to go from your transmitter to an aircraft and back again, it has actually travelled one hundred and eighty-six miles in that time. Therefore, the aircraft it bumped into is ninety-three miles away. All clear so far?'

Beside Virginia, Madge gave a faint groan.

Their lecturer went on genially. He was talking now about something called a cathode ray tube and was drawing a trumpet-shaped diagram on the blackboard.

'We need to be able to *see* our echoes as they come back to us, and this is what we use. The returning echoes make electron beams in this tube shoot from the cathode at the narrow end to a screen at the wide end where we can see and interpret what they are telling us . . .'

He turned back to the blackboard. 'You will see a green light running across the screen like this.' The chalk shrieked wince-makingly as he drew it. 'This is called the time base. As each radio wave leaves your transmitter and goes out into space, so a pulse starts across your screen from left to right. If that wave strikes an aircraft it rebounds and is picked up by the receiver. This will deflect your time base down into a little V-shaped depression that you will be able to see, like this. And above your trace you will have a calibrated scale measure in miles to give you your range.' He looked encouragingly over his shoulder with a small smile. 'Believe it or not, you will also learn how to take a bearing and height reading on your echo, and even to estimate numbers of aircraft.'

Madge groaned again.

From the innocuous beginning, the course progressed relentlessly. They were taught to convert wavelengths to frequencies and frequencies to wavelengths, about the difference between current and voltage, about magnetic fields, about cathodes and anodes, and exactly how the magical tube produced its trace . . . and after every lecture they had to hand in their notebooks for security. There were stringent tests at the end of each phase. Madge found it hard, but managed to stay the course; others were not equal to it and left. Virginia passed all tests easily.

They were shown a cathode-ray tube in operation. It was encased in a large steel cabinet so that only the screen was visible and an RAF corporal, seated in front and wearing headphones and a mouthpiece, demonstrated for them. Virginia watched, fascinated, as the bright green trace on the screen registered an echo. The corporal read off the range from the marker above the trace and rotated the goniometer control knob with his left hand to give, first, a bearing on the aircraft and then its height. Eventually, they learned to operate the tube themselves. For the practical part of their training they were divided into watches and into night shifts as well as day, and they plotted the dummy tracks onto a perspex plotting table with a chinagraph pencil. It was all a long way from the bat and the lamp post.

A lecturer explained how what they had learned would be put to use.

'We have a chain of radio direction finding stations all round the coast, as a defence against the enemy. We call them Chain Home, or CH stations, and their object is to provide an early warning of attack. Some use a high beam from very tall masts, others are designed to spot low-flying aircraft, and some are for guiding our fighters from the ground to intercept the enemy. They are all part of a big defensive network. I will take the area controlled by 11 Group, Fighter Command, as an example.'

He sketched a rough map of the south coast of England on the blackboard, from the Thames Estuary to the Isle of Wight, and chalked in six crosses.

'These are all Chain Home stations.'

He drew a line inland from each cross so that they all converged at a point, like wheel spokes. 'And here is Fighter Command HQ at Stanmore. Information on enemy aircraft is detected at long range by the CH stations and passed to filter rooms at Fighter Command HQ where it is sifted by Filter Officers, and courses, heights and numbers of aircraft accurately established and identified.' He marked more crosses on the map and drew lines radiating outwards from the wheel's centre to them. 'The sifted information is then passed on by tellers to plotters at Group HQ, Bentley Priory, here, and in these Sector Ops Rooms. Some of you may have been on the receiving end in previous postings. This may seem rather a long way round to you, but the actual time lag from CH to Sector is very short indeed. Controllers very quickly form a clear picture of the enemy aircraft approaching our shores and are able to act accordingly with the squadrons at their disposal. So, you can see that you will be operating an extremely potent weapon against the enemy. And, incidentally, one which enabled us to win the Battle of Britain.'

At the end of the course RAF and WAAF marched together at the passing out parade. Virginia had never been much good at drill, but she marched better than she had ever done – swinging her arms smartly in time and holding her head high. Both Madge and she were posted to the same Chain Home station on the south coast, only a few miles away from RAF Colston, but before they had to report they were given leave. Virginia went home to Wimbledon.

She was shocked by all the Blitz damage in London since

her last leave, and by the new gaps in Alfred Road where more houses had been hit. Again, she tried to persuade her mother to move to the country.

'I've told you before, Virginia, that I have no intention of letting the Germans drive me out of my home and leaving it to the mercy of burglars. Besides, they seem to have given up the raids. What's that peculiar badge that you're wearing on your arm?'

Virginia fingered her new sparks badge. 'It's a special sort of one they gave us at the end of the course.'

'It looks like some horrible insect. What was this course, anyway?'

'They were just teaching us a new way of doing clerical work.'

'Well, you'd think they could find something rather better for you to do than that – a girl of your background and education. If you had gone into the WRNS I'm sure it would have been quite different. And now they're suddenly sending you off somewhere else, for no good reason that I can see. It all seems very unsatisfactory. I sometimes wonder if the RAF knows what it's doing.'

'Oh, I think they do, Mother,' Virginia said. 'I think they know very well.'

The Chain Home station where she was posted was surrounded by a high metal fence and by a thicket of barbed wire. Four gigantic transmitter towers stood in line at the westerly end of the site, and four smaller receiver towers at the easterly end. The taller ones rose more than two hundred feet into the air, dwarfing the nearby village, and could be seen for miles; it seemed ironical when what they did was so secret.

Like the other WAAFS on the site, Virginia and Madge were billeted in the village and they found themselves staying with a Mrs Parsons, an elderly widow. Her small cottage also housed a budgerigar and a large black cat who passed much of its day staring at the caged bird with its yellow eyes – motionless but for the twitching of its tail. Every shelf and every surface in the cottage displayed Mrs Parsons' collection of spindly blown-glass ornaments – souvenirs, she told them, from trips along the south coast when her husband was alive. They both lived in fear of knocking them off and breaking them.

It was soon clear that nobody in the village had any idea of the true nature of the work done on the station. There were rumours that the huge towers could shoot death rays at the Germans, but Mrs Parsons had her own ideas.

'I can guess what you're doing, dears. You're making bad weather to keep the Germans away. That's right, isn't it? Don't worry, I shan't breathe a *word*. You just carry on.'

'We'll carry on letting her think that,' Madge said later, snorting with laughter. 'Though heaven knows why we'd need to be making bad weather in *this* country!'

Security at the site was very strict and passwords were constantly changed. They worked in windowless blocks, camouflaged and protected by blast walls, and in a world of Stygian gloom. Three watches rotated all round the clock and when on watch they were supposed to rest hourly from the strain of staring at the flickering green tube trace and switch to other watch duties – plotting, telling, tracking all the plots, or recording them in the log. In practice, they often spent much longer in front of their screen, operating the tube. The tall towers with their far-ranging, all-seeing eyes were never off-duty.

A spell of hot, clear weather did not shake Mrs Parsons' faith in them.

'It's on purpose, isn't it? To *lure* them over? Make them *think* it's all right?'

The budgerigar twittered in its cage. Madge put a finger to her lips.

On their day off they went on a long bicycle ride, making the most of the chance to be out in the sunlight and fresh air. Madge rode a bike as Virginia walked – at full steam ahead. She swooped round a blind corner in the middle of the road and had to swerve to avoid two bikes being ridden from the opposite direction. Virginia watched in horror as she careered across the road and fell over the handlebars headfirst into a ditch. She jumped off her bike and ran to her.

'*Madge!* Are you all right?'

Madge lay face down in the ditch, bottom sticking up, her skirt nearly to her waist, so that stocking-tops, suspenders, large thighs and grey summer-weight WAAF knickers were all clearly on view. Her shoulders were shaking hard and at first Virginia thought she was crying, until she realized that she was actually laughing.

'Golly Moses, I took a real header! Lucky there's no water in here.'

'Gee, I hope she's not hurt . . .'

Virginia turned her head to see Neil Mackenzie standing behind her and another Canadian soldier staring anxiously over his shoulder. It had all happened so quickly that she hadn't noticed who had been riding the other bikes. She pulled down Madge's skirt hurriedly.

'She's all right, thank you.'

She hoped they would go on their way, but they came forward and helped Madge to her feet, apologizing. Madge was still laughing and saying it was all her fault, while they were saying it was all theirs. Then Madge recognized Neil.

'I know *you!* We've met before . . . at the Sally Ann canteen. You're Ginny's friend. Fancy bumping into you again!'

They all laughed and after that Virginia knew there was no hope of continuing their ride alone. They went on together in a foursome – Madge in front with the other Canadian whose name was Tom, apparently, and Neil weaving alongside her behind them.

He grinned at her. 'Seems like we're always runnin' into each other. Never reckoned I'd ever see you again, though. I asked a WAAF I met who was from Colston and she said you'd been posted.'

'I went on a training course.'

'You back at Colston now, then?'

She shook her head. 'At a different station.'

'Near here?'

'Oh, several miles away.'

'Well, that new badge you're wearing gives me a clue, but I guess it's all mighty secret, so I won't ask any more questions.' He started whistling cheerfully.

They stopped at a country pub and sat outside on a bench in the sun. Madge asked for half a pint of bitter.

'Go *on*, Ginny, try it,' she said. 'It'll build you up.'

She gave way weakly, not wanting to argue about it in front of the two Canadians, but the beer, when it came, tasted horrible to her and she couldn't drink enough to quench her thirst.

'I'll get you somethin' else,' Neil said, seeing her trying to pretend that she liked it. 'Don't drink it.'

He went off into the pub again and came back with a glass of lemonade for her. She was grateful to him for that.

'How are your family?' she asked politely as he sat down beside her again at the end of the bench. She remembered the snapshot he had shown her of them all.

'They're doin' great, far as I know. Heard from Mum a week or two back. It's real hot there now. They've been at our cottage, takin' a vacation.'

'How nice.' They had vacations, not holidays.

'Well, it's not really what *you'd* call a cottage – more like a cabin, I s'pose. All made of wood, with just a coupla rooms – no electricity or anythin' like that . . . real simple. Lots of people have them for vacations. There's some great lookin' country not too far from Hamilton . . . pine forests, lots of lakes. Our place is about an hour's drive – fifty or sixty miles, I guess – and it's right on a lake. Great fishin'. Trout, pickerel, bass . . . they just jump right out. We cook 'em on an open fire. They taste real good. We go huntin' too – mostly rabbits,

411

some quail . . . Once in a while we've gone deer huntin' in the fall. Some people go after moose and bears too, but I don't like killin' animals like that.'

'*Bears?*'

'Sure.' He nodded, and smiled at her expression. 'There's lots of 'em, an' you want to watch out for 'em too. It's a mighty wild place, Canada. You ought to come and see it one of these days – when the war's over. We'd take you to the cottage. Dad and I were buildin' another two rooms onto it, but then the war came before we'd finished. I guess we'll get it done when I get back.'

She could hear a wistful note in his voice. 'You must miss it all a lot.'

'Yeah. I sure do. I try not to think too much about it, but sometimes you get kinda homesick. It seems a long way away. Not that I don't like England,' he added quickly. 'It's a wonderful country – especially in summer. All this green . . . and everythin' real pretty and old, like it's out of a storybook. I had a picturebook when I was a kid with things in it just like I've seen over here . . . cute little olden time houses with thatched roofs and a yard full of all kinds of flowers.'

'I'm afraid England doesn't really look at her best at the moment,' she said, thinking of the wartime greyness of everything – allotments instead of gardens, cabbages and potatoes instead of flowers, no time or materials or labour for painting and repairs, and ugly scars everywhere from bomb damage.'

'That's not your fault. You've been at war nearly two years and you've had a real struggle this last one on your own. The Jerries've been givin' you a heck of a lickin' . . . I've seen what they've done to London. Southampton, too. I guess most of the big cities've caught it. I sure can't wait for the chance to get back at 'em for you.'

She had noticed something different about him while he had been speaking – there were three stripes on his arm where there had been only two, which meant that

412

he had been promoted to sergeant. Something else struck her as well, looking at his face. A whole year had passed since she had first met him speeding round the corner of the lane, and in that time he had turned into a man. She had seen the same thing happen with rookies in the RAF; after a while they lost the raw look of schoolboys. She wondered if she herself looked any different from when she had first joined: whether she looked more grown-up and assured. When she was working on duty she felt full of self-confidence; it was only in other situations, like this one, that the feeling seemed to desert her. She couldn't think of anything interesting or clever to say, and all her shyness and clumsiness returned. Madge could be clumsy too – three of Mrs Parsons' blown-glass ornaments had already come to grief – but she was never at a loss for words. At this moment she and Tom were talking about a dance the Canadians were going to give. Instead of living in tents on a camp site they had now taken over a boys' school, apparently.

'Great place for a party,' Tom was saying. 'And we've got a great band, too. We'll lay on the transport. You'll both have a real good time.'

'You're coming, too, Ginny,' Madge told her in the same tone she had used about the beer.

'You don't have to,' Neil said quietly. 'Don't let her bully you. But I sure hope you will.'

That was probably why she went in the end – because he had been so understanding about it and not tried to press her. The boys' preparatory school was a huge Victorian building near the sea, with a big assembly hall that seemed to be full of people. Tom had been quite right about their band – it was far better than the station band at RAF Colston. The only trouble was that she didn't really know how to dance.

'I was hopin' you'd teach me,' Neil said easily. 'I'm a real clod-hopper. I've never learned. Say, why don't we give it a try, though . . . see how we go? We can always chicken out.'

She put a tentative hand on his shoulder and her other hand in his; he put his arm around her waist. She was nearly as tall as him – but not quite. Being so tall had made her few previous attempts at dancing a misery since her partners had all been shorter. She had stumbled round the floor in an agony of embarrassment, looking over the tops of their heads. Now, instead, she looked at her feet, trying to keep them from treading on Neil's toes. She suspected that he was better at dancing than he had pretended, and was going slowly only out of kindness, keeping to her pace, rather as he had done on the bike ride. Everyone else seemed to be whirling round, and there was a great deal of whooping and yelling.

He steered her to a quieter corner. 'Sorry, some of these guys are a pretty wild bunch.'

She had heard that before about Canadians. One of the RAF had once told her that they didn't switch electric lights off, they shot them out. The evening got a lot wilder and the noise worse, and some of the men got very drunk. Neil never left her side.

Finally, the band stopped playing and a sudden quietness came over the big room as the lights were dimmed and a spotlight switched on. Into the silence came the harsh skirl of bagpipes. A solitary, kilted piper stepped into the circle of light and the crowd fell back as he began a slow, measured march around the floor.

Virginia glanced at Neil's face as he stood beside her and saw how moved he was by the pipes' lament; she found the sound chillingly sad.

Madge had had too much to drink and another of the blown-glass ornaments fell by the wayside as she blundered through the darkened cottage on their return. She tripped over the cat who yowled and spat indignantly, and eventually collapsed on her bed, giggling.

'Don't look so worried, Ginny! I'm not drunk – just

a teeny bit squiffy. Never drunk Canadian whisky . . . or *any* whisky.'

She clutched her head in both hands. 'Golly, I hope I don't have a hangover in the morning. I'll never be able to read the bloody trace.'

She pulled off her clothes anyhow and fell headlong into bed. Virginia thought she had gone straight to sleep, but after a moment she said in a muffled voice: 'Tom says Neil's absolutely loony about you. Did he ask you to go out again?'

Virginia had gone red. 'Yes.'

'So . . . what did you say?'

'Well, I said I might.'

Made grunted. 'Should hope so too. Jolly nice chap.' She turned over heavily. 'Funny old Ginny . . . you never know what's good for you.'

Soon she began to snore.

Anne waited for Kit outside the Piccadilly Circus entrance of Swan and Edgars. She watched people going by: Londoners looking as drab and war-weary as their city. Faces were pinched and pale, clothes worn and shabby. Those in uniform looked much better: better fed, smarter and brighter. The ATS girl standing near her, obviously waiting for someone as well, was positively blooming with health and vitality. But then, unlike the civilians she had probably not had to endure the months of bombing – the nightly raids, the broken sleep snatched in shelters or huddled with hundreds of others in the depths of the Tube, the struggle to get to work and back somehow . . . and all on meagre civilian rations. The Blitz might be over but she could see that it had left its mark on more than buildings.

She tried to remember how the Circus had looked before the war when the lights came on after dark; when Eros had shot arrows airily from his plinth in the centre and the advertisements had dazzled the eyes. *Ever-Ready Batteries Are Marvellous, Defy The Rain* –

Wear a Telemac, Wrigleys After Every Meal, the big *Bovril* sign, and *Gordon's Gin*, and *Schweppes Tonic Water*, and the Guinness Time clock with *Guinness Is Good For You, Gives You Strength* underneath. Would the lights ever go on again?

A sailor was greeting the ATS girl. He was laughing as he swung her round, lifting her in his arms. The girl was laughing with him and they looked so happy and so much in love that it hurt her to see it. She turned away quickly and saw Kit striding towards her, tall and good-looking in his army uniform. There were two pips on his shoulder now.

He gave her a hug and smiled down at her. 'Hallo, Assistant Section Officer.'

'Hallo, yourself, Lieutenant.' She hugged him back.

'Congrats on the commission. Jolly well done.' He tweaked the soft crown of her new cap. 'That uniform's awfully smart. You look terrific in it.'

'Thanks.'

'Let's go and celebrate with a drink at the Ritz.'

As they walked down Piccadilly he squeezed her arm. 'Well, how does it feel – being an officer?'

'I haven't had much time to find out. The best thing so far is wearing comfortable shoes. I went and bought these myself and they're bliss. They actually *fit*.'

He laughed. 'You'll find there are other advantages.'

'Like not having to clean my own buttons and shoes? That'd be the next best thing.'

'What was the Officers' School like?'

'The place itself was jolly nice. They've taken over a big country house near Gerrards Cross – not far from home. The course was pretty deadly, though. Endless boring lectures on organization and admin. And on and on about King's Regs, Air Force Law, office procedure, hygiene, pay and allowances, etiquette . . . all that sort of rubbish. Everyone taking masses of notes and swotting away and being frightfully goody-goody. Some old bat from the Directorate came down to spout at us about duty and leadership, and how to inspire devotion in your followers. According to her discipline is "the cheerful obedience to orders recognized as reasonable". The trouble is I still don't think half of them *are* reasonable.'

'Same old Anne.'

'Well, I managed to pass all the tests and exams in the end. Quite a lot of them didn't.'

'Good for you.'

'You should have seen me taking drill . . . yelling at the squad like a RAF sergeant! We all had to take turns at it. That part was quite fun, actually. Drill is the bedrock of all training. Did you know that?'

'It rings a faint bell.'

An RAF sergeant coming along the pavement towards them, saluted them briskly. Anne returning the salute with Kit, almost giggled at the strangeness of it. They crossed Piccadilly and went under the arcade into the Ritz. In spite of the sandbags, the firebuckets, the blackout, the rationing and the presence of so many service uniforms, the hotel had somehow kept up the pretence that there was no such thing as a war on. Inside, its gilded splendour was undimmed. Teacups still tinkled in the Palm Court and a dowager in a long gown and ropes of pearls raised her lorgnettes at them.

Kit ordered champagne recklessly and when it came, lifted his glass to her. 'To you, twin. Congratulations.'

He had done that out on the terrace on the night of their eighteenth birthday dance two years ago. The toast then had been to them both . . . *and to the future . . . whatever it may bring*. She remembered his words very well. She had feared that future and, as it had turned out, with good reason. She lifted her own glass.

'To *us*, Kit. You and me.'

She looked at him carefully as she drank. Outwardly he was like his old self. The arm didn't appear to be troubling him any more, and he was smiling easily at her. But she knew him too well to be deceived. He had not really got over Villiers' death. That dead look still lay somewhere at the back of his eyes. We've both suffered now, she thought. Both of us have changed. I have too. I pretend to be the same old Anne, as he says, but inside I'm not at all. And I never will be again.

Kit leaned forward to light her cigarette. 'So, you're spending all your leave here in London?'

'Lucy Strickland asked me to stay. Her parents have a super place in Chester Square. You remember her, don't you? She was in my house at St Mary's and her brother Alex was at Eton. She used to come to the Fourth.'

'I think so. Rather a jolly sort of girl. Lots of fair hair and teeth. Piano legs.'

'That's her.'

'The parents were a bit disappointed you didn't go home, old bean.'

'I know. But I couldn't, Kit. I just couldn't face it.'

'Because of Michal?'

For a moment she couldn't answer. Just to hear his name spoken aloud again brought back all her grief and misery. It caught at her throat and she had to fight back tears.

Kit said gently: 'I was really sorry about him, twin. It was rotten, bloody luck.'

She swallowed hard. 'I didn't go home because I didn't want to see them – not yet. If it hadn't been for them Michal and I would have been married. We'd've had some sort of life together, however short. I would have had his name . . . perhaps his baby. Instead, there's *nothing*. I can't forgive them for that. I was a fool to listen to them when they wanted us to wait. I'll always regret it.'

'I can imagine how you feel. But I dare say they meant it for the best – or what they saw as the best thing for you.'

She said fiercely: 'It wasn't that. They were against my marrying Michal because he was Polish. Especially Mummy. You know what she's like, Kit. Her idea of the perfect husband for me has always been some blue-blooded English moron. She hoped like anything that Michal would be killed. I *know* she did. She's jolly glad it happened . . .'

Her voice had risen and an army major sitting near turned his head to stare. Kit touched her arm. 'Steady on, old thing. Don't work yourself up into a lather. I never met Michal, but I wish I had. He must have been a pretty good sort of bloke.'

She blew her nose. 'He was. He was wonderful. The Poles gave him a medal after he was killed, you know – their Cross of Valour. I just wish he could have had it when he was alive.'

'I know. That seems to happen rather a lot these days.'

'There'll never be anyone else like him for me, Kit.'

'Not like him – no. But someone else who's different, perhaps. One day.' He looked at her gravely. 'We both have something we bitterly regret. The only difference between us is that what happened to you wasn't your fault.'

'Oh, Kit, you're not still blaming yourself over Villiers?'

'I shall blame myself to the end of my days. But I've come to terms with the fact that, at heart, I'm a coward. I've faced it. I just live in hope that one day I shall get the chance to make amends in some way. To atone for my cowardice.'

'But you *mustn't* think like that. It's all wrong. You couldn't help what happened. The Germans killed him. *They* were to blame, not you.'

He gave her a brief smile. 'Let me be the judge of that, twin. And drink up your champagne.'

She watched him anxiously as they talked of other things; he made no further reference to Villiers and she dared not bring up the subject again. He seemed to chat on easily.

'I was hoping they'd send us to Crete but now we've been kicked out of there, it'll probably be North Africa. We don't seem to be doing exactly brilliantly there either. Rommel's having it all his own sweet way. Anything to get away from another English winter . . .' He looked across Anne's shoulder. 'Good lord, there's Isobel Bingham. She used to be Atkinson's girlfriend, you know, but it looks like she's with some RAF type now.'

Anne turned her head. 'That's Johnnie Somerville.'

'You know him?'

'I suppose you could say that. I met him at Colston. He's with one of the auxiliary squadrons – fearfully rich, snobby lot. At least they all used to be but a lot of the original ones have got killed. He's a bit of a pain. Frightfully pleased with himself.'

'The name's vaguely familiar.'

'He was at Eton, about five years ahead of you. Remember I asked you about him once? He won all those cups . . . Wet Bob and held the long jump record, or something.'

'Of course! *That* Somerville. Hallo, he seems to have spotted you. They're coming over.'

Isobel Bingham was dressed in pale blue taffeta and her hair was carefully curled. She had a sweet, eager smile.

There was no avoiding the introductions and the hand-shakes, and Anne was further dismayed to hear Kit suggesting that they all join forces. It was too late to kick him; Johnnie was already holding a chair for Isobel who sat down, arranging her taffeta skirts carefully and smiling sweetly round.

'We're celebrating Anne's commission,' Kit said, oblivious of her glowering lack of enthusiasm.

Johnnie smiled at her. 'I'd noticed. Congratulations. I always said you were wasted.'

'I'm thinking of joining the WAAF myself,' Isobel said brightly. 'It all sounds rather fun.'

It was bad enough that they had intruded on her drink with Kit, but even worse when Johnnie later proposed that they all had dinner together.

Isobel clasped her hands eagerly. 'Oh, yes, do let's go round to Quags. Hutch is singing there and he's absolutely super!'

Anne wondered sourly what Sergeant Beaty would have made of her as a recruit. She tried to catch Kit's eye, but he seemed perfectly happy with the idea and there was nothing to do but go along with it. She would have much preferred to spend the evening alone with him. Tomorrow he was going home for the rest of his leave and after that he might be posted overseas. It could be months and months before they saw each other again.

It was still broad daylight when they walked down St James's to Jermyn Street and along Bury Street to Quaglinos. The warm summer's evening should have lifted her spirits but she felt depressed and out-of-sorts now – reminded of Michal and worried for Kit.

Kit, on the other hand, seemed to be enjoying himself. She watched him later dancing with Isobel as though he hadn't a care in the world. Would he really blame himself for Villiers' death to the end of his days? What had he meant exactly by making amends? By atoning for his cowardice? What sort of nightmare of guilt and suffering was still tormenting him beneath the surface?

'Dance?' Johnnie said, stubbing out his cigarette.

'If you insist.'

'I always have to, where you're concerned.'

She went reluctantly onto the small dance floor, and put her hand in his. He looked down at her.

'This isn't the place to say it, Anne, but I heard about Racyñski and I'm extremely sorry.'

'Thanks, but I'd sooner not talk about it.'

'Then we won't.' He was silent for a moment. 'What do you think of Isobel?'

'Much too sweet for you. Not your usual type, is she?'

'Well, I got a bit tired of actresses and mannequins. They're only really interested in themselves.'

'That must be a bore if there are two of you like that.'

He smiled. 'Isobel makes a pleasant change. She never argues or sulks, and she thinks I'm absolutely terrific.'

'I can see why you like her then. Does she always smile like that?'

'Always at me, and invariably at everybody else too. She's a very nice girl. Our mothers are old friends and I've known her since she was in nappies.'

'I shouldn't make that a public announcement or she might stop smiling. She's probably perfect for you. You ought to please both your mothers and marry her.'

'I'll bear it in mind.'

'I think it's in hers.'

He laughed. 'I like your twin. I can see a strong resemblance. You're very close, aren't you?'

'Yes, but we don't get a chance to see much of each other at the moment. We just happened to have some leave at the same time and arranged to meet up in London. It was lucky.'

'How long are you staying in London?'

'I've got another six days.'

'Good. I'm here for two more, so you'll be able to have dinner with me.'

'Why on earth should I want to do that?'

'Because I'll take you somewhere very nice and you'll have a very good dinner. You can still get one in London, if you know where to go. You could even have steak tartare, if you like.'

She grinned. 'No, thanks. A cooked steak wouldn't be bad, though. Thick and juicy, with lots of fried potatoes.'

'I guarantee it.'

'Hmm. What would Isobel say?'

'Isobel won't know.'

'It would only be for the sake of the food. That's all I ever seem to think about these days.'

'I didn't imagine it would be for any other reason. Where are you staying?'

'In Chester Square. With an old schoolfriend, Lucy Strickland.'

'I know the Stricklands well. I'll pick you up around seven tomorrow evening.'

Later on, Hutch sang at the piano. As she listened to him, Anne was glad of the dimmed cabaret lighting. The words, half-spoken, half-sung in his intimate, confiding way, went straight to her heart. The tears that were never very far away since Michal had been killed, welled up again and spilled over. She gulped and fumbled for her handkerchief, but couldn't find it in either tunic pocket. Then, through the blur, she saw a man's white silk one held out under her nose. Johnnie had quietly passed her his own.

Anne and Kit left the restaurant before the other two, who were still dancing. There was no moon or stars to help light the city for either the Germans or the inhabitants and it was pitch black outside.

Kit took hold of her arm. 'I'll try and get you a taxi. I'm kipping down at Atkinson's and it's easy walking distance from here. If the worst comes to the worst you can come there with me.'

He shouted into the impenetrable darkness of Bury Street. Further along, they could hear others yelling for taxis too. It was like some kind of party game – a variation on blind man's buff.

Miraculously, the twin pinpoints of a taxi's headlights slid to a stop beside the whitened kerb. Kit felt for the door.

'In you get. I'll go home and see the parents in the morning. I'll give them your love and say you're fine.'

She groped for him and hugged him tightly.

'Take care of yourself, Kit. Please don't go on blaming yourself. Promise you'll try to forget all about it.'

'I can't promise that.'

'Then promise you'll write, at least, and let me know how you are?'

'I swear. Whenever I can. You too. Happy landings, twin. It'll all come all right in the end.'

She fumbled her way in and gave the address to the driver. Kit closed the door after her and as the taxi carried her away, she twisted round to try and see him through the tiny back window, but it was much too dark.

'*Johnnie Somerville*! You lucky thing! He's super!'

'Don't you start, Lucy. He's nothing of the kind. He's actually a conceited bastard.'

'Oh, I've always *drooled* over him, but he's never looked my way.'

'I'm only going out with him to get a decent dinner.'

'Well, you'll certainly have that. He must know all the best restaurants. Ah me! Pots of money, a flat in Belgravia, that divine car, and those dreamy looks! The father's a baronet, you know, so he'll be Sir John one of these fine days. Quite a catch.'

'Well, you can stop sighing like that, Lucy. I'm not going fishing. I'm eating.'

He arrived to collect her in the green Lagonda and wearing mufti. He was one of the few men, she thought grudgingly, who looked equally good out of uniform; the suit had probably cost a small fortune, not to mention the shirt, tie and shoes. They certainly hadn't come from anywhere near The Fifty Shilling Tailors. It was rather sickening to watch Lucy and her mother fawning over him.

'Are all women like that with you?' she asked as they drove off.

'Most of them. Except you, of course.'

'My God . . .'

He took her to a small French restaurant hidden away down in a Mayfair basement and, as he had promised, there was thick, juicy steak – the best she had ever tasted.

'I like the dress,' he said. 'Blue always suits you.'

'I got it in Harrods this morning. I spent far too much on it and it'll have to last me the rest of the war, I should think. Specially now they're rationing clothes.'

'You look lovely in it. It was worth every penny.'

'Don't go on about it . . . How much longer do you think the war's going to drag on for, anyway?'

He shrugged. 'Who knows? Years, probably. If the Americans come in, then it'll be much shorter. We're going to have a hell of a job finishing it on our own.'

'Do you think they will?'

'Only if they have a good enough reason. Otherwise, why should they want to get involved?'

'I think they jolly well ought to help us. Don't they *want* Hitler beaten?'

'Europe's a long way away to most of them, you know. And at least they're lending us arms now.'

'Pity the Germans don't drop a few bombs on *them* to wake them up a bit more. It's funny how the Jerries have left us alone lately. Lucy's father thinks it's the calm before the storm and that they're planning to try a massive invasion again soon.'

'I don't believe they'll ever manage to invade England. Not now. It's too late. And it's too difficult, thanks to the Channel. By the way, where are you being posted?'

'East Thorpe in Norfolk. It's a bomber station. They're putting me in Ops Intelligence. I haven't the least idea yet what exactly I'm supposed to be doing there. Typical RAF.'

'You'll find the bomber chaps a bit different from us.'

'In what way?'

'Saner. Quieter. More sober.'

'Not so show-off and swanking around, you mean. Perhaps they'll even be able to stand upright on their own two feet, without having to lean against their 'plane, or something.'

He smiled. 'You can't lean against a bomber so easily. I wouldn't change places with them for anything. Trundling along at a snail's pace for hours on end . . . an absolute sitting duck for the Huns.'

'There's a whole crew of them together,' she pointed

out. 'It must make it less frightening than being all on your own.'

Johnnie shook his head. 'I don't agree. I'd far sooner have some control over my own destiny.'

How did Michal feel? I can't remember him ever talking about that. Was there any time for fear when he was plummeting down alone in the Hurricane towards the sea? Was he trapped in the cockpit, or too badly wounded to get out? Was he conscious, or mercifully unconscious like I've always prayed hard he was whenever I think about it and picture it happening in my mind. Like now.

She put down her knife and fork, her appetite gone. 'Aren't you ever frightened, then?'

'Only if I let myself think about what might happen – and mostly there isn't time, except on the ground. We've converted to Spitfires now and they're pretty nimble which gives one a fair bit of confidence. I suppose the thing one is most afraid of is being badly burned or disabled. I'd far sooner be dead if that happens.'

'Don't say that,' she said bitterly. 'Anything's better than someone being dead.'

'I'm sorry, Anne. That was extremely crass of me.'

She fiddled with her knife. 'Anyway, *you* seem to live a charmed life, so I wouldn't worry.'

'I'm not counting on it, I assure you. If I end up in some grim hospital ward, will you promise to come and visit me and cheer me up?'

'That will be Isobel's job.'

'I have a strange feeling that she might not be very good at it. Promise you will?'

'If I can. But it won't happen. I told you, you're much too lucky.'

'Spoiled rotten, I believe you once said, if I remember rightly. Now, which of these delectable desserts are you going to choose?'

'None of them, thanks. I couldn't manage it.'

426

'You disappoint me, Anne. I thought better of you and your stomach.'

He drove her back to Chester Square and saw her to the Strickland's front door, finding the right house number in the darkness with his torch.

'I hope I see you again, Anne. Somewhere. Some day. Somehow.'

She was feeling for the doorbell. 'I doubt if our paths will cross. Not very likely. Oh, I nearly forgot . . . here's your handkerchief back. I had it washed. Thanks for the loan.'

Their hands touched briefly as he took it from her. Although he was standing very close, it was so black that she could scarcely see him at all.

'It won't be the end of everything, Anne. You'll find that out eventually. It will get better, as time goes by.'

The sympathy in his voice made her feel like crying again. If he said another word, she'd start. To her relief she heard the front door opening and the Strickland's elderly manservant quavering a greeting.

'Well . . . thanks for the dinner, anyway. Good night.'

She went inside quickly and the door closed behind her.

'But, soft! What light through yonder window breaks? It is the east and Juliet is the sun!'

Felicity, standing near her office window, turned round in amazement.

'*Speedy!* How on earth did you get here?'

He flourished a hand. 'With love's light wings did I o'er perch these walls. Actually, I cadged a lift in a Lizzie that just happened to be coming this way.'

'I thought you were still miles away, up north.'

'So I was 'til recently. We've been playing nanny to the navy for months. Very cold and very boring. Now we're down south again, lending a hand on the land in the Garden of England, so to speak. Making little jaunts across the moat to see what we can do to annoy the Jerries in France.'

It was a year since she had last seen him but he hardly seemed to have changed at all. The only difference was that he looked less tired, she thought, and that his cap was even more battered than usual. Fit for the dustbin. The red, white and blue check scarf was still in place, and he was wearing a heavy sheepskin flying jacket. He rubbed his hands together, beaming at her with all his heart-lifting sunniness.

'Well, is Juliet going to invite Romeo to the Mess for a warming tot or two? To celebrate our reunion.'

She held out the file of papers that she had been busy looking at. 'I'm supposed to be dealing with all these . . .'

He came forward, took the file from her and tossed it onto her desk. 'No time for all that bumph now. I've only got a couple of hours here. Gather ye rosebuds while ye may. Make use of time, let no advantage slip . . . and all the rest of it.'

He held her arm and steered her firmly out of the office.

The late November day was grey and cold and the strong winds had blown most of the dead leaves from the trees round the station. A young WAAF hurried past them, saluting with her head bent. Speedy smiled at her, and she looked back over her shoulder.

As it was close to lunchtime the Officers' Mess ante-room was crowded. People came up to Speedy and slapped him on the back. As they sat down he looked round happily.

'Rather like coming home. Always was my favourite station . . . always will be. Even the Old Man had a kind word for me when I passed him in the corridor at HQ. He seems to have sprouted a few more grey hairs since I last saw him.'

'He has a hard job.'

Speedy cocked his head at her. 'Do I detect a slight change of heart in that direction? A thawing of the ice between you?'

'Well, he's not quite as bad as I first thought.'

'Matter of fact, he's a damned sight better than most. You should have seen the one we had last up north. Frightful stickler. Strutted round like a turkey cock. We had a name for him, but I couldn't repeat it in your company. He had this stupid idea that station security was slack, so he got two chaps to dress up as German airmen – full Luftwaffe rig: caps, boots, iron crosses, the whole shooting match – and told them to walk about the camp and see what happened. Well, of course, nobody took a blind bit of notice of them. There they were, goose-stepping all over the place and everyone politely saluting them!'

Felicity choked on her drink. 'I don't believe it!'

'Absolute gospel, Titania. Turned out everybody had thought they were dressed up for a play. Anyway, the Station Master, whose other name I won't mention, was hopping mad and there was the most almighty dust-up. Didn't see the funny side at all. Everybody confined to camp for a week. Bread and water. Rack and thumbscrews. Then a couple of weeks later we had these two Turkish air force blokes arrive. Odd sort of uniform they wear – long coats, funny hats, boots, that sort of thing . . . So, of course, every few minutes they're getting arrested and flung into the guardhouse. They got quite browned off with it.'

She laughed helplessly. 'Oh, Speedy, you're such a tonic!'

He grinned at her. 'Good story, isn't it? I swear it's true. Next time it'll probably be a couple of Ruskies wearing fur hats . . . I'll be sorry to miss that.' He drank some beer and shook his head. 'Can't get used to the Russians being on our side now. Bit like having a grizzly bear for company.'

'The poor Russians . . . They've suffered terribly. And the Germans are so near Moscow.'

'Not much we can do about it. Just have to hope they

can hang on somehow until the weather gets really bad. Remember what happened to Napoleon? Jolly nippy, those Russian winters. Even worse than Scotland. I'm surprised Adolf didn't look that up in his history book. I say, who's that corker of a WAAF who's just come in?'

Felicity turned her head. 'A new Code and Cypher officer.'

'Good lord! Brains *and* beauty! Just like you, Titania. How ever many more of you are there?'

'Nearly five hundred of us. On this station.'

He smiled at her. 'I'll never forget the day you first arrived. Just the two of you. Beauty and the Beast.'

'Nor shall I,' she said with feeling.

Just what exactly are you women supposed to be doing here, Company Assistant Newman? Perhaps you can explain that to me.

Speedy raised his beer mug. 'Here's to woman! Would that we could fall into her arms without falling into her hands.'

'Who said that one?' she asked, smiling too.

'No idea. Snodgrass used to mutter it sometimes. Mark you, he was a confirmed bachelor. Unlike me.'

He had to go soon after, back with the Lysander that had brought him. And when he had gone the station seemed to her a greyer and duller place.

At the beginning of December Ken had a very bad asthma attack and went into hospital. His health had deteriorated steadily over the past weeks and Winnie had noticed a change for the worse every time she saw him. She hitched a lift to the hospital in Ipswich. Ken was in a bed at the far end of a ward full of old men and she was shocked by his appearance. At first she scarcely recognized him. He seemed to have shrunk; to look like somebody else. His features had altered into another form, like a stranger's, and only his eyes remained the same. They lit up at the sight of her.

'Winnie . . . oh, Winnie.'

He grasped her hand tightly in his as she sat down beside his bed. He was breathing harshly and painfully and his skin had a funny blue-ish tinge. When he tried to sit up she pushed him back gently.

'Don't, Ken. You'll be more comfortable against the pillows.'

'I can't see you properly.'

'I'll move closer, so's you can.'

She pulled the chair nearer and sat holding his hand in hers. It felt cold though his forehead was beaded with sweat. It was a Sunday evening and there were other visitors in the ward. An old woman in a headscarf sat silently beside the next door bed. Its occupant lay quite still, eyes closed, mouth wide open, breathing with a horrible whistling sound.

'She comes every day,' Ken said in a whisper. 'But he never says anything. I don't think he even knows she's there.'

The place appalled Winnie – the rows of sick old men, the smell of disinfectant and ether, the ugly green-tiled walls and the harsh lighting, with death lying in wait in the shadows.

'Ken, do they say you have to stay here? Couldn't you go home? I could look after you. I could get special leave – '

'The doctor says it's for the best, just for a while. And what you're doin's much more important.'

'But it isn't, Ken. I'd much sooner look after you, so's you didn't have to be in here.'

'I won't let you, Winn, and that's that.' His voice was quiet but very firm. 'I want you to stay with the WAAF. They need you. And you might be able to work with the 'planes one day, just like you said . . . you never know.'

'They put a notice up the other day, asking for WAAFS to train as flight mechanics.'

She hadn't meant to tell him but it had slipped out.

'There you are, then. That's wonderful! You goin' to put in for it?'

She shook her head. 'No, I'm not.'

'Why ever not? It's what you've always wanted to do.'

'It'd mean me goin' away for trainin', and I'm not goin' to do that while you're ill. And they might post me anywhere.'

'Listen, Winnie,' he looked up at her. 'I'm goin' to go on bein' ill. And I don't want you to miss a chance like that because of me. I want you to put in for it.'

'No, Ken, I won't. No matter what you say, I won't.'

She stayed until a bell rang for the end of visiting time, somehow keeping up a cheerful front. As she walked away down the ward, she turned to smile and wave and saw Ken lift his hand weakly in reply.

An Army lorry stopped to give her a lift back to camp. She sat up beside the driver who whistled 'Tipperary' loudly in the darkness of the cab. He seemed in very good humour.

'Reckon 'itler's 'ad it now, after wot's 'appened. Saved our bloody bacon an' all, if you'll pardon my French.'

'What do you mean? What's happened?'

'Blimey, 'aven't you 'eard? It was on the wireless. The Japs attacked the American fleet. Sunk nearly all their ships. Some place called Pearl 'arbour. That means the Yanks'll bloody 'ave to join the war.'

She went home before Christmas. She had never thought of the shop as her home, and still less so now that Ken was not there. To have sat alone with Mrs Jervis would have been miserable. And she could visit Ken just as easily from there. He seemed no better, but no worse. The old man in the next bed had been replaced by another one.

At home all the talk was of the Americans joining the war, and of rumours in the Pig and Whistle that they would be coming over to build aerodromes in England.

432

'So long's it's not on my land, I don't mind,' her father had grunted.

He'd been doing quite well from the war lately, she knew. Far better than before it. He'd bought a whole lot more ewes, and a three-furrow plough, and a brand new baler.

Gran wasn't sure where America was, so Winnie fetched an old atlas to show her. She peered at the map.

'S'posin' there wurnt no wind?'

'Wind, Gran?'

She jabbed the blue with a sooty finger. 'Fur crossin' all that sea.'

'Boats have engines now, Gran. And I expect they'll come in aeroplanes, too. If they can fly all the way across the Atlantic with them.'

'They speak English?'

'They learned it from us, Gran. They used to be a colony, remember?'

'Huh! I furgot. Whoi've they bin waitin' round all this time, then? I'll give 'em a piece o' moi mind when they get here.'

Ken came home for Christmas but he was very weak. Everything had become an effort for him. He only had enough energy to sit in a chair during the day, or to lie on his bed. In February he caught influenza and when he had another serious asthma attack he had to be rushed into hospital again. It had snowed heavily and the roads were bad. By the time that Winnie had managed to get to the hospital he had sunk into unconsciousness. The nurses had pulled screens around his bed and his mother was already sitting beside him, bolt upright on the chair, her hands clasping the black handbag on her lap. She turned her head briefly.

'You're here at last, then.'

'I came as soon as I could, Mrs Jervis. I got a lift but the car got stuck in the snow . . .'

'You're too late, I'd say. He was asking for you a while back. Now he won't even know you're here.'

Winnie fetched another chair and sat on the other side of the bed. She took Ken's hand in hers and it felt cold and lifeless. She kept her eyes on his face, searching in anguish for some sign of awareness. There was none. His eyes remained shut. Once or twice she thought she saw his lips move but when she bent close there was only the rasp of his breathing, and when she spoke his name there was no response at all. When he had asked for her she had not been there and now he had gone beyond her reach. She had failed him when it mattered most.

It snowed all day long, the white flakes falling thickly like goose feathers outside the high window above Ken's bed. Beyond the screens she could hear the sounds from the ward – someone groaning, another calling out feebly for a nurse, the rustle of starched uniforms, the squeaky tread of feet up and down the linoleum.

When it began to get dark the nurses drew the blackout blinds across the windows and switched on the electric lights. Mrs Jervis's face, in shadow, looked carved from stone.

Ken died so quietly that at first they did not even realize that he had gone. He slipped silently away from them into another world. Winnie wept, but Mrs Jervis remained dry-eyed and tight-lipped.

'He's gone to his rest,' she said, as though to herself. 'The Lord be thanked for that. He's suffered enough.'

He was buried a few days later in the churchyard at Elmbury, in a grave dug in the cold and snowy ground. Most of the village turned out for the ceremony, shivering in shawls and scarves in a bitter wind.

Afterwards, at the shop, Mrs Jervis said stiffly to Winnie: 'He'd no money to leave, but I suppose you'll be wanting to take some of his things.'

'I'd like one of his bird books, if that's all right. And the photograph of him on the mantelpiece. Nothin' else. I'll move my things out.'

There was never any suggestion that she would go on living at the shop with her mother-in-law. Neither of them would have considered the idea. Winnie went up to the bedroom that she and Ken had shared but where they had never been truly man and wife. His Home Guard helmet hung on a hook behind the door and Colonel Foster's pike was still propped in the corner. She looked at them sadly. Poor Ken who had wanted so much to do his bit.

She found the book that she had given him for his eighteenth birthday, *Wild Birds of the British Isles*, which had been his favourite, and put it with her own things in her suitcase. Inside the book she tucked the snapshot of him that she had taken from the mantelpiece. He had pinned the picture of the bearded reedling on the wall close to the bed so that he could look at it while he was lying there. *I saw a whole flock of them this summer . . . When you're better you must go out bird-watchin' again.* He had never gone, and now he never would. He would never see the reed beds again, or hear the wind in the long grasses, or feel the sun warm on his face, or watch the birds flying across the fens . . .

She unpinned the picture, folded it carefully, and put it inside the book with the photo. It was all that she had left of Ken – the book, the photo and the picture. At twenty he was dead and buried. And at twenty she was a widow. She shut the suitcase and went downstairs.

When she returned to RAF Mantleham she put in her application to train as a flight mechanic.

Sixteen

The Wellington crew looked washed out with fatigue and pinched with cold. It was a look that Anne had come to know well over the past months. When a crew came back from ops, it was always the same. They would tramp into the room and slump down in the chairs round the de-briefing table, blinking under the lights and rubbing their reddened eyes. Their hands would clutch at the mugs of hot, rum-laced cocoa and they would light up cigarettes or pipes, and make the odd tired joke or two – if they had any energy left. She would smile at them and laugh at the jokes, and generally behave as though this were a perfectly ordinary interview about something quite mundane, and not an interrogation on the past hours of acute discomfort, deadly danger and horrible fear that they had endured flying in the dark over enemy territory, and somehow survived. She would plough through all the questions that it was her job to ask, and they would be determined to cut it as short as possible so that they could get away to their breakfast eggs and then lie down in blissful sleep and forget all about Hamburg or Münster or Wilhelmshaven, or wherever they had been that night.

She looked down at the form on the table in front of her and the six men yawned and fidgeted as she went through the list. Yes, they'd dropped their bombs bang on the primary target; yes, the weather over the target had been clear – for once; and yes, they had been attacked by enemy fighters.

'Can you tell me about that?'

The Wimpey's skipper massaged both his ears. He was still partly deaf from the noise of the engines and under the glare of the electric light his face looked ashen. There were black rubber marks on his cheeks from the oxygen mask and a red soreness round his mouth. His Irvin jacket collar was turned up about his neck; beneath it a dingy white polo-neck sweater. He was thawing out slowly.

'Couple of them jumped us when we were crossing the Dutch coast coming back. Near Leiden. We were hit in the starboard wing. Nothing too serious, luckily. Jock thinks he got one of them, don't you, Jock?'

The tail gunner took his pipe out of his mouth. 'Aye. I saw one engine on fire and he was going down. I'm not too sure if it was a 110 or a JU88. I didn't get a good enough look. The other laddie pushed off.'

The pilot said: 'Bags of flak, as usual. Some of it where there wasn't supposed to be any.'

She pushed the map across the table. 'Can you show me where exactly?'

The interrogation went on. Had they seen any other enemy fighters? What about searchlights? Was there anything special or unusual about the enemy anti-aircraft defences? Had they noticed any lights on the ground? Had they seen any other aircraft go down?

'The kite behind us went down in flames,' the skipper said laconically, scratching his head.

She wrote down all the details painstakingly. Sometimes, when the answers came too pat from a crew, she had the suspicion that they had agreed earlier between themselves what they were going to say so that they could get the de-briefing over quickly. When she had finished they stood up with relief, scraping their chairs. The navigator stumbled groggily. Their average age, she supposed, was about twenty: the same age as herself. She did not think that she would have the courage to do what they did.

The skipper came round to her as she was collecting her papers together.

'Any news of Digger yet?'

She shook her head. 'Nothing so far, Mike. Sorry.'

437

He nodded and turned away.

Digger was the skipper of A-Apple, one of the two Wellington bombers that had so far failed to return from the night's operation. Its crew was entirely made up of men from the Commonwealth – Digger and another Australian, two New Zealanders, a Rhodesian and a Canadian.

Anne had sat in on the briefing the day before. The crews, as always, had been confined to camp all day and any communication with the outside world forbidden. The briefing room was kept locked and guarded until the time came for them to troop in. The window blinds were drawn and a curtain concealed the big wall map on the stage at the end of the room. The crews always sat together at the long tables, chatting idly while they waited for the show to start – like an audience in the stalls of a theatre. Different ranks, different types, different backgrounds, different nationalities and from all kinds of schools and jobs and professions – but bonded together in a small, special unit where none of those differences counted and the only thing that mattered was their loyalty to each other. They were like links forged into a circular chain, each dependent on the rest for its whole strength. Some crews were good, and some were not so good. Some were lucky and rarely saw any flak, whereas others were not so lucky and always seemed to catch it. Some flew a tour of ops completely unscathed and others invariably returned with their aircraft holed like a sieve. The really unlucky ones didn't return at all. Some arrived at the station one day and were reported missing the next, before they'd had time to unpack. Sometimes a crew's luck simply ran out. Occasionally she had a premonition that they were fated and was proved right.

There had been twenty crews in the briefing room and the usual tension in the air, in spite of the casual chit-chat, while they waited for the Station Commander and the squadron COs to arrive. That was the signal for the curtain to be drawn back and allow them to see the red tape pinned across the map to the target and back. Essen. There had been an audible collective intake of breath. The Ruhr. Happy Valley. Heavy enemy defences. Coning searchlights. Walls of flak. Swarms of night fighters. She had seen it all in their faces beneath the grey haze of tobacco smoke that hung over them like a pall, and she had wondered, as she often did, which of them would not return. Which ones, come the morning, would be there to eat their operational eggs and bacon, and which would not? Digger had caught her eye and grinned; his luck had held so far, cross fingers. It was more likely to be the sprog crew she had noticed sitting at the back and studiously taking notes. Their inexperience, plus being stuck with the worst aircraft as new boys, saw to that, and everyone always said that the first three ops were the riskiest. Their skipper looked about nineteen and she had been able to tell, even from a quick glance at a distance, that he was desperately nervous. Or, maybe it would be the crew of C-Charlie with the spare bod in place of a sick gunner – that was supposed to be unlucky.

She had avoided looking at any more faces. The trick was not to think about it at all. To join in the game of make-believe that everybody on the station played – that brave young men were not dying almost nightly and that all of them would be there for breakfast when the new day dawned.

The Group Captain, better known as Sunshine because of the complete lack of any such thing in his nature, had started off the performance up on the stage in his customarily chilling manner.

'Primary industrial target . . . a blow at the very vitals of the enemy . . . steel works and armaments . . . striking at the morale of both the enemy civilian populations and the industrial workers . . . all the might of aerial bombardment . . . bringing them to their knees . . . maximum effort expected from all crews . . .'

When he had finished his harangue, the squadron COs had had their little say, followed by Navigation, Bombing,

Signals, Intelligence and Met. Any questions had been asked and answered. Then the crews had synchronized their watches and collected their rice paper flimsies, to be eaten if there was any danger of the information they contained falling into enemy hands. To add to the illusion of some *Boys' Own* adventure, they were issued with escape kits containing foreign banknotes, a silk scarf that was also a map of northern Europe and a brass RAF button that was a compass in disguise. They had handed in their personal papers and snapshots, and anything that might give help to enemy intelligence if they were to fall into their hands, dead or alive, and had been doled out their cans of orange juice, barley sugar, Wrigleys chewing gum and two keep-awake pills. Then they had gone off to have their flying supper – the Last Supper some of the cynics among them called it.

Later, when they had been ferried out to dispersal, she had gone to stand by the beginning of the runway together with a little group of ground crew, WAAFS and other personnel, to see them off. It was an unfailing ritual, whatever the weather – the waving Godspeed, the thumbs-up, the station's display of solidarity and encouragement.

The twenty Wellingtons had taken off at two-minute intervals, beginning their lumbering run at the green signal from the Watch Office. The group had waved to each one as it roared past them, loaded with petrol, incendiaries, explosives and ammunition, to clamber slowly up into the sky, the red and green wing tip lights gradually fading away, together with the howl of the Bristol engines. When the last one had gone and silence had fallen, the waiting had begun – catnapping on a bed and listening all the while, even in her sleep, for the distant drone that heralded the bombers' home-coming.

There had been one Early Return: B-Baker had turned back over the North Sea with engine trouble. The rest of them had returned safely from Essen, except for A-Apple and C-Charlie. They had circled noisily above the station while they waited to land, rattling the windows. Then the crews had arrived in the trucks from dispersal for their de-briefing. The sprog crew had made it back all right in their ropey kite; she saw their young pilot looking dazedly euphoric, as though he could scarcely believe it.

After the de-briefing Anne wrote up her reports for teleprinting through to Group. When she had finished she went outside. Dawn had come up on the new day and there was still no news of Digger and A-Apple, or C-Charlie, the crew with the spare bod. She looked up at an empty sky. The weather seemed set fair, as though it was going to be a nice March day with a good hint of spring. Don't think about the two missing crews, or whether they would ever see it. *They come and they go*, one of the older WAAFS had said to her when she had arrived. *You have to get used to it.* She could see the bombers standing out at dispersal in the distance, and the midget figures of the ground crews moving about. A Wimpey was progressing majestically round the perimeter track towards the hangars, displaying the stout-bellied outline that had given the aircraft its nickname after Popeye's hamburger-eating friend, J. Wellington Wimpey. Someone was cycling along behind the bomber, weaving from side to side in its wake. Station life was going on as usual.

She had met Digger at a mess party a few weeks before. The tall Australian, in his royal blue uniform, had walked up to her on his hands, upside down.

'I'm from Down Under. Care for a dance?'

He had an Aussie accent she could have cut with a knife and he was one of the craziest people she had ever met. And one of the worst dancers. But he had made up for the bad dancing by making her laugh more than she'd laughed for months and months.

She found out that he had volunteered for the Air Force at the very beginning of war, even though he lived on the other side of the world. Like so many of them. When she had asked him why, he had grinned.

'When people ask me that I always say I had to come and help the Old Country in her hour of need, didn't I? That makes it sound good. If I told the truth it'd be more like it seemed like it might be a hell've a good party and I didn't want to miss it.'

He had talked about his home in Mosman, Sydney where his parents had a house near the water.

'It's a bonza place. You'd love it. Sun, sailing, swimming . . .'

'Sharks?'

'You've got to watch for them, but they don't come in very often.'

'Once would be enough. I don't know anything much about Australia, I'm afraid.'

'Well, you know we walk about upside down, don't you?'

'Yes, I realize that. And you have koala bears, kangaroos, gum trees and Sydney Harbour Bridge. That's about all I can think of.'

He had laughed. 'Oh, my word! We'll have to change all that.'

Soon after he had taken her up for her first flight, smuggling her on board his Wellington for a cross-country. She had sat beside him in the cockpit and been thrilled by the sudden charge down the runway for take-off, by the exhilarating feeling of speed as the ground rushed past in a blur, and then the sudden, extraordinary lightness as the heavy bomber lifted clear of the concrete and began its climb up into the sky. Digger had grinned as she had clutched at the sides of her seat and given a reassuring thumbs-up sign. The earth had become a hazy, patchwork place far, far below and the clouds, so near, like outsize puffs of cottonwool. The noise of the engines had been deafening, and the aircraft, for all its size, seemed cramped and uncomfortable. She had tried to imagine what it must be like to fly in it on ops for hours on end.

She went on staring up into the empty sky and thinking

about Digger for quite a while before she went back into the Ops Room.

News had just come in from Signals of A-Apple. The Wellington had made an emergency landing at an aerodrome on the south coast, on one engine, but all the crew were safe. She breathed a huge sigh of relief. There was no news of C-Charlie and they were posted missing. The sick gunner must have been thanking his lucky stars.

Later on, Anne biked over to the WAAF site. It was half a mile away from the main buildings and housed a growing contingent of WAAFS from a variety of trades – Code and Cypher, Meteorology, Radio and Instrument Mechanics, Photography, Maps . . . the list had expanded still further. Sometimes she thought back, wryly, to the early days when they had been allowed to do so little.

Like RAF Colston, Denton had been a pre-war base that had grown rapidly as the war progressed. The main station buildings were brick-built and comfortable, the outlying ones, including the Waafery, prefabricated huts put up in haste. She had survived another winter in a bedroom heated by a temperamental coke stove. The WAAF officers had breakfast on their site but messed with the RAF for other meals, and not without resentment from some of the men. When she had first arrived and walked into the ante-room she had overheard one grumble to another: 'This is getting to be a hell of a place . . . all these bloody women in the Mess.'

She had quickly got used to eating with the men, but was still sometimes amazed at being saluted by airmen as well as by airwomen, and at being addressed as ma'am. It was still strange to be giving orders and reprimands, instead of always receiving them.

She had learned her job in Ops Intelligence more or less as she went along. There were two other WAAF officers besides herself and two WAAF sergeants. They worked in three watches, alternating the longest fourteen-hour stretch from early evening until nine the next morning, so that she now had twenty-eight hours off to recover until she was due back on duty. The next watch had taken over and in Operations Intelligence their day would begin with Group phoning through with the gen on the target for the coming night, if ops were on. They would be given the name of the target, the number of aircraft needed, the bomb load, routes, diversionary attacks, call signs and flashing beacon letters of the day, and any other vital information. Instructions would be typed up ready for the briefing later in the day and the room prepared and locked. And so it would begin all over again . . . the loaded Wellingtons taking off with their crews, the waving Godspeed and safe return, the waiting for them to come back. Sometimes an op was scrubbed, even at the last moment, and usually because of the weather, but with it looking so clear it was unlikely today.

From dropping leaflets, Bomber Command had gone on to dropping bombs on German cities – civilian and industrial targets alike. She knew that in the darkness and over invariably obscured targets, the crews rarely knew where their bombs actually fell – whether on a steel works or armaments factory, or on a children's home or hospital. If any of them felt squeamish about it, they never said so; any more than they ever talked about feeling afraid. She knew that they were afraid – most of them. She had seen them mooching about the station during the daytime before ops, trying to kill the waiting time. Back in the summer, when she had first arrived, she had watched them playing cricket, or lounging around on the grass, smoking and talking. Sometimes they tried to sleep. At briefings she had seen the nervous twitches, the shaking hand lighting yet another cigarette, and heard them being sick in the lavatories afterwards if the target was a tough one. Once, the MO had taken her aside and asked her to sit with a tail gunner who had collapsed on landing back from his first op. He had been a Lancashire lad, small and thin, like most of those who had to squash themselves into the lonely confines of the rear turret, far from the rest of the crew, without even the comfort of a parachute as a forlorn hope, and with an open panel in front of them onto the bitter cold of the night skies. The gunner had been stiff, not only with cold, but with terror. They had carried him to a bunk where he lay as rigid as a plank of wood, unable to move or speak. She had sat beside him, holding his hand, and it had been like holding a block of ice. Very slowly and gradually she had felt him relax, muscle by muscle, and return to normal. He had even managed to smile as he had thanked her. A few days later he had been posted missing with the rest of his crew on a raid over Wilhelmshaven.

Some never betrayed any fear, but nearly all were openly superstitious. Spare bods, certain aircraft, unlucky beds, WAAFS going too near the bomber before an op, drinking their thermos coffee before the target . . . there were all kinds of jinxes. One pilot always touched her right shoulder as he left the briefing room, and she knew of a navigator who had to turn round three times and touch his Wimpey's tail before he would climb in. Others carried special scarves, lucky cigarette lighters, lucky coins or mascot toys. Some of the fighter pilots at Colston had done that but Johnnie had been right when he had said that the bomber boys were different. There was no room for individual swashbuckling and, except for the ones like Digger, they were mostly quieter, though not necessarily any more sober. The crews drank together, never mind their different ranks, and went out on the town together. Their war was different. When they went to fight it was a long drawn-out ordeal of hours, not a matter of minutes. It asked, she came to understand, for different qualities and a different kind of courage.

A new crew arrived to replace the one that had gone missing with C-Charlie. When the pilot came into the Officers' Mess, she recognized him at once. The last time she had seen him he had been wearing a top hat and tails. The uniform was different now and the spots that had afflicted him then had gone, but it was undoubtedly

Latimer. And he blushed when he saw her, just as much as he had blushed on that summer's day in June at Eton . . . so long ago.

'Good lord,' he stammered. 'I knew you were in the WAAF, but I never imagined you'd be *here!* I say, that's absolutely marvellous! Simply wonderful!'

'Kit told me you were with bombers but I never expected to run across you either.'

'How is Kit? I haven't heard anything of him for ages.'

'He's been sent to North Africa — I'm not sure quite where exactly. When I last heard he was all right.' *This place is nothing but sand, twin. I should have brought my bucket and spade.* 'Did you hear that Villiers was killed in France?'

He nodded. 'Yes. Jolly bad luck. Frightful shame. Parker-Smiley bought it too, you know. He was flying Stirlings. His kite got shot down over France, apparently.' Latimer gestured helplessly, his soft spaniel's eyes sad. 'Rotten show.'

Little Parker-Smiley who had been afraid of the dark, flying on a night bombing raid. She said with the determined brightness that she had acquired in recent months: 'Do you know, I've never known your Christian name. I've only ever heard you called Latimer.'

'Oh.' He blushed again and smiled. 'It's Henry.'

She smiled back at him, but with a heavy heart. He had thirty trips ahead of him in order to do his tour and she would be waving him off now with the others, and wondering whether he was going to come back.

He had been on five ops over Germany when he summoned up the courage to ask her to go out to dinner in King's Lynn. She accepted but against her better judgement. The look in his eyes and the way he followed her with them told her that he was still what Kit would have called smitten, but she hadn't the heart to refuse.

He drove an Alvis, a cut above and in considerably better condition than most of the pilots' cars.

'A twenty-first birthday present from my parents,' he told her on the way. 'Awfully decent of them. I manage to scrounge the odd bit of petrol now and then.'

'A lot of the chaps pinch the aviation stuff.'

'I know. I expect I'll end up doing that.' He clashed the gears as he changed down. 'Sorry about that . . . it's funny, but I could fly before I could drive. Only just learned.'

'I've come across several pilots like that. They know how to drive huge bombers all over the skies, but not cars on the ground. Is that your mascot?'

She nodded at the small toy rabbit dangling above the dashboard, dressed in a green waistcoat and wearing a spotted bow tie.

'Yes. Meet Hannibal. My sister gave him to me. He comes on ops with us.'

'How brave of him!'

'Yes, isn't it – considering the pilot. I scraped through training. Always thought I'd be washed out. Hannibal likes a front seat. I hang him up in the cockpit so that he can see what's going on.'

She had a pretty good idea now of what sort of thing the rabbit would have seen 'going on' – not so much from things she had been told at the official de-briefings as from listening to the crews talking at other times. Hannibal's little black button eyes would have widened in fright to see the flak coming up at him – shells exploding like fireworks in starry bursts of yellow and white and orange-red. He would have been dazzled and scared by searchlights slithering over the cockpit, groping for him like blind men's fingers. He would have peered down in awe at the fires blazing away in the city below and been horrified to catch sight of a Wimpey silhouetted blackly against those flames as it spiralled downwards. He would have craned to count the parachutes mushrooming forth – one, two, three . . . and then turned his head, appalled, to see another Wimpey trapped in the tips of those long, white fingers and ringed by murderous flak. He would

447

have watched it helplessly and in horror as the bomber blossomed suddenly into a bright fireball that blew apart and fell to earth like red rain. Away from the target area and the starry flak, he would have been shocked again to see a dark shadow appear below the wing, spurting yellow blobs and streams of silver tracer. The night sky would have see-sawed about him as the bomber corkscrewed frantically to get away from the enemy fighter. He would have shut his eyes and opened them later in relief to see the glimmer of white wave caps and the blessed sight of the English coastline . . . the succession of flashing red beacons marking the homeward track . . . and, at last, the flarepath at Denton winking its welcome in the dark.

'What are your crew like?' she asked.

'The very best,' he said and there was a great pride in his voice. 'I've never met such marvellous chaps. I was lucky to team up with them. You know, they put you in a big room at OTU and let you all sort of mill about and choose each other. Amazing how well it works, really. My navigator just walked up to me and said: "I'm looking for a skipper who can fly a Wimpey without making me throw up . . ." Then the others somehow joined us. We're a pretty mixed bag – Welsh, Scots, Lancashire, my family's from the West Country and our tail gunner's a real East End cockney, so we're from all over. As a matter of fact, I was a bit worried to begin with as I'm the only one who's been to public school. I was afraid they might think I was toffee-nosed, or something . . . the way I spoke. But it hasn't been like that at all. They rag me a bit, sometimes, but we all get along terribly well.'

Eton going to war on equal terms with the Council schools, Anne thought. The playing fields joining forces with the asphalt and the city streets. Perhaps some good will come out of it in the end. It wasn't just a question of different schools and backgrounds, though. They were such different types – from the crazy, tough extroverts like Digger to the shy, sensitive, thoughtful ones like Latimer. She wondered how he felt about dropping bombs on civilians, as well as military targets, and whether it worried him. When she asked him he thought for a moment as he was driving along, and then said seriously:

'I was in London during the Blitz once, when I was on leave. I walked around all over the place, looking at all the bomb damage . . . all the ruins of wonderful old buildings, and the homes smashed to rubble. Then, when I travelled on the Tube I saw all those poor people sheltering down there – sleeping on the platforms, on the stairs, everywhere . . . huddled together in those awful conditions, driven down there like animals. I think the homeless were actually *living* there. I had to step over them, there were so many and so close together, and I nearly trod on an old woman by mistake – she was all in black and looked like a pile of rags. When I apologized she smiled up at me – no teeth and her hair in curlers, a hideous old thing really – and she said: "*Good old RAF! Give it to 'em back for us. Let 'em 'ave a taste of their own medicine.*" And then everyone round her started calling out the same sort of thing to me . . . So, I promised them I would.'

She could picture the scene well – the shy young RAF pilot standing there, probably blushing like mad, and the bloody but unbowed Londoners, all urging him on.

'Actually,' Latimer went on with a dry smile. 'When I started on ops I found I was much too frightened to think about anything at all except pulling the plug and getting away as fast as possible. I don't think many of us have room for noble thoughts, one way or the other.'

'I don't blame you. I'd be scared stiff,' she said, with feeling.

'One thing I'll never quite get used to,' he continued, 'is the contrast between being here in the English countryside during the day and then that same night finding myself in the middle of all that hell and horror over Germany . . . then you come back again and it's all so normal and peaceful – as though what had happened

449

over there was just some ghastly nightmare. It's very strange.'

'It must be.' She remembered the dazed look on the sprog skipper's face; as though he were waking up from a bad dream.

Latimer said earnestly, 'You can't imagine how much it means to us to see you there when we get back – you're always smiling, always just the same, always behaving as though everything were perfectly all right . . .'

They had dinner at a restaurant in King's Lynn. Taking a peek at the menu prices, she hoped that Latimer did not have to rely exclusively on his RAF pay. Kit had spoken once of his family – an ancient one with large estates somewhere down in Dorset. She tried to recall the brief encounter with his parents at the Fourth, but could only dredge up a vague impression of a tall, Edwardian-looking man and a rather pretty woman in something pale grey, with a large hat to match. There had been a small girl, too, hanging shyly back behind them – presumably the sister who had presented Hannibal and made his smart outfit. She wondered whether Latimer, like most other bomber crews, had already written them a 'last letter' and left it ready and obvious in his drawer.

'How are your parents?' Latimer asked politely, during the course of the meal.

She shrugged. 'Fine, as far as I know. I haven't actually seen them since Christmas.'

She had gone home on leave then – but reluctantly. Even though time had passed, she found that her resentment towards them, and especially her mother, had not. She had brought up Michal's name many times, deliberately. *Michal was given a posthumous medal, you know . . . Michal had one of the highest scores in his squadron . . . Michal always said that . . . Michal and I . . .* On Boxing Day people had come for drinks and her mother had carefully invited the army officer son of near neighbours who had happened to be on leave too – Harrow, Sandhurst, good regiment, the *right* background,

450

the right everything. She had taken a bitter satisfaction in ignoring him completely. And she had worn Michal's ring and pinned the Polish eagle brooch to her dress. In uniform, she always wore his ring hidden on a thin chain round her neck and the brooch pinned inside her tunic above the RAF wings she had taken from his best blue and sewn to the lining. *Wear it inside your tunic where no-one can see. Next to your heart.*

She looked up to see Latimer's eyes on her.

'I heard that you were engaged and that your fiancé was killed in action,' he said awkwardly. 'I'm awfully sorry.'

'I can't seem to get over it,' she said, and tears were threatening yet again, suddenly and without warning. She managed to swallow them down.

'What will you do after the war, Henry?'

He smiled quietly. 'That's a long way ahead. I don't know really. Go up to Cambridge and read law, I suppose, like I was supposed to do – if they'll still have me. Then join my uncle's firm in London, perhaps. It's going to seem jolly dull, after all this.'

'Yes,' she said, 'I suppose it will.'

Driving back, in the darkness of the car, he said suddenly:

'The thing is I've had this feeling lately . . . well, it's more than a feeling really, it's like a certainty – that I'm for the chop. So, I don't think much about what's going to happen after the war.'

She said urgently: 'You mustn't think like that. You'll get through it all right. You've got a wonderful crew, and that means everything.'

'I know. But it's really a matter of luck, isn't it? I've come to that conclusion. So there's not much you can do about it. And statistically, an awful lot of us are dead men. I'm fairly sure that I'm going to be one of them – sooner or later. At first I used to believe that it would always be the other chap – the one you saw blown up, or falling out of the sky, or crashing in flames, and felt guiltily glad that it wasn't you . . . But lately I've known it would be *my* turn eventually. It's a bit frightening not knowing where, or when, or how, but I seem to have accepted it more or less now.'

She put a hand on his arm. 'I've heard other aircrew talk like this, Henry, and it hasn't happened to them. They've all finished their tour.' *Not true. Not true. None of them had.*

When he stopped the car later he said hesitantly: 'Would you mind terribly if I kissed you – just this once?'

'Of course not.' *How can I possibly say 'No'?*

He was wryly apologetic afterwards.

'Sorry – I'm not much good at it. To be honest, it's the first time I've ever kissed a girl. I hope it won't be the last.'

'Ayers Rock,' Digger said. 'Alice Springs. Heard of those?'

Anne shook her head. 'Sorry.'

'Stone the crows! What a sheila! Come on now, you can do better than that. What *have* you heard of?'

She thought hard for a moment. 'The Great Barrier Reef.'

'OK. That's better. What else?'

There was another Mess party in full swing; another thrash to help blot out the very thought of ops – all scrubbed that night because of bad weather. Digger had come in search of her and they were standing drinking and talking.

She closed her eyes. 'Wait a mo . . . Botany Bay. Convicts.'

'Sore point there. What about Ned Kelly?'

'I think I've heard of him. He was a horse-thief, wasn't he? They hanged him.'

'A dinkum Aussie!' Digger's piercing blue eyes crinkled at the corners as though he was still looking into the Australian sun. 'What else?'

'Aboriginals.'

'Another sore point. Think of something different.'

'Captain Cook.'

'He was a bloody Pom!'

'Didn't he discover you?'

'That's no excuse. What else?'

There was a long pause while Anne racked her brains. The pilot watched her, eyes narrowed, cigarette drooping from the corner of his mouth.

'The duck-billed platypus.'

Digger roared with laughter. 'That's bonza! Good on you, Annie!'

She laughed too and caught Henry Latimer's eye across the room. He smiled and lifted his hand. She thought he looked quite cheerful. Four more ops done. So far, so good.

Some New Zealanders had started a sort of Maori war dance, all in a line, whooping and stamping their feet. They whooped and stamped faster and faster until they finally ended up in a tangled heap on the floor.

'Drunken Kiwi savages,' Digger said good-humouredly, aiming a kick at the squirming mass. The music started up again with a catchy quickstep number. He stuck out a hand towards Anne. 'Come on, you Pommy popsie. Let's dance.'

Winnie was sent to the RAF flight mechanic training school at Hednesford in Staffordshire. The train journey from Suffolk, crawling north-west in stages across England, took all day. She had to change three times and missed her connection once so that she had to wait more than two hours for the next train. The trains were all crowded, unheated and dirty. There were no empty seats and she had to stand in the corridor all the way. On the final leg of her journey, when she was sitting wearily on her kitbag, a soldier came to stand near her and tried to strike up a conversation.

'Goin' on leave, then?'

She shook her head. He offered a cigarette, which

she refused, and leaned his shoulders back against the window, heavy army boots braced against the rocking and swaying of the train. He lit his cigarette.

'Posted then?'

She gave in and told him. There was no harm in it, after all, and he looked friendly and nice. She wasn't sorry to have someone to talk to.

'Could you tell me when we get to Brindley Heath, please? I can't always hear the station when they call it out.'

He nodded. 'Stupid idea takin' all the names down, if you ask me. Jerry can read a map, same as anyone else. 'e won't need flippin' station signs to tell 'im where 'e 'is. Just makes it flippin' 'ard for us lot. 'alf the time you can't 'ear 'em sing out, the other 'alf you can't understand what the locals are sayin' anyway . . . What sort've WAAF are you, then? What d'you do?'

'I used to be a clerk, but I've just re-mustered. I'm going to train as a flight mechanic.'

He stared. 'A what?'

'A flight mechanic.'

'You mean, servicin' the 'planes an' all that?'

'That's right.'

'You're not 'avin' me on?' He was half-laughing, half-incredulous.

'No. They're short of men, you see. So they're trainin' us.'

He whistled and shook his head. 'Blimey! Don't say we've come to that. I flippin' 'ope 'itler don't get to 'ear of this or 'e'll know we're on our flippin' uppers.'

She forgave him because he meant no offence. And because he was so cheerful and funny the rest of the journey passed quickly. At Brindley Heath he carried her heavy kitbag off the train for her.

'Strewth, what you got 'in 'ere, darlin'? The kitchen stove'n all?' He set it down on the wooden platform. 'There you are, sunshine. Sorry I can't carry it all the way. Best of luck, an' if I ever go in one of your 'planes

454

you make sure you tighten all them nuts.' He chucked her under the chin. 'Keep smilin'.'

He waved to her from the window and gave her a thumbs-up and a cheery grin as the train drew away.

She swung the kitbag up, staggering under its weight, and went to ask a porter for directions to the camp. She could barely understand a word he said, but set off up a steep hill in the direction of his pointing finger, burdened like a mule with her kitbag over her shoulder, her respirator slung across her chest and her helmet and folded gas cape on her back. It was very cold and getting dark and halfway up the hill, just as she was beginning to wonder if she would manage to make it to the top, a farmer came by with a horsedrawn cartload of potatoes and stopped to give her a lift. She clambered up thankfully beside him. When she told him, too, that she was going to train as a flight mechanic on aircraft engines he laughed even more than the soldier on the train.

'That's a good one! I'll come'n be a pilot!'

He set her down near the camp entrance and she could hear him still chuckling to himself as the grey horse clip-clopped off down the road.

RAF Hednesford was on high ground – a bleak and windswept place surrounded by a high wire fence that made it look like a prison. There were rows and rows of camouflaged Nissen huts, curved like hen coops. The WAAF huts were a mile from the main gates. There were thirty girls to each hut with a corporal in the small room at the end, and most of the Nissens leaked whenever it rained. The walls and windows streamed constantly with condensation. There were linoleum floors, tortoise stoves giving off a meagre heat, and double bunk beds without ladders. Winnie, allotted a top bunk, had to scramble up and jump down and when she was lying in her bunk her head came unpleasantly close to the curving tin roof. The only comforting thought was that it was the end, and not the beginning of winter.

She was given another embarrassing medical examination and an undignified Free From Infection inspection for fleas, lice, scabies or any other catching diseases. Then she was issued with trousers, a battle dress top, RAF overalls and a black beret, like the one that she had worn before there were WAAF caps. The trousers, she soon discovered, itched horribly.

Most of the other girls in her intake had come straight from initial training and had been in all kinds of civilian jobs before joining up. A few, like herself, had re-mustered from other trades. The girl in the bunk immediately below hers was called Hilda. She came from Lancashire and had just completed her initial training at Morecambe.

'It was hell,' she told Winnie cheerfully. 'Square bashing up and down the sea front in a force ten gale, with everyone looking on and criticizing us. Then PT in our blackouts with half the old men in Morecambe leering at us. And the landlady at our billet was *evil*! She'd had the RAF before, you see, so she didn't want us. We weren't like her nice boys. "I don't want you, but I've got to have you," she told us. "So you'll behave yourselves." She had a great long list of rules pinned up on the wall: wipe your feet when you come in, no noise, no singing, in bed by 10.00 p.m., windows open whatever the weather, bedrooms left spotless in the morning . . . Oooh, she did make our life a misery! Some of the girls cried every night. We had to pay her five shillings a week and she half-starved us! Three tinned plums on a plate for our tea and two slices of bread and butter. That's all we had. The kitchen was down in the basement and the food would come up in one of those little lifts. Rattle, rattle, rattle it went and the tinned plums would appear and we'd all *groan* . . . We had to go down and do the washing up afterwards too. Insult to injury.'

'It sounds dreadful,' Winnie said.

'We were all *miserable*. Mind you, one or two of the girls deserved a bit of chasing. I never knew people could be so dirty. Filthy habits some of them had. They never washed or changed their clothes, dirty STs left about . . . And they didn't know how to eat at table. One girl broke her bread into her soup and ate it with a knife and fork. It takes all sorts, I suppose. You're Engines, not Airframes, aren't you? Like me. That's good.'

Apart from the WAAFS, there was a large intake of RAF trainees, including some Poles and Czechs, and a large contingent from the Fleet Air Arm. Most of the men seemed amused by the presence of the WAAFS. A few were dead against them. None expected the girls to reach the same standard as themselves, or to be capable of the same workload.

To begin with the Engine and Airframe mechanics attended classes together. They learned about metals, how to file and make simple joints, how to handle tools and to identify all the different types of screw heads, bolts, hammers, hack-saws, chisels and files. They were introduced to precision instruments and taught the basics of riveting and simple carpentry. Then they separated. The Airframe trainees went away to learn about the complicated structure of modern aircraft, while the mysteries of the internal combustion engine were explained to the Engine mechanics, starting with a simple motor cycle engine.

'Right now, who can tell me what this is?'

The RAF sergeant instructor pointed with his stick at a part of the section of motor cycle engine on the bench in front of him.

Winnie put up her hand. 'It's a cylinder.'

'Correct.' The stick moved on. 'And this?'

'A piston.'

'Correct again. Well done. A cylinder and a piston. Both very important parts of the internal combustion engine, as I am about to show you.' The instructor tapped with his stick again. 'If you introduce a mixture of petrol vapour and air into this cylinder in the ratio fifteen parts of air to one part of petrol, compress it and ignite it with an electric spark then the temperature and pressure rises and the *piston* is forced down the cylinder. I want you to learn and remember four magic words: Induction, Compression, Power and Exhaust.'

He went on talking about revs and strokes and conrods; about the combustion chamber, crankshafts, inlets and outlets; about swept volume and clearance volume, mixture, magnetos, Top Dead Centre and Bottom Dead Centre, valve lag and valve lead, compression ratios . . . The technical words, strange to most of the trainees, were already familiar to Winnie from everything that Taffy had taught her.

Her first sight of a Merlin engine out on a workbench thrilled her. At last she was going to be allowed, not only to touch it, but dismantle parts of it and reassemble them back into their places.

The class instructor, watching her working away happily in her beret and outsize RAF overalls, with grease streaks on her face and dirt under her fingernails, put her down as a natural. It was rare in women in his experience so far and he was still trying to get used to the idea of having them in his class. They were painstaking and conscientious, he had discovered, and very thorough, and they had some advantages over the men, like small hands and lots of patience, but they did not usually have that inborn feeling for engines that was far more than mere competence. He smiled at Winnie and she smiled back. Pretty with it, he thought drily. Even rarer.

Winter began to turn very slowly into spring. The long, hard training absorbed Winnie completely. She scarcely noticed the changing weather, the bad food, the awful conditions, the ill-tempered hut corporal who was always shouting '*Move!*' Her absorption in her work led her to fall down on other things. When it was her turn to polish the brown linoleum in the hut, which showed every mark, the corporal was never satisfied. And at Kit Inspection she was frequently reprimanded by the WAAF officer. A WAAF sergeant would read aloud from a list as the items laid out on her bed were checked.

'Coat, great, one. Overalls, blue, two. Gloves, knitted, one pair. Panties, three. Knickers, three. Vests, WAAF, three. Shirts, poplin, three?'

Winnie pointed nervously. 'One there, one on and one in the wash.'

'Collars, poplin, six. Skirts, two. Slacks, blue, one. Stockings, lisle, four?'

There were only three pairs and the Section Officer was seriously displeased.

'Last time you had lost your housewife, Jervis. If you can't find them, they'll have to come out of your pay.'

'Yes, ma'am.'

She was not careless in her work, however. Her notes and diagrams were models of neatness and accuracy and the other WAAFS often copied from them. When they were studying in the hut in the evenings Hilda would sing out from her lower bunk,

'I can't make head or tail of this. Let me see your diagram, Winnie.'

'Which one?'

'The Hurricane fuel system. And the oil system too. Mine are both in a mess and I can't read half what I've written.'

They were tested every week on what they had been taught and if they failed more than once on a test they were taken off the course. As time passed, faces disappeared from the classes.

Winnie and Hilda rehearsed questions and answers with each other.

'Give me one disadvantage of a single carb, Hilda.'

'Hmm. Hang on a mo. Oh, yes, I know. It doesn't atomize or emulsify fuel.'

'That's right.'

'My turn to ask you. Let's see . . . what tools would you use to check the bore of a cylinder?'

'An inside micrometer.'

'That was too easy. What about this, then. Describe a Merlin coolant pump.'

459

Winnie said at once: 'It's a centrifugal impeller pump bolted beneath the wheel case and driven from lower vertical drive. The pump is in two pieces. The lower half contains two coolant inlets, a drain tap and a Morganite thrust pad. The upper half contains two outlets, two lead-bronze lined bushes, a packin' gland, a gland nut and a grease cap. The gland prevents coolant leakage – '

'All right, all right! You know it backwards. Now ask me something nice and simple.'

'Where do you enter up fuel, oil and coolant after servicin'?'

'Form 700. Ask me another one like that. It gives me confidence.'

'Who's the last person to sign Form 700 before a flight?'

'The pilot. Make it harder than that, Winn.'

Winnie turned the pages of her notebook. 'All right. What's meant by high tensile steel?'

'Steel that's capable of taking a tensile strength of fifty tons or more. Give me another one.'

'Name two types of piston rings.'

'Compression rings and scraper rings. Compression rings are to make a gas tight joint. Scraper rings to prevent excess oil passing the piston and going into the cylinder head. Now ask me something even harder.'

'What can you tell me about superchargin'?'

'Ouch! Well, I did ask for it. Hum. Well, here goes. Supercharging consists of supplying a greater weight of mixture to the induction system than would be induced by normal means, with the object of increasing the power output . . . OK? Now let's have a break before our brains get addled.'

Hilda fetched her ukulele from her locker and began to strum quietly, sitting on her bunk. It was raining hard outside, drumming an accompaniment on the Nissen hut roof. She was a good-natured girl with short, straight dark hair. Everything about her looked square. She had a square jaw, square-shaped hands and feet, but her ready smile transformed her plain face into something near beauty. She had told Winnie all about her home life in Rochdale. Her mother had worked in a mill, her father on the trams. Hers was a northern town world of back-to-back terraced houses, cobbled streets, black pudding, jam and chip butties, chimneys, smoke, soot and Lancashire rain. Her childhood had been spent playing in the streets. She had scorned dolls and played cricket and football with the boys instead. At fourteen her mother had taken her along to the local factory to queue for a job. The factory made paper tubes for the cotton to wind on to. She had worked there for four years until it burned down. Then she'd joined the Civil Defence when war broke out and was put into the ambulance corps where she learned first aid.

'I was doing that when I got a letter On His Majesty's Service, and that was that. I *had* to join up. I wasn't a volunteer, like you, Winnie, but I didn't mind. I liked the idea – specially when I found out I could train as a flight mech. That was a bit of luck. I was always playing with my brother's meccano set – I could build better things than him. He used to bash me for that.'

If she found book-learning more difficult than Winnie, Hilda was first class at the practical side. And she could play the ukulele very well indeed. The whole hut rocked and sang to her tunes. Winnie, lying with her arms behind her head and the dank tin roof inches from her nose, listened contentedly to her playing *Tiptoe Through The Tulips*. The camp was a dreadful place, so cold and bleak, and she had discovered that the high wire fence was a relic from when it had been a POW camp in the First World War, but she had never felt happier in her life. At last she was doing what she had always wanted to do and it was just as satisfying as she had always imagined it would be.

Towards the end of the course, they learned the starting procedure for all types of aircraft. And they practised how to swing a propeller on a small 'plane like a Tiger Moth, and how to nip smartly out of the way before their arm was cut off, or their head bashed in.

'He who swings and runs away, lives to swing another day,' their instructor chanted grimly. 'He who swings and stands about gets his big fat head a clout.'

And they learned how to run-up an aircraft.

When it was Winnie's turn to climb into the Hurricane cockpit, her heart was thumping hard and her hands felt sweaty with nerves. They'd raised the bucket seat so that she could see out and put some old cushions on it in place of the parachute that the pilot would sit on. As she climbed in, the two airmen ready to tail-squat were looking as though they thought it was all a huge joke. She lowered herself into the seat and stared at the instrument panel in front of her. She remembered it well from the time Taffy had shown her, and since then she had carefully memorized everything. The mechanic standing by the trolly acc. was grinning up at her and, as she glanced at him, he gave her the all-clear. She stretched out her hand towards the panel and began reciting the notes that she had learned by heart, under her breath.

Set fuel cock to Main Tanks ON. Throttle half an inch open. Propeller control fully forward. Supercharger control – moderate. Radiator shutter – open. Winnie licked her dry lips. *Work the Ki-gas priming pump until the fuel reaches the priming nozzles . . .*

She looked towards the mechanic again and shouted out as she put her hand the on the ignition switch: 'Contact!' Her voice sounded high and squeaky to her ears. He was still grinning. Winnie drew a deep breath.

Switch ignition ON and press the starter button. Turning periods must not exceed twenty seconds, with a thirty-second wait between each. Work the priming pump as rapidly and vigorously as possible while the engine is being turned. With normal air temperature and normal fuel it should start after about four strokes . . .

The propeller blades jerked suddenly as the Merlin engine spluttered into life. Ch-ch-ch-ch it went as Winnie held her breath. Then it exploded into a full-throated roar and the blades went from milling slowly into a spinning blur. The Hurricane, firing on all twelve cylinders, trembled and vibrated round her. Winnie released the starter button and screwed down the priming pump. She opened up slowly to one thousand revs. Black and acrid exhaust fumes were drifting back over the open cockpit, which meant that she'd over-primed.

Warm up to at least fifteen degrees centigrade oil temperature and sixty degrees centigrade coolant.

She tried the magnetos in turn and checked pressures and temperatures. Then she opened up steadily to twenty-eight hundred revs. The crescendo roar of the Merlin rose to an ear-splitting level and the fighter juddered and rocked, like a living thing straining to be free. Winnie forced herself to keep calm and think clearly. She checked the ammeter and the constant speed propeller – fine, coarse, fine. *Keep your eye on the revs, the oil pressure, coolant temperature and fuel pressure . . .* Help! She'd nearly forgotten to read the boost pressure! She tested the mags in turn again, making sure there was not more than fifty revs drop with each, and then throttled back and allowed the engine to idle for a few minutes.

When she climbed down to earth again her legs felt wobbly.

The instructor nodded. 'Not bad. Not bad at all.'

Their final exam was both written and oral. In the written paper, Winnie read the first question anxiously.

What is the function of a solenoid switch?

She picked up her pen and began to write: *A solenoid switch enables light leads to be used to the cockpit switch. When the button is pressed the circuit is completed in the heavy duty leads and so to the electric starter.* Winnie drew a diagram and labelled it neatly. She looked at the next question.

How does a propeller work?

She wrote on steadily.

463

At the oral test her examiner had cold eyes and an even colder manner. He made no attempt to put her at her ease; quite the reverse. He picked up something from the bench and held it in front of her.

'What's this?'

'It's a condenser, sir.'

'What is its purpose?'

'To help the rapid collapse of the primary circuit, sir. And to minimize arcin' at the contact break points.'

He picked up something else. 'What about this?'

'A cylinder head, sir.'

'How many cylinders does a Rolls Royce Merlin engine have?'

'Twelve, sir. In two banks of six.'

'And what's this?'

'A carburettor, sir.'

'What type?'

Winnie hesitated for a moment. The cold eyes watched her impatiently.

'I think it's a Claudel Hobson, sir.'

'You *think*? Aren't you sure?'

She swallowed. 'Yes, I am sure, sir.'

'And what engine, for example, do you *think* it might have come from?' His voice was sarcastic.

'A Bristol Pegasus, sir.'

'Hmm. If an engine overheats where would you look for trouble?'

'In the coolin' system, sir. There might not be enough coolant. The pump could be defective, or there might be a restriction. Or the rad shutters might be closed.'

'Or?'

'Or I'd look at the cowling shutters, sir – on an air-cooled engine. They might be closed.'

'Hmm. Suppose your engine's running irregularly – misfiring and losing power during normal running. What could be wrong then?'

'Shortage of fuel, perhaps, sir? The air vent to the tank might be choked, or the pump defective. I'd check those.

464

Or there might be water in the fuel. Or it could be dirty jets, or plugs. I'd clean them.'

'What else? If it's none of those things?'

Winnie thought hard. 'Well, there might be an airleak in the system somewhere. Or a mag defect. Or the mixture control might be defective.'

Coldly. 'What else?'

She searched her mind desperately. *What else could be wrong?* The examiner was frowning. He glanced at his watch. She remembered suddenly.

'Oh, yes, there could be a valve stuck open, sir.'

The questions went on and on. What was this? What was that? What was it from? What was its function? How did it work? How would she fit this, clean that, test the other? Assemble these, please. The examiner gave no sign as to whether or not she had given him the right answers, or done the right thing in the right way. When he dismissed her without a word of encouragement or thanks, she was sure that she must have failed.

The results came through and she found that she had not only passed, but done so quite easily with sixty-five per cent marks. And with her success came reclassification to aircraftwoman first class. She had risen from Trade Group IV to Group II which meant an increase in pay to three shillings and fourpence a day.

She would have been completely happy but for her posting. She and two other newly-qualified WAAF flight mechanics – two Engines and one Airframes – were to go to an operational training unit near Dundee in Scotland. She looked it up on the map and it seemed a very long way away.

Hilda had been posted to an initial flying training school in Nottinghamshire. Winnie wished that she were coming to Scotland with her. They said goodbye and wished each other luck before they went home on leave – Hilda to Lancashire and Winnie to Suffolk.

As she walked into the farm kitchen, Gran said, as though she had never been away:

'They be comin'.'

Winnie lowered her kitbag wearily. The journey had taken all day and she had had to walk the last two miles from the bus stop outside the Pig and Whistle.

'Who, Gran?'

'Them thare Amuricans. They be a-goin' t' knock down trees an' hedges over at Josh Stannard's. 'Tis all flat thare. 'Twill be fur Amurican flyin' machines. Turrible mess, they'll be makin'. Thass what I've hared. I doan't hode wi' it.'

Gossip came to Gran. Sitting in her chair close by the range – even in summer – she somehow heard it all.

Winnie couldn't imagine Americans in Suffolk. Where they lived everything was so new and clean. In the films the sun was always shining, the sky blue and the colours so bright. The people all wore beautiful, glamorous clothes. They drove those big cars and lived in houses with big rooms and kept their food in huge refrigerators, and hung those starched, white, frilly curtains at the windows. What would they make of the grey skies, the rain and the mud, and everything being so small and old and shabby?

'What'll they think of Elmbury, Gran? Whatever'll they think of us?'

Gran snorted. 'Huh! 'Tis more like what're *we* goin' t' think o' *them*?'

'Münster,' Sunshine barked, glaring round the briefing room as though daring anybody to contradict him.

'Christ, another bloody snorter!' Anne heard someone mutter behind her.

'Vital rail junction between Germany's northern coastal ports and the heavy industries and munition plants of the Ruhr valley . . . marshalling yards . . . hundreds of tons of armaments and war materials . . . factories making Messerschmitt and Focke-Wulf parts . . . military garrison . . . strategic importance . . .'

'OK. OK.' The voice muttered again. 'No need to go on about it.'

Anne glanced over her shoulder from her seat in the front row. She couldn't identify the voice but all the faces she saw looked drained and weary. Two scrubs in succession had taken a toll on nerves, and last night's op had been a shaky do, to say the least. Three Wimpeys lost, complete with crews.

When the Group Captain had finished, people came and went on the stage. The Met man, when it came to his turn, spoke vaguely of low stratocumulus over the North Sea and uncertainty about the weather over the target.

The same voice grumbled behind her. 'Bloody useless wanker! Don't know why they don't just ring up the bloody Huns and ask them what the weather's like over there . . .'

The crews filed out of the briefing room collecting their rice-paper flimsies, their escape kits and their orange juice, chewing gum, barley sugar and wakey-wakey pills.

'Can I have your egg if you don't come back?' she heard one of them say to another.

Latimer's crew passed her and she smiled at them all; the spry little rear gunner gave her a huge wink. Latimer looked back as he went out and raised his hand with a smile. Eighteen done. Only twelve more to go.

She went down to stand by the beginning of the main runway. It was dusk and she watched the procession of laden Wimpeys trundling round the peri track towards her. One by one they swung round onto the run-way, the most senior first. B-Baker, T-Tommy, K-King, D-Dog, S-Sugar, E-Easy thundered off in turn and staggered away into the darkening sky. She waved to them all, along with the rest of the faithful little band of personnel and ground crew. A-Apple was next and she watched the Wimpey lift and climb away. *Good luck, Digger* . . .

Latimer's, C-Charlie, swung round into position, waiting for the signal from the Watch Tower. She stood on tiptoe and waved as hard as she could. *I hope he's seen me.*

The green signal flashed out and C-Charlie began its

take-off run with a howling shriek of engines, and a thumbs-up from the rear gunner as the bomber gathered speed away from her. She followed it with her eyes as it tore on towards the far end of the runway and then sighed with relief as it began to rise at last, wallowing a little, and to clamber upwards slowly and painfully, like an old lady climbing very steep stairs. Hannibal would be there, up in his front row seat, watching what was going on; seeing the concrete and grass slip away beneath him.

Beside her, one of the ground crew said suddenly: 'Crikey, I don't like the sound of that bloody engine . . .'

She strained after the bomber. Its left wing dropped suddenly and the Wimpey seemed to fall sideways out of the sky. The wing hit the ground first and the bomber cartwheeled over on its back and burst into flames.

She stood frozen in horror, her hand still lifted in farewell. The fire-engines and a bloodwagon were tearing pointlessly towards the terrible inferno.

Very slowly, her hand sank to her side.

Seventeen

The Station Warrant Officer at RAF Kirkton, near Dundee, happened to be looking out of a window as three girls walked by. He stared, and went on staring. They were dressed in RAF blue battle dress blouses and slacks and wore black berets on their heads. He had never seen anything like it. He opened the window and leaned out.

'Ooh the 'ell are you lot?'

They stopped dead. The one nearest to him, a pretty girl with short, curly hair, went scarlet.

'We're flight mechs, sir. We've just arrived.'

He looked at them incredulously and clapped his hand to his forehead. 'God 'elp us all!' he said, and slammed the window shut.

Winnie gulped. The other two, Irene and Phyllis, laughed. Irene tossed her head.

'I'm not going to let them bother me. We've been sent here and they'll just have to put up with us.'

The Chief Technical Officer appeared as astonished as the SWO. He scratched his head as they stood before his desk.

'I don't know what I'm going to do with you three. We've never had WAAF flight mechs here before.'

They waited patiently while he went on scratching his head. At last, he made up his mind.

'Well, I'll give you a chance to prove yourselves. But if any of you aren't up to scratch you'll find yourselves sent back where you came from.'

They were split up and sent to different places on the aerodrome.

'Diluting us,' Phyllis said scornfully. 'Afraid we'll contaminate them, or something.'

Winnie was sent to a flight out at dispersal where she was greeted with more stares and consternation. Only one of the ground crew showed any friendliness. He came over, wiping his hands on a piece of oily rag and grinning broadly. His hair was carrot red and he wore his forage cap perched so far over on the side of his head that she couldn't see how it stayed on.

'What're you doing here, love?'

'I'm a flight mechanic,' she told him. 'Engines. I've just done the course and been sent here.'

He whistled. 'Blimey . . . what's Chiefy going to think? He hates women.'

When Flight Sergeant Jock McFarlane came out of his office he took just one look at her.

'You can take yourself off, lassie. I'm not having you out here. I'm counting ten and I don't want to see you when I've finished.'

She could barely understand his Scottish accent and his ice-blue eyes terrified her. So did the sight of the three stripes and crown on his sleeve. But she stood her ground.

'Squadron Leader Ryan said I was to come here, Flight.'

He glared at her ferociously, fists on hips. 'Och, he did, did he? Well, we'll soon see about that, my girl.'

He went away to see about it, but the squadron leader won the battle and she stayed. She was issued with men's overalls so big that she had to tie them up round her waist with locking wire, and she was given the worst, the dirtiest and the most tedious jobs to do. She cleaned oil filters, scraping away painstakingly at the rubbery deposits before washing them in petrol; she polished the perspex on the cockpits; she refuelled the aircraft tanks from the bowsers, clambering out on the wing in the wind and getting cold petrol all over her hands; she drained oil from engine sumps and on blustery days the oil spattered her face and hair; she held tools for the men and fetched and carried for them, shutting her ears to their bad language.

'Sorry, Winn,' they'd say. 'Forgot you was there . . .'

Because she was so doggedly willing they soon gave up resenting her. Before long they began to tease her instead. Bob, a corporal fitter and one of the oldest of the gang, sent her off to the stores.

'Go and ask them for three size seven sky hooks and a long rest.'

She was puzzled. 'What are those?'

He looked impatient: sarcastic. 'Thought you said you'd done your training. You don't mean to tell me you've never learned about sky hooks and long rests? You've heard of a spanner, I suppose?'

''Course I have.'

'Just wondered. Off you go, then, and be quick about it.'

She pedalled away round the peri track on her bike. It was more than a mile to the stores and raining hard. By the time she arrived she was soaking wet. When she asked for the tools the stores sergeant looked at her hard.

'You tryin' to be funny, or somethin'?'

'No, Sarge.'

'There's no such thing as sky 'ooks. Or a long rest either — 'cept on leave, an' you won't be 'avin' *that* yet. *Long rest*, see? Someone's been 'avin' you on. Takin' the mickey. You want to get yer number dry.'

When she cycled back to dispersal they were all laughing, even Ginger the carrot-haired one, who had once asked her to fetch him a left-handed screwdriver.

When the NAAFI van came round she would fetch them their char and wads.

'NAAFI's up!' they'd shout. 'Winn, be a love . . .'

She took it all in good part and kept well out of Chiefy's way. His cold eye was often upon her, she knew that, watching and waiting for any excuse to be rid of her.

'Shift yourself, woman,' he'd say. 'Out of my way!'

471

Everything she was given to do she did well, no matter how menial or dull the task. And she did it better, she guessed, than any of the men ever did. At Chiefy's bellow of *Two Six!* she was always there at once to help push or pull or lift, whatever was needed. Hands raw and red from petrol, ingrained with grease, the fingernails black-rimmed and ragged, and with her face streaked with dirt, she worked with a will and as hard, or harder, than any of them.

At first they wouldn't let her tail-squat when the aircraft were being ground-tested, saying it was no job for a woman. She watched them lying across the tailplane, keeping it down with their weight, and could see nothing very difficult or dangerous about it. Her chance to find out what it was like finally came when there was a flap on and everyone else was busy. The erk who was going on with her chivalrously gave her the starboard side where he told her there would be less blast from the propeller.

'You've got to keep down flat, see, so's the slipstream goes over you. Keep yer 'ead well down an' yer eyes shut, 'cos of the stones an' stuff blowin' about. An' 'ang on tight, for God's sake.' He eyed her doubtfully. 'I just 'ope you're 'eavy enough.'

She positioned herself as he had shown her, facing aft across the Hurricane's tailplane, and lay with her feet off the ground, gripping the fin with her right hand and the leading edge with her left. She shut her eyes tight. The Merlin engine started up with its ch-ch-ch clatter and exploded into a roar. The roar increased steadily until it hurt her ears and the prop blast felt so strong she thought it would sweep her clean away. Her hair was blowing all over the place and a hail of small stones spattered her back and legs. She screwed her eyes tighter shut as the fitter in the cockpit took the engine up as far as the gate, testing for mag drop and boost, and wished she could shut her ears. The smell of exhaust gas was choking her and the tailplane was juddering and jumping beneath her as it tried to lift off from the ground. She clung on to it desperately. Then suddenly the fitter throttled back, the revs died and he switched off. The prop blades windmilled to a stop.

She slid off the tail, her ears still singing, weak at the knees. The airman put his arm round her shoulders and gave her a squeeze.

'Thought we was both takin' to the air fer a minute there . . . You want to eat up yer porridge before next time.'

From a distance she watched the pilots – young men at the final stage of their training before they went operational. She saw them going to and fro from the crew room, parachute harnesses clinking and clanking, and she envied them as they climbed into their aircraft and taxied out to take off and climb away into the sky. One or two were nervous, she thought. It showed in the way they walked and moved, in the way they lit their cigarettes with hands that trembled just a little, and laughed just a bit too loudly. Once, she was allowed to help strap one of them in.

'The woman's touch,' Chiefy said caustically. 'Mebbe it'll remind the laddie of his mother and calm his puir wee nerves.'

The pilot looked very young. He had very smooth, pink cheeks like a schoolboy. Not more than nineteen, Winnie thought, feeling as maternal as Chiefy had intended, with her twenty-one years.

As he climbed up onto the Hurricane ahead of her his foot slipped on the wing. He corrected his balance quickly but there was a tinge of red in his face as he lowered himself into the cockpit. She hopped up after him and stood on the wing-root to help him with his harness straps, handing them over his shoulders from the back for him to fasten in front. She noticed how his hands shook as he did so, and the small beads of sweat on his forehead.

She gave the windscreen an extra little polish with the rag tucked in her string belt and smiled at him encouragingly. 'All right now, sir?'

He nodded and tried to smile too, but his face looked stiff with fright. He shouldn't be doing this if it scares him so much, she thought. Really he shouldn't. She dropped back onto the ground and went to stand ready to pull the chock away on one side. Titch, the mechanic at the trolly acc, was waiting patiently for his signal. It was some time coming from the cockpit and he caught Winnie's eye and raised his own heavenwards. When the Hurricane had started up at last, he nipped smartly under the wing to pull the lead from the socket. Winnie waited for her signal from the pilot and then moved forward to pull the rope, dragging the chock clear of the fighter's wheel. She watched the Hurry as it moved off and went on watching it anxiously as it turned to begin the take-off run. It seemed a long time before the wheels left the ground and it wobbled unsteadily into the sky.

Titch sniffed. 'Bloody awful pilot, that one.' He dragged the trolly acc off in disgust.

Later on, she saw the Hurricane return. It made an awkward approach, one wing dipped, and to her eyes it was too high up and going too fast for the landing. On touchdown it bounced hard several times and slewed round sharply. One of the undercarriage legs collapsed and the port wingtip buckled as it scraped along the ground. Then the nose tipped forward, crumpling the propeller blades like the petals of a flower. Her ground crew watched in grim silence.

The WAAF quarters were in a damp and dismal house on the edge of the aerodrome. It had stood empty for many years and the boiler, a Victorian monster in the cellar, seldom heated the bathwater above lukewarm, and then only in the middle of the day. In the mornings it was stone cold. There was nowhere to dry their wet clothes. Winnie tried laying her battledress trousers under her biscuits at night but in the morning they were still damp. The three flight mechanics shared a room together.

'Just as well,' Phyllis pointed out. 'The way those others

hold their noses when we're around.'

They reeked of oil and petrol. The smell clung to their skin, their hair and their clothes and the water was never hot enough to wash it away properly, or get rid of the grime from their hands. The five inches of tepid bathwater that they were allowed made little difference. In the Airwomen's Mess the other WAAFS edged pointedly away from them and went to sit elsewhere. A group of admin clerks complained to the officer when she came round the tables.

'Do we have to have *them* in here, ma'am? They're so dirty!'

To their delight and gratitude the section officer responded coldly. 'Most certainly you do. And I would remind you all that flight mechanics are classified as Group Two, whereas you yourselves are only Group Four. Your work may be cleaner but it is nowhere near as skilled.'

Irene smirked into her meat pie. 'Little do they know that there's nothing skilled about what we do. We're just blooming dogsbodies.'

She spent most of her time cleaning and polishing cockpit perspex. 'They won't let me touch much else. I scrape off bits of dead birds and squashed flies all day long . . . Then I sweep out the hangar.'

Phyllis passed her days removing split pins from magnetos and, because she was a big girl, tail-squatting. 'I don't know what we did all that training for,' she would say morosely. 'Honest, I don't.'

Sometimes, though, Ginger let Winnie help him on the engines, when Flight Sergeant McFarlane wasn't looking.

'Here Winn, you can have a go at this. Your 'ands are small-like so you'll reach it better'n me.'

She'd undo a screw or tighten a nut or get at some awkward part of the engine. Ginger watched her.

'It's a right shame Chiefy won't let you do more, Winnie. You're that quick with it.'

475

During a spell of cold, wet weather when there was little flying, Ginger gathered up some firewood and made a brazier out of an old tin can. They lit it in a small dugout shelter near the dispersal huts and he brewed up cocoa and condensed milk and water in an old saucepan over the fire for the two of them. One day he brought some bread, too, and a lump of margarine which he produced from his overall pocket.

'Nicked it from the cookhouse this morning. We'll make us some toast.'

Outside, the Scottish rain drifted across the aerodrome in grey sheets, but inside the shelter they were dry and quite warm. Ginger took his screwdriver out of his belt, stuck a piece of bread on it and held it over the fire. When it had toasted on both sides he spread it with margarine for her.

'There you are, love. A feast fit for a queen.'

He never talked much about himself and she didn't like to ask questions. All she knew was that he came from a village in North Yorkshire and had left home at fourteen to earn his own living. After working in a factory and then a garage he had ended up in the RAF and trained, like herself, as a flight mechanic on engines. Soon after she had first arrived he had asked her about the wedding ring she wore.

'Got a husband, then?'

'He died last February.'

He had clicked his tongue in sympathy. 'RAF, was he? Active service?'

'No, he was ill. He couldn't ever join up.'

'Poor bloke. He must've been bloody choked about that.'

She had been touched that he had understood how Ken had felt.

The toast tasted smoky but good. Ginger poured her out some more cocoa and she curled her hands round the tin mug.

'Have you ever wished you were a pilot, Ginger?'

He shook his head. 'Not me. I like workin' on engines best. That's what I like. Feet on the ground.'

'I feel sorry for the pilots when they're nervous.'

'Nothin' to what they'll feel like when they go operational. Sooner them than me, that's what I say.'

'I don't think I'd be nervous – not for the flyin' part, I mean. Have you ever been up in a 'plane, Ginger?'

'Been up on test flights when I was with bombers, before this.'

'What's it like?'

He screwed up his freckled face. 'Don't rightly know how to describe it. It's noisy, for a start. An' you go up and down all the time, so it feels unsteady. You can see everythin' for miles down below, if it's clear and everythin's little – like toys. Funny sort of feeling, really ... seein' it from a long way off an' not bein' part of it any more. Can't say I cared for it. We went right through some clouds once and that was just like a whole lot of cotton wool. Bumped all over the place, she did, the Wimpey.'

She said wistfully: 'I wish I could go up.'

'You want to get one of the instructors to take you in a trainer. Why don't you ask them?'

But she didn't think she'd ever have the nerve. Instructors seemed like gods to her. They had never even spoken to her, scarcely glanced in her direction.

She munched her smoky toast and drank some more of the cocoa. 'Do you think we'll win the war, Ginger?'

'"Course we will. Mind you, back in '40 I wasn't quite so sure for a bit, but now we've got the Yanks in it too we'll be all right.'

'They're buildin' a big bomber station near where I live in Suffolk – the Americans.'

'You'll want to watch out for them when you go on leave then. From what I hear they'll be after all the girls.'

'I've never seen an American – except at the pictures.'

'You will. Bound to. So just you remember what I said and watch out.'

Winnie drained her mug. 'What're you goin' to do when the war's over, Ginger?'

He had the answer ready to that one. 'Run my own garage, that's what and make a pile of brass. An' you can 'ave a job in it any time you like, love.'

'Chiefy wouldn't give me a job anywhere. He jumped down my throat again this morning. I don't know what I'd done wrong.'

'You don't want to take any notice of him, Winnie. 'is bark's worse than 'is bite. 'e can't 'elp this thing 'e's got against women. The wife ran off with a sailor, or somethin', so now 'e 'ates them all. Bit stupid, I reckon. I mean, women are all different, aren't they? Same as blokes are all different.'

He fished in his pocket, pulled out a packet of Woodbines and shook it dolefully. 'Only one left. Swop me some more of your fag coupons for sweet ones?'

''Course I will.'

'Thanks, love.' Ginger lit the last cigarette and stuck it in the corner of his mouth. 'I keep tellin' you, you want to go and see Chiefy an' 'ave it out. Stand up for yourself, like. Tell 'im straight out you want to do proper jobs, like you was trained for, same as the rest of us. He's no right to keep you down. From what I've seen, you'd be just as good as any of us, 'cept for liftin' the 'eavy stuff.'

'Thanks, Ginger.'

He grinned at her. 'I'm only tellin' the truth, love. That's all.'

Somehow she found the courage to go and see the Flight Sergeant. He looked up from some forms.

'What do you want, then?'

She took a deep breath. 'I want to do some proper work on the engines, please, Flight. Like I've been trained to do. Will you let me try at least? Give me a chance to show you that I can do it?'

He stared at her for a moment with his cold blue eyes; she met them bravely. There was silence in the office while they looked at each other. Then he threw down his pencil.

'All right then, I'll give you a chance. But only one, mind. You can try taking a cylinder head off.'

'I can do that all right, Flight.'

'Mebbe. Mebbe not. We'll soon see.'

A fitter was detailed to stand over her while she worked, checking every step as she removed the cylinder head and replaced it with a new one. When she had finished he said surprised:

'You did that well, Winnie. Nice and quick and neat. I thought you'd take all day.'

Flight Sergeant McFarlane came over. 'All right. So far, so good,' he grunted. 'Now let's see what a mess you make of a DI.'

She carried out her part of the Daily Inspection on the Hurricane with meticulous care, just as she had been taught on the training course. First, she checked the propeller blades for damage and inspected the aircraft outside for any sign of oil or coolant leaks. Then she removed the cowling and examined all pipe fittings, joints and clips and went over all the electrical leads, control rods and couplings. She checked the flexible drive and all the nuts and bolts, and the engine mounting bolts and bearers, and looked over the cowling frames for cracks. When that was done she checked oil, fuel and coolant levels and topped up the air compressor with castor oil.

The Hurricane's rigger, responsible for the airframe, watched her and chuckled. 'You don't want to take it too serious, love.' He walked casually round the aircraft and aimed a kick at one of the tyres. 'Nothing wrong with this kite, see.'

Next she ran up the engine and checked the dial temperatures and pressures and the mag-drop. Replacing the cowling afterwards might have defeated her if Ginger hadn't shown her the trick of it and how to bang home the fasteners with the flat of her hand. When she had finally finished she made sure the chocks were placed correctly in front of the wheels, with the string neatly round the front, as Ginger had once shown her. 'So's you can pull 'em away nice 'n easy.'

She went into the office to sign the Form 700. Chiefy McFarlane looked at her through narrowed eyes.

'You're saying that aircraft's serviceable, then?'

'Yes, Flight.'

'You've checked *everything*?'

She nodded.

'What about the air intake?'

She went bright red, realizing that she had forgotten it. How could she have been so stupid? So careless? Chiefy must have been watching her through the window. She hurried back to inspect that the intake was free from any obstruction and returned to the office.

He glowered at her as she signed the form. 'If I find anything's wrong I'll eat you alive.'

As she reached the door he yelled after her suddenly, jabbing a finger at the form.

'Come back here, woman! You've signed in the wrong bloody place!'

When the day's work was done the fitter who had watched her change the cylinder head stopped by her.

'We're off down the Lamb and Flag tonight, Winnie. Want to come along?'

It was the first time they had asked her to join them. She blushed.

'Thanks, Bob. I'd like that.'

She bicycled the four miles to the pub with them and drank half a pint of bitter.

Ginger nudged her. 'You're one of the gang now,' he said.

'Mother, this is Neil Mackenzie.'

Virginia watched her mother anxiously as she extended a hand. She was looking at Neil with the same expression she wore when the butcher gave her an unsatisfactory piece of meat.

'How do you do, Mr Mackenzie.'

'Pleased to meet you, ma'am.'

As Neil sat down he nearly knocked over a small table. He looked uneasy and out of place in the genteel sitting-room. Mother, seated straight-backed in her chair, went on looking at him in the same way.

'I hear you come from *Canada*, Mr Mackenzie.'

She made it sound as though it were some very remote and uncivilized part of the world.

'Call me Neil, please . . . That's right, Mrs Stratton. I'm from Hamilton, near Toronto.'

'I'm afraid I'm not acquainted with your country.'

'Well, I guess it's a long way away.'

'It is indeed. And you are in the Canadian army?'

'Sure thing. Came over in the summer of '40.'

'I see. May I ask how you came to meet my daughter?'

He grinned. 'Oh, we bumped into each other on a bike ride . . . Matter of fact, I nearly rode right into her goin' round a corner too fast. I guess it was fate.'

'Fate?'

'That we met. Though we didn't see each other again for a while – not 'til we sat opposite in a Salvation Army canteen in town. Fate again! Then we went 'n bumped into each other again on another bike ride.' He turned his head to smile at Virginia. 'Since then we've been meetin' whenever we can.'

'Really?'

Virginia watched and listened helplessly. She knew already that it had been a terrible mistake to bring Neil home – a vain and foolish hope that her mother might take to him and make him welcome. Instead it was going to be like the dreadful time when she had invited Molly from school home to tea – only worse. Far worse. Neil seemed unaware of it. He was sitting back easily in his chair, one leg crossed over the other and resting on his knee – slouching her mother would no doubt be thinking. She had drawn herself up regally. With a sinking heart Virginia saw that the table was elaborately laid with the best white tablecloth, silver cutlery and damask napkins.

Her mother rose to her feet. 'Luncheon is ready, Virginia. I expected you some time ago. Perhaps you will help me carry the dishes through. Mr Mackenzie can wait here.'

In the kitchen her mother did not trouble to lower her voice.

'I expected an officer at least, Virginia. And a gentleman. Not a sergeant and a *Colonial!* That speech! Those casual manners! What *can* you be thinking of?'

'Please, Mother! He'll hear you.'

'Just as well if he does. He has quite a nerve, in my opinion. You should never have encouraged someone of his type. I hope you're not taking him seriously in any way.'

'He's just a friend.'

'Well, I don't know why you insisted on bringing him home. There's no room for him here.'

'He had nowhere to go on leave. He'll sleep on the sofa, if that's all right. We've only got forty-eight hours. And I wanted you to meet him.'

'I can't imagine why. However, since he's here, I suppose I shall just have to make the best of it.'

Lunch was torture for Virginia. She saw her mother staring pointedly at the way Neil used his knife and fork, and at the gravy stain that appeared on the tablecloth beside his plate. The stew was grey and tasteless but Neil ate heartily and finished before either of them. He wiped his mouth on his napkin.

'I hope you have had sufficient, Mr Mackenzie.' Her mother dabbed at the corner of her mouth with hers. 'I'm afraid our rations in this country are rather meagre. I dare say you are more fortunate in the Colonies.'

'My folks send me food parcels, and we do pretty well at the camp. I guess we're lucky compared to you British. I brought some canned ham and fruit with me for you, Mrs Stratton. Hope you'll accept it.'

'We have learned how to make do with the little we have, thank you, Mr Mackenzie. In this country we prefer not to take handouts.'

'Sure. I understand. I didn't mean any offence.'

The pudding was awful – a pallid blancmange that hadn't set properly. Again, Neil seemed to enjoy every mouthful, though Virginia could hardly eat hers.

'You should visit Canada one day, Mrs Stratton. It's a great country. You'd like it.'

'I hardly think it likely that I shall ever go there, Mr Mackenzie. And I don't think it would appeal to me.'

'You never know 'til you try. When I first got here I was real homesick. Now, I've gotten over it . . .'

Her mother's face was frozen.

After lunch Virginia took Neil for a walk in the park down the road. They sat for a while by the lake in the sunshine, watching a mother and her small boy feeding the ducks with stale bread. Neil twisted his cap round in his hands.

'I guess your mum thinks I'm a real backwoodsman, Ginny.'

She said miserably: 'I'm so sorry about the way she is. She's never met a Canadian before. She doesn't really mean it.'

'I think she *does* mean it. It don't matter to me, though. Only I can see it hurts you, an' that makes me mad. I heard how she spoke to you when you were out in the kitchen.'

'I'm sorry,' she said again, close to tears. 'I hoped you wouldn't hear.'

'I don't care what she said about me. As a mother, I guess she's got every right to be concerned . . . but is she always like that with you? Treatin' you that bad?'

She lifted her shoulders. 'She's been awfully bitter about everything ever since my father left her, I think. She can't seem to help the way she is.'

'Why did he go?'

'For another woman, she says. I don't really know. I've never seen or heard from him since. But Mother doesn't seem to have got over it, even though it was a long time ago. And she's never really got used to living in a small flat. We had a big house near the Common once, but it all had to go when Father's company failed. He was made bankrupt and that's when he left – or soon after. You can understand why Mother's bitter.'

'Sure. But it wasn't your fault, Ginny. It wasn't anything to do with you. Just you remember that. You've got your own life. Say, look at that little guy! He's real cute.'

She looked at the small boy feeding the ducks, but through a blurred mist of tears. He was throwing little pieces of crust haphazardly into the water with funny, jerky movements, and the ducks were flapping and splashing and quacking about after them. She had so wanted Neil's visit to go right, but everything had gone wrong. Now, he would probably never want to see her again. He would probably believe that she felt like Mother, when what she felt was quite the opposite.

She wiped her eyes quickly with the back of her hand. 'Neil, you don't believe I think like Mother, do you?'

He turned back from watching the boy and smiled at her. 'About me being only a sergeant and a Colonial? No, Ginny, I know you don't. You're not made like that. But I guess she's right that I'm not good enough for you.'

She stared at him in anguish. 'Don't say that, Neil! Please don't.'

They looked at each other and his smile faded. He took hold of her hand and said earnestly: 'Trouble is, Ginny, I don't know for sure how you *do* feel about me. I mean, we've been seein' each other all these months, off 'n on, but you've never given me a clue . . . never let on what you're thinkin' . . . never let me get close in any way . . . You told your mum I was just a friend – I heard that too, couldn't help it. Is that the way you feel?'

She turned her head away. 'That's what we are, aren't we – friends?'

'I hoped we were more 'n that. A whole lot more. I wasn't goin' to say a thing yet, but I'm scared now that if I don't maybe I'll go and lose you for some crazy reason to do with your mum. I love you, Ginny. Have done ever since I first saw you that day on the bike when I came harin' round that corner . . . First of all I didn't think I had a chance with you, but lately I've begun to think different. But I knew I had to take it real slow. See, I want us to get engaged, Ginny. To get married, soon as we can. To go back and live in Canada one day, when the war's over. I'll take good care of you, I swear it. An' my folks'll love you. What d'you say?'

The tears began again, trickling down her cheeks.

'Gee, Ginny, if it's that bad an idea . . .'

'No, no.' She shook her head. 'I'm crying because I'm so happy.'

He laughed and caught her against him. It was the first time she had ever been kissed. Presently he said:

'I'll speak to your mum as soon as we go back.'

She pulled away from in alarm. 'No, not yet, Neil. Let's keep it to ourselves for a little while longer. Please.'

'All right,' he said reluctantly. 'If that's what you want. But we'll have to tell her in the end.'

He put his arm around her and drew her close against him. The little boy and his mother had gone and the ducks were paddling quietly on the lake. The sunlight shimmered across the surface of the water. I don't want anything to spoil this for us, she thought. Not yet. She rested her head on his shoulder and closed her eyes tiredly. Not yet.

'Kookaburras and wattle?' Digger said, leaning against the bar in the Black Bull.

Anne shook her head. 'What on earth are those?'

'First one's an Aussie bird. Second's a yellow flower. Grows everywhere.'

'I've heard of the Outback,' she said. 'You've got a lot of that.'

'Too right. How about dingoes. Heard of those?'

'They're wild dogs, aren't they? *Up jumped dingo, yellow dog dingo . . .* that's from some poem or other.'

Digger lifted his beer mug. 'Don't know about the poem, but you're right there too. Nasty, savage creatures you wouldn't want to meet.' He took a long swallow.

'Bondi beach,' she said, suddenly inspired. 'Surfing.'

He looked over the mug admiringly. 'My word, you're getting better all the time.'

'Sheep. Gold. Opals. Pineapples. Sugar cane.'

He whistled. 'You've been cheating. Looking things up.'

'No, I haven't. I swear it. I just remembered what we learned at school. Tasmania and apples.'

'Good on you! What about wine?'

'Wine? You mean you have vineyards? I don't remember learning about that.'

'Oh, my word, yes. It's good wine, too. Good as German or French any day. I'll bet you thought we drank Fosters all the time.'

'Fosters?'

He groaned in mock despair. 'You mean to say you've never heard of Fosters? That's terrible! Best beer there is.' He took another swig. 'Better than this Pommy muck. Heard of The Wet?'

'Is that another beer?'

He laughed. 'Strewth, no! It's the rainy season in Australia. Comes down in bloody torrents.'

'We have that all the year round.'

'All right, try these. King's Cross and Paddington.'

'They're in London.'

'They're in Sydney, too.'

'Couldn't you think of your own names?'

'Yeah. Woollamaloo, Wagga Wagga, Wollongong.'

'I like those. They sound lovely.'

'Matter of fact, we pinched those from the Abos.'

Digger drained his mug and pushed it across the counter towards the landlord. 'Same again, sport.' He winked at Anne over his shoulder. 'Have to keep it filled up 'case they run out.'

'Stuttgart,' Sunshine snapped, making it sound like a bad sneeze. 'That is our target for tonight, gentlemen.'

'*Our* target, you mean,' someone in the row behind Anne whispered resentfully. '*You* don't have to bloody go. All that bloody way.'

She looked at the red tape stretched across the map on the wall behind the Group Captain – representing something like five hundred long miles there and five hundred long miles back.

Sunshine was glowering round the briefing room. 'Industrial area . . . diesel-engine and ignition factories . . . penetration into Southern Germany . . . impose ARP measures over a wide area . . . high morale value . . . maximum effort expected.'

She listened to him giving his usual harangue. All available aircraft on the station were being bombed up. It was going to be a big one.

Digger and his crew were sitting near the front, to her left. Digger was looking carefully unconcerned, smoking a cigarette and leaning back in his chair. Twenty-nine ops behind him and only this one to go, and it had to be a snorter.

When the briefing was over he passed close to her as he left the room.

'Didgeridoo,' she said.

'Stone the crows!' He grinned. 'Never thought of that. That one deserves a gong.' He tugged a button off his tunic and pressed it into her palm. 'Here you are. The Wollongong. Aussie medal for the best Pommy sheila I ever knew.'

The long wait began. She lay on her bed, sleeping in short bouts, listening for the distant sound of engines that would herald the bombers' return. This was the hardest part. Sunshine, no doubt, would be peacefully asleep and dreaming of promotion and medals (his own), but many on his station and under his command would be watching, listening and waiting as the hours of darkness dragged by.

After dawn they began to come back, the faint drone of the first arrivals swelling gradually to a roar when they circled above the aerodrome. One, she could hear, was in bad trouble, flying on a single faltering engine. She held her breath as it passed over very low; after a few moments a horrible thudding whoomph shook the building. As the first crews stumbled into the de-briefing room she saw without asking a single question that it had been a very shaky do. Their faces told the story before they began to talk of murderous flak, marauding night fighters and kites going down in flames.

Six of them failed to return, among them Digger and his crew. She waited for a long while with the squadron CO, sitting in the empty room with the sound of the clock ticking away hope. There were no late stragglers and there was no news.

She skipped breakfast and went outside, still hoping against all likelihood for the sight of A-Apple or any of the others in the sky. She fingered the black Australian Air Force button in her pocket.

Oh, Digger, I've thought of a whole lot more that I was going to tell you . . . swagmen, billabongs, tuckerbags, billies, coolibah trees and Waltzing Matilda.

Virginia watched the ladybird crawling slowly across the back of her hand and wondered if insects had any feelings at all. Or did they go through their short lives in a state of blissful ignorance of such things – feeling and caring nothing, driven only by conditioned reflex and blind instinct. Sometimes she wished that she had none. That she could live without always dreading this and fearing that and being so nervous about the other. It spoiled everything. Now, at this moment, sitting in the shade in a corner of the field, the bikes propped against the tree, she was happy – happier perhaps than she had ever been in her life. But that happiness was still tinged with a gnawing fear that it might not last. That Neil could not really love her as much as he said, that he might not really want to marry her, that something somehow would go wrong . . . She looked at him lying on his back on the grass close by, his hands behind his head, his eyes shut, and could not trust her good fortune. It had taken a long while for her to overcome her shyness with him and she could remember the very instant when it had finally dawned on her that she was in love with him. He had taken her to watch him play in an ice hockey match in Brighton between Canadian and British servicemen. Two teams had been scratched together and somehow equipped. She had watched from the edge of her seat as the players tore round the rink at breakneck speed chasing the tiny puck. There had been horrifying collisions, spills and thrills and the best thrill had been when Neil had scored one of the goals. He had swept down the side of the rink, flicking the puck before him and veered across to shoot straight past the keeper into the goal mouth. She had been on her feet with the rest of the Canadians in the crowd, yelling and clapping, though she knew she should have been supporting the other side. The match had ended in victory for the Canadian team, after a fierce struggle, and to her relief, Neil had come off the ice unscathed. He had looked up to where she was sitting, laughing and waving. As she waved back she had realized suddenly how she felt about him and the knowledge had filled her with both happiness and trepidation.

'Penny for your thoughts, Ginny.'

He had opened his eyes and was watching her.

'Nothing really . . . I was just remembering the match in Brighton.'

'That was great.'

'You scored that goal.'

'Yeah.' He propped himself up on one elbow. 'Wish we could spend more time together, Ginny – have more days like that one, and today . . . Don't know when our next chance'll be. Looks like somethin's up. I reckon things're goin' to be busy for a while.'

Her stomach fluttered in fright. 'How do you mean?'

He tugged at the grass by his hand, frowning. 'Couldn't tell you even if I knew, which I don't. But somethin's cookin' all right. We're doin' all these manoeuvres an' exercises an' all that stuff the whole time. It's gotta be for somethin' special.'

She stared at him in dismay. 'Will it be dangerous?'

'Now, don't you go worryin'. I wouldn't've said anythin' only you might've started wonderin' if you didn't hear from me for a bit.' He smiled at her. 'Might get to thinkin' I'd gone off with some other girl.'

It was just what she probably would have thought, in her fatalistic way. He saw the look on her face and put his hand on her arm.

'Don't ever think like that, Ginny. It'll never be true. You'll always be my girl. Don't worry about a thing. We're goin' to get married and when this war's over we're goin' to settle down in Canada and be happy for the rest of our lives.'

He leaned over and kissed her cheek and then her mouth. He went on kissing her longer and more fiercely than he had ever done before, pressing her down onto the grass. She clasped him tightly in her arms.

This can't be wrong, she thought dazedly, because we love each other. The air felt cool against her skin and Neil's mouth was warm. It's the war, she thought, the ghastly, horrible war. Even if it *is* wrong, I simply don't care.

'He's off his feed,' Mrs Parsons said. 'Something's the matter with him.'

She was standing by the budgerigar's cage as Virginia and Madge came in, peering anxiously at the bird. The

490

black cat sat watching from a chair with his yellow eyes. Madge took a brisk look.

'Seems all right to me.'

Mrs Parsons shook her head. 'He's not. I can tell. Look at the way his feathers are all droopy. And he's not touched his seed.'

Virginia said: 'Perhaps he's just feeling down in the dumps today.'

'Maybe he heard the news.' Mrs Parsons made little kissing noises through the bars. 'Enough to put anyone out of sorts.'

'What news?'

'Haven't you heard, dear? It was on the wireless. We landed a whole lot of troops over the other side of the Channel, at some French port. They were mostly Canadians, it said.'

'*Canadians?*'

'Well, some of them speak French, don't they? I expect that's why they sent them. Ever so many of them got killed, though, by the sound of it. Poor boys. I don't know what good they thought it would do . . .' She bent towards the cage again. 'If he's not better by tomorrow, I think I'll definitely take him to the vet.'

Virginia stood quite still, hands hanging at her sides. The room went dark around her and there was a singing sort of sound in her ears, then it went light again. Mrs Parsons was blowing more kisses through the birdcage bars, making little popping noises with her mouth. Madge was looking across at her anxiously and with pity in her eyes. Madge knew, just as she knew. *Somethin's up . . . we're doin' all these manoeuvres an' exercises . . . it's gotta be for somethin' special.*

She turned and stumbled blindly from the room.

Eighteen

The woman sitting on the other side of Felicity's desk was dressed all in grey – grey felt hat, grey coat, grey gloves clutching the large handbag on her lap. Her hair was grey too, blending almost invisibly with the shapeless hat. The expression on her pale face was uncomprehending.

'I was told Gwynneth was seriously ill . . . now you say she isn't, and I've come all this way.'

'Your daughter *was* very ill, Mrs Morgan, and we were very concerned about her. I'm very relieved to be able to tell you that the doctor has taken her off the critical list as of this morning. I am sorry to have alarmed you like this.'

'Well, I may as well see her since I'm here. Where is she then?'

'She's in our sick quarters at present. We'll be moving her to a civilian hospital as soon as she's strong enough.'

'*Civilian* hospital? Why can't the RAF look after her? She must have caught whatever it is from someone in the Service.'

Felicity looked down at the pen she was holding in her fingers. She turned it round several times before replying.

'Your daughter asked me to have a word with you before you saw her, Mrs Morgan. To explain the situation to you.'

The woman's face sharpened with suspicion. 'What situation? What's happened? What's Gwynneth been doing?'

Felicity met her hostile stare. 'She's had a baby, Mrs Morgan. A boy. He was born yesterday.'

'A *baby*! How could she? There must be some mistake.'

'There's no mistake, I'm afraid. He was very premature but the doctor believes he will survive, I'm thankful to say. Unfortunately, Gwynneth didn't tell anyone about her condition – no-one at all.'

Not even you, Felicity thought, watching her mother's outraged expression. *Especially not you.* ACW Morgan had clung to her hand, weeping and trembling. 'Don't tell her, *please*, ma'am . . . she'll kill me.'

She had done her best to calm her. 'I'll *have* to tell her, but I'll speak to her before she sees you so she'll have time to get used to the idea.'

The airwoman had moved her head miserably from side to side on the pillow. 'She'll *never* get used to it. *Never*.'

'You mean to tell me,' Mrs Morgan was saying through tight lips, 'that you let such a disgusting thing happen? You're responsible for the girls in your charge, aren't you? Supposed to be.'

'I'm extremely sorry, Mrs Morgan – '

'*Sorry!* Being sorry isn't going to help. Our family's disgraced. Humiliated. I'll never be able to hold my head up again . . .'

'Surely the most important thing is that Gwynneth is going to be all right. It was touch and go, you know. She lost a great deal of blood.'

A passing WAAF sergeant had heard moaning coming from a boiler room and found Morgan lying on some sacks in a dark corner. The baby had been born and the girl was haemorrhaging badly. It seemed incredible that she had somehow managed to keep her secret, even from NCOs like Beaty who were always on the look out for trouble.

Mrs Morgan drew herself up in her chair. 'You can spare me the details, thank you. Gwynneth's life is ruined anyway. No respectable man will look at her now. She'll have to marry the father, whatever he's like.'

'Unfortunately that won't be possible.'

493

'Why not? He must be made to marry her. *Ordered* to.'

'He was killed in action six months ago. He was a sergeant pilot. Your daughter told me all about it, Mrs Morgan. They were going to get married when she learned about the baby, but he was killed before they could do so.' Felicity paused again. 'They were very much in love, I'm sure of that . . . and these things do happen in wartime. It's no excuse, but time can seem so precious when so many young men are being killed every day.'

'Are you telling me that loose, immoral behaviour is all right just because there's a war on? Where I live we have different standards, I can tell you.'

A village in the wilds of Wales. Strict chapel. Unbending and unforgiving of those who strayed from the path.

'I can understand your distress, Mrs Morgan, and please believe me that I feel very responsible for what has happened and regret it deeply. But your daughter is in great distress, too, and she needs your love and understanding – '

'Gwynneth knows very well what I think about such things. And her father won't have her over the threshold again.'

'You can't mean that.'

'I assure you that I do. She's made her bed and now she must lie on it.'

Mrs Morgan rose to her feet; she clasped the handbag to her chest, as though to ward off any contamination from her surroundings.

'But you'll see your daughter, at least, Mrs Morgan. And your grandson.'

Her face was implacable. 'As far as I'm concerned, I no longer have a daughter. And I have no grandson.'

The door closed behind her. Felicity watched through the window as she walked away towards the main gate – a grim, grey figure, stiff-backed and unrelenting. Remembering her own mother and her loving care and understanding, she felt very sorry for ACW

Morgan. There seemed no alternative for her but to go to some bleak home for unmarried mothers. She would be discharged from the WAAF on compassionate grounds, of course, and the Church of England Moral Welfare Council would do what they could to help, but Mrs Morgan would probably be proved right – her daughter's life was ruined. And she held herself responsible for it. Somehow she had failed in her duty towards Morgan. *A WAAF officer is responsible for the welfare and well-being of the airwomen under her charge.* That was one of the very first things she had been taught in training. And yet how could she have prevented such a thing happening? You could arrange all the lectures you liked about moral behaviour and chastity and venereal disease, but that was no proof against two people in love snatching time together during a war.

As she stared out of the window at the trees blowing in the wind and the brown autumn leaves bowling across the ground, another thought occurred to her. The baby would have two sets of grandparents, assuming the sergeant pilot's mother and father were alive. Morgan had told her his name and she would be able to find out their address from records. If she were to write to them and tell them what had happened, they might be very glad to learn that their dead son had left a son of his own . . .

As she mulled this over in her mind, Group Captain Palmer came into view, striding along the path towards the entrance to Station HQ. She drew back from the window, not wanting him to catch sight of her standing there idly. Two WAAFS passing him saluted smartly. She remembered his fury in the early days when he had received all manner of salutations from waves to curtsies. Thinking back to how undisciplined they had been then, she could hardly blame him. But since then they had shown what they could do. WAAFS were now working in all kinds of trades and they had been able to replace men in almost every field – as electricians, meteorologists, armourers, welders, wireless and instrument mechanics, even as flight mechanics. She thought of nice Winifred Briggs who had so wanted to become one and wondered whether she had managed to achieve her ambition yet.

Group Captain Palmer had disappeared round the corner and would soon be passing her office door on the way to his. She no longer shivered when he did so. Their confrontations were now conducted on a very civil basis. He still remained a distant and awe-inspiring figure but he was unfailingly polite to her. Since that first terrible bombing raid on the station in the summer of 1940 there had been no more harsh words. It had been gloriously gratifying to hear him eat those words but she had not made the mistake of showing it. He had earned her respect by doing so and since then she had seen him in a rather different light. There was a rumour going round that he would probably soon be posted elsewhere, in which case she would have to adapt to a new station commander. A daunting thought. Better the devil you know . . . She listened to the devil's footsteps going briskly past in the corridor. He seemed such a lonely man but then it was a lonely job, as Speedy had pointed out, and his wife was always away in London. There were times when she felt quite sorry for him. Even times when she wanted to cheer him with a smile and some encouraging words, but except for that evening of the bombing raid when he had dropped his guard briefly and seemed almost human, he had never been that approachable again.

Speedy . . . He had been constantly in her thoughts ever since she had received the letter from Sinbad. *I thought I ought to let you know that Speedy went missing on a rhubarb over France. Nobody actually saw him go down, so we don't know what happened exactly. He hasn't been reported as KIA or POW yet, so there's still hope that he may be hiding up somewhere over there and will get back eventually. I am very sorry to give you this news but I thought you would want to be told. By the way, I'm looking after George for the time being.*

He had signed it Michael Sailer and for a moment or two she couldn't think who on earth he was. That had been two months ago and there had been no more news, but she had not given up hope. Speedy seemed indestructible. It was impossible to believe that he would not, any day, come breezing into her office, calling her some ridiculous name and reciting some absurd quotation as he twirled his battered cap on his finger and smiled his most charming smile. While there is life there's hope, he would certainly have said, and she could not believe him dead. There was another saying, though, that could equally apply: hope for the best, but prepare for the worst.

She sat down at her desk and began to draft out a letter to the sergeant pilot's parents.

The two men coming up the steps to the Mess as Anne was leaving were still wearing flying clothes. She looked at them curiously, not recognizing their uniform. Their caps were khaki with leather peaks and high in front, almost like the German ones. They wore flat-looking Mae Wests over short leather jackets, and fawn trousers tucked into flying boots. One of them was carrying his oxygen mask and he caught hold of Anne's arm as she passed him.

'Say, miss, can you tell us, is this place the Officers' Mess?'

He was chewing gum as he spoke. American. That explained it. Tales were told of American servicemen's casual customs and dress — how they slapped senior officers on the back, saluted sloppily, slouched about. This was her first encounter with the species. The one who had stopped her was tall and fair with bright blue eyes, the other darker and smaller. Our new and powerful allies, she thought. Without them we'll never win the war. I must be very nice to them.

She smiled at them both. 'Yes, this is the Mess.'

The fair one was still chewing. 'We just didn't want to make any mistakes round here.'

497

You're about to make one right now, she thought — going into the Mess dressed like that. Aloud she said: 'Are you on a visit?'

He laughed. 'I guess you could say that, though it wasn't scheduled. We were up slow-timin' a new engine and we had some real problems with it, so we kinda had to drop in, ain't that so, Frank?'

The darker one shook his head ruefully. 'Matter of fact we weren't even too sure where we were.'

'You're at East Thorpe.'

'So they tell us. There's a heck of a lot of bases in this area . . . it's going to take some getting used to.' He smiled at her. 'I'm Frank Wallace, United States Army Air Force. And this is Scott Cullen, my co-pilot.'

'How do you do. I'm Anne Cunningham, British Women's Auxiliary Air Force.'

The co-pilot was looking her up and down; his gaze rested finally on her shoulder. 'I can't figure out your Air Force yet. What's that bar on your coat mean?'

'I'm an Assistant Section Officer.'

He grinned. 'Well you can assist me any time.'

His skipper said apologetically: 'Take no notice. Scott's from New Jersey. He's never learned any manners.'

'That's all right.' She smiled at him. 'And where do you come from?'

'Chicago, Illinois.'

'You're both a long way from home.' She had no idea where either place was on the map.

'Sure feels like it,' Scott Cullen said heavily.

'Where are you based?'

'Rudwick St Mary. I guess it's not far from here. You certainly have some great names . . . real quaint.'

'What aircraft do you fly?'

'B24s. Bombers. Libs . . . you British call them Liberators.'

'I don't think I've ever seen one.'

'You will,' the co-pilot assured her kindly. 'You'll be seein' a whole lot of 'em from now on. Great ships.'

498

He was watching a WAAF officer approaching the steps, one of the prettiest in the camp, and followed her with his eyes into the Mess. A faint whistle came from his lips. 'Well, I guess, we'll be stickin' around for an hour or so while they fix things up . . . Let's go get somethin' to eat.'

His skipper smiled at Anne, half-apologetically again. 'Thanks for the help. I sure hope we run into you again.'

She hesitated, not wanting to sound bossy, but surely it was better to warn them. 'Actually, it isn't done to wear flying gear in the Mess. I thought I'd mention it . . . so you know another time. You can always leave things in the cloakroom inside.'

'Oh.' He looked embarrassed. 'Thanks for telling us.'

As she walked away she heard the co-pilot say in an exaggerated Oxford accent: 'Not the done thing, old boy. I say, we nearly put up a jolly frightful black. Damned bad show . . .'

'Mrs Paxton to see you, ma'am.'

The woman shown into Felicity's office by a WAAF sergeant, was in complete contrast to Mrs Morgan. Instead of drab grey, she was dressed in warm cherry red and wore a wonderfully frivolous-looking fur hat. And she was smiling. She came forwards with her arms extended, her face alight.

'Where is he? I can't wait to see him! Where's my grandson? And my daughter? I've come to take both of them home.'

Sometimes, Felicity thought later, when she had left Mrs Paxton cradling the baby in her arms and laughing delightedly with his mother, things did work out all right in the end. She walked back to HQ with a light heart, feeling that she had done something to set right the wrong. And in a few days she would be going home on leave. For a while she would be able to forget all about her cares and responsibilities – to stop worrying about whether she was being completely conscientious, scrupulously fair, totally devoted to her duty. As she passed the open door of Robbie Robinson's office, the squadron leader called out,

'CO wants a word, my dear. In his office.'

Group Captain Palmer looked up as she entered. She was relieved to find that it was nothing more critical than the arrangements for the Station Dance.

'Another Christmas nearly here, Section Officer, and we still find ourselves at war, unfortunately.'

'Perhaps it will be over by next year, sir – now that the Germans are in retreat in North Africa.'

He shook his head. 'I wish I thought so, but I'm afraid we've got a long way to go yet – on all fronts. Still, there's some light at the end of the tunnel, and we must press on regardless, as they say. Keep our chins up. You have some leave due, isn't that right?'

'Yes, sir. I'm going home next Thursday.'

'Norfolk, isn't it? You'll be looking forward to that, I'm sure. Are you taking the train?'

'Yes, sir. To London, and then on.'

He cleared his throat. 'It so happens that I'm going to London myself by car on Thursday. My driver and I could give you a lift as far as there, if it would help. Rather more comfortable than the train. And more reliable these days.'

Train journeys had become a nightmare. Miserable hours could be spent waiting on icy platforms for trains that were either very late or never came at all. And, when and if they did arrive, they were invariably crowded and little warmer than the platform, and they crawled like snails across the countryside.

'That's very kind of you, sir. If you're sure it's no trouble.'

He was moving some papers around on his desk, no longer looking at her. 'None at all, Section Officer. None at all.'

* * *

Anne came across the two American pilots that she had met on the Mess steps in the bar of the Black Bull. She had gone to the pub with one of the Wimpey crews and during the evening a large group of American Air Force servicemen came in with the two pilots among them. She watched with interest as they ordered drinks in some confusion and pulled wads of notes and handfuls of change from their pockets, dumping it on the counter for the barmaid to sort out. There was a lot of talk and laughter.

'Bloody Yanks!' the Wimpey navigator said. 'They pay them the earth and they come over here and throw their money around like there was no tomorrow.'

There may not be, though, she thought. I don't blame them, or anyone, for living for today. For spending everything they've got. For seizing every chance. At that moment the one that she remembered was called Frank Wallace caught sight of her and she smiled and waved. After a while he wove his way through the crush to her side, beer in hand.

'Say, this is great.' He looked down at her, pleased. 'I've been wondering how the heck I could get to meet you again. I was planning another engine failure, if necessary.'

'Did you find your way back all right?'

'Yeah. We got back to base OK. We're kinda getting used to it all now. Getting to know our way round a lot better. Round the pubs too. Someone told us this was a good place to go and it sure seems popular. Is it always this crowded?'

'Usually. It's our station local.'

'I really like your English pubs. They're wonderful.'

'How do you like our English beer?'

'Let's just say I'm getting used to that as well.'

'And our money?'

He groaned. 'I'll never get used to *that*. I just can't seem to get the hang of it. Pounds, shillings, pence . . . that's sort of OK. But then you've got half-crowns, sixpences, threepenny bits, halfpennies, farthings . . . it's darn complicated, you've got to admit. I've got pockets weighted down with the stuff because I keep handing over pound notes to save having to figure it all out. What the heck's a florin, by the way?'

'Two shillings. Twenty shillings in a pound. Twelve pennies in a shilling. It's quite simple, really.'

'Not to me it isn't.'

'Have you come across guineas yet?'

'Jeez . . . something else to worry about?'

'A guinea is one pound and one shilling. It's a snobby way of charging for something. Three guineas for a Paris hat. That sort of thing.'

'Well, I guess I won't be buying any of those, so I don't need to remember it. Smoke?' He was holding out a packet of cigarettes.

She looked at the brand. 'Philip Morris? I've never tried American cigarettes before. Thanks.'

He lit it for her. 'Look, keep the pack. I've got plenty more back at the base. I know you're short of everything.'

'Thanks.'

That was another thing she'd heard about the Americans: that they were exceedingly generous. Especially with women. She looked at two of them leaning across the bar and chatting up the barmaid, who was clearly enjoying it. They were no longer the objects of intense curiosity that they had been when they had first appeared in the area, but they still drew attention and stood out from the rest. It wasn't only the louder voices and the strange accent, or even the different uniform – the leather jackets, the better quality and cut of the cloth – it was also the casual, easy way they moved and talked. The wise-cracking, gum chewing confidence, the appreciative way of looking the girls over, the surprisingly good manners . . . And they seemed so much better fed and healthier than us, she thought. So clean and groomed and full of energy. After three years of war, we all look pale and pasty and shabby and tired.

The American pilot, seeing the direction of her gaze said: 'I guess you think we're a pretty loud-mouthed bunch.'

'The RAF can be quite loud, too. When they get going.'

'I don't know . . . you British are very reserved. I'm just beginning to learn about your famous understatements. When one of your guys says it was a bit tricky on a mission what he *really* means is that he ended up with half an engine, one wing and all the crew jumped out.'

She laughed. 'It's true they won't often admit how bad it was . . . not in so many words. You have to drag it out of them. That's part of my job, as a matter of fact. Interrogating air crews after ops.'

He looked intrigued. 'That so? Then you must know pretty much what goes on. What it's like?'

'I doubt if anyone could really know what it's like without actually going on ops, do you? Have you yet?'

He drew on his cigarette. 'Done a couple've missions over France. Nothing like the distance most of your guys are doing. How the heck they do it all in the dark, I'll never know. I sure admire them.'

'I think they admire you for going in broad daylight when the Germans can't miss seeing you.'

'Yeah, we're finding out about that the hard way,' he said. 'On the other hand, it's a damn sight easier to hit a target when you can see it – weather permitting. I can tell you the weather's a real problem. Most of us learned to fly in clear skies back in the US. It's a whole new ballgame over here. It's all we can do to find our way there and back sometimes and not go ramming each other on the way.'

She changed the subject away from war. Most airmen from overseas, in her experience, wanted to talk about home: that faraway, beloved place that they all dreamed of going back to one day when it was over.

'You said you came from Chicago?'

'That's right. The windy city. Hog butcher to the world.'

'Sorry?'

'Windy because it's right on Lake Michigan and, boy, does it blow sometimes . . . Hog butcher because of the slaughter houses. It's where most of the cattle from the Great Plains end up.'

'How about gangsters?'

He laughed. 'You don't want to believe everything you see in the movies. Sure we have them – Al Capone, John Dillinger - but they have more in New York. I come from a nice quiet part on the north shore called Evanston. We're a pretty law-abiding lot.'

'How did you get into the Air Force?'

'Volunteered. We all did. I guess I've always liked the idea of learning to fly. I was at Northwestern, majoring in engineering, but that'll have to wait now 'til the war's over. Got sent to Georgia first for primary, then Texas for basic and California, out in the desert, for advanced. We formed into crews at Grand Island in Nebraska – that's where I met up with Scottie.'

She looked across at the co-pilot who had a rosy-cheeked Land Girl pinned against the wall. 'He seems to be settling in all right.'

'Yeah.' He grinned. 'He'd settle in anywhere, so long as there were pretty girls.'

'Did you fly over? It must be an awful long way.'

He shook his head. 'We came over by ship. That was some voyage! Zig-zagging all the way and all the guys being sick as dogs.'

'I like your uniform,' she told him, head on one side as she considered the dark olive shirt and pale tie, the brown leather jacket. 'Specially the jacket.'

'We call them A2s. They're pretty comfortable.'

She peered at the round patch on the front of his jacket. It showed a brightly painted bird carrying a bomb in its yellow beak. 'What on earth's that?'

'Squadron patch.'

'We don't have those in the RAF.'

'You're more conservative, I guess. You don't paint things on your airplanes either.'

'What sort of things?'

He grinned again. 'Girls, mostly. Not wearing too much. It kind've cheers the guys up.'

The leather jacket gave no clue to his rank. 'I'm a Second Lieutenant,' he said when she asked him. He pronounced it oddly as lootenant and she giggled.

'Sorry, but that sounds funny. We don't say it like that. We say *left*enant.'

'You don't say a lot of things like us, and I'm having a hard time learning them all. There's a whole bunch of different words – petrol for gas, lift for elevator, trousers for pants, bill for check, windscreen for windshield, bonnet for hood, boot for trunk . . .'

'Still, we more or less understand each other.'

'I sure hope so,' he said, smiling slowly. 'Would you come out with me some place, some time, Anne? Let me take you to dinner, or the movies, or wherever you'd like to go?'

She looked down at her glass.

'The thing is I made up my mind not to go out with one person any more – to stick to going with groups, like this evening. I'm here with one of the crews.'

Don't get involved any more, she'd told herself – not even just as good friends like with Jimmy, and Latimer and Digger . . . she was practically a chop girl. Anyone she got friendly with bought it.

'Are those the guys right behind you who keep looking at me like they'd like to drop me over Germany on their next trip?'

She laughed. 'Some of them resent Americans a bit. They think you're overpaid, overfed and taking all their women. We've been warned about you, you know. The Queen Bee delivered a lecture.'

'Queen Bee?'

'The head WAAF at the station.'

'What did she say?'

'She said: "Americans have a big country and they have big mouths. They also have lots of money and they're going to think you WAAFS are there for their entertainment, so do be careful." Her very words.'

'Ouch!' He ducked his head. 'So, you won't come out with me then?'

'It's better not. Honestly.'

'It's not because of what your Queen Bee said, though, is it?' He met her eyes. 'You're afraid of getting to know someone who might get himself killed, isn't that so?'

'My fiancé was killed in action in 1940. And I've had a lot of friends who've been lost. I don't seem to be able to get used to it.'

'I'm sorry,' he said. 'Real sorry. Me and my big American mouth. Let me buy you another drink to make up – your glass is empty and it's not nearly Time yet.'

'That's jolly nice of you. I'll have half a bitter, please.'

'Coming right up.' The American dug into his pocket and produced a handful of coins that would have added up to nearly a week of her pay. He held them out helplessly. 'But first you'll have to tell me what the hell to give them.'

She laughed and bent her head over his palm.

'Warm enough, Section Officer?'

'Yes, thank you, sir.'

This was certainly better, Felicity thought, than waiting around on a cold platform. The staff car was warm and comfortable and the WAAF driver was steering it smoothly and swiftly towards London. Nonetheless, she found it hard to relax, sitting beside Group Captain Palmer.

'Appalling weather,' he said. 'All this rain . . .'

She watched the sodden fields flashing past. At home there would probably be floods and the Rectory would be damp and freezing. She was still longing to be there. It was already getting dark – in fact, the winter day had never been properly light – and the second half of the journey, by train from London, was going to be depressing, sitting in a blacked-out compartment under a weak, blue light, stopping and starting . . .

'Liverpool Street, isn't it?'

He had turned his head away from his own window towards her; the goldtrimmed peak of his cap shaded his face.

'Yes, sir. If you could drop me at any tube station . . .'

'We'll take you there.'

'There's no need, sir,' she said, embarrassed.

'I'm not due at the Ministry until first thing in the morning, so it makes no odds.'

'Thank you, sir.'

In the close confines of the back seat, the bulky sleeve of his greatcoat was touching hers; she moved her arm away.

At Liverpool Street he sent the driver away and insisted on carrying her suitcase to the platform, which embarrassed her even more. The station was crowded, as all stations seemed to be in wartime. Service people with heavy kitbags slung over their shoulders and civilians hurrying home from work formed an ever-changing kaleidoscope. There were long queues everywhere – at the ticket counters, the kiosks, the canteens, the left luggage. People were sitting in rows on the benches or on their luggage, some asleep. They passed a soldier with his girl locked in his arms: the girl was crying.

At the barrier she was told that the train had been cancelled. An unexploded bomb had been discovered somewhere on the line and there would be no more trains reaching Norwich that night. The ticket collector seemed almost triumphant about it. Feebly, she felt close to tears. Every day, every hour of her leave was precious.

Group Captain Palmer said: 'Have you somewhere to stay in London?'

'I'll have to book into a hotel, sir.'

'We'll find somewhere reasonable for you.' He was taking charge of the situation quietly and firmly. He put his hand under her arm, guiding her away from the barrier. 'But first of all you need a drink and something to eat.'

He knew most of the best restaurants in London and had his wife to thank for that. She had no idea how to cook and hated to eat at home anyway. He took Felicity to a small place in Knightsbridge where the cuisine was excellent and the surroundings unpretentious. It was one of Caroline's least favourite and the one he most preferred. Looking at his WAAF officer seated on the other side of the table, he thanked God silently for the unexploded bomb. While she was studying the menu, head bent, he had a chance to savour the situation. For once it wasn't a desk between them and there was no need, surely, for service protocol. They were both off-duty. He wished she would stop calling him 'sir' and relax a little.

She lifted her head with a slight smile. 'It all looks wonderful.'

'The chef's rather good. I can recommend almost everything. What would you like?'

She chose fish and he ordered from the head waiter who knew him well from previous visits but was the soul of discretion. No reference was made to his wife.

'Do you live in London, sir . . . when you're not at Colston?'

She was making polite conversation – no different from in the Officers' Mess, in their usual surroundings.

'Partly. We have a house here, and one in Gloucestershire. Or my wife has, to be more accurate. They belong to her.' He turned his wineglass round and round by its stem. 'As a matter of fact, I've always more or less considered the RAF to be my home.'

'You've been in the service a long time, haven't you, sir? I remember your saying.'

Caroline had been right, he must seem like Methuselah

to her. How could he seriously imagine that he could hold any interest for her at all, other than the compulsory one as her commanding officer?

'Yes,' he said shortly. 'A fair while.'

'You like the life, though, don't you, sir?'

It *is* my life, he almost answered. I have nothing else I care about. Except you. And I can never have that. Aloud he said: 'It has its drawbacks, of course, but on the whole it's a good life. Worthwhile.'

'You do a wonderful job, sir. Everyone admires you.'

He looked at her, surprised. It never occurred to him that he might be admired. Respected, yes. Feared, certainly. But not admired. She had spoken warmly and honestly, and he felt himself reddening. He cleared his throat.

'One does one's best. I couldn't do the job without the help of the WAAF, and that's a fact that I'm happy to acknowledge.'

It was her turn to blush. 'Thank you, sir. It's good of you to say so.'

'Not really. It's the truth, as it so happens, though, as you may remember it wasn't always my view.'

She laughed suddenly and so did he, with a faint hope stirring in his heart as they laughed together.

'Will you stay in when the war's over?' he asked.

'I haven't really thought about it, sir. Perhaps they'll disband the WAAF anyway – like they did after the last war.'

He smiled. 'I rather doubt that. I think we can say that you have proved your worth beyond dispute.'

She smiled too and put up her hand to tuck a wisp of hair behind one ear. The small, womanly gesture made him catch his breath. He longed to see how her hair would look loose about her face instead of in that neat roll she always wore. He pictured himself taking out the pins, freeing it with his fingers . . . He picked up his wineglass again quickly. As he did so, the sight of the four rings on his sleeve reminded Felicity of what she had been in danger of forgetting – who and what he was. He had shown another side to his character: a completely different sort of man that she had not realized existed beneath the austere exterior – shy, unsure of himself and, she suddenly understood, very lonely. She looked at him with new eyes and then away quickly as he met her gaze.

She tried to cover the uneasy moment by speaking briskly: 'It's very kind of you, sir . . . this dinner. It wasn't necessary. I could have managed perfectly well.'

'I don't doubt it, but I'm glad you didn't deny me the pleasure. Do you think that as we're off duty you could forget the "sir" for a while?'

The colour came into her cheeks again. 'Oh . . .'

'Please try. And I'll drop the "Section Officer". Just for this evening.'

She returned his smile rather nervously, he thought. And who could blame her? He spent most of his time putting the fear of God into people and keeping a clearly-marked distance from them, and she must be thinking that he was going soft in the head. It was a long while since he had acted the ogre with her but he had never dared to lower his guard further in case she might begin to suspect how he felt about her. He was not her only admirer on station, he knew; he had seen several young officers trying their luck but, apart from Speedy Dutton she seemed to have no serious interest in any of them. Dutton, he'd heard, had gone missing over France and he could not suppress the uncharitable wish that he'd stay there. It would be typical of him, though, to turn up again like a bad penny.

She managed not to say 'sir' more than once or twice during the rest of the meal, but it was clearly an effort. He kept the conversation as light as he could – well away from the war, from the station and from anything to do with service life. For a while he allowed himself the pretence that they were just a normal dinner couple with nothing standing between them, and for a while he almost convinced himself. It might have been the good food and the wine, or even just the pleasant atmosphere of the little restaurant, but he thought she was almost feeling that way too towards the end of the meal. He spun it out for as long as he dared, ordering liqueurs, drinking very slowly, delaying signalling for the bill, but, finally, she began to look anxiously at her watch.

'I ought to telephone my father to let him know I won't be there tonight or he'll be worried.'

'Of course. We'll ask if you can do it from here.'

But the restaurant's telephone was out of order.

'There's a quiet hotel not far away that I thought would suit you,' he suggested. 'You'll be able to telephone from there.'

He shone his torch along the whitened kerb edge for her as they walked in the direction of the Brompton Road. Just as they reached it the air raid siren suddenly went, its eerie rising and falling wail sounding shockingly loud in the dark.

'False alarm, I'm sure,' Palmer said. 'Some unidentified aircraft causing a bit of a panic. But we'd better take cover, just in case. My house is only across the road and there's a very safe cellar there.'

Caroline's house, he should have said, he reminded himself. His RAF pay could never have run to the Georgian house in the Georgian square in Knightsbridge. He unlocked the front door and shone his torch into the blackness of the hall.

'I'll have to do the blackout before we can turn on any lights. Can you see enough to come up the stairs?'

She followed him up to the first floor, guided by the torch beam, and into what was probably the drawing-room. The searchlights' white beams were criss-crossing the sky beyond the long windows but there was no noise of any aircraft. She could hear Group Captain Palmer moving about and the rattle of blackout blinds coming down over the windows, and then the swish of heavy curtains being drawn across. She waited in the darkness as the torchlight bobbed across the room and then he switched on chandelier lights. She gasped.

'What a beautiful room!'

The furniture was French, the upholstery pale blue, the rugs Chinese, the wallpaper watered silk. She saw her reflection in a huge gilt-framed looking-glass over the mantelpiece and her WAAF uniform was completely incongruous in its surroundings.

'Yes,' he said. 'My wife has excellent taste and the means to indulge it.' He switched on some table lamps and turned off the glittering chandelier. 'We could stay up here for a moment, if you like . . . so long as we don't hear any aircraft or ack-ack. Unless you prefer to go down to the shelter at once.'

She had had more than enough of sitting in shelters. 'I'd prefer to stay here, I think, sir.'

It was 'sir' again, he noted. 'Let me take your coat.'

He helped her off with it and draped it over the back of a chair beside her suitcase. He switched on the electric fire that stood in the grate. 'Would you like a drink?' He moved towards the drinks cabinet that he knew would be very well stocked.

'No, thank you, sir.' She seemed very ill at ease.

'I think I'll have another brandy . . .'

When he turned round from pouring it he saw that she was staring at the large oil painting of Caroline that hung on the wall. She had been painted wearing a long white muslin gown and carrying a big straw *bergère* hat with blue satin ribbons. The background was sunlit meadows and blue skies with fleecy white clouds.

'That's a lovely portrait of your wife.'

'Yes,' he said heavily. Caroline's affair with the artist had lasted six months before she had tired of him. She had spent a great deal of time in some Chelsea attic and taken to wearing flowing garments. Her Bohemian phase. 'She's away in Gloucestershire at the moment.'

With her latest lover, no doubt. Not that he cared a

damn. He drank some of the brandy. 'Would you like to try that phone call now?'

Tactfully, he left her alone in the room. She got through to Trunks on the white telephone and the connection was surprisingly quick. Her father's voice sounded faint, though. He would be holding the instrument gingerly, she guessed, and speaking from too far away. It was the only real modern convenience in the rectory and he had resisted its installation for a long time before parish needs won the day. She explained what had happened, but she didn't mention the air raid warning, or where she was.

She was replacing the receiver when Group Captain Palmer came back into the room.

'Did you get through all right?'

'Yes, thank you, sir.'

'I hope he wasn't too worried.'

She shook her head with a wry smile. 'I think he'd forgotten I was coming. He's very absent-minded. My mother used to keep track of everything for him, but now it's rather chaotic.'

'Has she been dead many years?'

'Eleven. She died when I was fourteen.'

He did not need reminding that she was only twenty-five to his forty-four. 'How very sad for you. You must miss her very much.' He could scarcely remember his own parents. They had both died a long time ago of fever in India and he had never seen much of them when they were alive. They had faded into the dim, distant past along with aunts and uncles, teachers and schoolfriends whom he hadn't seen for years and years. He retrieved his glass of brandy.

'Sure you won't have a drink?'

'No, thank you, sir.'

There was an awkward silence. She had remained standing behind one of the blue brocade chairs, keeping it as a barrier between them. The situation, he realized, was hopeless. She was probably deeply embarrassed by it and only wished to be gone. He tried to smile jovially.

'Well, looks like it was a false alarm . . . I expect the All Clear will go any minute. As soon as it does I'll take you round to that hotel. It's quite near.'

'Thank you, sir. You've been very kind.'

I'm not kind at all, he wanted to say. I'm in love with you. As passionately in love as any young man could be and more deeply than I knew was possible. If I had the guts I'd tell you so here and now, but I haven't because I'm so afraid that you'd be appalled and disgusted, or worse, amused. And that you'd ask to be posted away and I'd never see you again.

There was another long silence. They stood facing each other and she saw the desperate look in his eyes. In the restaurant she had felt pity for him, and understanding, but now she began to feel something much more than that and it was so surprising and so overwhelming that she could neither move nor speak. They went on staring at each other in silence.

The All Clear went suddenly, sounding its long steady note. It was the first time he had ever been sorry to hear it. He put down his glass and picked up her greatcoat from the chair.

'We can leave now.'

He held out the coat for her and she slid her arms into the sleeves, her back to him. When she turned round she began to thank him again and then faltered as she saw his expression. Before he could stop himself he had grasped her by both shoulders and pulled her towards him. Her mouth felt as soft as he had always imagined it to be, and as sweet. He let her go abruptly.

She grabbed at her suitcase and fled from the room. He followed her down the stairs slowly and wretchedly, knowing that he had lost her. She had reached the front door when he was halfway down and was struggling with the difficult catch in the dimness of the hallway.

He said, but without any hope, 'Felicity, please don't go.'

She turned and looked up at him.

'I love you,' he said humbly. 'Stay with me. Please.'

He held his breath because she had stopped trying to open the door. After a long, long moment she set down the suitcase on the floor.

Nineteen

Winnie had never known cold like it – not even in the worst winters in Suffolk, working on the farm. Out at dispersal the wind was merciless and chilled her to the bone. She had been issued with a leather jerkin and oilskins to wear over her overalls and had added a thick pullover, scarf and mittens from the Comforts Fund; the oilskins kept out the worst of the wet but nothing could keep out the bitter cold. The only warm place was close to the stove in the wooden hut where she tried unsuccessfully sometimes to thaw out her frozen fingers.

The day now began in pitch dark. She dressed hurriedly in clothes still damp from the day before and went out to wipe the rain or frost from the saddle of her bike before cycling the two miles to the camp for breakfast. She drank the hot tea and took the bacon sandwich with her, eating it as she biked out to dispersal. As dawn broke she was helping to take the covers off the picketed aircraft. After a hard night frost it was a slippery, dangerous job scrambling up onto the wings and the closed cockpits gave no good handholds. The canvas covers were stiff and unwieldy in already numb fingers and flapped violently like loose sails in the wind.

One morning, when she was doing a plug change, one of the plugs slipped from her cold fingers and fell down into the engine. She tried frantically to retrieve it but it had fallen into an inaccessible place and there seemed nothing for it but to confess to Chiefy. The twenty-four plugs all had to be accounted for on a change and a loose one could not be left somewhere in an engine where it might do damage. Winnie was close to tears. She had come so far

516

without making any serious mistakes and Chiefy, though he would never show it, seemed better disposed towards her than he had ever been. One small sparking plug would soon change all that. It would be back to cleaning oil filters, and fetching and carrying.

It was Ginger who came to her rescue with a bit of wire and a magnet which he produced, magician-like, from the pocket of his dungarees. After a bit of jiggling and fiddling around down in the engine the plug reappeared, as though by magic too, clamped firmly to the magnet.

'Useful trick to know,' he told her. 'And another one is to shove a bit of rag under where you're working then if you drop a plug or something it'll land on that.'

She wasn't sure how she'd have managed without Ginger. He helped her in all sorts of ways, showing her the quickest and best methods, the good short cuts and the bad ones. And warning her of the dangers.

'Always watch out for the props, love. You can't see 'em when they're spinnin'. Walk into one and it'll cut you to little pieces. Ever 'ad a dekko at Shorty's right 'and?'

Winnie shook her head. Shorty was a very tall, gangly aircrafthand on general duties.

'Not much of it left. Used to be a flight mech 'til the silly sod swung a prop one day and left is 'and stuck up in the air. Sliced all the fingers off neat as sausages.'

They went on brewing cocoa up on Ginger's tin-can brazier down in the dugout, out of the wind, and whenever he could he nicked food from the cookhouse for her. Once he brought some empty beer bottles and filled them with boiling water so that she could tuck them inside her battledress for warmth. Another time he presented her with a little copper brooch in the shape of a Spitfire that he'd made out of a penny. She pinned it to her dungarees.

'It's lovely, Ginger. Thanks.'

'Now there's a real beauty of a 'plane for you,' he told her. 'Makes the poor old Hurry look like a workhorse.'

'I still like the Hurricanes best. I don't know why, but I do. Better than any of them.'

They talked about a pilot who kept complaining of a mag drop where none existed.

'Don't want to worry about that, sweetheart,' Ginger said, spearing another piece of stolen bread on his screwdriver. 'Chiefy says he's yellow. Any excuse not to go up.'

And they talked of a new rigger.

'Dim as a ruddy Toc H lamp,' was Ginger's scornful verdict. 'They should've sent us another WAAF. We'd've been a sight better off.'

'Tell that to Chiefy.'

'I did.'

'Whatever did he say?'

'Can't repeat that. But that's just 'is way. Thinks a lot of you now, you know. Though you'd never guess it, and he'd make sure you never did. Remember that French-Canadian laddie caused all that trouble about you t'other day?'

Winnie nodded. She held her hands over the fire and rubbed them together. 'He didn't want to fly my Hurry, did he? Not a bit.'

Ginger grinned. 'I was in Chiefy's office when 'e come in and shouts there's a woman sittin' in 'is cockpit. "Yes," says Chiefy, all innocent-like, "that's my flight mech and she's warming the engine up for you, sir." So this bloke goes mad and starts to stamp about the place and yell that 'e's not flyin' any aircraft some bloody woman's been fiddlin' about with . . . Chiefy waits 'til 'e's finished, then 'e says, quiet as anythin' but very firm-like, that there's no other aircraft available. An' then 'e says that 'e'll be a lot safer in that particular one than any other 'cos you take more trouble than all the men put together.'

Winnie put her hands over her cheeks. 'Did he really say that?'

'True as I'm sittin' 'ere,' Ginger told her, spreading the toast with marg for her. 'Mind you, pigs'd fly 'fore 'e ever said anythin' of the kind to you. But I 'eard it with my own ears.'

That was another thing Ginger did for her: boosted her spirits, encouraged her, made her feel that she wasn't doing so badly after all.

The incident with the French-Canadian pilot had shaken her for a bit. He had been shockingly rude to her and she had watched him take off, in tears, and waited anxiously for over an hour until he returned and landed safely. He had strode past her on his way to the crew room without a glance or word.

Most of the pilots were pleasant enough, though. Some, she thought, treated you rather like a piece of equipment — as though you weren't really there at all. She didn't think they meant it, it was just that they had other things on their mind than being nice to the flight mech who looked after their aircraft.

One of a new intake of pilots was specially charming. Nothing wrong with his nerves, Winnie thought thankfully, as she went to help him. No nervous stumble as he sprang up into the cockpit. No shaky hands as she passed him the straps over his shoulders for fastening. No white, strained face. He smiled at her and thanked her nicely. The blue silk scarf that he wore round his neck exactly matched his eyes. She hopped down off the Hurricane's wing root and watched as he taxied out. No imaginary mag drops either. He took off quickly and smoothly. Nothing to worry about there.

When the pilot returned she was helping Ginger put back an obstinate engine cowling, sitting astride it to weigh it down for him. She lifted her head to watch the Hurricane make its approach and then fly low across the 'drome and flick into a showy roll. Ginger looked up from the cowling at the noise.

'Playing silly buggers. They'll 'ave his goolies off for that.'

They both watched as the fighter climbed away, stall-turned and came down for another low run over the 'drome. Halfway across it went into a second roll, but more clumsily this time. Something went wrong and the Hurricane seemed to hang motionless in the air for a moment before plunging straight into the ground. Winnie stared in horror as fire engines and the blood wagon tore across the grass towards the wreck.

'Stupid sod,' Ginger said. 'Dead before 'e's got a chance to get hisself killed.'

One wet, cold and miserable day an RAF sergeant stopped Winnie when she was biking back from dispersal.

'There's someone asking for you at the guard'ouse, Jervis.'

'For *me*?'

'That's wot I said. Better get over there and see 'oo it is.'

She pedalled over and there, waiting for her and soaking wet from the rain, was Taffy.

'Would you like to tell me what's wrong, my dear? Or shouldn't I ask?'

Felicity looked up. Her father was smiling at her gently from his chair on the other side of the fire-place.

'Wrong?'

'You've been sitting gazing into the fire for a very long time, as though you were somewhere else. And since you've been home it's been very obvious to me that something's troubling you. I can see that you're unhappy. That something *is* very wrong. Perhaps talking about it might help.'

'I can't tell you, Father.'

'Why not? Are you afraid it might shock me? I can assure you it won't. I'm quite unshockable. But I might be able to give you some advice, perhaps. It's a man, I imagine. The one who telephoned you yesterday. And today. Are you in love with him?'

She nodded.

'Then you should be happy. Not unhappy. So long as he's in love with you, too, and I'm quite sure he is.'

'He's married, Father.'

There was a pause. 'Ah, I see . . . My poor child. What a misfortune for you. We can't help whom we fall in love with but such a situation can only bring you terrible heartache. Is he in the RAF?'

'Yes.'

'At your station?'

'Yes. He says he's been in love with me for a long time, but he never showed it. I never knew . . . had no idea. I never dreamed of such a thing. He's older, you see. And married. I never thought of him that way . . . until recently.'

'Quite rightly.'

'His wife –' She swallowed. 'His wife has been unfaithful to him for years. They've only stayed together for appearances.'

'Those whom God hath joined together . . .'

'I know, I *know*,' she said in anguish. 'But it isn't a proper marriage any longer.'

'It is still a marriage and they have both made solemn vows to each other. You must not be a party to anything that might encourage them to break those vows, Felicity. You must ask to be moved away – put yourself out of reach of temptation.' He leaned forward and put his hand on her arm. 'Believe me, this can only bring you great unhappiness otherwise. You cannot build a good life on such an unsure foundation. And you must not try to take away another woman's husband, whatever the circumstances. You must see that.'

She did see it. She saw it very clearly and she knew that her father was right. But she could not forget that night in London. And all the time she thought of him.

There had been no hotel. She had stayed with him all night and had woken in his arms and knowing that she loved him in return. It had happened against all logic or reason or wisdom and she could not see how she could undo it. Ever.

Taffy had hitch-hiked all the way from Essex where he was stationed now and had walked the last five miles to the camp in the pouring rain. Water dripped off him onto the guardroom floor, forming puddles, but he did not seem to notice or care. He looked at her with his intense gaze.

'I've got leave,' he told her. 'I've found myself a room at the Lamb and Flag.'

'How did you know I was here?'

'I'm stationed not far from your home, Elmbury. We're just near the Suffolk border. So, one day I rode over there on my bike to see what it was like and where you lived. I asked about you in the pub and they told me your husband had died. They told me where the farm was too, so I went and knocked on the door and your mother said about you doing the training at Hednesford and being sent up here. I came as soon as I could.'

She wished he hadn't. 'It's a long way to come,' she said, flustered. 'You shouldn't have.'

'I told you I wouldn't let you go . . . that I'd find you wherever you were.'

She went out with him to the Lamb and Flag, catching the evening bus down. She hadn't wanted to at all but seeing as he'd come all that way and got so wet, it was very hard to refuse. In the bus he put his arm round the back of her seat and in the pub he went on gazing at her.

'You've changed a bit, Winnie. Seems like you've got a lot more sure of yourself. And you're lovelier than ever. You've got your wish, haven't you? You're a flight mech now, like you always wanted. How are you getting on?'

'Not so bad,' she said. She told him about Chiefy and about Ginger and all the gang.

'This Ginger,' he said. 'What's he to you, then?'

'He's a friend,' she answered stiffly, thinking that it was none of his business. 'He's helped me a lot.'

Taffy drank his beer with his eyes still on her face. He was thinking of the small back bedroom he had upstairs in the pub, and wondering how it had been with that weak and failing husband of hers . . . thinking of how he would show her what it could be like, if she'd give him the chance.

'Don't look at me like that, Taffy.'

'Sorry.' He lowered his eyes. 'Funny seeing you drinking beer. It was always orange juice.' He took hold of one of her hands, examining the ingrained grease, the grazes and half-healed cuts, the split nails, the reddened, chapped skin. He turned it over. 'Seems a pity, really, you spoiling your hands like this.' He lifted it to his lips but she snatched it quickly away. Watch it, he said to himself. Don't frighten her and you'll get there in the end.

On her day off they went into Dundee on the bus. She hadn't wanted to, but, again, she didn't like to refuse. In an odd way it was a comfort to see someone from the old days at Colston – if only it didn't have to be Taffy. She tried to remember that he had been a help too, like Ginger, and had taught her a lot. She had reason to be grateful to him. It was raining again and so they spent a long time sitting in a café, eating fish and chips and drinking tea.

'There's not much to do here, really,' Winnie said, feeling she ought to apologize for the bleakness of it all. The cold, the rain, the seedy little café with its smeary oilskin tablecloths pockmarked with cigarette burns. 'Some evenings there's a dance, but that's all. Except for the pictures.'

'I'll take you to the flicks,' he told her.

'I expect you'll've seen the film.'

'Doesn't matter. It'll be dry and warm.'

And dark, he added inwardly.

He made sure they were in the back row of the stalls. It was an Old Mother Riley film that he'd seen before but he didn't care. He scarcely looked at the screen. His eyes were on Winnie's profile – on the curve of her cheek, the soft outline of her mouth. Very carefully he put his arm round her shoulders. He felt her stiffen and as he touched the back of her neck very lightly, she hunched her shoulders.

'Don't, Taffy, please.'

'No harm in that, is there?'

He kept his arm round her and after a while shifted a little sideways so that his head was nearly touching hers. She leaned sharply away from him.

'It's all right, Winnie, there's nothing to fret about.'

But she sat so rigidly that he dared not make any further move in case she took flight. He burned with frustration in the darkness. He had had such hopes, such dreams about her . . . of how glad she would be to see him and how she would realize at long last what she had been missing. Now that feeble husband of hers was dead there was nothing to stand in his way. Nothing for her to feel guilty about. He was a good lover, he knew that. Women had always told him so – showed him so. He had imagined making love to Winnie many times and he longed to make it reality. Never before had he had any difficulty in getting a woman whom he wanted and he wanted Winnie more than he had ever wanted any of them.

They caught the last bus back to the camp. It was full of other RAF and WAAF and reeked of beer and cigarettes, of cheap perfume and damp greatcoats. Taffy pulled Winnie into a seat near the back where other couples were sitting with their arms round each other. As the bus jerked away from the stop the single dim blackout bulb was switched off and the necking began.

Taffy didn't say anything; he didn't speak a word. He simply turned to her as she shrank against the window and started to kiss her.

At the front of the bus the airmen had begun singing loudly.

524

When this lousy war is over,
Oh! how happy I shall be!
When I get my civvy clothes on,
No more soldiering for me . . .

She was struggling but he was taking no notice at all. It was just like it had been in the stores shed that Christmas at Colston, only this time there was no escape and he was going on and on, and worse and worse.

No more church parades on Sunday,
No more asking for a pass,
I shall tell the old Flight Sergeant
Where to stuff his blinking pass.

She could feel his hand sliding underneath her skirt now and his fingers on the bare skin of her thigh above her stocking top. She pushed his hand away but after a while it came back again. And all the while he went on kissing her, his tongue deep in her mouth. The bus veered round a sharp corner and swayed on through the blackness. The singing had become a roar.

AC2s are common.
AC1s are rare.
LACs are plentiful,
You'll meet them anywhere . . .

Her head was pressed back so hard against the window blind that she could not turn it away, nor could she get her hands against his chest to push him off; he was holding her too tightly.

Corporals they are stinkers.
Sergeants they are too.
But the Station Warrant Officer
Is a bastard through and through.

525

At last the bus jolted to a stop and the light came on. A girl's voice hissed frantically at the very back: 'Christ, Bert, we're there! Help do me up, quick!' Taffy let Winnie go and she rubbed her mouth, trembling. She stumbled after him off the bus past grinning, leering faces.

The rain had turned to sleet, driving into their faces as they walked to the guardhouse. When he tried to take her arm she shook him off. As they reached the gate he said contritely: 'I'm sorry, Winnie. I didn't mean to be like that . . . couldn't help myself, see. I love you. More than I've ever loved any girl. I want you more than I've ever wanted anyone. I can't help it . . . You could love me, too, if only you'd let yourself. You know you could – '

'*Stop it!*' She turned on him furiously. 'I don't want to hear any more. I don't love you and I *never* will. Can't you understand that?' The taste of him was still in her mouth and the feel of his hands still crawled on her skin. She shivered with revulsion.

But he went on fiercely, relentlessly. 'I'll *make* you love me, Winnie. I won't give up. I'll write to you and I'll come and see you when you're home on leave.' He gripped her arm tightly and forced her round to face him. 'Promise me you'll let me know when you're home next. Promise me you'll write and tell me. *Promise.*'

'No,' she said. 'I *won't* promise. I don't want to see you ever again.'

'You'll see me again all right, Winnie. I swear it. I told you, I'll never give up.'

She tugged her arm free of him and ran off through the camp gateway without a backward glance. Taffy stood for a moment, looking after her, then he turned up the collar of his greatcoat against the sleet and trudged off to the Lamb and Flag. And every step of the way he thought of Winnie.

'Turn on the lamp, please, Virginia. I can't see to count these stitches.'

Virginia rose to switch on the standard lamp close by

her mother's chair and then returned to her own seat and picked up her knitting. She was turning the heel of a thick woollen sock and her mother was halfway through a balaclava helmet. Sometimes she wondered whether all the knitted garments being produced in almost every home in Britain found wearers in the services or whether there was an enormous storehouse somewhere piled to the roof with sweaters and scarves, socks and gloves and balaclava helmets, all knitted with varying degrees of skill but all with patriotism in every stitch. It was rumoured that the saucepans appealed for by the Government to turn into Spitfires and Hurricanes, Blenheims and Wellingtons lay unused in great metal mountains. Who would wear her socks? Some serviceman fighting in the cold of Northern Europe or on the Atlantic, or on a convoy to Russia? She hoped they would give him some warmth and comfort, whoever he was.

They listened to the nine o'clock news on the wireless, as usual. The Chindits had crossed into Burma, the Russian Army were advancing on Rostov, the American forces were fighting fiercely in the Guadalcanal . . .

Her mother began another row. 'Those Americans . . . There were two of them outside the newsagents today, chewing gum and slouching about. I thought they were Canadians at first by the way they spoke. If it wasn't for the uniform it would be impossible to tell the difference. They both appear to be quite uncivilized. I'm glad you never brought that Canadian sergeant here again. A very rough diamond, I thought.'

Virginia's hands went very still and the sock hung motionless from its heel. 'I couldn't bring him here again, Mother, because he was killed last August. He died when they raided Dieppe.'

'Oh. You didn't tell me.'

'Why should I? You wouldn't have cared. You made it very clear that you didn't like him.'

'There's no need to use that tone of voice, Virginia. I really don't know what's got into you these days. It must

527

be the bad influence of the WAAF. I never wanted you to join. You should never have associated with anyone like that. I brought you up to have some standards.'

She put her knitting down on her lap. 'No, Mother, you brought me up to be stupidly snobbish, like yourself – to have all the *wrong* standards. You think that just because someone speaks or eats or behaves differently, or comes from a different background then they're not worth anything. That's not true and I found it out long ago. Neil was a wonderful person – decent and kind and brave – and I loved him. We were engaged and we were going to be married as soon as we could and live in Canada after the war was over. And I was glad that we'd be far away from you. I'll never forgive you for the way you treated him when he came here. *Never.*'

'Have you gone quite mad, Virginia? You couldn't possibly have married him. It would have been a ridiculous mistake and you would have lived to regret it. There's no need to make all this fuss. It wasn't my fault that he was killed. I hear that raid on Dieppe was completely useless. No point to it at all. I sometimes wonder if Mr Churchill knows what he's doing.'

Virginia stood up, clutching the sock to her breast. 'I'm not going to listen to you any more. I'm not going to listen to anything you say again in my whole life. I'm not surprised Father left you. You probably drove him to it.'

'*Virginia!* That's a wicked thing to say, and to your own mother! After all I've done for you . . . You will apologize this instant.'

'No, I won't. I'm not a bit sorry. I meant every word of it.' She picked up her knitting bag and put the sock and needles away. Her mother was gaping at her, white and shocked. 'I'm going to bed now. I have to leave very early in the morning so I won't disturb you. And I'm not sure if I shall ever come here again.'

She went out and slammed the sitting-room door behind her.

* * *

The snow lay thick and white over the aerodrome and the wind whipped it up into stinging flurries that made Winnie blink as she drew the nozzle of the de-icing equipment along the leading edge of the Hurricane's wing. The cold fluid trickled back down her arm, finding its way under her sleeve and leaving an uncomfortable sticky trail. It was a horrible job and she hated it. She blinked hard again and wiped the snow away from her face. It clung to her wool mittens in frozen little lumps like burrs that she would have to pick off. Her fingers looked like purple sausages and were too cold to feel any longer; her throat felt as though it were on fire. She had had a bad sore throat for several days that had started after she'd been out helping to clear the runways, and got steadily worse. She'd been to the sickbay and they'd given her something to gargle with, but it hadn't helped much. Today her limbs ached, too, and the glands in her neck were swollen right up. She swallowed hard.

The sound of an aircraft approaching made her look up and she saw that it was coming in to land – a big, two-engined one that must be visiting. From habit, she tried to identify it and, as it came closer, saw that it was a Hampden. She watched it land and lumber down the runway and then went back to the de-icing job and finished it somehow. After that, she gave Ginger a hand changing a radiator, holding the fairing bath for him while he undid the screws.

He clicked his tongue at her. 'You look that bad, Winnie. You ought to be in bed.'

'I'm all right. It's just this sore throat,' she croaked. 'It'll go soon.'

The Hampden was trundling noisily round the peri track.

'Well, if it's not better by tomorrow, mind you report sick. I don't want to see you out here in this weather. You'll go and make yourself really ill.'

'All right.'

She helped him lower the radiator, wondering how

much longer she'd be able to keep going. Her throat hurt so much now that she could hardly swallow at all. Ginger looked at her anxiously.

'You go and sit down in the 'ut for a while, love.' He tucked her scarf higher round her neck. 'Get yourself a bit warm. I'll finish this off. NAAFI van'll be round in a tick so you can 'ave a nice hot cuppa.'

She went and sat on her toolbox in the hut, close to the coke stove and with her arms wrapped round her body. She felt dreadful. Worse than ever. If it went on like this she'd have to do like Ginger said. She couldn't remember ever feeling ill like this in her life; she'd never had anything worse than a cold. Chiefy would probably think she was putting it on just to stay in the hut by the stove . . . After a while she went to peer out of the window. The visiting Hampden had parked close by and shut down its engines – Peggy eighteens, she remembered from the training course. She also remembered the instructor's warning about the Pegasus engine's nasty habit of suddenly kicking over and spinning a few revs after they'd been switched off.

'NAAFI up!' someone shouted outside.

She saw the NAAFI van drive up and people started running towards it from all directions. You had to be quick off the mark if you didn't want to be at the back of the queue. Ginger flung open the hut door.

'Bung us your mug, sweet'eart. I'll get yours for you. You stay there in the warm.'

She watched him as he ran, a mug in each hand, in the direction of the van. The Hampden stood in his path and she saw him duck under its starboard wing, close to the engine nacelle, taking a short cut. Then, all of a sudden, his body arced high up into the air as the Pegasus kicked over without any warning and its propeller caught him. His head went one way, his limbs another and what was left of Ginger fell to the ground in a bloody, mangled mess. The enamel mugs rolled over and over across the concrete.

Winnie ran out of the hut. She stood there with her hands to her cheeks and her mouth opened in a scream that went on and on and on. It was Chiefy who caught her in his arms and turned her face into his chest, away from the sight, and, as she slumped against him, picked her up and carried her away.

The head floated above her, its eyes looking at her from behind a pair of hornrimmed spectacles. Like Ginger's head it had no body. Winnie tried to speak to it but her throat seemed to have closed up completely. She was lying on a bed somewhere, she knew that. The room was dim and behind the floating head there was a green screen.

Its mouth was moving now, making sounds that she could vaguely hear but not really understand. The head disappeared and then another head appeared, wearing a white cap. She made another great effort to speak.

'Ginger . . . Ginger . . .'

'It's all right,' the second head told her. 'I'm here. Go to sleep.'

Winnie drifted away.

She was in the isolation hospital for a month, lying flat on her back and wavering deliriously between life and death. At last she turned towards life. She was not allowed any visitors but when she was feeling better a WAAF officer came to see her. She was plump and smiling, in a uniform that was too tight for her, and she sat on the end of Winnie's bed, making the springs creak.

'Well, you did give us a fright being so ill, dear. You've had diphtheria, you know. What a to-do! Everyone confined to camp in quarantine for three weeks. We were quite worried about you. Lots of people have been asking after you — you're a very popular girl. How are you feeling now, then?'

'Better, thank you, ma'am.'

'Jolly good! That's the spirit.'

The officer didn't mention Ginger at all. She just went on talking cheerfully.

'Now, we're giving you a month's sick leave so you'll be able to go home and convalesce and get into tip-top shape again.'

Suffolk and home. 'Thank you, ma'am.'

'And how would you feel if we arranged a transfer for you down south — somewhere in Suffolk, if possible, nearer your home? Would you like that?'

'As a flight mech, ma'am?'

'Rather! You're much too good to lose, so I hear. Flight Sergeant McFarlane has been singing your praises no end.'

Chiefy being so kind. Chiefy holding her tight in his arms and comforting her . . . Don't think about Ginger. Not now. Not yet. Not until you can think about it without wanting to start screaming again and cry and cry for what had happened.

Winnie said weakly: 'Thank you, ma'am.'

She turned her head away and closed her eyes.

Twenty

The Fordson chugged steadily across the ten-acre field, hauling the plough. As Winnie neared the headland on the far side, she stood up on the axle and looked back at the furrows left behind her. They were dead straight. She had marked the field carefully with sticks before starting, measuring forty paces in from the side at each end. If there was one thing Dad couldn't abide it was crooked furrows for people to see over the hedge. And he still thought the horses could do it better. Prince and Smiler would follow straight to a handkerchief tied on the stick; only sometimes they'd ramble a bit in the way a tractor never would, so long as you drove it right. It was very bouncy going along and the iron seat was hard as anything but she'd tied an old sack filled with straw on top, like a cushion, to make it more comfortable.

She'd done half of the field and the sun was high in the sky. Time to stop for a bite and a bit of a rest. She switched off the ignition and turned off the petrol tap and the engine petered to a stop. She climbed down and took her sandwich out of the tool box on the side, and sat down by the hedge to eat it. The rooks were cawing away loudly, fussing over their nests in the elms behind her, but otherwise it was peaceful and the sun felt warm. Hot almost. It was hard to remember how cold it had been in the winter. The hedges were all coming out and she could see the new leaves on the trees. She felt a lot better now. Stronger in every way. She could think of Ginger without crying. The trick was not to think about how he'd died but only to remember him alive . . . to blot out the nightmare completely, as though it had never happened. She wished she could have talked to Ken about Ginger. It would have been a comfort to hear him say in his quiet way: *It wasn't your fault, Winn. You couldn't've known he'd go and do the very thing he'd warned you against*. But Ken was in his grave in the churchyard and she would never hear his voice again. Mrs Jervis had sold the shop to someone else and gone to live with a sister somewhere in Sussex. Everything had changed.

She ate some more of the cheese sandwich and squinted along the furrows, viewing them from a different angle. Dead straight. Dad grumbled even more these days. Mostly it was about the Ministry of Agriculture who kept telling him what to grow. They'd told him to plough up some of the pasture, too, and he'd been furious about that. But the truth was he was making quite a bit of money out of the war. Most of the farmers must be. The country needed all the food they could provide.

When Dad wasn't grumbling about the Ministry it was usually about the Americans – about the way they'd taken over good farmland for their airfields and chopped down so many trees and made a real mess of the countryside. And he grumbled all the time about how their 'planes frightened the animals and stopped them producing. And how they drove their lorries and jeeps about too fast and often on the wrong side of the road. And how they'd taken over the Pig and Whistle and were drinking it dry of whisky and beer. But he was making good money out of the Americans too, selling them bacon and chickens and eggs and butter. And they stood him plenty of drinks in the Pig and Whistle, so Gran said. Gran heard lots of stories about the Yanks, even though she never left the house.

'Some o' them've got black skins,' she had told Winnie, nodding her head. 'Black as coal, so I hear. They say as they've got tails too, though I don' see as how they could have . . . couldn' sit down, could they?'

'Of course they haven't got tails, Gran. They'd be just the same as us but with another colour skin. I saw some in a lorry an' they didn't look much different.'

'Huh. Wonder if it comes off?'

'What?'

'The black o' course. When they wash.'

Winnie had laughed. 'It's not like that black you're always gettin' on your face, sittin' close to the fire all the time. You can't wash it off, or I 'spect they would. I should think they'd sooner be white if they could be.'

'I haard the white ones all be millionaires, thass what they say.'

'Who says, Gran?'

'Folks.'

She would never say who had passed on the gossip, but people came to the back door all the time for eggs and milk, so there was never a shortage of informants.

The peace was suddenly shattered by the noise of a big aircraft taking off. Winnie turned her head to see a bomber rising from the direction of the American Air Force base across the fields. Dad would fuss again about losing unborn lambs if the ewes took fright, but at least he hadn't lost any of his land, not like poor Josh Stannard who'd lost most of his farm. She watched the big bomber climbing slowly upwards. It was a Flying Fortress. A Boeing B17. Four Wright engines, twelve hundred horsepower each. She'd learned all that from old Ebenezer Stannard who'd been allowed to stay in his cottage on the edge of the base and spent his hours watching the bombers come and go. Not as nice looking as the Lancaster. It was a lumpy sort of thing, bristling with guns; there was even a gun turret hanging down underneath. But then the Americans went on daylight ops, so they'd need them. As it passed over the field she could see the big white American star on its side and a coloured picture painted up near the nose that looked like it was of a girl in a bathing suit, and not much of one either. Most of their bombers had pictures on them like that. What would Ginger have made of

535

it? He'd liked 'planes to be 'planes and not messed around with like they were toys. He'd warned her once about the Yanks. She'd discovered already that they were even worse than the RAF. One day, when she'd biked over to take a look at the new airfield, a jeep with four of them in it had passed her on the road and slowed down. They'd been such a nuisance that she'd had to stop. She'd stood on tiptoe to peer over the hedge and had seen how trees had been felled and other hedges rooted up. Where spring crops should have been growing was a sea of sticky brown mud, crossed by ribbons of grey concrete. The perimeter track ran along within fifty yards or so of where she was standing and she could just see the threshold of the main runway. Close by there was a concrete hardstand where men were working on a Flying Fortress. She had studied them unobserved for some time. They were dressed in grey-green overalls and wearing funny kinds of caps with the brims turned up. They chewed gum as they worked and when one of them shouted out to another she could hear the twangy way they talked – just like in the films. It was odd to hear it in real life.

She followed the bomber with her gaze as it climbed away and flew out of sight, and then she stood up, brushing her hands free of crumbs. Time to get back to work again before Dad came to the gate and started yelling across at her.

Nora Gibson came over one evening. She lived down the lane and had joined the Women's Land Army. She came dressed up in her uniform, the brim of the brown hat pulled down over one eye and her big bosom looking bigger still in the tight green jersey. She followed Winnie out to the barn when she went to bottle-feed two orphan lambs, and sat on an upturned pail, watching her and talking all the while.

'I've got a smashin' new boyfriend, Winn. He's a Yank.

One of those up at the base. Rear gunner, he is. Mum takes in washin' for some of them – that's how I got to know him. You never saw such good-lookin' blokes . . . like film stars, they are. And they've got such lovely manners and say such nice things to you. And they've got all this money . . .'

'What's that got to do with it, Nora?'

Nora flicked a piece of straw from her breeches. 'Well, it makes a difference. You can't help likin' it . . . least, I can't. And they're so generous with it. Buzz is always givin' me chocolate and chewin' gum, and he gives Mum tins of ham and fruit and things like that. Last time he gave me a lipstick. A lovely bright pink, it is, an' my old one was all finished.'

'That's a funny name – Buzz.'

'Short for Buster, or somethin' like that. Lots of them have those sort of names – like Chuck 'n Hank 'n Tex. But they're such fun, Winnie, you've no idea . . .' Nora sighed. 'Not like most of our boys – *they're* so dull.'

'I don't think they're dull,' Winnie said. The smaller of the lambs had given up the effort of sucking. If she didn't persuade it to keep going, it would soon give up on life too. She picked it up and held it close against her, coaxing the teat back into its mouth. It began again, but feebly. 'I think they're just as good as the Americans. Better.'

'You ever met a Yank, then?'

'No, but I've seen them around. They make a lot of noise, seems to me, and look like they show off a lot too. Dad says they act like they'd already won the war for us when they're in the pub. I don't think I'd like them much.'

'You can't say that 'til you've met one – it's not fair. You ought to come to one of their dances. I've never had such fun.' Nora's eyes were shining. 'There was this wonderful band playin' an' you should see the way they dance. They do what's called jitterbuggin'. It's fast as anythin' an' they throw the girls right over their shoulders. Buzz is teachin' me.'

The lamb was sucking a bit more strongly now and waggling its little tail. Winnie tilted the bottle carefully. 'Doesn't sound much fun to me, bein' thrown around . . .'

'Oh, Winnie, you're so old-fashioned sometimes! It's the new way people dance. Why don't you come and see for yourself? There's a dance on Saturday and I'm goin'. Come with me. They send one of their trucks over to the war memorial to pick us up, so we don't have to worry about gettin' there and back. The wolf wagon they call it,' Nora giggled.

'I don't think so, thanks, Nora.'

'You're scared!'

'No, I'm not. I just don't want to go.'

'But it'd do you good, Winnie. After being so ill, an' everythin'. You have to go back soon, don't you?'

'Next week. They've posted me to Flaxton.'

'That's only a few miles away. Better 'n Scotland. What sort of place is it?'

'It's a Conversion Unit for bomber crews. They re-train them onto new aircraft.'

'Bombers! Fancy you workin' on those big engines, Winnie. Must be so difficult.'

'Not when you've been taught how.'

'You should've been a Land Girl like me, then you wouldn't've had to learn a thing. Milkin' cows, muckin' out, pullin' turnips, pickin' sprouts, cleanin' ditches . . .' Nora rolled her eyes. 'Sometimes it gets me down. Still, it's my birthday on Saturday and there's the dance to look forward to then. Say you'll come to it, Winnie. Go on! For *my* sake.'

Winnie set the lamb down gently and watched it wobble off to rejoin the other one. 'All right then, Nora, seein' as it's your birthday an' that, I s'pose I can't say no.' She didn't want Nora thinking she was afraid.

*　　*　　*

She heard the music long before she saw the band. It sounded loud enough to wake the dead – a whole lot of brass instruments blasting some tune out at top speed. She could hear it clearly in the cloakroom where they'd gone first to take off their coats. Nora was in her Land Army uniform, which she said Buzz liked a lot, and she went straight to the mirror to put on some more of the bright pink lipstick that he'd given her. Winnie didn't think it went very well with the green and brown but she didn't say anything. She was in civvies herself – the old cotton frock she'd worn when she'd gone off to Colston. She stood waiting for Nora and listening to two ATS talking to each other in put-on American accents. They kept giggling and nudging each other. She already wished that she hadn't come.

Nora grabbed her arm; her mouth was a glistening pink bow. 'Come on, let's find Buzz.'

It was like being thrust into a foreign land. There were Americans everywhere – smooth American uniforms, loud, drawling American voices, back-slapping, gum-chewing, hands-in-pockets, bold-eyed Americans . . . She hurried after Nora who was heading in the direction of the music. It was growing louder at every step and by the time they reached the entrance to the big hall where the dance was being held, she felt like clapping her hands over her ears.

In front of her a seething mass of dancers twisted and writhed and leaped about. She watched them in amazement. Nora was jigging from side to side, swinging her arms to the beat of the music. A small and wiry airman bounded up to her.

'Hiya, doll!'

'Winnie . . . this is Buzz.'

'Hi there, sugar. How ya doin'?' He nodded to her and clicked his fingers at Nora. 'Come'n, baby, let's dance.'

He jerked Nora away into the mass and Winnie backed nervously against a wall. The music was getting even louder, the dancing even more frenzied. The brass players in the band had leaped to their feet and were trumpeting and sawing up into the air and down at their feet, and the drummer was flailing about him like a madman. She could feel the whole floor shaking beneath her. It made her dizzy to watch the men spinning their partners back and forth and round and round. She stared at a couple whirling towards her – a tall, fair airman dancing with a blond girl in a mauve dress and high-heeled shoes. They were so good that people were making room for them. Winnie gasped as the American tossed the girl clean over his shoulder. There was a flash of her suspenders and knickers for all to see and an even clearer view as she slid on her back along the floor straight between his legs. It had brought them close to the wall and as he jerked the girl to her feet again and swung her round, he winked broadly at Winnie standing a few feet from him, open-mouthed.

The music changed at last to a slower, quieter tune and what she supposed must be a sergeant asked her to dance – only he wore his stripes upside down on his arm. To her relief he made no attempt to throw her around. The music was still too loud to hear much of what he was saying and the little she did hear she couldn't understand very well. He told her that he was from somewhere called Minnesota and she nodded politely without the least idea where that was. At the end of the dance she escaped back to her corner against the wall.

After a short pause the band struck up again, fast and furiously, and, to her horror, the fair one that she had watched dancing with the girl in mauve suddenly appeared before her and caught her by the hand. In panic she tried to pull herself free.

'Please . . . I can't . . . I don't know how.'

'Sure you do. Nothin' to it. I'll show you.'

He dragged her relentlessly onto the floor, ignoring her pleas and protests. 'We'll just take it nice 'n easy. You'll soon get it.'

He took both her hands in his and swung her this way

540

and that. Scarlet in the face, Winnie struggled to keep time with the music. He grinned at her.

'You're doin' great . . . See, I told you it was easy. Don't worry 'bout a thing.'

He put one hand on her waist and suddenly spun her round like a top. Winnie found herself being propelled back and forth, and roundabout. She had never felt so embarrassed or so foolish in her life. Stiff and awkward, stumbling and blushing furiously, she had no alternative but to make the best of it and pray for the music to stop. But it seemed to go on for ever, and the American went on twisting and turning her until she felt so dizzy she would have fallen down if he hadn't held on to her tightly. The room whirled about her, other people dissolving into blurs. As the music swelled to a final, blasting crescendo, he put his hands on her waist again and lifted her high into the air above his head.

Her feet back on the ground and the music stopped at last, Winnie stood with her eyes shut, trying to stem the dizziness. She began to stagger off the floor, but he blocked her way.

'Hey – don't run away yet. You were doin' fine.'

He was grinning at her again. Laughing, more like, she thought bitterly. He'd made a fine fool of her, that's what he'd done. She lurched sideways as though she were drunk and he put out his hand to steady her.

'Gee, I'm sorry. Guess I should've been more careful. Look, this number's real slow . . .'

She found herself being propelled round the floor again, but gently this time. The music was blessedly quiet and the band had stopped jumping about. Her sense of balance returned but not her sense of humour. Inside she was still indignant at the cavalier way he'd behaved. She could tell by the way he was looking down at her, though, that he hadn't a clue how cross she was.

'Saw you standin' over by the wall when I was dancin' a while back . . . lookin' like you was real shocked by everythin'. Real startled. I said to myself, what's a pretty girl like that doin' standin' there all alone, an' nobody lookin' after her? That ain't right. I'll have to do somethin' 'bout that, soon as I get the chance. I ain't seen you here before. What's your name?'

'Winifred Jervis,' she said coldly.

'Cute name. Where're you from?'

'Elmbury.'

'That so? Funny, I ain't never seen you. I figured I knew all the girls round here.'

I bet he does, she thought, and he must think he's God's gift to them. 'I'm generally away.'

'Doin' what?'

'I'm a WAAF.'

'Oh, yeah . . . I've met some of those. There's a whole bunch here tonight. Part of the RAF, ain't that so? How come you're not in uniform like the rest?'

'I'm on leave.'

'How long for?'

'Two more days.'

'That all? Gee, that's a shame. Where're you stationed?'

She felt like saying: It's none of your business. She was tired of all the questions, and he was too cocky by half.

'I'm being posted to Flaxton,' she muttered.

He grinned. 'Hey, that's not far, is it? I've been over there a coupla times. Great little pub. What d'you do in your Air Force? Type? Work the telephones? Somethin' like that?'

'I'm a flight mechanic,' she said stiffly. 'I work on the engines.'

He whistled and his blue eyes widened at her. 'No kiddin'? I didn't know the RAF had girls doin' that. Gee . . . that sure *is* somethin'. How d'you learn to do a thing like that?'

'I went on a training course.'

He was still looking amazed, and the wind seemed to have been taken momentarily out of his sails – much to her satisfaction. Only momentarily, though.

542

'I'm a waist gunner,' he told her, as though there were nothing better to be. 'Know what that is?'

'I know what a gunner is. I'm not sure what the waist bit means.'

'Means I'm in the middle of the ship. There's two of us. Back to back, firin' opposite ways through a hole in the side. B17s. Flyin' Fortress to you, I guess. You ever seen one?'

'Yes,' she said. 'I've seen them flyin' over. I thought they were rather ugly.' Why on earth did he call a 'plane a ship?

He stared. 'Jeez . . . you can't mean that.'

'Yes, I do,' she said defiantly. 'They're not nearly as nice-lookin' as a Lancaster. Or a Wellington. Or even a Stirling.'

He shook his head in wonder. 'I guess we all think our own are the best, but a B17 ugly . . . I sure ain't never heard that said before.' He cocked his head at her. 'You know, it just don't seem right to me, lettin' girls do your job. Just not right . . .'

'Why not?'

'Dunno. It ain't natural, I s'pose.'

She said tartly: 'We can do just as well as men, you know, 'cept for the heavy liftin'. We're just as good.'

He let go of her and lifted both hands in mock surrender. 'OK, OK. Sure you can . . .' He took hold again. 'Say, I didn't tell you my name. It's Virgil. Virgil Gillies.'

It sounded odd to her, but then they all seemed to have odd names. Over his shoulder she had spotted Nora and Buzz clasped in each other's arms, rotating slowly, eyes shut.

'I'm from Ohio,' he told her. 'Place called Clyde. I guess you ain't heard of it.'

She wondered whether they always told you where they were from – whether you wanted to know or not. She'd no more idea where Ohio was than Minnesota. And she didn't care either.

543

'That's 'bout four thousand miles from here, I reckon,' he went on. 'Seems a long ways.'

She felt almost sorry for him about that. Such a distance was unimaginable to her. It must be dreadful, she thought, to be so far away from home.

'It's a state in the Mid-West,' he was telling her now. 'I guess it's not so big like some of our other states, but it's a whole lot bigger 'n Suffolk. I figure you'd get Suffolk into Ohio twenty times over.'

'I don't know why you'd want to.'

'Been over here a month already. Still tryin' to get used to the place. Everythin' so small . . . all squashed up together . . . you sure ain't got much room on this little island o' yours.'

'You've taken up a lot of space.'

'Well, I guess we Yanks won't be stickin' around too long. Won't take no time, I reckon. We'll soon have those Jerries on the run. I'm gonna blow 'em right outta the skies, soon 's I get the chance.'

'Haven't you been on an op yet, then?'

'Mission, I guess you mean? Nope. Any day now, though. An' I sure can't wait. Hermann Goerin', here I come!'

'I s'pose you think it'll be a piece of cake?'

'Cake? I don't get you . . .'

'It's an RAF sayin' – it means very easy. Nothin' to it.'

'Well, see, I reckon we ain't goin' to have much trouble – not with the Forts. We got ten guns on 'em an' they ain't peashooters, like your guys'. We'll get those fighters – zap, zap! Swot 'em down like flies.'

'Is that what you're goin' to do?' she said sarcastically. 'Just like that? You really think so?'

'Sure. That Lancaster of yours you think's so great ain't got guns like ours. I reckon if they didn't go at night when it's dark they'd never get there at all. No, sir! An' your guys can't see what the heck they're doin' when they do get there. Bombs all over the place . . . hittin' everythin' 'cept the target. But, see, in daylight we can drop our bombs right on the nail – right in the pickle barrel – wham, wham *wham*!'

She said nothing, though she could think of all sorts of things she'd like to have said. The stories told about how the Americans boasted were true, then, and this one hadn't even been on a single op yet. He'd come over thinking he knew it all – that there was nothing to it. He'll learn, she thought. He'll soon find out. If he hadn't been so cocky, she might almost have felt sorry for him about that too.

He was looking at her differently now, smiling at her in a meaning sort of way.

'I'd sure like to see you again, Winifred.'

How many more of them had those bright eyes, that clear healthy skin, those straight white teeth? They didn't seem like real people to her. No more real than the film stars she'd seen up on the screen. She'd sooner the RAF any time – never mind that they weren't as good-looking or as well-dressed, or as well-paid.

'I'm married,' she told him, inspiration coming to her. She held up her left hand to show her wedding ring.

'That's no bar to seein' you. Not in my book.'

'It is in mine.'

'Where's your husband, then?'

'In Elmbury,' she said truthfully.

When the music stopped he tried to keep her with him but she escaped into the crowd and hid in the cloakroom. She spent most of the remaining evening there. Her head was aching from the heat and noise and she longed to go home. She listened to some WAAFS comparing the dance with ones on their station. 'Who wants beer and stale sandwiches and some scratched old records, when there's this?' one of them said scornfully as she powdered her nose. 'Poor old RAF, they can't compete.'

Before the end Winnie glimpsed the waist gunner again. He was dancing with the same blond girl as before and tossing her around as though she weighed no more than a feather.

The truck that took them back to Elmbury was full of girls who'd had a good time. They were carrying the things they'd been given – showing them round like trophies: nylon stockings, tins of meat and fruit, sweets, chewing gum, bright lipsticks like Nora's ... Some she knew from the village, but others she'd never seen before – service girls, Land Girls and strangers in cheap shiny clothes. There was a lot of giggling and shrieking as the truck veered round a sharp bend. It reminded her of the day she'd first gone to Colston, except that she wasn't feeling sick – just indignant.

Out of the darkness Nora said: 'I saw you with Virgil Gillies. Smashin' dancer, isn't he? An' ever so good-looking – just like a cowboy in the films.'

'I didn't notice.'

'You are funny, Winnie! All the girls are after him! He was huntin' everywhere for you later, askin' where you'd gone, so you must've made ever such a hit with him. Wish he'd fancy me ... He's in the same crew as Buzz, did he tell you? Waist gunner.'

'Oh yes, he told me all about what he did, an' what he's goin' to do.'

'Did he tell you what they call their 'plane?'

'No.'

Nora tittered and dug her elbow in Winnie's side. 'Sassy Sally that's what they call her. They give them all names like that, an' paint pictures of girls an' things on the nose.'

'I know. I've seen them.'

'You ought to see Sassy Sally! She's got no clothes on at all. Not a stitch! The only thing she's wearin' is a flower in her hair. An' she's sort of stretched out ... ever so naughty, really.'

Winnie was silent. Over the tailgate she could see the moon shining brightly in a clear night sky. What ops would the RAF be on tonight? Where would they be going to drop their bombs 'all over the place'? Somewhere far into Germany, probably. Dusseldorf, Frankfurt, Stuttgart, Cologne, Berlin . . .? And how many of them would never come back, to add to all the rest? She wished she'd given that American a piece of her mind: told him just what she thought of him and his big talk.

'Well,' Nora asked. 'What did you think of the Yanks?'

'They're just like I thought they'd be,' she said.

On the next day, the last one of her leave, she went to answer a knock on the back door and found Taffy standing there.

'You didn't let me know you were home,' he said. 'But I found out.'

'You shouldn't have come,' she told him. 'I said I don't want to see you any more.'

He took no notice. 'You've been ill, haven't you? They told me that too in the pub.' He searched her face. 'You look pale.'

'I'm better now. I'm leavin' tomorrow.'

Gran, nosy as ever, called out from her chair. 'Who's yew talkin' wi', Winnie? Who's that thare?'

In the end he stayed to tea, though she tried to stop it. He sat in Ken's old place, eating her mother's cake and scones, and, except for Gran who watched him beadily and in silence, they all liked him, she could tell. He was charming to Mum, nice to Ruth and Laura, and he listened to her father grumbling about the Americans.

'Winnie went to a dance at the Americans base,' Ruth said brightly.

'Did she now?' Taffy's eyes turned on her.

She wouldn't tell him exactly where she was being posted, but Ruth told him that too.

'Flaxton's not far at all,' he said to her as he left after tea. 'There'll be no reason why we can't see each other now.'

'Yes there will. I don't want to see you. Why won't

you understand that? An' I don't want you to come here again.'

He looked at her with his burning eyes. 'You don't know what you do want, Winnie. Or what's good for you. You never have. But *I* do. I've always known.'

She opened the door for him. 'Please go now.'

He stopped on the threshold. 'Why did you go to that dance, Winnie? You're not that sort of girl . . . like the ones who go with Yanks. Don't go again.'

'I'll do as I please. You've no right to tell me anythin'.'

She shut the door on him indignantly. Gran looked up as she went back into the kitchen.

'He've a silver tongue thet thare furrin fellah. An' bad eyes. Yew moind 'm, Winnie. Thass what oi say. Yew moind 'm right well.'

The daffodils were in full bloom in the rough grass at the end of the lawn, making a brilliant yellow splash against the new green, but David Palmer scarcely noticed them. He stood staring out of the drawing-room window of his wife's Gloucestershire house where he felt as alien as he did in her house in London. Behind him he could hear the clink of bottle on glass as Caroline poured herself another gin. He waited until he knew she had sat down again and then turned round to face her.

'I have something to say, Caroline. I want a divorce. As soon as it can be arranged.'

He saw the astonishment on her face. Her mouth dropped open and the hand holding her glass froze halfway to her mouth. Then, slowly, her expression was replaced by a different one – of hard-edged amusement. She took a sip of her drink and considered him, her head on one side.

'Are you serious, David?'

'Perfectly. I'm sorry, but I don't imagine you'll be exactly heartbroken at the idea. Our marriage hasn't meant anything to either of us for a very long time. I would think you'd be quite relieved to be rid of me.'

She smiled at him, that acid-sweet smile he knew so well. 'Now, there you are quite mistaken. I don't choose to be rid of you at all. I happen to like being married to you, in spite of your bloody RAF. I don't want a divorce and I've no intention of losing you to some other woman. That's what this is all about, isn't it, David? You'd never have considered it otherwise – not in a million years. It's that prissy little WAAF officer at Colston, isn't it? The one you've always fancied. I suppose you've been having an affair and she wants you to marry her now.'

'As it happens Section Officer Newman is no longer at Colston.'

'I dare say she isn't. But that doesn't stop you two, does it? Did you get her sent away so it was easier for you to carry on on the quiet? To save your precious reputation?'

He thought for a moment of Felicity's pale and determined face when she had told him that she wanted to be posted away. He had begged her to stay. Pleaded with her. And then she had said that she did not want to see him again.

'I'll get a divorce,' he had told her, in despair. 'We could be married . . .'

'No,' she had said. 'I couldn't bear to be responsible for breaking up your marriage.'

'You wouldn't be. It was finished long ago.'

'It doesn't make any difference,' she had told him. 'It would mean you breaking your vows . . . and it would be because of me. And a divorce could ruin your career and that means more to you than anything.'

'Not more than you,' he had told her quietly. 'Not now.'

He had spoken with perfect truth. He had caught a glimpse now of another life than the RAF – one he had never really known existed. Never thought about. Never dreamed of. Never hoped for. And with that glimpse he had realized that life being married to Caroline was no longer tolerable. It had become insupportable to him. He

549

must get a divorce, and then he would wait and hope and pray that one day he would be able to persuade Felicity to change her mind. He looked at his wife.

'You must think what you like, Caroline, but that's not so.'

She began to laugh, but it was a laugh without mirth and with a note of triumph. 'You randy old goat! She's young enough to be your daughter. You ought to be ashamed of yourself.'

With a sinking heart he realized that she was enjoying the situation. He had foolishly imagined that she would probably welcome a divorce. Now he saw that it had been naïve of him in the extreme to think so. She was enjoying not only the situation, but the power he had now given her over him.

He said evenly: 'Our marriage is a sham, Caroline, and you know it. I'll give you all the evidence you need to divorce me. It can be arranged – '

'Oh, I know all about that, darling. You pay someone to be in a hotel room with you and the maid comes in and sees you – it's done all the time. But I'm not letting you get away with that.'

He watched her lighting a cigarette in her casual way – holding the table lighter in both hands and blowing a thin stream of smoke upwards.

'I'm asking you to be reasonable, Caroline. You've had lovers for years and I've turned a blind eye. It wouldn't be difficult for me to find the evidence to bring a case for divorce against you.'

She was still holding the heavy silver lighter, weighing it in one hand. 'If you try that, David, I'll defend it. And I'll cross-petition and make damned sure that your little WAAF's name is dragged all across the newspapers. I can see the headlines, can't you? RAF Station Commander cross-petitioned over affair with WAAF . . . Married Group Captain accused by wife of adultery with WAAF officer under his command . . .' She put down the lighter on the table beside her. 'It'd ruin your career, and you know it. That's what really surprises me about this. You always minded about your career more than anything else. The bloody RAF always came first with you. I didn't think you had it in you to risk losing that. A divorce – especially a messy one – will mean you'll never make it to the top. Still waters run deep, I suppose. You must love her a lot.'

He moved away from the window and stood looking down at her. 'I don't love you, and you don't love me. What's the point of all this, Caroline? Why can't we call it a day?'

She smiled up at him sweetly again. 'Why? Because I'm your wife, David. And you're my husband. For better, for worse, remember? And I happen to want it to stay that way.'

In the early summer of 1943 Virginia and Madge were sent on another special and secret training course. The RAF instructor was young and very keen. He kept bouncing on his heels and rubbing his hands together.

'This is a top secret new device that could turn the tide of the war in our favour. And its name is *Oboe*.' He paused for effect and then bounced on his heels again and rubbed his hands again. 'Basically,' he went on, radiating his enthusiasm round the room like an RDF beam, 'this is a blind bombing aid. The idea is to help our bomber chaps get to the target accurately without actually having to *see* it themselves. Up 'til now it's not been unknown, I regret to say, for them to miss the target altogether, or bomb the wrong jolly one. All a bit hit and miss, really. But we're going to change all that. You all understand about Radio Direction Finding . . . well, this is the same principle, different application. A wonderful new box of tricks to use against the enemy.'

He picked up a piece of chalk and drew a long line with a flourish across the blackboard behind him. 'Here we have a beam laid by a ground station.' He marked a cross at the start of the line. 'And here we have an aircraft flying along precisely at the end of the beam.' He drew a misshapen 'plane at the end of the line. 'Bit like a conker on a piece of string being whirled about a child's head. Now . . . here we have *another* beam laid by a second ground station . . .' He flourished the chalk again. 'We call these two stations cat and mouse and where their beams cross, at the *exact* point of intersection, our aircraft must release its bombs. Smack on target! No chance of visual error, you see. *Offensive* radar, that's the difference. We're not just using it to defend ourselves by spotting the enemy popping over here, but taking it into *their* territory as an offensive weapon.'

He had turned round from the blackboard and was doing some more heel-bouncing and hand-rubbing.

'On recent tests over France it has proved extremely accurate. And we have the perfect aircraft to carry *Oboe* for us – the Mosquito! The Mosquito can fly at three hundred and fifty miles per hour – too fast for the Germans fighters to catch easily – and it can mark from twenty-eight thousand feet, to get the utmost range. *And* it's capable of carrying a four-thousand-pound bomb. A wonderful tool in our hands. The Mosquito will be spearheading the Pathfinder force who are going to mark these targets accurately for the bombers following along behind.' He rubbed his hands together and beamed another smile round. 'In other words, the hit-and-miss days of bombing are over on any target within *Oboe*'s range. And *you* are going to make sure it's always a hit.'

'East Kent!' moaned Madge at the end of the course. 'Stuck out on the cliffs, miles from anywhere again. No transport. Nothing to do. No fun at all.'

They were given leave before reporting for duty. But Virginia did not go home. Instead she went to stay with Madge and her family in the small house in Brighton where the sitting-room had been turned into her dentist father's waiting-room and the dining-room was the surgery. The remaining space was cramped, but Madge's parents and her smaller brother made her feel welcome and nobody seemed to care very much about how the table was laid or whether they kept their elbows off it. She and Madge went to the cinema twice and they walked along the seafront behind the barbed wire and sat in the sun eating ice-cream cornets. Once, they went past the ice rink where she had watched Neil playing in the hockey match.

In her diary she wrote: *I shall never forget him. There will never be anybody else for me, I know there won't. I still can't forgive Mother for the way she treated him. I don't know if I ever shall. Why, oh why did Neil have to die?*

While Madge lay sleeping peacefully, Virginia lay wide awake, remembering.

Twenty-One

The phone in the rectory hall was ringing. Felicity went from the kitchen to answer it, but as she lifted the earphone off the hook, the roar of a bomber passing overhead drowned the caller's voice. She waited until the noise had died away.

'Hallo? I'm sorry, I couldn't hear you.'

'Is that you, Titania?'

Her heart leaped. '*Speedy!* Is that really you?'

'I just asked you the same thing, Titania.'

She started to laugh. 'Well, it *is* me. But, Speedy, oh Speedy . . . I don't believe it! Where have you been all this time? What happened to you? Where are you now? Are you all right?'

'Which one shall I answer first?'

'Are you all right?'

'Never better. Lost a spot of weight, that's all. I've been wandering about France for months on end. Managed to pop back via Spain eventually. I'll tell you all about that later.'

'But where are you now? You haven't told me that.'

'Norwich. Not a million miles from you. Fifteen, to be exact. I looked you up on the map. They've given me a nice bit of leave, so I came up here in search of you. Took me a while to track you down . . . when did they shunt you off to the bomber boys in Yorks?'

'A while ago. I'm on a forty-eight.'

'I know. They told me. So, I thought I had a chance of seeing you. Thought I might nip over today – if that's all right.'

'Of course it is. You must stay the night. I don't have to go back 'til tomorrow.'

'Never thought I'd hear you ask me to do that, Titania.'

'And meet my father,' she added firmly.

There was a sigh at the other end of the line. 'Best behaviour and all that . . . I'm on my way.'

He arrived in the red MG, string trailing, and swept up the driveway in a flurry of gravel with George sitting beside him in the passenger seat. Seeing him, back from the dead and as jaunty as ever, made her feel like bursting into tears. He sprang out of the car, George at his heels, and swept her, without hesitation, into his arms, holding her tightly against him. George was barking excitedly. She managed to free herself eventually and held him at arm's length. He was thinner, certainly, but otherwise looked fit and well. The same old Speedy with the same bright and laughing eyes.

'I still can't quite believe it,' she said at last. 'I'd almost given you up.'

'Given me up?' He looked at her in mock horror. 'While there is life there's hope.'

'I knew you'd say that, but I didn't even know you *were* still alive.'

'Would have dropped you a line, Titania, but there's not much of a postal service between Frogland and England at the moment.'

George was snuffling at her ankles and wagging his tail. She bent to pat him. He had lost weight, too, probably from pining. She looked up and smiled at Speedy.

'Come in and meet Father.'

She led him towards the study and opened the door. 'Father, this is Flight Lieutenant Ian Dutton.'

Before supper the two of them walked in the tangled wilderness that had once been the rectory garden. They wandered along the overgrown herbaceous border where delphiniums, lupins, canterbury bells and poppies had struggled through to bloom among the weeds. George followed them, exploring with his nose in the undergrowth.

'Tell me what happened, Speedy . . . in all these months.'

'Long story, Titania. I'll give you the bare bones. We were doing a sweep over France – we've got Spits now, you know, instead of Hurries. Jolly good little bus. Climbs like a rocket. Very nippy. Though I was rather fond of the old Hurry . . . Anyway, I was tootling along, minding my own business, as usual, when all of a sudden someone started shooting at me. Jerry ack-ack where I didn't expect it. Pretty unsporting of them. Either they were good shots or they were lucky because they scored a bullseye. The kite went up in flames and I had to hop out smartly. Touched down right in the middle of a field of cabbages . . . never knew the French were that keen on them, but still. There was this old Frenchman digging away in a corner as I floated down but he didn't even look up.'

Felicity laughed. 'Last time it was a girl.'

'Wasn't so lucky second time around. I undid the parachute and sort of bundled it up in my arms and carried it over to the Frenchman. I thought I'd ask to borrow his spade, see, so I could bury it. I did the old *je suis aviateur anglais* bit and bowed very politely, then I couldn't remember the French for spade. So, I did a sort of mime – digging and so on.'

'Did he understand you?'

'Well, he may have done, but he started to spout a whole gabble of French at me that didn't sound very friendly and he made some rather insulting gestures. So, no help there. I pushed off sharpish and went and hid in a wood for a while. Got out my little escape kit, but that wasn't much help either.'

'What do they give you?'

'Bit rum, I thought . . . There was a booklet entitled *Instruction and Hints for Fishing* and a fishing hook. I suppose that would have come in handy if I'd landed near a river or pond but I couldn't spot one in the immediate vicinity. And then there was a safety pin, which I'm glad to say I didn't need – not a tear in the old blue.'

'What about a map?'

Speedy sighed. 'Turned out to be of Norway. Not much use in France. So, I lay low 'til it got dark and then set off in what my compass button had vouchsafed was a northerly direction, to see if I could find a friendly farmhouse for some grub. I was feeling a bit peckish by that time. Not a morsel since breakfast the day before, you see. The first two or three wouldn't let me in or even give me a crust. Kept flapping their arms and aprons at me, telling me to go away. I was rather hurt, I can tell you. Anyway, I pressed on regardless in true RAF spirit and came to a village. Knocked on the first door and did the *aviateur anglais* routine yet again and, hey presto, this old crone beckons me in. Could've knocked me down with a feather. No beauty, she, I have to say. All in black, not a tooth in her head and a moustache like my Uncle Arthur, but she was all smiles and nods and made me sit down at the kitchen table while she got out a jolly decent bottle of *vin rouge* . . . I felt considerably better after a few glasses.'

Felicity imagined the scene with amusement: the old peasant woman nodding and smiling as she kept pouring out wine for Speedy, undoubtedly at his most charming.

'What happened then, Speedy?'

He picked a stick up off the grass and lobbed it ahead for George who scampered rheumatically in pursuit.

'Well, after a while the son came home. No oil painting either, but he spoke passable English. He soon sorted the whole thing out. Off with the old RAF togs and on with some very smelly blue overalls and a pair of boots I think he'd been wearing to clean out the pigs. I was a bit choked about having to give mine up, I must say.' He kicked mournfully at the long grass.

'Needs must when the devil drives.'

'My thoughts precisely, Titania. In fact I muttered

557

those very words to myself as I handed them over to Pierre. Hung on to my gong and wings, though, so all was not lost.'

They had reached the end of the border and strolled on in the golden sunlight, past the dilapidated summer house and towards a bench set against the kitchen garden wall where Albertine had rampaged unchecked and smothered the brickwork with its pink flowers. They sat down and George collapsed at their feet, tongue lolling, flanks heaving. It was warm in the sun. Speedy leaned forward, arms resting on his knees, hands clasped, and looked about him.

'Wonderful place this . . . peaceful, unspoiled . . .'

'Rather a jungle, I'm afraid. It was lovely once.'

'I like it this way: the long grass, the flowers all jumbled up, roses all over the shop. Perfect on a summer evening like this. Listen to that bird singing.'

'It's a blackbird. He's on the top of the apple tree.'

Speedy craned his neck. 'Can't see the little blighter. He's warbling away like fury . . . Sure it's not a *blue*bird? One of those ones that are supposed to be going to zoom around over the White Cliffs of Dover one of these fine days? Never seen one yet, I must say, and I've flown over there enough times myself. Don't think we even have them, do we? Jolly good song, though. Some Yank wrote it, apparently. Hence the bluebirds, I suppose. Never seen the place. Chap didn't have a clue we didn't even have them in this country.'

'It's symbolic, isn't it? The bluebird of happiness.'

He smiled at her sideways. 'Matter of fact, Titania, I've heard some of the RAF call you WAAFS bluebirds . . . for that very reason. You bring happiness.'

'Not always,' she said.

'Tomorrow, just you wait and see . . .'

'I want to hear what happened next,' she told him quickly. 'What did you do, dressed in your French disguise?'

'They moved me onto another house in some other

558

village. Rather an attractive widow, as a matter of fact – teeth all present and correct and not a whisker. I stayed there for a few days. Quite pleasant, I have to admit.'

'I'm sure it was.'

'Don't look at me like that, Titania. I behaved at all times like a perfect English gentleman.'

'Hum. That can mean anything. And after the French widow?'

'Not so much fun. They parked me with the *curé* in the next village. Well, you know me and God bods . . . not really my line at all – excepting your father, of course. Still, the old boy turned out to be rather good at poker and he had some quite special brandy stashed away out of sight of the marauding Huns. I positively warmed to him by the time I had to leave. Almost converted me.'

'Never.'

'I said, *almost*. And you won't believe this either, but they dressed me up as a nun to move me on to the next place. A *bonne soeur* they called it.'

She put her hand over her mouth. 'Oh, Speedy!'

'All very well for you to laugh. He jests at scars that never felt a wound . . . Our old friend Romeo, I believe. I can tell you, Titania, that I've spent a jolly rum sort of time over there. Real cloak and dagger stuff – hiding from the Huns. All kinds of disguises. Wigs. False beards. Forged papers. The whole caboodle. I've biked miles. Walked miles. Gone on train journeys sitting bang next to Jerry soldiers . . .' He paused and glanced at her again. 'Not sure I should tell you about the oddest hiding place of all. Not really fit for your ears.'

'You may as well.'

He grinned. 'Well, one of my last ports of call was what I shall politely call a house of ill repute. By this time I'd been joined by another RAF type – pilot officer by the name of Butterworth. He tagged along for the last couple of months. Nice chap, really, but hadn't been around much, if you get my meaning. Only nineteen and still wet behind the ears. Anyway, the two of us were hidden in this particular house – '

'How convenient.'

'Jolly good place for a chap to hide, actually. The thing is that the Huns somehow got wind of something and raided the place. Butterworth and I were called upon to do a pretty fair imitation of paying guests, as you might say, only poor old Butters was such an innocent the Frogs were frightened he'd give himself and them away, so they dressed him up in women's clothes and stuck him in one of the rooms.'

She laughed. 'You're not making all this up, are you Speedy? I never know whether to believe you or not.'

'Absolute gospel, I swear it. Made rather a good-looking popsie, as a matter of fact. He was damned lucky none of the Huns took a fancy to him. They got us to the Spanish border after that and then it was a long slog over the Pyrenees. Butterworth and I finally showed up at the British Consulate at Figueras, a trifle the worse for wear. They put us up at the Embassy for a while, so we went to the odd cocktail party and did a fair bit of line-shooting before we managed to cadge a lift back by air. Home sweet home.' He sighed deeply and leaned back against the bench. 'Still can't quite believe I'm here. Back in jolly old England. And with you. Can't tell you how much I thought about you in France – but then, as you know, I always do . . .'

She saw that he was perfectly serious now and wished that he weren't. Fond as she was of him, there was a world of difference between that and being in love with him – a huge gulf that she didn't think she could ever cross. But everything would have been so wonderfully simple and happy if it had happened with Speedy. There would have been none of this terrible heartache and misery. None of this guilt and despair. None of this wishing for what could never be. She hadn't seen David for nearly six months now – not since she had told him that what had scarcely begun was finished.

His sadness had been hard to bear and it had taken all her strength to keep to her resolution. Now she was far away at RAF Pickerton in Yorkshire, while he had been posted recently to Fighter Command HQ at Bentley Priory. It was very unlikely that their paths would ever cross again.

She stood up. 'Come and see our church, Speedy. It's well worth looking at.'

He got to his feet slowly. 'So am I, Titania. If only you would.'

The willow trees overhanging the river bank and trailing their long, pale leaves in the water, gave a prettily dappled shade. Sunlight filtered through translucent green and sparkled in bright blobs on the water's surface. Anne, admiring the effect, let her fingers trail too, dangling one hand over the side of the punt. The river water felt blissfully cool and her fingertips made tickly little furrows as the punt glided along. She leaned back against the cushion. It seemed a very long time ago since she had last been in a punt. One summer, before the war, her parents had taken her to visit a cousin who was up at Cambridge. They had gone to his rooms – a mullion-windowed den up a stone staircase at the corner of the quad. Kit had been there too so that he could compare Cambridge with Oxford. Afterwards Cousin Hugo had taken them out on the Cam. They had punted along the Backs and up the river to Grantchester where they had had, not Rupert Brooke's honey tea, but a picnic lunch with cold salmon, strawberries and cream and Pimms. It had been a perfect, baking hot summer's day – just like this one. There had been lots of other punts on the river, propelled by undergraduates in straw boaters, with girls in cotton frocks and floppy sun hats lazing back against the cushions and trailing their hands over the sides, as she was doing now. She could remember the sound of their laughter and voices across the water . . .
I say, Frobisher, watch where you're going! Head down,

Fiona! I'm taking us under that branch . . . oh God, you silly clot! I did warn you . . . A wind-up gramophone had been playing in one of the punts and she had listened to *Deep Purple* floating away down the river.

The weather was the same, and so was the scenery, but all the rest had changed. Gone were the dashing young men and the pretty girls, the laughter and the loud voices and the music. There were no picnicking parties on the banks, no wicker hampers, no pitchers of fruity Pimms. The church clock at Grantchester might stand at ten to three but there would be nobody there for tea. The quads in Cambridge were deserted and military lorries rumbled through the streets. Kit was in Africa, Cousin Hugo had been killed at Dunkirk and in his place at the punt's stern was an American pilot in uniform. She had never meant to come out with Frank Wallace. After the time she had met him in the Black Bull and refused to do so she had kept on meeting him there again. And he had kept on asking her.

'I'd sure like to see Cambridge,' he'd said one evening in the smoke-filled, beer-soaked bar. 'I want to know if it's all it's cracked up to be.'

'It's not far. You can get there by train.'

'I'd need a native guide. Someone to show me round and make sure I didn't miss anything.'

'Don't look at me. I've only been there once for the day and that was years ago.'

'Yeah, but you were born and bred in this country. You know all about its treasures.'

'I can give you a list. Christ's College, Trinity, Clare, Queen's . . . well, all the colleges, really. The Bridge of Sighs, King's College Chapel – '

He had interrupted her, shaking his head. 'Won't do. Not the same thing at all – going round with a long list in my hand.' Big sigh. 'Well, I guess I'll just have to give it a miss if you won't take pity on me.'

In the end she'd given in. 'You realize this is against my golden rule.'

'I know,' he'd said. 'But I've got a rule too. No strings, so no worries. That's the deal.'

I'm a fool to do this, though, she'd thought to herself on the train journey. I don't really believe that there's such a thing as a chop girl – that's just men's superstition, like not letting women go near an aircraft or down mines, but I do know that I don't want to get close to anyone else who's going to get killed and the Yanks are losing plenty. He's got about the same chance of survival as a snowball in hell at the moment. I don't want to get to know him or care what happens to him.

They bought a guidebook and walked round Cambridge, seeing all its glories – the ancient colleges, the quadrangles, the Gothic wonder of King's, the Backs where the smooth green lawns swept down to the banks of the Cam. After lunch at the Anchor pub they'd hired the punt, to realize another of Frank's dreams.

It was an odd experience, Anne thought, as they drifted along the river, to see England through a foreigner's eyes, especially one from the New World. To watch him marvel over things taken for granted by the natives. There seemed nothing very remarkable to her about colleges being founded in the thirteenth and fourteenth centuries – beautiful as they were. Hundreds of ordinary village churches all over the country must be equally old. But Frank had stood spellbound, drinking it all in. Seeing his enchantment had made her glad, after all, that she'd agreed to come.

She smiled at him. 'Where did you learn to punt, Frank?'

He grinned. 'Here and now. I'm doing it by the seat of my pants. Any moment now I'll fall in.'

'Hope you can swim.'

'Sure I can.' He fed the pole upwards through his hands again. 'This is just great . . . beautiful . . . it's all just like I always imagined.'

'Pity you're not seeing it in peacetime. As it was.'

He dug the pole down again. 'That's what everybody

keeps on telling me about everything over here. You British all say: oh, but you should have seen it before the war – it looked so much better then. England doesn't look her best now . . . You all seem ashamed that things are a bit shabby, but that doesn't seem anything to be ashamed of to me. Just the opposite. You've been fighting a war for nearly four years, and most of that time you've been going it alone. If it shows, then that's something to be proud of, not apologize for.'

'Oh, we apologize for everything. It's a national habit. Even when someone steps on our foot we apologize to *them* for having it trodden on.'

He laughed. 'I know. I've found that out.'

'Well, you're the first American I've heard say nice things like that. Usually they tell you how they've come over to win the war for you.'

'You've been meeting the wrong guys. We've come over to give you a hand. So far we haven't done a hell of a lot, but give us time.'

He had taken off his jacket, rolled up his shirtsleeves and loosened his tie. The uniform jacket lay on the cushion opposite her, together with her own. American Air Force olive beside RAF blue. Rather symbolic really. It was a combined effort now. Round the clock. The RAF bombed Germany by night and the Yanks went over in the day and dropped a whole lot more bombs. But the RAF losses had been horrific and everyone said the Americans were having a really rough time without a fighter escort that could go with them the whole way. She wondered what on earth that must be like – going on ops in broad daylight, clearly visible for miles, and with only their own guns for protection. A bit like driving a loaded sledge through a pack of ravening wolves?

The punt glided gently on upstream, through meadows deep in buttercups, on towards Grantchester. Anne changed hands and cooled the other one. Frank was a pretty decent chap. *Very* decent, in fact. Good-looking and attractive too, like so many of the Americans. Had they left all the ugly ones behind on purpose? *Send the best-lookers we've got to impress them over there. Yes, Mr President.* And they seemed so clean and smelled so nice. Hard to resist, and lots of girls didn't bother to try. But she and Frank had a deal and she, for one, was going to stick to it.

At Grantchester they moored the punt and walked into the village. They strolled around and looked at the old church and at its clock, and found the Old Vicarage where Rupert Brooke had written his verses. June roses were in full bloom in gardens and rambled riotously over walls. Then they wandered slowly back to the punt and sat for a while on the river bank in the shade of an alder tree.

She picked up his cap off the grass. It looked as beaten up as most RAF ones after several years hard service. 'This looks pretty worn.'

'Fifty mission crush, we call that. Guys take out the grommets and then kick them around 'til they look good and old. I wore mine in the shower and then stamped all over it. Did that the day I got here.'

'The RAF do things like that to theirs, too.'

'I guess we're not so very different. Nobody wants to look a rookie.'

She put the cap down beside him again. 'How many missions have you flown, Frank?'

'Thirteen. Twelve more to go. Twenty-five to a tour, for us.'

'Then home?'

'I guess so. Or maybe some other assignment over here. I don't know. I don't even think about it. I figure the odds aren't that great on finishing it anyhow.'

He lay back on the bank and put his hands behind his head, lacing them for a pillow. She glanced down at him and then away. He was much, much too nice to die. Her throat tightened at the thought. Christ, she was starting to worry about him – just like she'd sworn she wouldn't.

'We ought to be getting along, Frank.'

'Do you mind if we stay here for a bit? It's real peaceful.'

'If you like.'

It was the same old thing, she said to herself, staring sadly at the river. When you knew they could buy it any day you went along with whatever made them happy. And you looked them straight in the eye to show you weren't actually thinking anything of the kind or feeling sorry for them, though they probably knew very well that you were. And, if they wanted to, you let them talk about it.

After a moment he sighed and said, 'Sometimes I can't figure out what's real any longer . . . *this* here and now or being on a mission. I guess you could say *that's* reality and this is just make-believe. They sure are two different worlds.'

Latimer had said much the same thing, only in another way. Anne stopped lobbing small bits of twig into the water and waited.

'This is just pretending the other isn't happening,' he went on. 'Real life isn't peaceful and beautiful like this. Or it sure ain't in wartime. Reality's guys getting shot to pieces, blown out of the sky in front of you, pulped in gun turrets . . . It's tasting fear like you were eating it because the same thing could happen to you any moment. It's hours of tiredness and cold and aching arms. Shifting that punt pole was a cinch for me after the muscle it takes to keep a B24 in tight formation without running into the other guys, hour after hour. There's ships each side of you, and sometimes above and below as well . . . you've gotta keep correcting the whole damn time. Toughest trip we ever had – we'd got shot up real bad and lost power in a couple've engines – I had to holler out for some help to land real quick. You know: *Hallo Darky* . . .'

She nodded. It was the emergency call for aircraft in need of help.

'We were in big trouble. Matter of fact, I thought there was no way we were going to make it down somewhere in time. I kept on calling and then, all of a sudden, this

English girl's voice came out of nowhere, answering me. "Hallo, Yank," she said – very calm and clear, very British – one of your WAAFS, I guess. "What is your emergency?" She sounded cool as a cucumber, as though everything was just fine, and it sure helped. They got us down OK. Made it seem like it was no problem.'

Anne was silent. *They got us down* OK would probably have really meant one of those terrifying landings like she'd seen, coming in on a wing and a prayer – underpowered, controls damaged, skidding and slithering skew-whiff down the runway, liable to burst into flames any second. Horrible.

'Anne.' He had reached out and touched her wrist. As she turned he met her eyes. 'Remember the deal? No strings, so no worries.'

The light was turning to soft gold as they punted slowly downstream. It gilded the brickwork and stone of the college walls along the Backs where the shadows were lengthening across the lawns. As Frank helped her out of the punt he kept her hand in his for a moment.

'Thanks for this day, Anne. It's meant a heck of a lot to me. More than I can say.'

She smiled up at him. 'You're welcome, Yank.'

Twenty-Two

The Lancaster came in to land almost over the top of Winnie's head. She clutched on to her beret, looking up into the darkness, as the long black belly and outstretched wings swept by above her. The bomber touched down beyond with a big thud and a loud squeal of rubber against tarmac. She saw it bounce high and then bounce twice again before it settled to earth and rolled on down the runway. Bit of a shaky landing, but then the crew was a new one on the course and the pilot was still learning how to handle a heavy four-engined bomber. At least he'd got the kite down in one piece and without bending it.

She knew that it was very dangerous to stand so near the runway, but she often did so when she had finished the job of setting out the flarepath. She looked forward to when it was her turn to drive the station tractor up and down each side of the runway, trailing the load of gooseneck flares, and putting them out, one by one, at intervals all the way along. When it was done she would stand and gaze at the glimmering pathway. A way to the stars, that's how it looked to her. A magic stairway of lights that would take the bombers and their crews up into the night skies, towards those stars, and then bring them down to earth again.

She had waited, alone and unobserved, in the darkness by the edge of the runway, listening for them to come back from night exercises. It made her spine tingle when they roared in so close overhead. At first she had thought it was the most thrilling thing she had ever done – but that had been before she had flown in one.

She'd liked RAF Flaxton from the moment she had

arrived there, and not only because it was in her native county. The heavy bomber conversion unit trained air crews to fly Lancasters and, from the start, she'd liked the Lancaster too. It had always looked lovely in the air, in her eyes, and she thought it was every bit as beautiful on the ground. Majestic. Mighty. Valiant – like its crews. Forgiving, too, they always said, which was just as well considering the mess some of them made flying her when they first started. She had fallen in love with the bomber the way she had fallen in love with the Hurricane fighter. And the four engines were Merlins – like they'd been on the Hurricanes and Spitfires, so she'd felt at home straight away with those.

She had been the very first WAAF flight mechanic at the unit. The technical wing commander had looked her over uncertainly when she had reported for duty.

'I feel as though we should put you in a glass case, ACW Jervis. Or wrap you in cotton wool.'

'I want to work, sir.'

He had smiled at her, amused. 'And so you shall.'

The flight sergeant in charge was Scottish – just like Chiefy at Kirkton – and he had given her the same jaundiced eye until she had proved she could do the jobs. The men had teased her the same, too, but she knew all about 'long rests' and 'sky hooks' and 'left-handed' screwdrivers now, and after a while they stopped. It was very different working on a big bomber, though. Luckily, she had a good head for heights because it was a long way down to the ground from the wing of a Lancaster, or from a gantry.

'Seeing as you're servicing this aircraft, lassie,' the flight sergeant had told her, soon after she'd arrived. 'You'll be going up when she's tested. That way we make sure the work's done properly and nobody cuts any corners – not when it could be their neck too.'

And so, at last, her dream had come true.

It had been a grey, overcast day when she'd climbed up the ladder into K-King, heart thumping with excitement, and had made her way forwards and upwards along the fuselage incline, from tail to nose. Ahead, a pool of light flooded the cockpit but it was dark in the main body of the aircraft and she had learned the hard way before to keep her head down and take care to avoid the sharp metal edges and projections all along its length. Getting over the great mainspar, where the wings joined the fuselage, was like clambering over a farm gate.

She had stood behind the flight engineer's seat and had watched anxiously as the engines were started up in turn – first the port inner, then the starboard inner, then the port outer and the starboard outer. The last one had been giving plug trouble and she had heaved a sigh of relief when it fired and ran steadily. As the pilot and flight engineer had worked through the checks, all four engines bellowing at full stretch, she had kept scanning the dials for any sign of trouble, but all had been on top line.

Her heart had still been thumping away as they had taxied slowly round the peri track, but when the pilot had swung the Lanc round to face the long, long stretch of runway that would take them up into the skies, it had seemed to move from her chest to her mouth. She had watched his hand push the throttles forward and K-King had started to roll. The roar of the engines had blotted out all other sound and she would have put her hands over her ears if she had not needed them to hold onto the back of the seat. The bomber had gone faster and faster. Grass had flown by in a green streak and then a clutch of buildings in a grey blur. She had felt the tail lift off and realized that the Lanc was balancing on its main wheels as it tore down the runway. The group of trees standing like a huge race jump at the far end were coming closer and closer. Out of the corner of her eye she had seen the pilot easing the control wheel back towards him and, at that moment, K-King had suddenly risen like magic into the air. Winnie had gaped at the sight of the runway dropping away beneath and at the treetops, slipping past below the wings and, as they had climbed slowly upwards she had seen Suffolk spread out below her like a huge patterned carpet . . . cornfields, pasture, woods, hedges, farms, houses and winding roads, and, in the distance, the cold silver glint of the North Sea.

And then the patterned carpet had vanished abruptly as the bomber had flown into cloud. A thick fog had enveloped them, shrouding the cockpit, blotting out everything from sight. The Lancaster had climbed on blindly through the grey and when the nose had suddenly burst into a world of brilliant sunlight and dazzling blue skies, Winnie had blinked in astonishment and gasped in awe.

K-King had soared around in that sparkling air, wheeling majestically like a great bird of prey, and the sensation of it had taken Winnie's breath away. Somewhere – hidden far below that dense barrier of cloud – people were going about their earthbound, humdrum, ordinary lives, but up in the crystal clear blue had been a world of endless space and freedom.

Now she no longer stood gazing up into the skies and wondering what it was like up there. Now, she knew.

In summer it could sometimes be as uncomfortable working on the aircraft as it had been in winter. Chiefy was a real stickler for rules and regulations and she had to wear her collar and tie even in the hottest weather. 'I'm not having half-naked women in my hangar,' he'd said. Whereas she had shaken with cold up at Kirkton, she now ran with sweat and was parched with thirst.

Sometimes, when they were off duty in the cool of the evening, she would bike down to the Fox and Grapes in the village with the others to have half a bitter or a cider. On one of these evenings she met the American waist gunner again.

She noticed the group of American airmen as soon as she entered the bar – heard their accents and saw the olive uniforms. They had taken over the far corner, making it their own territory, and were teasing the barmaid. Then, to her dismay, she saw Virgil Gillies among them, and Buzz, Nora's boyfriend. She shrank back behind the RAF corporal fitter beside her. Buzz, though, spotted her. He waved and sang out loudly.

'Hi there, sugar! Come on over 'n say hello.'

The Americans all turned to look in her direction.

'You know them?' the fitter said, surprised, and with a touch of disapproval.

'Not really.'

'Well, they seem to know you all right. All of them.'

There was a chorus coming from the corner now, hailing her, hands beckoning, faces grinning at her. She knew her own face must be red as a beetroot and she wanted to run out of the bar and get back on her bike and pedal away as fast as she could, but the only way to stop them was to go over, like they wanted. She felt a traitor, knowing how a lot of the RAF were about the Yanks and English girls, and inside she was as angry as she'd been when the gunner had made her dance.

They crowded round her, hemming her in, dwarfing her, offering her drinks, telling her their names. One of them bowed and held out an open packet of cigarettes with a picture of a camel on it.

'Howdy, ma'am. I'm Hank.'

'He's from Texas,' someone else said. 'That's why he talks funny.'

Virgil Gillies looked down at her, grinning wider than any of them. 'Gee, I've been comin' here, hopin' I'd see you, ain't that so, Buzz?'

'Sure is. An' who spotted her? I reckon she was tryin' to hide from you, pal. Figure she's smarter than most of 'em.'

'Lay off it, Buzz.'

'OK, OK. Hey, fellas, back off now . . . We saw her first.'

She found herself manoeuvered further into a corner. Buzz melted away and she was left with the waist gunner.

'I found out you ain't married,' he said. 'Least not any more. Got Buzz to ask his girl, seein' as she lives in the same place as you. She told him all about you. He passed it on to me.'

'It was none of your business,' she told him coldly.

'Wanted to know if I'd got a chance. First time I saw you standin' there on your own at the dance, I figured you was the girl for me.'

He was teasing her – just the way they always teased girls, the Americans. Sweet-talked them. Led them on.

'Don't say things like that. I don't like it an' it's silly.'

'It ain't if I mean it, an' I do.' His eyes travelled over her pointedly. 'You're sure cute in that uniform. What's your rank?'

'I'm an aircraftwoman, first class.'

'You sure are!' He laughed. 'I'm a sergeant now, since I last saw you.' He lifted his arm to show her the three stripes on his sleeve. 'Reckon I'll soon make staff sergeant.'

'They're the wrong way up.'

'No, they ain't. That's the way we wear them – to be different from your guys. Did it on purpose after we got independent from you, so I've heard. Kind've a poke in the eye, I guess.'

She looked at him coldly. 'How many Jerry fighters've you blown out of the skies – like you said you would?'

'Yeah, well, it's a lot tougher 'n I figured.– I gotta admit that.' He shook his head. 'They keep on comin' at us from every which way . . . ain't sure I've clobbered any of 'em yet. An' if it's not the fighters, it's the flak – so thick sometimes you could walk on it. Those Jerries aim real good. We've lost a whole lotta guys. Seems like not many of us'll be goin' home . . .'

Most of her anger evaporated at his words and she felt rather ashamed of the rude way she had spoken to him. Whatever the Americans were like, they were fighting and dying just the same as the RAF. They'd come over to try and help. She stared down at her glass uncomfortably. He

573

was busy lighting a cigarette now – not from a packet with a camel on it, but one with a circle. She wondered if they were very different from English cigarettes. They smelled luxurious, somehow. Gran would have seized the whole lot from him if she got the chance. With the shortage of cigarettes she was having to do without some days, which made her crabbier than ever. Somehow she'd got hold of some American chewing gum – though she wouldn't let on how – and when she ran out of cigarettes, she'd sit chomping and champing away with the few teeth she'd got left.

He lifted his head, snapping the lighter shut. 'Nora told Buzz your folks've got a farm. That right?'

'Yes.' None of his business either.

'Same as me.' He looked pleased for some reason. 'Born and bred on one. My folks've got a spread near Clyde, Ohio. Think I already told you I come from thereabouts. My grandpa settled the land. Hundred and sixty acres. Corn, wheat, oats, alfalfa . . . an' we've got some cows an' some chickens, few pigs . . . how about your folks' place?'

'It's not as big as that,' she said shortly. He was off bragging again. 'It's only fifty acres. We've got cows and chickens too, and pigs – well, only one pig really, 'less she's got a litter. But we've got a flock of sheep. An' we grow turnip 'n swedes 'n worzles 'n beet. An' we grow oats 'n corn as well.'

'Yeah, but your corn's what we call wheat,' he told her. 'I found that out seein' it grow round here an' talkin' with the farmer at the base. What *we* call corn, *you* call maize.'

'I didn't know that,' she said, muddled. 'I've never seen maize. Dad doesn't grow it. And what's alfalfa?'

'Animal feed crop. Roots go down real deep . . . get full of goodness, see.'

'I've never seen that either,' she admitted.

'There's lots o' things *I* ain't never seen 'fore I got over here.'

574

'Such as?' she asked suspiciously. Any moment now he was probably going to start grumbling about the weather, or the food, or the money – like people said the Americans did.

'Real old houses. Ain't never seen anythin' old as you've got here. I guess the oldest building I knew's our barn, but that's not more'n seventy years old. My grandpa built it when he first settled there last century.'

'Our barn's five hundred years old,' she said, unable to help telling him so.

'Son of a gun! That's *real* old. How come it's still standin'?'

'They built them very strong. Good as houses. The beams are very thick.'

'I'd sure like to see it . . . must be somethin'.'

'What else hadn't you seen?' She was feeling quite gracious now, seeing as he'd been so impressed by the barn.

He raised his glass. 'Beer like this – watery an' with straw in it.'

'It's *meant* to look cloudy like that.'

He peered sideways into the depths of the glass. 'That so? With all those bits floatin' around? Beats me why they serve it warm, though. It'd sure taste a whole lot better chilled.'

'It's meant to be warm like that too,' she said stiffly.

'OK, if you say so.' He drank some and grimaced, wiping his mouth with the back of his hand. 'Hey, I just remembered somethin' else I ain't never seen before. Square eggs.'

'Square eggs?' She looked at him blankly.

'Dried ones. At the base, they mix 'em up and cook 'em in tins and serve 'em up cut in squares – so we call 'em square eggs. They stink real bad – make a buzzard gag.'

'Fresh eggs are very scarce here.'

'That's what they keep tellin' us. Brussels sprouts ain't, though. We sure get plenty o' those. Jeez, they're worse 'n square eggs. How come you grow so many?'

'We like them.' In fact, she hated them too when they went soggy and yellow.

He shook his head in wonder. 'Can't figure out why. Now, fish 'n chips – they're great. Best food you got over here, I reckon.'

'Most food's rationed,' she reproved him. 'There *is* a war on, you know.'

He gave her a wry smile. 'I'd kinda noticed that. Sorry, didn't mean no offence. I know you folks've been doin' without for years. They told us all 'bout the tough time you've been havin'. Gave us a little handbook called *A Short Guide to Great Britain*. I guess we just don't know nothin' yet. But I sure do miss some of the things we have back stateside – peanut butter, chocolate milk shakes, maple syrup, T-bone steaks, apple pie . . .'

It sounded a funny sort of list to her.

''Nother thing I ain't seen before's rain like there is here,' he went on cheerfully. 'Never seen so much as when I first got here. Nor mud so bad neither. Been enough to swallow a man whole up at the base.'

'Don't you have rain in Ohio?' There he went, complaining about the weather.

'Sure we do. Couldn't grow crops, else. But it ain't like here. Reckon that's why England's so green. Real pretty, your countryside . . . all the grass, 'n trees 'n flowers, an' I ain't never seen hedges, like you got here. Wish we had those back in Ohio.'

He had a way of making her cross and then saying something nice, which flustered her. She didn't know what to make of him. He kept reminding her of one of those cowboys she'd seen in the Western films. He was tall and broad-shouldered like they were. She could picture him riding into town down a dusty main street, getting off his horse, looping the reins round a rail and walking up the steps to the saloon bar. He'd be wearing a broad-brimmed cowboy hat and guns sticking out of each holster and a kerchief tied the wrong way round his neck. She could see him pushing open the swing doors and they'd go flipping back and forth behind him as he strolled over to the bar and ordered something out of the corner of his mouth. The bartender, in shirt sleeves and a dark waistcoat, would slide a little glass along the counter top towards him and he'd toss back the contents in one gulp. There'd be a long mirror at the back of the bar and he'd catch sight of the villain's reflection as he sat at a table in the saloon, playing cards and smoking a thin sort of cigar. He'd be wearing a black hat and a fancy waistcoat and there'd be a gun sticking out of his holster, too. Their eyes would meet in the mirror, and narrow, and the cowboy would turn round very slowly, fingering his gun . . . The villain would draw first, from under the table, but the cowboy'd be faster and there'd be a bullet hole in the fancy waistcoat in the blink of an eye. The piano would have stopped strumming and he'd stand there in the hushed saloon, gun smoking. He'd blow on it and put it casually back in the holster. Then he'd call for another drink and toss that one back in one gulp as well before pushing his way out of the swing doors to get back on his horse and canter away into the sunset . . .

The waist gunner put his hand on the wall above her head. 'Nora told Buzz everyone calls you Winnie. That's cute. Mind if I do?'

'If you like.' What else could she say, trapped against the wall. It was easy to picture him blazing away with a machine gun in a B17, too, she thought. Not much different, really, from the cowboy.

'It'd be great to see that old barn of yours someday,' he said. 'An' the farm. Meet your folks. Ain't never been in a real English home . . .'

'I don't get there very often.'

'Must do sometimes.' He grinned down at her. 'It ain't far. We could fix it so's I came over then.' His blue gaze seemed guileless. 'Your folks like ham, and peaches, and pineapple? I got cans o' them. An' I can get plenty o' gum, 'n candy, 'n cigarettes . . .'

Winnie hesitated. She'd been going to find some other

excuse, but then she heard Gran urging her on. *No harm in thet thare. Think o' yar ould Gran.* Smoking was one of the few pleasures she had left – that and gossip. And she liked chewing gum too. Candy meant sweets – she knew that – and Gran loved sweets. She always finished her ration almost as soon as she got it. She owed it to Gran. It was Gran who'd made Mum and Dad let her join the WAAF. Thanks to her she wasn't stuck milking cows or cleaning out pigsties, like Nora, or doing the same boring thing over and over again in a factory all day long. Thanks to Gran she was working with 'planes and flying in them, just like she'd always wanted.

'All right,' she said at last. 'But Dad's not very fond of Americans.'

He smiled slowly. 'I got a bottle o' scotch too.'

The Code and Cypher officer stopped Anne in the corridor. She was an ex-debutante with a double-barrelled name who reminded her irritatingly of Susan in the far-off Colston days.

'I say, you know Johnnie Somerville, don't you?'

'Unfortunately. What about him?'

'I just had a letter from a friend. Apparently he got shot up the other day and crash-landed. They took him to some hospital in East Grinstead. A special burns place. Frightful shame, isn't it? He was awfully good-looking.'

Anne had been going to hurry on, but now she stopped. 'Was he badly burned?'

'Pretty badly, by the sound of it. Jolly rotten luck . . .'

The girl walked on down the corridor and Anne stood there for a moment. *I'd far sooner be dead.* That's what he'd told her when she'd had dinner with him in London. She'd been rather scathing in return, she remembered. *You live a charmed life. It won't happen, you're much too lucky.* But Johnnie's luck, it seemed, had finally run out.

*   *   *

As she sat in the darkness of the transmitting room, Virginia would imagine the Pathfinder Mosquito flying high and fast through the night skies over enemy territory. Her eyes were fixed on the screen, but in her mind's eye she carried the image of the pilot and navigator listening intently to the signal reaching their ears. If they strayed to right or left of the circular flight path, the continuous note would turn to dots or dashes to tell them so. The other transmitting station, far away in East Anglia, would be tracking the Mosquito too and waiting for the last ten minutes of flying time to the target. Then they would send out Morse letter signals and, in the closing seconds, a succession of pips. On the final pip the pilot would release the target indicators and their coloured flares would mark the spot for the heavy bombers that followed.

She rubbed her hands quickly over her eyes. The long hours spent staring at the radar screen made them sore and she often had a headache by the end of the watch. But it seemed a small price to pay compared with the price so often paid by the men flying over Nazi Germany. And when she was concentrating so hard she could forget everything else, including the latest letter from her mother – bitter as ever.

You needn't trouble to come home on your next leave. You've made it very clear that you've no wish to do so. In my opinion you have grown up into a very selfish and ungrateful person. I have only ever wanted the best for you, but I might as well have saved myself the trouble and worry. It was for your own good entirely that I tried to discourage you from a most unsuitable connection and one day, when you have come to your senses, you will find you have cause to thank me for that.

I will never thank you for it, Mother, she had thought, as she read the letter. *Never*. I shall always hold it against you.

There had been some Canadian Army engineers working for a while at the camp site. Just to see the Canada flash on their shoulders and hear their voices had pained her.

'Do you know a place called Hamilton,' she had asked one of them. 'It's near Toronto.'

He'd shaken his head. 'I come from Edmonton. You know someone from Hamilton?'

'I did – once.'

Once, but no more. Virginia rubbed her eyes again and concentrated hard on the screen.

'Took yar toime a comin' over here, yew Amuricans,' Gran greeted Virgil Gillies from her chair by the range.

He grinned at her, quite untroubled. 'I guess so, ma'am, but then I reckon we was worth waitin' for.'

'Huh! Tis us'll be the judge o' that.'

Winnie could see Gran's eyes fix beadily on the green canvas bag that he was carrying.

'What's in thet thare?'

'Things I figured might come in handy for you folks.'

'What sort o' things?'

He set the bag on the table and unzipped it. 'Can of ham.' He took it out and held it aloft.

'Huh. What else?'

He fished again and produced more tins. 'Pineapple, peaches, grapefruit . . .'

'Huh. That all?'

'No, ma'am.' He dug deeper. 'Chocolate . . . candy . . . gum . . .' The pile on the table was growing. He dug deeper still and drew a long cardboard carton from the very bottom of the bag. 'Luckies.'

Gran's eyes flickered. She had been watching him like a child watching a conjuror, her eyes following each emerging item in turn, and now she inspected the assortment before her suspiciously. Her tobacco-stained forefinger jabbed the air.

'Them thare'ss Amurican cigarettes?'

'Sure are.' Virgil picked up the carton and offered it to her. 'Special for you, ma'am.'

Quick as a flash Gran had the Lucky Strikes on her lap, buried in the folds of her black gown. 'Thet thare chewin' gum . . .'

The Wrigleys packets disappeared too and she graciously accepted a bar in a brown and silver wrapper. She held it up, turning it this way and that.

'Whass this'm?'

'That there's a Hershey bar, ma'am. Chocolate. Made in Pennsylvania.'

'Hmm.' The bar vanished into her gown. 'Oi'll troi one o' these here cigarettes . . .' She tugged at the carton.

Virgil extracted a packet for her and bent to light the cigarette that she stuck in the corner of her mouth as attentively as if Gran had been a great beauty and not a cantankerous old woman. She puffed away for a moment, eyes closed, tasting.

'Ain't bad. Ain't good, neither. But t'aint bad.'

She squinted up at the young American through a curl of smoke, considering him. 'Reckun yew's a sight better'n thet tibby husband o' Winnie's . . . weren't no good fur naun. Or thet thare pesky Welsh fellah.' She stretched her mouth sideways at him in what was Gran's version of a smile. 'Reckun yew'll do right well.'

To Winnie's chagrin, her mother also seemed as taken by Virgil as she was by the tins of fruit and ham. She kept on thanking him and exclaiming over them as though they were made of solid gold. And Ruth and Laura clustered round him, squealing with delight at all the sweets and chocolate bars. Ruth hung onto his arm, gazing upwards, and he picked her up by the waist and swung her round high up in the air, making her squeal a whole lot more. Then Laura jumped up and down, begging him to do the same to her.

Dad wasn't so easy to please, though, as she'd known. He stomped into the kitchen for his midday meal, grunting away like Susie and acting at first like there was no visitor there. But the bottle of Johnnie Walker whisky went some way to thawing him – she could tell that by the way his eyes kept returning to where he'd set it on the dresser, and halfway through eating his rabbit stew he'd relented enough to start complaining yet again about the Yanks in the Pig and Whistle, which also meant having to acknowledge that there was one of them sitting at his table.

'Time us farmers get there of an evenin', place's near dry,' he said bitterly. 'Drink like fish they do.'

It was a clear case of the pot calling the kettle black, but Dad wouldn't see that.

'Sure am sorry about that, sir,' Virgil glanced at the bottle standing sentinel on the dresser. 'I figure least thing I can do's see you ain't goin' to run dry here.'

Dad grunted again, but it was a milder grunt than when he'd come in. Ruth was still gazing across the table at Virgil. Winnie saw him give her a big wink, and she giggled and looked down at her lap and went pink. Laura started to giggle too, a big smear of Hershey chocolate about her mouth.

After the rabbit stew there was apple pudding with thick cream. Virgil reached the chunks of apple beneath the suet crust.

'Gee, ma'am, I ain't never tasted nothin' so good since I left home.'

Mum went as pink as Ruth. 'I make it with plums too. I've got some bottled, so next time you're here I'll cook that for you, Mr Gillies.'

'Call me Virgil, please. An' I'd sure appreciate it. Ain't nothin' like home cookin'.'

'Where's your home . . . Virgil?'

They listened while he told them about the farm back in Ohio – about the one hundred and sixty acres and the wood-built farmhouse with the creek running close by, and about the seventy-year-old barn that his grandfather had built.

'See, the Government was givin' out land free then, an' my grandpa homesteaded back in the 1880s. Went out there with my grandma an' worked the land from nothin'.

Then my pa and ma took over when they died. Reckon I'll do the same when it comes to my turn – if I make it back. Guess I'll try to get a whole lot more land, grow more crops . . .'

Dad put down his spoon with a clatter. 'Seen my corn? Best lookin' crop I've had in years. We'll be harvestin' in a few weeks.'

'Be glad to give you a hand, sir . . . long as I'm still around.'

Winnie could tell that Dad was weighing up the thought of having a Yank on his fields against the thought of having another much-needed pair of strong hands and, with any luck, another bottle of Johnnie Walker. He wouldn't have noticed the 'long as I'm still around', or thought what it meant if he had. The flying and the fighting, the living and the dying went on somewhere up in the skies and so long as it didn't interfere with the farm or the animals he took no account of it. Bombers and fighters came and went over his head and he shook his fist at them if they made too much noise, but he never troubled to count them or to wonder how many had failed to come back.

The extra pair of hands and the whisky won. Dad nodded grudgingly. 'Reckon you'd come in useful.'

After the meal was over Winnie was hustled out to show Virgil round the farm. She could never remember so much fuss being made over a visitor. She wondered uneasily how it would all compare with the hundred and sixty acres in Ohio. Everything in America, it seemed, was bigger and better than in England. Not that she cared – except for pride's sake. In his eyes, she supposed, it would all seem small and old-fashioned, and now that she tried to see things as he might, she noticed the shabbiness and the untidiness as well. The Fordson had left thick tracks of mud all across the yard, the flint wall had tumbled down at one end and the cow byres had been patched up with planks, any old how. She suddenly felt ashamed of the rusty, cast-off machinery and tools lying about in corners, of the broken cart, lopsided on three wheels, of the dung heap covered in flies. Even the farmhouse looked dingy. Its plaster walls were cracked and grimy and fat green cushions of moss grew over the thatched roof. She couldn't remember when the window frames had last been painted, it was so long ago.

Rusty, lying by his kennel, muzzle on forepaws, thumped his tail and followed them with his eyes as they passed.

'Got a coupla dogs back home,' Virgil observed. 'Different kind, though.'

'He's a sheepdog. Dad uses him to round up the flock.' But she blushed as she said it. Rusty was getting too slow and blind to do more than pant after the sheep, who mostly knew their own way without him.

The sheep and the cows and the two Suffolks were all out in the fields, but Susie was in her sty, snuffling and grunting over some choice morsel. Winnie picked up the long stick she kept by the wall and leaned over to scratch her back.

Virgil leaned over too. 'Hi there, Gorgeous! Ain't never seen a black an' white pig like you.'

'She's an Essex Saddleback.'

'That so? I guess the white part's the saddle. Well, she sure is a fine old lady. Kinda small, though. Reckon ours're a whole lot bigger'n that.'

'She's supposed to be that size,' Winnie said coldly. 'It's the breed. She had ten piglets last time.' And don't tell me yours have fourteen, she thought to herself.

'They still around?'

She shook her head. 'They all went to market, 'cept one. He's hangin' up on a hook. We're only allowed to kill two pigs a year. Mum cures them for ham.'

'Ma does the same. Better 'n out've a can, huh?'

Winnie was surprised. Somehow she had pictured his mother, all neat and trim in a pretty apron, taking things out of one of those big refrigerators she'd seen in American kitchens in films – not going through the long, messy process of curing a pig.

'I've never tried ham out of a tin,' she said.

'Aint' like home-cured. Or home-anythin'.'

'Mum boils the trotters,' she volunteered. 'They get a kind of jelly over them when they're cold. Do you have those?'

He shuddered. 'Ugh! Won't touch that kinda stuff. Me, I like real meat. Steaks an' things.'

'She boils the head, too,' Winnie went on gleefully, seeing his disgust. 'Takes out the eyes and the brains first, then boils it down. Then she mashes it all up and lets it go cold. That's called brawn. It's a bit like jelly too. Haven't you ever eaten that?'

'Jeez, no! I'll bet you eat it with Brussels sprouts. You Limeys . . . you'll eat anythin'. An' there's another thing you call different – like corn. Jelly's somethin' you spread on bread to us. You mean jello.'

'No, I don't,' she said indignantly. 'I mean jelly. Stuff that wobbles. It's *jam* you spread on bread.'

'Ain't jam 'less it's got lots o' fruit all mixed up in it.'

'Yes it is. It's jam. You don't put jelly on bread. It's our language. We started it. It's you that's got it all wrong.' She turned her back on him, scratching some more at Susie.

'OK,' he conceded. 'We'll call it quits. It's jelly over here. But in America you're goin' to have to call it jello.'

'I shan't ever be goin' there, so I won't have to do any such thing.'

'Sure you will, when the war's over . . .'

She was still scratching at the sow's back, not looking at him. 'All those things you brought today . . . seemed all wrong to me. Like you felt you had to. Like a bribe, or somethin'. I thought it'd be all right – just for Gran's sake. For the cigarettes, see, an' she likes the sweets and gum, too, but I don't want you to bring any more. It's not right.'

'Well, I guess you could call it a kind of bribe,' he said

slowly. 'But then I reckon we'd all've got along just fine without that stuff — maybe even your pa, come harvest time. An' I can't see anybody bribin' your gran. She figures things out for herself. Ain't nobody goin' to make her do nothin' she don't want to. Or think any different. An' what's so wrong with us Yanks sharin' what we've got around a bit? Seems to me that's only fair. So quit fussin', Winnie, an' show me that old barn o' yours.'

There might be bigger barns in America, she thought, and maybe even better, but there wouldn't be one older. Virgil stood with his hands on his hips, looking admiringly about him at the ancient stones and up at the massive roof timbers.

'Oh boy! Five hundred years old! That's a helluva long time . . . a whole lot've harvests. Gee, the folks back then — well, they must've been walkin' around wearin' those old costumes, like you see in the movies about the old days . . . only they was wearin' them for real. Know what I mean?'

She did know exactly what he meant because she often thought of that too — wondered if their ghosts watched her as she went about the place, and if their spirits lived on somehow in the old walls.

He went on staring about him. 'An' they'd've been seein' just what I'm seein' now. Same stones, same timbers . . .'

Honesty prevailed this time. 'Well, bits of it 've been mended. You can see new wood over there where the windbrace rotted, an' there's some of the roof timbers are different, if you look hard.'

'Ain't nothin'. Reckon most've it's just like it was when some guy put it all together.' He craned his neck upwards. 'There's birds nestin' high up there.'

'Swallows. They come back here every summer. Don't know how they find it.' She tilted her head as well, noticing patches of daylight gleaming among the cobwebs. 'There's a few tiles missin' too. Dad keeps meanin' to do somethin' 'bout them.'

'Don't make no never mind,' he said. 'Sure is the darnedest old barn I ever seen.' He took his gaze off the roof and looked instead at her. 'An' you're the prettiest girl I ever seen. You were cute in that Air Force uniform, but that outfit sure beats everythin'.'

She went pink in the cheeks. The old blue bib-and-braces dungarees were what she always wore about the farm. So was the checked shirt. And both of them were darned and patched. There he was sweet-talking again, and she didn't want it.

'An' don't say that's dumb,' he went on as she opened her mouth, ''cos I'm tellin' you that's so. That husband o' yours . . . what was his name?'

'Ken.'

'He killed in the war?'

'No, he was ill. He had asthma and a weak heart.'

'You married long?'

'Bit more than a year.'

'Tough luck on the guy,' he said. 'Sure feel sorry for him, losin' out like that. The other guy your grandma talked about . . . Welsh, she said. Where's he fit in?'

She took hold of a broom and swept some straw against the wall. 'I don't know what you mean.'

'Sure you do. He your boyfriend now?'

She found some more straw to sweep up. 'It's nothin' to do with you.'

'Yeah, but I'm real curious, see. Your grandma said he was pesky. Now that's a word we use just the same's you, I figure. Means a doggone nuisance, back where I come from. That what he is?'

'He's just someone in the RAF I knew where I was stationed once, that's all.'

'Still hangin' around, though?'

'I told you – it's nothin' to do with you.' She propped the broom back against the wall. 'The cows'll be comin' in soon. I ought to go an' help Jack with the milkin'.'

'Give you a hand, if you like.'

She looked at him doubtfully, standing there in his smart, smooth, American uniform. 'Do you know how?'

'Sure I do.' He was laughing at her expression. 'I'm just a country boy – remember?'

They passed the lean-to shed where the tractor was kept and he spotted it through the open doorway.

'Gee, there's a Fordson . . . mind if I take a peek?'

Dad didn't treat her kindly, Winnie thought sadly. The orange paint was scraped and scratched all over and there were some bad dents.

'We've got a John Deere,' Virgil said.

'Bigger an' better, I suppose.'

'Bigger, sure, but then we ain't got little fields like yours, so we have to use big ploughs – an' that means big tractors to pull 'em. Stands to reason.'

Dad had left the tap switched over to TVO again, she noticed, and he'd probably try to start it like that. She turned it to petrol. No sense saying anything to him; he'd only be grumpy about it, and it wouldn't make any difference.

Virgil watched her. 'You're real handy with machines, ain't you, Winnie? It comes natural to you. Still seems funny to me, though, a pretty girl like you messin' about with engines.'

She straightened up. 'I don't see why. What's funny about it?'

He shrugged. 'Guess I'm just not used to it. Reckon there's no reason why not . . . Now, if you looked more like a man – same as some women I've seen in uniform – wouldn't seem so strange. But seein' you're pretty as you are makes it hard to figure out. I mean our ground crews 're tough as hell . . . out in all weathers, workin' all hours.'

'It's not so hard as on an operational station,' she said. 'They don't let us on those yet . . . at least I don't think so. I've never heard of a WAAF mechanic on one.'

He grinned. 'Guess they don't trust you enough.'

She said hotly: 'We're just as good as the men. Some

588

of the RAF say we're more reliable. More conscientious
. . . that's what a lot of them say.'

He was still grinning. 'I like it when you get cross,
Winnie. Makes you go all pink and look prettier than
ever. I won't tease you no more . . . ain't fair. I'm glad
you're good with machines – comes in real handy. Me,
I'm pretty good with 'em too. Cars, tractors, all kinds o'
engines 'n things. Take real good care o' my gun . . .
make sure there ain't nothin' goin' to go wrong with it
on a mission.'

He raised both arms and swung an imaginary machine
gun from side to side, traversing the top of the Fordson's
engine cover. She stared.

'Have you shot any Jerry fighters down yet?'

He dropped his arms. 'Got one the other day. Boy, that
was a great feelin'. Got some of our own back for what
they'd been doin' to our guys . . . Jeez, those fighters
come at us from all round the clock . . . they sure ain't
beginners. Got lucky with this one an' blew his wing off
an' down he went. Ain't easy, though. You're slippin'
and slidin' around with all the empty shells droppin'
on the floor, and you keep bumpin' the guy on the
other side . . . tough to get a good aim 'n keep firin'
real steady.'

'How many crew do you have?'

'Ten. Pilot, co-pilot, bombardier, navigator, flight
engineer, radio operator, ball turret gunner, two waist
gunners 'n a tail gunner.' He ticked them off on his
fingers. 'Some of those guys man guns too.'

'There's only seven in a Lanc. What do you need all
those for?'

'We've got more guns, like I told you before. So we
need more guys to fire 'em. Else there ain't no point
havin' them.'

'The Lanc carries more bombs than you.'

'Sure. Goin' at night they don't need all the guns, so
they can carry more weight. But we drop our bombs
where they're s'posed to go.' He shook his head. 'Aw,

shucks . . . come 'n, Winnie, it was meant to be quits, remember? Let's go find those cows.'

Tulip, Buttercup, Cherry and Daisy were already in their stalls in the milking parlour. They swung their heads round.

'Hiya, girls!' Virgil said, chewing on a piece of gum. 'Which one's gonna be first?'

Jack, grinning from ear to ear, went to fetch him some overalls and Winnie waited, not without hope, for Virgil to fall off the one-legged stool, or miss the bucket, or for Buttercup, who could be touchy, to kick him. But none of those things happened. He went on chewing gum, balanced easily on the stool, and Buttercup went on chomping cud placidly as though she'd been acquainted with him for years, and the milk went squirting straight into the bucket – ping, ping. As she watched, disconcerted, he gave her a big wink.

At tea-time there were sweetcakes and butter and a jar of jam that Mum had saved for a special occasion. And she'd put the cloth on the table as though it were a Sunday. They opened one of the tins of peaches and had them too. Virgil mixed up the peaches with everything else, all on one plate, which made them stare – except for Gran who was too busy guzzling to notice anything.

When it was time for him to go he lifted up Ruth and Laura once more and swung them round, and gave Dad that funny sort of casual American salute that was almost a wave. When it came to her turn he just grinned and said: 'I'll be seein' you, Winnie.'

He'd come on a bike and freewheeled away down the lane, bearing the dozen fresh eggs that her mother had pressed on him in the canvas bag, propped across the handlebars.

Gran demanded to see the atlas again. She'd forgotten where America was. 'Near Lunnon, is't?'

'No, Gran, it's nowhere near London. It's a long way away – across the sea, remember? Like I showed you before.'

Winnie fetched the atlas and opened it at the picture of the world and placed it on Gran's lap. 'There it is, see. All that big yellow bit.'

'Huh! Doan't look much tew me. Little doddy place.' Ash toppled off the end of the American cigarette and landed in the middle of its country of origin. Gran's jaw was going up and down and Winnie realized that she was chewing gum as well as smoking.

'Well, the map's only on a small scale, Gran. Look, there's England. You could fit us into America hundreds of times over, I should think.'

'Whass all them thare loines?'

'They must be the states. America's divided up into them. Bit like our counties, only they're much bigger. Suffolk'd be a lot smaller than any of their states – you can tell that, see, if you look how little Britain is. They went and joined them all up to make one big country and called themselves the United States of America. I remember learnin' that at school. O' course they belonged to us once – before then. That's why they speak English . . . well, sort of.'

Gran was frowning and scattering more ash. Winnie could see that she was having a hard time grasping it all. But then Gran had never left Suffolk. She'd never been to London. And she'd only been to Ipswich once and that was thirty years ago. Come to that, it was a long time since she'd been down to the village. She didn't know how big any place was outside Elmbury. She couldn't compare anything with anything. Winnie stared at the map. Now that she looked closely, she could see how huge America was, and what a long, long way away from England. It must be thousands of miles across the Atlantic and then thousands more across all that land that stretched as far as the Pacific Ocean. Virgil had once said how many miles it was to Ohio but she had forgotten now. Scotland had seemed such a long way away to her, but compared with America it was no distance at all.

'Thet Amurican o' yurs . . . where's he live?'

'He's not mine, Gran. I didn't ask him here. He asked himself.'

'Huh!'

Winnie turned the atlas pages. 'Look, Gran. This shows you all the states close-up – see. He lives in one called Ohio. We'll find it.'

But she had to search all over before she could. In the mid-west, she thought he'd said, but it looked nearer the east to her and not really in the middle at all. She couldn't see Clyde marked anywhere. Gran made a stab at the state of Ohio with her finger.

'Funny sort o' name. Sounds Oirish. Ain't as big as some, but looks like there's plenty o' room . . . plenty o' room.' She looked up at Winnie beadily, puffing away on her cigarette. 'He askin' hisself here agin?'

'Dad said he could come and help with the harvest, if he wanted. 'Course he might not be able to.'

'Whoi not?'

'He's a gunner in one of those big American 'planes you've seen flyin' over, Gran. They go an' drop bombs on the Germans an' some of them don't come back.'

'What they want to stay thare fur?'

'They get shot down by the Germans. They get taken prisoner . . . or killed.'

'Huh!' Gran slammed the atlas shut and pushed it away. She picked up the empty teacup she had kept beside her and held it out to Winnie. 'Think oi'll tek a drop o' thet thare whisky now. So's I c'n drink hiss health.'

Twenty-Three

The hospital smelled of ether and disinfectant, mingled with some other frightening odour. Burned flesh? Anne shuddered. She stopped a nurse near the entrance.

'Could you tell me where I could find Flight Lieutenant Somerville, please?'

The nurse was plump and pretty, and in a hurry. She smiled.

'It's *Squadron Leader* Somerville . . . go down that corridor and turn right. You'll find the ward straight ahead.'

'Thanks.'

Anne walked on. Squadron Leader? That was news. She passed an open doorway and caught a quick and horrifying glimpse of two rows of beds containing mummy-like forms, of drips and sling pulleys and cages and, incongruously, many vases of bright flowers. A wireless was blaring out some dance music. One of the forms raised a white, bandaged arm and waved at her. She waved back. The hospital smell had intensified sickeningly. At the end of the corridor she turned right and saw another ward ahead. A sister, starched and brisk, stopped her.

'Squadron Leader Somerville? Last bed on the left. You can have ten minutes, but please don't tire him unnecessarily. He had an operation yesterday.'

She took a deep breath and walked down the length of the ward. It was no more than a hut — just like the RAF ones — with walls painted a depressing dark green and cream, but she had never seen a hospital ward that had a piano, or a barrel of beer where a dressing-gowned

593

mummy in a wheelchair was drawing himself a pint. A wireless was playing loudly here, too, and there were vases of flowers on every table – their scent fighting a losing battle with the hospital smells. And these beds contained more white-bandaged figures, and, even more gruesome, others without bandages so that she could see the hideously disfigured faces – the raw red flesh, the flaps of skin hanging loose, the swollen, misshapen features, holes where there should have been noses, slits where there should have been eyes . . . A letter-box opening gaped and twisted in her direction and she realized that it was what was left of a mouth and that its owner was trying manfully to smile at her. She smiled back, swallowed hard, and walked on.

Johnnie was lying against the pillows and his hands were two fat white cocoons resting on the covers before him. When he turned his head slowly towards her she saw that only one side of his face was bandaged and that he still had two eyes, a nose and a mouth. The relief was so great that she nearly laughed aloud.

'Good Christ, Anne! What the hell are you doing here?'

'Keeping my promise. Visiting you. Remember? God knows why.' She held out a bunch of asters. 'I've brought you these.'

She hoped he wouldn't notice that her hand was shaking. In fact, she seemed to be shaking all over. Nausea, horror, shock, disgust, pity, dread and then, finally, the intense relief had all chased each other through her in the past few minutes and left her close to collapse.

'A bottle of whisky would have been better.'

'You'll have to make do with flowers instead. Your nanny would have told you to mind your manners and be grateful for what you're given.'

'I don't like to tell you the answer I'd give her at the moment. Sit down. No, not on that chair. Here, on the bed.'

'What about that ward sister? Won't she mind?'

'Sod her.'

She perched on the edge of the bed. 'How are you, then?'

'How do I look?'

'Actually, not so bad. I was afraid you might be a lot worse.'

'Well, I'm absolutely and totally bloody. Fed up to the back teeth.'

She pointed to the two white cocoons. 'Do they hurt?'

'Don't ask bloody silly questions, Anne. Of course they do. Like hell. They never stop hurting.'

'Sorry. What happened?'

He leaned back on the pillow. 'Some blasted Jerry got me. I managed to make it back but the kite was too shot up to do a decent landing and it went up in flames . . . I should have baled out if I'd had any sense, but the Channel didn't look particularly inviting. Still, as you can see if you look around you, I'm one of the luckier ones.'

'Yes, you are. *Very* lucky. I'd already noticed.'

He gave a snort of laughter. 'I might have known you wouldn't have come to wipe my fevered brow and whisper gentle womanly comforts in my ear.'

'Well, compared with some of the others you look pretty OK to me.'

'Thank you,' he said with sarcasm. 'A trifle blemished, of course, but the quacks tell me they'll be able to patch up my face in time. There's some wizard here who works miracles.'

'Well, you were too good-looking for your own good. Vanity's your middle name.'

'It's Charles, actually. Anne, you're just the sort of visitor they don't encourage. You're supposed to be bolstering my ego, not deflating it.'

'Do you want me to go?'

'No, you can stay and make yourself useful and light me a cigarette. There are some in the drawer there.'

She found a packet of Players and a lighter in the bedside cabinet drawer, lit one and placed it between his lips.

He drew on it and looked up at her quizzically. 'Thanks. As a matter of fact, I don't really give a damn about the face. The hands are another matter, though. One rather needs them to fly with.' He lifted the cocoons. 'And the last time I saw these they looked like two very overcooked bits of steak. No gloves, you see. Bloody stupid.'

'The sister said you had an operation yesterday.'

'*Yet* another, she should have said. And more to come. Still, they seem to think they'll be able to make them work – eventually.'

'Then there's no need to worry.'

He smiled for the first time. 'You remind me of my mother when I fell off my bike, aged about five and cut my knee open badly. The bone was showing through, all white and gleaming, and I yelled when she put disinfectant on it because it hurt a lot. She said: "Don't make such a fuss! It's nothing that won't mend perfectly well." I still bear the scar to this day. I'll show it to you sometime, if you like.'

'No thanks.'

'Oh well . . . How are the bomber lot in Norfolk?'

'Dying.'

'I imagine they are, the poor bastards. Not a job I've ever envied.'

'Who would? Can you manage that cigarette?' She leaned forward to rescue it from the corner of his mouth. He looked at her tunic sleeve.

'It's Section Officer Cunningham, I see. You've gone up in the world.'

'So have you. I didn't know. Squadron Leader's pretty impressive.'

'I'm glad I impress you at last.'

'It's Isobel you need to impress. Weren't you planning to marry her? I thought I'd find her at your bedside, smiling sweetly and attentive to your every need.'

'She came here once and damned nearly passed out. Can't stand hospitals, apparently, and this particular one has some rather gory sights, as you will have observed. It was all too much for her. I told her not to come again. I'm rather relieved to be rid of her. All that adoring adulation was positively boring. And I never had any intention of marrying her.'

'You're a complete swine . . . you know that?'

'You like to think so. Anyway, now you're here *you* can attend to my needs instead. Will you get me some beer from the splendid barrel over there?'

'Is that there all the time?'

'Certainly. We're open all hours. And it never runs dry. You'll find a pint mug in the cupboard.'

She went to draw the beer and returned with a brimming mugful.

'You'll have to give it to me,' he said. 'I can't hold it with these hands.'

She took the cigarette away from his lips and stubbed it out, and held the beer for him to drink, then she sat down on the end of the bed again. 'Say when you want some more.'

The patient in the next bed began to groan and thrash about. His face was completely swathed in bandages with holes left for his nose and mouth and he kept jerking his head from side to side on the pillow. A sour sweet smell came from the bed. Someone turned up the wireless.

'Bomber boy,' Johnnie said laconically. 'His Halifax caught fire doing a wheels up – same as me. He was the only one they got out. Not much face left. They gave him a new upper lip the other day and it's gone septic.'

She listened uneasily to the groaning. 'Can't they do something for him? He sounds in awful pain.'

'I expect some nurse will come along to give him a shot, if it's time. Otherwise he'll just have to grin and bear it for a while – as it were.'

'That sounds pretty hard-hearted.'

'Well, that's the way it is in this ward. If we were

597

soft-hearted we'd all be wringing our hands the whole time – those of us who have hands to wring. More beer, please.'

She put the mug to his lips again. The groans behind her had become pitiful sobs. In her distress she let some of the beer spill down Johnnie's pyjamas.

'Steady on, Anne,' he said. 'Don't go to pieces like Isobel. That's not like you at all.'

A nurse came hurrying down the ward, carrying a kidney dish. She bent over the writhing form in the next bed. After a moment the sobbing stopped.

'Wonderful stuff morphine,' Johnnie observed.

He was leaning back on the pillows again and looking chalk-white.

'God,' she said. 'Your hands don't hurt like that, do they?'

'I've no idea. We don't have such a thing as a pain thermometer to pass round. At the moment it's rather like being stabbed with red hot skewers.'

She stood up. 'I'd better go.'

'You'd better not!'

'That sister said I could stay only a short time. She was rather fierce about it. Said I wasn't to tire you.'

'I never get tired of you, Anne.'

'Don't twist words.'

'Don't go.' He looked up at her with a bitter smile. 'Do you know the worst thing about being in this bloody place?'

'I can guess. Being out of things.'

'Astute girl. Exactly. It's lying here and hearing fighters go overhead and thinking of the lucky bastards flying them while I'm stuck here in this stinking butcher's shop, missing it all.'

'You'll be back flying eventually.'

'The war'll bloody well be over by then. Some of these chaps have been in here for months. Years even.'

'Patience is a virtue. Surely your nanny taught you that?'

'I'm glad you're not sorry for me – like Isobel. I don't think I could have borne that. You'll come again?'

'It'll be difficult. This is only a forty-eight and I have to get back. The trains always take for ever. Not sure when I'll get a decent amount of leave next . . . and you're miles away. Anyway, you must have masses of visitors.'

'Not many that I want to see. Are you going to take that beer away with you?'

She had forgotten that she was still holding the mug. 'Do you want some more?'

He shook his head. 'You can leave it on the side there. A nurse will come round and minister to me soon.'

'They're all very pretty.'

'Specially chosen to cheer us up and make us feel the same handsome, attractive, devil-may-care chaps we once were . . .' He looked at her. 'You've cheered me up more than any of them, Anne. Thanks for keeping your promise.'

She walked away down the ward between the rows of beds, smiling resolutely at their occupants as she passed them. At the doorway she turned to look back. Johnnie lifted one of the white cocoons in farewell.

It was much quieter than usual in the Fox and Grapes.

'Where're all the bloody Yanks, then?' the corporal fitter asked the landlord.

'Lyin' all over Germany, by the sound of it,' was the reply. 'They lost a whole lot of bombers today. Some big raid . . . Nearly four hundred went and sixty didn't come back. That's the rumour.'

'Blimey! Maybe that'll teach 'em it's not so bloody easy. Be a bit more peaceful round here, too. Might even be some beer left for us, eh, mate?'

Winnie listened, shocked. Sixty bombers missing . . . Ten crew to each, Virgil had said. That was six hundred men. Some might have parachuted to safety, but most would probably be dead. She had never cared much for the fitter and now she liked him even less for his callous words. She wanted to tell him just what she thought of him for them, but it would only have started him and the others off again – teasing her about Americans. They'd given her a hard time after she'd gone over to the American corner in the pub that evening. *Where's the nylons, then, Winnie? Didn't know you was after a millionaire, love. You know what they say about girls who go with Americans, Winnie – one Yank and they're off* . . . She hadn't been down to the Fox and Grapes since, afraid that Virgil Gillies and Buzz and the rest of them would be there and that the same thing would happen again. This evening, though, the RAF lads had made out they were offended she wouldn't join them, and so she'd gone too.

The barmaid had red-rimmed eyes and kept dabbing at them with a handkerchief taken from her bosom. Winnie wondered if she was crying for all the missing Americans, or if she knew which bombers hadn't come back and was crying for one. If she had the nerve and the chance, she might be able to ask her if she knew whether *Sassy Sally* had gone on the raid, and whether she had come back . . .

'You're very quiet, Winnie,' the fitter said nastily. 'You wondering about your Yank? I reckon he won't be walking in here this evening. You'll just have to make do with us.'

The rabbits were running out from the corn. Winnie, following after the binder round the ten-acre field and stooking the sheaves it dropped, could see them bolting from the circle left standing in the middle where they'd taken refuge as the corn was cut. Old Ebenezer Stannard's two terriers were straining at their leashes and yapping excitedly. He stooped to release them and they streaked after the rabbits. One of them caught up with one near the edge of the field and there was a squealing and a snapping and then the squealing stopped abruptly. Winnie made another stook and then rested for a moment. The island of corn was growing steadily smaller as Dad went round and round on the Fordson, with Jack sitting on the binder behind. She knew he'd far sooner have been driving Prince and Smiler, but he wouldn't let her do the job – not with other people watching.

She wiped her hand across her forehead and let the breeze cool her down a bit. They were lagging far behind with the sheaves but it couldn't be helped, they were so shorthanded this harvest. Mr Stannard had hurt his back and couldn't come over as he usually did and the labourer he'd sent was even older than Jack. The two boys from the village who were supposed to be helping her with the sheaves were playing about more than they were working. It was lucky she'd had some leave due or Dad wouldn't have managed at all.

She chewed on a bit of straw, watching the binder's sails turning. Gran had kept on and on about Virgil Gillies since she'd got home.

'That thare Amurican . . . 'tis toime he came.'

'I don't know if he can, Gran.'

'Whoi not?' she'd demanded.

'Well, lots of their bombers were lost on a big raid last week. He might have been in one of them.'

'Doan't sinnify . . . he moit not. Whoi doan't yew go an' ask, gal?'

But Winnie couldn't bring herself to go up to the base and ask the American guards at the main gate whether or not Virgil Gillies was missing. She was too shy to do it. Nora might have known, because of Buzz, but she was away working on another farm and busy with the harvest too. Whenever a B17 went over low she tried to read the name on its nose and to see if it had a painting of a girl wearing nothing but a flower in her hair, like Nora had told her, but though several of them had girls looking rather like that, none of them was *Sassy Sally*. They had other names – *Honey Girl, Calamity Jane, Delectable Duchess, Sleepy Time Gal, Red Hot Riding Hood* . . .

'He've good strong shoulders on 'm,' Gran had muttered. 'Puts me in moind o' Gideon.'

She often boasted about how strong Grandad had been. How he could swing a scythe nine feet and pitch whole sacks of grain on a fork up over the wagon eaves to load them. But Gran thought they still cut the corn with scythes and threshed it with a flail in the barn, like in the old days, though Winnie had tried to explain that it was different now.

Gran could remember all sorts of other things from the past. She'd go on about the gibbet on the Common with its cage swinging in the wind, about tales of smugglers out on the marshes, about the mail coach passing through the village, sounding its horn, and the gentry's carriages bowling by. She remembered when there had been a pig-pole in every cottage garden for the pig's carcass and when folks used horn lanterns and rushlights. Grandad Gideon had worn a smock and a tall beaver hat shaped like a chimney pot, and she'd worn a bonnet and shawl and pattens on her feet for the mud.

Winnie went on chewing the straw and cooling down a bit. Gran believed in all kinds of strange old superstitions too – that it would rain if you killed a black beetle, that if you burned eggshells you'd bind the hens, that you could cure warts by rubbing them three times with a bean which you then buried. She'd cured Dad of a wart on his hand once like that. And she believed that toads could bite and that pigs could see the wind and horses see ghosts, and that if you put horse hairs into the river they'd turn into eels. And she could always tell by the way the fire burned and how the smoke went up the chimney what the weather was going to do. Mum said she was lucky they didn't still burn witches.

There was only a small patch of corn left standing now – a little doddy bit, Gran would have called it – and all the rabbits had fled. But there were a whole lot of sheaves waiting to be stooked and she was aching with weariness already. She turned, shielding her eyes against the bright sun, as she heard someone shouting from across the field. There was a figure standing by the gate – a tall figure dressed in uniform. She blinked and went on staring as it vaulted over the gate and came striding along the edge of the field towards her. She waited, as though rooted to the spot.

'Hi there, Winnie!'

Virgil came up to her, grinning, his jacket hooked by his thumb over his shoulder. 'Came just like I said I would. Sorry I couldn't make it sooner. I only just got leave.'

She was still staring. She didn't know what to say to him. *I thought you must be dead – we all did, except Gran* . . . she couldn't very well say that.

He looked down at her puzzled. 'You OK, Winnie? Look like you'd seen a ghost . . .' He took the straw slowly out of her mouth and dropped it on the ground. 'Hey, I guess you thought you *had*. You figured I'd had it – like all those other guys . . . you hear about that?'

'We weren't sure,' she said. 'Gran kept asking about you. We didn't know.'

'Brought her some more Luckies. More scotch for your dad too. An' more cans o' fruit. Know you said like I shouldn't but I just reckoned it'd come in handy – same as me.' He looked around the ten-acre and whistled. 'Sure seems like you could do with some help round here.'

He stripped off his tie and shirt and started work then and there, and they worked until the very last of the daylight had gone and the harvest moon was rising over the fields and shining down on all the stooks of corn.

Gran had waited up long past her bedtime. She received the carton of Lucky Strikes regally.

'Took yar toime agin'.'

Virgil grinned at her. 'Yeah, but like I told you before, ma'am, we're worth waitin' for.'

She gave him one of her fearsome smiles. 'Yew moit jest be an' all.'

603

Since there was no spare bedroom in the house he slept outside in the barn.

'Don't worry me none, ma'am,' he told Winnie's mother. 'Straw makes a great bed . . .'

Winnie, in her attic room, watched the moonlight shining in through the little window onto the end of her bed, and thought of him there across the yard. She'd been so thankful when she'd seen it was him at the gate – and not just because of his helping with the harvest. She'd been happy that he was still alive and when he'd come striding over towards her, her heart had started beating faster, just like it did when she stood close by the runway watching the Lancs come in. And she'd kept on sneaking looks at him while he was working away in the field, stripped to the waist and lifting the corn sheaves as though they weighed nothing – like he'd lifted that blond girl at the dance. If Gran could have seen him she'd have started off about Grandad again. And if she, Winnie, wasn't very careful she'd turn into one of those girls at the dance, going on about the Yanks the whole time. *One Yank and they're off* . . . that's what the fitter had said to her in his nasty way, and she'd known very well what he meant.

It was hot again the next day and she was up early to help Jack milk the cows. She looked out of the window and saw that Virgil was already up too and washing at the old pump in the yard, ducking his whole head under the gush of water as he worked the handle. By the time she got to the milking parlour he was there, balanced on the one-legged stool, his wet head pressed against Tulip's flank, the milk pinging steadily into the pail.

'Mornin', Winnie.'

At breakfast he put jam on his porridge and stirred it in with his spoon, and then he cut up all his bacon and eggs into pieces and set down his knife across the side of his plate to eat them just with his fork, and a slice of bread and jam at the same time too. Ruth and Laura watched him, wide-eyed, and when he winked at them they collapsed into giggles.

After breakfast Prince and Smiler were brought clip-clopping into the stackyard to be harnessed up to the wagon. Virgil was impressed.

'Finest farm horses I ever seen,' he said. 'Biggest too. Never seen such hooves. Must be real strong.'

'They're Suffolk Punches,' Winnie told him proudly. At last there was something bigger and better on the farm than he had in America, not counting the barn. In Grandad's day the wagon's paint would have been bright red and yellow, not all faded and peeling like it was now, but she thought that it still made a beautiful sight to see the two Suffolks pulling it out to the fields, their heads nodding and long tails swishing.

Near midday the workers rested in the shade and ate thick sandwiches. Virgil tried some of Jack's home-brewed beer and said it was much better than the watery stuff in the pubs.

'Gran used to brew 'fore she got old,' Winnie said, chewing her spam sandwich. 'But Mum won't do that any more. She says Dad has enough beer down at the Pig 'n Whistle. She baked this bread, though, an' made the butter. She churns every week on Tuesdays.'

'It's real good,' Virgil said. 'An' those hens o' yours lay good eggs. They ain't heard o' square ones. Ma bakes bread too, but she buys butter at the store. Guess it's easier.'

'Mmm. It's hard to make the butter come sometimes when the weather's hot. Mum has to churn early in the morning then, 'fore it gets warm. She makes barley wine, too. Have you ever drunk that?'

'Nope. Maybe I'll get to try some.'

'It's quite strong. Gran likes it a lot. We always drink some at Christmas.'

'Christmas . . .' he shook his head. 'That's a long ways off. Can't think about that. Can't even think 'bout Thanksgivin'.'

'Thanksgivin'? What's that?'

'Gee, don't tell me you ain't never heard o' Thanksgivin'?'

'No. What is it?'

'Gee,' he said, shaking his head again. 'I kinda thought you'd know all about that – seein' how it's to do with you folks. You know . . . those Puritan guys o' yours back in history that crossed the Atlantic in that old tub . . . you musta heard of 'em?'

She frowned. 'Oh, you mean the Pilgrim Fathers? I remember we were taught about them at school. They sailed from Plymouth, I think, 'cos they didn't like the way things were in England, and went to America.'

'Check! Called it the same name on our side when they finally made it over. Guess they couldn't think of anythin' else. Well, seems they had a hell 've a time findin' any food there to start with, an' it was so damn cold their first winter that a whole bunch o' them died. So when they had a good harvest the next year, I guess they thought it was really somethin' to celebrate an' they had a great big feast – turkey an' cranberries an' pumpkins, an' all that stuff. See, the turkeys had been runnin' around wild when they arrived an' they started catchin' 'em to eat. Then they grew all the rest. An' they asked the local Indians round too, seein' as they'd been real helpful givin' 'em seeds an' such like.'

'They don't seem very helpful in films.'

'Well, that was 'fore they'd cottoned on we was goin' to grab all their land. So, that was the first Thanksgivin' an' we have one regular every year now an' eat the same kinda stuff those Pilgrim guys ate. Have it last Thursday in November – right around the time the snows come back home.'

'You get snow?' She was amazed. She'd imagined Ohio to have wonderful weather the whole year round – not like England. Endless sunshine and blue skies, like in Hollywood.

'Sure do . . . boy, can it snow sometimes! In a bad

winter it c'n stay right through March. Worse 'n anythin' you'd get here, I reckon. An' in summer it can get real hot, an' we get big thunderstorms an' tornados.'

'Goodness . . . *tornados!* Like the one in *The Wizard of Oz?*'

'Yeah. Just like that, 'cept we don't get no witches flyin' by. That was Kansas though. Ohio looks different. Where I live we've got rollin' bits with woods and creeks. Real pretty in parts.'

She was curious about this far-off land of his. 'What sort of wild animals do you have? Are there foxes?'

'Sure there are. An' skunks, an' racoons, 'n chipmunks, 'n possums.'

'We don't have any of those,' she said.

'You've got rabbits same as us, though. We've got more rabbits 'n we know what to do with, 'cept shoot.'

'Do you have the same sort of birds as us?'

He considered her question a moment. 'Ain't too sure 'bout that. Think I've seen some here look the same. We've starlin's, an' woodpeckers, an' owls, an' bluebirds – '

'Bluebirds? *Really* blue?'

'Sure. Real bright blue.' He held out his hands several inches apart. ''Bout this big.'

'We don't have those. Least I don't think so. Ken, my husband, had lots of bird books an' I never saw one in those. It's funny 'cos in that song Vera Lynn sings she goes on 'bout there bein' bluebirds over the white cliffs of Dover one day, an' there couldn't be.'

'Well, I guess the guy who wrote it got that wrong.'

She remembered something Taffy had once said to her. 'P'raps he just meant bluebirds of happiness, sort of thing. When the war's over.'

'Yeah. Guess so. That'd be it.'

Virgil lit a cigarette and lay back, staring up into the cloudless sky. 'Sure is good to be down here for a bit, though, an' not up there.'

'That raid must've been a very bad one,' Winnie said cautiously, seeing he must be thinking about it.

'Oh boy . . .' he moved his head slowly from side to side. 'Guess we all knew we were in for it, soon as we got to the briefin'. This is goin' to be a tough job, they said, and they sure weren't kiddin' us.'

He drew on the cigarette and went on staring up into the sky. She stole a look sideways at him. Gran had been right about the strong shoulders. They were burned brown now by the sun and his fair hair was dark with sweat from pitching the sheaves up onto the wagon.

'I ain't never seen so many Jerry fighters as on that mission,' he said, almost to himself. 'Soon as our escorts'd turned back they showed up – dozens of 'em. MEs and FWs – even saw an old Dornier. Seemed like they'd put up everythin' they could find to stop us. They lined up an' they came in real fast, rollin' as they fired.' He turned his hand over. 'I saw three ships go down just on one pass . . . An' they kept on doin' that to us all the way over. Chutes goin' down all over the sky – theirs an' ours together – an' stuff sailin' past us . . . doors 'n bits o' wings, 'n worse . . . I was firin' away, up to the ankles in empty cases, so was Matt – he's the other waist gunner. Thought I got a couple, but it's sure hard to tell sometimes. They can fool you – puff out smoke like they're hit an' goin' down, then round they come again.'

The village boys were throwing clods of earth at each other and tumbling about. Jack had his hat over his eyes and was probably asleep. Prince and Smiler were swish-swishing the flies away with their tails. The sun glared down.

Virgil brushed a fly away absently. 'They jumped us goin' back too. Gave us hell again. I saw a coupla Forts just blown clean to pieces. No chutes then . . . An' all the way back we could see the smoke 'n flames from the wrecks down on the ground. Reckon we could've found our way home by them. Jeez, were we glad to see our fighter boys show up, and then the English coast! When we landed Buzz knelt down an' kissed the ground. Know just how he felt. Nearly did the same myself.'

She looked at him again, troubled. 'Will you have to go on more raids like that?'

'Guess so. Gotta fly the mission.'

At the end of the day she tried to thank him for his help, for Dad wouldn't, but he brushed her words aside.

'Weren't nothin', Winnie. Only wish I could stay an' help finish the job, but I gotta go back tomorrow.'

They were walking across the yard in the darkness. The moon looked like a huge orange hanging over the farmhouse. Rusty rattled his chain softly.

'Before the war,' she said, 'we always used to have a supper in the barn when the harvest was over – horkey, we call it. It's like a thank-you to everyone who helped gettin' it in. A kind of feast.'

'With turkey an' that sort of thing?'

'Oh, no, nothin' like that. We'd have things like rabbit pie an' those jellied pigs' trotters I was tellin' you about.'

'Then I ain't sorry I'm missin' it.'

'We don't have it any more anyway, not since the war started. It was fun, though. Jack used to play the fiddle an' people danced . . . not like your sort o' dancin', o' course, more like hoppin' about.'

'Well, I guess that's pretty much all we do too,' he said. 'Hop about.' He stopped walking. 'Remember that dance? I already told you, Winnie – moment I saw you standin' there I knew you was the girl for me. You thought I was kiddin', but I wasn't. I've had all kinds o' dreams an' plans for you 'n me when the war's over . . .' He sighed. 'But right now I figure there ain't no sense in dreamin' or plannin' anythin' no more. The way I see it, I ain't got a prayer o' gettin' through this tour.'

Her mother's voice called out sharply to her from the back door.

'Guess she don't trust me out here with you in the dark.'

She could tell by his voice that he was smiling a bit. Dad would soon start bellowing for her too.

'I'd better go in . . .'

'Reckon you had.' He moved towards her and put his hands on her shoulders. 'In a moment.'

Twenty-Four

It seemed to Felicity, walking down Bond Street after a visit to the tailors for a new uniform fitting, that London no longer carried her battle scars wearily, but flaunted them with pride. The stoic 'London Can Take It' had became the 'London Can Dish It Out', and it showed on people's faces and in the way they held themselves. The landings in Italy and the Italian surrender had boosted spirits and she had walked past a bookshop earlier that had filled its windows optimistically with guide books for Rome, Naples and Milan. Somewhat prematurely, as the Germans were now demonstrating, but it had been a small sign that perhaps the tide was turning at long last. There had been rumours all summer of a landing being planned across the Channel in France as well. Everyone had hoped it might happen in August, but the month had come and gone and now it was late October and nobody expected it to happen before the spring. There were other signs too, though, like the bookshop. Crates of oranges had appeared in greengrocers – fruits of the African victory – and were on sale to children, many of whom would never have seen one.

The biggest sign of all was the presence of the Americans. They were everywhere in London – on every corner and every street, gazing into shop windows, cramming into taxis, sauntering along, snapping right and left with their cameras, and arm-in-arm with the English girls. They looked like conquerors already. The fact was, though, that their noses had been badly bloodied lately. There had been huge American losses on the daylight bombing raids over Germany and that nice-looking young airman from the

New World who was standing and staring about him at grimy old London would probably never set eyes on his own homeland again.

The newsvendors' placards were carrying stark warnings in big letters: *New German Secret Weapon! Terror Rocket Threat!* There had been vague rumours in the papers for months about some kind of rocket that could be lobbed over from France, but nobody seemed very worried about it. 'So long as they don't come and drop no more of them bloody bombs, who bloody cares?' she'd overheard someone say on a bus. 'Can't do much damage from that far away.'

A tall American GI, loping along, bumped into her and apologized with a charming smile, touching his cap and addressing her as ma'am. Some of them are real heart-throbs, she thought. No wonder our girls are bowled over like ninepins.

As she reached Piccadilly she turned the corner and nearly collided with another man in uniform, but this time an RAF Air Commodore. She saluted quickly and would have hurried past him if he had not caught at her arm.

'Felicity!'

'Hallo, sir.'

David Palmer was staring at her. 'What on earth are you doing here? I thought you were miles away, up in Yorkshire.' He was looking as though he could hardly believe his eyes.

'I'm on leave, on my way home.'

'I wish I'd known you were going to be in London.' He was still holding on to her arm. 'Look, at least we could have a drink together. No harm in that, don't you agree?'

He steered her firmly along. He was taking charge, just as he had done once before at Liverpool Street Station, and she felt equally helpless. She found herself sitting opposite him in a corner of a cocktail bar, with a sherry set before her. He looked a little greyer and older and he wore his new rank well, as she would have expected.

He was smiling at her wryly. 'Forgive me for abducting you, Felicity. I'm so glad to see you . . . if only for a moment. It's incredible to have run into you like this. You're a flight officer now . . . congratulations. I'm not a bit surprised.'

'And to you, on your promotion.'

He waved that aside impatiently. 'How have you been? How are you getting on in Yorkshire?'

She hesitated. 'Actually, I've just been posted down to Bomber Command HQ. They wanted someone and a WAAF officer there remembered me from my training course.'

'Is that what *you* wanted?'

'I wasn't sorry to leave the Station. So many were being killed. It was tragic.'

He nodded. 'It's hard to have to watch it happening to fine young men. I could never get used to it at Colston. But I miss being on an operational station, for all that.' His eyes were fixed intently on her face. 'Do you remember that day you first came to Colston and I treated you so appallingly? That haunts me. I'm ashamed of it.'

She remembered it very well. How she had stood in front of him, perspiring, pink in the face, and terrified. *Just exactly what are you women supposed to be doing here, Company Assistant Newman? Perhaps you can explain that to me.*

'It was difficult for you.'

'No, it wasn't. I was just a dyed-in-the-wool misogynist. A blinkered old fool. I know better now, but I must have made life very hard for you then and I regret that very much.'

'It was hard for everyone at the beginning.'

'All the more reason why I should have helped you.' He smiled at her gently. 'It's getting on for a year since we last met, Felicity, and I've thought of you every single day. Is there any hope that you'll change your mind about us?'

She almost weakened – but only for a moment. I mustn't, she told herself desperately. It would ruin his career and the RAF is his life. He would never have been promoted if he'd been involved in a sordid divorce case over a WAAF. Because I love him, I can't let that happen. And I can't steal another woman's husband, no matter what she's like.

'I can't,' she said stiffly. 'I'm sorry, but there's no hope.'

'I understand,' he said quietly. 'Just tell me, though, is there someone else now? Dutton, for instance? He was always very keen. I used to watch him with you.'

It was better to let him think so. 'I see Speedy quite a bit, as a matter of fact.'

He looked down at the table between them and fiddled with his glass. 'Well, I suppose it's not very surprising. Dutton's a young man. Your age.'

She stood up, making herself look and sound brisk and indifferent. 'I really must go, or I'll miss my train . . .'

'Yes, of course.'

He helped her on with her coat and they went outside into the street. It had started to rain.

He touched her arm. 'Take care of yourself, Felicity.'

'You too, David,' she said. She turned and walked quickly away.

The young army captain sitting opposite Anne kept on trying to catch her eye. In a moment he'll go and say something, she thought, and I don't feel in the least like talking. She stared out of the train window, deliberately avoiding his gaze. I'm sick of the war, she thought. Sick to the stomach with the whole ghastly business. Now Frank's dead too – just like I knew he would be, and *he* knew he would be. Killed over Germany on some stupid raid that probably won't have made any difference to winning the war. The thought of it made her want to cry buckets and yell out loud that it wasn't bloody fair. He was so nice. Why couldn't he have gone back home to Chicago and had a life, instead of it being ended horribly like that. Nobody ever died anything but horribly on those raids. And why couldn't Latimer have lived? Or Digger? Or Jimmy? Or any of them? The hundreds of decent, nice young men who would never have proper lives. Twenty-something wasn't very long to live. Not much of an innings. And Michal . . . better not to think about him at the moment or she would really start crying and disgrace herself in front of the rest of the carriage – the two tweedy spinsters, the stuffy-looking old colonel, though he had gone to sleep, the three RAF penguins and the young captain, who was *still* trying to catch her eye – bother him! Why couldn't he leave her in peace?

London had given way to the suburbs and now they were getting into the country. It all looked grey-brown and wintry. November was halfway through and there were hardly any leaves left on the trees – just a few dead ones that would blow away with the next strong wind. Soon it would be Christmas again. Another bloody Christmas! Awful camp concerts, tatty decorations, officers dishing round the turkey to other ranks, false bonhomie, false merry-making – for what was there to be merry about, with everyone dying like flies? And then a few days later it would be 1944. Another bloody year of war notched up.

The train slowed to a stop in the middle of nowhere and stayed there, engine hissing away up front. This was the fourth time since they'd left Paddington. It was the usual business. Stop-start. Start-stop. You never knew what was going on. And it was freezing cold in the carriage. Naturally, the heating wasn't working. Or if it had been it would probably have roasted them alive. One or the other. Her feet felt like blocks of ice and there was probably another two or three hours to go. She wriggled her toes uncomfortably.

Why was she doing this anyway? Giving up precious leave to go and stay with the Somervilles? *Dear Anne,* Lady Somerville had written in a very nice, flourishing hand. *Johnnie is home for a while, in between operations on his hands, and he's very down in the dumps. He tells me that of all his hospital visitors, you cheered him up the most. Would you come and stay with us when you next get some leave? I think he'll be here for some time. He doesn't know that I'm writing to you – for some reason he won't ask you himself, so I decided to. I would be in your debt if you would come. Yours sincerely, Mary Somerville.*

She'd been rather flattered, in a way. And maybe a bit curious to see the Gloucestershire pile. And not that keen to go home and face the parade of suitable young officers who would be dragged round for drinks by her mother. Oddly, she didn't mind seeing Johnnie again too much, though whether she'd be able to cheer him, as his mother hoped, was another matter. They'd be more likely to end up rowing.

The train jerked forward and crawled a few yards before it stopped again. Just teasing us, she thought. Raising our hopes that we might get there before tomorrow, only to dash them again.

The captain leaned forward. 'I say, excuse me, but aren't you Anne Cunningham? Kit's sister?'

She looked at him reluctantly. 'Yes, do I know you?'

He flushed. 'Well, not exactly. We did meet once, but I'm sure you won't remember. It was at the Fourth one year. I'm Alastair Crawford.'

'I'm sorry. There were so many of you always . . .'

'Oh, I didn't expect you would remember. It was only for a moment. But Kit had a photo of you in his room, and of course you're so like him. I thought it must be you. Actually, I saw Kit quite recently. In Alex.'

He had her full attention now. 'How was he?'

'Fine. Absolutely fine. I ran across him in a bar . . . we just had a few words, that's all. Of course he didn't know I was going to run into you too, like this, or he'd have sent some sort of message.' He laughed. 'Didn't know it myself. Extraordinary coincidence.'

And he's a captain, she thought, God save us. 'Are you here on leave?'

'Yes. On my way home to the parents. I get out at the next stop – if we ever get there. Simply frightful these trains, aren't they?'

She wondered if he knew about Villiers, and Latimer and Parker-Smiley, and heaven knew how many more of those gilded youths who'd swanned about Eton on those sunlit, summer days. How many were now lying in cold, dark graves, or in no graves at all?

'How did Kit look?'

'Oh, jolly well, really. We were all pretty chuffed out there at getting our own back – '

'Did he say anything about getting home soon?'

'No, didn't mention anything like that. Careless talk, anyway, I suppose. But I expect he'll get back before too long. Is it a long time since you saw him?'

'Yes,' she said. 'It's more than two years.'

'Gosh, that must be awful. I mean, I should think you were pretty close – being twins.' He beamed at her. 'You do look awfully alike.'

The train jerked forward again and this time gathered speed. She leaned back and smiled at him kindly. He'd given her news of Kit, however little. If he was getting out at the next stop, she didn't mind talking until then.

Lady Somerville met her at the station in a pony and trap. 'It'll be a bit chilly, hope you don't mind. There's no petrol, of course, for this sort of thing, so we use old Dolly. She used to be Johnnie's years ago.'

Old Dolly was a fat skewbald who moved at her own pace, ignoring any gentle inducement with the whip. And Johnnie's mother was a surprise. Anne had pictured some frighteningly elegant woman; instead she was dressed in slacks and an old tweed hacking jacket, with a scarf tied round her head. But she was beautiful in the understated, unfading way of very aristocratic English women. And she had Johnnie's blue eyes. Or rather, he had hers.

She made more chucking noises at Dolly's broad back,

which were disregarded, and smiled sideways at Anne. 'Thank you for coming. I told Johnnie what I'd done this morning and, of course, he was furious with me for it. I can't think why. As soon as I saw you, I knew I had done just the right thing.'

'How is he?'

'Better, I think. At least his face is getting better. Really not bad at all. He was very lucky about that. I say that to myself every day when I remember some of those other poor young men in that ward . . . In time I expect we'll hardly notice it, and it doesn't seem to worry him, which is the main thing. It's the hands that are the trouble. They're still giving him a lot of pain at times and he gets so frustrated that he can't go back and fly again immediately – thank goodness. They've done several operations on them and he's got more to be done before they're finished. Our GP and the district nurse are coping meanwhile.'

'Can he use them?'

'Oh, yes. Just not very well. And they don't look very pretty, but what does that matter so long as he still has hands? And they *will* work. He's supposed to do exercises with them but he gets bored and discouraged. You know how impatient men can be. I'm hoping that's where you'll come in – to make him persevere.'

'Well, I'll try.'

'Oh, I think he might listen to you,' Mary Somerville said with a small smile. 'You might make all the difference.'

The Gloucestershire pile was very impressive. When it came into view shortly after they had passed through a large gateway, Anne's jaw almost dropped. The huge and very beautiful Georgian mansion was built of golden Cotswold stone and stood serenely in a dip in the land. She could see rows of tall windows and a porticoed entrance. The driveway leading to it swept through iron railed parkland and looked about two miles long. Dolly, scenting home, suddenly increased her pace to a smart trot. They clattered into the stableyard round the side of the house and an elderly, gaitered groom appeared, looking like a character out of a nineteenth-century novel. He touched his cap.

'This is Gribble,' Lady Somerville said. 'He's been with us for years.' And as two black labradors also appeared: 'And these are Samson and Delilah. We'll go in through the back, if you don't mind. We never use the front these days.'

The passageway was lined with a jumble of wellington boots, and coats and hats hanging anyhow on hooks. It was glacially cold. They passed warren-like kitchen quarters that reminded Anne a little of the ones at Colston, and went past the green baize door.

Her WAAF shoes rang on the flagstone floor in the hall, as she followed Lady Somerville. She had time to take in some rather amazing pieces of antique furniture and a row of what looked like old masters, and then a magnificent staircase curving upwards. At the top stood Johnnie.

'Don't you dare ask me what I'm doing here,' she said. His mother seemed to have disappeared.

He came down slowly towards her. 'I know what you're doing here. You've come to cheer me up at my dear Mamma's request. I apologize that you've been dragged all the way here for such a boring task.'

'It certainly seems like it's going to be pretty boring, if you're being difficult.' He was within a few steps of her now and the light had fallen on his face. 'You're looking rather healthy. And the face is fine.'

In fact, it had given her a bit of a shock to see how it had marred his smooth good looks. The side that had been under the bandages was a patchwork of angry red and dead white skin. His hands, hanging at his sides, were still bandaged, but the fingers were visible – swollen and liver-coloured.

He smiled. 'It's good of you to come, Anne. I'll try to behave and entertain you.'

619

'I think I'm supposed to be entertaining *you*, aren't I?'

'How long can you stay?'

'I've got seven days. If I can stand it.'

'I'm beginning to feel brighter already,' he said.

He showed her round the house, opening doors onto rooms where the furniture stood shrouded with dust sheets and the window blinds were down.

'Pity you can't see it as it was before the war. We've shut most of it up for the duration. Nearly all the staff have gone. There's only a couple of women who come in from the village, and Gribble in the stables, and an even older gardener. My mother's learned to cook – she rather enjoys it.'

'It's a beautiful house,' she said. 'Have your family lived here long?'

'Only four generations. Newcomers, really. I love the place . . . After the war, I imagine we'll try to open it all up again, but I'm not sure if it will ever be quite the same again. I've a feeling those pre-war times are gone for good. Perhaps that's not such a bad thing, in a way.'

'The end of privilege and all that?'

'You're quite a radical at heart, aren't you, Anne? Well, I don't think the Nazi regime is the only one that's going to find itself replaced. It's going to be quite a different sort of world, for better or worse.'

'Better, of course.'

'I hope you're right.'

The weather was dry but they stayed indoors on most days because the cold wind pained his hands. They sat by a logfire in the snuggery, playing snakes and ladders and draughts, gin rummy and poker.

'Good exercise for your fingers,' she told him cheerfully. 'Picking up and putting down.'

'Sadist.'

He had propped his hand of cards up against his knee and, as he fumbled clumsily with them, they all toppled onto the carpet. He swore violently.

'I might as well have a bunch of bananas. Those damned exercises don't seem to make any difference.'

'That's because you're not giving them a chance. They will – if you do them properly.'

'All very well for *you* to talk, Anne . . . and, by the way, I think you must be cheating. I usually win.'

But he smiled as he said it.

One afternoon, when the wind had dropped, they went for a walk across the parkland with Samson and Delilah bounding along in attendance. He kept his hands carefully in his pockets.

'I like your mother,' she told him, striding along.

'And she likes you. I'm sorry my father isn't here. He'd have enjoyed meeting you. But he spends a lot of time in London at the moment, doing some sort of liaison work. In his element, so far as I can tell. He flew in the Flying Corps in the Great War, you know. Camels and Gladiators. Chestful of medals. Loved every moment of it. He still flies my Moth – or did until this war started.'

'I'd forgotten you'd got a 'plane as well as everything else. Where do you keep it?'

'In one of the barns. I'll bring it out when the war's over and take you up.'

They had reached the top of a steep incline and turned to look at the view of the house and surrounding countryside.

'Has your father ever come up here with you and said all this will be yours one day, my son?'

He smiled. 'Something of the kind. It's been dinned into me from a fairly early age that I have a responsibility. There's a fair number of people to consider – tenant farms, tied cottages, and all that kind of thing. It must be a bit of a nightmare for my father having just one son – especially these days. I sometimes think it must be much worse for our parents than for us, in the thick of things – or at least as I *used* to be.'

'And will be again. If you do your exercises.'

'You were supposed to entertain me, not bully me. You

621

remind me of my dear old nanny. You haven't met her, of course, have you? I'll take you to see her. She lives in a cottage on the estate.'

She was sitting by the fireside in a room that was crowded with pictures from the past — photographs of other people's children that she undoubtedly thought of as her own. Her hair was snowy white and she had the sort of sloping, comforting bosom that must have pillowed many a small, weary head. When Johnnie bent to kiss her cheek she reached up to touch his burned face with her fingers and took his bandaged hands in her own, clucking over them like a mother hen. Anne noticed how bright and sharp her eyes were behind her spectacles and, with them turned upon her, found herself hoping that her fingernails were clean and her hair properly brushed.

She insisted that they stay for tea and went off to the small kitchen, waving away offers of help. Anne looked at a large photo of Johnnie as a small boy, dressed in a sailor suit and with angelically fair hair. It was prominently displayed.

'I bet you were her favourite,' she whispered. 'How sickening.'

There were other photos of him, at different ages — from the baby in a lace christening robe to the young Etonian in tails. And there was one taken with his three sisters — he at about ten years old, the girls already grown-up.

'Rosemary, Henrietta and Sarah.' He pointed them out for her.

'They're all beautiful, like your mother. Aren't they all married now?'

'Lord, yes. Married with sprogs. I'm an uncle eight times over already. Rosemary lives up in Scotland — married to a landowner there. Henrietta lives in London and Sarah in Hampshire. Their husbands are army, navy and air force respectively. Thank God, they've all survived, so far. You must meet them one day.'

They drank their tea and ate up the fish paste sandwiches under an eagle eye.

'A clean plate is a healthy plate, isn't that right, Nanny?'

'I'm glad to see you haven't forgotten, Master John. And we must think of all the starving children in Europe.'

'I thought she was going to ask you if you had a clean handkerchief as we were leaving,' Anne said later.

'I wouldn't put it past her. She'd have called that after me as I was scrambling if she could, and told me to sit up straight in the cockpit and keep my elbows in. By the way, did you notice the way she was looking you over to see if you had good child-bearing hips? She's waiting to be brought out of retirement.'

'Don't be ridiculous!'

'I've never seen you blush before, Anne. This is something quite new.'

'Well, it was a jolly stupid sort of joke.'

'I wasn't joking,' he said.

'Does anyone play that very grand grand piano?' she asked him after dinner on her last evening, when they were alone in the drawing-room by the fire, drinking brandy.

'My mother. She plays extremely well, as a matter of fact, though she'd never admit it.'

'I wish I'd asked before she went to bed. How about you?'

'I used to strum.'

'Used to?'

He raised his hands mutely.

'Why don't you try,' she said. 'It would – '

'Be good exercise for them. I know. How I've suffered at *your* hands this week, Anne.' He went over to the piano, sat down and lifted the lid. Then, very slowly, he picked out the scale of C major with one finger – up and then down again. 'There.'

She got up to join him and leaned her elbows on the top. 'You can do better than that.'

'How are you so sure?'

'Because you're not even trying.'

He picked out a few more notes that became a tune.

'I know that one.' She smiled.

'I know you know it. You were singing it when I first saw you.'

'When you second saw me, actually.'

'I don't count the other time. I really don't remember it very well. According to you, I was behaving badly.'

'You behaved pretty badly the second time – barging in to that dressing-room and acting as though I was supposed to swoon at your feet. And the next time, after that, you abducted me.'

'The only course of action with someone like you, Anne.' He played some more notes idly with his right hand and then added chords with his left. She half-spoke, half-sang a soft accompaniment.

> Look for the silver lining
> When e'er a cloud appears in the blue.
> Remember somewhere the sun is shining
> And so the right thing to do is make it shine for
> you . . .

He stopped. 'Sorry. I can't play any more.'

'Are your hands hurting?'

'Yes, as a matter of fact. Like hell, this evening.'

She said contritely: 'I didn't realize.'

'How could you?'

'But they are getting better, aren't they? You'll be able to play properly again one day. I can tell you're very good, but you won't admit it – like your mother.'

He banged the lid shut. 'Blow the bloody piano! It's *flying* I care about. When am I going to be able to do that again?'

'What's the rush?'

'You're not a fighter pilot, Anne, or you wouldn't have asked that.'

'Sorry.'

'It's me that should be sorry,' he said. 'I'm being boorish yet again. I've learned bad ways in the hospital. Nanny would have given me a ticking-off and a long lecture about being gracious to guests, especially ones who are trying very hard to be helpful.' He smiled at her. 'I love you in that blue dress. You wore it when we went out to dinner in London.'

'How observant of you. It's not really warm enough for winter though . . .' She tweaked her cardigan closer round her shoulders.

'Come and sit by the fire again and I'll pour us both some more brandy.'

'I'm already rather tiddly or I wouldn't have started singing.'

'Does it matter? And I'm glad you did. It reminded me of that evening, seeing you up on that stage . . .'

She went back to the fireside and he recharged their glasses and handed hers to her.

'Cigarette?'

'Thanks.'

He lit it for her and leaned against the mantelpiece.

'You were still very upset over Racyñski's death that time we met in London. Have you got over it?'

'It's not an illness – like measles or chicken pox.'

'I know, but it takes time to recover, in the same way.'

'Well, I haven't. It still makes me completely miserable, if you want to know. And I still think about him all the time.'

'I doubt if that's what he would have wanted. Would he?'

I do not want you to be sad for me . . . remember me sometimes, but only with a smile. She had re-read Michal's letter countless times and it was stained with many tears.

'I can't help it.'

'Perhaps you should try harder, Anne. Like I should try harder with my exercises. We could both do better, as they say in school reports.'

'They said a lot more in mine . . . Anyway, it's really nothing to do with you.'

'I think it is. You see, I've been hoping that you were slowly coming round to the idea that I wasn't quite so appalling as you first thought. That you might even be prepared to give us a chance.'

'Us?'

'Us,' he repeated. 'You and me. Hasn't that possibility ever occurred to you?'

She looked up at his face, and then quickly down at her glass. 'No, actually, it hasn't.'

'I'm not sure I believe you, Anne. You wouldn't have come here if you weren't ready to think about it.'

'I wish I hadn't.'

'Don't you realize how I feel about you? I thought you must do by now. I've been in love with you for a long time, almost ever since I first saw you singing up on that stage – all right, since the *second* time I saw you. I would have told you before but you'd taken such a dislike to me, and then there was Racyñski . . . I didn't think you'd listen.'

'And I won't listen now, so please don't go on,' she said in agitation. She put down her drink and threw her cigarette into the fire. 'This is crazy and I can't think straight. That wine at dinner and all this brandy . . . I'd better go to bed.'

She stood up and staggered a little, and as she did so, he caught her against him.

'If you won't listen, Anne, then maybe this will convince you.'

After a moment, she said unsteadily: 'That wasn't fair.'

'All's fair in love and war.'

She retreated out of his arms. 'I'm going to bed.'

Her attempt at a dignified exit from the drawing-room was rather spoiled by colliding with one of the chairs, and she realized that she must be a lot more sloshed than she had thought. Far too much of Sir William's five-star brandy had gone down her throat than was good for her. She put out a hand to steady herself and proceeded carefully. When she had reached the top of the hall staircase, Johnnie called up from its foot.

'You're going the wrong way.'

Damn and blast, she thought, I'll never get the hang of this place.

'It's down *this* corridor.'

He had materialized beside her and put his arm under hers. When they had reached the door of her bedroom, he opened it for her and then followed, shutting it behind him.

'What do you think – ' she began indignantly, but the words were stifled abruptly by his mouth.

The next thing she knew, she was lying on the bed and Johnnie was still kissing her, and all kinds of things had been happening. Her blue frock seemed to be half off already. She thought muzzily: Why am I letting this happen? Why aren't I trying to stop him? God, I'm even *helping* him get the rest of it off . . . And she was actually helping him with *his* clothes now – fumbling with buttons that he couldn't manage easily with his burned hands. Her arms had found their own way around him and she was kissing him back as though she loved him. Later on she thought quite clearly: I don't want him to stop, anyway. I most definitely don't want him to stop at all.

In the morning he came to her room as she was packing. She fancied he looked triumphant. Pleased with himself.

'I'm sorry about last night.' He didn't look in the least sorry.

'So am I.' She folded her cardigan, avoiding his eyes. 'You knew I'd had too much to drink. That was a cad's trick.'

'Well, you know what a cad I am.'

She laid the cardigan in her suitcase. 'Anyway, let's just forget it. It won't happen again.'

'I've no intention of forgetting it.' He moved closer. 'And I want to go on doing the same for many years to come.'

She looked up. '*What?*'

He was smiling. 'I want you to marry me, Anne. I'm asking you if you will?'

After a moment's silence, she said: 'Are you trying to do the decent thing, or something? Because it's certainly not necessary. I'm not that feeble, and, as you probably realized, it wasn't the first time for me.'

'My dear Anne, cads don't do the decent thing. And if I'd asked every girl I've ever been to bed with to marry me, I'd have had a string of wives already.'

'I'm sure you would,' she said coldly. 'And I'm not your dear Anne. And I never will be. Now, if you'll excuse me, I've got to finish this packing before your mother takes me to the station. I've got a stinking hangover, which isn't helping much.'

'Is that your answer, then – no?'

'Looks like it, doesn't it?'

He seemed almost angry. 'Forgive me, Anne, but I had the distinct impression last night that you felt very differently about me . . .'

She flushed and turned back to the suitcase. 'Well, you were wrong. You're still the same conceited Johnnie, aren't you? You can't imagine anyone not wanting you – or actually saying "No" to you. You're not disappointed, you're amazed and very put out. Well, I'm saying "No". No, no, NO.'

Except for the burns on his face, he was very pale. 'I see. Then there's nothing more to be said, is there?'

'I can't think of anything – except goodbye.'

There was another silence. At last he said: 'Very well. But if you change your mind, Anne, let me know.'

'I won't.'

Her head was splitting now and she felt close to tears. It had all gone sour, somehow, and she hadn't really meant that to happen. His proposal had stunned her. And then he had enraged her. And now she was utterly confused. When he had left the room she sank slowly down onto the bed and held her aching head in her hands.

'Peaches,' said Virgil. 'Pineapples, apricots, pears, cranberries, fruit juice . . .' The cans appeared one by one from the green canvas bag that he had set on the kitchen table. 'Chocolate, hard candy, gum.' A wink in Gran's direction. 'Luckies. And scotch.'

'Is that all?' Ruth asked.

'Mebbe. Let's see . . .' He shut his eyes and made a circular motion with his right hand over the bag. 'Abracadabra . . .'

'What is it?' she squealed, hands clasped. 'Is it a rabbit?'

'*Presto!*'

Laura shrieked. 'It's a great big dead chicken!'

'That ain't no chicken, honey. It's a turkey. Don't tell me you ain't never seen a turkey?'

Winnie stared at the big fat bird. It was drawn and plucked but with its head still attached and dangling gruesomely over the edge of the table. 'Where ever did you get it?'

'Well, they was havin' them for Thanksgivin' at the base an' one of the cooks is a buddy of mine . . . They ain't never goin' to miss one.'

'What's Thanksgivin'?' Ruth asked.

'Gee, sweetheart, I'd forgotten you folks don't know 'bout that.' He sat down and lifted her onto his knee. Laura edged close too. 'Well, see, once upon a time — way back in the bad old days – these guys called Puritans, 'cos they behaved real good, got into a boat at Plymouth, England, an' set sail for America . . .'

While the turkey was cooking, Winnie went out to the yard to see to the animals. Virgil went with her, carrying a bucket of potato peelings for Susie. He tipped it over the sty wall into her trough and watched her gobbling away.

'Reminds me of mealtimes back at the base.'

'Thanks for the turkey, Virgil,' Winnie said awkwardly. 'But you shouldn't've done that . . . or brought all those other things. You don't have to.'

'You always say that, Winnie, an' I know I don't have to. I *want* to. I don't see it same as you, so let's just call it quits an' not argue any more. 'Sides your Ma's cookin' it for me to eat too, an' that's real nice of her. I'll have two Thanksgivin's.' He leaned on the sty wall, admiring Susie. 'Atta girl! You sure can shovel it in quick.'

She noticed suddenly that there was a curve of tape shaped like a rocker under the stripes on his arm. 'Have you been promoted – is that what that thing means?'

'Yep. Staff sergeant. Told you I would be.'

She was surprised he hadn't mentioned it long before. 'Is that quite high up?'

'Gettin' on. Should make technical sergeant by the end of my tour – if I live long enough. I guess you'll be gettin' promotion soon, too – a girl like you.'

She looked doubtful. 'I don't know about that. I might be made LACW if I do well on the con course I'm goin' on – that's leadin' aircraftwoman.'

'Con course?' He turned his head towards her. 'What's that?'

'Conversion course. To become a fitter.'

She couldn't help sounding a bit proud about it. Chiefy had been full of praise. 'If anyone's earned it, you have, lassie,' he'd told her. 'You're as good as any of the lads. No reason why you won't make a fitter.' It was a big step forward from being just a flight mechanic. She'd learn a whole lot more on the course and, if she passed it all right, she'd be given more responsibility and be allowed to do more difficult things . . . to take charge of engine changes, to dismantle and reassemble, and carry out bigger inspections. There'd be more pay, too. And maybe she'd even be made a corporal one day, though she couldn't imagine herself telling others what to do all the time.

'First I've heard you mention it,' Virgil said. 'That mean you'll be goin' away?'

She nodded. 'They're sendin' me to RAF Halton.'

'Where's that?'

'In Buckinghamshire. Sort of west of London.'

'How long for?'

'Eight weeks, I think.'

'Gee . . . I'm real glad for you, Winnie. It's great you're doin' that. But I'm sure goin' to miss you.' He shook his head and looked depressed.

She never knew how much of what he said was just sweet-talk. She'd heard so many tales about the way the Yanks fooled the English girls. How they showed photos they said were of their sisters, when they were really of their sweethearts or wives back home. How they promised marriage when they were married already, and how they talked about taking girls back to America after the war, but never meant a word of it. One of the WAAFS in her hut at Flaxton had had to leave because she was having a baby. The father was one of the Yanks at Virgil's base, but he'd been posted away suddenly and she'd never heard from him again. Girls were taken in all the time and made fools of – or so it seemed to her. It was easy for the Americans when they knew they'd be leaving, sooner or later, and they must laugh like anything among themselves. When Virgil had started to kiss her that time out in the yard, in the dark, she'd wriggled free of him and run indoors. She didn't want him thinking that she was easy like the other girls, or that he could lead her up the garden path like them.

'You'll be goin' home soon, anyway, won't you?' she said. 'Soon as you've finished your tour?'

'Well, see, I figured I'd volunteer for another one,' he said slowly. 'Reckon I'd like to stick around a bit longer.

631

I'm a good gunner an' I guess they'd be glad to have me, seein' the way they keep losin' 'em.'

She looked at him, dismayed. 'But that'd be twenty-five more ops.'

'Thirty — that's what the guys do now. But that's OK by me. Funny, when I first got over here, couldn't wait to get back stateside. Now, I ain't in so much of a hurry. An' I guess it wouldn't be straight off. I'd get some leave. Look around some.'

'I wish you wouldn't volunteer, Virgil,' she said earnestly. 'I hope they don't let you do it.'

He smiled. 'Well now, Winnie, I'm sure glad to hear you say that. Didn't figure you'd care much, one way or the other.'

Susie had cleared out the trough and was grunting at them, hoping for more. Virgil picked up the long stick and scratched her back. Winnie leaned on the sty wall and pointed.

'There's a spot just there where she loves it.'

He grinned. 'I know all about things like that.'

Winnie went red and straightened up. 'I ought to go and help Mum.'

Her mother had put on the best tablecloth and fetched out the barley wine. 'Seein' as it's this American thing, whatever it's called,' she told Winnie. 'I thought maybe we ought to make it a bit special an' make Virgil feel at home.'

Dad was already making himself feel well at home with the Johnnie Walker and Winnie could tell by the colour of his face and the level in the bottle that he'd been doing it for some time. Gran was smoking like a chimney and chewing gum too. Ruth and Laura were sticky with sweets. She helped to set the table. The turkey smelled wonderful. They were going to have the tinned cranberries with it like Virgil said they did in America and instead of pumpkin pie her mother had put the other tinned fruit together in a bowl.

When they sat down round the table it felt like

Christmas. Ruth and Laura wore ribbons in their hair and Gran had a clean lace bib on her dress, though it didn't stay that way for long once she'd started eating. Virgil tasted the barley wine and choked a bit. He wiped his mouth.

'Gee . . . that's kinda strong stuff.'

'I made it myself,' her mother told him proudly, pouring him some more.

'Great brew, ma'am.'

Gran drank hers out of a beaker and she was on her third one. Dad always had a tankard and Winnie had lost count of his, on top of all the whisky. She watched him anxiously. When he got going there was no stopping him. She'd often come across him lying in the corner of the barn on a Sunday morning when he was sleeping off a Saturday evening at the Pig and Whistle and sounding like he was driving twenty pigs to market.

Towards the end of the meal, to her embarrassment, he struggled to his feet and stood clutching the edge of the table with one hand while his other raised his tankard.

'Thish bein' a speshul occasion,' he began. 'An' there bein' one of our gallant allies in our midsht . . .'

Gallant allies! Winnie thought. I've heard him call them something quite different. Unlike a lot of men, drink could make Dad quite friendly and very sentimental. She glanced across at Virgil who was, apparently, all ears.

'. . . calls for a toasht,' Dad was saying, and moving to and fro like a sapling in the wind.

Gran stirred irritably. 'Get on wi' it, Josh. Say yar piece an' sit down.'

'I'm comin' to it.' The tankard wavered and some of the brown-gold barley wine splashed over onto the best tablecloth. Dad steadied himself. 'Ladies an' shentlemen, I give you a toasht. God blesh . . . God blesh . . . wass its name?'

'America, sir?' Virgil suggested helpfully.

Dad nodded. 'Thass it. God blesh America . . . an' all who sail in her.'

His hand slipped off the table as he drank. He grabbed at the edge, missed it and toppled forward, landing face down in the remains of his fruit salad.

Gran had drained her beaker. 'Amen,' she said, and gave a loud belch.

PART 4

RECKONING

Twenty-Five

Kit was sitting on the nursery window seat, reading a book – just as he'd been doing the last time they had both been home on leave together. When Anne had opened the door he had lifted his head and smiled at her, and then as she came into the room he stood up. He put his hands on her shoulders and kissed her cheek.

In the old days it would have been a casual wave or a 'wotcha', or some such greeting. Now, she thought, and with regret, they had moved on to another stage in their lives – one where there were now social niceties to be observed between them. He had only arrived home a few hours before her and was still wearing his uniform. There were three captain's pips now on his uniform and he looked older, heavier and rather distinguished. The boy he had been seemed to have vanished completely to be replaced by the man he had become. She felt immensely proud of him, and yet rather sad.

She looked round the old nursery. It still bore the scars of the evacuees, but everything was in its place, just as she always pictured it in her mind – the rocking horse, her dolls' house, the books on the shelves, the tall brass-rimmed guard in front of the gas fire . . . We don't belong here any more, though, she thought. It's stayed the same but we've gone on to become something that doesn't fit here any longer. We're only visitors now. The door has shut behind us and we can never go back.

She glanced at the book that Kit had left open on the window-seat: *The Just So Stories*.

'I was reminding myself how the rhinoceros got its skin,' he said.

In the past, the story had always made her feel itchy all over. She picked up the book and looked at the familiar illustration of the smooth-skinned rhinoceros gazing greedily at the Parsee and his cake on the shores of the Red Sea. He'd stolen the cake and eaten it all up and when he'd unbuttoned his skin and taken it off in a heatwave the Parsee had punished him by filling it with dry, stale, tickly cake-crumbs. And when he'd put it on again the rhinoceros had scratched and rubbed and rolled until it had gone into great folds . . . Just looking at the picture made her feel itchy again, in exactly the same way. The shut door opened a crack, like magic, but only for a moment before it slammed shut again. She put the book down and smiled at Kit.

'You're looking well. How was North Africa?'

'Hot. Sandy. Rather dirty.'

'We sound as though we're talking about a holiday resort. It must have been pretty good hell out there.'

'I've known worse.' He held out his open cigarette case. 'At least we achieved the object in the end – this time.'

She took a cigarette and bent her head to his lighter. She supposed he was referring to Dunkirk and heard the edge in his voice. Surely he had come to terms with what had happened there by now? It was all so long ago. Just one horror in an endless succession of horrors in this interminable war.

She said brightly: 'Anyway, jolly well done, all of you. You gave us a much-needed boost to morale.'

'The RAF haven't been doing so badly over here, from all accounts.'

'Hideous losses in Bomber Command.'

He nodded. 'So I gather. You must hate that.'

She sat down slowly on the window seat. 'I do. So many of them have died, Kit. So many. And you can't pretend it's not happening when you're doing my job. You see them go and not come back. There's no fooling yourself, or getting away from it. Lately, I've begun to feel I can't stand it any longer, which is pretty feeble,

I suppose. It's just so sad and depressing . . .' She drew on the cigarette. 'Anyway, I'm putting in to re-muster to Admin. Apparently they're short of officers so there's a good chance I might be able to. It'll mean another training course with a lot of prissy types, but at least I won't have anything to do with actual ops any more.'

He raised an eyebrow at her. 'You in Admin, Anne? Inspections, charges, jankers . . . not really your style, I'd have thought.'

She grinned. 'I know. In Ops. Int. we always look down on the admins. They aren't even allowed in the room. They get frightfully miffed and jealous.'

'You won't like being one of them.'

'There's method in my madness, though. I've been thinking, you see . . . when we invade Europe they're going to need admins along with them at some stage and I'm volunteering to go the minute that happens. The bombers'll be stuck over here, still bombing.'

'Travel broadens the mind?'

'Absolutely. When do you think it's going to happen, Kit? And where?'

'This summer. Has to be. And somewhere between the Pas de Calais and Brest – it's anybody's guess. Personally, I'm putting my chips down on Normandy, but that's just a hunch.'

'Will you be going?'

'I bloody well hope so.'

She knew better now than to say anything, for what was there to say? I wish you didn't have to, Kit. I couldn't bear it if you were killed too, as well as all the others. You've survived France and you survived North Africa, by a miracle, can't you just stay somewhere nice and safe for the rest of the war? He had no choice in the matter, and neither had she. She turned aside to flick her cigarette ash out of the nursery window and stared at the sunlit garden. The lawn had the lush new green of spring and the herbaceous border was coming to life. Nineteen forty-four was already three months old and this year she would be twenty-three. It was hard to remember what it had been like when there had been no war on, and hard to imagine how it would be when peace came again. She'd leave the WAAF, of course. There'd be no point in staying in. And then what? A boring secretarial course? Some kind of job in London? The War Office, perhaps? Or the Foreign Office? No, not the Foreign Office. That was where Johnnie had been going. If she wasn't careful she'd find herself taking letters from him, and that wouldn't do at all.

She turned back from the window. 'I met someone you knew at Eton called Alastair Crawford last November. We were both on a train going to Gloucestershire. He'd just come back from North Africa and said he'd run into you in a bar in Alex.'

'Crawford?' Kit perched on the edge of the fender, legs stuck out in front of him. 'Yes, I remember us coming across each other. How did he know you were you?'

'Recognized me from that photo you used to have in your room, and from us looking alike. He was on his way home on leave.'

'And where were you on your way to?'

'To stay with the Somervilles, actually.'

'Johnnie Somerville? I thought you couldn't stand him.'

'I was on a mission of mercy. He was burned crash-landing his Spitfire last year and spent ages in hospital. Got pretty fed up and for some reason his mother thought I might be able to cheer him up. I can't think why she picked on me.'

Kit smiled at the floor. 'Oh, I can. Did Ma know? She'd have been in seventh heaven, planning your wedding.'

'That's why I didn't tell her. And she'd have been horribly disappointed. I haven't seen him since.'

'Why not?'

'Because I didn't want to.'

'Pity. I rather liked him. But it's your affair, twin.' Kit reached out with one foot and prodded Poppy. The rocking horse creaked gently to and fro. 'Is it because of Michal? Haven't you got over him yet?'

'Everyone always makes it sound like an illness. Something that will go away so you'll feel better. I don't *want* Michal to go away. I want to remember him.'

'Fine. But don't let the past spoil the future for you.'

'Nor you.' She held his gaze steadily. 'You won't either, will you, Kit?'

'I don't think about the future.'

'The war won't last for ever. What will you do when it's all over? Go up to Oxford, like you would have done?'

He stubbed out his cigarette in the *Present from Swanage* mug. 'I told you, I don't think about it.'

She watched him uneasily, knowing him so well. 'You're still blaming yourself over what happened to Villiers and the others, aren't you?'

'Guilt's not an illness either, Anne. It won't simply go away, as you so rightly pointed out. There's no real cure for it. I've learned to live with it, though, in a manner of speaking, but not enough to care a row of beans about what happens to me, now or in the future. I really don't mind whether I live or die. In fact, to be perfectly honest, I rather hope I die. I'm too much of a coward to do the deed myself so perhaps some kind Jerry will oblige. It would be no more than justice done, in my view.'

He seemed quite calm. Deadly serious.

'You can't really mean that, Kit?'

'Yes, I do. And I'm only telling you so that if it does happen, you'll be glad for me, not sorry.'

'Kit . . .' Tears were trickling down her cheeks. 'Don't say things like that.'

He stood up and passed her his handkerchief. 'Forget I did. I'm sorry. Let's go down and see what Ma has in store for us.'

She wiped her eyes and sniffed. 'Some ghastly people are coming for drinks. There'll be at least two very suitable and deadly boring men for me and probably somebody's drippy daughter for you.'

'Well, we won't tell her she's wasting her time.' He put an arm round her shoulders. 'Come on, old bean. Let's go and face the music and smile.'

'Shall I do the blackout now, Mother?'

'As you wish.'

Virginia rose and went over to the sitting-room windows and began pulling down the blinds. The reply had been cold and indifferent. It was the tone Mother had been using throughout her leave – her way of showing her hurt at the whole year that Virginia had stayed away. Stiff and stilted letters had passed between them, like between strangers, and when Virginia had at last come home it had been made very clear that her outburst had not been either forgotten or forgiven. Her punishment was the cold speech, the long silences, the tight lips, the turned shoulder. She had found to her surprise that she no longer cared very much. The long absence had made her see Mother as someone to be pitied for her narrow, lonely life and her silly snobbery.

Virginia began to draw the curtains over the blinds. Mother, of course, had completely ignored her promotion. Corporal would not be worth comment; nothing less than an officer would do. Well, she might soon be made sergeant and then, after that, there was a good chance of becoming an officer. Mother would never believe the progress that she had made, how sure of herself she felt, how much she had changed. One day it would be Assistant Section Officer Stratton. Then Section Officer. Then Flight Officer, then Squadron Officer . . .

'Don't tug at the curtains like that, Virginia. It's quite unnecessary. You'll damage them.'

Once she would have said she was sorry; now she said nothing. She finished the job and then switched on the lamps and then she sat down and picked up her knitting. There was silence in the sitting-room, except for the clicking of the needles.

*　　*　　*

Winnie enjoyed every moment of the Fitters' Course at RAF Halton and even the journey there went without a hitch. She found her way on the Underground in London, and took the train out to Wendover, passing through the gentle countryside of Buckinghamshire. The camp had been built in peacetime, like Colston, and the quarters were of solid redbrick with highly-polished wood floors. There was much more spit-and-polish than there had been at Flaxton or at Kirkton, and the WAAF officers were real sticklers. She had to polish her buttons and shoes until they shone like glass, and the smallest fault was picked on. At church parade the officer walked all round her, inspecting her minutely, and reported her for not having one stocking seam quite straight and for leaving the little button on the slit in her greatcoat unfastened. But she didn't mind because everything else was worth it.

Every morning they marched to a pipe-band down to the lecture rooms and workshops and so the day began on a bright note. The course was far more thorough and detailed than the flight mechanics' one had been. She learned about metals and metallurgy, about how to crack-test and shock-load test, and how to do precision checks and pressure tests. She was taught how to replace a fuel pump, dismantle a crankcase, check a cylinder block for leaks, test a suspect thermostat, remove and fit a propeller . . . Her gen book filled steadily with her notes as the days passed. In the workshops everything was stripped down to the last nut and bolt and checked in every possible way for wear and tear and damage.

'There's no *near enough* with what's acceptable,' the instructor impressed on them from the start. 'You're working to thousandths of an inch and it's got to be exact. If you strip down an engine and adjust it and replace it *precisely* according to what's laid down in the book, then every part and every component will work sweet as a song when it's all reassembled.'

Winnie found that very satisfying.

At the end of the course she passed out as Leading

Aircraftwoman Jervis with a mark of eighty per cent, and she sewed her props on her sleeve with pride. When she was told to put in for an area where she would like to be sent, she wrote down Suffolk and to her delight she was posted back to Flaxton.

'Thought we'd got rid of you,' Chiefy said when he saw her arrive. 'You're like a bad penny.'

But later on she found out that he had asked specially to have her back. She was put to work on engines in the Maintenance hangar and though some of the men in the gang pulled her leg at first, and others resented her new status, they all got used to her after a while and she was accepted. There were several more WAAF flight mechs at the station now so she was no longer such an oddity

Quite often she would see the American B17s flying over but she could never tell if it was the *Sassy Sally* because they were always too far away; in any case she would have a different crew by now. There goes Texas an' Minnesota, she said to herself as she watched the bombers, remembering names of the states. An' Maine an' Georgia, an' Oklahoma an' Tennessee, Kentucky an' Idaho . . . Virgil had told her the crews came from all over America.

He'd written a letter to her when she was at Halton, saying that he had finished his tour and had been given thirty days leave. He was off to take a look around, he'd said. She'd got a postcard from London with a picture of Buckingham Palace on it and an X marked on one of the windows that he said was his room. Then there had been more cards from Oxford, from Stratford-upon-Avon, from Wales and Somerset, Devon and Cornwall. The last one had been from a remote place in Scotland. He had said nothing in any of them about whether he was ever coming back to Suffolk to do another tour and she thought that he must have been sent back to America after all.

When the weather got better and the evenings lighter, she sometimes biked down to the Fox and Grapes with the rest of the gang. There seemed to be more Americans than ever going there. Once she met Nora who was with an American army sergeant. Buzz, she told Winnie, in a whispered aside had gone back home at the end of his tour. She had introduced the grinning sergeant whose hair, at odds with his name which was Curly, looked like bristles on a brush. He came from somewhere called Wyoming, Nora hissed, and he said he had a big ranch. Privately, Winnie doubted it. She'd heard that a lot of them pretended things like that.

One evening when she was there, watching a darts match in progress in a corner of the bar, she felt a hand touch her shoulder. She turned her head and saw Taffy standing there behind her.

'Hallo, Winnie,' he said softly. 'Remember me?'

She went bright red. 'I'm with some others . . .'

'Just so long as you're not with one of these Yanks.'

'That's got nothin' to do with you.'

'Everything about you has to do with me.'

He moved round, putting himself between her and the others who were watching the darts match, isolating her. His eyes hadn't left her face and she looked away from their gaze.

'I told you, I don't want to see you any more.'

'But I don't believe you. Look how you blushed just now when you saw it was me. You wouldn't have done that if I didn't mean something to you.'

She looked round desperately for escape. He frightened her. He'd always frightened her. Confused her. Sometimes she had the feeling that she wouldn't be able to hold out against him for ever.

The bar was so crowded now that it was difficult to move. If she just left the pub Taffy would only come after her and it was a four-mile bike ride back to the station in the dark.

'Leave me alone,' she said pleadingly. 'You don't mean anythin' to me.'

But he moved even closer still so that she had to lean

backwards to keep her distance. 'Oh yes I do, girl. You know I do.'

There was a stir by the entrance as yet more people came in. It was another group of Americans. She could see their olive uniforms and hear their drawl. 'Six beers, bud!' one of them called out to the bar, and there was laughter and back-slapping as they joined the others there. 'Bloody Yanks,' a cockney voice said near her. 'They'll drink the bleedin' place dry.'

Then she saw Virgil. He must have been one of the last to enter because he was standing just inside the doorway, on the step, and looking round.

'Excuse me,' she said to Taffy very firmly. 'There's a friend of mine over there.'

She squeezed her way towards him, ducking under drinking arms and edging between people. Someone spilled beer all over her shoulder and a cigarette end burned her hand. Virgil saw her before she reached him and pushed through to meet her.

'Gee, Winnie . . .' He was grinning down at her.

'You're back,' she said unnecessarily.

'Looks like it. Howya doin', then?'

'All right, thanks.' She rubbed her burned hand surreptitiously behind her back. 'How 'bout you?'

'Fine 'n dandy. I'm doin' another tour, like I told you I wanted. Thought first off they was gonna send me back stateside, but they're short of good waist gunners over here. Keep on losin' them all the time. Worst place to be in the ship.'

She said, troubled: 'Are you still with the *Sassy Sally*?'

'Nope. Got another Fort now. Matter o' fact, she's named for you.'

She stared at him. '*Me?*'

'Yeah, *you*.' He grinned. 'Called her *Wattagal Winnie!* I told the other guys 'bout you an' they kinda liked the idea. Got this picture painted of you on the nose.'

'A picture of me?' She went very red, thinking of the naked women she'd seen fly over.

646

He read her face and laughed. 'Oh, it ain't like *Sassy Sally* or some of the others . . . I told the guy that did it 'bout the way you look in those blue dungarees an' that checked shirt you wear on the farm, an' how your hair's all curly, an' 'bout those blue eyes of yours, an' he painted a real pretty picture of you like that, an' put the name underneath. You've done a coupla missions already.'

'Oh . . .' Her blushed deepened even more. She felt both embarrassed and overwhelmed. An American bomber named after her! 'It's very nice of you all.'

'It's great havin' you with us.' He pointed to her shoulder suddenly. 'What happened there?'

'Someone spilled beer over me.'

'Didn't mean that. What's the new badge mean?'

'Leadin' aircraftwoman.'

'That since you done that course?'

She nodded. She would have liked to tell him about the eighty per cent marks but that might have sounded like boasting. He was gazing at her admiringly.

'Like I said, watta gal!'

She saw then that he had something new on his arm too. The sergeant's chevron was different, with two rockers beneath the wrong-way-up stripes.

'What about you an' that?'

He looked casual, almost modest. 'Technical sergeant – that's what that is. An' that's 'bout as far as I c'n go as a gunner. Still, it ain't bad. My folks'll be pleased. Gee, it's good to see you again. I've been in here a coupla times this week, hopin' I'd find you. Just wrote you a letter, but I wasn't sure if you'd been posted some place else now, so I ain't sent it yet. You get that other one I wrote you a while back? An' all those postcards?'

She nodded again. 'Thanks. I couldn't write back 'cos I didn't know where you were.'

'I was movin' all over the place. Had a swell time in London first. Went to the theatre, saw the sights, found some great clubs for dancin' . . .'

She thought of him as she'd first seen him, jitterbugging

647

with the blond girl in the mauve dress and high heels.
'How was Buckingham Palace?'

He grinned. 'Real fancy. He's a great guy, your King.
Say, I didn't know the Jerries'd dropped bombs on them
too? Strikes me he an' the Queen ought to be sent away
some place safe. Canada, maybe.'

'Oh, they'd never leave us,' she said. 'Never.'

'Guess they know best. Wouldn't want to leave much
if I was them either. It sure is a beautiful country. I ain't
never seen such pretty places, an' I sure loved those great
big old houses, an' the castles, an' all that kinda stuff . . .
Never knew you had mountains before. Got right up as
far as Scotland. Couldn't understand what in heck they
was sayin' but we got along just fine.'

A hand fell on her shoulder. Taffy had appeared beside
her. 'I'm taking you home, Winnie.' His fingers dug in
hard. 'Come on.'

Virgil looked at Taffy and then back at Winnie. 'You
with this guy?'

She hesitated. Several other RAF had gathered behind
Taffy. The last thing she wanted was to cause a scene,
or any trouble.

'No, but it's all right. I was goin' anyway.'

Virgil said slowly: 'Well, that's OK by me, if you want
to. But it ain't OK if it's only because this guy wants you
to. You want to stay, you stay.'

Taffy took hold of her arm and began to pull her
away. 'You keep away from her, Yank. She's coming
with me. She doesn't want anything to do with bloody
Yanks. She's not that kind of girl.'

Virgil looked at him again. 'Reckon I know what kind
of girl Winnie is, an' it ain't the sort that likes bein' pushed
around . . . I figure you oughta let go of her, mister. Let
her make up her own mind what she wants to do.'

Some of the Americans had turned round now and
were standing behind Virgil, listening and watching. The
RAF moved into a semi-circle round Taffy. One of them
growled: 'That's his girl, mate. Piss off!'

Winnie said quickly: 'I ought to go, Virgil . . . I must get back.'

But Virgil was barring the way. 'Just a moment, honey. If you don't want to go with this guy, then I'm stoppin' him takin' you. An' I figure if he's got to drag you outta here, then that's 'cos you ain't real keen on goin' with him. So, I'm tellin' you, mister, to let go of the lady right now.'

Taffy bunched his fist. 'Get out of my way, Yank!'

'I ain't doin' that. Not 'til you take your hands off her.'

'Then you bloody asked for it!'

Taffy dropped Winnie's arm and swung his closed fist. Virgil staggered back as it caught him in the face. Silence had fallen suddenly in the bar. Everyone stood quite still. Winnie held her breath. Virgil stood wiping the blood slowly from his nose, and then he went for Taffy.

The room exploded into uproar as Americans and RAF fell on each other. Glasses were smashed, tables and chairs overturned. The women screamed as the men crashed about, swinging punches, falling down and rolling over and over on the floor, grappling together. It was like a saloon fight scene from a Western.

Winnie backed against the wall and watched in horror. She had lost sight of Virgil who was somewhere beneath a heaving pile of bodies. She shut her eyes as fists were raised and blows fell, and then opened them again to find Virgil and Taffy locked in furious combat at her feet. Behind the bar, drowned out by the noise, the landlord was mouthing into his telephone.

Presently there was a loud squeal of jeep brakes outside and a group of American Military Police, truncheons flailing, burst into the Fox and Grapes.

'Here's to your very good health, Squadron Officer Newman.'

'And to yours, Squadron Leader Dutton.' Felicity raised her glass. 'You look awfully well.'

Speedy not only looked well but positively respectable. That was surely a new RAF cap, and what had happened to the old check scarf? The dishevelled young flying officer whom she had first met more than four years ago seemed to be gradually disappearing with passing time and promotion. She wondered whether he, too, saw a very different person sitting opposite him now from the new and nervous WAAF officer that she had been.

He beamed at her and looked suddenly exactly the same old Speedy. 'All the better for seeing you, my dear, as the Wolf said to Red Riding Hood. And how is life treating you in your exalted station at Bomber HQ?'

'I'm not very exalted. It's mostly routine admin. Quite dull, really. I feel quite remote from the reality of what's going on up in the skies, sometimes. Though that was a blessing at first, I must say.' She put down her wine glass. 'What have *you* been up to since I last saw you?'

He waved a hand airily. 'This and that. The odd sweep here and there. Spot of escort duty playing little friend to the Yanks as they set forth on their kamikaze raids. We try to swot the Jerries away from them only we can't go with them all the way – that's the big snag. Not enough juice. After that they're on their own, poor blighters. The Huns give 'em hell when we've scarpered. I wouldn't be in their shoes for all the tea in China.'

He had turned up unexpectedly, as he usually did, and swept her off to dinner. The restaurant was a rather dreary place and the waitress ancient and very slow, but she smiled at Speedy as she set the plates in front of them and he winked at her in return. When she had waddled away he prodded doubtfully at his food. 'I say, I hope this isn't horse, or something.'

'I don't know how you'd tell. It probably tastes just like anything else.'

He chewed hard for a moment, considering. 'Definitely an old nag, I'd say. Well past its prime. Lucky you had the fish, Titania. A very wise choice. Thank God the war will soon be over. First thing to be done when we've popped over the Channel is to liberate Paris so we can get a decent meal again. I bet if the French are eating horses as well as frogs, they're making sure they're not nags like this one. I'll take you out to dinner in Gay Paree, Titania. It beats High Wycombe any day.'

She laughed. 'I think it's going to be quite a while before you can do that.'

'Well, thanks to the Yanks the writing's on the wall for Adolf. Say another six months, or a year, and he'll be cashing in his chips.'

'I hope you're right, Speedy. Will you stay in the RAF after the war?'

'Hard to say at the moment. Depends what Civvy Street holds for the likes of me. Can't do much else besides fly a kite.'

'You once told me that you were going to sell encyclopedias to housewives and then buy a thirty-foot yacht and sail round the world.'

'Did I really say that? Jolly good idea, in a way, but somehow it's lost its appeal.' He put down his knife and fork. 'The fact is, I was rather hoping that you might be part of the future.'

Her heart sank at his words and at the earnest look on his face. 'Oh, Speedy . . .'

'You know how I feel about you — never made any bones about it. No point. The thing is, there comes a time when even a chap like me wants to settle down . . . Any chance you might marry me one fine day, do you think? I'm not such a bad bloke, when you get to know me properly.'

She looked down at the dry little piece of white fish on her plate, wishing that he hadn't spoken. She was so fond of Speedy and enjoyed his company so much — he was like a tonic. If she married him perhaps she might come to love him too, quite easily — there was so much that was lovable about him. But she wasn't sure that it could ever be the love he deserved and needed. It wouldn't be fair on him, or fair of her to be tempted just because she was often lonely and miserable – to risk his happiness, as well as hers. One day he would meet the girl who would be right for him.

'I'm sorry, Speedy. Truly sorry.'

His face fell. And then he grinned at her cheerfully. 'Well, no harm in asking. Faint heart ne'er won fair lady, or whatever the saying is.'

'Your heart's never been faint, Speedy. You're one of the best and bravest people I know.'

He looked pleased. 'Really? I say . . .' He twirled the stem of his wineglass. 'Shouldn't pry, of course. Nothing to do with me, but is there someone else? Pretty well bound to be with a girl like you.'

'There is someone,' she said slowly. 'But it can never come to anything.'

'How so?'

She looked down at her plate again. 'Because he's married.'

'Oh. Well, that's a bit of a snag, it must be said.' He looked at her hopefully. 'You don't think you'll get over him – eventually.'

'I don't seem to have done yet, and it's been a long time.'

'Do you mind my asking, do I know the chap?'

'Yes, as a matter of fact.'

'Wouldn't be old Palmer, would it? Our CO at Colston? By any chance?'

She could feel the colour rushing into her face. 'I can't say.'

'Wouldn't be surprised if it was. Always thought he was rather keen on you. Can't blame him. Tricky situation, though.'

'Don't ask me any more.'

'Wouldn't dream of it.' He put his hand on hers and squeezed it gently. 'I want what will make *you* happy, Titania. That's all. Just remember that. And if I can ever help in anyway, you've only to give the old word.'

She lifted her head and smiled at him mistily. 'Oh Speedy, you're an angel. An absolute angel.'

'Funny thing but no-one's ever called me that before. Lots of other things, but never that.' He let go of her hand abruptly. 'Now eat up your fish and I'll finish my horse, then we'll call Desdemona over and see what she's got for pudding.'

'Spam,' said Virgil. 'Soap, coffee, tomato juice, peas, bacon, sugar, gum, Life-Savers, Hershey bars.' He produced them with a flourish from his canvas bag and set them on the kitchen table. 'Luckies for you, ma'am.' He gave them to Gran who was waiting expectantly. 'Couldn't get scotch this time so I've brought bourbon. Think your Dad'll mind?'

Winnie shook her head. She didn't think Dad would care as long as it could be drunk. She had watched Virgil with the same embarrassment that she always felt when he brought things for them. He was reaching into the bag again and held aloft a fistful of something filmy. 'Nylon stockings! Three pairs. One for you ma'am.' He presented them to Gran who examined them with deep suspicion. Winter and summer alike she wore thick black wool stockings that wrinkled round her ankles.

'Doan't look decent tew me.'

'And for you, ma'am.' Virgil gave the second pair to Winnie's mother who drew one on over her hand and exclaimed at its sheerness. The third pair he gave to Winnie.

'For next time you come dancin' with me.'

He winked at her and she went pink and looked at the stockings. They were so thin she couldn't imagine how they'd be strong enough to wear at all. But the girl in mauve at the dance had been wearing ones like this. Perhaps he'd given them to her as well.

When he'd found out that she was home on leave, Virgil had biked over from the base with the canvas bag slung across the handlebars. Ruth and Laura had scampered down to the gate to meet him and he'd swung them both up high in turn and then carried Laura on his shoulders up the path, while holding Ruth by the hand. At tea they sat on each side of him, clamouring for his attention. They love him, Winnie thought, watching. How sad they'll be when he has to go home. Or if anything should happen to him . . . But she wouldn't let herself think about that at all.

After tea she and Virgil went out to the barn to look at the ewes waiting to lamb. There were still some bruises on his face and a strip of sticking plaster at the corner of his temple.

'I'm very sorry about what happened at the Fox an' Grapes,' she said. 'It was all my fault. I hope you didn't get into a lot of trouble over it.'

'Shucks, no . . . weren't nothin'. Long as you ain't mad at me.'

'Mad at you?' She didn't quite understand his meaning.

'Angry. I figured maybe I'd got it all wrong an' you was really with that guy – '

'I wasn't with him at all,' she said vehemently. 'He's just someone who was at the same station as me a long time ago. He's always botherin' me.'

'He that pesky Welsh guy your grandma was talkin' about once?'

She nodded.

He gave her a sideways grin. 'Well, I guess he won't be botherin' you again no more. An' if he does, you just let me know.'

She wanted to thank him for what he'd done – for the way he'd stood firm and rescued her from Taffy. He'd acted just like one of those cowboys in films who were on the good side, and he'd fought for her just like they did. It gave her a funny sort of feeling to think about it: grateful and glad and shy. But she didn't know how to begin to say any of this.

She opened the small door in the end of the barn.

'Maisie's due to lamb,' she told him. 'An' it's her first time, so things might not go so well. I've been worryin' a bit for her.'

There were some ewes standing about in the straw, munching hay. They swung their heads round to stare, but without any pause in the rhythmical working of their jaws. Their bodies bulged with unborn lambs.

'Hi girls!' Virgil said breezily. 'Howya all doin'?'

Maisie, lying in the far corner didn't look as though she was doing at all well. Her sides were heaving and she lifted her head and bleated piteously as they approached. Winnie knelt in the straw and Virgil crouched on his haunches beside her.

'Everythin' OK?'

She shook her head. 'I should've come sooner and not left her so long . . .'

'What's wrong?'

'I think the lamb's stuck. Look, you can see. Its head's out an' so's one foot, but the other one's still inside.'

He looked and saw the dark head of the lamb protruding wetly from the ewe's body. Its eyes were closed and beneath the chin he could make out the pointed black tip of one little cloven hoof. He whistled softly.

'Gee, my folks don't have sheep back home. I ain't never had nothin' to do with 'em. What the heck do we do now?'

Winnie was rinsing her hands in a bucket of water. 'I'll have to push the head back in and try to get hold of the other leg an' bring it forward. When a lamb's born it ought to come out with both feet forward together, like it was divin'. That way there's enough room. An' bein' Maisie's first makes it harder. Could you hold her still and talk to her a bit while I try?'

'Sure.' He gripped hold of the ewe's shoulders, his fingers sinking deep into the oily wool. She bleated loudly again and threshed her stick-like legs about. He was amazed at their thinness. They seemed much too frail to support the weight of her body.

'OK, Maisie, girl, take it easy now. You're doin' great. Easy . . . easy.'

The ewe looked up at him trustingly. She had strange pale eyes, he noticed, with pupils in a black horizontal bar.

'Makin' sheeps' eyes at me, huh, Maisie? Don't be fooled, sister. My flyin' jacket's made of someone like you.'

She gave another pathetic, pain-filled bleat. Winnie, he saw, had her hand deep inside her. The lamb's head had disappeared; he wondered how the hell it could breathe.

'How's it comin'?'

Her brow was furrowed in concentration, her bottom lip caught between her teeth. 'I think I've got it . . . the other leg. If I can just get it forward . . .'

'Maisie's doin' OK this end, ain't you, Beautiful? Atta girl!'

The ewe groaned and bleated helplessly. Jeez, he thought, what happens if Winnie can't shift it? This one's gonna be in big trouble, an' junior too. He stroked one of Maisie's ears, not knowing how else to comfort her. She groaned again and struggled hard and he had to use all his strength to pin her down. The other ewes were munching away, watching indifferently. Callous broads, he thought. Wait 'til it's your turn.

Winnie said suddenly: 'I've got it, Virgil! I've got it! It's goin' to be all right. Look, it's comin' . . .'

He turned his head in time to see the lamb slither out into the world. It slid down onto the straw and lay there, bloody and glistening with membrane. He thought at first that it was dead and then, to his huge relief, he saw its flank flutter. Steam rose from the small, wet body and Winnie wiped it gently with a wisp of straw.

'It's a ewe lamb.'

He swallowed. 'Congratulations.'

He looked across the lamb at Winnie, kneeling there. Her hands and arms were bloodstained and there was more blood on the bib of her dungarees and a long smear of it across her cheek. She smiled at him happily and he thought that he had never seen her look so lovely.

'We've got to get Maisie up,' she said. 'She's got to look after her. Can you help me?'

'Sure.'

They hauled the ewe to her feet. Maisie nosed at her newborn lamb and began licking it. She seemed to be recovering fast from her ordeal and Virgil saw that the lamb was already starting to make feeble, jerky little efforts to struggle up.

'How come it's black when Mom's white?'

'All Suffolks are born that colour. She'll turn white later, 'cept her face. She'll look just like Maisie.'

Winnie started rinsing her hands in the bucket and then dried them with some straw. The lamb was on its feet now, wobbling unsteadily. The ewe butted gently with her nose, guiding it. It staggered and lurched against her and then, with another butt in the right direction, found the teat and began sucking.

Winnie watched them. 'I think they're goin' to be all right now. We don't need to worry.'

'You did great,' he said. 'Just *great*.'

She turned her head to smile at him again and saw the way he was looking at her. Her smile faded. He took a couple of steps forward and stopped. He waited, arms hanging loose at his sides, his eyes fixed on her face. The ewes watched them both, chomping.

It was up to her, and she knew it. She took a small step towards him. Virgil stayed quite still where he was. She took another step. And then another. And then several more all at once, in a rush. He caught her tightly in his arms.

Twenty-Six

A gust of wind snatched at Madge's cap and whisked it from her head. It bowled away up the grassy incline towards the cliff top with Madge lumbering in pursuit and making frantic grabs at it with her hands. She caught up with it only a few yards from the edge, pinning it down at last with one foot. Virginia, watching from below, saw her look out over the Channel and then turn and shout something, but the wind carried her words away. She began to make frantic beckoning signals to Virginia, pointing and then jumping up and down.

They often walked along the cliffs above Walmer in the light evenings; it helped the sore eyes and aching heads from the hours spent in the darkened room and there was a wonderful view of the sea. It was more than the view, though, that was making Madge so excited. Virginia ran up the rest of the slope to join her, hanging on to her own cap.

The sea below heaved cold and grey and flecked with white, the horizon lost in murky mist and cloud. There was nothing remarkable about rough weather in the Channel, even in summer, but Madge was not pointing at the big waves, or the white horses, but at the huge fleet of small ships that were gathered there. She had a huge grin on her face and was shouting against the wind.

'They're going to invade! They're going to land in France! It's happening at last!' She jumped about again, waving her cap in the air. 'Hip-hip *hooray*!'

But Virginia didn't cheer too, or jump about with excitement like Madge. Instead she stood and stared at the great armada. It stretched away into the sea mist

658

as far as she could see, probably all the way down the coast for miles. Thousands of men in small ships would have to cross that treacherous expanse of water and fight their way ashore on mined and fiercely defended beaches. Thousands of them would probably die. Neil had done what they were trying to do and it had failed tragically.

Please God, she prayed, let them succeed this time.

They've gone and posted me back to Colston, Anne wrote to Kit, though heaven only knew when he'd get the letter. *I'm going back where I started. Except that last time I was Aircraftwoman Cunningham, the lowest form of life, and this time I'll be Flight Officer Cunningham (I bet that's a surprise). I'll be inspecting instead of being inspected, dishing out jankers instead of doing it. You'll probably be quite right and I'll hate it, but you know what they say about poachers making the best gamekeepers.* She finished the letter: *Take care of yourself.* That was a laugh! What hope was there of him doing any such thing in France? At D-Day plus fifteen the allies were still struggling to get a solid foothold there. Nobody had ever said it would be easy, but nobody seemed to have thought that it would be quite so difficult either. Nobody had expected the Germans to have had so much fight left in them.

And nobody had expected the Germans to start attacking London with a new and horrible weapon. There had been rumours, but there were rumours about all sorts of things, and most of them were untrue. Now, out of the blue, the Jerries had begun launching flying bombs that came over all on their own, without any pilot. Unsporting people called it, as though war were a game of cricket. The buzz bombs came at all hours, by day or by night, and when their engines stopped they simply crashed to the ground and blew up. It was hard to shoot them down, or deflect them – though fighters tried with their wingtips and sometimes succeeded – and as nobody could stay in a shelter all the time, survival in London had become a game of chance. People carried on with their daily lives hoping that if a flying bomb appeared overhead it would keep on going and fall on somebody else.

She was on her way to Victoria Station by taxi, crossing London to catch the train to Colston, when the air raid siren sounded. As she got out of the taxi at the railway station to pay the driver she saw a flying bomb approaching. It looked like a toy 'plane buzzing along about three hundred feet in the air, spurting a little tail of flame and making a spluttering growl. Everyone around had frozen like statues where they stood. Nobody moved. Everybody watched and listened. And when the spluttering stopped suddenly they all flung themselves to the ground with their arms over their heads, or crouched in doorways. The taxi driver leaped from his cab and pulled Anne down with him underneath it. 'Better safe than sorry, miss.' A moment later there was a violent explosion that shook the ground and dust and debris and shattered glass fell like rain. She crawled out from under the taxi, brushing herself down, and retrieved her scattered coins. The dust still in the air had made the day as dark as dusk. Only a few streets away ambulance sirens were wailing. Around her, people were picking themselves up off the ground and emerging from their doorways and then carrying on almost as though nothing had happened.

The taxi driver grinned at her. 'We've got used to 'em, miss. 'itler can stuff 'is doodlebugs.'

It was very strange to be back at RAF Colston. It was a bigger and busier place than she remembered – swarming with RAF and WAAF. Very young-looking airwomen saluted her smartly in immaculate uniforms. How different it had all been in the beginning. She thought of Gloria teetering along in her high-heeled sandals, of Pearl with the flask of whisky in her handbag, Sandra carrying her travelling rug, Enid weeping constantly, Winnie curtseying to an apoplectic CO, the airmen whistling and laughing from barrack room windows . . . The new Station Commander, a young Group Captain, leaned over backwards to accommodate WAAF needs, and there was a brand new Waafery with well-equipped recreation rooms and a large, sunny Mess that had curtains at the windows and flowers on the tables.

The WAAF sergeant who entered her office looked as efficient as all the rest. Anne looked, and looked again – closer.

'*Pearl!* I'd no idea you were back here. How wonderful! When were you posted here?'

'Six months ago, ma'am.'

She was ma'am now, not love or ducks or duckie any more. There was a gulf between them. An uncrossable chasm in RAF Regulations and it was sad.

'How are you, Pearl?'

'Very well, thank you, ma'am.'

She was still plump but instead of the riot of red curls tumbling over her forehead, there was one dark and restrained wave.

'Whatever happened to Autumn Glory, Pearl?'

'It's Rich Mahogany now, ma'am.'

'And that engagement ring on your finger? Is that Mr Right at last?'

There was a faint smile – a glimmer from the past. 'Mr He'll Do, like I always said. He's a RAF sergeant.'

'Congratulations.'

'Thank you, ma'am.'

Anne leaned her arms across the desk. 'Remember the old days, Pearl? I was just thinking about them now . . . Corporal Fowler in the kitchens, Sergeant Baker trying to teach us drill, how hopeless we were at everything? Remember that Sergeants' Mess dance when Enid got drunk and we carried her back? And that time you and I tried on all the fur coats at that Officers' Mess do? And the teacups, Pearl . . . remember how you read them for us and most of it came true?'

'Oh, yes, ma'am. I remember it all.'

'So do I,' Anne said. 'So do I.'

They smiled a conspiratorial smile at each other. There was a small silence and then Anne straightened up in her chair.

'Well, sergeant,' she said briskly. 'What did you want to see me about?'

Further along the South Coast, another WAAF flight officer, seated behind another desk, was looking at the sergeant on the other side sympathetically.

'I'm sorry, my dear, to have had to give you such bad news. So very sorry.'

She was a much older woman: one of those who had been in the Women's Royal Air Force in the First World War and rejoined for the Second. She did her best to act as surrogate mother to the young WAAFS away from home, seeing it as her special role by reason of her age. This made the job of telling one of them that her real mother was dead all the more unpleasant. It was by no means the first time she had had to do so. She had known a number of airwomen who had lost their mothers in the Blitz, but that had been near the beginning of the war. This was supposed to be near the end. Paris had been liberated. The Allies were pressing eastwards. And yet here she was telling this girl that her mother had just been killed by a flying bomb that had fallen directly on her home.

'If it's any comfort to you, she wouldn't have known anything about it. It was a direct hit. It would all have been over in a second.'

She watched Sergeant Stratton carefully as she spoke. She seemed totally stunned. Devastated. She had not yet said a word but sat staring down at her lap, her shoulders and head bowed. It was a great pity all ways round. The girl had been doing so well. When she had first come across her she had been a shy and very diffident sort of person – rather clumsy in her manner, though never in her job. But lately she had blossomed and acquired so much more confidence. She had made a sound corporal and was proving an excellent sergeant – responsible, efficient and unusually dedicated. She could easily become a good officer, given time, and make a real career in the WAAF. It would be a great shame if this tragedy were to set her back – knock the prop from under her, as it were.

The flight officer went on. 'Of course, we'll arrange compassionate leave for you at once. You should be able to catch the early afternoon train to London . . .' She looked down at the file on her desk. 'Your mother was a widow, I see.'

Virginia nodded. The face-saving lie had been perpetuated even in WAAF records.

'Do you have any brothers or sisters?'

She shook her head.

'Any aunts or uncles? Cousins?'

'I have a great-aunt who lives in Bexhill, that's all. I'm not sure if she's still alive, though.'

The flight officer said kindly: 'Would you like me to find out for you? You could go and stay with her for a few days, perhaps – '

Virginia thought of the gloomy, mothball-smelling house. 'No, thank you.'

'Are there any friends of your mother? Older people who might rally round?'

'My mother had no friends.'

'Oh. I see.' The flight officer didn't really see at all. A warm, outgoing person herself, she could not easily imagine someone having no friends. The one thing she did see clearly, though, was that Sergeant Stratton was now apparently completely alone in the world – so far as a family was concerned. It was very fortunate, she thought, that the girl had the WAAF. In her considerable experience, the service could sometimes fill that gap quite well.

She said gently: 'We'll do everything we can to help you, my dear.'

*   *   *

The house in Alfred Road had been almost flattened by the flying bomb. Only a small part of one wall remained standing; the rest was an uneven, towering mound of rubble. She saw that the houses on each side had been badly damaged, too, and all along the street windows had been shattered and tiles broken. The force of the explosion must have been enormous. Two small boys were picking through the ruins, clambering over piles of bricks. When they saw Virginia standing at what had once been the gateway, they ran away with their hands full of prized pieces of twisted metal.

She walked up the path and through the gap where the front door had been. The brown linoleum was still there on the hallway floor, covered in a thick layer of dust, and she could see the bottom part of the hat-stand sticking out from under debris. Horribly, one of her mother's hats was lying close to it, covered in dust, too, but undamaged. She edged her way round the splintered wreckage of the staircase, trying to see into the rest of the flat. Part of the gas stove was visible where the kitchen had been and one of the blue and white checked curtains had draped itself over a fallen rafter. The sitting-room had been completely buried beneath its ceiling and the upstairs floor. The armchair with the tattered floral cover and the enamel-topped table with two legs missing must have come from Mrs Hickey's flat above. One of the neighbours had stopped her and told her that Mrs Hickey had escaped because she had been out when the buzz bomb had fallen. Until that moment she hadn't even thought about her. All she had been able to think about was that she had never really made up the quarrel with her mother, and now she would never be able to. *My mother has no friends.* Until now she had never considered what that meant. Now she saw that it must have meant many long hours of loneliness. She, Virginia, had been the only friend her mother had had and she had first deserted her and then rejected her. And she had died all alone.

The undertaker was grave-faced and kind. He took all the arrangements out of her hands; she had only to choose the coffin – what kind and what price. He turned the pages of a folder apologetically, murmuring about types of wood and different handles, and she sat staring blankly at the different pictures. Later he found her a cheap bed-and-breakfast place not far away.

The cemetery was vast. The graves stood in unending rows of sad grey stone and sombre black marble, decked discordantly with gaudy flowers. She had thought that she was the only mourner in the small chapel where the priest said prayers over her mother's coffin, but when she turned to follow it out to the graveside, she saw a man and woman standing in the back pew – a middle-aged couple who were complete strangers to her. Relatives she had not known about? Friends, after all? The man stepped forward as she reached the pew.

'Virginia?'

She paused. He had grey hair and a pepper and salt moustache, and he was dressed in a dark suit and wearing a black tie.

'I'm your father . . .' he gestured helplessly with one hand. 'Forgive me for coming here like this. I wanted to pay my respects. To give you some support. To see if you were all right . . .' He turned to the woman beside him. 'This is Dorothy.'

She must be That Woman. She couldn't be his wife because Mother had never agreed to a divorce. *So long as I live I'll make sure he can never marry that woman.* She was nothing like the siren she had always imagined. She was rather overweight and her hair was grey, too. There was nothing glamorous about her at all.

The man took her arm gently – she could not yet think of him as her father. 'We won't trouble you. We're only here to help.'

After the burial, when the coffin had been lowered into the deep, dark hole, they asked her if she would like to go back with them to have some tea.

'We're quite near,' the woman told her. 'I made some sandwiches — just in case.'

She felt that it would be rude to refuse or waste the food if she had gone to that trouble.

It was a pleasant house in a shady suburban avenue. The furniture was rather shabby and the sitting-room a bit untidy — a piece of knitting left out on a chair, a newspaper open on the table, a cardigan hanging over the arm of the sofa. Mother would never have countenanced any of those things. There was also, she noticed, a framed photograph of herself as a child on the mantelpiece, taken when she must have been about five.

Her father said, seeing her noticing it: 'It's the only one I have. You're not so very different now.'

Dorothy had gone to the kitchen to make a pot of tea and fetch the sandwiches and she was left alone with him. He smiled ruefully and lifted his hands in another helpless gesture.

'I don't know much about you, sad to say. I didn't even know you were in the WAAF. I've tried to find things out, but it wasn't easy. Your mother never answered the questions I asked in my letters . . . would never tell me anything about you. I used to walk up and down Alfred Road, hoping to catch a glimpse of you. I only saw you twice. Once when you were coming home from school with your satchel on your back — from the high school — and another time, a few years ago, when you were grown-up. You were walking up that hill from the tube station — coming home from work, I think.' He hesitated. 'I wanted very much to stop you and say hallo and tell you who I was, but I knew it would cause trouble. Your mother always said I wasn't fit to have anything to do with you . . . living in sin with another woman. She was probably quite right, though it's never seemed like sin to me.'

'I wish you *had* said hallo. I always thought you didn't care about me.'

'Oh, Ginny . . .' he looked at her sadly. 'I've always

666

cared about you. But I thought it was best for you if I stayed away. There would have been terrible scenes with your mother that might have harmed you . . . She never forgave me, as you must know. She was full of bitterness, and I suppose I can't blame her. I failed her when the firm collapsed and we lost all our money, and then I deserted her for someone else. Someone whom I love and who has never expected anything of me but that love . . . Oh, you won't be able to understand all this. Why should you? You probably feel as letdown and deserted and bitter as she did.'

Virginia said slowly: 'I let her down too and deserted her as well in the end. I joined the WAAF when she didn't want me to go away, and then I quarrelled with her and didn't go home for a year. We never really made it up.'

Her eyes filled with tears and he came over to her and put his hand on her arm.

'Don't blame yourself ever, Ginny,' he told her in a quiet voice. 'You were perfectly right to go and join up. I don't know what the quarrel was about, but I do know what she was like. She was her own worst enemy, but I don't think she ever realized that, or ever would have done. Sometime, when you feel like it, I want you to talk about it more and we'll sort it all out together.'

Dorothy came in carrying a tray, followed by a large tortoise-shell cat that wound itself round Virginia's ankles. The sandwiches were rather thick and she had left the crust on. She poured the tea and passed them with a sweet smile.

'I do hope you'll come and see us again, Virginia, whenever you feel like it. We'd like it so much, your father and me, if you'd try to think of this as a home. Somewhere to come to whenever you want. The door will always be open for you, won't it, Harry?'

Her father looked across at her. 'Always,' he said.

'So, you two want to get married?'

'That's right, sir.'

Virgil had answered the question easily and with confidence but the American major did not seem at all impressed. Winnie thought that he had hard, cold eyes and that his mouth, thin and tight, looked like a trap. The eyes moved sideways away from Virgil and settled on her.

'How old are you?'

'Twenty-three, sir.'

'British?'

'Yes, sir.' What else would she be?

'Serving in the British Women's Air Force?'

'The Women's Auxiliary Air Force, sir.'

He said impatiently: 'Whatever it is . . . what as?'

'I'm ground crew, sir. A fitter, on engines.'

He looked taken aback for a moment. 'You don't say?'

I *do* say, she thought to herself indignantly. An' I work on four-engined Lancs, doin' major inspections, an' engine an' prop changes, an' things like that. *And* I've been made corporal because they're pleased with me – so there! Out loud, though, she said nothing. She looked down at her lap until his next question brought her head up again sharply.

'Are you pregnant?'

She felt Virgil tense angrily beside her and answered quickly before he could. 'No, I'm not, sir.' Her face was red with embarrassment, her indignation growing by the minute. The American officer was looking at her as though he thought she might be no better than a tart. Then he looked away again.

'You got another girl back home, Gillies? An American girl waiting for you?'

'No, sir.'

'A lot of people back there would say you ought to wait 'til you get home and marry one of your own kind. They've been writing to the newspapers all over the US protesting about the way you young men are marrying other girls overseas.'

'I reckon that's up to me, sir. I'm willin' to fight for the folks back home an' risk my neck for them, but I ain't willin' to have them tell me who I ought to marry. I figure that's my business, not theirs.'

'Well, what do your own folks think of you wanting to marry a foreigner?'

Virgil said levelly: 'They're pleased, sir. They're sendin' a ring for her. See, I've written them a lot 'bout Winnie. She's from a farm, same as me. Her folks have one too, round here. She's my kind all right.'

The cold eyes moved back to her again. 'The farmer's daughter, huh? And what do *your* folks think of you wanting to marry an American?'

She hesitated. The truth, if she told it to him, was that Mum and Dad didn't much want her to because it would mean going so far away – even though they liked Virgil, specially Mum. Gran was the only one who'd been really pleased. Gran liked Virgil a lot, and not just because he brought her cigarettes and gum and things. It was because he was strong and Gran liked strong men. Strong in mind as well as body. Gran would have been like one of those women in films who went across America in a covered wagon out West.

'They don't mind, sir.'

'But they're not jumping for joy?'

'America's a long way from England, sir.'

'It sure is . . . and not only in distance. Ever been there?'

'No, sir.' He might as well have asked her if she'd ever been to the moon. It was about as likely.

'I guess you think it's just like you've seen in the movies?'

'I don't know, sir.'

'Well, some of it is and some of it isn't. But we've got the highest standard of living in the world. It's a great country.'

'So's England, sir,' she said stoutly.

He stared at her. 'England's gotten pretty tired and

beat. Lots of people over here would give their eye teeth to go and live in America because they know it's a real good place to be. Some of them would do anything to get there.'

She didn't like this man one bit. She didn't like what he'd said about England, and was he trying to say that she was only marrying Virgil so she could go and live in America?

She looked him straight in the eye. 'I don't want to leave England at all, sir, but if I marry Virgil I have to go wherever he goes. I don't care about America havin' the highest standard of livin' in the world, or about all those big cars an' modern houses with refrigerators an' things like that. I want to marry Virgil because I love him, not 'cos I want to go an' live in America.'

She stopped, appalled at her outburst. She'd sounded angry and defiant, and she'd probably gone and spoiled their chances. He'd never give them permission now.

The major looked at her in silence for a moment. 'I guess that's so,' he said and his thin lips moved in what might have been a sort of smile. He turned away.

'You going to be able to support her, Gillies?'

'We'll live on my folks' farm to start with, sir. Goin' to build ourselves a place of our own there. Soon as I can I'm goin' to buy more land next door, an' one day I'll take over from my pa –'

'OK. OK. You realize being married won't give you any special privileges, or special living arrangements? That when you go back to the US she won't be allowed to go with you? She'd have to wait over here 'til it's peacetime before she can sail?'

'Yes, sir. We know that.'

The major leaned back in his chair and propped his chin on his clasped hands. 'You were wounded recently, Gillies. And got your fingers frostbitten. You've been off flying status for a couple of months as a result. How did you get frostbite? Take your gloves off, or something? Only a fool does that in those temperatures, or a guy whose

670

mind's not on the job . . . thinking of other things. That's one reason we don't like servicemen marrying – they get distracted. Make mistakes. Worry more about their wives and kids than their buddies.'

'It was a pretty rough mission, sir,' Virgil said coolly. 'The Merseburg raid, July seventh. A lot of FWs attacked us on the way into the target. We took a cannon hit in the waist and my buddy was hurt pretty bad in the leg. He was lyin' on the floor an' bleedin' a lot. I got the bleedin' stopped with a tourniquet, but I had to take my gloves off to inject the morphine syrette. You can't handle them little things with your flyin' gloves on.'

'Hmm. How did you manage to get yourself wounded?'

'Later on, during the run, sir. The Krauts were puttin' up a pretty good box barrage an' we took a near miss. Some of the shrapnel came through the roof an' got me in the arm an' side an' broke a coupla ribs.'

Winnie felt like jumping to her feet and telling the major just what she thought of him for talking as though it was Virgil's fault that he'd got frostbitten and wounded. He wasn't looking a bit sorry about it. He was still leaning back in his chair, tipped on its legs against the wall. He'd clasped his hands behind his head now and was staring hard. She clenched her fists in her lap.

At last he let the chair fall forward and dropped his hands onto his desk.

'All right, Gillies. I'm going to give you permission to marry this young lady, but not until you finish your tour. You've got to do that first.' He gave the same sort of dry half-smile in Winnie's direction again. 'I hope you're good enough for her. And I sure hope you make it.'

Twenty-Seven

On the eighth of September, 1944, the first of the German
V-2 rockets fell on London. Unlike the V-1 flying bombs,
they gave no warning, arriving like a bolt from the blue
with the sound of a distant express train that culminated
in a shattering explosion. There was no defence against
them and their destructive power was greater than any
weapon before.

Because of this new menace, David Palmer had expected
his wife to be out of London, either in Gloucestershire or
staying with one of her country friends. Her war work
for the Red Cross seemed infinitely flexible. However,
when he let himself into the hallway of the house in
Knightsbridge he heard the sound of voices and laughter
coming from the drawing-room above. For a moment he
contemplated leaving and finding a hotel to stay the night
in instead, but, as he hesitated, Caroline appeared at the
top of the staircase.

'*David!* What a surprise! I thought you were in the
wilds of Middlesex.'

There was a glass in her hand and he could tell, even
from a distance, that she was slightly drunk. And he
knew that she was far from pleased to see him. She was
entertaining and he was a kill-joy, a party spoiler. Her
friends upstairs would be equally dismayed by his arrival.
It was too late to turn and go, though. He climbed the
staircase slowly and reached her.

'Hallo, Caroline.' He removed his cap and brushed her
cheek quickly with his.

'Hallo, stranger.'

He had not seen her for several months. She had cut

her hair much shorter and was wearing an emerald green cocktail gown that he remembered from years ago. Even Caroline had to make-do-and-mend.

'You're putting on weight, David.'

'Am I?' He probably was. He was getting on for fifty now. The middle of middle-aged. He didn't much care.

'Actually,' she was looking at him with her head on one side, 'it rather suits you. So does the grey hair. And all that gold braid. You're quite the distinguished top brass now, aren't you, darling?' She slid her arm through his. 'Come and meet everyone.'

He went, reluctantly, into the drawing-room where five other people were gathered – two more women and three men, neatly paired, he saw. The women were similarly dressed to Caroline, the men all in uniform. There was a naval lieutenant, an RAF squadron leader who was looking considerably embarrassed, and a tall, good-looking American Air Force colonel – very likely the donor of the nylon stockings that Caroline was wearing. By the look of them, they were at least four or five drinks ahead of him. He shook hands with them in turn. The American colonel eyed him speculatively. One of the women started giggling and spilled some of her gin and tonic over the carpet. The squadron leader's face was flushed, though whether from gin or nervousness, he wasn't sure. He supposed that he must present a fairly intimidating figure . . . the unsmiling Air Commodore, and stone cold sober. He went to the drinks cabinet and poured himself a whisky. In spite of the shortages, it was, as usual, well-stocked. He never asked Caroline where it all came from – preferred not to think about it.

She was holding out her own glass for him to re-fill. 'We've got tickets for a new show, darling. You could meet us afterwards for dinner, if you like.'

He poured her drink. 'I don't think so, thank you. I've already eaten anyway. And I've got some papers to look at before a meeting first thing at the Ministry.' He sensed the collective sigh of relief behind his turned back.

'How boring of you, David. And how typical. Don't you *ever* have any fun?'

She was needling him on purpose, as she always did when she had been drinking. He handed her the replenished glass.

'There hasn't been much time for fun lately. Things have been pretty busy.'

She made a face. 'God, I'll be so glad when this *bloody* war's over . . . It will be soon, won't it? I thought when they landed in France it would all be finished in a few weeks, but they don't seem to be making much progress. And that fiasco over trying to take that bridge – '

'They're doing their best,' he said quietly. 'These things take time. The Germans are putting up a lot of resistance. Fighting very hard.'

'*And* sending these frightful rocket things over now! Can't the RAF stop them doing that, at least? Why can't you bomb the place they're coming from, or something?'

'We already have.'

'Why didn't you blow it to pieces?'

'It's not as simple as that.'

A lot of damage had been done to the secret weapon establishment at Peenemunde last year, he knew, though at the cost of many lives. Forty bombers had been shot down. The RAF and the Americans had been successful in destroying flying bomb storage depots and their big launch sites, but the V-2 rockets were sent from tiny launching pads and were much more difficult to deal with.

He said: 'I really don't think you should be in London, Caroline, if you can possibly help it. You ought to try to arrange to leave as soon as you can. It would be much safer.'

'Don't be silly, darling. You know I can't stand being in the country for long. I'm enjoying London. It's getting to be fun again.' She glanced at the colonel who had been listening with interest. 'Anyway, I can't think why the

RAF don't do bombing raids in daylight. How can they ever hit anything in the dark? Why don't you do like the Americans. Vic says they nearly always hit the target.'

Palmer looked at the American. 'I think Colonel Schaeffer would agree that daylight bombing presents plenty of problems of its own.'

'Sure does,' the colonel said easily. 'And we were dropping like flies before we got the Mustang. Now that little beauty goes all the way with our boys, I reckon the tables are turned on the Luftwaffe. Pretty soon we're going to wipe them out of the skies. I guess that fighter's the pawn that's changed the whole game.'

'There you are, David. The American Air Force is doing your job for you.'

'Well, I wouldn't say that exactly, Caroline . . .' the colonel demurred.

'Nor would I,' the squadron leader said loudly. He had flushed even deeper and took a large swallow from his glass.

'I think you're all simply *wonderful*,' the girl who had giggled breathed. '*Terribly* brave. *All* of you.' She gave David a coy look.

He felt tired and depressed by them and wished they would go soon so that he didn't have to carry on with this ludicrous conversation. To his relief, the other woman looked at her watch and announced that they would be late for the theatre if they didn't hurry.

'You're not coming, sir?' the squadron leader asked politely.

'David says he's got work to do,' Caroline said, draining her drink. 'All work and no play makes him a very dull boy.' She waved at him from the drawing-room doorway. 'Don't expect me back early. We'll probably go on somewhere after dinner. Have a boring evening, darling . . .'

When they had gone he sat down with his whisky and leaned his head against the back of the chair. He closed his eyes and thought of the evening when he had brought Felicity here. It was a year since they had met by chance in Piccadilly and he had heard nothing of her during that time. Nor had he tried to contact her in any way. What was the point? It would only embarrass her. And probably annoy her, too. If she had ever really felt anything for him – and he believed that she once had, remembering that night – then it had been over long since. She was probably married to Dutton by now, maybe even with a child on the way . . . He thought for a moment of what might have been – of the kind of home he might have had with her, of the children they might have had, of how life might have been. And then stopped himself abruptly. There's no fool like an old fool he reminded himself wryly.

He poured another drink and settled down to work on the papers. Around eleven o'clock he went to bed in one of the spare rooms and fell asleep almost at once. Sometime during the night he was awakened by a loud explosion some distance away. It was not until early in the morning, though, when a policeman came to the front door, that he learned that a V-2 rocket had landed close by the restaurant where Caroline and her friends had gone after the theatre. The explosion had killed them all.

Anne stood in the middle of Kit's room. She looked round it very slowly, taking an inventory, registering all that was left of him.

She looked at the model cars on the shelves, the Eton Eight oar on the wall, the Wet Bob trophies and the balsa wood airplane models hanging from their strings. After a while she walked over to the chest-of-drawers and stared at the row of leavers' photographs propped against the wall and their smiling faces. Only Atkinson and Stewart were still alive, so far as she knew. The rest were all dead. And now Kit was dead too.

When she had been given the news at Colston she had coped very well, carrying on with her duties and working away at her desk. It was not until Pearl had come into her office and completely ignoring their new conduct of behaviour, had simply put her arms around her, that she had broken down and wept for him.

Her parents had been devastated, but Anne felt as if a part of her had died with Kit – as though that part lay buried with him in the grave somewhere in France. He had been her other half and the loss was terrible to bear. She had been left to carry on a life without him – to ride on alone.

He had died bravely, they said. So bravely that he was to be given a posthumous Military Cross. He and a small detachment of thirty men had held a vital bridge for more than eight hours, against overwhelming enemy odds and under heavy shell fire. He had gone to the aid of one of his men who was lying wounded in the open and had succeeded in dragging him to shelter before he himself had been caught by machine-gun fire. The debt that Kit had always believed he owed had been paid in full.

She took one last look round the room and then went out, closing the door behind her.

The sexton's wife wielded her broom briskly down the nave, sweeping a little rustling accumulation of dead leaves before her.

'I don't know how so many of them get in here. I s'pose they must blow in whenever the door's opened.' She paused and leaned on her broom. 'That's a lovely tree you're doing there, dear.' She was swathed in layers of clothing against the bitter cold, a long, knitted scarf wrapped several times round her neck beneath a hat like a tea-cosy. Her breath vaporized in clouds as she spoke. 'It's nice you're home on leave to do it this year.'

'Do you think it looks all right?' Felicity stepped back for a better view of the church Christmas tree. 'Some of the ornaments got broken last year, unfortunately, and of course we can't replace them.'

The glass baubles were stored away carefully in a cardboard box in the vestry and brought out each year.

The parish children loved them and this Christmas there would be more London evacuees again, sent to safety from the V2s this time. She wanted the tree to look good for them.

Mrs Prewitt began to herd the dead leaves up against a pillar. 'Maybe we'll be able to soon. I got some peanuts at the greengrocer's the other day and put them by for a treat. I heard someone in the queue say we might be getting oranges too. I think I've forgotten what an orange looks like. And a banana.'

'Have you any news of Peter?'

Mrs Prewitt shook her head. 'He's somewhere in France with the rest of them. What I say to myself, and to Stanley, is that he's got this far all right and there's not much further to go, is there? It won't be long now.'

She had evidently not heard about the Germans' surprise offensive in the Ardennes – history repeating itself frighteningly as they advanced through the same forests as in 1940, before Dunkirk.

'I'm sure it won't, Mrs Prewitt,' she said firmly. '*Next* Christmas it will be peace. And Peter will soon be home again now.'

Mrs Prewitt's face beneath the knitted tea-cosy hat lit up. She clasped the broom handle to her breast.

'Oh . . . what a day that'll be!'

When she had finished decorating the Christmas tree to her satisfaction, Felicity walked back through the churchyard gate to the Rectory. Last night's frost was still hard and crisp beneath her feet, the afternoon light fading fast. As she entered the hallway her father came to the door of his study.

'There's someone to see you in here, my dear. I've lit the fire.'

It would be one of the parishioners. Mrs Clark about the church jumble sale, or perhaps Mrs Anstruther with one of her eternal grumbles about the flower rota . . . She took off her overcoat and went into the study.

David Palmer, standing beside the fireplace, saw the

shock register on her face as she caught sight of him. She went very pale and then very pink, and stood looking much the same as she had done on the other side of his desk that first day at Colston.

'I'm sorry to come here like this, Felicity. Please forgive me.'

She found her voice and some of the colour receded. 'That's all right. I'm just a bit surprised, that's all. How did you know I was here?'

He smiled slightly. 'I found out. It wasn't difficult. I wanted to see you. Your father seemed to think that you might be willing to see me, when I explained why just now.'

'Oh . . .' She looked round but her father had left the room and closed the door after him. 'Well, won't you sit down? I'm sorry it's so cold in here. I'm afraid the house is always freezing. The fire doesn't seem to make much difference. And of course the weather's been bitter. I really think we might have a White Christmas, don't you? There was a thick frost this morning – '

She was gabbling on and he interrupted her gently. 'I haven't come here to talk about the weather, Felicity. I've come to talk about us.'

'Us? But there's nothing to say.'

'Caroline's dead,' he said. 'She was killed by a V2 in London three months ago. I don't suppose you knew.'

She shook her head. 'No. I'm sorry.'

'I shouldn't be coming here like this, so soon, I know, but I was so afraid that if I waited for what they call a decent interval, I might lose any chance . . .' He paused. 'And I would never have come at all if somebody else hadn't given me good reason to hope that you might still feel something for me. I'd given that up, you see. I thought you would have long forgotten me . . .'

He saw that she had no idea to whom he was referring and ploughed on recklessly.

'About a week ago I had a letter from Speedy Dutton. He'd heard about Caroline's death – I think it was reported in some of the newspapers. He wrote to me about you. He told me enough to make me realize that there *was* some hope . . . I suppose you could say he betrayed a confidence, but he did so with the best intentions, do you see?'

She did see. Speedy was not only an angel, but Cupid as well. She turned away.

He misinterpreted the turned back, the bent head, the silence. 'I'm so sorry . . . I shouldn't have come here, I realize that. It's all been a mistake and it was very stupid of me. Inexcusable.' He picked up his cap. 'I'll leave at once.'

She turned round then and he saw that there were tears in her eyes and that she was trying to smile at him.

'You'll stay to tea, at least?' she asked. 'Father would be so pleased. And so would I.'

He put down the cap again slowly.

'I'd like that very much,' he said.

'Ooh, it's *lovely*, Winnie!' Nora held up the new suit on its hanger admiringly. 'However did you manage it with the coupons?'

'Mum saved up for me, an' Gran hardly uses hers. We got it in a shop in Ipswich.'

'I like the hat, too.' Nora tried on the little hat and looked at her reflection in the mirror over the washstand in Winnie's attic room. She tipped it at a rakish angle and patted the bunch of false flowers. 'You've got to wear it like this, see . . . so's it looks really smart.'

She looked so funny wearing the hat with her Land Army jersey and breeches that Winnie started giggling. She hung the suit carefully back in the wardrobe and stroked one of the soft wool sleeves. It was the smartest thing she'd ever had.

Nora was tweaking the hat veil over her face. 'I'm glad you're not gettin' married in uniform like lots of people do.'

'Virgil will be.'

'That's different. It looks right on a man. An' the Yanks' uniforms are smashin'. Virgil'd look dreamy, anyway, whatever he wore. He's gorgeous. An' ever so brave, too, doin' all those missions. I was afraid he'd never get through, Winnie? Did you worry a lot?'

''Course I did.' But worry wasn't enough of a word to describe the terror that she'd felt during the past weeks – the daily dread of bad news, the miserable agony of waiting until Virgil had done his final mission and come home safely.

Nora bent to peer closer into the mirror. 'This hat'll go just right with the suit, an' they're ever such a pretty colour. 'Course you couldn't wear white again, you bein' married before, an' all.'

Winnie knew what she meant by *an' all*. Only there hadn't been any an' all with Ken, though she wasn't going to tell Nora that – not unless she wanted the whole village to know too. The trouble was she hadn't told Virgil either, and she knew she ought to have done so he'd understand that she didn't know about things he'd expect her to know all about . . . She'd started to try to explain several times, but she'd felt so embarrassed and awkward. Americans were so different – lots of girls said that. They weren't shy and fumbling like most English boys. So, they probably didn't expect the girl to be shy either. Specially if she'd been married before. She'd got to tell him, somehow.

Nora was still admiring herself in the mirror. 'An' it's nice you're bein' married in the church again. Properly, not in a registry office. Do they have churches in America? I can't remember seein' any in films.'

''Course they have churches – they're just not as old as ours. Virgil says he's got one near where he lives an' it's the same sort of thing, only it's built of wood, not stone.' Winnie closed the wardrobe door. 'I'm so pleased you can come tomorrow, Nora. An' there's goin' to be a party after at the hall. Mum's doin' sandwiches an' jellies an' Virgil says they're goin' to get a whole lot of food from the camp, includin' *ice-cream!*'

681

Nora turned round. 'Oooh, Winnie!'

'An' one of the cooks at the base is a friend of Virgil's an' he's made us a real wedding cake with marzipan an' icin' on the top, not just cardboard.'

'Oooh!'

'An' there's goin' to be a band from the base, too, so you'll be able to dance.'

Nora's eyes were shining through the hat veil. 'Boy, are we goin' to have fun!'

'I'm sorry Curly isn't here.'

'I'm not really.' Nora pulled a face. 'He didn't have a ranch, you know. I found out.'

'I 'spect he just wanted to impress you.'

'Well, he needn't have done that. I didn't mind him not havin' a ranch so much. But I did mind him pretendin' about it, tellin' me a big fib. So, I said I didn't want to see him any more. Then he went off to fight in France with the rest of them an' I felt a bit bad about bein' like that to him when he'd probably go an' get killed.'

She sank down on Winnie's bed with a sigh. She was still wearing the hat. 'They'll all be goin' soon, Winnie. The Air Force lot won't stay here when the war's finished. They'll be movin' out, same as the soldiers, an' goin' back home. It's goin' to be *awful* without them . . . I don't know how I'm goin' to stand it. It was all colour an' fun when they came an' it's goin' to be all grey and dreary again when they're gone, just like it was before.' She heaved another sigh. 'You're so lucky, marryin' a Yank. Just think you'll be goin' off to live in America. You'll get away from dull old Elmbury.'

'I'll miss it, though, Nora. It isn't so dull to me really. Anyway, I won't be goin' for a while. When the war's over the boats'll all be full of troops goin' home first. It'll be a long time before I can get on one I should think.'

'Imagine that . . .' Nora rolled her eyes. 'Sailin' away across the sea to a new life on the other side of the world! It's ever so excitin' an' romantic. I wish *I* were doin' that.'

'P'raps you will. P'raps you'll meet someone tomorrow. There's lots of Americans comin'.'

'Oooh . . .' Nora brightened. She took off the little hat and handed it over. Then she got up and bent to look out of the attic window.

'Oh, Winnie, it's *snowin'*! Isn't that lovely? You're goin' to have a white weddin' after all.'

'Dearly beloved, we are gathered together here in the sight of God . . .'

The vicar was looking down his nose a bit as he recited the words in his thin voice. Winnie knew that he didn't approve of her marrying an American, or of his church being full of them either. Lots of them had turned out to give Virgil a good send-off because he'd done the two tours.

Dad was swaying slightly on the other side of her. He'd had to fortify himself from the bottle of Johnnie Walker on the kitchen dresser before they set off, and when he'd held out his arm to her at the church he'd hissed: 'I'm not doin' this *again* for you, Winnie. This is the last time.' He hated getting dressed up and all the fuss. She had walked down the aisle more holding *him* up than the other way around. Virgil had been there, waiting for her and the way he'd smiled at her had made her knees go as wobbly as Dad's.

'. . . *into which holy estate these two persons present come now to be joined.*' The vicar, mouth pursed, turned reluctantly to Virgil.

After the service she walked down the aisle on Virgil's strong arm, between the rows of smiling faces that made up for the vicar's long one, and to what wheezing notes Miss Hobson, the village school teacher, could coax out of the old organ. On her left hand was the gold wedding ring, sent from America, that had belonged to Virgil's grandmother – the one who'd gone out west to homestead the new land in Ohio, and on her right was the amethyst ring that had been hers too. It gave Winnie a proud feeling to be wearing them when they had belonged to someone like that.

Ten American servicemen from the base and ten WAAFS from Flaxton had formed a guard of honour outside the church for them. The sun was shining, making the snow sparkle, and the sky was clear and blue. In the far corner of the churchyard the red berries in the holly wreath she had laid on Ken's grave that morning stood out brightly. *He would have been glad for me,* she thought with certainty. *I know he would.*

As they reached the lych-gate there was the sound of a heavy bomber approaching. All eyes turned upwards as a B17 came into view, flying low. It roared straight over the church and dipped its wings in salute, and everyone could see *Wattagal Winnie!* in big letters on the nose and the painting of her in her blue dungarees and checked shirt.

'That's for you,' Virgil said, grinning at her.

'Oh, no,' she told him. 'It's for *you*. For what you've done.'

'Well, I guess, it's for both of us.' He put his arm round her shoulders.

Union Jacks and Stars and Stripes were strung together round the walls of the village hall and bunches of holly and mistletoe hung from the rafters. Up on the cramped little stage the band was getting ready, unpacking instruments and setting up music stands. Chairs had been placed in a regimented row at the edge of the room and near the door three trestle tables had been laden with food – with sandwiches and bridge rolls, cold turkey, spam and ham, big bowls of tinned fruit, shiny red, green and yellow jellies, blancmanges, biscuits, chocolates, candy and great tubs of American ice-cream. And from the centre of all this rose the glistening white three-tiered edifice of the wedding cake. To go with the feast there were jugs of orangeade, bottles of home-made wine donated from village larders, and a barrel of beer from the Pig and Whistle.

As the Elmbury villagers and the WAAFS from Flaxton crowded into the hall there was a long moment's silence in

684

appreciation of the sight that met their gaze. Then, with one accord, they fell upon the tables. The Americans, hanging back politely, watched in wonder.

Later, when the band began to play – softly at first – Virgil gathered Winnie in his arms. 'Told you from the first you was the girl for me,' he said in her ear. 'Now you'll always be mine.'

The lower the level in the beer barrel and bottles sank, the higher the noise level in the hall rose. And the faster the band played. Young and old took to the floor. Winnie, having a breather for a while, saw that even Dad was hopping about with Mum, waving his hands in the air. The WAAFS and the village girls were jiving wildly with the Americans and Nora squealed like a pig going to market as she was pitched over her partner's broad shoulder.

'Gee . . .' The sergeant standing beside Winnie was chewing gum and clicking his fingers as he stared at the scene in disbelief. 'This old joint's really jumpin'!'

Gran had found herself a chair strategically close to the trestle tables and the plate on her lap was piled high with samples of everything within her reach. Winnie went to sit beside her. She smelled strongly of the camphor used to keep the moths away from her best dress, and the lace bib that had been clean on that morning was well-spotted now. Her black straw bonnet was tied with a ribbon under her chin and must have been very old.

'You all right, Gran?' Winnie shouted in her ear.

'Whoi wouldn't oi be? T'ain't the fust party oi've bin ta, yew know. Gideon an' me liked a bit o' fun an' dancin' at Chrissmus.'

She was tapping her foot to the music and Winnie saw that she had put on the nylon stockings that Virgil had given her instead of her black woollen ones – only they were on the wrong way round, with the seams in front and the heels hanging like pouches round her ankles.

''Tis good to see our boys enjoyin' thareselves so finely.'

She meant the Americans, Winnie realized. Our boys, she'd called them. Other people in the village called them that too, in spite of the vicar. They weren't *those Yanks* any more. They were *our boys*.

She watched Virgil dancing with Ruth, bending down to teach her how to jive, twisting her gently this way and that. Laura was jumping about close by, wanting to be taught too. As he swung Ruth round he caught sight of Winnie and gave her a huge wink just like the one he'd given her the very first time she'd seen him at the dance.

Gran had been quaffing her elderberry wine and now she jabbed a bridge roll in Virgil's direction. 'Knew he was the one fur yew, soon as I set eyes on'm. Alus puts me in moind o' Gideon.'

Winnie knew why. Virgil was not only tall and strong like Grandad had been, he was very brave too, and Grandad must have had plenty of courage. He had gone off to fight on the North-West Frontier in India in his youth and been wounded, and been given a medal that Gran kept in a matchbox. Virgil had been wounded too and he had been given two medals for what he'd done. She'd sewn the ribbons on for him and she'd never felt so proud of anyone.

They went to Cambridge for their honeymoon and because of the snow and the slow train it was very late by the time they arrived at the Garden House Hotel. The manager looked at them with open suspicion, fingering the register.

'I'm not sure that we have a room after all, sir.'

Virgil leaned one arm on the reception counter. 'This here's my wife, 'case you was wonderin', mister. We're just married. She's done me the honour.'

The manager smiled then. He turned the book round and pushed it forward. 'Congratulations, sir. I'm sorry . . . we get so many who aren't.'

He brought a bottle of champagne and two glasses up to their room and opened it for them with a flourish. 'May I wish you both every happiness.'

'Nice guy,' Virgil said when he had left the room, wishing them a good night. 'I ain't never drunk champagne before.' He was taking off his jacket and loosening his tie.

Nor had Winnie but she took several big swallows. It was now or never. 'Virgil, there's somethin' I've got to tell you.'

He picked up his glass. 'Sure . . . fire away.'

'Well . . . well . . . well . . .'

'Aw, come on, honey,' he grinned. 'Can't be that bad.'

She swallowed some more champagne and burped. 'Well, you know I told you that Ken, my first husband died . . .'

'No disrespect to him, but I sure hope he did else we're breakin' the law, an' that guy downstairs is gonna want his champagne back.'

'Yes, he did. Just like I told you. But you see, before that he was ill – for a long time.'

'Yeah, I remember you said. Poor guy.'

'Right from the day we got married he was poorly. He had a bad chest an' cough, an' he was very weak 'cos of his heart. I knew he was dyin' – that's really why I married him. We were goin' to wait 'til after the war otherwise.'

'Gee. Kind've a tough situation.'

She nodded. 'The thing is Ken was so poorly most of the time that he never . . . we never . . . he never . . .'

Virgil put down his glass slowly, staring at her. Then he went and put his hands on her shoulders. 'Wait a second, Winnie. Am I receivin' you right? You tryin' to tell me he ain't *never* made love to you? That it?'

'That's it.'

'Jeez . . . I feel real sorry for the guy, but to tell the truth I'm kinda glad too. Can't help feelin' like that. So, you ain't never – '

She shook her head.

'With nobody?'

'No.'

'Not even that Welsh guy?'

'*Specially* not him.' She shivered. 'He tried, though.'

'Wish I'd punched him harder.' There was a smile lurking round the corners of Virgil's mouth. 'An' I guess you've been worryin'. Thinkin' I'd figure you'd know the score?'

'Somethin' like that.'

'Well, you ain't got nothin' to worry 'bout, Winnie. Never had. But I'm glad you told me.' The smile broadened. 'Say, that's a real cute hat, but I can't get at you with all that nettin' in the way. You plannin' on keepin' it on all night?'

'Oh.' She took off the little hat and veil.

'That's better.' He bent and kissed her gently. 'Ain't nothin' to be scared of, see.'

After a moment or two he said: 'This suit you're wearin' sure is pretty too, but I reckon it's 'bout time that came off as well.'

He unbuttoned the jacket for her, and then the blouse underneath, and then her skirt, and soon she was standing there in her petticoat.

'Mum made this for me,' she faltered, looking at the floor. 'It's parachute silk. We got some damaged from Flaxton.'

'It's real pretty too.' He lifted her chin and held it in his hand, looking into her eyes. 'But I ain't gonna let you keep that on neither.'

He picked her up easily and cradled her against him, and kissed her again. 'Nor what's under there. Fact is, Winifred Gillies, I ain't lettin' you keep anythin' on at all.'

The Dakota gathered speed down the runway and rose into the air. Anne watched RAF Northolt and England drop away in a hazy pattern of little houses and roads and fields, with splashes of new spring green and the bright glint of a river.

The American army officer in the seat beside her leaned across. 'Isn't that Windsor Castle down there?'

'Yes, that's right.'

'I went to see it once,' he said. 'Wonderful place. And that famous school there where they wear top hats and tails . . .'

'Eton.'

My brother went there, she wanted to tell him. We used to visit him and every summer they have this wonderful day in June . . . But she couldn't bring herself to talk about Kit to a stranger. He was nice looking and polite and very friendly, and he'd helped her to get her luggage on board, but she couldn't talk to him about Kit.

She watched the castle fade into the distance and presently the Dakota flew into cloud and England vanished from view. Liberated Brussels lay ahead. It was only the second time that she had been abroad in her life – the first was a family holiday in France – and she felt as eager about it as she had then. She had volunteered to be sent to Europe soon after D-Day but it had been early March before her posting had come through. The Americans had just crossed the Rhine that very day. It had been announced on the wireless and the newspapers had carried the simple headline: *They're Over!* Cologne had been taken. The Allies were advancing fast. And in the Far East the Yanks had been setting fire to Japanese cities with incendiary bombs. The final act of the war was being played out. Some of the newspapers had printed photographs of the ruins of Cologne. She had been shocked, at first, by the total devastation, by the mountains of rubble and by the carnage until she had reminded herself of what the Luftwaffe had done to London and English cities.

The American was offering her a cigarette. Philip Morris – the same brand that Frank had smoked. He reminded her quite a bit of Frank; he had similar coloured eyes and the same direct look. That brass thing on his shoulder meant that he was a major, if she'd got it right.

'Will you be based in Brussels?' he asked.

She nodded. 'At our 2nd TAF HQ there.'

'That'll be in the Rue de la Loi.'

'Do you know Brussels, then?'

'Pretty well. I've been there on and off ever since your people liberated it.'

He'd know where to go and where not to go, how to get things done and how not to get things done – all the gen. She bent her head towards his lighter flame.

'Do tell me *all* about it.'

Brussels was lovely old buildings and cobbled streets and squares and very grateful Belgians. We're liberators, she thought, as yet another one smiled at her. They've lived through five years of German occupation, and that's something we've never had to suffer – though we came close to it. The civilians looked hungry and poorly-nourished and she felt embarrassed by the good service rations. There was, naturally enough, a flourishing Black Market.

The 2nd Tactical Air Force Headquarters was in a tall building in the Rue de la Loi known as the Palais Résidence, while RAF airmen and WAAF airwomen were billeted in separate blocks in a large barracks in the city called the Caserne Baudouin, previously occupied by the Luftwaffe. The walls inside the barracks were decorated with huge paintings of Dorniers and Heinkels and Messerschmitts in dramatic flight and the Mess had well-polished refectory tables. The Germans had considerately installed a completely new plumbing system that worked wonderfully and as Anne made a tour of inspection of the airwomen's quarters she marvelled at the shining taps that gushed forth constant hot water, compared with the lukewarm dribblings in many WAAF ablutions in England. Here were no cracked basins or missing plugs, no slimy duckboards or sacking partitions, no rust-streaked baths painted with a black line to mark the permitted five inches of tepid water. The WAAF slept in light and airy dormitories and on good beds, though one airwoman complained to her.

'I don't like the idea that I'm sleeping in some German's bed, ma'am. It gives me goose-pimples.' She was a wireless operator and had a plain, rather sour face that reminded Anne of Maureen. 'I don't think it's right.'

And that was just the sort of thing that Maureen had always said. *It's disgusting. It oughtn't to be allowed.* And Gloria had always teased her, like the time when they thought England was going to be invaded any moment. *Storm troopers . . . just think of that, Maureen, something for you to look forward to. You'll be 'aving the bloody time of your life.* If Gloria had been here she would have given a tart answer: *Pity he's not still in it. Might take that lemon look off your face.* Anne found that she was starting to smile and hurriedly changed her expression.

'I'm afraid you'll just have to be sensible about it, airwoman. We can't provide a different bed specially for you. We mustn't allow our personal feelings to interfere in any way with the job we're here to do. There's still a war to be won.'

The American major from the Dakota drove her round in a jeep, pointing out the sights. The city seemed to have escaped serious damage and the shops stocked goods unobtainable in England. They're going to recover much quicker than us, she thought. It will probably be years before we finish re-building and rationing and making-do-and-mending.

One residential street was blocked by a huge bonfire in the roadway. People were carrying furniture out of a house and tossing it onto the fire – chairs, carpets, cupboards, pictures. Anne watched in astonishment as two men added a valuable-looking table to the flames.

'What on *earth* are they doing?'

'The house belongs to a collaborator,' the major told her. 'You'll see that happening quite often. The citizens are taking their revenge on anyone who got too friendly with the Nazis during the Occupation. And the POWs are coming back. They often know who denounced them to the Gestapo . . .' He turned the jeep round. 'Speaking of returning POWs, some Belgian friends of mine have asked me to a party this evening. It's to celebrate the release of their son. Would you like to come?'

'Will it be a good party?'

He smiled at her. 'I guarantee it.'

If a good party was to be measured by the amount of noise that everyone there was making, then he was right. The long drawing-room was crowded with people shouting at each other in French and English. She was introduced to the major's friends and to their army captain son, a pale young man who seemed overwhelmed by the fuss being made of him. She talked to him for a while, dredging up some rusty school French, and then to a British army lieutenant who seemed to resent her being in Brussels at all.

'You WAAFS have had it pretty easy, haven't you?'

'Easy?' She eyed his flushed, perspiring face.

'All very well for you. I mean to say, us chaps came over here the hard way. My lot landed in Normandy on D-Day plus thirteen.'

'Really,' she said coldly. 'What kept you?'

She moved away from him and headed for the far corner of the room where someone had sat down to play a grand piano. The pianist, a Belgian civilian, was playing with his eyes half shut, a cigarette drooping from his lips, his hands drifting over the keys. She leaned on the lid and listened while he picked his way softly through a song, and sang a few of the words with him.

He squinted at her through a spiral of smoke. 'You like to sing, mademoiselle?'

'Love to.'

'Ah . . .' He played a few bars of another song. 'You know this one?'

'Of course. Everybody knows that.'

'Alors . . . chantez.'

She began by singing only to him, leaning on the

piano, and he watched her, smoking his cigarette and
accompanying her quietly.

> *There'll be bluebirds over*
> *The white cliffs of Dover*
> *Tomorrow, just you wait and see.*
> *There'll be love and laughter*
> *And peace ever after*
> *Tomorrow, when the world is free . . .*

People standing near had turned to listen and gradually
the room fell silent.

> *The shepherd will tend his sheep*
> *The valley will bloom again.*
> *And Jimmy will go to sleep*
> *In his own little room again . . .*

It was then that she saw Johnnie. He was standing on
the far side of the room, leaning against a wall (as usual)
watching her. The jolt of seeing him so unexpectedly sent
the blood rushing into her face and almost put her off her
stride. She collected herself just in time.

> *There'll be bluebirds over*
> *The white cliffs of Dover*
> *Tomorrow, just you wait and see.*

Everyone was applauding and a woman nearby was
actually wiping away tears. The pianist leaned towards
her.

'You sing again mademoiselle?' He fingered the keys
encouragingly.

But she shook her head. Johnnie was making his way
across the room; there was no escape. She waited until
he reached her.

'You sing awfully well, Anne. I remember telling you that once before, long ago. And you're wearing that blue dress. It brings back memories too.' He smiled.

She ignored that. 'What are you doing here in Brussels?'

'I might ask the same of you. Did you desert your bomber boys?'

'I changed horses. I'm admin now. They posted me here two weeks ago.'

He looked amused. 'Admin? Not really your style, I'd have thought.'

'That's exactly what Kit said.'

'How is he?'

'He was killed last November in France.'

His face changed. 'I'm so very sorry, Anne. That's dreadful news. I know you were very close.'

'Well, there we are . . . I always had a feeling it would happen. Right from the first. Have you got a cigarette? I could do with one.'

He produced the gold case and lighter. The gold signet ring was back on his hand but she saw that the fingers still looked painfully red and crabbed, though the burns on the side of his face had faded so that they were not so noticeable.

'Are you back on ops now?' she asked him.

'I have been. The powers that be finally decided that I could hold more than a cigarette and a cocktail glass.'

Even so, he was doing both awkwardly, she thought, and it had taken several attempts to work the lighter.

'Do your hands still hurt?'

'Sometimes. There'll be more work to do on them eventually, so I'm told, but they function pretty well and that's the main thing.'

'You were lucky.'

'So you have frequently told me.'

'The war will soon be over anyway. You'll be handing in the Spits.'

'I'm going to regret that. The Moth won't seem quite

694

the same. Actually, I haven't done any flying for a while. They sent me off on a long lecture tour of America.'

'What on earth did you talk about?'

'The RAF. Told them what fine chaps we are . . . how hard we've been fighting . . . all that sort of thing. Drumming up sympathy and goodwill. When I got back they roped me in for liaison work over here. I've been in Ghent for the past month.'

'Liaison work?'

'I read French and German at Oxford.'

She'd forgotten that, and that he'd been bound for the Foreign Office. 'Another gong, I see. Congratulations.'

'Consolation prize.'

'Hmm. The DSO's usually a bit more than that. When did you get to be so modest?'

'Since you taught me to be. It's hellishly hot and crowded in here, Anne. Let's go out onto that balcony over there and get some air. Then we can talk without having to shout.'

'I'm supposed to be here with someone.'

'Someone?'

'A very nice American major. I met him on the 'plane coming over. He's been showing me around.'

'Well, he won't miss you for a moment.'

French windows opened onto a narrow balcony overlooking the street. The party chatter and music faded behind them; the early April night was cool and still. Anne leaned on the railings. Johnnie was silent for a moment, smoking.

'I've a suggestion to make, Anne. A proposition.'

She turned her head suspiciously. 'What?'

'That we start all over again. Pretend that this is the first time we've met. There you were singing, just like before, and I'm asking you to have dinner with me, just like before.'

'And I'm refusing, just like before.'

'So you're turning down my proposal flat?'

'We've had a similar conversation once before, I think.'

'I remember it well. Have you nothing more to say?'

'I can't think of anything.'

He tossed his cigarette away. 'The fact is, Anne, you've never let yourself *think* at all where I'm concerned. You've had this preconceived notion about me from the very first and you won't let yourself change it. You're stubborn as hell. You came very close to it in Gloucestershire – I thought you had – and then you suddenly backed away. I'm asking you, for the very last time, to give it another try.'

'You're giving me once last chance to have the honour of falling at your feet?'

He said, exasperated: 'That's not what I meant. You know perfectly well how I feel about you. Why are you so set against me?'

She straightened up. 'That's what you've never been able to understand, isn't it, Johnnie? How I could possibly resist you.'

'You didn't – once. Far from it.'

'And I've regretted it ever since.'

They faced each other in the darkness. At last he spoke in a cool tone.

'If that's really your final answer, Anne, then I accept it. The subject is closed for ever. And now you'd better go and find your American major. He might be wondering where you are.'

She found him in conversation with a Belgian couple and drew him aside. 'Do you mind if we go soon? I'm rather tired.'

'Sure . . .'

As they left, she saw Johnnie talking to a pretty, dark-haired woman – smiling down at her, laying on the charm with a trowel. Well that's that, she thought, turning away. End of story. Finis. Over and out.

Twenty-Eight

Virginia watched the rocket climbing high into the sky above the cliffs. It exploded in an umbrella of coloured stars that fell towards the sea below. Then a second one rose up from the direction of the town, and another, and another, sounding like gunfire.

But the guns were silent now. The war in Europe was over. Mr Churchill had broadcast to the nation, announcing it officially, and everyone on the camp had gone mad, cheering and hugging each other, laughing and crying. Madge had gone off into the town to join the crowds there, but Virginia had come up onto the cliffs by herself to think.

It had been drizzling all morning but the weather had cleared now and she thought she could just make out the faint smudge on the horizon that was France. Neil was buried over there and one day she would go and find his grave. One day she might even go to Canada and meet his family. His mother had written, inviting her.

Everyone had plans for peacetime. Madge wanted to get demobbed as soon as possible and work as a stewardess on a passenger airliner and travel all over the world. 'How about you, Ginny?' she'd asked.

'Well, I thought I might stay on in the WAAF for a bit.'

Madge had looked at her as though she was loopy. 'You don't want to do that. Not when the war's over. It won't be the same at all.'

Virginia walked along the cliff path, head bent. What else was there to do? Go back to the Falcon Assurance Company and turn into another Miss Parkes, spending the rest of her life among the filing cabinets? Live alone in a bed-sit and cook out of tins on a gas ring? 'We want you to come and live with us,' Dorothy and Father had said every time she went to visit them, but that wouldn't be right. Visiting was one thing, living there was another. They had their life and she had hers – such as it was, or would be. She was sure that she would never marry now and so she must somehow make her own way.

She stopped for a moment, staring at the ground. If she stayed on in the WAAF she could make a real career of it. Try for the commission she'd always dreamed about. Set herself to get as high as she could – maybe even to the top. The WAAF wouldn't be disbanded now. It had proved itself too useful. Women had been accepted in the service. Madge was right – it wouldn't be the same after the war, but there would be a new role for them to play in the postwar world. There would be work to be done. New goals to achieve. A whole new life. A purpose. A future.

She lifted her head and walked on with it held high.

The church bells were ringing out victoriously over London. The sound, not heard for five and a half long years, carried far across the rooftops in peal after glorious peal.

Felicity stood by the open hotel window, listening. Drinking it in. Later, as darkness fell, the lights would be coming on – shining in the streets, floodlighting buildings, pouring out of windows all over the city. No more blackout! No more *put that light out*! London was going to a glittering blaze of celebration tonight.

She peered downwards to watch a long line of people approaching down the middle of the road. They were wearing red, white and blue paper hats and were dancing, one behind the other, hands on the waist of the one in front, doing the Conga. The line snaked its way along, legs shooting out in unison, right, then left, right then left, like a prancing centipede. It was led by a young man wearing a policeman's helmet and playing the trumpet. He was holding it high, his head tipped back, as though he were some modern-day Pied Piper. He reminded her of Speedy; and of Whitters and Dumbo, and all of them, as they had been. There was a telegram in her pocket: *'Tis better to have loved and lost than never to have loved at all. Snodgrass.*

She turned round. 'Let's go out later, David.'

'There'll be huge crowds.' He was opening a bottle of champagne, easing out the cork with both thumbs.

'But it'll be fun. Let's join in and see all the lights when they come on.'

'All right.'

He smiled at her across the room. They had been married the day before, quietly in a registry office in London, and if she had suggested that they went to Timbukto in the morning he would have done his best to arrange it for her. One place that he would not take her, though, was the house in Kensington. After Caroline's death he had shut it up, and the one in Gloucestershire too, and he had no wish to re-open either, or for them to be any part of this new beginning. Eventually, he supposed, he would have to sell both and he knew what he was going to do with the proceeds. He was going to give the whole damn lot to the RAF Benevolent Fund – for those who had been badly wounded and maimed during this war, and for the dependents of those who had died. He had not the slightest doubt that Felicity would agree. Caroline's money would do some good in the end. He and Felicity would find a place of their own. Something quite different. Somewhere to spend leaves, to raise a family, perhaps, if they were so fortunate. He looked at his wife standing at the window, marvelling at his present good fortune, and hoped he wasn't too old to make a decent father.

The cork popped and he filled two glasses and carried them over. More people were coming along the street below, marching and waving Union Jacks and singing raucously.

There'll always be an England,
And England shall be free
If England means as much to you
As England means to me . . .

Palmer raised his glass. 'To victory.'

Felicity raised hers. 'And to the Royal Air Force.'

'And to the WAAF,' he countered. 'Thank God for you all. Each and every one.'

She smiled at that. 'And to us.'

'To us.' He was smiling too. He touched her glass lightly with his. 'May we live happily ever after.'

The RAF corporal singing *Scotland the Brave* at the top of his lungs, was doing so standing on a narrow ledge no more than a foot wide and six storeys high. He had climbed out of a window in the Palais Résidence, glass in hand, and was entertaining the crowd in the Place Dially below.

Drunken fool, Anne thought, watching him in horror from below. He's survived the war and now he's going to kill himself on VE Day. She could see faces at the window behind him, hands reaching out cautiously trying to grab hold of him. All around her in the crowd people were pointing and laughing and clapping, shouting up to him in different languages. At the end of his song he bowed unsteadily, teetering on the edge, and Anne held her breath. Then she put her hand over her eyes as he started to walk along the ledge towards the next window, holding his drinking glass aloft in one hand and balancing like a trapeze artist. The crowd had fallen silent. Anne kept her hand over her eyes until a great roar broke out. She expected the corporal to have toppled to his death but instead saw that he had reached the window and was being hauled headfirst over the sill to safety.

The square was now packed with people, swirling and eddying like a moving mass of water. Somewhere among them she caught a glimpse of a fair head that might have been Johnnie's, but it was lost to view almost immediately.

She had been rehearsing for some time what she would say to him if they should happen to meet again. 'I've been thinking, actually,' she was going to say very casually. 'Maybe we *should* give it a try . . . that is, if you still want to.' Or, she might say, equally casually: 'About that dinner invitation, if it's still on I could do with a square meal.' Or, 'I'm game, if you still are . . .' Something very offhand and throw-away so that he wouldn't know how hard she'd been kicking herself since the party, and in case *he'd* changed his mind. That's the sort of thing she'd say. *If* they ever met again.

She linked arms with a group of RAF and stepped out with them, doing the Lambeth Walk.

A Belgian civilian in a beret caught hold of her and pulled her into his arms, kissing her full on the mouth.

'You want zis flag?' He gestured to a Union Jack flying above a balcony window. 'I get for you.'

Before she could stop him he had scaled the wall and clambered up onto the balcony's rim to pluck the flag from its pole. When he had brought it down he presented it to her with a bow and kissed her again.

'*Vive l'Angleterre!*'

A chorus of *Land of Hope and Glory* had started up and was swelling across the square. She began to wave the flag in time and a Tommy soldier crouched down and hoisted her onto his shoulders, up above the heads of the crowd. This is conduct extremely unbecoming to a flight officer, she thought, but not caring, as he marched along with her. She held the Union Jack high in the air.

. . . how shall we extol thee, who are born of thee?

The swell had become a roar. The mass of faces surged towards her and other flags fluttered – the Belgian, the French Tricolour, the Stars and Stripes . . .

And then she saw Johnnie for certain. He was only yards away from her but separated by a solid body of people.

'Johnnie,' she yelled. '*Johnnie!*'

He heard her and turned his head. When he saw her brandishing her flag, he started laughing.

She forgot all her careful rehearsals, and she forgot her silly pride. '*Johnnie!*' She waved the flag frantically. '*I love you!*'

He was trying to fight his way towards her and she beat on the soldier's head to make him set her down. When she landed on her feet, the momentum of the crowd swept her still further away and she struggled helplessly against it. Suddenly, the flow ebbed and she was swept back in the other direction. The surge carried her along and, like a wave breaking onto a shore, dumped her unceremoniously in Johnnie's arms.

An RAF airman elbowed his mate, grinning. 'Cor, look at them two! Talk about a clinch! Effin' officers get all the bleedin' luck!'

Winnie leaned her arms on the top of the five-barred gate and looked out over the field, across the green corn towards the line of elm trees where the rooks circled, cawing, overhead, and to the church tower beyond. The bells were pealing – a forgotten and beautiful sound ringing out across the countryside. She gave a huge sigh, part happiness and part sadness. This was her England. Her country. At peace. But soon she would have to leave it and go to live in a vast and strange land far away across the sea. Sometimes her heart sank at the thought of it, but Virgil was there and where he was she wanted to be. They would be together and make their life on the farm in Ohio.

The baby moved inside her. She was sure it was a boy and it was funny to think that he would grow up an American and talk like them. But she could teach him about England. Tell him all about it. And one day perhaps he'd come back here to see it – not to fight in a war like his father. And maybe there'd be more sons, and a daughter too. When Pearl had read the tea leaves all that time ago she'd seen several children. *Four kids, or maybe even five*, that's what she'd said. *Long life and happiness*.

The breeze stirred her hair. The sun was warm on her upturned face. She closed her eyes.

She missed the WAAF badly but they wouldn't let her stay in any longer because of the baby. She missed the work and the companionship, and even the uniform. When she looked back, it had been a wonderful time from the very beginning. In spite of the war and of all the sad things that had happened, and in spite of all the difficulties and discomforts and dangers, they had been the happiest days of her life. She thought of the arrival at RAF Colston when she had been sick as a dog over the tailgate of the three-tonner. Anne, Pearl, Gloria, Enid, Sandra, Maureen and the rest had been there with her at the start of it all. She could picture it easily. Company Assistant Newman had given them that little speech of welcome and the airmen had been laughing and whistling at them from the windows. So much had happened since that first day. Everyone had tried so hard. Done their very best. And in the end they'd succeeded. The war had been won. The world was saved from Hitler and the Nazis. The lights would be going on again everywhere and everyone said it was all going to be different from now on. A better world.

The church bells had stopped and in the quietness she heard a different and familiar sound. She opened her eyes quickly and turned round, shielding them with her hand as she searched the skies.

A lone fighter was flying towards her, its small dark shape skimming low across the blue. The shape grew bigger and the throaty growl of its engine louder until, with a mighty roar, the Hurricane swept over her head and went into a triumphant victory roll. Winnie stood on the bottom rung of the gate and waved as it flew off into the distance and became a faint black speck. For some reason she found that she was crying.

THE END

A SELECTED LIST OF FINE NOVELS
AVAILABLE FROM CORGI BOOKS

☐	14058 9	MIST OVER THE MERSEY	Lyn Andrews	£5.99
☐	14060 0	MERSEY BLUES	Lyn Andrews	£5.99
☐	14096 1	THE WILD SEED	Iris Gower	£5.99
☐	14447 9	FIREBIRD	Iris Gower	£5.99
☐	14537 8	APPLE BLOSSOM TIME	Kathryn Haig	£4.99
☐	14566 1	THE DREAM SELLERS	Ruth Hamilton	£5.99
☐	14567 X	THE CORNER HOUSE	Ruth Hamilton	£5.99
☐	13872 X	LEGACY OF LOVE	Caroline Harvey	£5.99
☐	14686 2	CITY OF GEMS	Caroline Harvey	£5.99
☐	14535 1	THE HELMINGHAM ROSE	Joan Hessayon	£5.99
☐	14692 7	THE PARADISE GARDEN	Joan Hessayon	£5.99
☐	14332 4	THE WINTER HOUSE	Judith Lennox	£5.99
☐	14599 8	FOOTPRINTS ON THE SAND	Judith Lennox	£5.99
☐	14693 5	THE LITTLE SHIP	Margaret Mayhew	£5.99
☐	14492 4	THE CREW	Margaret Mayhew	£5.99
☐	14400 2	THE MOUNTAIN	Elvi Rhodes	£5.99
☐	14577 7	PORTRAIT OF CHLOE	Elvi Rhodes	£5.99
☐	14549 1	CHOICES	Susan Sallis	£5.99
☐	14636 6	COME RAIN OR SHINE	Susan Sallis	£5.99
☐	14606 4	FIRE OVER LONDON	Mary Jane Staples	£5.99
☐	14657 9	CHURCHILL'S PEOPLE	Mary Jane Staples	£5.99
☐	14504 1	THE GHOST	Danielle Steel	£6.99
☐	14502 5	THE LONG ROAD HOME	Danielle Steel	£6.99
☐	14640 4	THE ROMANY GIRL	Valerie Wood	£5.99